A DAUGHTER'S
A DAUGHTER
• AND OTHER NOVELS •

A MARY WESTMACOTT OMNIBUS

A DAUGHTER'S A DAUGHTER

•AND OTHER NOVELS•

A Daughter's a Daughter
Unfinished Portrait
The Burden

AGATHA CHRISTIE
writing as MARY WESTMACOTT

ST MARTIN'S MINOTAUR
NEW YORK

A DAUGHTER'S A DAUGHTER. Copyright © 1952 by Agatha Christie Mallowan Copyright ©
2000 by Rosalind Hicks UNFINISHED PORTRAIT Copyright © 1934 by Doubleday, Doran
and Company, Inc Copyright renewed 1961 by Agatha Christie Mallowan THE BURDEN
Copyright © 1956 by Agatha Christie Mallowan Copyright renewed 1984 by Rosalind Hicks
All rights reserved Printed in the United States of America . For information, address
St Martin's Press, 175 Fifth Avenue, New York, N Y 10010

www.minotaurbooks.com

Library of Congress Cataloging-in-Publication Data

Westmacott, Mary, 1890–1976.
    A daughter's a daughter and other novels a Mary Westmacott omnibus / Agatha Christie writing as Mary
Westmacott.—1st ed
       p. cm.
                                ISBN: 978-0-312-27472-6

    1. Domestic fiction, English. 2 Mothers and daughter- Fiction   3 Women—England— Fiction
4. Sisters—Fiction   I Title

PR6005 H66 A6 2001b
832'.912—dc21

                                                                                      2001049011

CONTENTS

· A DAUGHTER'S A DAUGHTER ·

BOOK ONE

Chapter One

1

Ann Prentice stood on the platform at Victoria, waving.

The boat train drew out in a series of purposeful jerks, Sarah's dark head disappeared, and Ann Prentice turned to walk slowly down the platform toward the exit.

She experienced the strangely mixed sensations that seeing a loved one off may occasionally engender.

Darling Sarah—how she would miss her. . . . Of course it was only for three weeks. . . . But the flat would seem so empty. . . . Just herself and Edith—two dull middle-aged women. . . .

Sarah was so alive, so vital, so positive about everything. . . . And yet still such a darling black-haired baby—

How awful! What a way to think! How frightfully annoyed Sarah would be! The one thing that Sarah—and all the other girls of her age—seemed to insist upon was an attitude of casual indifference on the part of their parents. "No *fuss*, Mother," they said urgently.

They accepted, of course, tribute in kind. Taking their clothes to the cleaners and fetching them and usually paying for them. Difficult telephone calls. ("If *you* just ring Carol up, it will be so much *easier*, Mother.") Clearing up the incessant untidiness. ("Darling, I did mean to take away my messes. But I have simply got to *rush*.")

"Now when I was young," reflected Ann. . . .

Her thoughts went back. Hers had been an old-fashioned home. Her mother had been a woman of over forty when she was born, her father older still, fifteen or sixteen years older than her mother. The house had been run in the way her father liked.

Affection had not been taken for granted, it had been expressed on both sides.

"There's my dear little girl." "Father's pet!" "Is there anything I can get you, Mother darling?"

Tidying up the house, odd errands, tradesmen's books, invitations and social notes, all these Ann had attended to as a matter of course. Daughters existed to serve their parents—not the other way about.

As she passed near the bookstall, Ann asked herself suddenly, "Which was the best?"

Surprisingly enough, it didn't seem an easy question to answer.

Running her eyes along the publications on the bookstall (something to read this evening in front of the fire) she came to the unexpected decision that it didn't really matter. The whole thing was a convention, nothing more. Like using slang. At one period one said things were "topping," and then that they were "too divine," and then that they were "marvelous," and that one "couldn't agree with you more," and that you were "madly" fond of this that and the other.

Children waited on parents, or parents waited on children—it made no difference to the underlying vital relationship of person to person. Between Sarah and herself there was, Ann believed, a deep and genuine love. Between her and her own mother? Looking back she thought that under the surface fondness and affection there had been, actually, that casual and kindly indifference which it was the fashion to assume now-adays.

Smiling to herself, Ann bought a Penguin, a book that she remembered reading some years ago and enjoying. Perhaps it might seem a little sentimental now, but that wouldn't matter, as Sarah was not going to be there . . .

Ann thought: "I shall miss her—of course I shall miss her—but it will be rather *peaceful.* . . ."

And she thought: "It will be a rest for Edith, too. She gets upset when plans are always being changed and meals altered."

For Sarah and her friends were always in a flux of coming and going and ringing up and changing plans. "Mother darling, can we have a meal early? We want to go to a movie." "Is that you, Mother? I rang up to say I shan't be in to lunch after all."

To Edith, that faithful retainer of over twenty years' service, now doing three times the work she was once expected to undertake, such interruptions to normal life were very irritating.

Edith, in Sarah's phrase, often turned sour.

Not that Sarah couldn't get round Edith any time she liked. Edith might scold and grumble, but she adored Sarah.

It would be very quiet alone with Edith. Peaceful—but very quiet. . . . A queer cold feeling made Ann give a little shiver. . . . She thought: "Nothing but quietness now—" Quietness stretching forward vaguely down the slopes of old age into death. Nothing, anymore, to look forward to.

"But what do I want?" she asked herself. "I've had everything. Love and happiness with Patrick. A child. I've had all I wanted from life. Now—it's over. Now Sarah will go on where I leave off. She will marry, have children. I shall be a grandmother."

She smiled to herself. She would enjoy being a grandmother. She pictured handsome spirited children, Sarah's children. Naughty little boys with Sarah's unruly black hair, plump little girls. She would read to them—tell them stories . . .

She smiled at the prospect—but the cold feeling was still there. If only Patrick had lived. The old rebellious sorrow rose up. It was so long ago now—when Sarah was only three—so long ago that the loss and the agony were healed. She could think of Patrick gently, without a pang. The impetuous young husband that she had loved so much. So far away now—far away in the past.

But today rebellion rose up anew. If Patrick was still alive, Sarah would go from them—to Switzerland for winter sports, to a husband and a home in due course—and she and Patrick would be there together, older, quieter, but sharing life and its ups and downs together. She would not be alone . . .

Ann Prentice came out into the crowded life of the station yard. She thought to herself: "How sinister all those red buses look—drawn up in line like monsters waiting to be fed." They seemed fantastically to have a sentient life of their own—a life that was, perhaps, inimical to their maker, Man.

What a busy, noisy, crowded world it was, everyone coming and going, hurrying, rushing, talking, laughing, complaining, full of greetings and partings.

And suddenly, once again, she felt that cold pang—of aloneness.

She thought: "It's time Sarah went away—I'm getting too dependent on her. I'm making her, perhaps, too dependent on *me*. I mustn't do that. One mustn't hold on to the young—stop them leading their own lives. That would be wicked—really wicked . . ."

She must efface herself, keep well in the background, encourage Sarah to make her own plans—her own friends.

And then she smiled, because there was really no need to encourage Sarah at all. Sarah had quantities of friends and was always making plans, rushing about here and there with the utmost confidence and enjoyment. She adored her mother, but treated her with a kindly patronage, as one excluded from all understanding and participation, owing to her advanced years.

How old to Sarah seemed the age of forty-one—whilst to Ann it was quite a struggle to call herself in her own mind middle-aged. Not that she attempted to keep time at bay. She used hardly any makeup, and her clothes still had the faintly countrified air of a young matron come to town—neat coats and skirts and a small string of real pearls.

Ann sighed. "I can't think why I'm so silly," she said to herself aloud. "I suppose it's just seeing Sarah off."

What did the French say? *Partir, c'est mourrir un peu. . . .*

Yes, that was true. . . . Sarah, swept away by that important puffing train, was, for the moment, dead to her mother. And "I to her," thought Ann. "A curious thing—distance. Separation in space. . . ."

Sarah, living one life. She, Ann, living another. . . . A life of her own.

Some faintly pleasurable sensation replaced the inner chill of which she had previously been conscious. She could choose now when she would get up, what she should do—she could plan her day. She could go to bed early with a meal on a tray—or go out to a theater or a cinema. Or she could take a train into the country and wander about . . . walking through bare woods with the blue sky showing between the intricate sharp pattern of the branches. . . .

Of course, actually she could do all these things at any time she liked. But when two people lived together, there was a tendency for one life to set the pattern. Ann had enjoyed a good deal, at second hand, Sarah's vivid comings and goings.

No doubt about it, it was great fun being a mother. It was like having your own life over again—with a great deal of the agonies of youth left out. Since you knew now how little some things mattered, you could smile indulgently over the crises that arose.

"But really, Mother," Sarah would say intensely, "it's frightfully serious. You mustn't smile. Nadia feels that the whole of her future is at stake!"

But at forty-one, one had learned that one's whole future was very seldom at stake. Life was far more elastic and resilient than one had once chosen to think.

During her service with an ambulance during the war, Ann had realized for the first time how much the small things of life mattered. The small envies and jealousies, the small pleasures, the chafing of a collar, a chilblain inside a tight shoe—all these ranked as far more immediately important than the great fact that you might be killed at any moment. That should have been a solemn, an overwhelming thought, but actually one became used to it very quickly—and the small things asserted their sway—perhaps heightened in their insistence just because, in the background, was the idea of there being very little time. She had learned something, too, of the curious inconsistencies of human nature, of how difficult it was to assess people as "good" or "bad" as she had been inclined to do in her days of youthful dogmatism. She had seen unbelievable courage spent in rescuing a victim—and then that same individual who had risked his life would stoop to some mean petty theft from the rescued individual he had just saved.

People, in fact, were not all of a piece.

Standing irresolutely on the curb, the sharp hooting of a taxi recalled Ann from abstract speculations to more practical considerations. What should she do now, at this moment?

Getting Sarah off to Switzerland had been so far as her mind had looked that morning. That evening she was going out to dine with James Grant. Dear James, always so kind and thoughtful. "You'll feel a bit flat with Sarah gone. Come out and have a little celebration." Really, it was very sweet of James. All very well for Sarah to laugh and call James "Your *pukka Sahib* boyfriend, darling." James was a very dear person. Sometimes it might be a little difficult to keep one's attention fixed when he was telling one of his very long and rambling stories, but he enjoyed telling them so much, and after all if one had known someone for twenty-five years, to listen kindly was the least one could do.

Ann glanced at her watch. She might go to the Army and Navy Stores. There were some kitchen things Edith had been wanting. This decision solved her immediate problem. But all the time that she was examining saucepans and asking prices (really fantastic now!) she was conscious of that queer cold panic at the back of her mind.

Finally, on an impulse, she went into a telephone box and dialed a number.

"Can I speak to Dame Laura Whitstable, please?"

"Who is speaking?"

"Mrs. Prentice."

"Just a moment, Mrs. Prentice."

There was a pause and then a deep resonant voice said:

"Ann?"

"Oh, Laura, I knew I oughtn't to ring you up at this time of day, but I've just seen Sarah off, and I wondered if you were terribly busy today—"

The voice said with decision:

"Better lunch with me. Rye bread and buttermilk. That suit you?"

"Anything will suit me. It's angelic of you."

"Be expecting you. Quarter-past one."

2

It was one minute to the quarter-past when Ann paid off her taxi in Harley Street and rang the bell.

The competent Harkness opened the door, smiled a welcome, said:

"Go straight on up, will you, Mrs. Prentice? Dame Laura may be a few minutes still."

Ann ran lightly up the stairs. The dining room of the house was now a waiting room and the top floor of the tall house was converted into a comfortable flat. In the sitting room a small table was laid for a meal. The room itself was more like a man's room than a woman's. Large sagging comfortable chairs, a wealth of books, some of them piled on the chairs, and rich-colored good-quality velvet curtains.

Ann had not long to wait. Dame Laura, her voice preceding her up the stairs like a triumphant bassoon, entered the room and kissed her guest affectionately.

Dame Laura Whitstable was a woman of sixty-four. She carried with her the atmosphere that is exuded by royalty, or well-known public characters. Everything about her was a little more than life-size, her voice, her uncompromising shelf-like bust, the piled masses of her iron-gray hair, her beak-like nose.

"Delighted to see you, my dear child," she boomed. "You look very pretty, Ann. I see you've bought yourself a bunch of violets. Very discerning of you. It's the flower you most resemble."

"The shrinking violet? Really, Laura."

"Autumn sweetness, well concealed by leaves."

"This is most unlike you, Laura. You are usually so rude!"

"I find it pays, but it's rather an effort sometimes. Let us eat immediately. Bassett, where is Bassett? Ah, there you are. There is a sole for you, Ann, you will be glad to hear. And a glass of hock."

"Oh, Laura, you shouldn't. Buttermilk and rye bread would have done quite well."

"There's only just enough buttermilk for me. Come on, sit down. So Sarah's gone off to Switzerland? For how long?"

"Three weeks."

"Very nice."

The angular Bassett had left the room. Sipping her glass of buttermilk with every appearance of enjoyment, Dame Laura said shrewdly:

"And you're going to miss her. But you didn't ring me up and come here to tell me that. Come on, now, Ann. Tell me. We haven't got much time. I know you're fond of me, but when people ring up, and want my company at a moment's notice, it's usually my superior wisdom that's the attraction."

"I feel horribly guilty," said Ann apologetically.

"Nonsense, my dear. Actually, it's rather a compliment."

Ann said with a rush:

"Oh, Laura, I'm a complete fool, I know! But I got in a sort of *panic*. There in Victoria Station with all the buses! I felt—I felt so terribly *alone*."

"Ye-es, I see . . ."

"It wasn't just Sarah going away and missing her. It was more than that . . ."

Laura Whitstable nodded, her shrewd gray eyes watching Ann dispassionately.

Ann said slowly:

"Because, after all, one is always alone . . . really—"

"Ah, so you've found that out? One does, of course, sooner or later. Curiously enough, it's usually a shock. How old are you, Ann? Forty-one? A very good age to make your discovery. Leave it until too late and it can be devastating. Discover it too young—and it takes a lot of courage to acknowledge it."

"Have you ever felt really alone, Laura?" Ann asked with curiosity.

"Oh, yes. It came to me when I was twenty-six—actually in the middle of a family gathering of the most affectionate nature. It startled me and frightened me—but I accepted it. Never deny the truth. One must accept the fact that we have only one companion in this world, a companion who accompanies us from the cradle to the grave—our own self. Get on good terms with that companion—*learn to live with yourself*. That's the answer. It's not always easy."

Ann sighed.

"Life felt absolutely pointless—I'm telling you everything, Laura— just years stretching ahead with nothing to fill them. Oh, I suppose I'm just a silly useless woman . . ."

"Now, now, keep your common sense. You did a very good, efficient, unspectacular job in the war, you've brought up Sarah to have nice manners and to enjoy life, and in your quiet way you enjoy life yourself. That's all very satisfactory. In fact, if you came to my consulting room I'd send you away without even collecting a fee—and I'm a money-grubbing old woman."

"Laura dear, you are very comforting. But I suppose, really—I do care for Sarah too much."

"Fiddle!"

"I am always so afraid of becoming one of those possessive mothers who positively eat their young."

Laura Whitstable said dryly:

"There's so much talk about possessive mothers that some women are afraid to show a normal affection for their young!"

"But possessiveness *is* a bad thing!"

"Of course it is. I come across it every day. Mothers who keep their sons tied to their apron strings, fathers who monopolize their daughters. But it's not always entirely their doing. I had a nest of birds in my room once, Ann. In due course the fledglings left the nest, but there was one who wouldn't go. Wanted to stay in the nest, wanted to be fed, refused to face the ordeal of tumbling over the edge. It disturbed the mother bird very much. She showed him, flew down again and again from the edge of the nest, chirruped to him, fluttered her wings. Finally she wouldn't feed him. Brought food in her beak, but stayed on the other side of the room calling him. Well, there are human beings like that. Children who don't want to grow up, who don't want to face the difficulties of adult life. It isn't their upbringing. It's *themselves*."

She paused before going on.

"There's the wish to be possessed as well as the wish to possess. Is it a case of maturing late? Or is it some inherent lack of the adult quality? One knows very little still of the human personality."

"Anyway," said Ann, uninterested in generalities, "you don't think I'm a possessive mother?"

"I've always thought that you and Sarah had a very satisfactory relationship. I should say there was a deep natural love between you." She added thoughtfully: "Of course Sarah's young for her age."

"I've always thought she was old for her age."

"I shouldn't say so. She strikes me as younger than nineteen in mentality."

"But she's very positive, very assured. And quite sophisticated. Full of her own ideas."

"Full of the current ideas, you mean. It will be a very long time before she has any ideas that are *really* her own. And all these young creatures nowadays seem positive. They need reassurance, that's why. We live in an uncertain age and everything is unstable and the young feel it. That's where half the trouble starts nowadays. Lack of stability. Broken homes. Lack of moral standards. A young plant, you know, needs tying up to a good firm stake."

She grinned suddenly.

"Like all old women, even if I am a distinguished one, I preach." She drained her glass of buttermilk. "Do you know why I drink this?"

"Because it's healthy?"

"Bah! I like it. Always have since I went for holidays to a farm in the country. The other reason is so as to be different. One poses. We all pose. Have to. I do it more than most. But, thank God, I know I'm doing it. But now about you, Ann. There's nothing wrong with you. You're just getting your second wind, that's all."

"What do you mean by my second wind, Laura? You don't mean—" she hesitated.

"I don't mean anything physical. I'm talking in mental terms. Women are lucky, although ninety-nine out of a hundred don't know it. At what age did St. Theresa set out to reform the monasteries? At fifty. And I could quote you a score of other cases. From twenty to forty women are biologically absorbed—and rightly so. Their concern is with children, with husbands, with lovers—with personal relations. Or they sublimate these things and fling themselves into a career in a female emotional way. But the natural second blooming is of the mind and spirit and it takes place at middle age. Women take more interest in impersonal things as they grow older. Men's interests grow narrower, women's grow wider. A man of sixty is usually repeating himself like a gramophone record. A woman of sixty, if she's got any individuality at all—is an interesting person."

Ann thought of James Grant and smiled.

"Women stretch out to something new. Oh, they make fools of themselves too at that age. Sometimes they're sex bound. But middle age is an age of great possibilities."

"How comforting you are, Laura! Do you think I ought to take up something? Social work of some kind?"

"How much do you love your fellow beings?" said Laura Whitstable gravely. "The deed is no good without the inner fire. Don't do things you don't want to do, and then pat yourself on the back for doing them! Nothing, if I may say so, produces a more odious result. If you enjoy visiting the sick old women, or taking unattractive mannerless brats to the seaside by all means do it. Quite a lot of people do enjoy it. No, Ann, don't force yourself into activities. Remember all ground has sometimes to lie fallow. Motherhood has been your crop up to now. I don't see you becoming a reformer, or an artist, or an exponent of the Social Services. You're quite an ordinary woman, Ann, but a very nice one. Wait. Just wait quietly, with faith and hope, and you'll see. Something worthwhile will come to fill your life."

She hesitated and then said:

"You've never had an affair, have you?"

Ann flushed.

"No." She braced herself. "Do you—do you think I ought to?"

Dame Laura gave a terrific snort, a vast explosive sound that shook the glasses on the table.

"All this modern cant! In Victorian days we were afraid of sex, draped the legs of the furniture, even! Hid sex away, shoved it out of sight. All very bad. But nowadays we've gone to the opposite extreme. We treat sex like something you order from the chemist. It's on a par with sulphur drugs and penicillin. Young women come and ask me, 'Had I better take a lover?' 'Do you think I ought to have a child?' You'd think it was a sacred duty to go to bed with a man instead of a pleasure. You're not a passionate woman, Ann. You're a woman with a very deep store of affection and tenderness. That can include sex, but sex doesn't come first with you. If you ask me to prophesy, I'll say that in due course you'll marry again."

"Oh no. I don't believe I could ever do that."

"Why did you buy a bunch of violets today and pin them in your coat? You buy flowers for your rooms but you don't usually wear them. Those violets are a symbol, Ann. You bought them because, deep down, you feel spring—your second spring is near."

"St. Martin's summer, you mean," said Ann ruefully.

"Yes, if you like to call it that."

"But really, Laura, I daresay it's a very pretty idea, but I only bought these violets because the woman who was selling them looked so cold and miserable."

"That's what *you* think. But that's only the superficial reason. Look down to the real motive, Ann. Learn to *know* yourself. That's the most important thing in life—to try and know yourself. Heavens—it's past two. I must fly. What are you doing this evening?"

"I'm going out to dinner with James Grant."

"Colonel Grant? Yes, of course. A nice fellow." Her eyes twinkled. "He's been after you for a long time, Ann."

Ann Prentice laughed and blushed.

"Oh, it's just a habit."

"He's asked you to marry him several times, hasn't he?"

"Yes, but it's all nonsense really. Oh, Laura, do you think—perhaps—I ought to? If we're both lonely—"

"There's no *ought* about marriage, Ann! And the wrong companion is worse than none. Poor Colonel Grant—not that I pity him really. A man who continually asks a woman to marry him and can't make her change her mind, is a man who secretly enjoys devotion to lost causes. If he was at Dunkirk, he would have enjoyed it—but I daresay the Charge of the Light Brigade would have suited him far better! How fond we are in this country of our defeats and our blunders—and how ashamed we always seem to be of our victories!"

Chapter Two

1

Ann arrived back at her flat to be greeted by the faithful Edith in a somewhat cold fashion.

"A nice bit of plaice I had for your lunch," she said, appearing at the kitchen door. "*And* a caramel custard."

"I'm so sorry. I had lunch with Dame Laura. I did telephone you in time that I shouldn't be in, didn't I?"

"I hadn't cooked the plaice," admitted Edith grudgingly. She was a tall lean women with the upright carriage of a grenadier and a pursed-up disapproving mouth.

"It's not like you, though, to go chopping and changing. With Miss Sarah, now, I shouldn't have been surprised. I found those fancy gloves she was looking for after she'd gone and it was too late. Stuffed down behind the sofa they were."

"What a pity." Ann took the gaily knitted woolen gloves. "She got off all right."

"And happy to go, I suppose."

"Yes, the whole party was very gay."

"Mayn't come back quite so gay. Back on crutches as likely as not."

"Oh no, Edith, don't say that."

"Dangerous, these Swiss places. Fracture your arms or your legs and then not set proper. Goes to gangrene under the plaster and that's the end of you. Awful smell, too."

"Well, we'll hope that won't happen to Sarah," said Ann, well used to Edith's gloomy pronouncements which were always uttered with considerable relish.

"Won't seem like the same place without Miss Sarah about," said Edith. "We shan't know ourselves, we'll be so quiet."

"It will give you a bit of a rest, Edith."

"Rest?" said Edith indignantly. "What would I want with a rest?

Better wear out than rust out, that's what my mother used to say to me, and it's what I've always gone by. Now Miss Sarah's away and she and her friends won't be popping in and out every minute I can get down to a real good clean. This place needs it."

"I'm sure the flat's beautifully clean, Edith."

"That's what you think. But I know better. All the curtains want to be took down and well shook, and them lusters on the electrics could do with a wash—oh! there's a hundred and one things need doing."

Edith's eyes gleamed with pleasurable anticipation.

"Get someone in to help you."

"What, me? No fear. I like things done the proper way, and it's not many of these women you can trust to do that nowadays. You've got nice things here and nice things should be kept nice. What with cooking and one thing and another I can't get down to my proper work as I should."

"But you do cook beautifully, Edith. You know you do."

A faintly gratified smile transformed Edith's habitual expression of profound disapproval.

"Oh, cooking," she said in an offhand way. "There's nothing to *that*. It's not what I call proper work, not by a long way."

Moving back into the kitchen, she asked:

"What time will you have your tea?"

"Oh, not just yet. About half-past four."

"If I were you I'd put your feet up and take a nap. Then you'll be fresh for this evening. Might as well enjoy a bit of peace while you've got it."

Ann laughed. She went into the sitting room and let Edith settle her comfortably on the sofa.

"You look after me as though I were a little girl, Edith."

"Well, you weren't much more when I first came to your ma, and you haven't changed much. Colonel Grant rang up. Said not to forget it was the Mogador Restaurant at eight o'clock. She knows, I said to him. But that's men all over—fuss, fuss, fuss, and military gentlemen are the worst."

"It's nice of him to think I might be lonely tonight and ask me out."

Edith said judicially:

"I've nothing against the colonel. Fussy he may be, but he's the right kind of gentleman." She paused and added: "On the whole you might do a lot worse than Colonel Grant."

"What did you say, Edith?"

Edith returned an unblinking stare.

"I said as there were worse gentlemen . . . Oh well, I suppose we shan't be seeing so much of that Mr. Gerry now Miss Sarah's gone away."

"You don't like him, do you, Edith?"

"Well, I do and I don't, if you know what I mean. He's got a way with him—that you can't deny. But he's not the steady sort. My sister's Marlene married one like that. Never in a job more than six months, he isn't. And whatever happens it's never his fault."

Edith went out of the room and Ann leaned her head back against the cushions and shut her eyes.

The sound of the traffic came faint and muted through the closed window, a pleasant humming sound like far-off bees. On the table near her a bowl of yellow jonquils sent their sweetness into the air.

She felt peaceful and happy. She was going to miss Sarah, but it was rather restful to be by herself for a short time.

What a queer panic she had had this morning . . .

She wondered what James Grant's party would consist of this evening.

2

The Mogador was a small rather old-fashioned restaurant with good food and wine and an unhurried air about it.

Ann was the first of the party to arrive and found Colonel Grant sitting in the reception bar opening and shutting his watch.

"Ah, Ann," he sprang up to greet her. "Here you are." His eyes went with approval over her black dinner dress and the single string of pearls round her throat. "It's a great thing when a pretty woman can be punctual."

"I'm three minutes late, no more," said Ann, smiling up at him.

James Grant was a tall man with a stiff soldierly bearing, close-cropped gray hair and an obstinate chin.

He consulted his watch again.

"Now why can't these other people turn up? Our table will be ready for us at a quarter-past eight and we want some drinks first. Sherry for you? You prefer it to a cocktail, don't you?"

"Yes, please. Who are the others?"

"The Massinghams. You know them?"

"Of course."

"And Jennifer Graham. She's a first cousin of mine, but I don't know whether you ever—"

"I met her once with you, I think."

"And the other man is Richard Cauldfield. I only ran into him the other day. Hadn't seen him for years. He's spent most of his life in Burma. Feels a bit out of things coming back to this country."

"Yes, I suppose so."

"Nice fellow. Rather a sad story. Wife died having her first child. He was devoted to her. Couldn't get over it for a long time. Felt he had to get right away—that's why he went out to Burma."

"And the baby?"

"Oh, that died, too."

"How sad."

"Ah, here come the Massinghams."

Mrs. Massingham, always alluded to by Sarah as "the Mem Sahib" bore down upon them in a grand flashing of teeth. She was a lean stringy woman, her skin bleached and dried by years in India. Her husband was a short tubby man with a staccato style of conversation.

"How nice to see you again," said Mrs. Massingham, shaking Ann warmly by the hand. "And how delightful to be coming out to dinner properly dressed. Positively I never seem to wear an evening dress. Everyone always says, 'Don't change.' I do think life is drab nowadays, and the things one has to do oneself! I seem to be always at the sink! I really don't think we can stay in this country. We've been considering Kenya."

"Lot of people clearing out," said her husband. "Fed up. Blinking government."

"Ah, here's Jennifer," said Colonel Grant, "and Cauldfield."

Jennifer Graham was a tall horse-faced woman of thirty-five who whinnied when she laughed. Richard Cauldfield was a middle-aged man with a sunburned face.

He sat down by Ann and she began to make conversation.

Had he been in England long? What did he think of things?

It took a bit of getting used to, he said. Everything was so different from what it was before the war. He'd been looking for a job—but jobs weren't so easy to find, not for a man of his age.

"No, I believe that's true. It seems all wrong somehow."

"Yes, after all I'm still the right side of fifty." He smiled a rather childlike and disarming smile. "I've got a small amount of capital. I'm wondering about buying a small place in the country. Going in for market gardening. Or chickens."

"*Not* chickens!" said Ann. "I've several friends who have tried chickens—and they always seem to get diseases."

"No, perhaps market gardening would be better. One wouldn't make much of a profit, perhaps, but it would be a pleasant life."

He sighed.

"Things are so much in the melting pot. Perhaps if we get a change of government—"

Ann acquiesced doubtfully. It was the usual panacea.

"It must be difficult to know what exactly to go in for," she said. "Quite worrying."

"Oh, I don't worry. I don't believe in worry. If a man has faith in himself and proper determination, every difficulty will straighten itself out."

It was a dogmatic assertion and Ann looked doubtful.

"I wonder," she said.

"I can assure you that it is so. I've no patience with people who go about always whining about their bad luck."

"Oh, there I do agree," exclaimed Ann with such fervor that he raised his eyebrows questioningly.

"You sound as though you had experience of something of the kind."

"I have. One of my daughter's boyfriends is always coming and telling us of his latest misfortune. I used to be sympathetic, but now I've become both callous and bored."

Mrs. Massingham said across the table:

"Hard-luck stories *are* boring."

Colonel Grant said:

"Who are you talking of, young Gerald Lloyd? He'll never amount to much."

Richard Cauldfield said quietly to Ann:

"So you have a daughter? And a daughter old enough to have a boyfriend."

"Oh yes. Sarah is nineteen."

"And you're very fond of her?"

"Of course."

She saw a momentary expression of pain across his face and remembered the story Colonel Grant had told her.

Richard Cauldfield was, she thought, a lonely man.

He said in a low voice:

"You look too young to have a grown-up daughter. . . ."

"That's the regulation thing to say to a woman of my age," said Ann with a laugh.

"Perhaps. But I meant it. Your husband is—" he hesitated—"dead?"

"Yes, a long time ago."

"Why haven't you remarried?"

It might have been an impertinent question, but the real interest in his voice saved it from any false imputation of that kind. Again Ann felt that Richard Cauldfield was a simple person. He really wanted to know.

"Oh, because—" she stopped. Then she spoke truthfully and with sincerity. "I loved my husband very much. After he died I never fell in love with anyone else. And there was Sarah, of course."

"Yes," said Cauldfield. "Yes—with you that is exactly what it would be."

Grant got up and suggested that they move into the restaurant. At the round table Ann sat next to her host with Major Massingham on her other side. She had no further opportunity of a *tête-à-tête* with Cauldfield, who was talking rather ponderously with Miss Graham.

"Think they might do for each other, eh?" murmured the colonel in her ear. "He needs a wife, you know."

For some reason the suggestion displeased Ann. Jennifer Graham, indeed, with her loud hearty voice and her neighing laugh! Not at all the sort of woman for a man like Cauldfield to marry.

Oysters were brought and the party settled down to food and talk.

"Sarah gone off this morning?"

"Yes, James. I do hope they'll have some good snow."

"Yes, it's a bit doubtful this time of year. Anyway, I expect she'll enjoy herself all right. Handsome girl, Sarah. By the way, hope young Lloyd isn't one of the party?"

"Oh no, he's just gone into his uncle's firm. He can't go away."

"Good thing. You must nip all that in the bud, Ann."

"One can't do much nipping in these days, James."

"Hm, suppose not. Still, you've got her away for a while."

"Yes. I thought it would be a good plan."

"Oh, you did? You're no fool, Ann. Let's hope she takes up with some other young fellow out there."

"Sarah's very young still, James. I don't think the Gerry Lloyd business was serious at all."

"Perhaps not. But she seemed very concerned about him when last I saw her."

"Being concerned is rather a thing of Sarah's. She knows exactly what everyone ought to do and makes them do it. She's very loyal to her friends."

"She's a dear child. And a very attractive one. But she'll never be as attractive as you, Ann, she's a harder type—what do they call it nowadays—hard-boiled."

Ann smiled.

"I don't think Sarah's very hard-boiled. It's just the manner of her generation."

"Perhaps so. . . . But some of these girls could take a lesson in charm from their mothers."

He was looking at her affectionately and Ann thought to herself with a sudden unusual warmth: "Dear James. How sweet he is to me. He really does think me perfect. Am I a fool not to accept what he offers? To be loved and cherished—"

Unfortunately at that moment Colonel Grant started telling her the story of one of his subalterns and a major's wife in India. It was a long story and she had heard it three times before.

The affectionate warmth died down. Across the table she watched Richard Cauldfield, appraising him. A little too confident of himself, too dogmatic—no, she corrected herself, not really. . . . That was only a defensive armor he put up against a strange and possibly hostile world.

It was a sad face, really. A lonely face . . .

He had a lot of good qualities, she thought. He would be kind and honest and strictly fair. Obstinate, probably, and occasionally prejudiced. A man unused to laughing at things or being laughed at. The kind of man who would blossom out if he felt himself truly loved—

"—and would you believe it?" the colonel came to a triumphant end to his story "—the Sayce had known about it all the time!"

With a shock Ann came back to her immediate duties and laughed with all the proper appreciation.

Chapter Three

1

Ann woke on the following morning and for a moment wondered where she was. Surely, that dim outline of the window should have been on the right, not the left. . . . The door, the wardrobe . . .

Then she realized. She had been dreaming; dreaming that she was back, a girl, in her old home at Applestream. She had come there full of excitement, to be welcomed by her mother, by a younger Edith. She had run round the garden, exclaiming at this and that and had finally entered the house. All was as it had been, the rather dark hall, the chintz-covered drawing room opening off it. And then, surprisingly, her mother had said: "We're having tea in *here* today," and had led her through a further door into a new and unfamiliar room. An attractive room, with gay chintz covers, and flowers, and sunlight; and someone was saying to her: "*You never knew that these rooms were here, did you? We found them last year!*" There had been more new rooms and a small staircase and more rooms upstairs. It had all been very exciting and thrilling.

Now that she was awake she was still partly in the dream. She was Ann the girl, a creature standing at the beginning of life. Those undiscovered rooms! Fancy never knowing about them all these years! When had they been found? Lately? Or years ago?

Reality seeped slowly through the confused pleasurable dream state. All a dream, a very happy dream. Shot through now with a slight ache, the ache of nostalgia. Because one couldn't go back. And how odd that a dream of discovering additional ordinary rooms in a house should engender such a queer ecstatic pleasure. She felt quite sad to think that these rooms had never actually existed.

Ann lay in bed watching the outline of the window grow clearer. It must be quite late, nine o'clock at least. The mornings were so dark now. Sarah would be waking to sunshine and snow in Switzerland.

But somehow Sarah hardly seemed real at this moment. Sarah was far away, remote, indistinct. . . .

What was real was the house in Cumberland, the chintzes, the sunlight, the flowers—her mother. And Edith, standing respectfully to attention, looking, in spite of her young, smooth, unlined face, definitely disapproving as usual.

Ann smiled and called: "Edith!"

Edith entered and pulled the curtains back.

"Well," she said approvingly. "You've had a nice lay in. I wasn't going to wake you. It's not much of a day. Fog coming on, I'd say."

The outlook from the window was a heavy yellow. It was not an attractive prospect, but Ann's sense of well-being was not shaken. She lay there smiling to herself.

"Your breakfast's all ready. I'll fetch it in."

Edith paused as she left the room, looking curiously at her mistress.

"Looking pleased with yourself this morning, I must say. You must have enjoyed yourself last night."

"Last night?" Ann was vague for a moment. "Oh, yes, yes. I enjoyed myself very much. Edith, when I woke up I'd been dreaming I was at home again. You were there and it was summer and there were new rooms in the house that we'd never known about."

"Good job we didn't, I'd say," said Edith. "Quite enough rooms as it was. Great rambling old place. And that kitchen! When I think of what that range must have ate in coal! Lucky it was cheap then."

"You were quite young again, Edith, and so was I."

"Ah, we can't put the clock back, can we? Not for all we may want to. Those times are dead and gone for ever."

"Dead and gone for ever," repeated Ann softly.

"Not as I'm not quite satisfied as I am. I've got my health and strength, though they do say it's at middle life you're most liable to get one of these internal growths. I've thought of that once or twice lately."

"I'm sure you haven't got anything of the kind, Edith."

"Ah, but you don't know yourself. Not until the moment when they cart you off to hospital and cuts you up and by then it's usually too late." And Edith left the room with gloomy relish.

She returned a few minutes later with Ann's breakfast tray of coffee and toast.

"There you are, ma'am. Sit up and I'll tuck the pillow behind your back."

Ann looked up at her and said impulsively:

"How good you are to me, Edith."

Edith flushed a fiery red with embarrassment.

"I know the way things should be done, that's all. And anyway, someone's got to look after you. You're not one of these strong-minded ladies. That Dame Laura now—the Pope of Rome himself couldn't stand up to her."

"Dame Laura is a great personality, Edith."

"I know. I've heard her on the radio. Why, just by the look of her you'd always know she was somebody. Managed to get married too, by what I've heard. Was it divorce or death that parted them?"

"Oh, he died."

"Best thing for him, I daresay. She's not the kind any gentleman would find it comfortable to live with—although I won't deny as there's *some* men as actually prefer their wives to wear the trousers."

Edith moved toward the door, observing as she did so:

"Now don't you hurry up, my dear. You just have a nice rest and lay-a-bed and think your pretty thoughts and enjoy your holiday."

"Holiday," thought Ann, amused. "Is that what she calls it?"

And yet in a way it was true enough. It was an interregnum in the patterned fabric of her life. Living with a child that you loved, there was always a faint clawing anxiety at the back of your mind. "Is she happy?" "Are A. or B. or C. good friends for her?" "Something must have gone wrong at that dance last night. I wonder what it was?"

She had never interfered or asked questions. Sarah, she realized, must feel free to be silent or to talk—must learn her own lessons from life, must choose her own friends. Yet, because you loved her, you could not banish her problems from your mind. And at any moment you might be needed. If Sarah were to turn to her mother for sympathy or for practical help, her mother must be there, ready. . . .

Sometimes Ann had said to herself: "I must be prepared one day to see Sarah unhappy, and even then I must not speak unless she wants me too."

The thing that had worried her lately was that bitter and querulous young man, Gerald Lloyd, and Sarah's increasing absorption in him. That fact lay at the back of her relief that Sarah was separated from him for at least three weeks and would be meeting plenty of other young men.

Yes, with Sarah in Switzerland, she could dismiss her happily from her mind and relax. Relax here in her comfortable bed and think about what she should do today. She'd enjoyed herself very much at the party last night. Dear James—so kind—and yet such a bore, too, poor darling! Those endless stories of his! Really, men, when they got to forty-five, should make a vow not to tell any stories or anecdotes at all. Did they even imagine how their friends' spirits sank when they began: "Don't know whether I ever told you, but rather a curious thing happened once to—" and so on.

One could say, of course: "Yes, James, you've told me three times already." And then the poor darling would look so hurt. No, one couldn't do that to James.

That other man, Richard Cauldfield. He was much younger, of course, but probably *he* would take to repeating long boring stories over and over again one day. . . .

She considered . . . perhaps . . . but she didn't think so. No, he was more likely to lay down the law, to become didactic. He would have prejudices, preconceived ideas. He would have to be teased. . . . He might be a little absurd sometimes, but he was a dear really—a lonely man—a very lonely man. . . . She felt sorry for him. He was so adrift in this modern frustrated life of London. She wondered what sort of job he would get. . . . It wasn't so easy nowadays. He would probably buy his farm or his market garden and settle down in the country.

She wondered whether she would meet him again. She would be asking James to dinner one evening soon. She might suggest he bring Richard Cauldfield with him. It would be a nice thing to do—he was clearly lonely. And she would ask another woman. They might go to a play—

What a noise Edith was making. She was in the sitting room next door and it sounded as though there were an army of removal men at work. Bangs, bumps, the occasional high whine of the vacuum cleaner. Edith must be enjoying herself.

Presently Edith peeped round the door. Her head was tied up in a duster and she wore the exalted rapt look of a priestess performing a ritual orgy.

"You wouldn't be out to lunch, I suppose? I was wrong about the fog. It's going to be a proper nice day. I don't mean as I've forgotten that bit of plaice. I haven't. But if it's kept till now, it'll keep till this evening. No denying, these fridges do keep things—but it takes the goodness out of them all the same. That's what I say."

Ann looked at Edith and laughed.

"All right, all right, I'll go out to lunch."

"Please yourself, of course. *I* don't mind."

"Yes, Edith, but don't kill yourself. Why not get Mrs. Hopper in to help you, if you must clean the place from top to toe."

"Mrs. Hopper, Mrs. Hopper! I'll Hopper her! I let her clean that nice brass fender of your ma's last time she came. Left it all smeary. Wash down the linoleum, that's all these women are good for, and anybody can do that. Remember that cut-steel fender and grate we had at Applestream? *That* took a bit of keeping. I took a pride in that, I can tell you. Ah well, you've some nice pieces of furniture here and they polish up something beautiful. Pity there's so much built-in stuff."

"It makes less work."

"Too much like a hotel for my liking. So you'll be going out? Good. I can get all the rugs up."

"Can I come here tonight? Or would you like me to go to a hotel?"

"Now then, Miss Ann, none of your jokes. By the way, that double saucepan you brought home from the Stores isn't a mite of good. It's too big for one thing and it's a bad shape for stirring inside. I want one like my old one."

"I'm afraid they don't make them anymore, Edith."

"This government," said Edith in disgust. "What about those china soufflé dishes I asked about? Miss Sarah likes a soufflé served that way."

"I forgot you'd asked me to get them. I daresay I could find some of them all right."

"There you are, then. That's something for you to do."

"Really, Edith," cried Ann, exasperated. "I might be a little girl you're telling to go out and have a nice bowl of her hoop."

"Miss Sarah being away makes you seem younger, I must admit. But I was only suggesting, ma'am—" Edith drew herself up to her full height and spoke with sour primness "—if you should happen to be in the neighborhood of the Army and Navy Stores, or maybe John Barker's—"

"All right, Edith. Go and bowl your own hoop in the sitting room."

"Well, really," said Edith, outraged, and withdrew.

The bangs and bumps recommenced and presently another sound was added to them, the thin tuneless sound of Edith's voice upraised in a particularly gloomy hymn tune:

> "This is a land of pain and woe
> No joy, no sun, no light.

Oh lave, Oh lave us in Thy blood
That we may mourn aright."

2

Ann enjoyed herself in the china department of the Army and Navy
Stores. She thought that nowadays when so many things were shoddily
and badly made, it was a relief to see what good china and glass and
pottery this country could turn out still.

The forbidding notices "For Export Only" did not spoil her appreciation of the wares displayed in their shining rows. She passed on
to the tables displaying the export rejects where there were always
women shoppers hovering with keen glances to pounce on some attractive piece.

Today, Ann herself was fortunate. There was actually a nearly complete breakfast set, with nice wide round cups in an agreeable brown
glazed and patterned pottery. The price was not unreasonable and she
purchased it just in time. Another woman came along just as the address
was being taken and said excitedly: "I'll have that."

"Sorry, madam, I'm afraid it's sold."

Ann said insincerely: "I'm so sorry," and walked away buoyed up
with the delight of successful achievement. She had also found some
very pleasant soufflé dishes of the right size, but in glass, not china,
which she hoped Edith would accept without grumbling too much.

From the china department she went across the street into the gardening department. The window box outside the flat window was crumbling into disintegration and she wanted to order another.

She was talking to the salesman about it when a voice behind her
said:

"Why, good morning, Mrs. Prentice."

She turned to find Richard Cauldfield. His pleasure at their meeting
was so evident that Ann could not help feeling flattered.

"Fancy meeting you here like this. It really is a wonderful coinci-
dence. I was just thinking about you as a matter of fact. You know,
last night, I wanted to ask you where you lived and if I might, perhaps,
come and see you? But then I thought that perhaps you would think it

was rather an impertinence on my part. You must have so many friends, and—"

Ann interrupted him.

"Of course you must come and see me. Actually I was thinking of asking Colonel Grant to dinner and suggesting that he might bring you with him."

"Were you? Were you really?"

His eagerness and pleasure were so evident that Ann felt a pang of sympathy. Poor man, he must be lonely. That happy smile of his was really quite boyish.

She said: "I've been ordering myself a new window box. That's the nearest we can get in a flat to having a garden."

"Yes, I suppose so."

"What are you doing here?"

"I've been looking at incubators—"

"Still hankering after chickens."

"In a way. I've been looking at all the latest poultry equipment. I understand this electrical stunt is the latest thing."

They moved together toward the exit. Richard Cauldfield said in a sudden rush:

"I wonder—of course perhaps you're engaged—whether you'd care to lunch with me—that is if you're not doing anything else."

"Thank you. I'd like to very much. As a matter of fact Edith, my maid, is indulging in an orgy of spring cleaning and has told me very firmly not to come home to lunch."

Richard Cauldfield looked rather shocked and not at all amused.

"That's very arbitrary, isn't it?"

"Edith is privileged."

"All the same, you know, it doesn't do to spoil servants."

He's reproving me, thought Ann with amusement. She said gently:

"There aren't many servants about to spoil. And anyway Edith is more a friend than a servant. She has been with me a great many years."

"Oh, I see." He felt he had been gently rebuked, yet his impression remained. This gentle pretty woman was being bullied by some tyrannical domestic. She wasn't the kind of woman who could stand up for herself. Too sweet and yielding a nature.

He said vaguely: "Spring cleaning? Is this the time of year one does it?"

"Not really. It should be done in March. But my daughter is away for some weeks in Switzerland, so it makes an opportunity. When she's at home there is too much going on."

"You miss her, I expect?"

"Yes, I do."

"Girls don't seem to like staying at home much nowadays. I suppose they're keen on living their own lives."

"Not quite as much as they were, I think. The novelty has rather worn off."

"Oh. It's a very nice day, isn't it? Would you like to walk across the park, or would it tire you?"

"No, of course it wouldn't. I was just going to suggest it to you."

They crossed Victoria Street and went down a narrow passageway, coming out finally by St. James's Park station. Cauldfield looked up at the Epstein statues.

"Can you see anything whatever in those? How can one call things like that *Art?*"

"Oh, I think one can. Very definitely so."

"Surely you don't *like* them?"

"I don't personally, no. I'm old-fashioned and continue to like classical sculpture and the things I was brought up to like. But that doesn't mean that my taste is right. I think one has to be educated to appreciate new forms of art. The same with music."

"Music! You can't call it music."

"Mr. Cauldfield, don't you think you're being rather narrow-minded?"

He turned his head sharply to look at her. She was flushed, a trifle nervous, but her eyes met his squarely and did not flinch.

"Am I? Perhaps I am. Yes, I suppose when you've been away a long time, you tend to come home and object to everything that isn't strictly as you remember it." He smiled suddenly. "You must take me in hand."

Ann said quickly: "Oh, I'm terribly old-fashioned myself. Sarah often laughs at me. But what I do feel is that it is a terrible pity to—to—how shall I put it?—close one's mind just as one is getting—well, getting old.

For one thing, it's going to make one so tiresome—and then, also, one may be missing something that matters."

Richard walked in silence for some moments. Then he said:

"It sounds so absurd to hear you talk of yourself as getting old. You're the youngest person I've met for a long time. Much younger than some of these alarming girls. They really do frighten me."

"Yes, they frighten me a little. But I always find them very kind."

They had reached St. James's Park. The sun was fully out now and the day was almost warm.

"Where shall we go?"

"Let's go and look at the pelicans."

They watched the birds with contentment, and talked about the various species of water fowl. Completely relaxed and at ease, Richard was boyish and natural, a charming companion. They chatted and laughed together and were astonishingly happy in each other's company.

Presently Richard said: "Shall we sit down for a while in the sun? You won't be cold, will you?"

"No, I'm quite warm."

They sat on two chairs and looked out over the water. The scene with its rarefied coloring was like a Japanese print.

Ann said softly: "How beautiful London can be. One doesn't always realize it."

"No. It's almost a revelation."

They sat quietly for a minute or two, then Richard said:

"My wife always used to say that London was the only place to be when spring came. She said the green buds and the almond trees and in time the lilacs all had more significance against a background of bricks and mortar. She said in the country it all happened confusedly and it was too big to see properly. But in a suburban garden spring came overnight."

"I think she was right."

Richard said with an effort, and not looking at Ann:

"She died—a long time ago."

"I know. Colonel Grant told me."

Richard turned and looked at her.

"Did he tell you how she died?"

"Yes."

"That's something I shall never get over. I shall always feel that I killed her."

Ann hesitated a moment, then spoke:

"I can understand what you feel. In your place I should feel as you do. But it isn't true, you know."

"It is true."

"No. Not from her—from a woman's point of view. The responsibility of accepting that risk is the woman's. It's implicit in—in her love. She wants the child, remember. Your wife did—want the child?"

"Oh yes. Aline was very happy about it. So was I. She was a strong healthy girl. There seemed no reason why anything should go wrong."

There was silence again.

Then Ann said: "I'm sorry—so very sorry."

"It's a long time ago now."

"The baby died too?"

"Yes. In a way, you know, I'm glad of that. I should, I feel, have resented the poor little thing. I should always have remembered the price that was paid for its life."

"Tell me about your wife."

Sitting there, in the pale wintry sunlight, he told her about Aline. How pretty she had been and how gay. And the sudden quiet moods she had had when he had wondered what she was thinking about and why she had gone so far away.

Once he broke off to say wonderingly: "I have not spoken about her to anyone for years," and Ann said gently: "Go on."

It had all been so short—too short. A three months' engagement, their marriage—"the usual fuss, we didn't really want it all, but her mother insisted." They had spent their honeymoon motoring in France, seeing the châteaux of the Loire.

He said inconsequentially: "She was nervous in a car, you know. She'd keep her hand on my knee. It seemed to give her confidence, I don't know why she was nervous. She'd never been in an accident." He paused and then went on: "Sometimes, after it had all happened, I used to feel her hand sometimes when I was driving out in Burma. Imagine it, you know. . . . It seemed incredible that she should go right away like that—right out of life. . . ."

Yes, thought Ann, that is what it feels like—incredible. So she had felt about Patrick. He *must* be somewhere. He *must* be able to make her feel his presence. He couldn't go out like that and leave nothing behind. That terrible gulf between the dead and the living!

Richard was going on. Telling her about the little house they had found in a cul-de-sac, with a lilac bush and a pear tree.

Then, when his voice, brusque and hard, came to the end of the halting phrases, he said again wonderingly: "I don't know why I have told you all this. . . ."

But he did know. When he had asked Ann rather nervously if it would be all right to lunch at his club—"they have a kind of Ladies' Annexe, I believe—or would you rather go to a restaurant?"—and when she had said that she would prefer the club, and they had got up and begun to walk toward Pall Mall, the knowledge was in his mind, though not willingly recognized by him.

This was his farewell to Aline, here in the cold unearthly beauty of the park in winter.

He would leave her here, beside the lake, with the bare branches of the trees showing their tracery against the sky.

For the last time, he brought her to life in her youth and her strength and the sadness of her fate. It was a lament, a dirge, a hymn of praise—a little perhaps of all of them.

But it was also a burial.

He left Aline there in the park and walked out into the streets of London with Ann.

Chapter Four

"Mrs. Prentice in?" asked Dame Laura Whitstable.

"Not just at present she isn't. But I should fancy she mayn't be long. Would you like to come in and wait, ma'am? I know she'd want to see you."

Edith drew aside respectfully as Dame Laura came in.

The latter said:

"I'll wait for a quarter of an hour, anyway. It's some time since I've seen anything of her."

"Yes, ma'am."

Edith ushered her into the sitting room and knelt down to turn on the electric fire. Dame Laura looked round the room and uttered an exclamation.

"Furniture been shifted round, I see. That desk used to be across the corner. And the sofa's in a different place."

"Mrs. Prentice thought it would be nice to have a change," said Edith. "Come in one day, I did, and there she was shoving things round and hauling them about. 'Oh, Edith,' she says, 'don't you think the room looks much nicer like this? It makes more space.' Well, I couldn't see any improvement myself, but naturally I didn't like to say so. Ladies have their fancies. All I said was: 'Now don't you go and strain yourself, ma'am. Lifting and heaving's the worst thing for your innards and once they've slipped out of place they don't go back so easy.' I should know. It happened to my own sister-in-law. Did it throwing up the window sash, she did. On the sofa for the rest of her days, she was."

"Probably quite unnecessary," said Dame Laura robustly. "Thank goodness we've got out of the affectation that lying on a sofa is the panacea for every ill."

"Don't even let you have your month after childbirth now," said Edith disapprovingly. "My poor young niece, now, they made her walk about on the fifth day."

"We're a much healthier race now than we've ever been before."

"I hope so, I'm sure," said Edith gloomily. "Terribly delicate I was as a child. Never thought they'd rear me. Fainting fits I used to have, and spasms something awful. And in winter I'd go quite blue—the cold used to fly to me 'art."

Uninterested in Edith's past ailments, Dame Laura was surveying the rearranged room.

"I think it's a change for the better," she said. "Mrs. Prentice is quite right. I wonder she didn't do it before."

"Nest-building," said Edith, with significance.

"What?"

"Nest-building. I've seen birds at it. Running about with twigs in their mouths."

"Oh."

The two women looked at each other. Without any change of expression, some intelligence appeared to be imparted. Dame Laura asked in an offhand way:

"Seen much of Colonel Grant lately?"

Edith shook her head.

"Poor gentleman," she said. "If you were to ask me, I'd say he's had his conger. French for your nose being put out of joint," she added in an explanatory fashion.

"Oh, congé—yes, I see."

"He was a nice gentleman," said Edith, putting him in the past tense in a funereal manner and as though pronouncing an epitaph. "Oh, well!"

As she left the room, she said: "I'll tell you one who won't like the room being rearranged, and that's Miss Sarah. She don't like changes."

Laura Whitstable raised her beetling eyebrows. Then she pulled a book from a shelf and turned its pages in a desultory manner.

Presently she heard a latchkey inserted and the door of the flat opened. Two voices, Ann's and a man's, sounded cheerful and gay in the small vestibule.

Ann's voice said: "Oh, post. Ah, here's a letter from Sarah."

She came into the sitting room with the letter in her hand and stopped short in momentary confusion.

"Why, Laura, how nice to see you." She turned to the man who had followed her into the room. "Mr. Cauldfield, Dame Laura Whitstable."

Dame Laura summed him up quickly.

Conventional type. Could be obstinate. Honest. Good-hearted. No humor. Probably sensitive. Very much in love with Ann.

She began talking to him in her bluff fashion.

Ann murmured: "I'll tell Edith to bring us tea," and left the room.

"Not for me, my dear," Dame Laura called after her. "It's nearly six o'clock."

"Well, Richard and I want tea, we've been to a concert. What will you have?"

"Brandy and soda."

"All right."

Dame Laura said:

"Fond of music, Mr. Cauldfield?"

"Yes. Particularly of Beethoven."

"All English people like Beethoven. Sends me to sleep, I'm sorry to say, but then I'm not particularly musical."

"Cigarette, Dame Laura?" Cauldfield proffered his case.

"No, thanks, I only smoke cigars."

She added, looking shrewdly at him: "So you're the type of man who prefers tea to cocktails or sherry at six o'clock?"

"No, I don't think so. I'm not particularly fond of tea. But somehow it seems to suit Ann—" he broke off. "That sounds absurd!"

"Not at all. You display perspicacity. I don't mean that Ann doesn't drink cocktails or sherry, she does, but she's essentially the type of woman who looks her best sitting behind a tea tray—a tea tray on which is beautiful old Georgian silver and cups and saucers of fine porcelain."

Richard was delighted.

"How absolutely right you are!"

"I've known Ann for a great many years. I'm very fond of her."

"I know. She has often spoken about you. And, of course, I know of you from other sources."

Dame Laura gave him a cheerful grin.

"Oh yes, I'm one of the best-known women in England. Always

sitting on committees, or airing my views on the wireless, or laying down the law generally on what's good for humanity. However, I do realize one thing and that is that whatever one accomplishes in life, it is really very little and could always quite easily have been accomplished by somebody else."

"Oh, come now," Richard protested. "Surely that's a very depressing conclusion to come to?"

"It shouldn't be. Humility should always lie behind effort."

"I don't think I agree with you."

"Don't you?"

"No. I think that if a man (or woman, of course) is ever to accomplish anything worth doing, the first condition is that he must believe in himself."

"Why should he?"

"Come now, Dame Laura, surely—"

"I'm old-fashioned. I would prefer that a man should have *knowledge* of himself and *belief* in God."

"Knowledge—belief, aren't they the same thing?"

"I beg your pardon, they're not at all the same thing. One of my pet theories (quite unrealizable, of course, that's the pleasant part about theories) is that everybody should spend one month a year in the middle of a desert. Camped by a well, of course, and plentifully supplied with dates or whatever you eat in deserts."

"Might be quite pleasant," said Richard, smiling. "I'd stipulate for a few of the world's best books, though."

"Ah, but that's just it. No books. Books are a habit-forming drug. With enough to eat and drink, and nothing—absolutely *nothing*—to do, you'd have, at last, a fairly good chance to make acquaintance with yourself."

Richard smiled disbelievingly.

"Don't you think most of us know ourselves pretty well?"

"I certainly do *not*. One hasn't time, in these days, to recognize anything except one's more pleasing characteristics."

"Now what are you two arguing about?" asked Ann coming in with a glass in her hand. "Here's your brandy and soda, Laura. Edith's just bringing tea."

"I'm propounding my desert meditation theory," said Laura.

"That's one of Laura's things," said Ann laughing. "You sit in a desert and do nothing and find out how horrible you really are!"

"Must everyone be horrible?" asked Richard dryly. "I know psychologists tell one so—but really—why?"

"Because if one only has time to know part of oneself one will, as I said just now, select the pleasantest part," said Dame Laura promptly.

"It's all very well, Laura," said Ann, "but after one has sat in one's desert and found out how horrible one is, what good will it do? Will one be able to change oneself?"

"I should think that would be most unlikely—but it does at least give one a guide as to what one is likely to do in certain circumstances, and even more important, *why* one does it?"

"But isn't one able to imagine quite well what one is likely to do in given circumstances? I mean, you've only got to imagine yourself there?"

"Oh Ann, Ann! Think of any man who rehearses in his own mind what he is going to say to his boss, to his girl, to his neighbor across the way. He's got it all cut and dried—and then, when the moment comes, he is either tongue-tied or says something entirely different! The people who are secretly quite sure they can rise to any emergency are the ones who lose their heads completely, while those who are afraid they will be inadequate surprise themselves by taking complete grasp of a situation."

"Yes, but that's not quite fair. What you're meaning now is that people rehearse imaginary conversations and actions *as they would like them to be*. They probably know quite well it wouldn't really happen. But I think fundamentally one *does* know quite well what one's reactions are and what—well what one's character is like."

"Oh, my dear child." Dame Laura held up her hands. "So you think you know Ann Prentice—I wonder."

Edith came in with the tea.

"I don't think I'm particularly nice," said Ann smiling.

"Here's Miss Sarah's letter, ma'am," said Edith. "You left it in your bedroom."

"Oh, thank you, Edith."

Ann laid down the still unopened letter by her plate. Dame Laura flashed a quick look at her.

Richard Cauldfield drank his cup of tea rather quickly and then excused himself.

"He's being tactful," said Ann. "He thinks we want to talk together."

Dame Laura looked at her friend attentively. She was quite surprised at the change in Ann. Ann's quiet good looks had bloomed into a kind of beauty. Laura Whitstable had seen that happen before, and she knew the cause. That radiance, that happy look, could have only one meaning: Ann was in love. How unfair it was, reflected Dame Laura, that women in love looked their best and men in love looked like depressed sheep.

"What have you been doing with yourself lately, Ann?" she asked.

"Oh, I don't know. Going about. Nothing much."

"Richard Cauldfield is a new friend, isn't he?"

"Yes. I've only known him about ten days. I met him at James Grant's dinner."

She told Dame Laura something about Richard, ending up by asking naively, "You do like him, don't you?"

Laura, who had not yet made up her mind whether she liked Richard Cauldfield or not, was prompt to reply:

"Yes, very much."

"I do feel, you know, that he's had a sad life."

Dame Laura had heard the statement made very often. She suppressed a smile and asked: "What news of Sarah?"

Ann's face lit up.

"Oh, Sarah's been enjoying herself madly. They've had perfect snow, and nobody seems to have broken anything."

Dame Laura said dryly that Edith would be disappointed. They both laughed.

"This letter is from Sarah. Do you mind if I open it?"

"Of course not."

Ann tore open the envelope and read the short letter. Then laughed affectionately and passed the letter to Dame Laura.

Darling Mother, (Sarah had written.)

Snow's been perfect. Everyone's saying it's been the best season ever. Lou took her test but didn't pass unfortunately. Roger's been coaching me a lot—terribly nice of him because he's such a big pot in the skiing world. Jane says he's got a thing about me, but I don't really think so. I think it's sadistic pleasure at seeing me tie myself into knots and land on my head in snowdrifts. Lady Cronsham's here with that awful S. American man. They really are *blatant*. I've got rather a crush on one of the guides—unbelievably handsome—but unfortunately he's used to everyone having crushes on him and I cut no ice at all. At last I've learned to waltz on the ice.

How are you getting on, darling? I hope you're going out a good deal with all the boyfriends. Don't go too far with the old colonel, he has quite a gay Poona sparkle in his eye sometimes! How's the professor? Has he been telling you any nice rude marriage customs lately? See you soon, Love, Sarah.

Dame Laura handed back the letter.

"Yes, Sarah seems to be enjoying herself. . . . I suppose the professor is that archaeological friend of yours?"

"Yes, Sarah always teases me about him. I really meant to ask him to lunch, but I've been so busy."

"Yes, you do seem to have been busy."

Ann was folding and refolding Sarah's letter. She said with a half sigh: "Oh dear."

"Why the Oh dear, Ann?"

"Oh, I suppose I might as well tell you. Anyway you've probably guessed. Richard Cauldfield has asked me to marry him."

"When was this?"

"Oh, only today."

"And you're going to?"

"I think so. . . . Why do I say that? Of course I am."

"Quick work, Ann!"

"You mean I haven't known him long enough? Oh, but we're both quite sure."

"And you do know a good deal about him—through Colonel Grant. I'm very glad for you, my dear. You look very happy."

"I suppose it sounds very silly to you, Laura, but I do love him very much."

"Why should it sound silly? Yes, one can see that you love him."

"And he loves me."

"That also is apparent. Never have I seen a man look so exactly like a sheep!"

"Richard doesn't look like a sheep!"

"A man in love *always* looks like a sheep. It seems to be some law of nature."

"But you do like him, Laura?" Ann persisted.

This time Laura Whitstable did not answer so quickly. She said slowly:

"He's a very simple type of man, you know, Ann."

"Simple? Perhaps. But isn't that rather nice?"

"Well, it may have its difficulties. And he's sensitive, ultra-sensitive."

"It's clever of you to see that, Laura. Some people wouldn't."

"I'm not 'some people.' " She hesitated a moment and then said: "Have you told Sarah yet?"

"No, of course not. I told you. It only happened today."

"What I really meant was have you mentioned him in your letters—paved the way, so to speak?"

"No—no, not really." She paused before adding: "I shall have to write and tell her."

"Yes."

Again Ann hesitated before saying: "I don't think Sarah will mind very much, do you?"

"Difficult to say."

"She's always so very sweet to me. Nobody knows how sweet Sarah can be—without, I mean, ever saying anything. Of course—I suppose—" Ann looked pleadingly at her friend. "She may think it *funny*."

"Quite likely. Do you mind?"

"Oh, *I* don't mind. But Richard will."

"Yes—yes. Well, Richard will have to lump it, won't he? But I should certainly let Sarah know about it all before she comes back. It will give her a little time to get used to the idea. When are you thinking of getting married, by the way?"

"Richard wants us to get married as soon as possible. And there really isn't anything to wait for, is there?"

"Nothing at all. The sooner you get married the better, I should say."

"It's really rather fortunate—Richard's just got a job—with Hellner Bros. He knew one of the junior partners in Burma during the war. It's lucky, isn't it?"

"My dear, everything seems turning out very well." She said again gently: "I'm very glad for you."

Getting up, Laura Whitstable went over to Ann and kissed her.

"Now then—why the puckered brow?"

"It's just Sarah—hoping she won't mind."

"My dear Ann, whose life are you living, yours or Sarah's?"

"Mine, of course, but—"

"If Sarah minds, she minds! She'll get over it. She loves you, Ann."

"Oh, I know."

"It's very inconvenient to be loved. Nearly everyone has found that out, sooner or later. The fewer people who love you the less you will have to suffer. How fortunate it is for me that most people dislike me heartily, and the rest only feel a cheerful indifference."

"Laura, that's not true. I—"

"Good-bye, Ann. And don't force your Richard to say that he likes me. Actually he took a violent dislike to me. It's not of the least consequence."

That night, at a public dinner, the learned man sitting next to Dame Laura was chagrined at the end of his exposition of a revolutionary innovation in shock therapy to find her fixing him with a blank stare.

"You've not been listening," he exclaimed reproachfully.

"Sorry, David. I was thinking of a mother and daughter."

"Ah, a Case." He looked expectant.

"No, not a case. Friends."

"One of these possessive mothers, I suppose?"

"No," said Dame Laura. "In this case it's a possessive daughter."

Chapter Five

1

"Well, Ann, my dear," said Geoffrey Fane. "I'm sure I congratulate you—or whatever one says on these occasions. Er—h'm. He's, if I may say so, a very lucky fellow—yes, a very lucky fellow. I've never met him, have I? I don't seem to recall the name."

"No, I only met him a few weeks ago."

Professor Fane peered at her mildly over the top of his glasses as was his habit.

"Dear me," he said disapprovingly. "Isn't this all rather sudden? Rather impetuous?"

"No, I don't think so."

"Among the Matawayala, there is a courtship period of a year and a half at least—"

"They must be a very cautious people. I thought savages obeyed primitive impulses."

"The Matawayala are very far from being savages," said Geoffrey Fane in a shocked voice. "Theirs is a very distinctive culture. Their marriage rites are curiously complicated. On the eve of the ceremony the bride's friends—er hum—well, perhaps better not to go into that. But it's really very interesting and seems to suggest that at one time the sacred ritual marriage of the Chief Priestess—no, I really must not run on. A wedding present now. What would you like as a wedding present, Ann?"

"You really don't need to give me a wedding present, Geoffrey."

"A piece of silver, usually, is it not? I seem to remember purchasing a silver mug—no, no, that was for a christening—spoons, perhaps? Or a toast rack? Ah, I have it, a rose bowl. But, Ann, my dear, you do know something *about* the fellow? I mean, he's vouched for—mutual friends, all that? Because one does read of such extraordinary things."

"He didn't pick me up on the pier, and I haven't insured my life in his favor."

Geoffrey Fane peered at her again anxiously and was relieved to find that she was laughing.

"That's all right, that's all right. Afraid you were annoyed with me. But one has to be careful. And how does the little girl take it?"

Ann's face clouded over for a moment.

"I wrote to Sarah—she's in Switzerland, you know—but I haven't had any answer. Of course, there's really been only just time for her to write, but I rather expected—" she broke off.

"Difficult to remember to answer letters. I find it increasingly so. Was asked to give a series of lectures in Oslo in March. Meant to answer it. Forgot all about it. Only found the letter yesterday—pocket of an old coat."

"Well, there's plenty of time still," said Ann consolingly.

Geoffrey Fane turned his mild blue eyes on her sadly.

"But the invitation was for last March, my dear Ann."

"Oh dear—but, Geoffrey, how could a letter stay all that time in a coat pocket?"

"It was my very old coat. One sleeve had become almost detached. That made it uncomfortable to wear. I—er—h'm—laid it aside."

"Somebody really ought to look after you, Geoffrey."

"I much prefer *not* to be looked after. I once had a very officious housekeeper, an excellent cook, but one of those inveterate tidiers-up. She actually threw away my notes on the Bulyano rainmakers. An irreparable loss. Her excuse was that they were in the coal scuttle—but as I said to her: 'a coal scuttle is not a wastepaper basket, Mrs.—Mrs.— ' whatever her name was. Women, I fear, have no sense of proportion. They attach an absurd importance to cleaning, which they perform as though it was a ritual act."

"Some people say it is, don't they? Laura Whitstable—you know her, of course—she quite horrified me by the sinister meaning she seemed to impute to people who wash their necks twice a day. Apparently the dirtier you are, the purer your heart!"

"In—deed? Well, I must be going." He sighed. "I shall miss you, Ann, I shall miss you more than I can say."

"But you're not losing me, Geoffrey. I'm not going away. Richard has a job in London. I'm sure you'll like him."

Geoffrey Fane sighed again.

"It will not be the same. No, no, when a pretty woman marries another man—" he squeezed her hand. "You have meant a great deal to me, Ann. I almost ventured to hope—but no, no, that could not have been. An old fogy such as I am. No, you would have been bored. But I am very devoted to you, Ann, and I wish you happiness with all my heart. Do you know what you have always reminded me of? Those lines in Homer."

He quoted with relish and at some length in Greek.

"There," he said, beaming.

"Thank you, Geoffrey," said Ann. "I don't know what it means—"

"It means that—"

"No, don't tell me. It couldn't possibly be as nice as it sounds. What a lovely language Greek is. Good-bye, dear Geoffrey, and thank you. . . . Don't forget your hat—that's not your umbrella, it's Sarah's sunshade—and—wait a minute—here's your briefcase."

She closed the front door after him.

Edith put her head out of the kitchen door.

"Helpless as a baby, isn't he?" she said. "And yet it's not that he's gaga, either. Clever in his own line, so I should think. Though I'd say as those native tribes as he's so keen about have downright nasty minds. That wooden figure he brought you along I put in the back of the linen cupboard. Needs a brassiere as well as a fig leaf. And yet the old professor himself hasn't got a nasty thought in his head. Not so old either."

"He's forty-five."

"There you are. It's all this learning as has made him lose his hair the way he has. My nephew's hair all came off in a fever. Bald as an egg he was. Still, it grew again after a bit. There's two letters there."

Ann picked them up.

"Returned postal packet?" Her face changed. "Oh, Edith, it's my letter to Sarah. What a fool I am. I addressed it to the hotel and no place name. I don't know what's the matter with me just lately."

"I do," said Edith significantly.

"I do the stupidest things. . . . This other one is from Dame Laura . . . oh, how sweet of her . . . I must ring her up."

She went into the sitting room and dialed.

"Laura? I just got your letter. It's really too kind of you. There's nothing I'd like better than a Picasso. I've always wanted to have a Picasso of my own. I shall put it over the desk. You are kind to me. Oh, Laura, I've been such an idiot! I wrote to Sarah telling her about everything—-and now my letter has come back. I just put Hotel des Alpes, Switzerland. Can you *conceive* of my being so foolish?"

Dame Laura's deep voice said:

"H'm, interesting."

"What do you mean by interesting?"

"Just what I said."

"I know that tone of voice. You're getting at something. You're hinting that I didn't really want Sarah to get my letter or something. It's that irritating theory of yours that all mistakes are really deliberate."

"It isn't my theory specially."

"Well, anyway, it isn't true! Here I am with Sarah coming home the day after tomorrow, and she won't know anything at all and I shall have to tell her in so many words, which really will be far more embarrassing. I simply shan't know how to begin."

"Yes, that's what you have let yourself in for by not wanting Sarah to get that letter."

"But I did want her to get it. Don't be so annoying."

There was a chuckle at the other end of the wire.

Ann said crossly:

"Anyway, it's a ridiculous theory! Why, Geoffrey Fane has just been here. He's just found an invitation to lecture in Oslo last March which he mislaid a year ago. I suppose you'd say he mislaid that on purpose?"

"Did he want to lecture in Oslo?" inquired Dame Laura.

"I suppose—well, I don't know."

Dame Laura said "Interesting," in a malicious voice and rang off.

2

Richard Cauldfield bought a bunch of daffodils at the florist's on the corner.

He was in a happy frame of mind. After his first doubts he was settling into the routine of his new job. Merrick Hellner, his boss, he found sympathetic—and their friendship, begun in Burma, proved itself a stable thing in England. The work was not technical. It was a routine administrative job in which a knowledge of Burma and the East came in handy. Richard was not a brilliant man, but he was conscientious, hardworking, and had plenty of common sense.

The first discouragements of his return to England were forgotten. It was like beginning a new life with everything in his favor. Congenial work, a friendly and sympathetic employer, and the near prospect of marrying the woman he loved.

Every day he marveled afresh that Ann should care for him. How sweet she was, so gentle and so appealing! And yet, sometimes, when he had been led to lay down the law somewhat dogmatically, he would look up to see her regarding him with a mischievous smile. He had not often been laughed at, and at first he was not sure that he liked it—but he had to admit in the end that from Ann he could take it and rather enjoy it.

When Ann said: "Aren't we pompous, darling?" he would first frown and then join in the laugh and say: "Suppose I was laying down the law a bit." And once he had said to her: "You're very good for me, Ann. You make me much more human."

She had said quickly: "We're both good for each other."

"There's not much I can do for you—except look after you and take care of you."

"Don't look after me too much. Don't encourage my weaknesses."

"Your weaknesses? You haven't any."

"Oh yes, I have, Richard. I like people to be pleased with me. I don't like rubbing people up the wrong way. I don't like rows—or fusses."

"Thank goodness for that! I'd hate to have a quarrelsome wife always scrapping. I've seen some, I can tell you! It's the thing I admire about you most, Ann, your being always gentle and sweet-tempered. Dearest, how happy we are going to be."

She said softly:

"Yes, I think we are."

Richard, she thought, had changed a good deal since the night she had first met him. He had no longer that rather aggressive manner of a man who is on the defensive. He was, as he had said himself, much more human. More sure of himself, and therefore more tolerant and friendly.

Richard took his daffodils and went up to the block of flats. Ann's flat was on the third floor. He went up in the lift after having been greeted affably by the porter who now knew him well by sight.

Edith opened the door to him and from the end of the passage he heard Ann's voice calling rather breathlessly:

"Edith—Edith, have you seen my bag? I've put it down somewhere."

"Good afternoon, Edith," said Cauldfield as he stepped inside.

He was never quite at his ease with Edith and tried to mask the fact by an additional bonhomie that did not sound quite natural.

"Good afternoon, sir," said Edith respectfully.

"Edith—" Ann's voice sounded urgently from the bedroom. "Didn't you hear me? Do *come!*"

She came out into the passage just as Edith said:

"It's Mr. Cauldfield, ma'am."

"Richard?" Ann came down the passage toward him looking surprised. She drew him into the sitting room, saying over her shoulder to Edith: "You *must* find that bag. See if I left it in Sarah's room?"

"Lose your head next, you will," said Edith as she went off.

Richard frowned. Edith's freedom of speech offended his sense of decorum. Servants had not spoken so fifteen years ago.

"Richard—I didn't expect you today. I thought you were coming to lunch tomorrow."

She sounded taken aback, slightly uneasy.

"Tomorrow seemed a long way off," he said, smiling. "I brought you these."

As he handed her the daffodils and she exclaimed with pleasure he suddenly noticed that there was already a profusion of flowers in the room. A pot of hyacinths was on the low table by the fire and there were bowls of early tulips and of narcissus.

"You look very festive," he said.

"Of course. Sarah's coming home today."

"Oh yes—yes, so she is. Do you know I'd forgotten."

"Oh, Richard."

Her tone was reproachful. It was true, he had forgotten. He had known perfectly the day of her arrival, but when he and Ann had been at a theater together the night before neither of them had referred to the fact. Yet it had been discussed between them and agreed that on the evening Sarah returned, she should have Ann to herself and that he should come to lunch on the following day to meet his stepdaughter to be.

"I'm sorry, Ann. Really it had slipped my memory. You seem very excited," he added with a faint note of disapproval.

"Well, homecomings are always rather special, don't you think?"

"I suppose so."

"I'm just going off to the station to meet her." She glanced at her watch. "Oh, it's all right. Anyway, I expect the boat train will be late. It usually is."

Edith marched into the room, carrying Ann's bag.

"In the linen cupboard—that's where you left it."

"Of course—when I was looking for those pillowcases. You've put Sarah's own green sheets on her bed? You haven't forgotten?"

"Now, do I ever forget?"

"And you remembered the cigarettes?"

"Yes."

"And Toby and Jumbo?"

"Yes, yes, yes."

Shaking her head indulgently, Edith went out of the room.

"Edith," Ann called her back and held out the daffodils. "Put these in a vase, will you?"

"I'll be hard put to it to find one! Never mind, I'll find something."

She took the flowers and went out.

Richard said: "You're as excited as a child, Ann."

"Well, it's so lovely to think of seeing Sarah again."

He said teasingly, yet with a slight stiffness:

"How long is it since you've seen her—a whole three weeks?"

"I daresay I'm ridiculous," Ann smiled at him disarmingly, "but I do love Sarah very much. You wouldn't want me not to, would you?"

"Of course I wouldn't. I'm looking forward to meeting her."

"She's so impulsive and affectionate. I'm sure you'll get on together."

"I'm sure we shall."

He added, still smiling: "She's your daughter—so she's sure to be a very sweet person."

"How nice of you to say that, Richard." Resting her hands on his shoulders, she lifted her face to his. "Dear Richard," she murmured as she kissed him. Then she added: "You—you will be patient, won't you darling? I mean—you see our going to be married may be rather a shock to her. If only I hadn't been stupid about that letter."

"Now don't get rattled, dearest. You can trust me, you know. Sarah may take it a bit hard at first, but we must get her to see that it's really quite a good idea. I assure you that I shan't be offended by anything she says."

"Oh, she won't *say* anything. Sarah has very good manners. But she does so hate change of any kind."

"Well, cheer up, darling. After all, she can't forbid the banns, can she?"

Ann did not respond to his joke. She was still looking worried.

"If only I'd written at once—

Richard said, laughing outright:

"You look exactly like a little girl who's been caught stealing the jam! It will be all right, sweetheart. Sarah and I will soon make friends."

Ann looked at him doubtfully. The cheerful assurance of his manner struck the wrong note. She would have preferred him to be slightly more nervous.

Richard went on:

"Darling, you really must *not* let things worry you so!"

"I don't usually," Ann said.

"But you do. Here you are, dithering—when the whole thing is perfectly simple and straightforward."

Ann said: "It's just that I'm—well, *shy*. I don't exactly know what to say, how to put it."

"Why not just say: 'Sarah, this is Richard Cauldfield. I'm getting married to him in three weeks' time.' "

"Quite baldly—like that?" Ann smiled in spite of herself. Richard smiled back.

"Isn't it really the best way?"

"Perhaps it is." She hesitated. "What you don't realize is that I shall feel so—so frightfully silly."

"Silly?" he took her up sharply.

"One does feel silly telling one's grown-up daughter that one's going to be married."

"I really can't see why."

"I suppose because young people unconsciously consider you as having done with all that sort of thing. You're *old* to them. They think love—falling in love, I mean—is a monopoly of youth. It's bound to strike them as ridiculous that middle-aged people should fall in love and marry."

"Nothing ridiculous about it," said Richard sharply.

"Not to *us*, because we *are* middle-aged."

Richard frowned. His voice, when he spoke, had a slight edge of asperity to it.

"Now look here, Ann, I know you and Sarah are very devoted to each other. I daresay the girl may feel rather sore and jealous about me. I understand that, it's natural, and I'm prepared to make allowances for it. I daresay she'll dislike me a good deal at first—but she'll come round all right. She must be made to realize that you've a right to live your own life and find your own happiness."

A slight flush rose in Ann's cheek.

"Sarah won't grudge me my 'happiness,' as you call it," she said. "There's nothing mean or petty about Sarah. She's the most generous creature in the world."

"The truth is that you're working yourself up about nothing, Ann. For all you know Sarah may be quite glad you are getting married. It will leave her freer to lead her own life."

"Lead her own life," Ann repeated the phrase with scorn. "Really, Richard, you talk like a Victorian novel."

"The truth of it is, you mothers never want the bird to leave the nest."

"You're quite wrong, Richard—absolutely wrong."

"I don't want to annoy you, darling, but sometimes even the most devoted mother's affection can be too much of a good thing. Why, I remember when I was a young man. I was very fond of my father and my mother, but living with them was often quite maddening. Always asking me how late I was going to be and where I was going. 'Don't forget your key.' 'Try and not make a noise when you come in.' 'You forgot to turn out the hall light last time.' 'What, going out *again* tonight? You don't seem to care at all about your home after all we've done for you.' " He paused. "I *did* care for my home—but oh God, how I wanted just to feel free."

"I understand all that, of course."

"So you mustn't feel injured if it turns out that Sarah hankers after her independence more than you think. There are so many careers open to girls nowadays, remember."

"Sarah's not a career type."

"That's what you say—but most girls do have a job, remember."

"That's very largely a question of economic necessity, isn't it?"

"What do you mean?"

Ann said impatiently:

"You're about fifteen years behind the times, Richard. Once it was all the fashion to 'lead your own life' and 'go out into the world.' Girls still do it, but there's no glamour about it. With taxation and death duties and all the rest of it, a girl is usually wise to train for something. Sarah has no special bent. She's well up in modern languages and she's been having a course of flower decoration. A friend of ours runs a floral decorating shop and she's arranged for Sarah to work there. I think she'll quite enjoy it—but it's just a job and that's all there is to it. It's no use talking so grandly about all this independence stuff. Sarah loves her home and she's perfectly happy here."

"I'm sorry if I've upset you, Ann, but—"

He broke off as Edith poked her head in. Her face had the smug expression of someone who has heard more of what is going on than she intends to admit.

"I don't want to interrupt you, ma'am, but you do know what time it is?"

Ann glanced down at her watch.

"There's still plenty of—why, it's exactly the same time as when I looked last." She held the watch to her ear. "Richard—it's stopped. What is the time really, Edith?"

"Twenty past the hour."

"Good heavens—I shall miss her. But boat trains are always late, aren't they? Where's my bag? Oh here. Lots of taxis now, thank goodness. No, Richard, don't come with me. Look here, stay and have tea with us. Yes, do. I mean it. I think it would be best. Really I do. I *must* go."

She rushed out of the room. The front door banged. The swing of her fur had whisked two tulips out of the bowl. Edith stooped to pick them up and rearranged them carefully in the bowl, saying as she did so:

"Tulips is Miss Sarah's favorite flower—always was—especially mauve ones."

Richard said with some irritation:

"This whole place seems to revolve round Miss Sarah."

Edith stole a swift glance at him. Her face remained imperturbable—disapproving. She said in her flat unemotional voice:

"Ah, she's got a way with her, Miss Sarah has. That you can't deny. I've often noticed as how there's young ladies who leave their things about, expect everything mended for them, run you off your feet clearing up after them—and yet there's nothing you won't do for them! There's others as gives no trouble at all, everything neat, no extra work made—and yet there you are, you don't seem to fancy them in the same way. Say what you like it's an unjust world. Only a crazy politician would talk about fair shares for all. Some has the kicks and some has the ha'pence, and that's the way it is."

She moved round the room as she spoke, setting one or two objects straight and shaking up one of the cushions.

Richard lit a cigarette. He said pleasantly:

"You've been with Mrs. Prentice a long time, haven't you, Edith?"

"More than twenty years. Twenty-two, it is. Come to her mother before Miss Ann married Mr. Prentice. He was a nice gentleman, he was."

Richard looked at her sharply. His ultra-sensitive ego led him to imagine that there had been a faint emphasis on the "he."

He said:

"Mrs. Prentice has told you that we are going to be married shortly?"

Edith nodded.

"Not that I needed telling," she said.

Richard said rather self-consciously, speaking pompously because he was shy: "I—I hope we shall be good friends, Edith."

Edith said rather gloomily:

"I hope so, too, sir."

Richard said, still speaking stiffly:

"I'm afraid it may mean extra work for you, but we must get outside help—"

"I'm not fond of these women that come in. When I'm on my own I know where I am. Yes, it will mean changes having a gentleman in the house. Meals is different to begin with."

"I'm really not a large eater," Richard assured her.

"It's the *kind* of meals," said Edith. "Gentlemen don't hold with trays."

"Women hold with them a good deal too much."

"That may be," Edith admitted. In a peculiarly lugubrious voice she added: "I'm not denying that a gentleman about the place cheers things up as it were."

Richard felt almost fulsomely grateful.

"That's very nice of you, Edith," he said warmly.

"Oh, you can rely on me, sir. I shan't go leaving Mrs. Prentice. Wouldn't leave her for anything. And anyway it's never been my way to quit if there's trouble in the offing."

"Trouble? What do you mean by trouble?"

"Squalls."

Again Richard repeated what she had said.

"Squalls?"

Edith faced him with an unflinching eye.

"Nobody asked my advice," she said. "And I'm not one to give it unasked, but I'll say this. If Miss Sarah had come back home to find you both married, and the whole thing over and done with, well, it might have been better, if you take my meaning."

The front doorbell rang and almost immediately the button was pressed again and again.

"And I know who that is right enough," said Edith.

She went out into the hall. As she opened the door two voices were heard, one male, one female. There was laughter and exclamations.

"Edith, you old pet." It was a girl's voice, a warm contralto. "Where's mother? Come on, Gerry. Shove those skis in the kitchen."

"Not in my kitchen, you don't."

"Where's mother?" repeated Sarah Prentice, coming into the sitting-room and talking over her shoulder.

She was a tall dark girl, and her vigor and exuberant vitality took Richard Cauldfield by surprise. He had seen photographs of Sarah about the flat, but a photograph can never represent life. He had expected a younger edition of Ann—a harder, more modern edition—but the same type. But Sarah Prentice resembled her gay and charming father. She was exotic and eager and her mere presence seemed to change the whole atmosphere of the flat.

"Oo, lovely tulips," she exclaimed, bending over the bowl. "They've got that faint lemony smell that is absolutely spring. I—"

Her eyes widened as she straightened up and saw Cauldfield.

He came forward, saying:

"My name's Richard Cauldfield."

Sarah shook hands with him prettily, inquiring politely:

"Are you waiting for mother?"

"I'm afraid she's only just gone to the station to meet you—let me see, five minutes ago."

"How idiotic of the pet! Why didn't Edith get her off in time? Edith!"

"Her watch had stopped."

"Mother's watches—Gerry—Where are you, Gerry?"

A young man with a rather good-looking discontented face looked in for a moment with a suitcase in each hand.

"Gerry, the human robot," he remarked. "Where do you want all these, Sarah? Why don't you have porters in these flats?"

"We do. But they're never about if you arrive with luggage. Take them all along to my room, Gerry. Oh, this is Mr. Lloyd. Mr.—er—"

"Cauldfield," said Richard.

Edith came in. Sarah caught hold of her and gave her a resounding kiss.

"Edith, it's lovely to see your dear old sourpuss face."

"Sourpuss face indeed," said Edith indignantly. "And don't go kissing me, Miss Sarah. You ought to know your place better than that."

"Don't be so cross, Edith. You know you're delighted to see me. How clean everything looks! It's all just the same. The chintzes and mother's shell box—oh, you've changed the sofa round. And the desk. It used to be over there."

"Your ma says it gives more space this way."

"No, I want it as it was. Gerry—Gerry, where are you?"

Gerry Lloyd entered saying: "What's the matter now?" Sarah was already tugging at the desk. Richard moved to help her, but Gerry said cheerfully: "Don't bother, sir, I'll do it. Where do you want it, Sarah?"

"Where it used to be. Over there."

When they had moved the desk and pushed the sofa back into its old position, Sarah gave a sigh and said:

"That's better."

"I'm not so sure about that," said Gerry, standing back critically.

"Well, I am," said Sarah. "I like everything to be just the same. Otherwise home isn't home. Where's the cushion with the birds on it, Edith?"

"Gone to be cleaned."

"Oh well, that's all right. I must go and see my room." She paused in the doorway to say: "Mix some drinks, Gerry. Give Mr. Coalfield one. You know where everything is."

"Sure thing." Gerry looked at Richard. "What will you have, sir? Martini, gin and orange? Pink gin?"

Richard moved with sudden decision.

"No, thanks very much. Nothing for me. I've got to be off."

"Won't you wait until Mrs. Prentice comes in?" Gerry had a likeable and charming manner. "I don't suppose she'll be long. As soon as she finds the train came in before she got there she'll come straight back."

"No, I must go. Tell Mrs. Prentice the—er—original appointment stands—for tomorrow."

He nodded to Gerry and went out into the hall. From Sarah's bedroom along the passage he could hear her voice talking in a rush of words to Edith.

Better, he thought, not to stay now. His and Ann's original plan had been the right one. She would tell Sarah tonight and tomorrow he would come to lunch and start to make friends with his future stepdaughter.

He was disturbed because Sarah was not as he had pictured her. He had thought of her as overmothered by Ann, as dependent on Ann. Her beauty and her vitality and her self-possession had startled him.

Up to now she had been a mere abstraction. Now she was reality.

Chapter Six

Sarah came back into the drawing room fastening up a brocaded house gown.

"I had to get out of that skiing suit. I really want a bath. How dirty trains are! Have you got a drink for me, Gerry?"

"Here you are."

Sarah accepted the glass.

"Thanks. Has that man gone? That's a good job."

"Who was he?"

"Never saw him in my life," said Sarah. She laughed. "He must be one of Mother's pickups."

Edith came into the room to pull the curtains and Sarah said:

"Who was he, Edith?"

"A friend of your mother's, Miss Sarah," said Edith.

She gave the curtains a sharp pull and then went to the second window.

Sarah said cheerfully: "Time I came home to choose her friends for her."

Edith said: "Ah," and pulled the second curtain. Then she said, looking hard at Sarah: "You didn't take to him?"

"No, I didn't."

Edith muttered something and went out of the room.

"What did she say, Gerry?"

"I think she said it was a pity."

"How funny."

"Sounded cryptic."

"Oh, you know what Edith's like. Why doesn't Mother come? Why does she have to be so vague?"

"She's not usually very vague. At least, I shouldn't have said so."

"It was nice of you to come and meet me, Gerry. Sorry I never wrote, but you know what life is. How did you manage to get off from the office early enough to get to Victoria?"

There was a slight pause before Gerry said:

"Oh, it wasn't particularly difficult under the circumstances."

Sarah sat up in a very alert way and looked at him.

"Now then, Gerry, out with it. What's wrong?"

"Nothing. At least, things haven't worked out very well."

Sarah said accusingly: "You said you were going to be patient and keep your temper."

Gerry frowned.

"I know all that, darling, but you've no idea what it's been like. Good God, to come home from somewhere like Korea where it's pretty fair hell, but at least most of the fellows are decent chaps, and then to get caught up in a money-grubbing City office. You've no idea what Uncle Luke is like. Fat and pursy with little darting eyes like a pig's. 'Very glad to have you home, me boy.' " Gerry was a good mimic. He wheezed out the words in an unctuous asthmatic way. " 'Er—ah—I hope now all this excitement's over, you'll come into the office and er—ah—really put your back into things. We're—er—short-handed—I think I can say there are—er excellent prospects if you're really serious over the job. Of course you'll start at the bottom. No—er, favors—

that's my motto. You've had a long spell of playing around—now we'll see if you can get down to it in earnest.' "

He got up and strolled about.

"Playing about—that's what the fat so-and-so calls active service in the Army. My word, I'd like to see him sniped at by a yellow Chinese Red soldier. These rich bleeders sitting on their arses in their offices, never thinking of anything but money—going on—"

"Oh, dry up, Gerry," said Sarah impatiently. "Your uncle just hasn't got any imagination. Anyway, you said yourself you've got to have a job and make some money. I daresay it's all very unpleasant, but what's the alternative? You're lucky, really, to have a rich uncle in the City. Most people would give their eyes to have one!"

"And why is he rich?" demanded Gerry. "Because he's rolling in the money that ought to have come to *me*. Why Great-uncle Harry left it to him instead of to my father who was the elder brother—"

"Never mind all that," said Sarah. "Anyway, by the time the money had come to you, there probably wouldn't have been any. It would all have gone in death duties."

"But it was unfair. You'll admit that?"

"Everything's always unfair," said Sarah. "But it's no good going on grousing about it. For one thing it makes you such a bore. One gets so tired of hearing nothing but people's hard-luck stories."

"I must say you're not awfully sympathetic, Sarah."

"No. You see what I believe in is absolute frankness. I think you ought either to make a gesture and get out of this job, or else stop grousing about it and just thank your stars you've got a rich uncle in the City with pig's eyes and asthma. Hullo, I do believe I hear mother at last."

Ann had just opened the door with her latchkey. She came running into the sitting room.

"Sarah darling."

"Mother—at last." Sarah enveloped her mother in a big hug. "What have you been doing with yourself?"

"It's my watch. It had stopped."

"Well, Gerry met me, so that was something."

"Oh hullo, Gerry, I didn't see you."

Ann greeted him cheerfully, though inwardly she felt annoyed. She had so hoped that this Gerry business would peter out.

"Let's have a look at you, darling," said Sarah. "You're looking quite smart. That's a new hat, isn't it? You look very well, Mother."

"So do you. And so sunburnt."

"Sun on the snow. Edith's awfully disappointed I didn't come home all swathed in bandages. You'd have liked me to have broken a few bones, wouldn't you, Edith?"

Edith, who was bringing in the tea tray, made no direct reply.

"I've brought in three cups," she said, "though I suppose Miss Sarah and Mr. Lloyd won't want any, seeing as they've been drinking gin."

"How dissipated you make it sound, Edith," said Sarah.

"Anyway, we offered what's-his-name some. Who is he, Mother? A name like Cauliflower."

Edith said to Ann: "Mr. Cauldfield said as he couldn't wait, ma'am. He'll be along tomorrow as previously arranged."

"Who is Cauldfield, Mother, and why does he have to come tomorrow? I'm sure we don't want him."

Ann said quickly: "Have another drink, won't you Gerry?"

"No, thank you, Mrs. Prentice. I really must be getting along now. Good-bye, Sarah."

Sarah went out with him into the hall. He said:

"What about a film this evening. There's a good continental one at the Academy."

"Oh, what fun. No—perhaps I'd better not. After all, it's my first evening home. I think I ought to spend it with mother. The poor pet might be disappointed if I rushed out at once."

"I do think, Sarah, that you're a frightfully good daughter."

"Well, mother's really very sweet."

"Oh, I know she is."

"She asks a terrible lot of questions, of course. You know, who one's met and what one's done. But on the whole, for a mother, she's really quite sensible. I tell you what, Gerry, if I find it's all right, I'll give you a ring later."

Sarah went back into the sitting room and started to nibble cakes.

"These are Edith's specials," she remarked. "Madly rich. I don't know how she gets hold of the stuff to make them with. Now, Mother, tell me all you've been doing. Have you been out with Colonel Grant and the rest of the boyfriends, and been having a good time?"

"No—at least yes, in a way . . ."

Ann stopped. Sarah stared at her.

"Is anything the matter, Mother?"

"The matter? No. Why?"

"You look all queer."

"Do I?"

"Mother, there *is* something. You really do look awfully peculiar. Come on, tell me. I've never seen such a guilty expression. Come on, Mother, what have you been up to?"

"Nothing really—at least. Oh, Sarah, darling—you must believe that it won't make any difference. Everything will be just the same, only—"

Ann's voice faltered and died. "What a coward I am," she thought to herself. "Why does a daughter make you feel so shy about things?"

Meanwhile Sarah was staring at her. Suddenly she began to grin the friendliest fashion.

"I do believe . . . Come on, Mother, own up. Are you trying to break it to me gently that I'm going to have a step-papa?"

"Oh, Sarah." Ann gave a gasp of relief. "*How* did you guess?"

"It wasn't so difficult as all that. I never saw anyone in such a frightful dither. Did you think I'd mind?"

"I suppose I did. And you don't? Really?"

"No," said Sarah seriously. "Actually I think you're quite right. After all, father died sixteen years ago. You ought to have some kind of sex life before it's too late. You're just at what they call the dangerous age. And you're much too old-fashioned to have just an affair."

Ann looked rather helplessly at her daughter. She was thinking how differently everything was going from the way she had thought it would go.

"Yes," said Sarah nodding her head. "With you it *has* to be marriage."

"The dear absurd baby," thought Ann, but was careful to say nothing of the kind.

"You're really quite good-looking still," went on Sarah with the devastating candor of youth. "That's because you've got a good skin. But you'd look heaps nicer if you'd have your eyebrows plucked."

"I like my eyebrows," said Ann obstinately.

"You're really awfully attractive, darling," said Sarah. "I'm really surprised you haven't got off before. Who is it, by the way? I'll have three guesses. One, Colonel Grant, two, Professor Fane, three that melancholy Pole with the unpronounceable name. But I'm pretty sure it's Colonel Grant. He's been hammering away at you for years."

Ann said rather breathlessly:

"It isn't James Grant. It's—it's Richard Cauldfield."

"Who's Richard Cauld—Mother, not that man who was here just now?"

Ann nodded.

"But you can't, Mother. He's all pompous and dreadful."

"He's not dreadful at all," said Ann sharply.

"Really, Mother, you could do a lot better than that."

"Sarah, you don't know what you're talking about. I—I care for him very much."

"You mean you're in love with him?" Sarah was frankly incredulous. "You mean you've actually got a *passion* for him."

Again Ann nodded.

"You know," said Sarah. "I really can't take all this in."

Ann straightened her shoulders.

"You only saw Richard for a moment or two," she said. "When you know him better, I'm sure you'll like him very much."

"He looks so aggressive."

"That was because he was shy."

"Well," said Sarah slowly, "it's your funeral, of course."

Mother and daughter sat silent for some moments. They were both embarrassed.

"You know, Mother," said Sarah, breaking the silence, "you really do need someone to look after you. Just because I go away for a few weeks, you go and do something silly."

"Sarah!" Anger flared up in Ann. "You're very unkind."

"Sorry, darling, but I do believe in absolute frankness."

"Well, I don't think I do."

"How long has this been going on?" demanded Sarah.

In spite of herself Ann laughed.

"Really, Sarah, you sound just like a heavy father in some Victorian drama. I met Richard three weeks ago."

"Where?"

"With James Grant. James has known him for years. He's just come back from Burma."

"Has he got any money?"

Ann was both irritated and touched. How ridiculous the child was— so earnest in her questions. Controlling her irritation she said in a dry ironical voice:

"He has an independent income and is fully able to support me. He has a job with Hellner Bros., a big firm in the City. Really, Sarah, anyone would think that *I* was *your* daughter, not the other way about."

Sarah said seriously: "Well, somebody has got to look after you, darling. You're quite unfit to look after yourself. I'm very fond of you, and I don't want you to go and do something foolish. Is he a bachelor or divorced or a widower?"

"He lost his wife many years ago. She died having her first baby and the baby died too."

Sarah sighed and shook her head.

"I see it all now. That's how he got at you. You always fall for sob stuff."

"Do stop being absurd, Sarah!"

"Has he got sisters and a mother—all that sort of thing?"

"I don't think he's got any near relations."

"That's a blessing anyway. Has he got a house? Where are you going to live?"

"Here, I think. There's heaps of room and his work is in London. You won't really mind, will you, Sarah?"

"Oh, *I* shan't mind. I'm thinking entirely of you."

"Darling, it's very sweet of you. But I really do know my own business best. I'm quite sure that Richard and I are going to be very happy together."

"When are you thinking of actually getting married?"

"In three weeks' time."

"In three weeks? Oh, you can't marry him as soon as that."

"There doesn't seem any point in waiting."

"Oh please, darling. Do put it off a little. Give me a little time to—to get used to the idea. Please, Mother."

"I don't know . . . we'll have to see . . ."

"Six weeks. Make it six weeks."

"Nothing's really decided yet. Richard's coming to lunch tomorrow. You—Sarah—you will be nice to him, won't you?"

"Of course I shall be nice to him. What do you think?"

"Thank you, darling."

"Cheer up, Mother, there's nothing to worry about."

"I'm sure you'll really both get very fond of each other," said Ann, rather weakly.

Sarah was silent.

Ann said, again with that gust of sudden anger:

"You might at least try—"

"I've told you you needn't worry." Sarah added after a moment or two: "I suppose you'd rather I stopped in tonight?"

"Why? Do you want to go out?"

"I thought I might—but I don't want to leave you alone, Mother."

Ann smiled at her daughter, the old relationship reasserting its sway.

"Oh, I shan't be lonely. As a matter of fact, Laura asked me to go to a lecture—"

"How is the old battle-ax? As indefatigable as ever?"

"Oh yes, just the same. I said no to the lecture, but I can easily ring her up."

She could, just as easily, ring Richard up. . . . But her mind shied away from the prospect. Better keep away from Richard until after he and Sarah had met on the morrow.

"That's all right, then," said Sarah. "I'll ring up Gerry."

"Oh, is it Gerry you're going out with?"

Sarah said, rather defiantly:

"Yes. Why not?"

But Ann did not take up the challenge. She said mildly:

"I just wondered. . . ."

Chapter Seven

1

"Gerry?"

"Yes, Sarah?"

"I don't really want to see this film. Can we go somewhere and talk?"

"Of course. Shall we go and have something to eat?"

"Oh, I couldn't. Edith has absolutely stuffed me."

"We'll go and get a drink somewhere then."

He cast a swift glance at her, wondering what had upset her. It was not until they were settled with drinks in front of them that Sarah spoke. Then she plunged abruptly:

"Gerry, mother's getting married again."

"Whew!" He was genuinely surprised.

"Hadn't you any idea of it?" he asked.

"How could I? She only met him since I've been away."

"Quick work."

"Much too quick. In some ways mother has really no sense at all!"

"Who is it?"

"That man who was there this afternoon. His name's Cauliflower or something like that."

"Oh, *that* man."

"Yes. Don't you agree that he's really quite impossible?"

"Well, I didn't really notice him much," said Gerry considering. "He seemed quite an ordinary sort of chap."

"He's absolutely the wrong person for mother."

"I suppose she's the best judge of that," said Gerry mildly.

"No, she isn't. The trouble about mother is that she's *weak*. She gets sorry for people. Mother needs somebody to look after her."

"Apparently she thinks so too," said Gerry with a grin.

"Don't laugh, Gerry, this is serious. Cauliflower is the wrong type for mother."

"Well, that's her business."

"I've got to look after her. I've always felt that. I know much more about life than she does, and I'm twice as tough."

Gerry did not dispute the statement. On the whole he agreed with it. Nevertheless he was troubled.

He said slowly: "All the same, Sarah, if she wants to get married again—"

Sarah broke in quickly:

"Oh, I quite agree to *that*. Mother *ought* to marry again. I told her so. She's been starved, you know, of a proper sex life. But definitely not Cauliflower."

"You don't think—" Gerry stopped uncertainly.

"Don't think what?"

"That you might—well, feel the same about anyone?" He was slightly nervous—but he got the words out. "After all, you can't really know that Cauliflower is the wrong sort for her. You've not spoken two words to him. Don't you think that perhaps it's really that you are—" it took courage to get the last word out, but he achieved it—"er—jealous?"

Sarah was up in arms at once.

"Jealous? *Me?* You mean stepfather stuff? My dear Gerry! Didn't I say to you long ago—before I went to Switzerland—that mother ought to marry again?"

"Yes. But it's different," said Gerry with a flash of perception, "just saying things from when they really happen."

"I've not got a jealous nature," said Sarah. "It's only mother's happiness I'm thinking about," she added virtuously.

"If I were you I wouldn't go monkeying about with other people's lives," said Gerry decidedly.

"But it's my own *mother*."

"Well, she probably knows her own business best."

"I tell you, mother's *weak*."

"Anyway," said Gerry, "there isn't anything you can do about it."

He thought Sarah was making a lot of fuss about nothing. He was tired of Ann and her affairs and wanted to talk about himself.

He said abruptly:

"I'm thinking about clearing out."

"Clearing out of your uncle's office? Oh, Gerry."

"I really can't stick it any longer. There's the hell of a fuss every time I turn up a quarter of an hour late."

"Well, you have to be punctual in offices, don't you?"

"Miserable lot of stick-in-the-muds! Fumbling away over ledgers, thinking of nothing but money, morning, noon, and night."

"But Gerry, if you chuck it, what will you do?"

"Oh, I'll find something," said Gerry airily.

"You've tried a lot of things already," said Sarah doubtfully.

"Meaning I always get the sack? Well, I'm not waiting for the sack this time."

"But Gerry, really, do you think you're wise?" Sarah looked at him with a worried, almost maternal, solicitude. "I mean he's your uncle and about the only relation you have, and you did say he was rolling."

"And if I behave prettily he may leave me all his money? I suppose that's what you mean."

"Well, you grouse enough about your Great-uncle what's-his-name not leaving his money to your father."

"If he'd had any decent family feelings I wouldn't need to go truckling to these City magnates. I think this whole country is rotten to the core. I've a good mind to clear out of it altogether."

"Go abroad somewhere?"

"Yes. Go somewhere where one has *scope*."

They were both silent, envisaging a nebulous life that had scope.

Sarah, whose feet were always more firmly on the ground than Gerry's were, said acutely:

"Can you do anything much without capital? You haven't got any capital, have you?"

"You know I haven't. Oh, I imagine there are all sorts of things one can do."

"Well, what can you do—actually?"

"Must you be so damned depressing, Sarah?"

"Sorry. What I mean is you haven't any particular training of any kind."

"I'm good at handling men, and at leading an outdoor life. Not cooped up in an office."

"Oh, Gerry," said Sarah and sighed.

"What's the matter?"

"I don't know. Life does seem difficult. All these wars have unsettled things so."

They stared gloomily in front of them.

Presently Gerry said magnanimously that he'd give his uncle another chance. Sarah applauded this decision.

"I'd better go home now," she said. "Mother will be back from her lecture."

"What was the lecture about?"

"I don't know. 'Where are we going and Why?' That sort of thing." She got up. "Thank you, Gerry," she said. "You've been very helpful."

"Try not to be prejudiced, Sarah. If your mother likes this fellow and is going to be happy with him, that's the main thing."

"If mother's going to be happy with him, then it's quite all right."

"After all, you'll be getting married yourself—I suppose—one of these days . . ."

He said it without looking at her. Sarah stared with absorption at her handbag.

"Someday, I suppose," she murmured. "I'm not particularly keen. . . ."

Embarrassment with a pleasurable tinge to it hovered in the air between them. . . .

2

Ann felt relieved in her mind during lunch on the following day. Sarah was behaving beautifully. She greeted Richard pleasantly and made conversation politely during the meal.

Ann felt proud of her young daughter with her vivid face, and her pretty manners. She might have known she could rely on Sarah—Sarah would never let her down.

What she did wish was that Richard could show to better advantage. He was nervous, she realized that. He was anxious to make a good impression, and as is so often the case, his very anxiety told against him. His manner was didactic, almost pompous. Being anxious to appear at ease, he gave the impression of dominating the party. The very deference that Sarah showed to him, heightened the impression he made. He was over-positive in his statements and seemed to indicate that no opinion was possible but his own. It vexed Ann who knew only too well the very real diffidence that there was in his nature.

But how could Sarah perceive it? She was seeing the worst side of Richard, and it was so important that she should see the best. It made Ann herself nervous and ill at ease and that, she soon saw, annoyed Richard.

After the meal was over and coffee had been brought, she left them on the excuse of having a telephone call to make. There was an extension in her bedroom. She hoped that, left together, Richard might feel more at ease and show more of his true self. It was she who was really the irritant. Once she had removed herself, things might settle down.

After Sarah had given Richard his coffee, she offered a few polite commonplaces and the conversation then petered out.

Richard braced himself. Frankness, he judged, was his best suit. He was favorably impressed on the whole with Sarah. She had shown no hostility. The great thing was to show her how well he understood the position. Before coming he had rehearsed what he meant to say. Like most things that have been rehearsed beforehand, they came out flatly and in an artificial manner. To make himself feel at ease he adopted a confident bonhomie that was wildly removed from his actual painful shyness.

"Look here, young lady, there are just one or two things I'd like to say to you."

"Oh, yes?" Sarah turned an attractive but at the moment quite expressionless face toward him. She waited politely and Richard felt more nervous still.

"I just want to say that I quite understand your feelings. This must all have come as a bit of a shock to you. You and your mother have always been very close. It's perfectly natural that you should resent somebody else coming into her life. You're bound to feel a bit sore and jealous about it."

Sarah said quickly in pleasant formal tones:

"Not at all, I assure you."

Unwary, Richard took no notice of what was, in effect, a warning. He blundered on:

"As I say, that's all quite normal. I shan't hurry you. Be as cool to me as you please. When you decide you're ready to be friends, I'll be ready to meet you halfway. What you've got to think of is your mother's happiness."

"I do think of that," said Sarah.

"Up to now, she's done everything for you. Now it's *her* turn to be considered. You want her to be happy, I'm sure. And you've got to remember this: you've got your own life to lead—it's all in front of you. You've got your own friends and your own hopes and ambitions. If you were to marry, or take up some job, your mother would be left all alone. That would mean great loneliness for her. This is the moment when you've got to put her first and yourself last."

He paused. He thought he had put that rather well.

Sarah's voice, polite but with an almost imperceptible undercurrent of impertinence, broke into his self-congratulations.

"Do you often make public speeches?" she inquired.

Startled, he said: "Why?"

"I should think you would be rather good at it," Sarah murmured.

She was leaning back now in her chair admiring her nails. The fact that they were carmine red, a fashion which he disliked intensely, added to Richard's irritation. He had recognized now that he was meeting hostility.

With an effort he kept his temper. As a result he spoke in an almost patronizing tone.

"Perhaps I was lecturing you a bit, my child. But I wanted to draw your attention to a few things you mightn't have considered. And I can assure you of one thing; your mother's not going to care for you any less because she cares for me, you know."

"Really? How kind of you to tell me so."

There was no doubt of the hostility now.

If Richard had abandoned his defenses, if he had said simply:

"I'm making an awful mess of this, Sarah. I'm shy and unhappy and it makes me say all the wrong things, but I'm terribly fond of Ann and I do want you to like me if you possibly can," it might perhaps have melted Sarah's defenses, since she was at heart a generous creature.

But instead, his tone stiffened.

"Young people," he said, "are inclined to be selfish. They don't usually think of anybody but themselves. But you've got to think of your mother's happiness. She's a right to a life of her own, and a right to take happiness when she finds it. She needs someone to look after her and protect her."

Sarah raised her eyes and looked him full in the face. The look in her eyes puzzled him. It was hard and there was a kind of calculation about it.

"I couldn't agree with you more," she said unexpectedly.

Ann came back into the room rather nervously.

"Any coffee left?" she asked.

Sarah poured out a cup carefully. She rose to her feet and handed the cup to her mother.

"There you are, Mother," she said. "You came back at just the right minute. We've had our little talk."

She walked out of the room. Ann looked inquiringly at Richard. His face was rather red.

"Your daughter," he said, "has made up her mind not to like me."

"Be patient with her, Richard, please be patient."

"Don't worry, Ann, I'm perfectly prepared to be patient."

"You see, it has come to her as rather a shock."

"Quite."

"Sarah has really a very loving heart. She's such a dear child, really."

Richard did not reply. He considered Sarah an odious young woman, but he could not very well tell her mother so.

"It will all work out," he said reassuringly.

"I'm sure it will. It only needs *time*."

They were both unhappy and they did not know quite what to say next.

3

Sarah had gone to her bedroom. With unseeing eyes she took clothes out of the wardrobe and spread them out on the bed.

Edith came in. "What are you doing, Miss Sarah?"

"Oh, looking through my things. Perhaps they need cleaning. Or mending or something."

"I've seen to all that. You've no need to bother."

Sarah did not reply. Edith took a quick look at her. She saw the tears welling up in Sarah's eyes.

"There, there, now, don't take on so."

"He's odious, Edith, quite odious. How could mother? Oh, everything's ruined, spoiled—nothing will ever be the same again!"

"Now, now, Miss Sarah. It's no good working yourself up.

Least said, soonest mended. What can't be cured must be endured."

Sarah laughed wildly.

"A stitch in time saves nine! And rolling stones gather no moss! Go away, Edith. Do go away."

Edith shook her head sympathetically and went away, shutting the door.

Sarah cried passionately, like a child. She was torn with misery. Like a child she saw blackness everywhere with nothing to redeem the gloom.

Under her breath she sobbed: "Oh, Mother, Mother, *Mother*. . . ."

Chapter Eight

1

"Oh, Laura, how pleased I am to see you."

Laura Whitstable sat down in an upright chair. She never lolled.

"Well, Ann, how's everything going?"

Ann sighed.

"Sarah's being rather difficult, I'm afraid."

"Well, that was to be expected, wasn't it?"

Laura Whitstable spoke with casual cheerfulness. But she looked at Ann with some concern.

"You're not looking very fit, my dear."

"I know. I don't sleep well and I get headaches."

"Don't take things too seriously."

"It's all very well to say that, Laura. You've no idea what it's like the whole time." Ann spoke fretfully. "The moment Sarah and Richard are left together for a moment, they quarrel."

"Sarah's jealous, of course."

"I'm afraid so."

"Well, as I said, that was to be expected. Sarah is still very much of a child. All children resent their mothers giving time and attention to somebody else. Surely you were prepared for that, Ann?"

"Yes, in a way. Although Sarah has always seemed so very detached and grown-up. Still, as you say, I was prepared for that. What I wasn't prepared for was Richard being jealous of Sarah."

"You expected Sarah to make a fool of herself, but thought that Richard might have a little more sense?"

"Yes."

"He's a man who's fundamentally unsure of himself. A more self-confident man would just laugh and tell Sarah to go to the devil."

Ann rubbed her forehead in an exasperated gesture.

"Really, Laura, you've no idea what it's like! They fall out about the silliest things and then they look at me to see which side I'm going to take."

"Very interesting."

"Very interesting to you—but it's not much fun for me."

"Which side *do* you take?"

"Neither if I can help it. But sometimes—"

"Yes, Ann?"

Ann was silent for a moment, then she said:

"You see, Laura, Sarah is cleverer than Richard about it all."

"In what way do you mean?"

"Well, Sarah's manner is always quite correct—outwardly. Polite, you know, and all that. But she knows how to get under Richard's skin. She—she torments him. And then he bursts out and becomes quite unreasonable. Oh, why can't they like each other?"

"Because there's a real natural antipathy between them, I should suppose. Do you agree with that? Or do you think it's only jealousy about you?"

"I'm afraid you may be right, Laura."

"What sort of things do they quarrel about?"

"The silliest things. For instance, you remember that I changed the furniture round, moved the desk and the sofa—and then Sarah moved it all back again, because she hates things changed . . . Well, Richard said suddenly one day:

'I thought you liked the desk over there, Ann.' I said I did think it gave more space. Then Sarah said, 'Well, I like it the way it always was.' And immediately Richard said in that domineering tone he sometimes puts on: 'It's not a question of what *you* like, Sarah, it's a question of what your mother likes. We'll arrange it the way she likes here and now.' And he moved the desk then and there and said to me: 'That's how you want it, isn't it?' So I more or less had to say 'Yes.' And he turned on Sarah and said: 'Any objections, young woman?' And Sarah looked at him and said quite quietly and politely: 'Oh, no. It's for mother to say. I don't count.' And you know, Laura, although I'd been backing up Richard, I really *felt* with Sarah. She loves her home and all the things in it—and Richard doesn't understand how she feels in the least. Oh dear, I don't know what to do."

"Yes, it's trying for you."

"I suppose it will wear off?"

Ann looked at her friend hopefully.

"I shouldn't count on that."

"I must say, you're not very comforting, Laura!"

"No good telling oneself fairy stories."

"It's really too unkind of them both. They ought to realize how unhappy they are making me. I really do feel *ill*."

"Self-pity won't help you, Ann. It never helps anybody."

"But I'm so unhappy."

"So are they, my dear. Give your pity to them. Sarah, poor child, is desperately miserable—and so, I imagine, is Richard."

"Oh dear, and we were so happy together until Sarah came home."

Dame Laura raised her eyebrows slightly. She was silent for a moment or two. Then she said: "You are getting married—when?"

"March 13th."

"Nearly two weeks still. You put it off—why?"

"Sarah begged me to. She said it would give her more time to get used to the idea. She went on and on at me until I gave way."

"Sarah . . . I see. And Richard was annoyed?"

"Of course he was annoyed. He was really very angry. He keeps saying that I've always spoiled Sarah. Laura, do you think that is true?"

"No, I don't. For all your love for Sarah you've never indulged her unduly. And up to now Sarah has always shown a reasonable consideration for you—as much, that is, as any egotistical young creature can."

"Laura, do you think I ought to—"

She stopped.

"Do I think you ought to do what?"

"Oh, nothing. But sometimes I feel I can't stand much more of this . . ."

She broke off as there was a sound of the front door of the flat opening. Sarah came into the room and looked pleased to see Laura Whitstable.

"Oh, Laura, I didn't know you were here."

"How's my godchild?"

Sarah came over and kissed her. Her cheek was fresh and cold from the outside air.

"I'm fine."

Murmuring something, Ann left the room. Sarah's eyes followed her. As they returned and met Dame Laura's, Sarah flushed guiltily.

Laura Whitstable nodded her head vigorously.

"Yes, your mother's been crying."

Sarah looked virtuous and indignant.

"Well, it's not *my* fault."

"Isn't it? You're fond of your mother, aren't you?"

"I adore mother. You know I do."

"Then why make her unhappy?"

"But I don't. I don't do *anything*."

"You quarrel with Richard, don't you?"

"Oh, *that!* Nobody could help it! He's impossible! If only mother could realize how impossible he is! I really think she will someday."

Laura Whitstable said:

"*Must* you try and arrange other people's lives for them, Sarah? In my young days it was parents who were accused of doing that to their children. Nowadays, it seems, it's the other way round."

Sarah sat down on the arm of Laura Whitstable's chair. Her manner was confiding.

"But I'm very worried," she said. "She's not going to be happy with him, you see."

"It's none of your business, Sarah."

"But I can't held *minding* about it. Because I don't want mother to be unhappy. And she will be. Mother's so—so helpless. She needs looking after."

Laura Whitstable imprisoned Sarah's two sunburnt hands in hers. She spoke with a forcefulness that startled Sarah into attention and something like alarm.

"Now listen, Sarah. Listen to me. *Be careful. Be very careful.*"

"What do you mean?"

Again Laura spoke with emphasis.

"Be very careful you don't let your mother do something she'll regret all her life."

"That's just what I—"

Laura swept on.

"I'm warning you. No one else will." She gave a sudden prolonged sniff, drawing in air through her nose. "I smell something in the air, Sarah, and I'll tell you what it is. *It's the smell of a burnt offering—* and I don't like burnt offerings."

Before they could say any more Edith opened the door and announced:

"Mr. Lloyd."

Sarah jumped up.

"Hullo, Gerry." She turned to Laura Whitstable. "This is Gerry Lloyd. My godmother, Dame Laura Whitstable."

Gerry shook hands and said:

"I believe I heard you on the wireless last night."

"How gratifying."

"Giving the second talk in the series 'How to Be Alive Today.' I was much impressed."

"None of your impudence," said Dame Laura, looking at him with a sudden twinkle.

"No, but I was, really. You seemed to have all the answers."

"Ah," said Dame Laura. "It's always easier to tell someone how to make a cake than to do it yourself. It's also much more enjoyable. Bad for the character, though. I am well aware that I get more odious every day."

"Oh, you don't," said Sarah.

"Yes, I do, child. I've almost reached the point of giving people good advice—an unpardonable sin. I shall go and find your mother now, Sarah."

2

As soon as Laura Whitstable had left the room, Gerry said:

"I'm getting out of this country, Sarah."

Sarah stared at him, stricken.

"Oh, Gerry—when?"

"Practically at once. Next Thursday."

"Where?"

"South Africa."

"But that's a long way," cried Sarah.

"It is rather."

"You won't come back for years and years!"

"Probably not."

"What are you going to do there?"

"Grow oranges. I'm going in with a couple of other chaps. Ought to be quite fun."

"Oh, Gerry, *must* you go?"

"Well, I'm fed up with this country. It's too tame and too smug. It's got no use for me and I haven't got any use for it."

"What about your uncle?"

"Oh, we're no longer on speaking terms; Aunt Lena's been quite kind, though. Gave me a check and some patent stuff for snake bites." He grinned.

"But do you *know* anything about growing oranges, Gerry?"

"Nothing whatever, but I imagine one soon picks it up."

Sarah sighed.

"I shall miss you. . . ."

"I don't suppose you will—not for long." Gerry spoke rather gruffly, avoiding looking at her. "If one's away at the other side of the world, people soon forget one."

"No, they don't. . . ."

He gave her a quick glance.

"Don't they?"

Sarah shook her head.

They looked away from each other, embarrassed.

"It's been fun—going about together," said Gerry.

"Yes . . ."

"People do quite well with oranges sometimes."

"I expect they do."

Gerry said, choosing his words carefully:

"I believe it's quite a cheery life—for a woman, I mean. Good climate—and plenty of servants—all that."

"Yes."

"But I suppose you'll go marrying some fellow . . ."

"Oh, no." Sarah shook her head. "It's a great mistake to marry too young. I don't mean to get married for ages."

"You think that—but some swine or other will make you change your mind," said Gerry gloomily.

"I've got a very cold nature," said Sarah reassuringly.

They stood, awkwardly, not looking at each other. Then Gerry, his face very pale, said in a choked voice:

"Darling Sarah—I'm crazy about you. You do know that?"

"Are you?"

Slowly, as though unwillingly, they drew closer together. Gerry's arms went round her. Timidly, wonderingly, they kissed. . . .

Strange, Gerry thought, that he should be so clumsy. He had been a gay young man and had had plenty of experience with girls. But this wasn't "girls," this was his own darling Sarah. . . .

"Gerry."

"Sarah . . ."

He kissed her again.

"You won't forget, darling Sarah, will you? All the amusing times we've had—and everything?"

"Of course I won't forget."

"You'll write to me?"

"I've got rather a thing about writing letters."

"But you'll write to me. Please, darling. I shall be so lonely. . . ."

Sarah pulled away from him and gave a shaky little laugh.

"You won't be lonely. There'll be lots of girls."

"If there are they'll be a lousy lot, I expect. But I rather imagine there will be nothing but oranges."

"You'd better send me a case from time to time."

"I will indeed. Oh, Sarah, I'd do anything for you."

"Well then, work hard. Make a success of your old orange farm."

"I will. I swear I will."

Sarah sighed.

"I wish you hadn't got to go just now," she said. "It's been such a comfort having you to talk things over with."

"How's Cauliflower? Do you like him any better?"

"No, I don't. We never stop having rows. But," her voice was triumphant, "I think I'm winning, Gerry!"

Gerry looked at her uncomfortable.

"You mean your mother—"

"I think she's beginning to see how impossible he is."

Sarah nodded her head in triumph.

Gerry looked more uncomfortable still.

"Sarah, I wish you wouldn't, somehow—"

"Not fight Cauliflower? I shall fight him tooth and nail! I won't give up. Mother's *got* to be saved."

"I wish you wouldn't interfere, Sarah. Your mother must know herself what she wants."

"I told you before, mother's weak. She gets sorry for people and her judgment goes. I'm saving her from making an unhappy marriage."

Gerry took his courage in both hands.

"Well, I still think you're just jealous."

Sarah cast him a furious look.

"All right! If that's what you think! You'd better go now."

"Now don't be mad with me. I daresay you know what you're doing."

"Of course I know," said Sarah.

3

Ann was in her bedroom sitting in front of the dressing table when Laura Whitstable came in.

"Feeling better now, my dear?"

"Yes. It was really very stupid of me. I mustn't let these things get on my nerves."

"A young man has just arrived. Gerald Lloyd. Is that the one—"

"Yes. What did you think of him?"

"Sarah's in love with him, of course."

Ann looked troubled. "Oh dear, I do hope not."

"No good your hoping."

"It can't come to anything, you see."

"He's thoroughly unsatisfactory, is he?"

Ann sighed. "I'm afraid so. He never sticks to anything. He's attractive. One can't help liking him but—"

"No stability?"

"One just feels he will never make good *anywhere*. Sarah is always saying what hard luck he's had, but I don't think it's only that." She went on: "Sarah knows so many really nice men, too."

"And finds them dull, I suppose. Nice capable girls—and Sarah is really very capable—are always attracted to detrimentals. It seems a law of nature. I must confess that I found the young man attractive myself."

"Even you, Laura?"

"I have my womanly weaknesses, Ann. Good night, my dear. Good luck to you."

4

Richard arrived at the flat just before eight. He was to dine there with Ann. Sarah was going out to a dinner and dance. She was in the sitting room when he arrived, painting her nails. There was a smell of peardrops in the air. She looked up and said: "Hullo, Richard," and then resumed operations. Richard watched her with irritation. He was rather dismayed himself at the increasing dislike he felt for Sarah. He had meant so well, had seen himself as the kindly and friendly stepfather, indulgent—almost fond. He had been prepared for suspicion at first, but had seen himself easily overcoming childish prejudices.

Instead it seemed to him that it was Sarah and not he who was in command of the situation. Her cool disdain and dislike pierced his sensitive skin and both wounded and humiliated him. Richard had never thought very much of himself, Sarah's treatment lowered his self-esteem still further. All his efforts, first to placate, then to dominate her, had been disastrous. He always seemed to say and do the wrong thing. Behind his dislike of Sarah there was growing, too, a rising irritation with Ann. Ann should support him. Ann should turn on Sarah and put her in her place, Ann should be on his side. Her efforts to play peacemaker, to steer a middle course, annoyed him. That sort of thing was no earthly use, and Ann ought to realize the fact!

Sarah stretched out a hand to dry, turning it this way and that.

Aware that it would have been better to say nothing, Richard could not stop himself remarking:

"Looks as though you'd dipped your fingers in blood. I can't think why you girls have to put that stuff on your nails."

"Can't you?"

Seeking for some safer topic, Richard went on:

"I met your friend young Lloyd this evening. He told me he was going out to South Africa."

"He's going on Thursday."

"He'll have to put his back into it if he wants to make a success out there. It's no place for a man who doesn't fancy working."

"I suppose you know all about South Africa?"

"All these places are much the same. They need men with guts."

"Gerry has plenty of guts," said Sarah, adding, "if you *must* use that expression."

"What's wrong with it?"

Sarah raised her head and gave him a cool stare.

"I just think it's rather disgusting—that's all," she said.

Richard's face went red.

"It's a pity your mother didn't bring you up to have better manners," he said.

"Was I rude?" Her eyes opened in an innocent stare. "I'm *so* sorry."

Her exaggerated apology did nothing to soothe him.

He asked abruptly:

"Where's your mother?"

"She's changing. She'll be here in a minute."

Sarah opened her bag and studied her face carefully. She began to touch it up, repainting her lips, applying eyebrow pencil. She had really made up her face some time ago. Her actions now were calculated to annoy Richard. She knew that he had a queer old-fashioned dislike of seeing a woman make up her face in public.

Trying to speak facetiously, Richard said:

"Come now, Sarah, don't overdo it."

She lowered the mirror she was holding and said:

"What do you mean?"

"I mean the paint and powder. Men don't really like such a lot of makeup, I can assure you. You simply make yourself look—"

"Like a tart, I suppose you mean?"

Richard said angrily:

"I didn't say so."

"But you meant it." Sarah dashed the makeup implements back in her bag. "Anyway, what the hell business is it of yours?"

"Look here, Sarah—"

"What I put on my face is my own business. It's no business of yours, you interfering Nosey Parker."

Sarah was trembling with rage, half crying.

Richard lost his temper thoroughly. He shouted at her:

"Of all the insufferable, bad-tempered little vixens. You're absolutely impossible!"

At that moment Ann came in. She stopped in the doorway and said wearily: "Oh dear, what's the matter *now*?"

Sarah rushed out past her. Ann looked at Richard.

"I was just telling her that she puts too much makeup on her face."

Ann gave a sharp exasperated sigh.

"Really, Richard, I do think you might have a little more sense. What earthly business is it of yours?"

Richard paced up and down angrily.

"Oh, very well. If you like your daughter going out looking like a tart."

"Sarah doesn't look like a tart," said Ann sharply. "What a horrid thing to say. All girls use makeup nowadays. You're so old-fashioned in your ideas, Richard."

"Old-fashioned! Out-of-date!—You don't think much of me, do you, Ann?"

"Oh, Richard, must we quarrel? Don't you realize that in saying what you did about Sarah, you're really criticizing *me*?"

"I can't say I think you're a particularly judicious mother. Not if Sarah is a specimen of your bringing up."

"That's a cruel thing to say and it's not true. There's nothing wrong with Sarah."

Richard flung himself down on a sofa.

"God help a man who marries a woman with an only daughter," he said.

Ann's eyes filled with tears.

"You knew about Sarah when you asked me to marry you. I told you how much I loved her and all she meant to me."

"I didn't know you were absolutely besotted about her! It's Sarah, Sarah, Sarah with you from morning to night!"

"Oh dear," said Ann. She went over to him and sat down beside him. "Richard, do try to be reasonable. I did think Sarah might be jealous of you—but I didn't think you'd be jealous of Sarah."

"I'm not jealous of Sarah," said Richard sulkily.

"But darling, you are."

"You always put Sarah first."

"Oh dear." Ann lay back helplessly and shut her eyes. "I really don't know what to do."

"Where do I come in? Nowhere. I simply don't count with you. You put off our marriage—simply because Sarah asked you to—"

"I wanted to give her a little more time to get used to the idea."

"Is she any more used to it now? She spends her whole time doing every earthly thing she can to annoy me."

"I know she's been difficult—but really, Richard, I do think you exaggerate. Poor Sarah can hardly say a word without your flying into a rage."

"Poor Sarah. Poor Sarah. You see? That's what you feel!"

"After all, Richard, Sarah's very little more than a child. One makes allowances for her. But you're a man—an adult human being."

Richard said suddenly, disarmingly:

"It's because I love you so, Ann."

"Oh, my dear."

"We were so happy together—before Sarah came home."

"I know. . . ."

"And now—all the time I seem to be losing you."

"But you're not losing me, Richard."

"Ann, dearest—you do still love me."

Ann said with sudden passion:

"More than ever, Richard. More than ever."

5

Dinner was a successful meal. Edith had taken pains with it, and the flat, with Sarah's tempestuous influence removed, was once again the peaceful setting it had been before.

Richard and Ann talked together, laughed, reminded each other of past incidents, and to both of them it was a welcome halcyon calm.

It was after they had returned to the drawing room and had finished their coffee and Benedictine that Richard said:

"This has been a wonderful evening. So peaceful. Ann dearest, if it could always be like this."

"But it will be, Richard."

"You don't really mean that, Ann. You know, I've been thinking things over. Truth's an unpleasant thing, but it's got to be faced. Quite frankly, I'm afraid that Sarah and I are never going to hit it off. If the three of us try to live together, life's going to be impossible. In fact, there's only one thing to be done."

"What do you mean?"

"To put it bluntly, Sarah's got to get out of here."

"No, Richard. That's impossible."

"When girls aren't happy at home, they go and live on their own."

"Sarah's only nineteen, Richard."

"There are places where girls can live. Hostels. Or as a P. G. with a suitable family."

Ann shook her head decidedly.

"I don't think you realize what you are suggesting. You are suggesting that because I want to marry again, I turn out my young daughter—turn her out of her home."

"Girls like being independent and living on their own."

"Sarah doesn't. It's not a question of her wanting to go off on her own. This is her home, Richard. She's not even of age."

"Well, I think it's a good sound scheme. We can give her a good allowance to live on—I'll contribute. She needn't feel skimped. She'll be happy on *her* own, and we'll be happy on *our* own. I can't see anything wrong with the plan."

"You're assuming that Sarah *is* going to be happy on her own?"

"She'll enjoy it. I tell you girls like independence."

"You don't know anything about girls, Richard. All you're thinking of is what *you* want."

"I'm suggesting what I think is a perfectly reasonable solution."

Ann said slowly: "You said before dinner that I put Sarah first. In a way, Richard, that's true. . . . It's not a question of which of you I love best. But when I consider you both—I know that it's Sarah whose interests have to come before yours. Because you see, Richard, Sarah is my responsibility. I've not done with that responsibility until Sarah is fully a woman—and she *isn't* fully a woman yet."

"Mothers never want their children to grow up."

"That's sometimes true, but I honestly don't think it's true of me and Sarah. I see, what you can't possibly see—that Sarah is still very young and defenseless."

Richard snorted.

"Defenseless!"

"Yes, that's just what I mean. She's unsure of herself, unsure of life. When she's ready to go out into the world, she'll *want* to go—and then I'll be only too ready to help her. But she's *not* ready."

Richard sighed. He said:

"I suppose one simply can't argue with mothers."

Ann said with unsuspected firmness:

"I'm not going to turn my daughter out of her home. To do that, when she didn't want to go, would be wicked."

"Well, if you feel so strongly about it."

"Oh, I do. But, Richard dear, if you will only have patience. Don't you see, it's not *you* who are the outsider, it's Sarah. And she feels it. But I know that, in time, she will learn to make friends with you. Because she really does love me, Richard. And, in the end, she won't want me to be unhappy."

Richard looked at her with a faintly quizzical smile.

"My sweet Ann, what an incurable wishful thinker you are."

She moved into the circle of his arm.

"Dear Richard—I love you. . . . Oh dear, I wish I hadn't got such a headache. . . ."

"I'll get you some aspirin. . . ."

It occurred to him that every conversation he had with Ann now ended in aspirin.

Chapter Nine

1

For two days there was an unexpected welcome peace. It encouraged Ann. Things after all were not so bad. In time, as she had said, everything would settle down. Her appeal to Richard had been successful. In a week's time they would be married—and after that, it seemed to her, life would be more normal. Sarah would surely cease to resent Richard so much, and would find more interest in outside matters.

"I really feel much better today," she observed to Edith.

It occurred to her that a day passing without a headache was now quite a phenomenon.

"Bit of a lull in the storm, as you might say," agreed Edith. "Just like cat and dog, Miss Sarah and Mr. Cauldfield. Taken what you might call a real natural dislike to each other."

"I think Sarah's getting over it a bit, though, don't you?"

"I shouldn't buoy yourself up with false hopes if I was you, ma'am," said Edith gloomily.

"But it can't go on like that always?"

"I shouldn't bank on that."

Edith, thought Ann, was always gloomy! She enjoyed predicting disasters.

"It *has* been better just lately," she insisted.

"Ah, because Mr. Cauldfield's been here mostly in the daytime when Miss Sarah's at her flower business, and she's had you to herself in the evenings. Besides, she's taken up with that Mr. Gerry going off to foreign parts. But once you're married, you'll have both of them here together. Tear you to pieces between them, they will."

"Oh, Edith." Dismay seized Ann. A horrible simile.

And so exactly what she had been feeling.

She said desperately: "I can't bear it. I *hate* scenes and rows and always have."

"That's right. Quiet and sheltered you've always lived, and that's the way it suits you."

"But what can I do about it? What would *you* do, Edith?"

Edith said with relish:

"No use repining. Taught as a child I was. '*This life is but a vale of tears.*' "

"If that's all you can suggest to console me!"

"These things are sent to try us," said Edith sententiously. "Now if only you were one of those ladies who enjoy rows! There's many that do. My uncle's second wife, for instance. Nothing she enjoys more than going at it hammer and tongs. Wicked tongue she's got—but there, once it's over, she bears no malice and never thinks twice about it again. Cleared the air, so to speak. Irish blood, *I* put it down to. Her mother came from Limerick. No spite in them, but always spoiling for a fight. Miss Sarah's got a bit of that. Mr. Prentice was half Irish, I remember your telling me. Likes to blow off steam, Miss Sarah does, but a betterhearted young lady never lived. If you ask me it's a good thing Mr. Gerry's taking himself off across the sea. He'll never settle down and go steady. Miss Sarah can do better than him."

"I'm afraid she's rather fond of him, Edith."

"I shouldn't worry. *Absence makes the heart grow fonder*, they say, but my Aunt Jane used to add onto that, 'of somebody else.' *Out of sight out of mind* is the truer proverb. Now don't you worry about her or anyone else. Here's that book you got from the library that you wanted so much to read, and I'll bring you in a nice cup of coffee and a biscuit or two. You enjoy yourself while you can."

The slightly sinister suggestion of the last three words was ignored by Ann. She said: "You're a great comfort, Edith."

On Thursday Gerry Lloyd left and Sarah came home that evening to have a worse quarrel than ever with Richard.

Ann left them and sought refuge in her own room. She lay there in the dark, her hands over her eyes, the fingers pressing on her aching forehead. Tears rolled down her cheeks.

She said to herself again and again under her breath: "I can't bear it. . . . I can't bear it. . . ."

Presently she heard the end of a sentence by Richard, almost shouted as he stormed out of the sitting room:

"—and your mother can't always get out of it by running away with one of her eternal headaches."

Then came the slam of the front door.

Sarah's footsteps sounded in the passage, coming slowly and hesitantly to her own room. Ann called out:

"Sarah."

The door opened. Sarah's voice, slightly conscience-stricken, said:

"All in the dark?"

"My head aches. Turn on the little lamp over in the corner."

Sarah did so. She came slowly toward the bed, her eyes averted. There was something forlorn and childish about her that struck at Ann's heart, although only a few minutes before she had felt violently angry with her.

"Sarah," said Ann. "Must you?"

"Must I what?"

"Quarrel with Richard the whole time? Haven't you got any feeling for me at all? Don't you realize how unhappy you're making me? Don't you want me to be happy?"

"Of course I want you to be happy. That's just *it!*"

"I don't understand you. You make me perfectly miserable. Sometimes I feel I can't go on. . . . Everything's so different."

"Yes, it's all different. He's spoiled everything. He wants to get me out of here. You won't let him make you send me away, will you?"

Ann was angry.

"Of course not. Who suggested such a thing?"

"He did. Just now. But you won't, will you? It's all like a bad dream." Suddenly Sarah's tears began to flow. "It's all gone wrong. Everything. Ever since I came back from Switzerland. Gerry's gone away—I shall probably never see him again. And you've turned against me—"

"I haven't turned against you! Don't say such things."

"Oh, Mother—Mother."

The girl flung herself down on her knees by the bed and sobbed uncontrollably.

She repeated at intervals that one word "Mother. . . ."

2

On Ann's breakfast tray the next morning was a note from Richard.

Dear Ann. Things really can't go on like this. We shall have to work out some kind of plan. I believe you will find Sarah more amenable than you think. Yours ever, Richard.

Ann frowned. Was Richard wilfully deceiving himself? Or had Sarah's outburst last night been largely hysterical? The latter was possible. Sarah, Ann felt sure, was suffering all the misery of calf love, and her first good-bye to the loved one. After all, since she disliked Richard so much, it might be that she really would be happier away from home. . . .

On an impulse Ann reached for the telephone and dialed Laura Whitstable's number.

"Laura? It's Ann."

"Good morning. This is a very early call."

"Oh, I'm at my wit's end. My head never stops aching and I feel quite ill. Things just can't go on like this. I wanted to ask your advice."

"I don't give advice. It's a most dangerous thing to do."

Ann paid no attention.

"Listen, Laura, do you think—possibly—it would be a good thing— if—if Sarah went to live by herself—I mean shared a flat with a friend— or something like that?"

There was a moment's pause and then Dame Laura asked:

"Does she want to?"

"Well—no—not exactly. I mean, it was just an *idea*."

"Who suggested it? Richard?"

"Well—yes."

"Very sensible."

"You do think it's sensible?" Ann said eagerly.

"I mean that it was very sensible from Richard's point of view. Richard knows what he wants—and goes for it."

"But what do *you* think?"

"I told you, Ann, I don't give advice. What does Sarah say?"

Ann hesitated.

"I haven't really discussed it with her—yet."

"But you've probably got some idea."

Ann said rather reluctantly: "I don't think she'd want to for a moment."

"Ah!"

"But perhaps I ought, really, to insist?"

"Why? To cure your headaches?"

"No, no," cried Ann, horrified. "I mean, entirely for her own happiness."

"That sounds magnificent! I always distrust noble sentiments. Elaborate, won't you?"

"Well, I've wondered whether perhaps I'm a rather clinging kind of mother. Whether it mightn't really be for Sarah's good to get away from me? So that she can develop her own personality."

"Yes, yes, very modern."

"Really, you know, I think she might quite *take* to the idea. I didn't at first, but now—Oh, do say what you think!"

"My poor Ann."

"Why do you say 'My poor Ann'?"

"You asked me what I thought."

"You're not being very helpful, Laura."

"In the sense you mean, I don't want to be."

"You see, Richard is really getting very hard to manage. He wrote me a kind of ultimatum this morning. . . . Soon he'll be asking me to choose between him and Sarah."

"And which would you choose?"

"Oh, don't, Laura. I didn't really mean it had come to that."

"It may do."

"Oh, you're maddening, Laura. You don't even try and help."

Ann banged down the receiver angrily.

3

At six o'clock that evening Richard Cauldfield rang up.

Edith answered the telephone.

"Mrs. Prentice in?"

"No, sir. She's out on that committee she goes to—an Old Ladies' Home or some such. She won't be back much before seven."

"And Miss Sarah?"

"Just come in. Do you want to speak to her?"

"No, I'll come round."

Richard covered the distance between his service flat and Ann's block of flats with a firm even tread. He had passed a sleepless night and had finally come to a definite resolution. Though a man who took a little time to make up his mind, once he had made it up, he stuck to his decision obstinately.

Things could not go on as they were. First Sarah and then Ann would have to be made to see that. That girl was wearing her mother out with her tantrums and her obstinacy! His poor tender Ann. But his thoughts of her were not entirely loving. Almost unrecognized, he felt a certain resentment against her. She was continually evading the point by her feminine artifices—her headaches, her collapse whenever a battle raged. . . . Ann had got to face up to things!

These two women. . . . All this feminine nonsense had got to *stop!*

He rang the bell, was admitted by Edith and went into the sitting room. Sarah, a glass in her hand, turned from the mantelpiece.

"Good evening, Richard."

"Good evening, Sarah."

Sarah said with an effort:

"I'm sorry, Richard, about last night. I'm afraid I was rather rude."

"That's all right." Richard waved a magnanimous hand. "We'll say no more about it."

"Will you have a drink?"

"No, thanks."

"I'm afraid mother won't be in for some time. She's gone to—"

He interrupted:

"That's all right. It's you I came to see."

"Me?"

Sarah's eyes darkened and narrowed. She came forward and sat down, watching him suspiciously.

"I want to talk things over with you. It seems to me perfectly clear that we can't go on as we are. All this sparring and bickering. It's not fair on your mother for one thing. You care for your mother, I'm sure."

"Naturally," said Sarah unemotionally.

"Then, between us, we've got to give her a break. In a week's time she and I are getting married. When we come back from our honeymoon, what sort of life do you think it is going to be, the three of us living here in this flat?"

"Pretty fair hell, I should think."

"You see? You recognize it yourself. Now I want to say right at the start that I don't put all the blame on you."

"That's very magnanimous of you, Richard," said Sarah.

Her tone was earnest and polite. He still did not know Sarah well enough to recognize a danger signal.

"It's unfortunate that we just don't get on. To be frank, you dislike me."

"If you must have it, yes, I do."

"That's all right. On my side, I'm not particularly fond of you."

"You hate me like poison," said Sarah.

"Oh, come now," said Richard, "I wouldn't put it as strongly as that."

"I would."

"Well, let's put it this way. We dislike each other. It doesn't matter much to me whether you like me or not. It's your mother I'm marrying, not you. I've tried to make friends with you but you won't have it. . . . So we've got to find a solution. I'm willing to do what I can in other ways?"

Sarah said suspiciously: "What other ways?"

"Since you can't stick life at home, I'll do what I can to help you lead your own life somewhere else where you can be a good deal happier. Once Ann is my wife, I'm prepared to provide for her entirely. There will be plenty of money over for you. A nice little flat somewhere, that you can share with a girl friend. Furnish it and all that—just exactly as you want it."

Her eyes narrowed still more, Sarah said: "What a wonderfully generous man you are, Richard."

He suspected no sarcasm. Inwardly he was applauding himself. After all, the thing was quite simple. The girl knew perfectly well which side her bread was buttered. The whole thing was going to settle itself quite amicably.

He smiled at her good-humoredly.

"Well, I don't like seeing people unhappy. And I realize, which your mother doesn't, that young people always hanker after going their own way and being independent. You'll be far happier on your own than living a cat-and-dog life here."

"So that's your suggestion, is it?"

"It's a very good idea. Everyone satisfied."

Sarah laughed. Richard turned his head sharply.

"You won't get rid of me as easily as that," said Sarah.

"But—"

"I won't go, I tell you. I won't go—"

Neither of them heard Ann's latchkey in the front door. She pushed open the door to find them standing glaring at each other. Sarah was shaking all over and repeating hysterically:

"I won't go—I won't go—I won't go—"

"Sarah—"

They both turned sharply. Sarah ran to her mother.

"Darling, darling, you won't let him send me away, will you? To live in a flat with a girl friend. I *hate* girl friends. I don't want to be on my own. I want to stay with you. Don't send me away, Mother. Don't—don't."

Ann said quickly, soothingly:

"Of course not. It's all right, darling." To Richard she said sharply: "What have you been saying to her?"

"Making a perfectly common-sense suggestion."

"He hates me, and he'll make you hate me."

Sarah was sobbing wildly now. She was a hysterical child.

Ann said quickly and soothingly:

"No, no, Sarah, don't be absurd."

She made a sign to Richard and said: "We'll talk about it some other time."

"No, we won't." Richard stuck his chin out. "We'll talk about it here and now. We've got to get matters straight."

"Oh, please." Ann moved forward, her hand to her head. She sat down on the sofa.

"No good getting out of it by having a headache, Ann! The question is, do I come first with you or does Sarah?"

"That's not the question."

"I say it is! All this has got to be settled once for all. I can't stand much more."

The loud tones of Richard's voice went through Ann's head setting every twinging nerve on fire in a flurry of pain. She had had a difficult committee meeting, had come home tired out, and now she felt that her life as at present lived was quite unendurable.

She said faintly: "I can't talk to you now, Richard. I really can't. I just can't stand anymore."

"I tell you it's got to be settled. Either Sarah gets out of here, or I do."

A faint quiver ran through Sarah's body. She lifted her chin, staring at Richard.

"My plan's a perfectly sensible one," said Richard. "I've outlined it to Sarah. She didn't seem to have much against it until you came in."

"I won't go," said Sarah.

"My good girl, you can come and see your mother whenever you want to, can't you?"

Sarah turned passionately to Ann, flinging herself down beside her.

"Mother, Mother, you won't turn me out? You won't, will you? You're my mother."

A flush rose in Ann's face. She said with sudden firmness:

"I shall not ask my only daughter to leave her home unless she wants to do so."

Richard shouted: "She would want to—if it weren't to spite me."

"That's the sort of thing *you* would think!" Sarah spat at him.

"Hold your tongue," shouted Richard.

Ann raised her hands to her head.

"I can't bear this," she said, "I'm warning you both, I can't bear it . . ."

Sarah cried appealingly:

"Mother . . ."

Richard turned on Ann angrily:

"It's no use, Ann. You and your headaches! You've got to choose, damn it all."

"Mother," Sarah was really beside herself now. She clung to Ann like a frightened child. "Don't let him turn you against me. Mother . . . don't let him . . ."

Ann, her hands still clutching her head, said: "I can't bear anymore. You'd better go, Richard."

"What?" He stared at her.

"Please go. Forget me . . . It's no use. . . ."

Again anger enveloped him. He said grimly:

"Do you realize what you're saying?"

Ann said distractedly: "I must have peace . . . I can't go on . . ."

Sarah whispered again: "Mother. . . ."

"Ann . . ." Richard's voice was full of incredulous pain.

Ann cried desperately: "It's no use . . . it's no *use*, Richard."

Sarah turned on him furiously and childishly:

"Go away," she said, "we don't want you, do you hear? We don't want you . . ."

There was a triumph in her face that would have been ugly if it had not been so childish.

He paid no attention to her. He was looking at Ann.

He said very quietly: "Do you mean this? I shan't—come back."

In an exhausted voice Ann said:

"I know . . . It just—can't be, Richard. Good-bye . . ."

He walked slowly out of the room.

Sarah cried: "Darling" and buried her head on her mother's lap.

Mechanically, Ann's hand stroked her daughter's head, but her eyes were on the door through which Richard had just gone out.

A moment later she heard the sound of the front door closing with a decisive bang.

She felt the same coldness she had felt that that day at Victoria Station together with a great desolation. . . .

Richard was walking down the stairs now, out into the courtyard and away down the street. . . .

Walking out of her life. . . .

BOOK TWO

Chapter One

1

Laura Whitstable looked affectionately through the windows of the Airway bus at the familiar streets of London. She had been away from London a long time, serving on a Royal Commission which had entailed an interesting and prolonged tour round the globe. The final sessions in the United States had been strenuous. Dame Laura had lectured and presided and lunched and dined, and had found difficulty in finding time to see her own personal friends.

Well, it was over now. She was home again, with a suitcase filled with notes and statistics and relevant papers, and with the prospect of a good deal more strenuous work ahead of her preparing for publication.

She was a woman of great vitality and enormous physical toughness. The prospect of work was always more alluring to her than the prospect of leisure, but unlike many people, she did not pride herself on the fact, and would sometimes disarmingly admit that the preference might be regarded as a weakness rather than a virtue. For work, she would say, was one of the chief avenues by which one escapes from oneself. And to live with oneself, without subterfuge, and in humility and content, was to attain the only true harmony of life.

Laura Whitstable was a woman who concentrated on one thing at a time. She had never been given to writing long newsy letters to friends. When she was absent, she was absent—in thought as well as in body.

She did conscientiously send highly-colored picture postcards to her domestic staff who would have been affronted if she had not done so. But her friends and intimates were aware that the first they would hear of Laura was a deep gruff voice on the telephone announcing that she was back again.

It was good to be home, Laura thought, a little later, as she looked round her comfortable mannish sitting room and listened with half an ear to Bassett's melancholy unimpassioned catalogue of small domestic disasters that had occurred in her absence.

She dismissed Bassett with a final "Quite right to tell me" and sank into the large, shabby leather-covered armchair. Letters and periodicals were heaped on a side table, but she did not bother about them. Everything urgent had been dealt with by her efficient secretary.

She lit a cigar and leaned back in the chair, her eyes half closed.

This was the end of one period, the beginning of another. . . .

She relaxed, letting the engine of her brain slow down and change over to the new rhythm. Her fellow commissioners—the problems that had arisen—speculations—points of view—American personalities— her American friends . . . gently, inexorably, they all receded, became shadowy . . .

London, the people she must see, the bigwigs whom she would bully, the Ministries to which she proposed to make herself a nuisance, the practical measures that she intended to take—the reports she must write . . . it all came clearly into her mind. The future campaign, the grueling daily tasks. . . .

But before that there was an interregnum, a settling in again. Personal relationships and pleasures. Her own personal friends to see—a revived interest in their troubles and joys. A revisiting of her favorite haunts—all the hundred and one pleasures of her intimate private life. Presents that she had brought home with her to be bestowed. . . . Her rugged face softened and she smiled. Names floated into her mind. Charlotte—young David—Geraldine and her children—old Walter Emlyn—Ann and Sarah—Professor Parkes . . .

What had happened to them all since she had been away?

She would go down to see Geraldine in Sussex—the day after tomorrow if that was convenient. She reached out for the telephone, got through, fixed a day and a time. Then she rang old Professor Parkes. Blind and almost stone deaf, he nevertheless seemed to be in the best of health and spirits and eager for a real furious controversy with his old friend Laura.

The next number she rang was that of Ann Prentice.

It was Edith who answered.

"Well, this is a surprise, ma'am. A long time it's been. Read a piece about you in the paper, I did, not above a month or two ago. No, I'm sorry, Mrs. Prentice is out. Nearly always out in the evening she is, nowadays. Yes, Miss Sarah's out, too. Yes, ma'am, I'll tell Mrs. Prentice you rang and that you're back again."

Restraining a desire to remark that it would have been harder for her to ring up if she hadn't been back again, Laura Whitstable rang off, and proceeded to dial another number.

During the ensuing conversations and the making of arrangements to meet, Laura Whitstable relegated to the back of her mind some small point which she promised herself to examine later.

It was not until she was in bed that her analytical mind questioned why something that Edith had said had surprised her. It was a moment or two before it came back to her, but at last she pinned it down. Edith had said that Ann was out and that she nearly always was out in the evenings, nowadays.

Laura frowned because it seemed to her that Ann must have changed very much in her habits. Sarah, naturally, might be supposed to go racketing around every evening of her life. Girls did. But Ann was the quiet type—an occasional dinner engagement—a cinema now and then—or a play—but not a nightly routine.

Lying in bed Laura Whitstable thought about Ann Prentice for some time . . .

2

It was a fortnight later that Dame Laura rang the bell of Ann Prentice's flat.

Edith opened the door, and her sour face changed ever so slightly, indicating that she was pleased.

She stood aside as Dame Laura entered.

"Mrs. Prentice is just dressing to go out," she said. "But I know she'll want to see you."

She ushered Dame Laura into the sitting room and her footsteps stumped along the passage toward Ann's bedroom.

Laura looked round the room in some surprise. It was completely transformed—she would hardly have known it for the same room, and just for a moment she toyed with the absurd idea that she had come to the wrong flat.

A few pieces of the original furniture remained, but across one corner was a big cocktail bar. The new decor was an up-to-date version of French Empire, with smartly striped satin curtains and a good deal of gilt and ormolu. The few pictures on the wall were modern. It looked less like a room in somebody's home, than like a "set" for a stage production.

Edith looked in to say:

"Mrs. Prentice will be with you in a moment, ma'am."

"This is a complete transformation scene," remarked Dame Laura, indicating her surroundings.

"Cost a mint of money, it did," said Edith with disapproval. "And one or two very odd young men there's been here seeing to it all. You wouldn't believe."

"Oh yes, I would," said Dame Laura. "Well, they seem to have made a very good job of it."

"Gimcrack," said Edith with a sniff.

"One must go with the times, Edith. I expect Miss Sarah likes it very much."

"Oh, it's not Miss Sarah's taste. Miss Sarah, she's never one for change. Never was. Why, you remember her, ma'am, didn't even like the sofa turned the other way! No, it's Mrs. Prentice that's so mad about all this."

Dame Laura raised her eyebrows slightly. It seemed to her again that Ann Prentice must have changed a good deal. But at that moment steps came hurrying down the passage, and Ann herself rushed in, her hands outstretched.

"Laura darling, how wonderful. I've been longing to see you."

She gave Laura a rapid and perfunctory kiss. The older woman studied her with surprise.

Yes, Ann Prentice had changed. Her hair, soft leaf-brown hair with a thread or two of gray, had been hennaed and cut in the latest and most extreme style. Her eyebrows had been plucked and her face was expensively made up. She was wearing a short cocktail dress adorned with a large and bizarre cluster of costume jewelry. Her movements were restless and artificial—and that, to Laura Whitstable, was the most significant change of all. For a gentle unhurried repose had been the chief characteristic of the Ann Prentice she had known two years ago.

Now she moved about the room, talking, fidgeting with small trifles and hardly waiting for an answer to what she said.

"It's such a long time—really ages—of course I've read about you occasionally in the paper. What was India like? They seem to have made a terrific fuss of you in the States? I suppose you had lovely food—beefsteaks—all that? And nylons! When did you get back?"

"A fortnight ago. I rang you up. You were out. I daresay Edith forgot to tell you."

"Poor old Edith. Her memory's not what it was. No, I think she did tell me, and I did mean to ring up—only you know what things are." She gave a little laugh. "One lives in such a rush."

"You usen't to live in a rush, Ann."

"Didn't I?" Ann was vague. "It seems impossible to avoid it. Have a drink, Laura. Gin and lime?"

"No, thanks. I never drink cocktails."

"Of course. Brandy and soda is your tipple. Here you are." She poured out the drink and brought it over, and then returned to get a drink for herself.

"How's Sarah?" asked Dame Laura.

Ann said vaguely:

"Oh, very well and gay. I hardly ever see her. Where's the gin? Edith! Edith!"

Edith came in.

"Why isn't there any gin?"

"Hasn't come," said Edith.

"I told you we must always have a reserve bottle. It's too sickening! You *must* see to it that we always have plenty of drink in the house."

"Enough comes in, goodness knows," said Edith. "A sight too much, to my way of thinking."

"That will do, Edith," cried Ann angrily. "Go round and get some."

"What, now?"

"Yes, now."

As Edith retreated, looking grim, Ann said angrily:

"She forgets everything. She's hopeless!"

"Well, don't work yourself up, my dear. Come and sit down and tell me all about yourself."

"There's nothing much to tell," Ann laughed.

"You're going out? Am I keeping you?"

"Oh no, no. My boyfriend's coming to fetch me."

"Colonel Grant?" asked Dame Laura, smiling.

"Poor old James? Oh no. I hardly ever see him nowadays."

"How's that?"

"These old men are really so terribly boring. James is a dear, I know—but those long rambling stories of his . . . I just feel I can't stand it." Ann shrugged her shoulders. "Awful of me—but there it is!"

"You haven't told me about Sarah. Has she got a young man?"

"Oh, lots of them. She's very popular, thank goodness . . . I really couldn't face having a daughter who was all wet."

"Not any particular young man, then?"

"We-ell. It's hard to say. Girls never tell their mothers anything, do they?"

"What about young Gerald Lloyd—the one you were rather worried about?"

"Oh, he went off to South America or somewhere. That's all washed up, thank goodness. Fancy your remembering that!"

"I remember things about Sarah. I'm very fond of her."

"Sweet of you, Laura. Sarah's all right. Very selfish and tiresome in many ways—but I suppose that has to be at her age. She'll be in presently and then—"

The telephone rang and Ann broke off to answer it.

"Hullo? . . . Oh it's you, darling . . . Why, of course, I'd love to . . . Yes, but I'll have to look in my little book . . . Oh, bother, I don't know where it is . . . Yes, I'm sure it's all right . . . Thursday, then . . . the *Petit Chat* . . . Yes, wasn't it? . . . Funny the way Johnnie passed out completely . . . Well, of course, we were all a bit tight . . . Yes, I do agree . . ."

She replaced the receiver, remarking to Laura with a note of satisfaction in her voice that belied the words:

"That telephone! It goes all day long."

"It's a habit they have," Laura Whitstable agreed dryly.

She added: "You seem to be leading a very gay life, Ann?"

"One can't vegetate, darling—oh, that sounds like Sarah."

Outside in the hall they heard Sarah's voice:

"Who? Dame Laura? Oh, splendid!"

She flung open the sitting-room door and came in. Laura Whitstable was struck by her beauty. The awkward touch of coltishness had gone, she was now a remarkably attractive young woman, with a quite unusual loveliness of face and form.

She looked radiant with pleasure at the sight of her godmother and kissed her warmly.

"Laura darling, how lovely. You do look wonderful in that hat. Almost Royal with a weeny touch of the militant Tyrolean."

"Impertinent child," said Laura, smiling at her.

"No, but I mean it. You really are a Personage, aren't you, pet?"

"And you're a very handsome young woman!"

"Oh, that's just my expensive makeup."

The telephone rang and Sarah picked it up.

"Hullo? Who's speaking? Yes, she's here. It's for you, Mother—as usual."

As Ann took the receiver from her, Sarah sat on the arm of Laura's chair.

"The telephone rings for Mother all day long," she said, laughing.

Ann said sharply:

"Be quiet, Sarah, I can't hear. Yes . . . well, I think so . . . but next week I'm terribly booked up . . . I'll look in my little book." Turning, she said, "Sarah, find my book. It must be by my bed . . ." Sarah went out of the room. Ann went on talking into the telephone. "Well, of course I know what you mean . . . yes, that sort of thing is an awful bind . . . Do you, darling? . . . Well, as far as I'm concerned I've had Edward . . . I . . . oh, here's my book. Yes . . ." she took it from Sarah, turning the pages . . . "No, I can't manage Friday . . . Yes, I could go on afterward . . . Very well then, we'll meet at the Lumley Smiths . . . Oh yes, I do agree. She's terribly wet."

She replaced the receiver and exclaimed:

"That telephone! I shall go off my head . . ."

"You adore it, Mother. And you adore gadding about, you know you do." Sarah turned to Dame Laura and demanded, "Don't you think Mother is looking awfully smart with that new hairdo? Years younger."

Ann said with a slightly artificial laugh:

"Sarah won't let me sink into graceful middle-age."

"Now, Mother, you know you like being gay. She's got far more boyfriends than I have, Laura, and she's seldom home before dawn."

"Don't be absurd, Sarah," said Ann.

"Who is it tonight, Mother? Johnnie?"

"No, Basil."

"Oh, sooner you than me. I really think Basil is pretty well the end."

"Nonsense," said Ann sharply. "He's very amusing. What about you, Sarah? You're going out, I suppose?"

"Yes, Lawrence is coming for me. I must rush and change."

"Go on, then. And Sarah—*Sarah*—don't leave your things all over the place. Your fur—and your gloves. And pick up that glass. It will get broken."

"Oh all right, Mother, don't fuss."

"Someone has to fuss. You never clear up anything. Really, sometimes I don't know how I stand it! No—take them *with* you!"

As Sarah went out, Ann sighed in an exasperated fashion.

"Really, girls are absolutely maddening. You've no idea how trying Sarah is!"

Laura gave her friend a quick sideways glance.

There had been a note of real bad temper and irritation in Ann's voice.

"Don't you get tired with so much rushing about, Ann?"

"Of course I do—dead tired. Still, one must do something to amuse oneself."

"You never used to have much difficulty amusing yourself."

"Sit at home with a good book and have a meal on a tray? One goes through that dull period. But I've got my second wind now. By the way, Laura, it was you who first used that expression. Aren't you glad to see it's come true?"

"I didn't exactly mean the social round."

"Of course you didn't, darling. You meant take up some worthy object. But we can't all be public characters like you, tremendously scientific and serious-minded. I like being gay."

"What does Sarah like? Does she like being gay too? How is the child? Happy?"

"Of course. She has a wonderful time."

Ann spoke lightly and carelessly, but Laura Whitstable frowned. As Sarah had gone out of the room, Laura had been disturbed by a momentary expression of deep weariness on the girl's face. It was as though for a moment the smiling mask had slipped—underneath it Laura thought she had glimpsed uncertainty and something like pain.

Was Sarah happy? Ann evidently thought so. And Ann would know.

"Don't fancy things, woman," said Laura Whitstable to herself, sternly.

But in spite of herself she felt uneasy and disturbed. There was something not quite right in the atmosphere of the flat. Ann, Sarah, even Edith—all of them were conscious of it. All of them, she thought, had something to hide. Edith's grim look of disapproval, Ann's restlessness and nervous artificial manner, Sarah's brittle poise . . . There was something wrong somewhere.

The front doorbell rang and Edith, her face grimmer than ever, announced Mr. Mowbray.

Mr. Mowbray darted in. There was no other term for it. It was the skimming motion of some gay insect. Dame Laura thought that he would play Osric well. He was young and affected in manner.

"Ann!" he exclaimed. "So you're wearing it! My dear, it's the greatest success."

He held off, his head on one side, studying Ann's dress, while Ann introduced him to Dame Laura.

He advanced upon her exclaiming with excitement:

"A *cameo* brooch. How absolutely *adorable!* I adore cameos. I've got a thing about them!"

"Basil has a thing about all Victorian jewelry," said Ann.

"My dear, they had imagination. Those heavenly heavenly lockets. Two people's hair all worked into a curl and a weeping willow or an urn. They can't do that hair work nowadays. It's a lost art. And wax flowers—I'm crazy about wax flowers—and little papier mâché tables. Ann, you must let me take you to see a really divine table. Fitted up inside with the original tea caddies. Wickedly wickedly expensive, but it's worth it."

Laura Whitstable said:

"I must be going. Don't let me keep you."

"Stay and talk to Sarah," said Ann. "You've hardly seen her. And Lawrence Steene won't be calling for her yet awhile."

"Steene? Lawrence Steene?" Dame Laura asked sharply.

"Yes, Sir Harry Steene's son. Most attractive."

"Oh, do you think so, darling?" said Basil. "He always seems to me rather *melodramatic*—a little like a bad film. But women all seem to go quite crazy about him."

"He's disgustingly rich," said Ann.

"Yes, there's that. Most rich people are so deadly unattractive. It hardly seems fair that anyone should have money and attraction."

"Well, I suppose we'd better go," said Ann. "I'll ring you up, Laura, and we'll arrange for a lovely long talk sometime."

She kissed Laura in a faintly artificial manner and she and Basil Mowbray went out.

In the hall Dame Laura heard Basil say: "What a wonderful Period Piece she is—so divinely grim. Why have I never met her before?"

Sarah rushed in a few minutes later.

"Haven't I been quick? I hurried and hardly did anything to my face."

"That's a pretty frock, Sarah."

Sarah whirled round. She was wearing a pale eau-de-nil satin that clung to the lovely lines of her figure.

"Like it? It was wickedly expensive. Where's Mother? Gone off with Basil? He's pretty terrible, isn't he, but he's very amusing and spiteful and he makes a sort of special cult of older women."

"He probably finds it pays," said Dame Laura grimly.

"What an old cynic you are—and horribly right, too! But after all, Mother must have *some* fun. She's enjoying herself madly, poor pet. And she really is awfully attractive, don't you think so? Oh dear, it must be terrible to grow old!"

"It's quite comfortable, I can assure you," said Dame Laura.

"It's all very well for *you*—but we can't all be Personages! What have you been doing all these years since we've seen you?"

"Generally throwing my weight about. Interfering with other people's lives and telling them how easy and pleasant and well and happy they will be if they do exactly as I tell them. In fact, making a nuisance of myself in an overbearing way."

Sarah laughed affectionately.

"Will you tell me just how to manage my life?"

"Do you need telling?"

"Well, I'm not sure that I'm being very clever about it."

"Anything the matter?"

"Not really . . . I have a lovely time and all that. I suppose really I ought to *do* something."

"What sort of thing?"

Sarah said vaguely:

"Oh. I don't know. Take something up. Train for something. Archaeology or shorthand and typing, or massage, or architecture."

"What a wide range! No special bent?"

"No—no, I don't think so. . . . This flower job is all right, but I'm a bit sick of it. I don't know what I want really. . . ."

Sarah wandered aimlessly about the room.

"Not thinking of getting married?"

"Oh, marriage!" Sarah made an expressive grimace. "Marriages always seem to go wrong."

"Not invariably."

Sarah said: "Well, most of my friends seem to have come apart. It's all right for a year or two and then it goes wrong. Of course if you marry someone with pots of money, I suppose it's all right."

"So that's your view?"

"Well, it's really the only sensible one. Love's all right in a way, but after all," Sarah went on glibly, "it's only based on sexual attraction, and that can't last."

"You seem as well informed as a textbook," said Dame Laura dryly.

"Well, it's true, isn't it?"

"Perfectly true," Laura replied promptly.

Sarah looked faintly disappointed.

"Therefore the only sensible thing is to marry someone—really well off."

A faint smile twisted Laura Whitstable's lips.

"That mightn't last either," she said.

"Yes, I suppose money is a bit uncertain these days."

"I didn't mean that," said Dame Laura. "I meant that the pleasure of having money to spend is like sexual attraction. One gets used to it. It wears off like everything else."

"It wouldn't with me," said Sarah positively. "Really lovely clothes . . . and furs—and jewelry—and a yacht—"

"What a child you are still, Sarah."

"Oh, but I'm not, Laura. I feel very old and disillusioned sometimes."

"Do you?" Dame Laura could not help smiling a little at Sarah's young and beautiful earnest face.

"I think really I ought to get out of here somehow," said Sarah unexpectedly. "Take a job or get married, or something. I get on Mother's nerves frightfully. I try to be nice, but it doesn't seem to work. Of course, I am difficult, I suppose. Life is odd, isn't it, Laura? One moment everything is such fun and you're enjoying yourself, and then it all seems to go wrong, and you don't know where you are and what you want to do. And there isn't anyone you can talk to. And sometimes I get a funny feeling of being scared. I don't know why or what of. . . . But just—*scared*. Perhaps I ought to be analyzed or something."

The front doorbell sounded. Sarah jumped up.

"That's Lawrence, I expect!"

"Lawrence Steene?" Laura asked sharply.

"Yes. Do you know him?"

"I've heard about him," said Laura. Her tone was rather grim.

Sarah laughed.

"No good, I'll be bound," she said, as Edith opened the door and announced: "Mr. Steene."

Lawrence Steene was tall and dark. He was about forty and looked it. He had rather curious eyes, almost veiled by the lids, and a languorous animal-like grace of movement. He was the sort of man of whom women are immediately conscious.

"Hullo, Lawrence," said Sarah. "This is Lawrence Steene. My godmother, Dame Laura Whitstable."

Lawrence Steene came across and took Dame Laura's hand. He bowed over it in a manner that was slightly theatrical and might almost have been impertinent.

"This is indeed an honor," he said.

"You see, darling?" said Sarah. "You really *are* Royalty! It must be great fun to be a Dame. Do you think I shall ever be one?"

"I should think it most unlikely," said Lawrence.

"Oh, why?"

"Your talents lie in other directions."

He turned to Dame Laura.

"I was reading an article of yours only yesterday. In the *Commentator*."

"Oh yes," said Dame Laura. "On the stability of marriage."

Lawrence murmured:

"You seemed to take it for granted that stability in marriage was to be desired. But to my mind it is the impermanence of marriage nowadays which constitutes its greatest charm."

"Lawrence has been married a good deal," put in Sarah mischievously.

"Only three times, Sarah."

"Dear me," said Dame Laura. "Not another case of brides in the bath, I hope?"

"He sheds them in the divorce court," said Sarah. "Much simpler than death."

"But regrettably more expensive," said Lawrence.

"I believe I knew your second wife when she was a girl," said Laura. "Moira Denham, am I right?"

"Yes, indeed."

"A very charming girl."

"I do agree with you. She was quite delightful. So unsophisticated."

"A quality for which one sometimes pays heavily," said Laura Whitstable.

She got up.

"I must go."

"We can drop you," said Sarah.

"No, thanks. I feel like a brisk walk. Good night, my dear."

The door shut briskly behind her.

"The disapproval," said Lawrence, "was marked. I'm a bad influence in your life, Sarah. The dragon Edith positively breathes fire from her nostrils whenever she lets me in."

"Hush," said Sarah. "She'll hear you."

"That's the worst of flats. No privacy . . ."

He had moved very close to her. Sarah moved away a little, saying flippantly:

"No, nothing's private in a flat, not even the plumbing."

"Where's your mother this evening?"

"She's out to dinner."

"Your mother is one of the wisest women I know."

"In what way?"

"She never interferes, does she?"

"No—oh no . . ."

"As I said—a wise woman. . . . Well, let's go." He stood back a minute looking at her. "You look your best tonight, Sarah. That's as it should be."

"Why all this fuss about tonight? Is it a special occasion?"

"It's a celebration. I'll tell you what we're celebrating later."

Chapter Two

It was some hours later when Sarah repeated her question.

They were sitting in the hazy atmosphere of one of London's most expensive nightclubs. It was crowded, insufficiently ventilated and, as far as could be seen, had nothing about it to distinguish it from any other nightclub, nevertheless it was, just for the time being, the fashion.

Once or twice Sarah had tried to approach the subject of what they were celebrating, but Steene had successfully parried her attempts. He was an adept in producing the right sense of heightened interest.

As she smoked and looked round her, Sarah said: "Lots of Mother's stuffy old friends think it's terrible that I'm allowed to come to this place."

"And still worse that you're allowed to come here with me?"

Sarah laughed.

"Why are you supposed to be so dangerous, Larry? Do you go about seducing innocent young girls?"

Lawrence shuddered affectedly and said: "Nothing so crude."

"What, then?"

"I'm supposed to participate in what newspapers call nameless orgies."

Sarah said frankly: "I've heard that you do have rather peculiar parties."

"Some people would call them that. The simple truth is that I'm not conventional. There's so much to be done with life if you've only got the courage to experiment."

Sarah kindled eagerly.

"That's what *I* think."

Steene went on:

"I don't really care about young girls much. Silly fluffy crude little things. But you're different, Sarah. You've got courage and fire—real fire in you." His eyes drifted meaningly over her in a slow caress.

"You've got a beautiful body, too. A body that can enjoy sensation—can taste—can feel. . . . You hardly know your own potentialities yet."

With an effort to hide her inner reaction, Sarah said lightly:

"You've got a very good line there, Larry. I'm sure it always goes down well."

"My dear—most girls bore me to distraction. You—don't. Hence—" he raised his glass to her—"our celebration."

"Yes—but what are we celebrating? Why all the mystery?"

He smiled at her.

"No mystery. It's quite simple. My divorce decree was made absolute today."

"Oh—" Sarah looked startled. Steene was watching her.

"Yes, it clears the way. Well—what about it, Sarah?"

"What about what?" said Sarah.

Steene spoke with a sudden telling savagery:

"Don't play the wide-eyed innocent with me, Sarah. You know well enough I—want you. You've known it for some time."

Sarah avoided his glance. Her heart was beating pleasurably. There was something very exciting about Larry.

"You find most women attractive, don't you?" she asked lightly.

"Only a very few nowadays. At the moment—only you." He paused and then said quietly and almost casually: "You're going to marry me, Sarah."

"I don't want to get married. Anyway, I should think you'd be glad to be free again without tying yourself up immediately."

"Freedom is an illusion."

"You're not a very good advertisement for matrimony. Your last wife was pretty unhappy, wasn't she?"

Lawrence said calmly:

"She cried almost incessantly for the last two months we were together."

"Because, I suppose, she cared for you?"

"So it seemed. She was always an incredibly stupid woman."

"Why did you marry her?"

"She was so exactly like an early Primitive Madonna. My favorite period of art. But that sort of thing palls on one in the home."

"You're a cruel devil, aren't you, Larry?" Sarah was half revolted, half fascinated.

"That's really what you like about me. If I were the type of man to make you a good, steady and faithful husband you wouldn't think twice about me."

"Well, you're frank, at any rate."

"Do you want to live tamely, Sarah, or dangerously?"

Sarah did not answer. She pushed a small piece of bread round her side plate. Then she said: "Your second wife—Moira Denham—the one Dame Laura knew—what—what about her?"

"You'd better ask Dame Laura." He smiled. "She'll give you chapter and verse. A sweet unsophisticated girl—and I broke her heart—putting it in the romantic vernacular."

"You seem a bit of a menace to wives, I must say."

"I didn't break my first wife's heart, I can assure you. Moral disapprobation was her reason for leaving me. A woman with a high standard. The truth of it is, Sarah, that women are never content to marry you for what you are. They wish you to be different. But at least you will admit that I do not conceal my real character from you. I like living dangerously, I like tasting forbidden pleasures. I have no high moral standards and I do not pretend to be what I am not."

He dropped his voice.

"I can give you a great deal, Sarah. I don't mean only what money can buy—furs to wrap round your adorable body, and jewels to put against your white skin. I mean that I can offer you the whole gamut of sensation. I can make you live, Sarah—I can make you *feel*. All life is experience, remember."

"I—yes, I suppose it is."

She was looking at him, half revolted, half fascinated. He leaned nearer to her.

"What do you really know of life, Sarah? Less than nothing! I can take you places, horrible sordid places, where you'll see life running fierce and dark, where you can feel—*feel*—till being alive is a dark ecstasy!"

He narrowed his eyes, watching the effect on her of his words. Then, deliberately, he broke the spell.

"Well," he said cheerfully, "we'd better get out of here."

He motioned the waiter to bring his bill.

Then he smiled at Sarah in a detached manner.

"Now I'm going to take you home."

In the luxurious darkness of the car, Sarah held herself taut and on the defensive, but Lawrence did not even attempt to touch her. Secretly she knew that she was disappointed. Smiling to himself, Lawrence was aware of that disappointment. Technically he knew a great deal about women.

He went up with her to the flat. Sarah opened the door with her key. She went into the sitting room, switching on the light.

"A drink, Larry?"

"No, thanks. Good night, Sarah."

She was impelled to call him back. He had counted on that.

"Larry."

"Yes?"

He stood in the doorway, his head turned over his shoulder.

His eyes swept over her with a connoisseur's approval. Perfect—quite perfect. Yes, he had got to have her. His pulses quickened a little, but he showed nothing in his face.

"You know—I think—"

"Yes?"

He came back toward her. They both spoke in low voices, mindful of the fact that Sarah's mother and Edith were presumably asleep nearby.

Sarah spoke in a hurried voice.

"You see, the fact is, I'm not really in love with you, Larry."

"Aren't you?"

Something in his tone made her voice hurry on, stammering a little.

"No—not really. Not properly. I mean, if you were to lose all your money and—oh, go and run an orange farm or something somewhere, I shouldn't think twice of you again."

"That would be very sensible."

"But that does show I'm not in love with you."

"Nothing would bore me more than romantic devotion. I don't want *that* from you, Sarah."

"Then—what do you want—?"

It was an unwise question—but she wanted to ask it. She wanted to go on. She wanted to see what—

He was very close beside her. Now, suddenly, he bent and kissed the nape of her neck. His hands went round her, holding her breasts.

She began to pull away—then yielded. Her breath came faster.

A moment later, he released her.

"When you say you don't feel anything for me, Sarah," he said softly, "you're a liar."

And with that, he left her.

Chapter Three

Ann had returned home some three-quarters of an hour before Sarah. On letting herself in with her latchkey, she was annoyed to see Edith's head, bristling with old-fashioned curling pins, poking out of her bedroom.

Of late, she had been finding Edith more and more irritating.

Edith said at once:

"Miss Sarah isn't in yet."

A kind of unspoken criticism behind Edith's observation annoyed Ann. She snapped back:

"Why should she be?"

"Out gallivanting to all hours—and only a young girl."

"Don't be absurd, Edith. Things aren't what they used to be when I was a young girl. Girls are brought up now to look after themselves."

"More's the pity," said Edith. "And come to grief as a result of it, likely as not."

"They came to grief in my girlhood, too," said Ann dryly. "They were unsuspecting and ignorant, and all the chaperonage in the world didn't stop them from making fools of themselves if they were that type of girl. Nowadays girls read everything, do anything, and go anywhere."

"Ah," said Edith darkly. "An ounce of experience is worth a pound of book learning. Well, if you're satisfied, it's none of my business—but there's gentlemen and gentlemen, if you take my meaning, and I don't take much to the one she's out with tonight. It's one of his type that got my sister Nora's second into her bit of difficulty—and no good crying your eyes out afterward when the harm's done."

Ann could not help smiling in spite of her irritation. Edith and her relations! Moreover the picture of the self-confident Sarah as a betrayed village maiden tickled her sense of humor.

She said: "Well, stop fussing and go to bed. Did you get that sleeping prescription made up for me today?"

Edith grunted.

"You'll find it by your bed. But starting off taking things to make you sleep won't do you no good. . . . Won't be able to sleep without them, that's the next thing you'll know. To say nothing of making you more nervy than you are already."

Ann turned on her furiously:

"Nervy? I'm not nervy."

Edith did not reply. She merely pulled down the corners of her mouth, and retired into her room with a long pronounced indrawn hiss of the breath.

Ann went on angrily into her own room.

Really, she thought, every day Edith gets more and more impossible. Why I put up with it I don't know.

Nervy? Of course she wasn't nervy. Lately she'd formed the habit of lying awake—that was all. Everyone suffered from insomnia at some time or another. Much more sensible to take some stuff and give yourself a good night's rest, than lie awake hearing the clocks strike with your thoughts going round and round like—like squirrels in a cage. Dr. McQueen had been quite understanding about it and had given her a prescription—something quite mild and innocuous—bromide, she believed it was. Something to calm you down and stop you thinking. . . .

Oh dear, how tiresome everybody was. Edith and Sarah—even dear old Laura. She felt a bit guilty about Laura. Of course she ought to have rung up Laura a week ago. Laura was one of her oldest friends. Only somehow, she hadn't wanted to be bothered with Laura—not just yet—Laura was sometimes rather difficult. . . .

Sarah and Lawrence Steene? Was there really anything in it? Girls always liked going about with a man who had a bad reputation. . . . It probably wasn't serious. And even if it was . . .

Calmed by bromide, Ann fell asleep, but even in sleep she twitched and tossed restlessly on her pillows.

The telephone by her bed rang as she was sitting up drinking her coffee the following morning. Lifting the receiver, she was annoyed to hear the gruff tones of Laura Whitstable.

"Ann, does Sarah go out much with Lawrence Steene?"

"Good gracious, Laura, do you have to ring up at this hour in the morning to ask me that? How should I know?"

"Well, you are the girl's mother, aren't you?"

"Yes, but one doesn't catechise one's children the whole time asking where they go and with whom. They wouldn't stand for it, to begin with."

"Come now, Ann, don't fence with me. He's after her, isn't he?"

"Oh, I shouldn't think so. His divorce hasn't gone through yet, I imagine."

"The decree was made absolute yesterday. I saw it in the paper. How much do you know about him?"

"He's old Sir Harry Steene's only son. Rolling in money."

"And with a notorious reputation?"

"Oh, that! Girls are always attracted by a man with a bad reputation—that's been so ever since the time of Lord Byron. But it doesn't really mean anything."

"I'd like to have a talk with you, Ann. Will you be in this evening?"

Ann said quickly:

"No, I'm going out."

"About six, then."

"Sorry, Laura, I'm going to a cocktail party. . . ."

"Very well, then, I shall come about five—or would you—" Laura Whitstable's voice held grim determination—"prefer that I came round *now*?"

Ann capitulated gracefully.

"Five o'clock—that will be lovely."

She replaced the receiver with a sigh of exasperation. Really, Laura was impossible! All these Commissions, and Unescos and Unos—they turned women's heads.

"I don't want Laura coming here all the time," said Ann to herself fretfully.

Nevertheless she received her friend with every sign of pleasure when the latter made her appearance. She chattered gaily and nervously while Edith brought in tea. Laura Whitstable was unusually unassertive. She listened and responded, but that was all.

Then, with conversation petered out, Dame Laura put down her cup and said with her usual forthrightness:

"I'm sorry to worry you, Ann, but as it happened, coming back from the States I heard two men discussing Larry Steene—and what they said wasn't particularly pleasant hearing."

Ann gave a quick shrug of her shoulders.

"Oh, the things one overhears—"

"Are often intensely interesting," said Dame Laura. "They were quite decent men—and their opinion of Steene was pretty damning. Then there's Moira Denham who was his second wife. I knew her before she married him and I knew her afterward. She was a complete nervous wreck."

"Are you suggesting that Sarah—"

"I'm not suggesting that Sarah would be reduced to a nervous wreck if she married Lawrence Steene. She has a more resilient nature. Nothing of the butterfly on the wheel about Sarah."

"Well, then—"

"But I do think she might be very unhappy. And there's one third point. Did you read in the papers about a young woman called Sheila Vaughan Wright?"

"Something to do with being a drug addict?"

"Yes. It's the second time she's been up in court. She was a friend of Lawrence Steene's at one time. All I'm saying to you, Ann, is that Lawrence Steene is a particularly nasty bit of goods—in case you don't know it already—but perhaps you do?"

"I know there's talk about him, of course," said Ann rather reluctantly. "But what do you expect me to do about it? I can't forbid Sarah to go out with him. If I did, it would probably drive her the other way.

Girls won't stand being dictated to, as you know very well. It would simply make the whole thing more important. As it is, I don't suppose for a minute there's anything serious in it. He admires her and she's flattered because he's said to be a bad lot. But you seem to be assuming that he wants to marry her—"

"Yes, I think he wants to marry her. He's what I would describe as a Collector."

"I don't know what you mean."

"It's a type—and not the best type. Supposing she does want to marry him. How would you feel about it?"

Ann said bitterly: "What would be the good of my feeling anything? Girls do exactly as they like and marry whom they please."

"But Sarah is very much influenced by you."

"Oh, no, Laura, you're wrong there. Sarah goes her own way entirely. I don't interfere."

Laura Whitstable stared at her.

"You know, Ann, I can't quite make you out. Wouldn't you be upset if she married this man?"

Ann lit a cigarette and puffed at it impatiently.

"It's all so difficult. Lots of men with bad reputations have made quite good husbands—once they've sown their wild oats. Looking at it in the purely worldly sense, Lawrence Steene is a very good match."

"That wouldn't influence you, Ann. It's Sarah's happiness you want, not her material property."

"Oh, of course. But Sarah, in case you haven't realized it, is very fond of pretty things. She likes luxurious living—far more than I do."

"But she wouldn't marry solely on that account?"

"I don't think so." Ann sounded doubtful. "Actually, I think she is definitely attracted by Lawrence."

"And you think money might tip the scales?"

"I don't *know*, I tell you! I think that Sarah would—well—hesitate before she married a poor man. Let's put it like that."

"I wonder," said Dame Laura thoughtfully.

"Girls nowadays seem to think and talk of nothing but money."

"Oh, *talk!* I've heard Sarah talk, bless her. All very reasonable and hard-boiled and unsentimental. But language is given you to conceal your thoughts as much as to express them. Whatever generation it is, young women talk to pattern. The question is, what does Sarah really *want?*"

"I've no idea," said Ann. "I rather imagine—just a good time."

Dame Laura shot her a quick glance.

"You think she's happy?"

"Oh, yes. Really, Laura, she has a wonderful time."

Laura said meditatively:

"I didn't think she looked quite happy."

Ann said sharply:

"All these girls look discontented. It's a pose."

"Perhaps. So you don't feel you can do anything about Lawrence Steene?"

"I don't see what I can do. Why don't *you* talk to her about it?"

"I shan't do that. I'm only her godmother. I know my place."

Ann flushed angrily.

"I suppose you think it's *my* place to talk to her?"

"Not at all. As you say, talking doesn't do much good."

"But you think I ought to do something?"

"No, not necessarily."

"Then what do you mean?"

Laura Whitstable looked thoughtfully across the room.

"I only wondered what was going on in your mind."

"In *my* mind?"

"Yes."

"Nothing's going on in my mind. Nothing at all."

Laura Whitstable withdrew her glance from the other side of the room and gave Ann a quick bird-like glance.

"No," she said. "That's what I was afraid of."

"I don't understand you in the least."

Laura Whitstable said:

"What's going on isn't in your mind. It's farther down."

"Oh, if you're going to talk nonsense about the subconscious! Really, Laura, you—you seem to be accusing me in some way."

"I'm not accusing you."

Ann got up and began to pace up and down the room.

"I simply don't know what you mean. . . . I'm devoted to Sarah. . . . You know how much she's always meant to me. I—why, I've given up everything for her sake!"

Laura said gravely: "I know that you made a big sacrifice for her two years ago."

"Well?" demanded Ann. "Doesn't that show you?"

"Show me what?"

"How absolutely devoted I am to Sarah."

"My dear, it wasn't I who suggested that you weren't! You're defending yourself—but not against any accusation of mine." Laura got up. "I must go now. I may have been unwise to come—"

Ann followed her toward the door.

"You see, it's all so vague—nothing one can take hold of—"

"Yes, yes."

Laura paused. She spoke with a sudden startling energy.

"The trouble with a sacrifice is that it's not over and done with once it's made! It goes on. . . ."

Ann stared at her in surprise.

"What do you mean, Laura?"

"Nothing. Bless you, my dear, and take a word of advice from me—in my professional capacity. Don't live at such a pace that you haven't time to think."

Ann laughed, her good temper restored.

"I shall sit down and think when I'm too old to do anything else," she said gaily.

Edith came in to clear away and Ann, with a glance at the clock, uttered an exclamation and went to her bedroom.

She painted her face with special care, peering closely in the glass. The new haircut was, she thought, a success. It certainly made her look much younger. Hearing a knock at the front door, she called out to Edith:

"Any post?"

There was a pause as Edith examined the letters, then she said:

"Nothing but bills, ma'am—and one for Miss Sarah—from South Africa."

Edith put a slight stress on the last three words, but Ann did not notice. She returned to the sitting room just as Sarah entered with her latchkey.

"What I hate about chrysanthemums is their beastly smell," Sarah grumbled. "I shall chuck Noreen and take a job as a mannequin. Sandra's dying to have me. It's better pay, too. Hullo, have you been having a tea party?" she asked, as Edith came in and gathered up a stray cup.

"Laura's been here."

"Laura? Again? She was here yesterday."

"I know." Ann hesitated a minute, then said: "She came to say that I oughtn't to let you go out with Larry Steene."

"Laura did? How very protective of her. Is she afraid I'll be eaten by a big bad wolf?"

"Apparently." Ann said deliberately: "It seems he has a very unsavory reputation."

"Well, everyone knows *that!* Did I see some letters in the hall?" Sarah went out and returned holding a letter with a South African stamp.

Ann said:

"Laura seems to think that I ought to put a stop to it."

Sarah was staring down at the letter. She said absently: "What?"

"Laura thinks I ought to put a stop to you and Lawrence going out together."

Sarah said cheerfully:

"Darling, what could you do?"

"That's what I told her," said Ann triumphantly. "Mothers are quite helpless nowadays."

Sarah sat down on the arm of a chair and opened her letter. She spread out the two pages and began to read.

Ann went on:

"One really forgets that Laura is the age she is! She's getting so old that she's really completely out of touch with modern ideas. Of course, to be honest, I *have* been rather worried about your going out with Larry Steene so much—but I decided that if I said anything to you, it would make it much worse. I know that I can trust you not to do anything really foolish—"

She paused. Sarah, intent on her letter, murmured:

"Of course, darling."

"But you must feel free to choose your own friends. I do think that sometimes a lot of friction arises because—"

The telephone rang.

"Oh dear, that telephone!" cried Ann. She moved gladly across to it, and picked up the receiver expectantly.

"Hullo. . . . Yes, Mrs. Prentice speaking. . . . Yes. . . . Who? I can't quite catch the name . . . Cornford, did you say? . . . Oh, C—A—U—L—D . . . Oh! . . . *Oh!* . . . how stupid of me. . . . Is it you, Richard? . . . Yes, such a long time. . . . Well, that's very sweet of you. . . . No, of course not. . . . No, I'm delighted. . . . Really, I mean it. . . . I've often wondered . . . What have you been doing with yourself? . . . What? . . . Really? . . . I'm so glad. My best congratulations. . . . I'm sure she's charming. . . . That's very nice of you . . . I should love to meet her. . . ."

Sarah got up from the arm of the chair where she had been sitting. She went slowly toward the door, her eyes blank and unseeing. The letter she had been reading was crushed up in her hand.

Ann continued: "No, I couldn't tomorrow—no—just wait a moment. I'll get my little book. . . ." She called urgently: "Sarah!"

Sarah turned in the doorway.

"Yes?"

"Where's my little book?"

"Your book? I've no idea."

Sarah was miles away. Ann said irritably:

"Well, do look for it. It must be somewhere. Beside my bed, perhaps. Darling, do *hurry.*"

Sarah went out of the room and returned a moment later with Ann's engagement book.

"Here you are, Mother."

Ann ruffled its pages.

"Are you there, Richard? No, lunch isn't any good. I suppose you couldn't come round for drinks on Thursday? . . . Oh, I see. I'm sorry. And lunch no good either? . . . Well, *must* you go by a morning train? . . . Where are you staying? . . . Oh, but that's just round the corner. I know, can't you both come round straight away and have a quick drink? . . . No, I was going out—but I've heaps of time. . . . That will be delightful. Come right away."

She replaced the receiver and stood absentmindedly staring into space.

Sarah said without much interest: "Who was that?" Then she added with an effort: "Mother, I've heard from Gerry. . . ."

Ann roused herself suddenly.

"Tell Edith to bring the best glasses in and some ice. Quickly. They're coming round for a drink."

Sarah moved obediently.

"Who is?" she asked, still without much interest.

Ann said: "Richard—Richard Cauldfield!"

"Who's he?" asked Sarah.

Ann looked at her sharply, but Sarah's face was quite blank. She went and called to Edith. When she returned Ann said with emphasis:

"It was Richard Cauldfield."

"Who's Richard Cauldfield?" Sarah looked puzzled.

Ann pressed her hands together. Her anger was so intense that she had to pause a minute to steady her voice.

"So—you don't even remember his name?"

Sarah's eyes had gone once more to the letter she was holding. She said quite naturally: "Did I know him? Tell me something about him."

Ann's voice was hoarse as she said, this time with a biting emphasis that could not be missed:

"*Richard Cauldfield.*"

Sarah looked up startled. Suddenly comprehension came to her.

"What! Not Cauliflower?"

"Yes."

To Sarah it was a huge joke.

"Fancy his turning up again," she said cheerfully. "Is he still after you, Mother?"

Ann said shortly: "No, he's married."

"That's a good job," said Sarah. "I wonder what she's like?"

"He's bringing her here for a drink. They'll be here almost at once. They're at the Langport. Tidy up these books, Sarah. Put your things in the hall. And your gloves."

Opening her bag, Ann surveyed her face anxiously in the small mirror. As Sarah returned she said:

"Do I look all right?"

"Yes, lovely." Sarah's reply was perfunctory.

She was frowning to herself. Ann shut her bag and moved restlessly about the room, altering the position of a chair, rearranging a cushion.

"Mother, I've heard from Gerry."

"Have you?"

The vase of bronze chrysanthemums would look better on the corner table.

"He's had awfully bad luck."

"Has he?"

The cigarette box here, and the matches.

"Yes, some sort of disease or something got into the oranges and then he and his partner got into debt and—and now they've had to sell up. The whole thing's a washout."

"What a pity. But I can't say I'm surprised."

"Why?"

"Something like that always seems to happen to Gerry," said Ann vaguely.

"Yes—yes, it does." Sarah was cast down. The generous indignation on Gerry's behalf was not so spontaneous now as it had been. She said halfheartedly: "It isn't his fault . . ." But she was no longer as convinced as she would once have been.

"Perhaps not." Ann spoke absently. "But I'm afraid he'll always make a nonsense of things."

"Are you?" Sarah sat down again on the arm of her chair. She said earnestly: "Mother, do you think—really—that Gerry never will get anywhere?"

"It doesn't look like it."

"And yet I know—I'm sure—there's a lot in Gerry."

"He's a charming boy," said Ann. "But I'm afraid he's one of the world's misfits."

"Perhaps," Sarah sighed.

"Where's the sherry? Richard always used to prefer sherry to gin. Oh, there it is."

Sarah said: "Gerry says he's going to Kenya—he and another pal of his. They're going to sell cars—and run a garage."

"It's extraordinary," commented Ann, "how many inefficients always end up running a garage."

"But Gerry was always a wizard with cars. He made that one he bought for ten pounds go wonderfully. And you know, Mother, it isn't that Gerry is really lazy or won't work. He does work—sometimes awfully hard. It's just, I think," she puzzled it out, "that his judgment's not very good."

For the first time, Ann gave her daughter her full attention. She spoke kindly but decisively.

"You know, Sarah, if I were you, I should—well, put Gerry right out of your mind."

Sarah looked shaken. Her lips quivered.

"Would you?" she asked uncertainly.

The electric bell rang, an insistent soulless summons.

"Here they are," said Ann.

She went and stood in a rather artificial attitude by the mantelpiece.

Chapter Four

Richard came into the room with that little extra air of confidence that he always assumed when he was embarrassed. If it hadn't been for Doris he wouldn't be doing this. But Doris had been curious. She'd gone on at him, pestered him, pouted, sulked. She was very pretty and young and, having married a man a good deal older than herself, she fully intended to see that she got her own way.

Ann came forward to meet them, smiling charmingly. She felt like someone playing a part on the stage.

"Richard—how nice to see you! And this is your wife?"

Behind the cover of polite greetings and nondescript remarks thoughts were busy.

Richard thought to himself:

"How she's changed . . . I'd hardly have known her. . . ."

And a kind of relief came to him as he thought:

"She wouldn't have done for me—not really. Too smart alto-gether . . . Fashionable. The gay kind. Not my sort."

And he felt a renewed affection for his wife, Doris. He was inclined to be besotted about Doris—she was so young. But there were times when he realized uneasily that that careful accent of hers was inclined to get on his nerves, and her continual archness was also a bit wearing. He did not admit that he had married out of his class—he had met her at a hotel on the south coast, and her people had plenty of money, her father was a retired builder—but there were times when her parents jarred on him. But less now than they had done a year ago. And he was coming to accept Doris's friends as the friends they would naturally make. It was not, as he knew, what he had once wanted . . . Doris would never take the place of his long dead Aline. But she had given him a second spring of the senses and for the moment that was enough.

Doris, who had been suspicious about this Mrs. Prentice and inclined to be jealous, was favorably surprised by Ann's appearance.

"Why, she's ever so old," she thought to herself with the cruel in-tolerance of youth.

She was impressed with the room and the furnishings. The daughter, too, was awfully smart and really looked quite like something in *Vogue*. She was a little impressed that her Richard had once been engaged to this fashionable woman. It raised him in her estimation.

To Ann, the sight of Richard had come as a shock. This man who was talking so confidently to her was a stranger. Not only was he a stranger to her, she was a stranger to him. They had moved, he and she, in opposite directions and there was now between them no com-mon meeting ground. She had always been conscious in Richard of dual tendencies. There had always been a strain of pompousness there, the tendency to a closed mind. He had been a simple man with interesting possibilities. The door had been shut on those possibilities. The Richard Ann had loved was imprisoned inside this good-humored, slightly pom-pous, commonplace British husband.

He had met and married this common predatory child, with no qualities of heart and brain, only an assured pink and white prettiness and a youthful crude sex appeal.

He had married this girl because she, Ann, had sent him away. Smarting with anger and resentment, he had fallen an easy prey to the first female creature who had laid herself out to attract him. Well, perhaps it was all for the best. She supposed he was happy. . . .

Sarah brought them drinks and talked politely. Her thoughts were quite uncomplicated, represented entirely by the phrase: "What a crashing bore these people are!" She was aware of no undercurrents. At the back of her mind was still a dull ache connected with the word "Gerry."

"You've had all this done up, I see?"

Richard was looking round.

"It's lovely, Mrs. Prentice," said Doris. "All this Regency is the latest thing, isn't it? What was it before?"

"Old-fashioned rosy things," said Richard vaguely. He had a memory of the soft firelight and Ann and himself sitting on the old sofa that had been banished to make way for the Empire couch. "I liked them better than this."

"Men are such frightful sticks-in-the-mud, aren't they, Mrs. Prentice?" simpered Doris.

"My wife is determined to keep me up-to-date," said Richard.

"Of course I am, darling. I'm not going to let you turn into an old fogey before your time," said Doris affectionately. "Don't you think he looks years younger than when you saw him last, Mrs. Prentice?"

Ann avoided Richard's eye. She said:

"I think he looks splendid."

"I've taken up golf," said Richard.

"We've found a house near Basing Heath. Isn't it lucky? Quite a good train service for Richard to go up and down every day. And it's such a wonderful golf course. Very crowded, of course, at weekends."

"It's enormous luck nowadays to get the house you're looking for," said Ann.

"Yes. It's got an Aga cooker and all wired for power and absolutely newly built on the latest lines. Richard hankered after one of these

terrible old falling-down decayed period houses. But I put my foot
down! We woman are the practical ones, aren't we?"

Ann said politely:

"I'm sure a modern house saves a lot of domestic bother these days.
Have you got a garden?"

Richard said: "Not really," just as Doris said: "Oh *yes.*"

His wife looked at Richard reproachfully.

"How can you say that, darling, after all the bulbs we've put in."

"Quarter of an acre round the house," said Richard.

For a moment his eyes met Ann's. They had talked together sometimes of the garden they would have if they went to live in the country.
A walled garden for fruit—and a lawn with trees. . . .

Richard turned hastily to Sarah:

"Well, young woman, what do you do with yourself?" His old nervousness of her revived and made him sound peculiarly and odiously
facetious. "Lots of wild parties, I suppose?"

Sarah laughed cheerfully, thinking to herself: "I'd forgotten how odious Cauliflower was. It's a good thing for Mother I settled his hash."

"Oh, yes," she said. "But I make it a rule not to end up in Vine
Street more than twice a week."

"Girls drink far too much nowadays. Ruin their complexions—
though I must say yours looks very good."

"You always were interested in cosmetics, I remember," said Sarah
sweetly.

She crossed to Doris who was talking to Ann.

"Let me give you another drink."

"Oh, no, thanks, Miss Prentice—I couldn't. Even this has gone to
my head. What a lovely cocktail bar you've got. It's all awfully smart,
isn't it?"

"It's very convenient," said Ann.

"Not married yet, Sarah?" said Richard.

"Oh, no. I have hopes, though."

"I suppose you go to Ascot and all those sort of things," said Doris
enviously.

"The rain this year ruined my best frock," said Sarah.

"You know, Mrs. Prentice," Doris turned again to Ann, "you're not a bit like what I imagined."

"What did you imagine?"

"But then men are so stupid at descriptions, aren't they?"

"How did Richard describe me?"

"Oh, I don't know. It wasn't exactly what he *said*. It was the impression I got. I pictured you somehow as one of those quiet mousy little women," she laughed shrilly.

"A quiet mousy little woman? How dreary that sounds!"

"Oh, no, Richard admired you *enormously*. He really *did*. Sometimes, you know, I've been quite *jealous*."

"That sounds most absurd."

"Oh, well, you know how one goes on. Sometimes when Richard is very quiet in the evening and won't talk I tease him by telling him he's thinking about you."

(Do you think of me, Richard? Do you? I don't believe you do. You try not to think of me—just as I try never to think of you.)

"If you're ever Basing Heath way, you *must* come and see us, Mrs. Prentice."

"That's very kind of you. I should love to."

"Of course, like everybody else, the domestic problem is our great trouble. Only dailies to be had—and so often unreliable."

Richard, turning away from his heavy-handed conversation with Sarah, said:

"You've still got your old Edith, I see, Ann?"

"Yes, indeed. We'd be lost without her."

"Jolly good cook she was. Very nice little dinners she used to turn out."

There was a moment's awkwardness.

One of Edith's little dinner—the firelight—the chintzes with their sprigs of rosebuds . . . Ann with her soft voice and her leaf-brown hair. . . . Talking—making plans . . . the happy future. . . . A daughter coming home from Switzerland—but he hadn't dreamt that *that* would ever matter. . . .

Ann was watching him. Just for a moment she saw the real Richard—her Richard—looking at her out of sad remembering eyes.

The real Richard? Wasn't Doris's Richard as real as Ann's Richard? But now her Richard had gone again. It was Doris's Richard who was saying good-bye. More talk, more proffers of hospitality—would they never go? That nasty greedy little girl with her affected mincing voice. Poor Richard—Oh, poor Richard!—and it was her doing. She had sent him to that hotel lounge where Doris was waiting.

But was it really poor Richard? He had a young pretty wife. He was probably very happy.

At last! They had gone! Sarah, politely seeing them out, came back into the room, uttering a terriffic "Whoof!"

"Thank goodness *that's* over! You know, Mother, you did have an escape."

"I suppose I did." Ann spoke like someone in a dream.

"Well, I ask you, would you like to marry him now?"

"No," said Ann. "I wouldn't like to marry him now."

(We've gone away from that meeting point there was in our lives. You've gone one way, Richard, and I've gone another. I'm not the woman who walked with you in St. James's Park, and you're not the man I was going to grow old with. . . . We're two different people—strangers. You didn't much care for the look of me today—and I found you dull and pompous. . . .)

"You'd be bored to death, you know you would," said Sarah's positive young voice.

"Yes," said Ann slowly. "It's quite true. I should be bored to death."

(I couldn't sit still now and drift on to old age. I must go out—be amused—things must happen.)

Sarah put a caressing hand on her mother's shoulder.

"No doubt about it, darling, what you really like is razzling. You'd be bored to death stuck in a suburb with a mingy little garden and nothin' to do but wait for Richard to come home on the 6.15, or tell you how he did the fourth hole in three! That's not your line of country at all."

"I should have liked it once."

(An old walled garden, and a lawn with trees, and a small Queen Anne house of rose-red bricks. And Richard would not have taken up golf, but would have sprayed rose trees and planted bluebells under the trees. Or if he had taken up golf, she would have been delighted he *had* done the fourth in three!)

Sarah kissed her mother's cheek affectionately.

"You ought to be very grateful to me, darling," she said, "for getting you out of it. If it hadn't been for me you'd have married him."

Ann drew away a little. Her eyes, the pupils distended, stared at Sarah.

"*If it hadn't been for you, I should have married him.* And now—I don't want to. He doesn't mean anything to me at all."

She walked to the mantlepiece, running her finger along it, her eyes dark with amazement and pain. She said softly:

"Nothing at all. . . . Nothing. . . . What a very bad joke life is!"

Sarah wandered over to the bar and poured herself out another drink. She stood there, fidgeting a little, and finally, without turning round, she spoke in a rather would-be detached voice.

"Mother—I suppose I'd better tell you. Larry wants me to marry him."

"Lawrence Steene?"

"Yes."

There was a pause. Ann said nothing for sometime. Then she asked: "What are you going to do about it?"

Sarah turned. She shot a swift appealing glance at Ann, but Ann was not looking at her.

She said: "I don't know. . . ."

Her voice held a rather forlorn frightened note, like a child's. She looked hopefully at Ann, but Ann's face was hard and remote. Ann said after a moment or two:

"Well, it's for you to decide."

"I know."

From the table close to her, Sarah picked up Gerry's letter. She twisted it slowly in her fingers, staring down at it. At last she said with the sharpness almost of a cry:

"I don't know *what* to do!"

"I don't see how I can help you," said Ann.

"But what do you *think*, Mother? Oh, do say something."

"I've already told you that he hasn't got a good reputation."

"Oh *that!* That doesn't matter. I should be bored to death with a model of all the virtues."

"He's rolling in money, of course," said Ann. "He could give you a very good time. But if you don't care for him I shouldn't marry him."

"I do care for him in a way," said Sarah slowly.

Ann got up, looking at the clock.

"Well then," she said briskly, "what's the difficulty? My goodness, I forgot I was going to the Eliots. I shall be frightfully late."

"All the same, I'm not sure—" Sarah stopped. "You see—"

Ann said: "There's no one else is there?"

"Not really," said Sarah. Again she looked down at Gerry's letter twisted in her hand.

Ann said quickly:

"If you're thinking of Gerry, I should put him right out of your head, Sarah. Gerry's no good, and the sooner you make up your mind to that, the better."

"I suppose you're right," said Sarah slowly.

"I'm quite certain I'm right," said Ann briskly. "Wash Gerry right out. If you don't care for Lawrence Steene, don't marry him. You're very young still. There's plenty of time."

Sarah walked moodily over to the fireplace.

"I suppose I might as well marry Lawrence. . . . After all, he's madly attractive. Oh, mother," it was a sudden cry—"what *shall* I do?"

Ann said angrily:

"Really, Sarah, you behave exactly like a baby of two! How can I decide your life for you? The responsibility rests with you and you only."

"Oh, I know."

"Well, then?" Ann was impatient.

Sarah said childishly:

"I thought perhaps you could—help me somehow?"

Ann said: "I've already told you that there's no need for you to marry *anyone* unless you want to."

Still with the childish look on her face, Sarah said unexpectedly: "But you'd like to get rid of me, wouldn't you?"

Ann said sharply:

"Sarah, how can you say such a thing? Of course I don't want to get rid of you. What an idea!"

"I'm sorry, Mother. I didn't really mean that. Only it's all so different now, isn't it? I mean we used to have such fun together. But nowadays I always seem to be getting on your nerves."

"I'm afraid I am rather nervy sometimes," said Ann coldly. "But after all, you're rather temperamental yourself, aren't you, Sarah?"

"Oh, I daresay it's all my fault," Sarah went on reflectively: "Most of my friends are married. Pam and Betty and Susan. Joan isn't but then she's gone all political." She paused again before going on. "It would really be rather fun to marry Lawrence. Glorious to have all the clothes and furs and things one wanted."

Ann said dryly: "I certainly think you'd better marry a man with money, Sarah. Your tastes are decidedly expensive. Your allowance is always overdrawn."

"I'd hate to be poor," said Sarah.

Ann took a deep breath. She felt insincere and artificial and she didn't quite know what to say.

"Darling, I don't really know how to advise you. You see, I do feel that this is so completely your own affair. It would be quite wrong for me to push you into it or to advise you against it. You *must* make up your mind for yourself. You do see that, Sarah, don't you?"

Sarah said quickly:

"Of course, darling—am I being a terrible bore?—I don't want to worry you. You might just tell me one thing. How do *you* feel about Lawrence?"

"I really haven't any feeling about him one way or the other."

"Sometimes—I feel just a bit—scared of him."

"Darling," Ann was amused, "isn't that rather silly?"

"Yes, I suppose it is . . ."

Slowly Sarah began to tear Gerry's letter, first in strips, then across and across. She threw the bits into the air and watched them float down like a snowstorm.

"Poor old Gerry," she said.

Then with a swift sideways glance she said:

"You do *mind* what happens to me, don't you, Mother?"

"Sarah! Really."

"Oh, I'm sorry—going on and on like this. I just feel awfully *queer* somehow. It's like being out in a snowstorm and not knowing which is the way home. . . . It's a frightfully queer feeling. Everything and everyone is different . . . You're different, Mother."

"What absolute nonsense, pet, I really *must* go now."

"I suppose you must. Does this party matter?"

"Well, I want particularly to see the new murals Kit Eliot has had done."

"Oh, I see." Sarah paused and then said: "You know, Mother, I really think I may be much keener on Lawrence than I think I am."

"I shouldn't be surprised," said Ann lightly. "But don't be in a hurry. Good-bye, my sweet—I must fly."

The front door shut behind Ann.

Edith came out of the kitchen and into the sitting room with a tray to clear away the glasses.

Sarah had put a record on the gramophone and was listening with a melancholy enjoyment to Paul Robeson singing "Sometimes I feel like a motherless child."

"The tunes you like!" said Edith. "Gives me the willies, that does."

"I think it's lovely."

"No accounting for tastes." Edith grunted crossly, as she observed: "Why can't people keep their cigarette ash in ashtrays. Flicking it all over the place."

"It's good for the carpet."

"That's always been said and it's no truer now than it ever was. And *why* you've got to scatter bits of paper all over the floor when the wastepaper basket's over by the wall—"

"Sorry, Edith. I didn't think. I was tearing up my past, and I wanted to make a gesture."

"Your past, indeed!" Edith snorted. Then she asked gently as she watched Sarah's face: "Anything wrong, my pretty?"

"Nothing at all. I'm thinking of getting married, Edith."

"No hurry for that. You wait until Mr. Right comes along."

"I don't believe it makes any difference who you marry. It's sure to go wrong anyway."

"Now don't you talk nonsense, Miss Sarah! What's all this about anyway?"

Sarah said wildly:

"I want to get away from here."

"And what's wrong with your home, I should like to know?" demanded Edith.

"I don't know. Everything seems to have changed. Why has it changed, Edith?"

Edith said gently:

"You're growing up, you see?"

"Is that what it is?"

"It might be."

Edith went toward the door with her tray of glasses. Then, unexpectedly, she put it down and came back. She patted Sarah's black head, as she had patted it years ago in the nursery.

"There, there, my pretty, there, there."

With a sudden change of mood Sarah sprang up and catching Edith round the waist, began to waltz wildly round the room with her.

"I'm going to be married, Edith. Isn't it fun? I'm going to marry Mr. Steene. He's rolling in money and he's madly attractive. Aren't I a lucky girl?"

Edith extricated herself, grumbling. "First one thing and then another. What's the matter with you, Miss Sarah?"

"I'm a little mad, I think. You shall come to the wedding, Edith, and I'll buy you a lovely new dress for it—crimson velvet, if you like."

"What do you think a wedding is—a Coronation?"

Sarah put the tray into Edith's hands and pushed her toward the door.

"Go on, you old darling, and don't grumble."

Edith shook her head doubtfully as she went.

Sarah walked slowly back into the room. Suddenly she flung herself down into the big chair and cried and cried.

The gramophone record drew to its close—the deep melancholy voice singing once more—

Sometimes I feel like a motherless child—a long way from Home . . .

BOOK THREE

Chapter One

Edith moved slowly and stiffly round her kitchen. She had been feeling what she called her "rheumatics" more and more lately, and it did not improve her temper. She still obstinately refused to delegate any of her household tasks.

A lady referred to by Edith as "*that* Mrs. Hopper," with a sniff, was allowed to come once a week and perform certain activities under Edith's jealous eye, but any further help was negatived by her with a venom that boded ill for any cleaning woman who dared to attempt it.

"I've always managed, haven't I?" was Edith's slogan.

So she continued to manage with an air of martyrdom and an increasingly sour expression. She had also formed the habit of grumbling under her breath most of the day.

She was doing so now.

"Bringing the milk at lunchtime—the idea! Milk should be delivered before breakfast, that's the proper time for it. Impudent young fellows, coming along whistling in their white coats . . . who do they think they are? Look like whippersnapper dentists to me . . ."

The sound of the latchkey in the front door arrested the flow.

Edith murmured to herself. "Now there'll be ructions!" and rinsed out a bowl under the tap with a vicious swishing motion.

Ann's voice called:

"Edith."

Edith removed her hands from the sink and dried them meticulously on the roller towel.

"Edith . . . Edith . . ."

"Coming, ma'am."

"Edith!"

Edith raised her eyebrows, pulled down the corners of her mouth and went out of the kitchen across the hall into the sitting room where Ann Prentice was tossing through letters and bills. She turned as Edith entered.

"Did you ring up Dame Laura?"

"Yes, of course I did."

Ann said: "Did you tell her it was urgent—that I *must* see her? Did she say she'd come?"

"Said she'd be round right away."

"Well, why hasn't she come?" demanded Ann angrily.

"I only telephoned twenty minutes ago. Just after you went out."

"It feels like an hour. Why doesn't she come?"

Edith said, in a more soothing tone:

"Everything can't happen right away. It's no good your upsetting yourself."

"Did you tell her I was ill?"

"I told her you was in one of your states."

Ann said angrily: "What do you mean—one of my states? It's my nerves. They're all to pieces."

"That's right, they are."

Ann threw her faithful retainer an angry glance. She walked restlessly over to the window, then to the mantelpiece. Edith stood watching her, her big awkward jointed hands, seamed with work, moving up and down on her apron.

"I can't stay still a moment," Ann complained. "I didn't sleep a wink last night. I feel terrible—terrible . . ." She sat down in a chair and put both hands to her temples. "I don't know what's the matter with me."

"I do," said Edith. "Too much gadding about. 'Tisn't natural at your age."

"Edith!" cried Ann. "You're very impertinent. You're getting worse and worse lately. You've been with me a long time and I value your services, but if you're going to presume you'll have to go."

Edith raised her eyes to the ceiling and assumed her martyr's expression.

She said: "I'm not going. And that's flat."

"You'll go if I give you notice," said Ann.

"You'd be more foolish than I think you are if you did a thing like that. I'd get another place easy as winking. Running after me they'd be, at these domestic agencies. But how would *you* get along? Nothing but daily women as likely as not! Or else a foreigner. Everything cooked in oil and turning your stomach—to say nothing of the smell in the flat. And those foreigners aren't so good on the telephone—get every name wrong, they would. Or else you'd get a nice clean pleasant-spoken woman, too good to be true, and you'd come back one day to find she'd made off with your furs and your jewelry. Heard of a case in Playne Court opposite only the other day. No, you're one as has to have things done the proper way—the *old* way. I cook you nice little meals and I don't go smashing your pretty things when I wash up, as some of these young hussies do, and what's more I know your ways. You can't do without me, and I know it, and I'm not going. Trying you may be, but everyone's got his cross to bear. It says so in Holy Writ, and you're mine and I'm a Christian woman."

Ann clasped her eyes and rocked to and fro with a moan.

"Oh, my head—my *head* . . ."

Edith's rigid sourness softened—a tenderness showed in her eyes.

"There, now. I'll make you a nice cup of tea."

Ann cried pettishly: "I don't want a nice cup of tea. I'd hate a nice cup of tea."

Edith sighed and raised her eyes to the ceiling once more.

"Please yourself," she said and left the room.

Ann reached for the cigarette box, took one out, lit it, puffed at it for a moment or two and then stubbed it out in the ashtray. She got up and started pacing about again.

After a minute or so she went to the telephone and dialed a number.

"Hullo—hullo—can I speak to Lady Ladscombe—oh, is that you,

Marcia darling?" Her voice assumed an artificially gay note. "How are you? . . . Oh, nothing really. I just thought I'd ring you up. . . . I don't know, darling—just felt frightfully blue—you know how one does. Are you doing anything tomorrow for lunch? . . . Oh, I see . . . Thursday night? Yes, I'm quite free. That would be lovely. I'll get hold of Lee or somebody and get up a party. That will be wonderful . . . I'll give you a ring in the morning."

She rang off. Her momentary animation subsided. Once again she began pacing about. Then, as she heard the doorbell, she stood still, poised in expectancy.

She heard Edith say:

"She's waiting for you in the sitting room," and then Laura Whitstable came in. Tall, grim, forbidding, but with the comfortable steadfastness of a rock in the middle of a heaving sea.

Ann ran toward her, crying out incoherently and with rising hysteria.

"Oh, Laura—*Laura*—I'm so glad you've come . . ."

Dame Laura's eyebrows went up, her eyes were steady and watchful. She laid her hands on Ann's shoulders and steered her gently to the couch where she sat down beside her, saying as she did so:

"Well, well, what's all this?"

Ann still sounded hysterical.

"Oh, I'm *so* glad to see you. I think I'm going mad."

"Nonsense," said Dame Laura robustly. "What's the trouble?"

"Nothing. Nothing at all. It's just my nerves. That's what frightens me. I can't sit still. I don't know what's the matter with me."

"H'm," Laura gave her a searching professional look. "You don't look too well."

Secretly she was dismayed by Ann's appearance. Under the heavy makeup Ann's face was haggard. She looked years older than when Laura had seen her last, some months ago.

Ann said fretfully: "I'm perfectly *well*. It's just—I don't know what it is. I can't sleep—not unless I take things. And I'm so irritable and bad-tempered."

"Seen a doctor?"

"Not lately. They just give you bromide and tell you not to overdo things."

"Very good advice."

"Yes, but it's all so absurd. I've *never* been a nervy woman, Laura, you know I haven't. I've never known what nerves were."

Laura Whitstable was silent for a moment, remembering the Ann Prentice of just over three years ago. Her gentle placidity, her repose, her enjoyment of life, her sweetness and evenness of temper. She felt deeply grieved for this friend of hers.

She said:

"It's all very well to say you've never been a nervy woman. After all, a man who has a broken leg has very likely never had a broken leg before!"

"But why should *I* have nerves?"

Laura Whitstable was careful in her answer.

She said evenly: "Your doctor was right. You probably do too much."

Ann said sharply:

"I can't sit at home moping all day."

"There's such a thing as sitting at home without moping," said Dame Laura.

"No," Ann's hands fluttered nervously. "I—I can't sit about and do nothing."

"Why not?" The question came sharp as a probe.

"I don't know." Ann's fluttering increased. "I can't be alone. I can't . . ." She threw a despairing glance at Laura. "I suppose you'd think I was quite mad if I said I was *afraid* of being alone?"

"Most sensible thing you've said yet," returned Dame Laura promptly.

"Sensible?" Ann was startled.

"Yes, because it's the truth."

"The truth?" Ann's eyelids fell. "I don't know what you mean by the truth."

"I mean that we shan't get anywhere without the truth."

"Oh, but you won't be able to understand. You've never been afraid of being alone, have you?"

"No."

"Then you just can't understand."

"Oh yes, I can." Laura went on gently: "Why did you send for me, my dear?"

"I had to talk to someone . . . I had to . . . and I thought perhaps you could *do* something?"

She looked hopefully at her friend.

Laura nodded her head and sighed.

"I see. You want a conjuring trick."

"Couldn't you do one for me, Laura? Psychoanalysis, or hypnotism, or *something*."

"Mumbo jumbo in modern terms, in fact?" Laura shook her head decisively. "I can't take the rabbits out of the hat for you, Ann. You must do that for yourself. And you've got to find out, first, exactly what's in the hat."

"What do you mean?"

Laura Whitstable waited a minute before saying: "You're not happy, Ann."

It was a statement rather than a question.

Ann replied quickly, too quickly perhaps.

"Oh yes, I am—at least I am in a way. I enjoy myself a good deal."

"You're not happy," said Dame Laura ruthlessly.

Ann made a gesture with her shoulders and her hands.

"Is anybody happy?" she threw out.

"Quite a lot of people are, thank God," said Dame Laura cheerfully. "*Why* aren't you happy, Ann?"

"I don't know."

"Nothing's going to help you but the truth, Ann. You know the answer quite well really."

Ann was silent a moment, then as though taking her courage in her hands, she burst out:

"I suppose—if I'm to be honest—because I'm growing old. I'm middle-aged, I'm losing my looks, I've nothing to look forward to in the future."

"Oh, my dear! Nothing to look forward to? You've excellent health, adequate brains—there is so much in life that one hasn't really time to attend to until one is past middle-age. I told you so once. Books, flowers, music, pictures, people, sunshine—all the interwoven inextricable pattern that we call Life."

Ann was silent a moment, then she said defiantly:

"Oh I daresay it's all a question of sex. Nothing else really matters when one isn't attractive to men any longer."

"That is possibly true of some women. It isn't true of you, Ann. You've seen the 'Immortal Hour'—or read it perhaps? Do you remember those lines: *'There is an Hour wherein a man might be happy all his life could he but find it?* You came near to finding it once, didn't you?"

Ann's face changed—softened. She looked suddenly a much younger woman.

She murmured: "Yes. There was that hour. I could have grown it with Richard. I could have grown old happily with Richard."

Laura said with deep sympathy:

"I know."

Ann went on. "And now—I can't even regret losing him! I saw him again, you know—oh, just about a year ago—and he meant nothing to me at all—*nothing*. That's what's so tragic, so absurd. It had all gone. We meant nothing to each other anymore. He was just an ordinary middle-aged man—a little pompous, rather dull, inclined to be fatuous about his new, pretty, empty-headed, meretricious little wife. Quite nice, you know, yet definitely boring. And yet—and yet—if we had married— I think we'd have been happy together. I *know* we should have been happy."

"Yes," said Laura thoughtfully, "I think you would."

"I was so near happiness—so near it—" Ann's voice trembled with self-pity—"and then—I had to let it all go."

"Had you?"

Ann paid no attention to the question.

"I gave it all up—for Sarah!"

"Exactly," said Dame Laura. *"And you've never forgiven her for it, have you?"*

Ann came out of her dream—startled.

"What do you mean?"

Laura Whitstable gave a venomous snort.

"Sacrifices! Blood sacrifices! Just realize for a moment, Ann, what a sacrifice *means*. It isn't just the one heroic moment when you feel warmed and generous and willing to immolate yourself. The kind of sacrifice where you offer your breast to the knife is easy—for it ends there, in the moment when you are *greater than yourself*. But most sacrifices you have to live with *afterward*—all day and every day—and that's *not* so easy. One has to be very big for that. You, Ann, weren't quite big enough . . ."

Ann flushed angrily.

"I gave up my whole life, my one chance of happiness, for Sarah's sake, and all you say is that it wasn't enough!"

"That isn't what I said."

"Everything's *my* fault, I suppose!" Ann was still angry.

Dame Laura said earnestly: "Half the troubles in life come from pretending to oneself that one is a better and finer human being than one is."

But Ann was not listening. Her unassimilated resentment came pouring out.

"Sarah's just like all these modern girls, wrapped up in herself. Never thinks of anybody else! Do you know that just over a year ago, when he rang up, she didn't even remember who Richard was? His name meant nothing to her—nothing at all."

Laura Whitstable nodded her head gravely with the air of one who sees her diagnosis proved correct.

"I see," she said. "I see . . ."

Ann went on: "What could I do? They never stopped fighting. It was nerve-racking! If I'd gone on with it there wouldn't have been a moment's peace."

Laura Whitstable spoke crisply and unexpectedly:

"If I were you, Ann, I should make up your mind whether you gave up Richard Cauldfield for Sarah's sake, or for the sake of your own peace."

Ann looked at her resentfully.

"I loved Richard," she said, "but I loved Sarah more. . . ."

"No, Ann, it isn't nearly as simple as that. I think that there was actually a moment when you loved Richard better than you loved Sarah. I think your inner unhappiness and resentment springs from that moment. If you'd given up Richard because you loved Sarah more, you wouldn't be in the state you are today. But if you gave up Richard out of weakness, because Sarah bullied you—because you wanted to escape from the bickering and the quarrels, if it was a defeat and *not* a renunciation—well, that's a thing one never likes admitting to oneself. But you did care for Richard very deeply."

Ann said bitterly:

"And now he means nothing to me!"

"What about Sarah?"

"Sarah?"

"Yes. What does Sarah mean to you?"

Ann shrugged her shoulders.

"Since her marriage I've hardly seen her. She's very busy and gay, I believe. But as I say, I hardly see anything of her."

"*I* saw her last night . . ." Laura paused, then went on: "In a restaurant with a party of people." She paused again and then said bluntly: "She was drunk."

"Drunk?" Ann sounded momentarily startled. Then she laughed. "Laura dear, you mustn't be old-fashioned. All young people drink a good deal nowadays, and it seems a party's hardly a success unless everybody's half-seas over, or 'high' or whatever you like to call it."

Laura was unruffled.

"That may be so—and I admit I'm old-fashioned enough not to like seeing a young woman I know drunk in a public place. But there's more than that, Ann. I spoke to Sarah. The pupils of her eyes were dilated."

"What does that mean?"

"One of the things it *could* mean is cocaine."

"Drugs?"

"Yes. I told you once that I suspected Lawrence Steene was mixed up with the drug racket. Oh, not for money—purely for sensation."

"He always seems quite normal."

"Oh, drugs won't hurt him. I know his type. They enjoy experimenting with sensation. His sort don't become addicts. A woman's different. If a woman's unhappy, these things get a hold on her—a hold that she can't break."

"Unhappy?" Ann sounded incredulous. "Sarah?"

Watching her closely, Laura Whitstable said dryly:

"You should know. You're her mother."

"Oh, *that!* Sarah doesn't confide in me."

"Why not?"

Ann got up, went over to the window, then came back slowly towards the fireplace. Dame Laura sat quite still and watched her. As Ann lit a cigarette, Laura asked quietly:

"What does it mean to you exactly, Ann, that Sarah should be unhappy?"

"How can you ask? It upsets me—terribly."

"Does it?" Laura rose. "Well, I must be going. I've got a committee meeting in ten minutes' time. I can just make it."

She went toward the door. Ann followed her.

"What do you mean by saying 'Does it?' like that, Laura?"

"I had some gloves somewhere—Now where did I put them?"

The bell of the front door sounded. Edith padded out of the kitchen to answer it.

Ann persisted: "You meant *something?*"

"Ah, here they are."

"Really, Laura, I think you're being horrible to me—quite horrible!"

Edith came in announcing with something that might almost have been a smile:

"Now here's a stranger. It's Mr. Lloyd, ma'am."

Ann stared at Gerry Lloyd for a moment as though she could hardly take him in.

It was over three years since she had seen him and Gerry looked a good deal more than three years older. He had a battered look about him, and his face showed the tired lines of the unsuccessful. He was wearing a rather rough country tweed suit, obviously a reach-me-down, and his shoes were shabby. It was clear that he had not prospered. The smile with which he greeted her was a grave one and his whole manner was serious, not to say perturbed.

"Gerry, this *is* a surprise!"

"It's good that you remember me, anyway. Three and a half years is a long time."

"I remember you, too, young man, but I don't suppose you remember me," said Dame Laura.

"Oh, but of course I do, Dame Laura. No one could forget *you*."

"Nicely put—or isn't it? Well, I must be on my way. Good-bye, Ann; good-bye, Mr. Lloyd."

She went out and Gerry followed Ann over to the fireplace. He sat down and took the cigarette she offered him.

Ann spoke gaily and cheerfully.

"Well, Gerry, tell me all about yourself and what you have been doing. Are you in England for long?"

"I'm not sure."

His level gaze, fixed on her, made Ann feel slightly uncomfortable. She wondered what was in his mind. It was a look very unlike the Gerry she remembered.

"Have a drink. What will you have—gin and orange—or pink gin—?"

"No, thanks. I don't want one. I came—just to talk to you."

"How nice of you. Have you seen Sarah? She's married, you know. To a man called Lawrence Steene."

"I know that. She wrote and told me. And I've seen her. I saw her last night. That's really why I've come here to see you." He paused for a moment and then said: "Mrs. Prentice, why did you let her marry that man?"

Ann was taken back.

"Gerry, my dear—*really!*"

His earnestness was unabated by her protest. He spoke seriously and quite simply.

"She isn't happy. You know that, don't you? She isn't happy."

"Did she tell you so?"

"No, of course not. Sarah wouldn't do a thing like that It wasn't necessary to tell me. I saw it at once. She was with a crowd of people—I only had a few words with her. But it sticks out a mile. Mrs. Prentice, why did you let such a thing happen?"

Ann felt her anger rising.

"My dear Gerry, aren't you being rather absurd?"

"No, I don't think so." He considered a moment. His complete simplicity and sincerity were disarming. "You see, Sarah matters to me. She always has. More than anything else in the world. So naturally I care whether she's happy or not. You know, you really shouldn't have let her marry Steene."

Ann broke out angrily:

"Really, Gerry, you talk like—like a Victorian. There was no question of my 'letting' or 'not letting' Sarah marry Larry Steene. Girls marry whoever they choose to marry and there's nothing their parents can do about it. Sarah chose to marry Lawrence Steene. That's all there is to it."

Gerry said with calm certainty:

"You could have stopped it."

"My dear boy, if you try to stop people doing what they want to do, it just makes them more obstinate and pigheaded."

He raised his eyes to her face.

"Did you try to stop it?"

Somehow, under the frank inquiry of those eyes, Ann floundered and stammered.

"I—I—of course he was much older than she was—and his reputation wasn't good. I did point that out to her—but—"

"He's a swine of the worst description."

"You can't really know anything about him, Gerry. You've been out of England for years."

"It's pretty common knowledge. Everybody knows. I daresay you wouldn't know all the unpleasant details—but surely Mrs. Prentice, you must have *felt* the kind of brute he is?"

"He was always very charming and pleasant to me," said Ann defensively. "And a man with a past doesn't always turn out such a bad husband. You can't believe all the spiteful things people say. Sarah was attracted by him—in fact she was determined to marry him. He's exceedingly well off—"

Gerry interrupted her.

"Yes, he's well off. But you're not the kind of woman, Mrs. Prentice, who just wants her daughter to marry for money. You were never what I'd call—well—worldly. You would just have wanted Sarah to be happy—or so I should have thought."

He looked at her with a kind of puzzled curiosity.

"Of course I wanted my only child to be happy. That goes without saying. But the point is, Gerry, that one can't *interfere*" She laboured the point. "You may think that what anyone is doing is all wrong, but you can't interfere."

She gazed at him defiantly.

He looked at her, still with that thoughtful, considering air.

"Did Sarah really want to marry him so much?"

"She was very much in love with him," Ann said defiantly.

When Gerry did not speak, she went on:

"I don't expect it's apparent to you, but Lawrence is exceedingly attractive to women."

"Oh yes, I quite realize that."

Ann rallied herself.

"You know, Gerry," she said, "you're really being quite unreasonable. Just because there was once a boy-and-girl thing between you and Sarah, you come here and accuse me—as though Sarah's marrying someone else was my fault—"

He interrupted her.

"I think it *was* your fault."

They stared at each other. Color rose in Gerry's face, Ann grew pale. The tension between them was strained to breaking point.

Ann got up. "This is too much," she said coldly.

Gerry rose too. He was quiet and polite, but she was aware of something implacable and remorseless behind the quietness of his manner.

"I'm sorry," he said, "if I've been rude—"

"It's unpardonable!"

"Perhaps it is, in a way. But you see I mind about Sarah. She's the only thing I do mind about. I can't help feeling that you've let her in for an unhappy marriage."

"Really!"

"I'm going to take her out of it."

"*What?*"

"I'm going to persuade her to leave that swine."

"What absolute nonsense. Just because there was once this girl-and-boy love affair between you two—"

"I understand Sarah—and she understands me."

Ann gave a sudden hard laugh.

"My dear Gerry, you'll find that Sarah has changed a good deal since you used to know her."

Gerry went very pale.

"I know she's changed," he said in a low voice. "I saw that. . . ."

He hesitated a moment, then said quietly:

"I'm sorry if you feel I've been impertinent, Mrs. Prentice. But you see, with me, Sarah will always come first."

He went out of the room.

Ann moved over to the drinks and poured herself out a glass of gin. As she drank it she murmured to herself:

"How dare he—how dare he . . . And Laura—*she's* against me too. They're all against me. It isn't fair . . . What have I done? Nothing at all. . . ."

Chapter Two

1

The butler who opened the door of 18 Pauncefoot Square looked superciliously at Gerry's ready-made rough suit.

Then, as his eyes were caught by the visitor's eye, his manner underwent reconsideration.

He would find out, he said, if Mrs. Steene was at home.

Shortly afterward Gerry was ushered into a large dim room full of exotic flowers and pale brocades, and here, after a lapse of some minutes, Sarah Steene came into the room, smiling a greeting.

"Well, Gerry! How nice of you to look me up. We were snatched away from each other the other night. Drink?"

She fetched him a drink and poured herself one, and then came to sit on a low *pouf* by the fire. The soft lighting of the room hardly showed her face. She had on some expensive perfume that he did not remember her using.

"Well, Gerry?" she said again, lightly.

He smiled back.

"Well, Sarah?"

Then with a finger touching her shoulder, he said: "Practically wearing the Zoo, aren't you?"

She had on an expensive wisp of chiffon trimmed with masses of soft pale fur.

"Nice!" Sarah assured him.

"Yes. You look wonderfully expensive!"

"Oh, I am. Now, Gerry, tell me the news. You left South Africa and went to Kenya. Since then, I've heard nothing at all."

"Oh, well. I've been rather down on my luck—"

"Naturally—"

The retort came swiftly.

Gerry demanded:

"What do you mean—naturally?"

"Well, luck always was your trouble, wasn't it?"

Just for a moment it was the old Sarah, teasing, hard-hitting. The beautiful woman with the hard face, the exotic stranger, was gone. It was Sarah, his Sarah, attacking him shrewdly.

And responding in his old manner, he grumbled:

"One thing after another let me down. First it was the crops that failed—no fault of mine. Then the cattle got disease—"

"I know. The old, old sad story."

"And then, of course, I hadn't enough capital. If only I'd had capital—"

"I know—I know."

"Well, dash it all, Sarah, it's *not* all my fault."

"It never is. What have you come back to England for?"

"As a matter of fact, my aunt died—"

"Aunt Lena?" asked Sarah, who was well acquainted with all Gerry's relatives.

"Yes. Uncle Luke died two years ago. The old screw never left me a penny—"

"Wise Uncle Luke."

"But Aunt Lena—"

"Aunt Lena has left you something?"

"Yes. Ten thousand pounds."

"H'm." Sarah considered. "That's not so bad—even in these days."

"I'm going in with a fellow who's got a ranch in Canada."

"What sort of a fellow? That's always the point. What about the garage you were starting with another fellow after you left South Africa?"

"Oh, that petered out. We did quite well to start with, but then we enlarged up a bit, and a slump came—"

"You needn't tell me. How familiar the pattern is! *Your* pattern."

"Yes," said Gerry. He added simply: "You're quite right, I suppose, I'm not really much good. I still think I've had rotten luck—but I suppose I've played the fool a bit as well. However, this time is going to be different."

Sarah said bitingly:

"I wonder."

"Come, Sarah. Don't you think I've learned a lesson?"

"I shouldn't think so," said Sarah. "People never do. They go on repeating themselves. What you need, Gerry, is a manager—like film stars and actresses. Someone to be practical and save you from being optimistic at the wrong moment."

"You've got something there. But really, Sarah, it will be all right this time. I'm going to be damn careful."

There was a pause and then Gerry said:

"I went and saw your mother yesterday."

"Did you? How nice of you. How was she? Rushing about madly as usual?"

Gerry said slowly: "Your mother's changed a lot."

"Do you think so?"

"Yes, I do."

"In what way do you think she's changed?"

"I don't quite know how to put it." He hesitated. "She's frightfully nervy, for one thing."

Sarah said lightly: "Who isn't in these days?"

"She used not to be. She was always calm and—and—well—sweet. . . ."

"Sounds like a line of a hymn!"

"You know what I mean quite well—and she *has* changed. Her hair—and her clothes—everything."

"She's gone a bit gay, that's all. Why shouldn't she, poor darling? Getting old must be absolutely the end! Anyway, people do change." Sarah paused for a minute before adding with a touch of defiance in her voice: "I expect *I've* changed, too. . . ."

"Not really."

Sarah flushed. Gerry said deliberately:

"In spite of the zoo," he touched the pale expensive fur again, "and the Woolworth assortment," he touched a diamond spray on her shoulder, "and the luxury setting—you're pretty much the same Sarah—" He paused and added: "*My* Sarah."

Sarah moved uncomfortably. She said in a gay voice:

"And you're still the same old Gerry. When do you go off to Canada?"

"Quite soon now. As soon as all the lawyer's business is cleared up."

He rose. "Well, I must be off. Come out with me some day soon, will you, Sarah?"

"No, you come and dine here with us. Or we'll have a party. You must meet Larry."

"I met him the other night, didn't I?"

"Only for a moment."

"I'm afraid I haven't time for parties. Come out for a walk with me one morning, Sarah."

"Darling, I'm really not up to much in the morning. A hideous time of day."

"A very good time for cold clear thinking."

"Who wants to do any cold clear thinking?"

"I think *we* do. Come on, Sarah. Twice round Regent's Park. And tomorrow morning. I'll meet you at Hanover Gate."

"You do have the most hideous ideas, Gerry! And what an awful suit."

"Very hard wearing."

"Yes, but the cut of it!"

"Clothes snob! Tomorrow, twelve o'clock, Hanover Gate. And don't get so tight tonight that you'll have a hangover tomorrow."

"I suppose you mean I was tight last night?"

"Well, you were, weren't you?"

"It was such a dreary party. Drink does help a girl through."

Gerry reiterated:

"Tomorrow. Hanover Gate. Twelve o'clock."

2

"Well, I've come," said Sarah, defiantly.

Gerry looked her up and down. She was astonishingly beautiful—far more beautiful than she had been as a girl. He noted the expensive simplicity of the clothes she was wearing, the big cabuchon emerald on her finger. He thought: "I'm mad." But he did not waver.

"Come on," he said. "We walk."

He walked her briskly, too. They skirted the lake and passed through the rose garden and paused at last to sit in two chairs in an unfrequented part of the park. It was too cold for there to be many people sitting about.

Gerry took a deep breath.

"Now," he said, "we get down to things. Sarah, will you come with me to Canada?"

Sarah stared at him in amazement.

"What on earth do you mean?"

"Just what I say."

"Do you mean—a kind of trip?" Sarah asked doubtfully.

Gerry grinned.

"I mean for good. Leave your husband and come to me."

Sarah laughed.

"Gerry, are you quite mad? Why, we haven't seen each other for nearly four years and—"

"Does that matter?"

"No." Sarah was taken off her balance. "No, I suppose it doesn't. . . ."

"Four years, five years, ten, twenty? I don't believe it would make any difference. You and I belong together. I've always known that. I still feel it. Don't you feel it, too?"

"Yes, in a way," Sarah admitted. "But all the same what you're suggesting is quite impossible."

"I don't see anything impossible about it. If you were married to some decent fellow and were happy with him, I shouldn't dream of butting in." He said in a low voice: "But you're not happy, are you, Sarah?"

"I'm as happy as most people, I suppose," said Sarah valiantly.

"I think you're utterly miserable."

"If I am—it's my own doing. After all, if one makes a mistake, one's got to abide by it."

"Lawrence Steene isn't particularly noticeable for abiding by his mistakes, is he?"

"That's a mean thing to say!"

"No, it isn't. It's true."

"And anyway, Gerry, what you suggest is quite, *quite* mad. Crazy!"

"Because I haven't hung round you and led up to it gradually? There's no need for that. As I say, you and I belong—and you know it, Sarah."

Sarah sighed.

"I was terribly fond of you once, I'll admit."

"It goes deeper than that, my girl."

She turned to look at him. Her pretenses fell away.

"Does it? Are you sure?"

"I'm sure."

They were both silent. Then Gerry said gently:

"Will you come with me, Sarah?"

Sarah sighed. She sat up, pulling her furs more closely about her. There was a cold little breeze stirring the trees.

"Sorry, Gerry. The answer is No."

"Why?"

"I just can't do it—that's all."

"People are leaving their husbands every day."

"Not me."

"Are you telling me that you love Lawrence Steene?"

Sarah shook her head.

"No, I don't love him. I never did love him. He fascinated me, though. He's—well, he's clever with women." She gave a faint shiver of distaste. "One doesn't often feel that anybody is really—well—bad. But if I felt that about anybody I'd feel it about Lawrence. Because the things he does aren't hot-blooded things—they're not things he does because he can't help doing them. He just likes experimenting with people and things."

"Then need you have any scruples about leaving him?"

Sarah was silent for a moment, then she said in a low voice:

"It's not scruples. Oh," she caught herself up impatiently, "how disgusting it is that one always trots out one's noble reasons first! All right, Gerry, you'd better know what I'm *really* like. Living with Lawrence I've got used to—to certain things. I don't want to give them up. Clothes, furs, money, expensive restaurants, parties, a maid, cars, a yacht. . . . Everything made easy and luxurious. I'm steeped in luxury. And you want me to come and rough it on a ranch miles from anywhere. I can't—and I won't. I've gone soft! I'm rotted with money and luxury."

Gerry said unemotionally:

"Then it's about time you were hauled out of it all."

"Oh, Gerry!" Sarah was halfway between tears and laughter. "You're so matter-of-fact."

"I've got my feet on the ground all right."

"Yes, but you don't understand half of it."

"No?"

"It's not only—just—money. It's other things. Oh, don't you understand? I've become a rather horrible person. The parties we have—and the places we go—"

She paused, crimsoning.

"All right," said Gerry calmly. "You're depraved. Anything else?"

"Yes. There are things—things I've got used to—things I just couldn't do without."

"Things?" He took her sharply by the chin, turned her head toward him. "I'd heard rumors. You mean—dope?"

Sarah nodded. "It gives you such wonderful sensations."

"Listen." Gerry's voice was hard and incisive. "You'll come with me, and you'll cut out all that stuff."

"Suppose I can't?"

"I'll see to that," said Gerry grimly.

Sarah's shoulders relaxed. She sighed, leaning toward him. But Gerry drew back.

"No," he said. "I'm not going to kiss you."

"I see. I've got to decide—in cold blood?"

"Yes."

"Funny Gerry!"

They sat silent for a few moments. Then Gerry said, speaking with rather an effort:

"I know all right that I'm not much good. I've made a mess of things all round. I do realize that you can't have much—faith in me. But I do believe, honestly I do, that if I had you with me I could put up a better show. You're so shrewd, Sarah. And you know how to ginger a fellow up when he's getting slack."

"I sound an adorable creature!" said Sarah.

Gerry insisted stubbornly:

"I know I can make good. It will be a hell of a life for you. Hard work and pigging it—yes, pretty fair hell. I don't know how I've got the cheek to persuade you to come. But it will be *real*, Sarah. It will be—well—*living*. . . ."

"Living . . . real . . ." Sarah repeated the words over to herself.

She got up and began to walk away. Gerry walked beside her.

"You'll come, Sarah?"

"I don't know."

"Sarah—darling . . ."

"No, Gerry—don't say any more. You've said it all—everything that needs to be said. It's up to me now. I've got to think. I'll let you know . . ."

"When?"

"Soon. . . ."

Chapter Three

"Well, here's a nice surprise!"

Edith, opening the door of the flat to Sarah, creased the sour lines of her face into a dour smile.

"Hullo, Edith, my pet. Mother in?"

"I'm expecting her any minute now. I'm glad you've come. Cheer her up a bit."

"Does she need cheering up? She always sound frightfully gay."

"There's something very wrong with your mother. Worried about her, I am." Edith followed Sarah into the sitting room. "Can't keep still for two minutes together and snaps your head off if you so much as make a remark. Organic, I shouldn't wonder."

"Oh, don't croak, Edith. According to you everyone is always at death's door."

"I shan't say if of you, Miss Sarah. Blooming, you're looking. Tch!— dropping your lovely furs about on the floor. That's you all over. Lovely they are, must have cost a mint of money."

"They cost the earth all right."

"Nicer than any the mistress ever had. You certainly have got a lot of lovely things, Miss Sarah."

"So I should have. If you sell your soul, you've got to get a good price for it."

"That's not a nice way to talk," said Edith disapprovingly. "The worst of you is, Miss Sarah, that you're up and down. How well I remember as though it was yesterday, here in this very room, when you told me you was hoping to marry Mr. Steene, and how you danced me round the room like a mad thing. 'I'm going to be married—I'm going to be married,' you said."

Sarah said sharply: "Don't—don't, Edith. I can't stand it."

Edith's face became immediately alert and knowledgeable.

"There, there, dearie," she said soothingly. "The first two years is always the worst, they say. If you can weather them, you'll be all right."

"Hardly a very optimistic view of marriage."

Edith said disapprovingly: "Marriage is a poor business at best, but I suppose the world couldn't get on without it. You'll excuse the liberty, no little strangers on the way?"

"No, there are *not*, Edith."

"Sorry, I'm sure. But you seemed a bit on edge like, and I wondered if that mightn't be the reason. Very odd the way young married ladies behave sometimes. My elder sister, when she was expecting, she was in the grocer's shop one day and it came to her sudden like as she must have a great big juicy pear as was there in a case. Seized it, she did, and bit into it then and there. 'Here, what are you doing?' the young assistant said. But the grocer, he was a family man, and he understood how it was. 'That'll do, sonny,' he says, '*I'll* attend to this lady'—and he didn't charge her for it, either. Very understanding he was, having thirteen of his own."

"How unlucky to have thirteen children," said Sarah. "What a wonderful family you have got, Edith. I've heard about them ever since I was a little girl."

"Ah, yes. Many's the story I've told you. Such a serious little thing as you were, and minding so much about everything. And that reminds me, that young gentleman of yours was round here the other day. Mr. Lloyd. Have you seen him?"

"Yes, I've seen him."

"Looks much older—but beautifully sunburnt. That comes from being so much in foreign parts. Done well for himself, has he?"

"Not particularly."

"Ah, that's a pity. Not quite enough drive to him—that's what's the matter with him."

"I suppose it is. Do you think Mother will be coming soon?"

"Oh, yes, Miss Sarah. She's going out to dinner. So she'll be home to change first. If you ask me, Miss Sarah, it's a great pity she doesn't have more quiet nights at home. She does far too much."

"I suppose she enjoys it."

"All this rushing around." Edith sniffed. "It doesn't suit her. She was always a quiet lady."

Sarah turned her head sharply, as though Edith's words had struck some chord of remembrance. She repeated musingly:

"A quiet lady. Yes, Mother was quiet. Gerry said so too. Funny how she's altered completely in the last three years. Do *you* think she's changed a lot, Edith?"

"Sometimes I'd say she wasn't the same lady."

"She used to be quite different . . . She used to be—" Sarah broke off, thinking. Then she went on: "Do you think mothers always go on being fond of their children, Edith?"

"Of course they do, Miss Sarah. It wouldn't be natural if they didn't."

"But is it really natural to go on caring about your young once they're grown up and out in the world? Animals don't."

Edith was scandalized. She said sharply:

"Animals indeed! We're Christian men and women. Don't you talk nonsense, Miss Sarah. Remember the saying: *A son's a son till he gets him a wife. But a daughter's a daughter all your life.*"

Sarah laughed.

"I know heaps of mothers who hate their daughters like poison, and daughters who've got no use for their mothers, either."

"Well, all I can say is, Miss Sarah, that I don't think that's at all nice."

"But much, much healthier, Edith—or so our psychologists say."

"Nasty minds they've got, then."

Sarah said thoughtfully:

"I've always been frightfully fond of Mother—as a person—not as a mother."

"And your mother's devoted to you, Miss Sarah."

Sarah did not answer for some seconds. Then she said thoughtfully: "I wonder . . ."

Edith sniffed.

"If you knew the state she was in when you had the pneumonia when you were fourteen—"

"Oh, yes, *then*. But now . . ."

They both heard the sound of the latchkey. Edith said:

"Here she is now."

Ann came in breathlessly, pulling off a gay little hat of multicolored feathers.

"Sarah? What a nice surprise. Oh dear, this hat has been hurting my head. What's the time? I'm terribly late. I'm meeting the Ladesburys at Chaliano's at eight. Come into my room while I change."

Sarah followed her obediently along the passage, and into her bedroom.

"How's Lawrence?" Ann asked.

"Very well."

"Good. Its ages since I've seen him—or you either for that matter. We must have a party sometime. That new revue at the Coronation sounds quite good—"

"Mother. I want to talk to you."

"Yes, darling?"

"Can't you stop doing things to your face and just listen to me?"

Ann looked surprised.

"Dear me, Sarah. You seem very much on edge."

"I want to talk to you. It's serious. It's—Gerry."

"Oh." Ann's hands fell to her sides. She looked thoughtful. "Gerry?"

Sarah said baldly:

"He wants me to leave Lawrence and go to Canada with him."

Ann breathed in once or twice. Then she said lightly:

"What absolute nonsense! Poor old Gerry. He really is too stupid for words."

Sarah said sharply:

"Gerry's all right."

Ann said: "I know you've always stuck up for him, darling. But seriously, don't you find you've rather outgrown him now that you see him again?"

"You're not helping me much, Mother," said Sarah. Her voice shook a little. "I want to be—serious about it."

Ann said sharply:

"You're not taking this ridiculous nonsense seriously?"

"Yes, I am."

Ann said angrily: "Then you're being stupid, Sarah."

Sarah said obstinately: "I've always cared for Gerry and he for me."

Ann laughed.

"Oh, my dear child!"

"I ought never to have married Lawrence. It was the greatest mistake I ever made."

"You'll settle down," said Ann comfortably.

Sarah got up and prowled up and down restlessly.

"I shan't. I shan't. My life's hell—pure hell."

"Don't exaggerate, Sarah." Ann's voice was acid.

"He's a beast—an inhuman beast."

"He's devoted to you Sarah," said Ann reproachfully.

"Why did I do it? Why? I never really wanted to marry him." She whirled round suddenly on Ann. "I shouldn't have married him if it hadn't been for *you*."

"Me?" Ann flushed angrily. "I had nothing to do with it!"

"You did—you did!"

"I told you at the time you must make up your own mind."

"You persuaded me it would be all right."

"What wicked nonsense! Why, I told you he had a bad reputation, that you were taking a risk—"

"I know. But it was the *way* you said it. As though it didn't matter. Oh, the whole thing! I don't care what words you used. The words were all right. *But you wanted me to marry him.* You *did*, Mother. I *know* you did! Why? Because you wanted to get rid of me?"

Ann faced her daughter angrily.

"Really, Sarah, this is the most extraordinary attack."

Sarah came up close to her mother. Her eyes, enormous and dark in her white face, stared into Ann's face as though she were looking there for the truth.

"I know what I'm saying is true. *You wanted me to marry Lawrence.*

And now it's turned out all wrong, now that I'm hellishly unhappy, you don't care. Sometimes—I've even thought you were *pleased* . . ."

"Sarah!"

"Yes, *pleased*." Her eyes were still searching. Ann was restless under that stare. "You *are* pleased. . . . You want me to be unhappy . . ."

Ann turned brusquely away. She was trembling. She walked away toward the door. Sarah followed her.

"Why? Why, Mother?"

Ann said, forcing the words through stiff lips:

"You don't know what you are saying."

Sarah persisted:

"I want to know why you wanted me to be unhappy."

"I never wanted you to be unhappy! Don't be absurd!"

"Mother . . ." Timidly, like a child, Sarah touched her mother's arm. "Mother . . . I'm your daughter . . . You ought to be fond of me."

"Of course I'm fond of you! What next?"

"No," said Sarah. "I don't think that you are. I don't think that you've been fond of me for a long time. . . . You've gone right away from me . . . somewhere where I can't get at you. . . ."

Ann made an effort to pull herself together. She said in a matter-of-fact voice:

"However much you care for your children, there comes a time when they have to learn to stand on their own feet. Mothers mustn't be possessive."

"No, of course not. But I think that when one is in trouble, one ought to be able to come to one's mother."

"But what do you want me to *do*, Sarah?"

"I want you to tell me whether I shall go away with Gerry or stay with Lawrence."

"Stay with your husband, of course."

"You sound very positive."

"My dear child, what other answer can you expect from a woman of my generation? I was brought up to observe certain standards of behavior."

"Morally right to stay with a husband, morally wrong to go away with a lover! Is that it?"

"Exactly. Of course, I daresay your modern friends would take quite a different view. But you asked me for mine."

Sarah sighed and shook her head.

"It isn't nearly as simple as you make it sound. It's all mixed up. Actually, it's the nastiest Me that would like to stay with Lawrence—the Me that's afraid to risk poverty and difficulties—the Me that likes soft living—the Me that has depraved tastes and is a slave to sensation. . . . The other Me, the Me that wants to go with Gerry isn't just an amorous little slut—it's a Me that believes in Gerry and wants to help him. You see, Mother, I've got just that something that Gerry hasn't got. There's a moment when he sits down and pities himself and it's just then that he needs me to give him a terrific kick in the pants! Gerry could be a really fine sort of person—he's got it in him. He just wants someone to laugh at him, and goad him and—oh, he—he just wants *me*. . . ."

Sarah stopped and looked imploringly at Ann. Ann's face was set like flint.

"It's no good my pretending to be impressed, Sarah. You married Lawrence of your own free will, no matter what you pretend, and you ought to stick to him."

"Perhaps . . ."

Ann pressed her advantage.

"And you know, darling," her tone was affectionate, "I don't feel that you're really cut out for a life of roughing it. It sounds all right just talking about it, but I'm sure you'd hate it when it came to the point, especially—" this, she felt, was a good touch—"especially if you felt you were hampering Gerry instead of helping him."

But almost at once she realized that she had made a false step.

Sarah's face hardened. She moved to the dressing table, took and lighted a cigarette. Then she said, lightly:

"You're quite the devil's advocate, aren't you, Mother?"

"What do you mean?"

Ann was bewildered.

Sarah came back and stood squarely in front of her mother. Her face was suspicious and hard.

"What's the real reason you don't want me to go off with Gerry, Mother?"

"I've told you—"

"The *real* reason. . . ." Very deliberately, her eyes boring into Ann's, Sarah said: "You're afraid, aren't you, *that I might be happy with Gerry?*"

"I'm afraid you might be very *un*happy!"

"No, you're not." Sarah shot the words out bitterly. "You wouldn't care if I was unhappy. It's my happiness you don't want. You don't like me. It's more than that. For some reason or other you hate me. . . . That's it, isn't it? You hate me. You hate me like hell!"

"Sarah, are you mad?"

"No, I'm not mad. I'm getting at the truth at last. You've hated me for a long time—for years. *Why?*"

"It's not true . . ."

"It *is* true. But why? It's not that you're jealous of me because I'm young. Some mothers are like that with their daughters, but not you. You were always sweet to me. . . . Why do you hate me, Mother? I've got to know!"

"I don't hate you!"

Sarah cried: "Oh, do stop telling lies! Come out into the open. What have I ever done to make you hate me? I've always adored you. I've always tried to be nice to you—and do things for you."

Ann turned on her. She spoke bitterly and with significance in her voice.

"You speak," she said, "as though the sacrifices had been all on your side!"

Sarah stared at her bewildered.

"Sacrifices? What sacrifices?"

Ann's voice trembled. She pressed her hands together.

"I've given up my life for you—given up everything I cared for—and you don't even remember it!"

Still bewildered, Sarah said: "I don't even know what you're talking about."

"No, you don't. You didn't even remember Richard Cauldfield's name. 'Richard Cauldfield?' you said. 'Who's he?'"

A dawning comprehension showed in Sarah's eyes. A faint dismay rose in her.

"Richard Cauldfield?"

"Yes, Richard Cauldfield." Ann was openly accusing now. "*You* disliked him. But *I* loved him! I cared for him very much. I wanted to marry him. But because of you I had to give him up."

"Mother . . ."

Sarah was appalled.

Ann said defiantly: "I'd a right to my happiness."

"I didn't know—you really cared," Sarah stammered.

"You didn't want to know. You shut your eyes to it. You did everything you could to stop the marriage. That's true, isn't it?"

"Yes, it's true . . ." Sarah's mind went back over the past. She felt just a little sick as she remembered her glib childish assurance. "I—I didn't think he'd make you happy. . . ."

"What right had you to think for another person?" Ann demanded fiercely.

Gerry had said that to her. Gerry had been worried by what she had been trying to do. And she had been so pleased with herself, so triumphant in her victory over the hated "Cauliflower." Such crude childish jealousy it had been—she saw that now! And because of it, her mother had suffered, had changed little by little into this nervy unhappy woman now confronting her with a reproach to which she had no answer.

She could only say, in an uncertain whisper:

"I didn't know . . . Oh, Mother, I didn't know. . . ."

Ann was back again in the past.

"We could have been happy together," she said. "He was a lonely man. His first wife had died with the baby, and it had been a great shock and grief to him. He had faults, I know, he was inclined to be pompous and to lay down the law—the sort of things young people notice—but underneath it he was kind and simple and good. We would have grown old together and been happy. And instead I hurt him badly—I sent him away. Sent him to a hotel on the south coast where he met that silly little harpy who doesn't even care for him."

Sarah drew away. Each word had hurt her. Yet she rallied to say what she could in her defense.

"If you wanted to marry him so much," she said, "you should have gone ahead and done it."

Ann turned on her sharply.

"Don't you remember the eternal scenes—the rows? You were like cat and dog together, you two. You provoked him deliberately. It was part of your plan."

(Yes, it *had* been part of her plan. . . .)

"I couldn't stand it, going on day after day. And then I was faced with an alternative. I had to choose—Richard put it like that—to choose between him and you. You were my daughter, my own flesh and blood. I chose you."

"And ever since then," said Sarah clear-sightedly, "you've hated me. . . ."

The pattern was completely clear to her now.

She gathered up her furs and turned away toward the door.

"Well," she said. "We know where we are now."

Her voice was hard and clear. From contemplating the ruin of Ann's life, she had turned to the contemplation of the ruin of her own.

In the doorway she turned and spoke to the woman with the ravaged face who had not denied that last accusation.

"*You* hate *me* for spoiling your life, Mother," she said. "Well, I hate *you* for spoiling mine!"

Ann said sharply: "I've had nothing to do with your life. You made your own choice."

"Oh, no, I didn't. Don't be a damned hypocrite, Mother. I came to you wanting you to help me not to marry Lawrence. You knew quite well that I was attracted by him, but that I wanted to get free of that attraction. You were quite clever about it. You knew just what to do and say."

"Nonsense. Why should I want you to marry Lawrence?"

"I think—because you knew I wouldn't be happy. *You* were unhappy—and you wanted me to be, too. Come now, Mother, spill the beans. Haven't you had a certain kick out of knowing that I'm miserable in my married life?"

In a sudden flash of passion Ann said:

"Sometimes, yes, I've felt that it served you right!"

Mother and daughter stared at each other implacably.

Then Sarah laughed, a harsh unpleasant laugh.

"So now we've got it! Good-bye Mother *dear*. . . ."

She went out of the door and along the passage. Ann heard the flat door close with a sharp sound of finality.

She was alone.

Trembling still, she reached her bed and flung herself down on it. Tears welled up in her eyes and flowed down her cheeks. ·

Presently she was shaken by a tempest of weeping such as she had not known for years.

She wept and she wept . . .

How long she had been crying she did not know, but as her sobs at last began to die down, there was a chink of china and Edith entered with a tea tray. She put it down on the table by the bed and sat down by her mistress, patting her shoulder gently.

"There, there, my lamb, my pretty. . . . Here's a nice cup of tea and you're going to drink it down whatever you say."

"Oh, Edith, Edith . . ." Ann clung to her faithful servant and friend.

"There, there, don't you take on so. It will be all right."

"The things I said—the things I said—"

"Never you mind. Sit up now. I'll pour out your tea. Now you drink it."

Obediently Ann sat up and sipped the hot tea.

"There now, you'll feel better in a minute."

"Sarah—how could I—?"

"Now don't you worry—"

"How could I say those things to her?"

"Better to say them than to think them, if you ask me," said Edith. "It's the things that you think and don't say that turn bitter as bile in you—and that's a fact."

"I was so cruel—so cruel—"

"I'd say that what has been wrong with you for a long time was bottling things up. Have a good row and get it over, that's what I say, instead of keeping it all to yourself and pretending there's nothing there. We've all got bad thoughts, but we don't always like to admit it."

"Have I really been hating Sarah? My little Sarah—how funny and sweet she used to be. And I've hated her?"

"Of course you haven't," said Edith robustly.

"But I have. I wanted her to suffer—to be hurt—like I was hurt."

"Now don't you go fancying a lot of nonsense. You're devoted to Miss Sarah, and always have been."

Ann said:

"All this time—all this time—running underneath in a dark current—hate . . . hate . . ."

"Pity you didn't set to and have it out sooner. A good row always clears the air."

Ann lay back weakly on her pillows.

"But I don't hate her now," she said wonderingly. "It's all gone—yes, all gone. . . ."

Edith got up and patted Ann on the shoulder.

"Don't you fret, my pretty. Everything's all right."

Ann shook her head.

"No, never again. We both said things that neither of us can ever forget."

"Don't you believe it. Hard words break no bones, and that's a true saying."

Ann said:

"There are some things, fundamental things, that can *never* be forgotten."

Edith picked up the tray.

"Never's a big word," she said.

Chapter Four

Sarah, when she arrived home, went to the big room at the back of the house which Lawrence called his studio.

He was there, unpacking a statuette that he had recently purchased—the work of a young French artist.

"What do you think of it, Sarah? Beautiful, isn't it?"

His fingers sensitively caressed the lines of the nude twisted body.

Sarah shivered a little, as though at some memory.

She said, frowning:

"Yes, beautiful—but obscene!"

"Oh, come now—how surprising that there is still that touch of the Puritan in you, Sarah. Interesting that it should persist."

"That figure *is* obscene."

"Slightly decadent, perhaps. . . . But very clever. And highly imaginative—Paul takes hashish, of course—that probably accounts for the spirit of the thing."

He put it down and turned to Sarah.

"You are looking very much *en beauté*—my charming wife—and you are upset over something. Distress always suits you."

Sarah said: "I've just had a terrific row with Mother."

"Indeed?" Lawrence raised his eyebrows in some amusement. "How very unlikely! I can hardly imagine it. The gentle Ann."

"She wasn't so gentle today! I was rather horrible to her, I admit."

"Domestic disputes are very uninteresting, Sarah. Don't let's talk about them."

"I wasn't going to. Mother and I are all washed up—that's what it amounts to. No, I want to talk to you about something else. I think I'm—leaving you, Lawrence."

Steene showed no particular reaction. He raised his eyebrows and murmured:

"I think, you know, that would be rather unwise on your part."

"You make that sound like a threat."

"Oh, no—just a gentle warning. And why are you leaving me, Sarah? Wives of mine have done it before but you can hardly have their reasons. I have not, for instance, broken your heart. You have very little heart where I am concerned and you are still—"

"The reigning favorite?" said Sarah.

"If you like to put it in that oriental manner. Yes, Sarah, I find you quite perfect—even the Puritan touch gives a spice to our—what shall I say—rather pagan mode of life? By the way, my first wife's reason for leaving me cannot apply either. Moral disapprobation could hardly be your strong suit, all things considered."

"Does it matter why I'm leaving you? Don't pretend that you'll really mind!"

"I shall mind very much! You are, at the moment, my most prized possession—better than all these."

He waved a hand round the studio.

"I meant—you don't *love* me?"

"Romantic devotion, as I once told you, has never appealed to me—to give or to receive."

"The plain truth is—there's someone else," said Sarah. "I'm going away with him."

"Ah! leaving your sins behind you?"

"Do you mean—"

"I wonder whether that will be as easy as you think. You've been an apt disciple. Sarah—the tide of life runs strongly in you—can you give up these sensations—these pleasures—these adventures of the senses? Think of that evening at the Mariana . . . remember Charcot and his Diversions. These things, Sarah, are not to be so lightly laid aside."

Sarah looked at him, and for a moment fear peeped out of her eyes.

"I know . . . I know . . . but one *can* give it all up!"

"Can one? You're rather deep in, Sarah. . . ."

"But I shall get out . . . I mean to get out. . . ."

Turning she went hurriedly out of the room.

Lawrence put down the statuette with a bang.

He was seriously annoyed. He was not yet tired of Sarah. He doubted that he would ever tire of her—a creature of temperament, capable of resistance—of struggle, a creature of enchanting beauty. A Collector's Piece of extreme rarity.

Chapter Five

"Why, Sarah," Dame Laura looked up from her desk in surprise.

Sarah was breathless and in a state of considerable emotion.

Laura Whitstable said:

"I haven't seen you for ages, goddaughter."

"No, I know . . . Oh, Laura, I'm in such a *mess*."

"Sit down." Laura Whitstable drew her gently to a couch. "Now then, tell me all about it."

"I thought perhaps you could help me. . . . Can one, does one—is it possible to stop taking things—when, I mean—when you've got used to taking them."

She added hastily:

"Oh, dear, I don't suppose you even know what I'm talking about."

"Oh, yes, I do. You mean dope?"

"Yes." Sarah felt an enormous relief at the matter-of-fact way in which Laura Whitstable reacted.

"Well, now, the answer depends on a lot of things. It's not easy—it's never easy. Women find it harder to break a habit of that kind than men do. It depends very much on how long you have been taking the stuff, how dependent you have got on it, how good your general health is, how much courage and resolution and willpower you have got, under what conditions you are going to pass your daily life, what you have to look forward to, and, if you are a woman, if you have someone at hand to *help* you in the fight."

Sarah's face brightened.

"Good. I think—I really think it will be all right then."

"Too much time on your hands isn't going to help," Laura warned her.

Sarah laughed.

"I shall have very little time on my hands! I shall be working like mad every minute of the day. I shall have someone to—to get tough with me and make me toe the line, and as for looking forward—I've got everything to look forward to—*everything!*"

"Well, Sarah, I think you've got a good chance." Laura looked at her—and added unexpectedly: "You seem to have grown up at last."

"Yes. I've been rather a long time about it . . . I realize that. I called Gerry weak, but *I'm* really the weak one. Always wanting to be bolstered up."

Sarah's face clouded over.

"Laura—I've been simply horrible to Mother. I only found out today that she'd really minded about Cauliflower. I know now that when you were warning me about sacrifices and burnt offerings I just wouldn't listen. I was so horribly pleased with myself, with my plan for getting rid of poor old Richard—and all the time I can see now I was just being jealous and childish and spiteful. I made Mother give him up; and then naturally she hated me only she never said so, but things just seemed to go all wrong. Today we had a terrific set-to—and shouted at each other, and I said the most beastly things to her, and blamed her for everything that had happened to me. Really, all the time, I was feeling awful about *her.*"

"I see."

"And now—" Sarah looked miserable—"I don't know *what* to do. If only I could make up to her in some way—but I suppose it's too late."

Laura Whitstable rose briskly to her feet.

"There is no greater waste of time," she said didactically, "than saying the right thing to the wrong person. . . ."

Chapter Six

1

With rather the air of someone who handles dynamite, Edith picked up the telephone receiver. She took a deep breath and dialed a number. When she heard the ringing at the other end, she turned her head uneasily over her shoulder. It was all right. She was alone in the flat. The brisk professional voice coming over the wire made her jump.

"Welbeck 97438."

"Oh—is that Dame Laura Whitstable?"

"Speaking."

Edith swallowed twice, nervously.

"It's Edith, ma'am. Mrs. Prentice's Edith."

"Good evening, Edith."

Edith swallowed again. She said obscurely: "Nasty things, telephones."

"Yes, I quite understand. You wanted to speak to me about something?"

"It's about Mrs. Prentice, ma'am. I'm worried about her, I really am."

"But you've been worried about her for a long time, haven't you, Edith?"

"This is different, ma'am. It's quite different. She's lost her appetite, and she sits about doing nothing. And often I'll find her crying. She's calmer, if you take my meaning, none of that restlessness she used to have. And she don't take me up sharp anymore. She's gentle and considerate like she used to be—but she's just got no heart in her—no *spirit* anymore. It's dreadful, ma'am, really it's dreadful."

The telephone said "Interesting," in a detached professional manner, which was not at all what Edith wanted.

"It would make your heart bleed, really it would, ma'am."

"Don't use such ridiculous terms, Edith. Hearts don't bleed unless they have received physical damage."

Edith pressed on.

"It's to do with Miss Sarah, ma'am. Proper dust-up they had, and now Miss Sarah's not been nigh the place for nearly a month."

"No, she's been away from London—in the country."

"I wrote to her."

"No letters have been forwarded to her."

Edith brightened a little.

"Ah, well, then, Once she's back in London—"

Dame Laura cut her short.

"I'm afraid, Edith, you'd better prepare yourself for a shock. Miss Sarah is going away with Mr. Gerald Lloyd to Canada."

Edith made a noise like a disapproving soda-water siphon.

"That's downright wicked. Leaving her husband!"

"Don't be sanctimonious, Edith. Who are you to judge other people's conduct? She'll have a hard life of it out there—none of the luxuries she's been accustomed to."

Edith sighed: "That does seem to make it a little less sinful . . . And if you'll excuse me saying so, ma'am, Mr. Steene always *has* given me the creeps. The sort of gentleman you could fancy has sold his soul to the devil."

In a dry voice Dame Laura said:

"Allowing for the inevitable difference in our phraseology, I'm inclined to agree with you."

"Won't Miss Sarah come and say good-bye?"

"It seems not."

Edith said indignantly: "I call that downright hard-hearted of her."

"You don't understand in the least."

"I understand how a daughter ought to behave to a mother. I'd never have believed it of Miss Sarah! Can't you do something about it, ma'am?"

"I never interfere."

Edith drew a deep breath.

"Well, you'll excuse me—I know you're a very famous lady and very

clever, and I'm only a servant—but this is a time that I think you
ought to!"

And Edith slammed down the receiver with a grim face.

2

Edith had spoken twice to Ann before the latter roused herself and
answered.

"What did you say, Edith?"

"I said as how your hair was looking peculiar round the roots. You
ought to do a bit more touching-up of it."

"I shan't bother anymore. It will look better gray."

"You'll look more respectable, I agree. But it will look funny if it's
half-and-half."

"It doesn't matter."

Nothing mattered. What could matter in the dull procession of day
that followed day? Ann thought, as she had thought again and again,
"Sarah will never forgive me. And she's quite right . . ."

The telephone rang and Ann got up and went to it. She said:
"Hullo?" in a listless voice, then started a little as Dame Laura's incisive
voice spoke at the other end.

"Ann?"

"Yes."

"I dislike interfering in other people's lives, but—I think that there
is something you perhaps ought to know. Sarah and Gerald Lloyd are
leaving by the eight o'clock plane for Canada this evening."

"What?" Ann gasped. "I—I haven't seen Sarah for weeks."

"No. She has been in a nursing home in the country. She went there
voluntarily to undergo a cure for drug-taking."

"Oh, Laura! Is she all right?"

"She's come through very well. You can probably appreciate that she
suffered a good deal. . . . Yes, I'm proud of my goddaughter. She's got
backbone."

"Oh, Laura." Words streamed from Ann. "Do you remember asking
me if I knew Ann Prentice? I do now. I've ruined Sarah's life through
resentment and spite. She'll never forgive me!"

"Rubbish. Nobody can really ruin another person's life. Don't be melodramatic and don't wallow."

"It's the truth. I know just what I am and what I did."

"That's all to the good then—but you've known it some time now, haven't you? Wouldn't it be as well to go on to the next thing?"

"You don't understand, Laura. I feel so conscience-stricken—so horribly remorseful . . ."

"Listen, Ann, there are just two things that I've no use for whatever—someone telling me how noble they are and what moral reasons they have for the things they do, and the other is someone going on moaning about how wickedly they have behaved. Both statements may be true—recognize the truth of your actions, by all means, but having done so, *pass on*. You can't put the clock back and you can't usually undo what you've done. Continue living."

"Laura, what do you think I ought to do about Sarah?"

Laura Whitstable snorted.

"I may have interfered—but I haven't sunk so low as to give advice."

She rang off firmly.

Ann, moving as though in a dream, crossed the room to the sofa and sat there, staring into space. . . .

Sarah—Gerry—would it work out? Would her child, her dearly loved child, find happiness at last? Gerry was fundamentally weak—would the record of failure go on—would he let Sarah down—would Sarah be disillusioned—unhappy? If only Gerry were a different type of man. But Gerry was the man that Sarah loved.

Time passed. Ann still sat motionless.

It was nothing to do with her any longer. She had forfeited all claim. Between her and Sarah yawned an impassable gulf.

Edith looked in on her mistress once, then crept away again.

But presently the doorbell rang and she went to answer it.

"Mr. Mowbray's called for you, ma'am."

"What do you say?"

"Mr. Mowbray. Waiting downstairs."

Ann sprang up. Her eyes went to the clock. What had she been thinking about—to sit there, half paralyzed?

Sarah was going away—tonight—to the other side of the world. . . .

Ann snatched up her fur cape and ran out of the flat.

"Basil." She spoke breathlessly. "Please—drive me to London Airport. As quick as you can."

"But Ann darling, what *is* all this about?"

"It's Sarah. She's going to Canada. I haven't seen her to say goodbye."

"But darling, haven't you left it rather *late?*"

"Of course I have. I've been a fool. But I hope it isn't *too* late. Oh, go on—Basil—quick!"

Basil Mowbray sighed, and started the engine.

"I always thought you were such a reasonable woman, Ann," he said reproachfully. "I really am thankful that I shall never be a parent. It seems to make people behave so oddly."

"You must drive *fast*, Basil."

Basil sighed.

Through the Kensington streets, avoiding the Hammersmith bottleneck by a series of intricate side streets, through Chiswick where traffic was heavy, out at last on the Great West Road, roaring along past tall factories and neon-lit buildings—then past rows of prim houses where people lived. Mothers and daughters, fathers and sons, husbands and wives. All with their problems and their quarrels and their reconciliations, "Just like me," thought Ann. She felt a sudden kinship, a sudden love and understanding for all the human race. . . . She was not, could never be, lonely, for she lived in a world peopled with her own kind. . . .

3

At Heathrow the passengers stood and sat in the lounge, awaiting the summons to embark.

Gerry said to Sarah:

"Not regretting?"

She flashed a quick look of reassurance at him.

Sarah was thinner and her face bore the lines that the endurance of pain puts there. It was an older face, not less lovely, but now fully mature.

She was thinking: "Gerry wanted me to go and say good-bye to Mother. He doesn't understand. . . . If I could only make up to her for what I did—but I can't . . ."

She couldn't give back Richard Cauldfield. . . .

No, the thing she had done to her mother was beyond forgiveness.

She was glad to be with Gerry—going forward to a new life with him, but something in her cried forlornly. . . .

"I'm going *away*, Mother, I'm going *away*. . . ."

If only—

The raucous note of the announcer made her jump. "Will passengers traveling by Flight 00346 for Prestwick, Gander and Montreal please follow the green light to Customs and Immigration. . . ."

The passengers picked up their hand luggage and went toward the end door. Sarah followed Gerry, lagging a little behind.

"Sarah!"

Through the outer door Ann, her fur cape slipping from her shoulders, came running toward her daughter. Sarah ran back to meet her, dropping her small traveling bag.

"Mother!"

They hugged each other, then drew back to look.

All the things that Ann had thought of saying, had rehearsed saying, on the way down, died on her lips. There was no need of them. And Sarah, too, felt no need of speech. To have said "Forgive me, Mother," would have been meaningless.

And in that moment Sarah shed the last vestige of her childish dependence on Ann. She was a woman now who could stand on her own feet and make her own decisions.

With an odd instinct of reassurance Sarah said quickly:

"I shall be all right, Mother."

And Gerry, beaming, said: "I'll look after her, Mrs. Prentice."

An Air official was approaching to herd Gerry and Sarah in the way they should go.

Sarah said in the same inadequate idiom:

"*You'll* be all right, *won't* you, Mother?"

And Ann answered:

"Yes, darling. I'll be quite all right. Good-bye—God bless you both."

Gerry and Sarah went through the door toward their new life and Ann went back to the car where Basil was waiting for her.

"These terrifying machines," said Basil, as an airliner roared along the runway. "Just like enormous malignant *insects!* They frighten me to *death!*"

He drove out on to the road and turned in the direction of London.

Ann said: "If you don't mind, Basil, I won't come out tonight with you. I'd rather have a quiet evening at home."

"Very well, darling. I'll take you back there."

Ann had always thought of Basil Mowbray as "so amusing and so spiteful." She realized suddenly that he was also *kind*—a kind little man and rather a lonely one.

"Dear me," thought Ann—"What a ridiculous *fuss* I have been making."

Basil was saying anxiously:

"But Ann, darling, oughtn't you to have something to *eat?* There won't be anything ready at the flat."

Ann smiled and shook her head. A pleasant picture rose before her eyes.

"Don't worry," she said. "Edith will bring me scrambled eggs on a tray in front of the fire—yes—and a nice hot cup of tea, bless her!"

Edith gave her mistress a sharp look as she let her in, but all she said was:

"Now you go and sit by the fire."

"I'll just get out of these silly clothes, and put on something comfortable."

"You'd better have that blue flannel dressing gown you gave me four years ago. Much cozier than that silly negligee affair as you call it. I haven't ever worn it. It's been put away in my bottom drawer. Took a fancy to be buried in it, I did."

Lying on the sofa in the drawing room, the blue dressing gown tucked snugly round her, Ann stared into the fire.

Presently Edith came in with the tray and arranged it on a low table by her mistress's side.

"I'll brush your hair for you later," she said.

Ann smiled up at her.

"You're treating me like a little girl tonight, Edith. Why?"

Edith grunted.

"That's what you always look like to me."

"Edith—" Ann looked up at her and said with a slight effort: "Edith—I saw Sarah. It's—all right."

"Of course it's all right! Always was! I told you so!"

For a moment she stood looking down at her mistress, her grim old face soft and kind.

Then she went out of the room.

"This wonderful peace . . ." Ann thought. Words remembered from long ago came back to her.

"The peace of God which passeth all understanding. . . ."

· UNFINISHED PORTRAIT ·

Foreword

My Dear Mary: I send you this because I don't know what to do with it. I suppose, really, I want it to see the light of day. One does. I suppose the complete genius keeps his pictures stacked in the studio and never shows them to anybody. I was never like that, but then I was never a genius—just Mr. Larraby, the promising young portrait painter.

Well, my dear, *you* know what it is, none better—to be cut off from the thing you loved doing and did well because you loved doing it. That's why we were friends, you and I. And you know about this writing business—I don't.

If you read this manuscript, you'll see that I've taken Barge's advice. You remember? He said, "Try a new medium." This is a portrait—and probably a damned bad one because I don't know my medium. If you say it's no good, I'll take your word for it, but if you think it has, in the smallest degree, that significant form we both believe to be the fundamental basis of art—well, then, I don't see why it shouldn't be published. I've put the real names, but you can change them. And who is to mind? Not Michael. And as for Dermot he would never recognize himself! He isn't made that way. Anyway, as Celia herself said, her story is a very ordinary story. It might happen to anybody. In fact, it frequently does. It isn't her story I've been interested in. All along it's been Celia herself. Yes, Celia herself. . . .

You see I wanted to nail her in paint to a canvas, and that being out of the question, I've tried to get her in another way. But I'm working in an unfamiliar medium—these words and sentences and commas and full stops—they're not my craft. You'll remark, I dare say, *que ça se voit!*

I've seen her, you know, from two angles. First, from my own. And second, owing to the peculiar circumstances of twenty-four hours, I've been able—at moments—to get inside her skin and see her from her own. And the two don't always agree. That's what's so tantalizing and fascinating to me! I should like to be God and know the truth.

But a novelist can be God to the creatures he creates. He has them in his power to do what he likes with—or so he thinks. But they do give him surprises. I wonder if the real God finds that too. . . . Yes, I wonder. . . .

Well, my dear, I won't wander on anymore. Do what you can for me.

Yours ever,

J. L.

BOOK ONE

THE ISLAND

There is a lonely isle
Set apart
In the midst of the sea
Where the birds rest awhile
On their long flight
To the South
They rest a night
Then take wing and depart
To the Southern seas . . .

I am an island set apart
In the midst of the sea
And a bird from the mainland
Rested on me . . .

Chapter 1

THE WOMAN IN THE GARDEN

Do you know the feeling you have when you know something quite well and yet for the life of you can't recollect it?

I had that feeling all the way down the winding white road to the town. It was with me when I started from the plateau overhanging the sea in the villa gardens. And with every step I took, it grew stronger and—somehow—more urgent. And at last, just when the avenue of palm trees runs down to the beach, I stopped. Because, you see, I knew it was now or never. This shadowy thing that was lurking at the back of my brain had got to be pulled out into the open, had got to be probed and examined and nailed down, so that I knew what it was. I'd got to pin the thing down—otherwise it would be too late.

I did what one always does do when trying to remember things. I went over the facts.

The walk up from the town—with the dust and the sun on the back of my neck. Nothing there.

The grounds of the Villa—cool and refreshing with the great cypresses standing dark against the skyline. The green grass path that led to the plateau where the seat was placed overlooking the sea. The surprise and slight annoyance at finding a woman occupying the seat.

For a moment I had felt awkward. She had turned her head and looked at me. An Englishwoman. I felt the need of saying something—some phrase to cover my retirement.

"Lovely view from up here."

That was what I had said—just the ordinary silly conventional thing. And she answered in exactly the words and tone that an ordinary well-bred woman would use.

"Delightful," she had said. "And such a beautiful day."

"But rather a long pull up from the town."

She agreed and said it *was* a long dusty walk.

And that was all. Just that interchange of polite commonplaces between two English people abroad who have not met before and who do not expect to meet again. I retraced my steps, walked once or twice round the Villa admiring the orange berberis (if that's what the thing is called) and then started back to the town.

That was absolutely all there was to it—and yet, somehow, it wasn't. There was this feeling of knowing something quite well and not being able to remember it.

Had it been something in her manner? No, her manner had been perfectly normal and pleasant. She'd behaved and looked just as ninety-nine women out of a hundred women would have behaved.

Except—no, it was true—she hadn't looked at my hands.

There! What an odd thing to have written down. It amazes me when I look at it. An Irish bull if there ever was one. And yet to put it down correctly wouldn't express my meaning.

She hadn't looked at my hands. And you see, I'm used to women looking at my hands. Women are so quick. And they're so soft-hearted I'm used to the expression that comes over their faces—bless them and damn them. Sympathy, and discretion, and determination not to show they've noticed. And the immediate change in their manner—the gentleness.

But this woman hadn't seen or noticed.

I began thinking about her more closely. A queer thing—I couldn't have described her in the least at the moment I turned my back on her. I would have said she was fairish and about thirty-odd—that's all. But all the way down the hill, the picture of her had been growing—growing——It was for all the world like a photographic plate that you develop in a dark cellar. (That's one of my earliest memories—developing negatives with my father in our cellar.)

I've never forgotten the thrill of it. The blank white expanse with the developer washing over it. And then, suddenly, the tiny speck that appears, darkening and widening rapidly. The thrill of it—the uncertainty. The plate darkens rapidly—but still you can't see exactly. It's just a jumble of dark and light. And then—recognition—you know what it is—you see that this is the branch of the tree, or somebody's face, or the back of the chair, and you know whether the negative is upside down or not—and you reverse it if it is—and then you watch the whole picture emerging from nothingness till it begins to darken and you lose it again.

Well, that's the best description I can give of what happened to me. All the way down to the town, I saw that woman's face more and more clearly. I saw her small ears, set very close against her head, and the long lapis-lazuli earrings that hung from them, and the curved wave of intensely blonde flaxen hair that lay across the top of the ear. I saw the contour of her face, and the width between the eyes—eyes of a very faint clear blue. I saw the short, very thick dark brown lashes and the faint penciled line of the brows with their slight hint of surprise. I saw the small square face and the rather hard line of the mouth.

The features came to me—not suddenly—but little by little—exactly, as I have said, like a photographic plate developing.

I can't explain what happened next. The surface development, you see, was over. I'd arrived at the point where the image begins to darken.

But, you see, this wasn't a photographic plate, but a human being. And so the development went on. From the surface, it went *behind*— or *within*, whichever way you like to put it. At least, that's as near as I can get to it in the way of explanation.

I'd known the truth, I suppose, all along, from the very moment I'd first seen her. The development was taking place in *me*. The picture was coming from my subconscious into my conscious mind. . . .

I *knew*—but I didn't know what it was I knew until suddenly it came! Bang up out of the black whiteness! A speck—and then an image.

I turned and fairly ran up that dusty road. I was in pretty good condition, but it seemed to me that I wasn't going nearly fast enough. Through the Villa gates and past the cypresses and along the grass path.

The woman was sitting exactly where I had left her.

I was out of breath. Gasping, I flung myself down on the seat beside her.

"Look here," I said. "I don't know who you are or anything about you. But you mustn't do it. Do you hear? You mustn't do it."

Chapter 2

CALL TO ACTION

I suppose the queerest thing (but only on thinking it over afterward) was the way she didn't try to put up any conventional defense. She might have said: "What on earth do you mean?" or "You don't know what you're talking about." Or she might have just *looked* it. Frozen me with a glance.

But of course the truth of it was that she had gone past that. She was down to fundamentals. At that moment, nothing that anyone said or did could possibly have been surprising to her.

She was quite calm and reasonable about it—and that was just what was so frightening. You can deal with a mood—a mood is bound to pass, and the more violent it is, the more complete the reaction to it will be. But a calm and reasonable determination is very different, because it's been arrived at slowly and isn't likely to be laid aside.

She looked at me thoughtfully, but she didn't say anything.

"At any rate," I said, "you'll tell me why?"

She bent her head, as though allowing the justice of that.

"It's simply," she said, "that it really does seem best."

"That's where you're wrong," I said. "Completely and utterly wrong."

Violent words didn't ruffle her. She was too calm and far away for that.

"I've thought about it a good deal," she said. "And it really *is* best. It's simple and easy and—quick. And it won't be—inconvenient to anybody."

I realized by that last phrase that she had been what is called "well brought up." "Consideration for others" had been impressed upon her as a desirable thing.

"And what about—afterward?" I asked.

"One has to risk that."

"Do you believe in an afterward?" I asked curiously.

"I'm afraid," she said slowly, "I do. Just nothing—would be almost too good to be true. Just going to sleep—peacefully—and just—not waking up. That *would* be so lovely."

Her eyes half closed dreamily.

"What color was your nursery wallpaper?" I asked suddenly.

"Mauve irises—twisting round a pillar—" She started. "How did you know I was thinking about them just then?"

"I just thought you were. That's all." I went on. "What was your idea of Heaven as a child?"

"Green pastures—a green valley—with sheep and the shepherd. The hymn, you know."

"Who read it to you—your mother or your nurse?"

"My nurse . . ." She smiled a little. "The Good Shepherd. Do you know, I don't think I'd ever seen a shepherd. But there were two lambs in a field quite near us." She paused and then added: "It's built over now."

And I thought: "Odd. If that field weren't built over, well, perhaps *she* wouldn't be here now." And I said: "You were happy as a child?"

"Oh, *yes!*" There was no doubting the eager certainty of her assent. She went on: "Too happy."

"Is that possible?"

"I think so. You see, you're not prepared—for the things that happen. You never conceive that—they might happen."

"You've had a tragic experience," I suggested.

But she shook her head.

"No—I don't think so—not really. What happened to me isn't out of the ordinary. It's the stupid, commonplace thing that happens to lots of women. I wasn't particularly unfortunate. I was—stupid. Yes, just stupid. And there isn't really room in the world for stupid people."

"My dear," I said, "listen to me. I know what I'm talking about. I've stood where you are now—I've felt as you feel—that life isn't worth living. I've known that blinding despair that can only see one way out—and I tell you, child—*that it passes.* Grief doesn't last forever. Nothing lasts. There is only one true consoler and healer—time. Give time its chance."

I had spoken earnestly, but I saw at once that I had made a mistake.

"You don't understand," she said. "I know what you mean. I *have* felt that. In fact, I had one try—that didn't come off. And afterward I was glad that it hadn't. This is different."

"Tell me," I said.

"This has come quite slowly. You see—it's rather hard to put it clearly. I'm thirty-nine—and I'm very strong and healthy. It's quite on the cards that I shall live to at least seventy—perhaps longer. And I simply can't face it, that's all. Another thirty-five long empty years."

"But they won't be empty, my dear. That's where you're wrong. Something will bloom again to fill them."

She looked at me.

"*That* is what I'm most afraid of," she said below her breath. "It's the thought of that that I simply can't face."

"In fact, you're a coward," I said.

"Yes." She acquiesced at once. "I've always been a coward. I've thought it funny sometimes that other people haven't seen it as clearly as I have. Yes, I'm afraid—afraid—afraid."

There was silence.

"After all," she said, "it's natural. If a cinder jumps out of a fire and burns a dog, he's frightened of the fire in future. He never knows when another cinder might come. It's a form of intelligence, really. The complete fool thinks a fire is just something kind and warm—he doesn't know about burning or cinders."

"So that really," I said, "it's the possibility of—happiness you won't face."

It sounded queer as I said it, and yet I knew that it wasn't really as strange as it sounded. I know something about nerves and mind. Three of my best friends were shell-shocked in the war. I know myself what it is for a man to be physically maimed—I know just what it can do to him. I know, too, that one can be mentally maimed. The damage can't be seen when the wound is healed—but it's there. There's a weak spot— a flaw—you're crippled and not whole.

I said to her: "All that will pass with time." But I said it with an assurance I did not feel. Because superficial healing wasn't going to be any good. The scar had gone deep.

"You won't take one risk," I went on. "But you will take another—a simple colossal one."

She said less calmly, with a touch of eagerness:

"But that's entirely different—entirely. It's when you know what a thing's like that you won't risk it. An unknown risk—there's something rather alluring about that—something adventurous. After all, death might be anything—"

It was the first time the actual word had been spoken between us. Death . . .

And then, as though for the first time a natural curiosity stirred in her, she turned her head slightly and asked:

"How did you know?"

"I don't quite profess to be able to tell," I confessed. "I've been through—well, something, myself. And I suppose I knew that way."

She said:

"I see."

She displayed no interest in what my experience might have been, and I think it was at that moment that I vowed myself to her service. I'd had so much, you see, of the other thing. Womanly sympathy and tenderness. My need—though I didn't know it—was not to be given—but to give.

There wasn't any tenderness in Celia—any sympathy. She'd squandered all that—and wasted it. She had been, as she saw herself, stupid about it. She'd been too unhappy herself to have any pity left for others. That new hard line about her mouth was a tribute to the amount of suffering she had endured. Her understanding was quick—she realized in a moment that to me, too, "things had happened." We were on a par. She had no pity for herself, and she wasted no pity on me. My misfortune was, to her, simply the reason of my guessing something which on the face of it was seemingly unguessable.

She was, I saw in that moment, a child. Her real world was the world that surrounded herself. She had gone back deliberately to a childish world, finding there refuge from the world's cruelty.

And that attitude of hers was tremendously stimulating to me. It was what for the last ten years I had been needing. It was, you see, a call to action.

Well, I acted. My one fear was leaving her to herself. I didn't leave her to herself. I stuck to her like the proverbial leech. She walked down with me to the town amiably enough. She had plenty of common sense. She realized that her purpose was, for the moment, frustrated. She didn't abandon it—she merely postponed it. I knew that without her saying a word.

I'm not going into details—this isn't a chronicle of such things. There's no need to describe the quaint little Spanish town, or the meal we had together at her hotel, or the way I had my luggage secretly conveyed from my hotel to the one she was staying at.

No, I'm dealing only with the essentials. I knew that I'd got to stick to her till something happened—till in some way she broke down and surrendered.

As I say, I stayed with her, close by her side. When she went to her room I said:

"I'll give you ten minutes—then I'm coming in."

I didn't dare give her longer. You see, her room was on the fourth floor, and she might override that "consideration for others" that was part of her upbringing and embarrass the hotel manager by jumping from one of his windows instead of jumping from the cliff.

Well, I went back. She was in bed, sitting up, her pale gold hair combed back from her face. I don't think she saw anything odd in what we were doing. I'm sure I didn't. What the hotel thought, I don't know. If they knew that I entered her room at ten o'clock that night and left it at seven the next morning, they would have jumped, I suppose, to the one and only conclusion. But I couldn't bother about that.

I was out to save a life, and I couldn't bother about a mere reputation.

Well, I sat there, on her bed, and we talked.

We talked all night.

A strange night—I've never known a night like it.

I didn't talk to her about her trouble, whatever it was. Instead we started at the beginning—the mauve irises on the wallpaper, and the lambs in the field, and the valley down by the station where the primroses were. . . .

After a while, it was she who talked, not I. I had ceased to exist for her save as a kind of human recording machine that was there to be talked to.

She talked as you might talk to yourself—or to God. Not, you understand, with any heat or passion. Just sheer remembrance, passing from one unrelated incident to another. The building up of a life—a kind of bridge of significant incidents.

It's an odd question, when you come to think of it, the things we choose to remember. For choice there must be, make it as unconscious as you like. Think back yourself—take any year of your childhood. You will remember perhaps five—six incidents. They weren't important, probably; why have you remembered them out of those three hundred and sixty-five days? Some of them didn't even mean much to you at the time. And yet, somehow, they've persisted. They've gone with you into these later years. . . .

It is from that night that I say I got my inside vision of Celia. I can write about her from the standpoint, as I said, of God. . . . I'm going to endeavor to do so.

She told me, you see, all the things that mattered and that didn't matter. She wasn't trying to make a story of it.

No—but I wanted to! *I* seemed to catch glimpses of a pattern that *she* couldn't see.

It was seven o'clock when I left her. She had turned over on her side at last and gone to sleep like a child. . . . The danger was over.

It was as though the burden had been taken from her shoulders and laid on mine. She was safe. . . .

Later in the morning I took her down to the boat and saw her off.

And that's when it happened. The thing, I mean, that seems to me to embody the whole thing. . . .

Perhaps I'm wrong. . . . Perhaps it was only an ordinary trivial incident. . . .

Anyway I won't write it down now. . . .

Not until I've had my shot at being God and either failed or succeeded.

Tried getting her on canvas in this new unfamiliar medium. . . .

Words. . . .

Strung together words. . . .

No brushes, no tubes of color—none of the dear old familiar stuff.

Portrait in four dimensions, because, in your craft, Mary, there's time as well as space. . . .

BOOK TWO

CANVAS

"Set up the canvas. Here's a subject to hand."

Chapter 1

HOME

Celia lay in her cot and looked at the mauve irises on the nursery wall. She felt happy and sleepy.

There was a screen round the foot of her cot. This was to shut off the light of Nannie's lamp. Invisible to Celia, behind that screen, sat Nannie reading the Bible. Nannie's lamp was a special lamp—a portly brass lamp with a pink china shade. It never smelled because Susan, the housemaid, was very particular. Susan was a good girl, Celia knew, although sometimes guilty of the sin of "flouncing about." When she flounced about she nearly always knocked off some small ornament in the immediate neighborhood. She was a great big girl with elbows the color of raw beef. Celia associated them vaguely with the mysterious words "elbow grease."

There was a faint whispering sound. Nannie murmuring over the words to herself as she read. It was soothing to Celia. Her eyelids drooped. . . .

The door opened, and Susan entered with a tray. She endeavored to move noiselessly, but her loud and squeaking shoes prevented her.

She said in a low voice:

"Sorry I'm so late with your supper, Nurse."

Nurse merely said, "Hush. She's asleep."

"Oh, I wouldn't wake her for the world, I'm sure." Susan peeped round the corner of the screen, breathing heavily.

"Little duck, ain't she? My little niece isn't half so knowing."

Turning back from the screen, Susan ran into the table. A spoon fell to the floor.

Nurse said mildly:

"You must try and not flounce about so, Susan, my girl."

Susan said dolefully:

"I'm sure I don't mean to."

She left the room tiptoeing, which made her shoes squeak more than ever.

"Nannie," called Celia cautiously.

"Yes, my dear, what is it?"

"I'm not asleep, Nannie."

Nannie refused to take the hint. She just said:

"No, dear."

There was a pause.

"Nannie?"

"Yes, dear."

"Is your supper nice, Nannie?"

"Very nice, dear."

"What is it?"

"Boiled fish and treacle tart."

"Oh!" sighed Celia ecstatically.

There was a pause. Then Nannie appeared round the screen. A little, old gray-haired woman with a lawn cap tied under her chin. In her hand she carried a fork. On the tip of the fork was a minute piece of treacle tart.

"Now you're to be a good girl and go to sleep at once," said Nannie warningly.

"Oh! Yes," said Celia fervently.

Elysium! Heaven! The morsel of treacle tart was between her lips. Unbelievable deliciousness.

Nannie disappeared round the screen again. Celia cuddled down on her side. The mauve irises danced in the firelight. Agreeable sensation of treacle tart within. Soothing rustling noises of Somebody in the Room. Utter contentment.

Celia slept. . . .

2

It was Celia's third birthday. They were having tea in the garden. There were éclairs. She had been allowed only one éclair. Cyril had had three. Cyril was her brother. He was a big boy—fourteen years old. He wanted another, but her mother said, "That's enough, Cyril."

The usual kind of conversation then happened. Cyril saying "Why?" interminably.

A little red spider, a microscopic thing, ran across the white table-cloth.

"Look," said his mother, "that's a lucky spider. He's going to Celia because it's her birthday. That means great good luck."

Celia felt excited and important. Cyril brought his questioning mind to another point.

"Why are spiders lucky, Mum?"

Then at last Cyril went away, and Celia was left with her mother. She had her mother all to herself. Her mother was smiling at her across the table—a nice smile—not the smile that thought you were a funny little girl.

"Mummy," said Celia, "tell me a story."

She adored her mother's stories—they weren't like other people's stories. Other people, when asked, told you about Cinderella, and Jack and the Beanstalk, and Red Riding Hood. Nannie told you about Joseph and his brothers, and Moses in the bulrushes. (Bulrushes were always visualized by Celia as wooden sheds containing massed bulls.) Occasionally she told you about Captain Stretton's little children in India. But Mummy!

To begin with, you never knew, not in the least, what the story was going to be about. It might be about mice—or about children—or about princesses. It might be anything. . . . The only drawbacks about Mummy's stories were that she never told them a second time. She said (most incomprehensible to Celia) that she couldn't remember.

"Very well," said Mummy. "What shall it be?"

Celia held her breath.

"About Bright Eyes," she suggested. "And Long Tail and the cheese."

"Oh! I've forgotten all about them. No—we'll have a new story." She gazed across the table, unseeing for the moment, her bright hazel eyes dancing, the long delicate oval of her face very serious, her small arched nose held high. All of her tense in the effort of concentration.

"I know—" She came back from afar suddenly. "The story is called the Curious Candle. . . ."

"Oh!" Celia drew an enraptured breath. Already she was intrigued—spellbound. . . . The Curious Candle!

3

Celia was a serious little girl. She thought a great deal about God and being good and holy. When she pulled a wishbone, she always wished to be good. She was, alas! undoubtedly a prig, but at least she kept her priggishness to herself.

At times she had a horrible fear that she was "worldly" (perturbing mysterious word!). This especially when she was all dressed in her starched muslin and big golden-yellow sash to go down to dessert. But on the whole she was complacently satisfied with herself. She was of the elect. She was *saved*.

But her family caused her horrible qualms. It was terrible—but she was not quite sure about her mother. Supposing Mummy should not go to Heaven? Agonizing, tormenting thought.

The laws were so very clearly laid down. To play croquet on Sunday was wicked. So was playing the piano (unless it was hymns). Celia would have died, a willing martyr, sooner than have touched a croquet mallet on the "Lord's Day," though to be allowed to hit balls at random about the lawn on other days was her chief delight.

But her mother played croquet on Sunday and so did her father. And her father played the piano and sang songs about "He called on Mrs. C and took a cup of tea when Mr. C had gone to town." Clearly *not* a holy song!

It worried Celia terribly. She questioned Nannie anxiously. Nannie, good earnest woman, was in something of a quandary.

"Your father and mother are your father and mother," said Nannie. "And everything they do is right and proper, and you mustn't think otherwise."

"But playing croquet on Sunday is wrong," said Celia.

"Yes, dear. It's not keeping the Sabbath holy."

"But then—but then—"

"It's not for you to worry about these things, my dear. You just go on doing your duty."

So Celia went on shaking her head when offered a mallet "as a treat."

"Why on earth—?" said her father.

And her mother murmured:

"It's Nurse. She's told her it's wrong."

And then to Celia:

"It's all right, darling, don't play if you don't want to."

But sometimes she would say gently:

"You know, darling, God has made us a lovely world, and He wants us to be happy. His own day is a very special day—a day we can have special treats on—only we mustn't make work for other people—the servants, for instance. But it's quite all right to enjoy yourself."

But, strangely enough, deeply as she loved her mother, Celia's opinions were not swayed by her. A thing was so because Nannie knew it was.

Still, she ceased to worry about her mother. Her mother had a picture of St. Francis on her wall, and a little book called *The Imitation of Christ* by her bedside. God, Celia felt, might conceivably overlook croquet playing on a Sunday.

But her father caused her grave misgivings. He frequently joked about sacred matters. At lunch one day he told a funny story about a curate and a bishop. It was not funny to Celia—it was merely terrible.

At last, one day, she burst out crying and sobbed her horrible fears into her mother's ear.

"But, darling, your father is a very good man. And a very religious man. He kneels down and says his prayers every night just like a child. He's one of the best men in the world."

"He laughs at clergymen," said Celia. "And he plays games on Sundays, and he sings songs—worldly songs. And I'm so afraid he'll go to Hell Fire."

"What do you know about a thing like Hell Fire?" said her mother, and her voice sounded angry.

"It's where you go if you're wicked," said Celia.

"Who has been frightening you with things like that?"

"I'm not frightened," said Celia, surprised. "I'm not going there. I'm going to be always good and go to Heaven. But"—her lips trembled—"I want Daddy to be in Heaven too."

And then her mother talked a great deal—about God's love and goodness, and how He would never be so unkind as to burn people eternally.

But Celia was not in the least convinced. There was Hell and there was Heaven, and there were sheep and goats. If only—if only she were *quite* sure Daddy was not a goat!

Of course there was Hell as well as Heaven. It was one of the immovable facts of life, as real as rice pudding or washing behind the ears or saying, Yes, please, and No, thank you.

4

Celia dreamt a good deal. Some of her dreams were just funny and queer—things that had happened all mixed up. But some dreams were specially nice. Those dreams were about places she knew which were, in the dreams, different.

Strange to explain why this should be so thrilling, but somehow (in the dream) it was.

There was the valley down by the station. In real life the railway line ran along it, but in the good dreams there was a river there, and primroses all up the banks and into the wood. And each time she would say in delighted surprise: "Why, I never knew—I always thought it was a railway here." And instead there was the lovely green valley and the shining stream.

Then there were the dream fields at the bottom of the garden where in real life there was the ugly red-brick house. And, almost most thrilling of all, the secret rooms inside her own home. Sometimes you got to them through the pantry—sometimes, in the most unexpected way, they led out of Daddy's study. But there they were all the time—although you had forgotten them for so long. Each time you had a delighted thrill of recognition. And yet, really, each time they were quite different. But there was always that curious secret joy about finding them. . . .

Then there was the one terrible dream—the Gun Man with his powdered hair and his blue and red uniform and his gun. And, most horrible of all, where his hands came out of his sleeves—there were *no* hands—only *stumps*. Whenever he came into a dream, you woke up screaming. It was the safest thing to do. And there you were, safe in your bed, and Nannie in her bed next you and everything All Right.

There was no special reason why the Gun Man should be so frightening. It wasn't that he might shoot you. His gun was a symbol, not a direct menace. No, it was something about his face, his hard, intensely blue eyes, the sheer malignity of the look he gave you. It turned you sick with fright.

Then there were the things you thought about in the daytime. Nobody knew that as Celia walked sedately along the road she was in reality mounted upon a white palfrey. (Her ideas of a palfrey were rather dim. She imagined a super horse of the dimensions of an elephant.) When she walked along the narrow brick wall of the cucumber frames she was going along a precipice with a bottomless chasm at one side. She was on different occasions a duchess, a princess, a goose girl, and a beggar maid. All this made life very interesting to Celia, and so she was what is called "a good child," meaning she kept very quiet, was happy playing by herself, and did not importune her elders to amuse her.

The dolls she was given were never real to her. She played with them dutifully when Nannie suggested it, but without any real enthusiasm.

"She's a good little girl," said Nannie. "No imagination, but you can't have everything. Master Tommy—Captain Stretton's eldest, he never stopped teasing me with his questions."

Celia seldom asked questions. Most of her world was inside her head. The outside world did not excite her curiosity.

5

Something that happened one April was to make her afraid of the outside world.

She and Nannie went primrosing. It was an April day, clear and sunny with little clouds scudding across the blue sky. They went down by the railway line (where the river was in Celia's dreams) and up the hill beyond it into a copse where the primroses grew like a yellow carpet. They picked and they picked. It was a lovely day, and the primroses had a delicious, faint lemony smell that Celia loved.

And then (it was rather like the Gun Man dream) a great harsh voice roared at them suddenly.

"Here," it said. "What are you a-doing of here?"

It was a man, a big man with a red face dressed in corduroys. He scowled.

"This is private here. Trespassers will be prosecuted."

Nurse said: "I'm sorry, I'm sure. I didn't know."

"Well, you get on out of it. Quick, now." As they turned to go his voice called after them: "I'll boil you alive. Yes, I will. Boil you alive if you're not out of the woods in three minutes."

Celia stumbled forward tugging desperately at Nannie. Why wouldn't Nannie go faster? The man would come after them. He'd catch them. They'd be boiled alive in a great pot. She felt sick with fright. . . . She stumbled desperately on, her whole quivering little body alive with terror. He was coming—coming up behind them—they'd be boiled. . . . She felt horribly sick. Quick—oh, quick!

They were out on the road again. A great gasping sigh burst from Celia.

"He—he can't get us now," she murmured.

Nurse looked at her, startled by the dead white of her face.

"Why, what's the matter, dear?" A thought struck her. "Surely you weren't frightened by what he said about boiling—that was only a joke—you knew that."

And obedient to the spirit of acquiescent falsehood that every child possesses, Celia murmured:

"Oh, of course, Nannie. I knew it was a joke."

But it was a long time before she got over the terror of that moment. All her life she never quite forgot it.

The terror had been so horribly *real*.

6

On her fourth birthday Celia was given a canary. He was given the unoriginal name of Goldie. He soon became very tame and would perch on Celia's finger. She loved him. He was her bird whom she fed with hemp seeds, but he was also her companion in adventure. There was Dick's Mistress who was a queen, and the Prince Dicky, her son, and the two of them roamed the world and had adventures. Prince Dicky was very handsome and wore garments of golden velvet with black velvet sleeves.

Later in the year Dicky was given a wife called Daphne. Daphne was a big bird with a lot of brown about her. She was awkward and ungainly. She spilled her water and upset things that she perched on. She never became as tame as Dicky. Celia's father called her Susan because she "flounced."

Susan used to poke at the birds with a match "to see what they would do," as she said. The birds were afraid of her and would flutter against the bars when they saw her coming. Susan thought all sorts of curious things funny. She laughed a great deal when a mouse's tail was found in the mouse trap.

Susan was very fond of Celia. She played games with her such as hiding behind curtains and jumping out to say Boo! Celia was not really very fond of Susan—she was so big and so bouncy. She was much fonder of Mrs. Rouncewell, the cook. Rouncy, as Celia called her, was an enormous, monumental woman, and she was the embodiment of calm. She never hurried. She moved about her kitchen in dignified slow motion, going through the ritual of her cooking. She was never harried, never flustered. She served meals always on the exact stroke of the hour. Rouncy had no imagination. When Celia's mother would ask her:

"Well, what do you suggest for lunch today?" she always made the same reply. "Well, ma'am, we could have a nice chicken and a ginger pudding." Mrs. Rouncewell could cook soufflés, vol-au-vents, creams, salmis, every kind of pastry, and the most elaborate French dishes, but she never suggested anything but a chicken and a ginger pudding.

Celia loved going into the kitchen—it was rather like Rouncy herself, very big, very vast, very clean, and very peaceful. In the midst of the cleanliness and space was Rouncy, her jaws moving suggestively. She was always eating. Little bits of this, that, and the other.

She would say:

"Now, Miss Celia, what do you want?"

And then with a slow smile that stretched right across her wide face she would go across to a cupboard, open a tin, and pour a handful of raisins or currants into Celia's cupped hands. Sometimes it would be a slice of bread and treacle that she was given, or a corner of jam tart, but there was always *something*.

And Celia would carry off her prize into the garden and up into the secret place by the garden wall, and there, nestled tightly into the bushes, she would be the Princess in hiding from her enemies to whom her devoted followers had brought provisions in the dead of night. . . .

Upstairs in the nursery Nannie sat sewing. It was nice for Miss Celia to have such a good safe garden to play in—no nasty ponds or dangerous places. Nannie herself was getting old, she liked to sit and sew—and think over things—the little Strettons—all grown-up men and women now—and little Miss Lilian—getting married she was—and Master Roderick and Master Phil—both at Winchester. . . . Her mind ran gently backward over the years. . . .

7

Something terrible happened. Goldie was lost. He had become so tame that his cage door was left open. He used to flutter about the nursery. He would sit on the top of Nannie's head and tweak with his beak at her cap and Nannie's would say mildly: "Now, now, Master Goldie, I can't have that." He would sit on Celia's shoulder and take a hemp seed from between her lips. He was like a spoiled child. If you did not pay attention to him, he got cross and squawked at you.

And on this terrible day Goldie was lost. The nursery window was open. Goldie must have flown away.

Celia cried and cried. Both Nannie and her mother tried to console her.

"He'll come back, perhaps, my pet."

"He's just gone to fly round. We'll put his cage outside the window."

But Celia cried inconsolably. Birds pecked canaries to death—she had heard someone say so. Goldie was dead—dead somewhere under the trees. She would never feel his little beak again. She cried on and off all day. She would not eat either her dinner or her tea. Goldie's cage outside the window remained empty.

At last bedtime came. Celia lay in her little white bed. She still sobbed automatically. She held her mother's hand very tight. She wanted Mummy more than Nannie. Nannie had suggested that Celia's father would perhaps give her another bird. Mother knew better than that. It wasn't just a *bird* she wanted—after all, she still had Daphne—it was *Goldie*. Oh! Goldie—Goldie—Goldie. . . . She *loved* Goldie—and he was gone—pecked to death. She squeezed her mother's hand frenziedly. Her mother squeezed back.

And then, in the silence broken only by Celia's heavy breathing, there came a little sound—the tweet of a bird.

Master Goldie flew down from the top of the curtain pole where he had been roosting quietly all day.

All her life Celia never forgot the incredulous wonderful joy of that moment. . . .

It became a saying in the family when you began to worry over anything:

"Now, then, *remember Dicky and the curtain pole!*"

8

The Gun Man dream changed. It got, somehow, more frightening.

The dream would start well. It would be a happy dream—a picnic or a party. And suddenly, just when you were having lots of fun, a queer feeling crept over you. Something was wrong somewhere. . . . What was it? Why, of course, the Gun Man was there. But he wasn't himself. One of the guests was the Gun Man. . . .

And the awful part of it was, he might be anybody. You looked at them. Everyone was gay, laughing and talking. And then suddenly you knew. It might be Mummy or Daddy or Nannie—someone you were just talking to. You looked up in Mummy's face—of course it was Mummy—and then you saw the light steely-blue eyes—and from the sleeve of Mummy's dress—oh, horror!—that horrible stump. It wasn't Mummy—it was the Gun Man. . . . And you woke screaming. . . .

And you couldn't explain to anyone—to Mummy or to Nannie—it didn't sound frightening just told. Someone said: "There, there, you've had a bad dream, my dearie," and patted you. And presently you went to sleep again—but you didn't like going to sleep because *the dream might come again.*

Celia would say desperately to herself in the dark night: "Mummy *isn't* the Gun Man. She isn't. She isn't. I *know* she isn't. She's *Mummy.*"

But in the night, with the shadows and the dream still clinging round you, it was difficult to be sure of anything. Perhaps *nothing* was what it seemed and you had always known it really.

"Miss Celia had another bad dream last night, ma'am."

"What was it, Nurse?"

"Something about a man with a gun, ma'am."

Celia would say:

"No, Mummy, not a man with a gun. The Gun Man. My Gun Man."

"Were you afraid he'd shoot you, darling? Was it that?"

Celia shook her head—shivered.

She couldn't explain.

Her mother didn't try to make her. She said very gently:

"You're quite safe, darling, here with us. No one can hurt you."

That was comforting.

9

"Nannie, what's that word there—on that poster—the big one?"

" '*Comforting*,' dear. 'Make yourself a comforting cup of tea.' "

This went on every day. Celia displayed an insatiable curiosity about words. She knew her letters, but her mother had a prejudice against children being taught to read too early.

"I shan't begin teaching Celia to read till she is six."

But theories of education do not always turn out as planned. By the time she was five and a half Celia could read all the story books in the nursery shelves, and practically all the words on the posters. It was true that at times she became confused between words. She would come to Nannie and say, "Please, Nannie, is this word 'greedy' or 'selfish'? I can't remember." Since she read by sight and not by spelling out the words, spelling was to be a difficulty to her all her life.

Celia found reading enchanting. It opened a new world to her, a world of fairies, witches, hobgoblins, trolls. Fairy stories were her passion. Stories of real-life children did not much interest her.

She had few children of her own age to play with. Her home was in a remote spot and motors were as yet few and far between. There was one little girl a year older than herself—Margaret McCrae. Occasionally Margaret would be asked to tea, or Celia would be asked to tea with her. But on these occasions Celia would beg frenziedly not to go.

"Why, darling, don't you like Margaret?"

"Yes, I *do*."

"Then why?"

Celia could only shake her head.

"She's shy," said Cyril scornfully.

"It's absurd not to want to see other children," said her father. "It's unnatural."

"Perhaps Margaret teases her?" said her mother.

"No," cried Celia, and burst into tears.

She could not explain. She simply could not explain. And yet the facts were so simple. Margaret had lost all her front teeth. Her words came out very fast in a hissing manner—and Celia could never understand properly what she was saying. The climax had occurred when

Margaret had accompanied her for a walk. She had said: "I'll tell you a nice story, Celia," and had straight away embarked upon it—hissing and lisping about a "Printheth and poithoned thweeth." Celia listened in an agony. Occasionally Margaret would stop and demand: "Ithn't it a nithe thtory?" Celia, concealing valiantly the fact that she had not the faintest idea what the story was about, would try to answer intelligently. And inwardly, as was her habit, she would have recourse to prayer.

"Oh, please, please, God, let me get home soon—don't let her know I don't know. Oh, let's get home soon—please, God."

In some obscure way she felt that to let Margaret know that her speech was incomprehensible would be the height of cruelty. Margaret must never know.

But the strain was awful. She would reach home white and tearful. Everyone thought that she didn't like Margaret. And really it was the opposite. It was because she liked Margaret so much that she could not bear Margaret to know.

And nobody understood—nobody at all. It made Celia feel queer and panic stricken and horribly lonely.

10

On Thursdays there was dancing class. The first time Celia went she was very frightened. The room was full of children—big dazzling children in silken skirts.

In the middle of the room, fitting on a long pair of white gloves, was Miss Mackintosh, who was quite the most awe-inspiring but at the same time fascinating person that Celia had ever seen. Miss Mackintosh was very tall—quite the tallest person in the world, so Celia thought. (In later life it came as a shock to Celia to realize that Miss Mackintosh was only just over medium height. She had achieved her effect by billowing skirts, her terrific uprightness, and sheer personality.)

"Ah!" said Miss Mackintosh graciously. "So this is Celia. Miss Tenterden?"

Miss Tenterden, an anxious-looking creature who danced exquisitely but had no personality, hurried up like an eager terrier.

Celia was handed over to her and was presently standing in a line of small children manipulating "expanders"—a stretch of royal-blue elastic with a handle at each end. After "expanders" came the mysteries of the polka, and after that the small children sat down and watched the glittering beings in the silk skirts doing a fancy dance with tambourines.

After that, Lancers was announced. A small boy with dark mischievous eyes hurried up to Celia.

"I say—will you be my partner?"

"I can't," said Celia regretfully. "I don't know how."

"Oh, what a shame."

But presently Miss Tenterden swooped down upon her.

"Don't know how? No, of course not, dear, but you're going to learn. Now, here is a partner for you."

Celia was paired with a sandy-haired boy with freckles. Opposite them was the dark-eyed boy and his partner. He said reproachfully to Celia as they met in the middle:

"I say, you wouldn't dance with me. I think it's a shame."

A pang she was to know well in after years swept through Celia. How explain? How say, "But I want to dance with you. I'd much rather dance with you. This is all a mistake."

It was her first experience of that tragedy of girlhood—the Wrong Partner!

But the exigencies of the Lancers swept them apart. They met once more in the grand chain, but the boy only gave her a look of deep reproach and squeezed her hand.

He never came to dancing class again, and Celia never learned his name.

11

When Celia was seven years old Nannie left. Nannie had a sister even older than herself, and that sister was now broken down in health, and Nannie had to go and look after her.

Celia was inconsolable and wept bitterly. When Nannie departed, Celia wrote to her every day short, wildly written, impossibly spelled letters which caused an infinitude of trouble to compose.

Her mother said gently:

"You know, darling, you needn't write every day to Nannie. She won't really expect it. Twice a week will be quite enough."

But Celia shook her head determinedly.

"Nannie might think I'd forgotten her. I shan't forget—ever."

Her mother said to her father:

"The child's very tenacious in her affections. It's a pity."

Her father said, with a laugh:

"A contrast from Master Cyril."

Cyril never wrote to his parents from school unless he was made to do so, or unless he wanted something. But his charm of manner was so great that all small misdemeanors were forgiven him.

Celia's obstinate fidelity to the memory of Nannie worried her mother.

"It isn't natural," she said. "At her age she ought to forget more easily."

No new nurse came to replace Nannie. Susan looked after Celia to the extent of giving her her bath in the evening and getting up in the morning. When she was dressed Celia would go to her mother's room. Her mother always had her breakfast in bed. Celia would be given a small slice of toast and marmalade, and would then sail a small fat china duck in her mother's wash basin. Her father would be in his dressing room next door. Sometimes he would call her in and give her a penny, and the penny would then be introduced into a small painted wooden money box. When the box was full the pennies would be put into the savings bank and when there was enough in the savings bank, Celia was to buy herself something really exciting with her own money. What that something was to be was one of the main preoccupations of Celia's life. The favorite objects varied from week to week. First, there was a high tortoiseshell comb covered with knobs for Celia's mother to wear in her back hair. Such a comb had been pointed out to Celia by Susan in a shop window. "A titled lady might wear a comb like that," said Susan in a reverent voice. Then there was an accordion-pleated dress in white silk to go to dancing class in—that was another of Celia's dreams. Only the children who did skirt dancing wore accordion-pleated dresses. It would be many years before Celia would be old enough to learn skirt dancing, but, after all, the day would come. Then there was a pair of real gold slippers (Celia had no doubt of there being such things) and there was a summerhouse to put in the wood, and there was a pony. One of these delectable things was waiting for her on the day when she had got "enough in the savings bank."

In the daytime she played in the garden, bowling a hoop (which might be anything from a stagecoach to an express train), climbing trees in a gingerly and uncertain manner, and making secret places in the midst of dense bushes where she could lie hidden and weave romances. If it was wet she read books in the nursery or painted in old numbers of the *Queen*. Between tea and dinner there were delightful plays with her mother. Sometimes they made houses with towels spread over chairs and crawled in and out of them—sometimes they blew bubbles. You never knew beforehand, but there was always some enchanting and delightful game—the kind of game that you couldn't think of for yourself, the kind of game that was only possible with Mummy.

In the morning now there were "lessons," which made Celia feel very important. There was arithmetic, which Celia did with Daddy. She loved arithmetic, and she liked hearing Daddy say: "This child's got a very good mathematical brain. She won't count on her fingers like you do, Miriam." And her mother would laugh and say: "I never did have any head for figures." First Celia did addition and then subtraction, and then multiplication which was fun, and then division which seemed very grown up and difficult, and then there were pages called "Problems." Celia adored problems. They were about boys and apples, and sheep in fields, and cakes, and men working, and though they were really only addition, subtraction, multiplication, and division in disguise, yet the answers were in boys or apples or sheep, which made it ever so much more exciting. After arithmetic there was "copy" done in an exercise book. Her mother would write a line across the top, and Celia would copy it down, down, down the page till she got to the bottom. Celia did not care for copy very much, but sometimes Mummy would write a very funny sentence such as "Cross-eyed cats can't cough comfortably," which made Celia laugh very much. Then there was a page of spelling to be learned—simple little words, but they cost Celia a good deal of trouble. In her anxiety to spell she always put so many unnecessary letters into words that they were quite unrecognizable.

In the evening, after Susan had given Celia her bath, Mummy would come into the nursery to give Celia a "last tuck." "Mummy's tuck," Celia would call it, and she would try to lie very still so that "Mummy's tuck" should still be there in the morning. But somehow or other it never was.

"Would you like a light, my pet? Or the door left open?"

But Celia never wanted a light. She liked the nice warm comforting darkness that you sank down into. The darkness, she felt, was friendly.

"Well, you're not one to be frightened of the dark," Susan used to say. "My little niece now, she screams her life out if you leave her in the dark."

Susan's little niece, Celia had for some time thought privately, must be a very unpleasant little girl—and also very silly. Why should one be frightened of the dark? The only thing that could frighten one was dreams. Dreams were frightening because they made real things go topsy-turvy. If she woke up with a scream after dreaming of the Gun Man, she would jump out of bed, knowing her way perfectly in the dark, and run along the passage to her mother's room. And her mother would come back with her and sit a while, saying, "There's no Gun Man, darling. You're quite safe—you're quite safe." And then Celia would fall asleep again, knowing that Mummy had indeed made everything safe, and in a few minutes she would be wandering in the valley by the river picking primroses and saying triumphantly to herself, "I knew it wasn't a railway line, really. Of course, the river's always been here."

Chapter 2

ABROAD

It was six months after Nannie had departed that Mummy told Celia a very exciting piece of news. They were going abroad—to France.

"Me too?"

"Yes, darling, you too."

"And Cyril?"

"Yes."

"And Susan and Rouncy?"

"No. Daddy and I and Cyril and you. Daddy hasn't been well, and the doctor wants him to go abroad for the winter to somewhere warm."

"Is France warm?"

"The south is."

"What is it like, Mummy?"

"Well, there are mountains there. Mountains with snow on them."

"Why have they got snow on them?"

"Because they are so high."

"How high?"

And her mother would try to explain just how high mountains were—but Celia found it very hard to imagine.

She knew Woodbury Beacon. It took you half an hour to walk to the top of that. But Woodbury Beacon hardly counted as a mountain at all.

It was all very exciting—particularly the traveling bag. A real traveling bag of her very own in dark green leather, and inside it had bottles, and a place for a brush and comb and clothes brush, and there was a little traveling clock and even a little traveling inkpot!

It was, Celia felt, the loveliest possession she had ever had.

The journey was very exciting. There was crossing the Channel, to

begin with. Her mother went to lie down, and Celia stayed on deck
with her father, which made her feel very grown up and important.

France, when they actually saw it, was a little disappointing. It looked
like any other place. But the blue-uniformed porters talking French were
rather thrilling, and so was the funny high train they got into. They were
to sleep in it, which seemed to Celia another thrilling thing.

She and her mother were to have one compartment, and her father
and Cyril the one next door.

Cyril was, of course, very lordly about it all. Cyril was sixteen, and
he made it a point of honor not to be excited about anything. He asked
questions in a would-be indolent fashion, but even he could hardly conceal his passion and curiosity for the great French engine.

Celia said to her mother:

"Will there *really* be mountains, Mummy?"

"Yes, darling."

"Very, very, *very* high?"

"Yes."

"Higher than Woodbury Beacon?"

"Much, much higher. So high that there's snow on top of them."

Celia shut her eyes and tried to imagine. Mountains. Great hills going
up, up, up—so high that perhaps you couldn't see the tops of them.
Celia's neck went back, back—in imagination she was looking up the
steep sides of the mountains.

"What is it, darling? Have you got a crick in your neck?"

Celia shook her head emphatically.

"I'm thinking of big mountains," she said.

"Silly little kid," said Cyril with good-humored scorn.

Presently there was the excitement of going to bed. In the morning,
when they woke up, they would be in the South of France.

It was ten o'clock on the following morning when they arrived at
Pau. There was a great fuss about collecting the luggage, of which there
was a lot—no less than thirteen great round-topped trunks and innumerable leather valises.

At last, however, they were out of the station and driving to the
hotel. Celia peered out in every direction.

"Where are the mountains, Mummy?"

"Over there, darling. Do you see that line of snow peaks?"

Those! Against the skyline was a zigzag of white, looking as though it were cut out of paper. A low line. Where were those great towering monuments rising up into the sky—far, far up above Celia's head?

"Oh!" said Celia.

A bitter pang of disappointment swept through her. Mountains indeed!

2

After she had got over her disappointment about the mountains, Celia enjoyed her life in Pau very much. The meals were exciting. Called for some strange reason Tabbeldote, you had lunch at a long table of all sorts of strange and exciting dishes. There were two other children in the hotel, twin sisters a year older than Celia. She and Bar and Beatrice went about everywhere together. Celia discovered, for the first time in her eight solemn years, the joys of mischief. The three children would eat oranges on their balcony and throw over the pips onto passing soldiers gay in blue and red uniforms. When the soldiers looked up angrily, the children would have dived back and become invisible. They put little heaps of salt and pepper on all the plates laid for Tabbeldote and annoyed Victor, the old waiter, very much indeed. They concealed themselves in a niche under the stairs and tickled the legs of all the visitors descending to dinner with a long peacock's feather. Their final feat came on a day when they had worried the fierce chambermaid of the upper floor to the point of distraction. They had followed her into a little sanctum of mops and pails and scrubbing brushes. Turning on them angrily and pouring forth a torrent of that incomprehensible language— French—she swept out, banging the door on them and locking it. The three children were prisoners.

"She's done us," said Bar bitterly.

"I wonder how long it'll be before she lets us out?"

They looked at each other somberly. Bar's eyes flashed rebelliously.

"I can't bear to let her crow over us. We must do something."

Bar was always the ringleader. Her eyes went to a microscopic slit of a window which was all the room possessed.

"I wonder if we could squeeze through that. We're none of us very fat. What's outside, Celia, anything at all?"

Celia reported that there was a gutter.

"It's big enough to walk along," she said.

"Good, we'll do Suzanne yet. Won't she have a fit when we come jumping out on her?"

They got the window open with difficulty, and one by one they squeezed themselves through. The gutter was a ledge about a foot wide with an edge perhaps two inches high. Below it was a sheer drop of five stories.

The Belgian lady in No. 33 sent a polite note to the English lady in No. 54. Was Madame aware of the fact that her little girl and the little girls of Madame Owen were walking round the parapet on the fifth story?

The fuss that followed was to Celia quite extraordinary and rather unjust. She had never been told not to walk on parapets.

"You might have fallen and been killed."

"Oh! No, Mummy, there was lots of room—even to put both feet together."

The incident remained one of those inexplicable ones where grownups fuss about nothing at all.

3

Celia would, of course, have to learn French. Cyril had a young Frenchman who came every day. For Celia a young lady was engaged to take her for walks every day and talk French. The lady was actually English, the daughter of the proprietor of the English bookshop, but she had lived her whole life in Pau and spoke French as easily as English.

Miss Leadbetter was a young lady of extreme refinement. Her English was mincing and clipped. She spoke slowly, with condescending kindness.

"See, Celia, that is a shop where they bake bread. A *boulangerie*."

"Yes, Miss Leadbetter."

"Look, Celia, there is a little dog crossing the road. *Un chien qui traverse la rue. Qu'est-ce qu'il fait?* That means, what is he doing?"

Miss Leadbetter had not been happy in this last attempt. Dogs are indelicate creatures apt to bring a blush to the cheek of ultra-refined young women. This particular dog stopped crossing the road and engaged in other activities.

"I don't know how to say what he is doing in French," said Celia.

"Look the other way, dear," said Miss Leadbetter. "It's not very nice. That is a church in front of us. *Voilà une église.*"

The walks were long, boring, and monotonous.

After a fortnight, Celia's mother got rid of Miss Leadbetter.

"An impossible young woman," she said to her husband. "She could make the most exciting thing in the world seem dull."

Celia's father agreed. He said the child would never learn French except from a Frenchwoman. Celia did not much like the idea of a Frenchwoman. She had a good insular distrust of all foreigners. Still, if it was only for walks. . . . Her mother said that she was sure she would like Mademoiselle Mauhourat very much. It struck Celia as an extraordinarily funny name.

Mademoiselle Mauhourat was tall and big. She always wore dresses made with a number of little capes which swung about and knocked things over on tables.

Celia was of opinion that Nannie would have said she "flounced."

Mademoiselle Mauhourat was very voluble and very affectionate.

"*Oh, la chère mignonne!*" cried Mademoiselle Mauhourat, "*la chère petite mignonne.*" She knelt down in front of Celia and laughed in an engaging manner into her face. Celia remained very British and stolid and disliked this very much. It made her feel embarrassed.

"*Nous allons nous amuser. Ah, comme nous allons nous amuser!*"

Again there were walks. Mademoiselle Mauhourat talked without ceasing, and Celia endured politely the flow of meaningless words. Mademoiselle Mauhourat was very kind—the kinder she was the more Celia disliked her.

After ten days Celia got a cold. She was slightly feverish.

"I think you'd better not go out today," said her mother. "Mademoiselle can amuse you here."

"No," burst out Celia. "No. Send her away. Send her away."

Her mother looked at her attentively. It was a look Celia knew well—a queer, luminous, searching look. She said quietly:

"Very well, darling, I will."

"Don't even let her come in here," implored Celia.

But at that moment the door of the sitting room opened and Mademoiselle, very much becaped, entered.

Celia's mother spoke to her in French. Mademoiselle uttered exclamations of chagrin and sympathy.

"*Ah, la pauvre mignonne,*" she cried when Celia's mother had finished. She plopped down in front of Celia. "*La pauvre, pauvre mignonne.*"

Celia glanced appealingly at her mother. She made terrible faces at her. "Send her away," the faces said, "send her away."

Fortunately at that moment one of Mademoiselle Mauhourat's many capes knocked over a vase of flowers, and her whole attention was absorbed by apologies.

When she had finally left the room, Celia's mother said gently:

"Darling, you shouldn't have made those faces. Mademoiselle Mauhourat was only meaning to be kind. You would have hurt her feelings."

Celia looked at her mother in surprise.

"But, Mummy," she said, "they were *English* faces."

She didn't understand why her mother laughed so much. That evening Miriam said to her husband:

"This woman's no good, either. Celia doesn't like her. I wonder—"

"What?"

"Nothing," said Miriam. "I was thinking of a girl in the dressmaker's today."

The next time she went to be fitted she spoke to the girl. She was only one of the apprentices; her job was to stand by holding pins. She was about nineteen, with dark hair neatly piled up in a chignon, a snub nose, and a rosy, good-humored face.

Jeanne was very astonished when the English lady spoke to her and asked her whether she would like to come to England. It depended, she said, on what Maman thought. Miriam asked for her mother's address. Jeanne's father and mother kept a small café—very neat and clean.

Madame Beaugé listened in great surprise to the English lady's proposal. To act as lady's maid and look after a little girl? Jeanne had very little experience—she was rather awkward and clumsy. Berthe now, her elder daughter—but it was Jeanne the English lady wanted. M. Beaugé was called in for consultation. He said they must not stand in Jeanne's way. The wages were good, much better than Jeanne got in the dressmaking establishment.

Three days later Jeanne, very nervous and elated, came to take up her duties. She was rather frightened of the little English girl she was to look after. She did not know any English. She learned a phrase and said it hopefully. "Good morning—mees."

Alas, so peculiar was Jeanne's accent that Celia did not understand. The toilet proceeded in silence. Celia and Jeanne eyed each other like strange dogs. Jeanne brushed Celia's curls round her fingers. Celia never stopped staring at her.

"Mummy," said Celia at breakfast, "doesn't Jeanne talk any English at all?"

"No."

"How funny."

"Do you like Jeanne?"

"She's got a very funny face," said Celia. She thought a minute. "Tell her to brush my hair harder."

At the end of three weeks Celia and Jeanne could understand each other. At the end of the fourth week they met a herd of cows when out on their walk.

"*Mon Dieu!*" cried Jeanne. "*Des vaches—des vaches! Maman, maman.*"

And catching Celia frenziedly by the hand, she rushed up a bank.

"What's the matter?" said Celia.

"*J'ai peur des vaches.*"

Celia looked at her kindly.

"If we meet any more cows," she said, "you get behind me."

After that they were perfect friends. Celia found Jeanne a most entertaining companion. Jeanne dressed some small dolls that had been given to Celia and sustained dialogues would ensue. Jeanne was, in turn, the *femme de chambre* (a very impertinent one), the maman, the papa (who was very military and twirled his mustache), and the three naughty children. Once she enacted the part of M. le Curé and heard their confessions and imposed dreadful penances on them. This enchanted Celia, who was always begging for a repetition.

"*Non, non, mees, c'est très mal ce que j'ai fait là.*"

"*Pourquoi?*"

Jeanne explained.

"I have made a mock of M. le Curé. It is a sin, that!"

"Oh, Jeanne, couldn't you do it once more? It was so *funny.*"

The softhearted Jeanne imperiled her immortal soul and did it again even more amusingly.

Celia knew all about Jeanne's family. About Berthe who was *très sérieuse*, and Louis who was *si gentil*, and Edouard who was *spirituel*, and *la petite* Lise who had just made her first communion, and the cat who was so clever that he could curl himself up in the middle of the glasses in the café and never break one of them.

Celia, in her turn, told Jeanne about Goldie and Rouncy and Susan, and the garden, and all the things they would do when Jeanne came to England. Jeanne had never seen the sea. The idea of going on a boat from France to England frightened her very much.

"*Je me figure,*" said Jeanne, "*que j'aurais horriblement peur. N'en parlons pas! Parlez-moi de votre petit oiseau.*"

4

One day, as Celia was walking with her father, a voice hailed them from a small table outside one of the hotels.

"John! I declare it's old John!"

"Bernard!"

A big jolly-looking man had jumped up and was wringing her father warmly by the hand.

This, it seemed, was a Mr. Grant, who was one of her father's oldest friends. They had not seen each other for some years, and neither of them had had the least idea that the other was in Pau. The Grants were staying in a different hotel, but the two families used to foregather after *déjeuner* and drink coffee.

Mrs. Grant was, Celia thought, the loveliest thing she had ever seen. She had silver-gray hair, exquisitely arranged, and wonderful dark-blue eyes, clear-cut features, and a very clear incisive voice. Celia immediately invented a new character, called Queen Marise. Queen Marise had all the personal attributes of Mrs. Grant and was adored by her devoted subjects. She was three times the victim of attempted assassination, but was rescued by a devoted young man called Colin, whom she at once knighted. Her coronation robes were of emerald green velvet and she had a silver crown set with diamonds.

Mr. Grant was not made a king. Celia thought he was nice, but that his face was too fat and too red—not nearly so nice as her own father with his brown beard and his habit of throwing it up in the air when he laughed. Her own father, Celia thought, was just what a father should be—full of nice jokes that didn't make you feel silly like Mr. Grant's sometimes did.

With the Grants was their son Jim, a pleasant freckle-faced schoolboy. He was always good-tempered and smiling, and had very round blue eyes that gave him rather a surprised look. He adored his mother.

He and Cyril eyed each other like strange dogs. Jim was very respectful to Cyril, because Cyril was two years older and at a public school. Neither of them took any notice of Celia because, of course, Celia was only a kid.

The Grants went home to England after about three weeks. Celia overheard Mr. Grant say to her mother:

"It gave me a shock to see old John, but he tells me he is ever so much fitter since being here."

Celia said to her mother afterward:

"Mummy, is Daddy ill?"

Her mother looked a little queer as she answered:

"No. No, of course not. He's perfectly well now. It was just the damp and the rain in England."

Celia was glad her father wasn't ill. Not, she thought, that he could be—he never went to bed or sneezed or had a bilious attack. He coughed sometimes, but that was because he smoked so much. Celia knew that, because her father told her so.

But she wondered why her mother had looked—well, queer. . . .

5

When May came they left Pau and went first to Argelès at the foot of the Pyrenees and after that to Cauterets up in the mountains.

At Argelès Celia fell in love. The object of her passion was the lift boy—Auguste. Not Henri, the little fair lift boy who played tricks sometimes with her and Bar and Beatrice (they also had come to Argelès), but Auguste. Auguste was eighteen, tall, dark, sallow, and very gloomy in appearance.

He took no interest in the passengers he propelled up and down. Celia never gathered courage to speak to him. No one, not even Jeanne, knew of her romantic passion. In bed at night Celia would envisage scenes in which she saved Auguste's life by catching the bridle of his furiously galloping horse—a shipwreck in which she and Auguste alone survived, she saving his life by swimming ashore and holding his head above water. Sometimes Auguste saved her life in a fire, but this was somehow not quite so satisfactory. The climax she preferred was when Auguste, with tears in his eyes, said: "Mademoiselle, I owe you my life. How can I ever thank you?"

It was a brief but violent passion. A month later they went to Cauterets, and Celia fell in love with Janet Patterson instead.

Janet was fifteen. She was a nice pleasant girl with brown hair and kindly blue eyes. She was not beautiful or striking in any way. She was kind to younger children and not bored by playing with them.

To Celia the only joy in life was some day to grow up to be like her idol. Someday she too would wear a striped blouse and collar and tie, and would wear her hair in a plait tied with black bow. She would have, too, that mysterious thing—a figure. Janet had a figure—a very apparent one sticking out each side of the striped blouse. Celia—a very thin child (described indeed by her brother Cyril when he wanted to annoy as a Scrawny Chicken—a term which never failed to reduce her to tears)—was passionately enamoured of plumpness. Someday, some glorious day, she would be grown up and sticking out and going in in all the proper places.

"Mummy," she said one day, "when shall I have a chest that sticks out?"

Her mother looked at her and said:

"Why, do you want one so badly?"

"Oh, yes," breathed Celia anxiously.

"When you're about fourteen or fifteen—Janet's age."

"Can I have a striped blouse then?"

"Perhaps, but I don't think they're very pretty."

Celia looked at her reproachfully.

"I think they're lovely. Oh, Mummy, do say I can have one when I'm fifteen."

"You can have one—if you still want it."

Of course she would want it.

She went off to look for her idol. To her great annoyance Janet was walking with her French friend Yvonne Barbier. Celia hated Yvonne Barbier with a jealous hatred. Yvonne was very pretty, very elegant, very sophisticated. Although only fifteen, she looked more like eighteen. Her arm linked through Janet's, she was talking to her in a cooing voice.

"Naturellement, je n'ai rien dit à Maman. Je lui ai répondu—"

"Run away, darling," said Janet kindly. "Yvonne and I are busy just now."

Celia withdrew sadly. How she hated that horrible Yvonne Barbier.

Alas, two weeks later, Janet and her parents left Cauterets. Her image faded quickly from Celia's mind, but her ecstatic anticipation of the day when she would have "a figure" remained.

Cauterets was great fun. You were right under the mountains here. Not that even now they looked at all as Celia had pictured them. To the end of her life she could never really admire mountain scenery. A sense of being cheated remained at the back of her mind. The delights of Cauterets were varied. There was the hot walk in the morning to La Raillière where her mother and father drank glasses of nasty tasting water. After the water drinking there was the purchase of sticks of *sucre d'orge*. They were twirly sticks of different colors and flavors. Celia usually had *ananas*—her mother liked a green one—aniseed. Her father, strangely enough, liked none of them. He seemed buoyant and happier since he came to Cauterets.

"This place suits me, Miriam," he said. "I can feel myself getting a new man here."

His wife answered:

"We'll stay here as long as we can."

She too seemed gayer—she laughed more. The anxious pucker between her brows smoothed itself away. She saw very little of Celia. Satisfied with the child being in Jeanne's keeping, she devoted herself heart and soul to her husband.

After the morning excursion Celia would come home with Jeanne through the woods, going up and down zigzag paths, occasionally tobogganing down steep slopes with disastrous results to the seats of her drawers. Agonized wails would arise from Jeanne.

"*Oh, mees—ce n'est pas gentille ce que vous faites là. Et vos pantalons. Que dirait Madame votre mère?*"

"*Encore une fois, Jeanne. Une fois seulement.*"

"*Non, non.* Oh, mees!"

After lunch Jeanne would be busy sewing. Celia would go out into the Place and join some of the other children. A little girl called Mary Hayes had been specially designated as a suitable companion. "Such a nice child," said Celia's mother. "Pretty manners and so sweet. A nice little friend for Celia."

Celia played with Mary Hayes when she could not avoid it, but, alas, she found Mary woefully dull. She was sweet-tempered and amiable but, to Celia, extremely boring. The child whom Celia liked was a little American girl called Marguerite Priestman. She came from a Western state and had a terrific twang in her speech which fascinated the English child. She played games that were new to Celia. Accompanying her was her nurse, an amazing old woman in an enormous flopping black hat whose standard phrase was, "Now you stay right by Fanny, do you hear?"

Occasionally Fanny came to the rescue when a dispute was in progress. One day she found both children almost in tears, arguing hotly.

"Now, just you tell Fanny what it's all about," she commanded.

"I was just telling Celia a story, and she says what I say isn't so—and it is so."

"You tell Fanny what the story was."

"It was going to be just a lovely story. It was about a little girl who grew up in a wood kinder lonesome because the doctor had never fetched her in his black bag—"

Celia interrupted.

"That isn't true. Marguerite says babies are found by doctors in woods and brought to the mothers. That's not true. The angels bring them in the night and put them into the cradle."

"It's doctors."

"It's angels."

"It isn't."

Fanny raised a large hand.

"You listen to me."

They listened. Fanny's little black eyes snapped intelligently as she considered and then dealt with the problem.

"You've neither of you call to get excited. Marguerite's right and so's Celia. One's the way they do with English babies and the other's the way they do with American babies."

How simple after all! Celia and Marguerite beamed on each other and were friends again.

Fanny murmured, "You stay right by Fanny," and resumed her knitting.

"I'll go right on with the story, shall I?" asked Marguerite.

"Yes, do," said Celia. "And afterward I'll tell you a story about an opal fairy who came out of a peach stone."

Marguerite embarked on her narrative, later to be interrupted once more.

"What's a scarrapin?"

"A scarrapin? Why, Celia, don't you know what a scarrapin is?"

"No, what is it?"

That was more difficult. From the welter of Marguerite's explanation Celia only grasped the fact that a scarrapin was in point of fact a scarrapin! A scarrapin remained for her a fabulous beast connected with the continent of America.

Only one day when she was grown up did it suddenly flash into Celia's mind.

"Of course. Marguerite Priestman's scarrapin was a *scorpion*."

And she felt quite a pang of loss.

6

Dinner was very early at Cauterets. It took place at half-past six. Celia was allowed to sit up. Afterward they would all sit outside round little tables, and once or twice a week the conjurer would conjure.

Celia adored the conjurer. She liked his name. He was, so her father told her, a *prestidigitateur*.

Celia would repeat the syllables very slowly over to herself.

The conjurer was a tall man with a long black beard. He did the most entrancing things with colored ribbons—yards and yards of them he would suddenly pull out of his mouth. At the end of his entertainment he would announce "a little lottery." First he would hand round a large wooden plate into which every one would put a contribution. Then the winning numbers would be announced and the prizes given—a paper fan—a little lantern—a pot of paper flowers. There seemed to be something very lucky for children in the lottery. It was nearly always children who won the prizes. Celia had a tremendous longing to win the paper fan. She never did, however, although she twice won a lantern.

One day Celia's father said to her, "How would you like to go to the top of that fellow there?" He indicated one of the mountains behind the hotel.

"Me, Daddy? Right up to the top?"

"Yes. You shall ride there on a mule."

"What's a mule, Daddy?"

He told her that a mule was rather like a donkey and rather like a horse. Celia was thrilled at the thought of the adventure. Her mother seemed a little doubtful. "Are you sure it's quite safe, John?" she said.

Celia's father pooh-poohed her fears. Of course the child would be all right.

She, her father, and Cyril were to go. Cyril said in a lofty tone, "Oh! is the kid coming? She'll be a rotten nuisance." Yet he was quite fond of Celia, but her coming offended his manly pride. This was to have been a man's expedition—women and children left at home.

Early on the morning of the great expedition Celia was ready and standing on the balcony to see the mules arrive. They came at a trot round the corner—great big animals—more like horses than donkeys.

Celia ran downstairs full of joyful expectation. A little man with a brown face in a beret was talking to her father. He was saying that the *petite demoiselle* would be quite all right. He would charge himself with looking after her. Her father and Cyril mounted; then the guide picked her up and swung her up to the saddle. How very high up it felt! But very, very exciting.

They moved off. From the balcony above, Celia's mother waved to them. Celia was thrilling with pride. She felt practically grown up. The guide ran beside her. He chatted to her, but she understood very little of what he said, owing to his strong Spanish accent.

It was a marvelous ride. They went up zigzag paths that grew gradually steeper and steeper. Now they were well out on the mountain side, a wall of rock on one side of them and a sheer drop on the other. At the most dangerous-looking places Celia's mule would stop reflectively on the precipice edge and kick out idly with one foot. It also liked walking on the extreme edge. It was, Celia thought, a very nice horse. Its name seemed to be Aniseed, which Celia thought a very queer name for a horse to have.

It was midday when they reached the summit. There was a tiny little hut there with a table in front of it, and they sat down, and presently the woman there brought them out lunch—a very good lunch too. Omelette, some fried trout, and cream cheese and bread. There was a big woolly dog with whom Celia played.

"*C'est presque un Anglais,*" said the woman. "*Il s'appelle Milor.*"

Milor was very amiable and allowed Celia to do anything she pleased with him.

Presently Celia's father looked at his watch and said it was time to start down again. He called to the guide.

The latter came smiling. He had something in his hands.

"See what I have just caught," he said.

It was a beautiful big butterfly.

"*C'est pour Mademoiselle,*" he said.

And quickly, deftly, before she knew what he was going to do, he had produced a pin and skewered the butterfly to the crown of Celia's straw hat.

"*Voilà que Mademoiselle est chic,*" he said, falling back to admire his handiwork.

Then the mules were brought round, the party was mounted, and the descent was begun.

Celia was miserable. She could feel the wings of the butterfly fluttering against her hat. It was alive—alive. Skewered on a pin! She felt sick and miserable. Large tears gathered in her eyes and rolled down her cheeks.

At last her father noticed.

"What's the matter, poppet?"

Celia shook her head. Her sobs increased.

"Have you got a pain? Are you very tired? Does your head ache?"

Celia merely shook her head more and more violently at each suggestion.

"She's frightened of the horse," said Cyril.

"I'm not," said Celia.

"Then what are you blubbing for?"

"*La petite demoiselle est fatiguée,*" suggested the guide.

Celia's tears flowed faster and faster. They were all looking at her, questioning her—and how could she say what was the matter? It would hurt the guide's feelings terribly. He had meant to be kind. He had caught the butterfly specially for her. He had been so proud of his idea in pinning it to her hat. How could she say out loud that she didn't like it? And now nobody would ever, *ever* understand! The wind made the butterfly's wings flap more than ever. Celia wept unrestrainedly. Never, she felt, had there been misery such as hers.

"We'd better push on as fast as we can," said her father. He looked vexed. "Get her back to her mother. She was right. It's been too much for the child."

Celia longed to cry out: "It hasn't, hasn't. It's not that at all." But she didn't because she realized that then they would ask her again, "But then what *is* it?" She only shook her head dumbly.

She wept all the way down. Her misery grew blacker and blacker. Still weeping she was lifted from her mule, and her father carried her up to the sitting room where her mother was sitting waiting for them.

"You were right, Miriam," said her father. "It's been too much for the child. I don't know whether she's got a pain or whether she's overtired."

"I'm not," said Celia.

"She was frightened of coming down those steep places," said Cyril.

"I wasn't," said Celia.

"Then what is it?" demanded her father.

Celia stared dumbly at her mother. She knew now that she could never tell. The cause of her misery would remain locked in her own breast forever and ever. She wanted to tell—oh, how badly she wanted to tell—but somehow she couldn't. Some mysterious inhibition had been laid on her, sealing her lips. If only Mummy knew.

Mummy would understand. But she couldn't tell Mummy. They were all looking at her—waiting for her to speak. A terrible agony welled up in her breast. She gazed dumbly, agonizingly, at her mother. "Help me," that gaze said. "Oh, do help me."

Miriam gazed back at her.

"I believe she doesn't like that butterfly in her hat," she said. "Who pinned it there?"

Oh, the relief—the wonderful, aching, agonizing relief.

"Nonsense," her father was beginning, but Celia interrupted him. Words burst from her released like water at the bursting of a dam.

"I 'ate it. I 'ate it," she cried. "It flaps. It's alive. It's being hurt."

"Why on earth didn't you say so, you silly kid?" said Cyril.

Celia's mother answered: "I expect she didn't want to hurt the guide's feelings."

"Oh, Mummy!" said Celia.

It was all there—in those two words. Her relief, her gratitude—and a great welling up of love.

Her mother had understood.

Chapter 3

GRANNIE

The following winter Celia's father and mother went to Egypt. They did not think it practicable to take Celia with them, so she and Jeanne went to stay with Grannie.

Grannie lived at Wimbledon, and Celia liked staying with her very much. The features of Grannie's house were, first, the garden—a square pocket handkerchief of green, bordered with rose trees, every tree of which Celia knew intimately, remembering even in winter: "That's the pink la France—Jeanne, you'd like that one," but the crown and glory of the garden was a big ash tree trained over wire supports to make an arbor. There was nothing like the ash tree at home, and Celia regarded it as one of the most exciting wonders of the world. Then there was the W.C. seat of old-fashioned mahogany set very high. Retiring to this spot after breakfast, Celia would fancy herself a queen enthroned, and securely secluded behind a locked door she would bow regally, extend a hand to be kissed by imaginary courtiers and prolong the court scene as long as she dared. There was also Grannie's store cupboard situated by the door into the garden. Every morning, her large bunch of keys clanking, Grannie would visit her store cupboard, and with the punctuality of a child, a dog, or a lion at feeding time, Celia would be there too. Grannie would hand out packets of sugar, butter, eggs, or a pot of jam. She would hold long acrimonious discussions with old Sarah, the cook. Very different from Rouncy, old Sarah. As thin as Rouncy was fat. A little old woman with a nutcracker wrinkled face. For fifty years of her life she had been in service with Grannie, and during all those been years the discussions had been the same. Too much sugar was being used: what happened to the last half pound of tea? It was, by now, a kind of ritual—it was Grannie going through her daily performance of the careful housewife. Servants were so wasteful! You had to look after them sharply. The ritual finished, Grannie would pretend to notice Celia for the first time.

"Dear, dear, what's a little girl doing here?"

And Grannie would pretend great surprise.

"Well, well," she would say, "you can't *want* anything?"

"I do, Grannie, I do."

"Well, let me see now." Grannie would burrow leisurely in the depths of the cupboard. Something would be extracted—a jar of French plums, a stick of angelica, a pot of quince preserve. There was always something for a little girl.

Grannie was a very handsome old lady. She had pink and white skin, two waves of white crimped hair each side of her forehead, and a big good-humored mouth. In figure she was majestically stout with a pronounced bosom and stately hips. She wore dresses of velvet or brocade, ample as to skirts, and well pulled in round the waist.

"I always had a beautiful figure, my dear," she used to tell Celia. "Fanny—that was my sister—had the prettiest face of the family, but she'd no figure—no figure at all! As thin as two boards nailed together. No man looked at her for long when *I* was about. It's figure the men care for, not face."

"The men" bulked largely in Grannie's conversation. She had been brought up in the days when men were considered to be the hub of the universe. Women merely existed to minister to these magnificent beings.

"You wouldn't have found a handsomer man anywhere than my father. Six foot tall, he was. All we children were afraid of him. He was very severe."

"What was your mother like, Grannie?"

"Ah, poor soul. Only thirty-nine when she died. Ten of us children, there were. A lot of hungry mouths. After a baby was born, when she was staying in bed—"

"Why did she stay in bed, Grannie?"

"It's the custom, dearie."

Celia accepted the mandate incuriously.

"She always took her month," went on Grannie. "It was the only rest she got, poor soul. She enjoyed her month. She used to have breakfast in bed and a boiled egg. Not that she got much of that. We children used to come and bother her. 'Can I have a taste of your egg, Mother? Can I have the top of it?' There wouldn't be much left for her after each child had had a taste. She was too kind—too gentle. She died when I was fourteen. I was the eldest of the family. Poor father was heart-broken. They were a devoted couple. He followed her to the grave six months later."

Celia nodded. That seemed right and fitting in her eyes. In most of the child's books in the nursery there was a deathbed scene—usually that of a child—a peculiarly holy and angelic child.

"What did he die of?"

"Galloping consumption," replied Grannie.

"And your mother?"

"She went into a decline, my dear. Just went into a decline. Always wrap your throat up well when you go out in an east wind. Remember that, Celia. It's the east wind that kills. Poor Miss Sankey—why, she had tea with me only a month ago. Went to those nasty swimming baths—came out afterward with an east wind blowing and no boa round her neck—and she was dead in a week."

Nearly all Grannie's stories and reminiscences ended like this. A most cheerful person herself, she delighted in tales of incurable illness, of sudden death, or of mysterious disease. Celia was so well accustomed to this that she would demand with eager and rapturous interest in the middle of one of Grannie's stories, "And then did he die, Grannie?" And Grannie would reply, "Ah, yes, he died, poor fellow." Or girl, or boy, or woman—as the case might be. None of Grannie's stories ever ended happily. It was perhaps her natural reaction from her own healthy and vigorous personality.

Grannie was also full of mysterious warnings.

"If anybody you don't know offers you sweets, dearie, never take them. And when you're an older girl, remember never to get into a train with a single man."

This last injunction rather distressed Celia. She was a shy child. If one was not to get into a train with a single man, one would have to ask him whether or not he was married. You couldn't tell if a man was married or not to look at him. The mere thought of having to do such a thing made her squirm uneasily.

She did not connect with herself a murmur from a lady visitor.

"Surely unwise—put things into her head."

Grannie's answer rose robustly.

"Those that are warned in time won't come to grief. Young people ought to know these things. And there's a thing that perhaps you never heard of, my dear. My husband told me about it—my first husband." (Grannie had had three husbands—so attractive had been her figure— and so well had she ministered to the male sex. She had buried them in turn—one with tears—one with resignation—and one with decorum.) "He said women ought to know about such things."

Her voice dropped. It hissed in sibilant whispers.

What she could hear seemed to Celia dull. She strayed away into the garden. . . .

2

Jeanne was unhappy. She became increasingly homesick for France and her own people. The English servants, she told Celia, were not kind.

"The *cuisinière*, Sarah, she is *gentille*, though she calls me a papist. But the others, Mary and Kate—they laugh because I do not spend my wages on my clothes, and send it all home to Maman."

Grannie attempted to cheer Jeanne.

"You go on behaving like a sensible girl," she told Jeanne. "Putting a lot of useless finery on your back never caught a decent man yet. You go on sending your wages home to your mother, and you'll have a nice little nest egg laid by for when you get married. That next plain style of dressing is far more suitable to a domestic servant than a lot of fal-lals. You go on being a sensible girl."

But Jeanne would occasionally give way to tears when Mary or Kate had been unusually spiteful or unkind. The English girls did not like foreigners, and Jeanne was a papist too, and everyone knew that Roman Catholics worshipped the Scarlet Woman.

Grannie's rough encouragements did not always heal the wound.

"Quite right to stick to your religion, my girl. Not that I hold with the Roman Catholic religion myself, because I don't. Most Romans I've known have been liars. I'd think more of them if their priests married.

And these convents! *All those beautiful young girls shut up in convents and never being heard of again.* What happens to them, I should like to know? The priests could answer *that* question, I dare say."

Fortunately Jeanne's English was not quite equal to this flow of remarks.

Madame was very kind, she said, she would try not to mind what the other girls said.

Grannie then had up Mary and Kate and denounced them in no measured terms for their unkindness to a poor girl in a strange country. Mary and Kate were very soft spoken, very polite, very surprised. Indeed, they had said nothing—nothing at all. Jeanne was such a one as never was for imagining things.

Grannie got a little satisfaction by refusing with horror Mary's plea to be allowed to keep a bicycle.

"I am surprised at you, Mary, for making such a suggestion. No servant of mine shall ever do such an unsuitable thing."

Mary, looking sulky, muttered that her cousin at Richmond was allowed to have one.

"Let me hear nothing more about it," said Grannie. "Anyway, they're dangerous things for women. Many a woman has been prevented from having children for life by riding those nasty things. They're not good for a woman's inside."

Mary and Kate retired sulkily. They would have given notice, but they knew that the place was a good one. The food was first class—no inferior tainted stuff bought for the kitchen as in some places—and the work was not heavy. The old lady was rather a tartar, but she was kind in her way. If there was any trouble at home, she'd often come to the rescue, and nobody could be more generous at Christmas. There was old Sarah's tongue, of course, but you had to put up with that. Her cooking was prime.

Like all children, Celia haunted the kitchen a good deal. Old Sarah was much fiercer than Rouncy, but then, of course, she was terribly old. If anyone had told Celia that Sarah was a hundred and fifty she would not have been in the least surprised. Nobody, Celia felt, had ever been quite so old as Sarah.

Sarah was most unaccountably touchy about the most extraordinary things. One day, for instance, Celia had gone into the kitchen and had asked Sarah what she was cooking.

"Giblet soup, Miss Celia."

"What are giblets, Sarah?"

Sarah pursed her mouth.

"Things that it's not nice for a little lady to make inquiries about."

"But what *are* they?" Celia's curiosity was pleasantly aroused.

"Now, that's enough, Miss Celia. It's not for a little lady like you to ask questions about such things."

"Sarah." Celia danced about the kitchen. Her flaxen hair bobbed. "What are giblets? Sarah, what are giblets? Giblets—giblets—giblets?"

The infuriated Sarah made a rush at her with a frying pan, and Celia retreated, to poke her head in a few minutes later with the query, "Sarah, what are giblets?"

She next repeated the question from the kitchen window.

Sarah, her face dark with annoyance, made no answer, merely mumbled to herself.

Finally, tiring suddenly of this sport, Celia sought out her grandmother.

Grannie always sat in the dining room, which was situated looking out over the short drive in front of the house. It was a room that Celia could have described minutely twenty years later. The heavy Nottingham lace curtains, the dark red and gold wallpaper, the general air of gloom, and the faint smell of apples and a trace still of the midday joint. The broad Victorian dining table with its chenille cloth, the massive mahogany sideboard, the little table by the fire with the stacked-up newspapers, the heavy bronzes on the mantelpiece ("Your grandfather gave £70 for them at the Paris Exhibition"), the sofa upholstered in shiny red leather on which Celia sometimes had her "rest," and which was so slippery that it was hard to remain in the center of it, the crocheted woolwork that was hung over the back of it, the dumbwaiters in the windows crammed with small objects, the revolving bookcase on the round table, the red velvet rocking chair in which Celia had once rocked so violently that she had shot over backward and developed an egg-like bump on her head, the row of leather upholstered chairs against the wall, and lastly the great high-backed leather chair in which Grannie sat pursuing this, that, and the other activity.

Grannie was never idle. She wrote letters—long letters in a spiky spidery handwriting, mostly on half sheets of paper, because it used them up, and she couldn't bear waste. ("Waste not, want not, Celia.") Then she crocheted shawls—pretty shawls in purples and blues and mauves. They were usually for the servants' relations. Then she knitted with great balls of soft fleecy wool. That was usually for somebody's baby. And there was netting—a delicate foam of netting round a little circle of damask. At teatime all the cakes and biscuits reposed on these foamy doilies. Then there were waistcoats—for the old gentlemen of Grannie's acquaintance. You did them on strips of huckaback toweling, running through the stitches with lines of colored embroidery cotton. This was, perhaps, Grannie's favorite work. Though eighty-one years of age, she still had an eye for "the men." She knitted them bed socks, too.

Under Grannie's guidance Celia was doing a set of washstand mats as a surprise for Mummy on her return. You took different-sized rounds of bath toweling, buttonholed them round first in wool, and then crocheted into the buttonholing. Celia was doing her set in pale blue wool, and both she and Grannie admired the result enormously. After tea was cleared away, Grannie and Celia would play spillikins, and after that cribbage, their faces serious and preoccupied, the classic phrases falling from their lips, "One for his knob, two for his heel, fifteen two, fifteen four, fifteen six, and six are twelve." "Do you know why cribbage is such a good game, my dear?" "No, Grannie." "Because it teaches you *to count*."

Grannie never failed to make this little speech. She had been brought up never to admit enjoyment for enjoyment's sake. You ate your food because it was good for your health. Stewed cherries, of which Grannie was passionately fond, she had nearly every day because they were "so good for the kidneys." Cheese, which Grannie also loved, "digested your food," the glass of port served with dessert "I have been ordered by the doctor." Especially was it necessary to emphasize the enjoyment of alcohol (for a member of the weaker sex). "Don't you like it, Grannie?" Celia would demand. "No, dear," Grannie would reply, and would make a wry face as she took the first sip. "I drink it for my health." She could then finish her glass with every sign of enjoyment, having uttered the required formula. Coffee was the only thing for which Grannie admitted a partiality. "Very Moorish, this coffee," she would say, wrinkling up her eyelids in enjoyment. "Very moreish," and would laugh at her little joke as she helped herself to another cup.

On the other side of the hall was the morning room, where sat Poor Miss Bennett, the sewing woman. Miss Bennett was never referred to without the poor in front of her name.

"Poor Miss Bennett," Grannie would say. "It's a charity to give her employment. I really don't believe the poor thing has enough to eat sometimes."

If any special delicacies were served at table, a share was always sent in to Poor Miss Bennett.

Poor Miss Bennett was a little woman with a wealth of untidy gray hair wreathed round her head till it looked like a bird's nest. She was not actually deformed, but she had a look of deformity. She spoke in a mincing and ultrarefined voice, addressing Grannie as Madam. She was quite incapable of making any article correctly. The dresses she made for Celia were always so much too large that the sleeves fell over her hands, and the armholes were halfway down her arms.

You had to be very, very careful not to hurt Poor Miss Bennett's feelings. The least thing did it, and then Miss Bennett would sit sewing violently with a red spot in each cheek and tossing her head.

Poor Miss Bennett had had an Unfortunate History. Her father, as she constantly told you, had been very well connected—"In fact, though perhaps I ought not to say so, but this is entirely in confidence, he was a very Great Gentleman. My mother always said so. I take after him. You may have noticed my hands and my ears—always a sign of breeding, they say. It would be a great shock to him, I'm sure, if he knew I was earning my living this way. Not but that with you, madam, it is different from what I have had to bear from Some People. Treated almost like a Servant. You, madam, *understand*."

So Grannie was careful always to see that Poor Miss Bennett was treated properly. Her meals went in on a tray. Miss Bennett treated the servants very haughtily, ordering them about, with the result that they disliked her intensely.

"Giving herself such airs," Celia heard old Sarah mutter. "And her nothing but a come-by-chance with a father she doesn't even know the name of."

"What's a come-by-chance, Sarah?"

Sarah grew very red.

"Nothing to hear about on the lips of a young lady, Miss Celia."

"Is it giblet?" asked Celia hopefully.

Kate, who was standing by, went off into peals of laughter and was wrathfully told by Sarah to hold her tongue.

Behind the morning room was the drawing room. It was cool and dim and remote in there. It was only used when Grannie gave a party. It was very full of velvety chairs and tables and brocaded sofas, it had big cabinets crammed to bursting point with china figures. In one corner was a piano with a loud bass and a week sweet treble. The windows led into a conservatory, and from there into the garden. The steel grate and fire irons were the delight of old Sarah, who kept them bright and shining so that you could almost see your face in them.

Upstairs was the nursery, a low long room overlooking the garden, above it an attic which housed Mary and Kate, and up a few steps, the three best bedrooms and an airless slit of a room belonging to Sarah.

Celia privately considered the three best bedrooms much grander than anything at home. They had vast suites in them, one of a dappled gray wood, the other two of mahogany. Grannie's bedroom was over the dining room. It had a vast four-poster bed, a huge mahogany wardrobe which occupied the whole of one wall, a handsome washstand and dressing table, and another huge chest of drawers. Every drawer in the room was crammed to repletion with parcels of articles neatly folded. Sometimes when opened the drawers would not shut, and Grannie would have a terrible time with them. Everything was securely locked. On the inside of the door, besides the lock were a substantial bolt and two brass cabin hooks and eyes. Once securely fastened into her apartment, Grannie would retire for the night with a watchman's rattle and a police whistle within reach of her hand so as to be able to give an immediate alarm should burglars attempt to storm her fortress.

On the top of the wardrobe, protected by a glass case, was a large crown of white wax flowers, a floral tribute at the decease of Grannie's first husband. On the right-hand wall was the framed memorial service of Grannie's second husband. On the left-hand wall was a large photograph of the handsome marble tombstone erected to Grannie's third husband.

The bed was a feather one, and the windows were never opened.

The night air, Grannie said, was highly injurious. Air of all kinds, indeed, she regarded as something of a risk. Except on the hottest days of summer she rarely went into the garden, such outings as she made were usually to the Army and Navy Stores—a four-wheeler to the station, train to Victoria, and another four-wheeler to the stores. On such occasions she was well wrapped up in her "mantle" and further protected by a feather boa wound tightly many times round her neck.

Grannie never went out to see people. They came to see her. When visitors arrived cake was brought in and sweet biscuits, and different kinds of Grannie's own homemade liqueur. The gentlemen were first asked what they would take. "You must taste my cherry brandy—that's what all the gentlemen like." Then the ladies were urged in their turn, "A little drop—just to keep the cold out." Thus Grannie, believing that no member of the female sex could admit publicly to liking alcoholic liquor. Or if it was in the afternoon: "You'll find it digests your dinner, my dear."

If an old gentleman who came should not already be in possession of a waistcoat, Grannie would display the waistcoat at present in hand and she would then say with a kind of sprightly archness: "I'd offer to make *you* one if I were sure your wife wouldn't object." The wife would then cry: "Oh, do make him one. I shall be delighted." Grannie would say waggishly: "I mustn't cause trouble," and the old gentleman would say something gallant about wearing a waistcoat worked "with her own fair fingers."

After a visit, Grannie's cheeks would be twice as pink, and her figure twice as upright. She adored the giving of hospitality in any form.

3

"Grannie, may I come and be with you for a little?"

"Why? Can't you find anything to do upstairs with Jeanne?"

Celia hesitated for a minute or two to find a phrase that satisfied her. She said at last:

"Things aren't very pleasant in the nursery this afternoon."

Grannie laughed and said:

"Well, to be sure, that's one way of putting it."

Celia was always uncomfortable and miserable on the rare occasions on which she fell out with Jeanne. This afternoon trouble had come out of the blue in the most unexpected manner.

They had been arguing about the correct disposition of the furniture in Celia's dolls' house, and Celia, arguing a point, had exclaimed: *"Mais, ma pauvre fille—"* And that had done it. Jeanne had burst into tears and a voluble flood of French.

Yes, no doubt she was a *pauvre fille*, as Celia said, but her family, though poor, was honest and respectable. Her father was respected all over Pau. M. le Maire even was on terms of friendship with him.

"But I never said—" began Celia.

Jeanne swept on.

"Doubtless *la petite* Mees, so rich, so beautifully dressed, with her parents who voyaged, and her frocks of silk, considered her, Jeanne, as an equal with a mendicant in the street—"

"But I never said—" began Celia again, more and more bewildered.

But even *les pauvres filles* had their feelings. She, Jeanne, had her feelings. She was wounded. She was wounded to the core.

"But, Jeanne, I love you," cried Celia desperately.

But Jeanne was not to be appeased. She got out some of her most severe sewing, a buckram collar for a gown she was making for Grannie, and stitched at it in silence, shaking her head and refusing to answer Celia's appeals.

Naturally Celia knew nothing of certain remarks made by Mary and Kate at the midday meal as to Jeanne's people being indeed poor if they took all their daughter's earnings.

Faced by an incomprehensible situation, Celia retreated from it and trotted downstairs to the dining room.

"And what do you want to do?" asked Grannie, peering over her spectacles and dropping a large ball of wool. Celia picked it up.

"Tell me about when you were a little girl—about what you said when you came down after tea."

"We used all to come down together and knock on the drawing-room door. My father would say, 'Come in.' Then we would all go in, shutting the door behind us. Quietly, mind you, remember always to shut the door quietly. No lady bangs a door. Indeed, in my young days, no lady ever shut a door at all. It spoiled the shape of the hands. There was ginger wine on the table, and each of us children was given a glass."

"And then you said—" prompted Celia, who knew this story backward.

"We each said in turn, 'My duty to you, Father and Mother.' "

"And they said?"

"They said, 'My love to you, children.' "

"Oh!" Celia wriggled in an ecstasy of delight. She could hardly have said why she enjoyed this particular story so much.

"Tell me about the hymns in church," she prompted. "About you and Uncle Tom."

Crocheting vigorously, Grannie repeated the oft-told tale.

"There was a big board with hymn numbers on it. The clerk used to give them out. He had a fine booming great voice. 'Let us now sing to the honor and glory of God. Hymn No.——' and then he stopped—because the board had been put up the wrong way round. He began again: 'Let us sing to the honor and glory of God. Hymn No.——' Then he said it a third time: 'Let us sing to the honor and glory of God. Hymn No.——,'ere, Bill, just you turn that 'ere board.' "

Grannie was a good actress. The cockney aside came out in an inimitable manner.

"And you and Uncle Tom laughed," prompted Celia.

"Yes, we both laughed. And my father looked at us. Just looked at us, that was all. But when we got home we were sent straight to bed and had no lunch. And it was Michaelmas Sunday—with the Michaelmas goose."

"And you had no goose," said Celia, awestruck.

"And we had no goose."

Celia pondered the calamity deeply for a minute or two. Then with a deep sigh, she said: "Grannie, make me be a chicken."

"You're too big a girl."

"Oh, no, Grannie, make me be a chicken."

Grannie laid aside her crochet and her spectacles.

The comedy was played through from the first moment of entering Mr. Whiteley's shop, a demand to speak to Mr. Whiteley himself: a specially nice chicken was required for a very special dinner. Would Mr. Whiteley select a chicken himself? Grannie was in turn herself and Mr. Whiteley. The chicken was wrapped up (business with Celia and a newspaper), carried home, stuffed (more business), trussed, skewered (screams of delight), popped in the oven, served up on a dish and then the grand climax: "Sarah—Sarah, come here, this chicken's *alive!*"

Oh, certainly there were few playmates to equal Grannie. The truth of it was that Grannie enjoyed playing as much as you did. She was kind, too. In some ways kinder than Mummy. If you asked long enough and often enough, she would give in. She would even give you Things that Were Bad for You.

4

Letters came from Mummy and Daddy—written very clearly in print.

My Darling Little Popsy Wopsums: How is my little girl? Does Jeanne take you on nice walks? How do you enjoy dancing class? The people out here have very nearly black faces. I hear Grannie is going to take you to the Pantomime. Is not that kind of her? I am sure you will be very grateful and do everything you can to be a helpful little girl to her. I am sure you are being a very good girl to dear Grannie who is so good to you. Give Goldie a hemp seed from me.

Your loving,
Daddy.

My own Precious Darling: I do miss you so much, but I am sure you are having a very happy time with dear Grannie who is so good to you, and that you are being a good little girl and doing everything you can to please her. It is lovely hot sunshine out here and beautiful flowers. Will you be a very clever little girl and write to Rouncy for me? Grannie will address the envelope. Tell her to pick the Christmas roses and send them to Grannie. Tell her to give Tommy a big saucer of milk on Christmas Day.

A lot of kisses, my precious lamb, pigeony pumpkin, from,

Mother.

Lovely letters. Two lovely, lovely letters. Why did a lump rise in Celia's throat? The Christmas roses—in the bed under the hedge—Mummy arranging them in a bowl with moss—Mummy saying, "Look at their beautiful wide-open faces." Mummy's voice . . .

Tommy, the big white cat. Rouncy, munching, always munching.

Home, she wanted to go home.

Home, with Mummy in it. . . . Precious lamb, pigeony pumpkin—that's what Mummy called her with a laugh in her voice and a sharp, short sudden hug.

Oh, Mummy—Mummy . . .

Grannie, coming up the stairs, said:

"What's this? Crying? What are you crying for? You've got no fish to sell."

That was Grannie's joke. She always made it.

Celia hated it. It made her want to cry more. When she was unhappy, she didn't want Grannie. She didn't want Grannie at all. Grannie made it worse, somehow.

She slipped past Grannie down the stairs and into the kitchen. Sarah was baking bread.

Sarah looked up at her.

"Had a letter from your mammy?"

Celia nodded. The tears overflowed again. Oh, empty, lonely world.

Sarah went on kneading bread.

"She'll be home soon, love, she'll be home soon. You watch for the leaves on the trees."

She began to roll the dough on the board. Her voice was remote, soothing.

She detached a small lump of the dough.

"Make some little loaves of your own, honey. I'll bake them along of mine."

Celia's tears stopped.

"Twists and cottages?"

"Twists and cottages."

Celia set to work. For twists you rolled out three long sausages and then plaited them in and out, pinching the ends well. Cottages were a big round ball and a smaller ball on top and then—ecstatic moment— you drove your thumb sharply in, making a big round hole. She made five twists and six cottages.

"It's ill for a child away from her mammy," murmured Sarah under her breath.

Her own eyes filled with tears.

It was not till Sarah died some fourteen years later that it was discovered that the superior and refined niece who occasionally came to visit her aunt was in reality Sarah's daughter, the "fruit of sin," as in Sarah's young days the term went. The mistress she served for over sixty years had had no idea of the fact, desperately concealed from her. The only thing she could remember was an illness of Sarah's that had delayed her return from one of her rare holidays. That and the fact that she was unusually thin on her return. What agonies of concealment, of tight lacing, of secret desperation Sarah had gone through must forever remain a mystery. She kept her secret till death revealed it.

COMMENT BY J. L.

It's odd how words—casual, unconnected words—can make a thing live in your imagination. I'm convinced that I see all these people much more clearly than Celia did as she was telling me about them. I can visualize that old grandmother—so vigorous, so much of her generation, with her Rabelaisian tongue, her bullying of her servants, her kindness to the poor sewing woman. I can see further back still to her mother—that delicate, lovable creature "enjoying her month." Note, too, the difference of description between male and female. The wife dies of a decline, the husband of galloping consumption. The ugly word tuberculosis never intrudes. Women decline, men gallop to death. Note, too, for it is amusing, the vigor of these consumptive parents' progeny. Of those ten children, so Celia told me when I asked her, only three died early and those were accidental deaths, a sailor of yellow fever, a sister in a carriage accident, another sister in childbed. Seven of them reached the age of seventy. Do we really know anything about heredity?

It pleases me, that picture of a house with its Nottingham lace and its woolwork and its solid shining mahogany furniture. It has backbone. They knew what they wanted, that generation. They got it and they enjoyed it, and they took a keen, full-blooded active pleasure in the art of self-preservation.

You notice that Celia pictures that house, her grandmother's, far more clearly than her own home. She must have gone there just at the noticing age. Her home is more people than place—Nannie, Rouncy, the bouncing Susan, Goldie in his cage.

Then her discovery of her mother—funny, it seems, that she should not have discovered her before.

For Miriam, I think, had a very vivid personality. The glimpses I get of Miriam enchant me. She had, I fancy, a charm that Celia did not inherit. Even between the conventional lines of her letter to her little girl (such "period pieces" those letters, full of stress on the moral attitude)—even, as I say, between the conventional admonitions to goodness, a trace of the real Miriam peeps out. I like the endearment—precious lamb, pigeony pumpkin—and the caress—the short, sharp hug. Not a maudlin or a demonstrative woman—an impulsive one—a woman with strange flashes of intuitive understanding.

The father is dimmer. He appeared to Celia as a brown-bearded giant—lazy, good-humored, full of fun. He sounds unlike his mother—probably took after his father, who is represented in Celia's narrative by a crown of wax flowers under glass. He was, I fancy, a friendly soul whom everybody liked—more popular than Miriam—but without her quality of enchantment. Celia, I think, took after him. Her placidity, her even temper, her sweetness.

But she inherited something from Miriam—a dangerous intensity of affection.

That's how I see it. But perhaps I invent. . . . These people have, after all, become my creations.

Chapter 4

DEATH

Celia was going home!

The excitement of it!

The train journey seemed endless. Celia had a nice book to read, they had the carriage to themselves—but her impatience made the whole thing seem interminable.

"Well," said her father. "Glad to be going home, poppet?"

He gave her a playful little nip as he spoke. How big and brown he looked—much bigger than Celia had thought. Her mother, on the other hand, was much smaller. Queer the way that shapes and sizes seemed to alter.

"Yes, Daddy, very pleased," said Celia.

She spoke primly. This queer swelling, aching feeling inside wouldn't let her do anything else.

Her father looked a little disappointed. Her cousin Lottie, who was coming to stay with them and who was traveling with them, said:

"What a solemn little mite it is!"

Her father said:

"Oh, well, a child soon forgets. . . ."

His face looked wistful.

Miriam said: "She hasn't forgotten a bit. She's just boiling over inside."

And she reached out her hand and gave Celia's a little squeeze. Her eyes smiled into Celia's—as though they two had a secret shared between them.

Cousin Lottie, who was plump and attractive, said:

"She hasn't much sense of humor, has she?"

"None at all," said Miriam. "No more have I," she added ruefully. "At least, John says I haven't."

Celia murmured.

"Mummy, will it be soon—will it be soon, Mummy?"

"Will what be soon, pet?"

Celia breathed: "The sea."

"In about five minutes now."

"I expect she'd like to live by the seaside and play on the sands," said Cousin Lottie.

Celia did not speak. How explain? The sea was the sign that one was getting near home.

The train ran into a tunnel and out again. Ah, there it was, dark blue and sparkling, on the left-hand side of the train. They were running along beside it, popping in and out of tunnels. Blue, blue sea—so dazzling that it made Celia shut her eyes involuntarily.

Then the train twisted away inland. Very soon now they would be *Home!*

2

Sizes again! Home was enormous! Simply enormous! Great big rooms with hardly any furniture in them—or so it seemed to Celia after the house at Wimbledon. It was all so exciting she hardly knew what to do first. . . .

The garden—yes, first of all it must be the garden. She ran madly along the steep path. There was the Beech Tree—funny she'd never thought about the Beech Tree before. It was almost the most important part of home. And there was the little arbor with the seat in the laurustinus—oh! it was nearly overgrown. Now to go up to the wood—perhaps the bluebells would be out. But they weren't. Perhaps they were over. There was the tree with the forked branch that you played Queen-in-hiding on. Oh! Oh! Oh! there was the little White Boy.

The Little White Boy stood in an arbor in the wood. Three rustic steps led up to him. He carried a stone basket on his head, and into his basket you placed an offering and made a wish.

Celia had indeed quite a ritual. The proceedings were as follows. You started from the house and crossed the lawn, which was a flowing river. Then you tethered your river horse to the rose arch, picked your offering, and proceeded solemnly up the path to the wood. You made your offering and wished and dropped a curtsey and backed away. And your wish would come true. Only you mustn't have more than one wish a week. Celia had always wished the same wish—inspired by Nannie. Wishbones, boy in wood, piebald horse, it was always the same—she wished to be good! It wasn't right, Nannie said, to wish for *things*. The Lord would send you what was necessary for you to have, and since God had behaved with great generosity in the matter (via Grannie and Mummy and Daddy) Celia adhered honorably to her pious wish.

Now she thought: "I must, I must, I must, I simply *must* bring him an offering." She would do it the old way—across the river of the lawn on the sea horse, tether the horse to the rose arch, now up the path, and now lay the offering—two ragged dandelions, in the basket and wish . . .

But alas, shades of Nannie, Celia forsook that pious aspiration which had been hers so long.

"I want to be always happy," wished Celia.

Then to the kitchen garden—ah! there was Rumbolt, the gardener—very gloomy-looking and cross.

"Hullo, Rumbolt, I've come home."

"So I see, missie. And I'll trouble you not to stand on the young lettuces as you're doing at the minute."

Celia shifted her feet.

"Are there any gooseberries to eat, Rumbolt?"

"They're over. Poor crop this year. There might be a raspberry or two—"

"Oh!" Celia danced off.

"But don't you be eating them all," called Rumbolt after her. "I want a nice dish for dessert."

Celia was moving between the raspberry canes eating vigorously. A raspberry or two—why, there were hundreds!

With a final sigh of repletion Celia abandoned the raspberries. Next to visit her private niche by the wall looking down on the road. It was hard now to find the entrance to it, but she got it at last—

Next, to the kitchen and Rouncy. Rouncy looking very clean and larger than ever, her jaws, as always moving rhythmically. Dear, dear Rouncy, smiling as though her face was cut in two, giving the old soft throaty chuckle . . .

"Well, I never, Miss Celia, you have got a big girl."

"What are you eating, Rouncy?"

"I've just been making some rock cakes for the kitchen tea."

"Oh! Rouncy, give me one!"

" 'Twill spoil your tea."

Not a real protest that. Rouncy's bulk is moving toward the oven even as she speaks. She wipes open the oven door.

"They're just done. Now, mind, Miss Celia, it's *hot*."

Oh, lovely home! Back into the cool dim corridors of the house, and there, through the landing window, the green glow of the beech tree.

Her mother, coming out of her bedroom, found Celia standing ecstatically at the top of the stairs, her hands pressed firmly to her middle.

"What is it, child? Why are you holding your tummy?"

"It's the Beech Tree, Mummy. It's so beautiful."

"I believe you feel everything in your tummy, Celia."

"I get a sort of queer pain there. Not a *real* pain, Mummy, a sort of nice pain."

"Then you're glad to be home again?"

"Oh, *Mummy!*"

3

"Rumbolt's gloomier than ever," said Celia's father at breakfast.

"Oh, how I hate having that man," cried Miriam. "I wish we hadn't got him."

"Well, my dear, he's a first-class gardener. The best gardener we've ever had. Look at the peaches last year."

"I know. I know. But I never wanted him."

Celia had hardly ever heard her mother so vehement. Her hands were pressed together. Her father was looking at her indulgently, rather in the same way that he looked at Celia herself.

"Well, I gave in to you, didn't I?" he said good-humoredly. "I turned him down in spite of his references and took that lazy lout of a Spinaker instead."

"It seems so extraordinary," said Miriam. "My dislike of him, and then our letting the house when we went to Pau, and Mr. Rogers writing that Spinaker had given notice and that he was getting another gardener who had excellent references, and coming home to find this man installed, after all."

"I can't think why you don't like him, Miriam. He's a little on the sad side, but a perfectly decent fellow."

Miriam shivered.

"I don't know what it is. It's *something*."

Her eyes stared out in front of her.

The parlor maid entered the room.

"Please, sir, Mrs. Rumbolt would like to speak to you. She's at the front door."

"What does she want? Oh, well, I'd better go and see."

He flung down his table napkin, went out. Celia was staring at her mother. How very funny Mummy looked—as though she were very frightened.

Her father came back.

"Seems Rumbolt never went home last night. Odd business. They've had several rows lately, I fancy."

He turned to the parlor maid who was in the room.

"Is Rumbolt here this morning?"

"I haven't seen him, sir. I'll ask Mrs. Rouncewell."

Her father left the room again. It was five minutes before he returned. As he opened the door and came in, Miriam uttered an exclamation, and even Celia was startled.

Daddy looked so queer—so very queer—like an old man. He seemed to have difficulty in getting his breath.

Like a flash her mother had jumped up off her seat and run round to him.

"John, John, what is it? Tell me. Sit down. You've had some terrible shock."

Her father had gone a queer blue color. He gasped out words with difficulty.

"Hanging—in the stable . . . I've cut him down—but there's no—he must have done it last night. . . ."

"The shock—it's so bad for you." Her mother jumped up, fetched the brandy from the sideboard.

She cried:

"I knew—I *knew* there was *something*—"

She knelt down beside her husband, holding the brandy to his lips. Her glance caught Celia.

"Run upstairs, darling, to Jeanne. It's nothing to be frightened about. Daddy's not feeling very well." She murmured in a lower tone to him: "She mustn't know. That sort of thing might haunt a child for life."

Very puzzled, Celia left the room. On the landing upstairs Doris and Susan were talking together.

"Carried on with her, he did, so they say, and his wife got wind of it. Well, it's always the quietest are the worst."

"Did you see him? Was his tongue hanging out?"

"No, the master said no one was to go there. I wonder if I could get a bit of the rope—they say it's ever so lucky."

"The master had a proper shock, and him with a weak heart and all."

"Well, it's an awful thing to happen."

"What's happened?" asked Celia.

"Gardener's hanged himself in the stables," said Susan with relish.

"Oh!" said Celia not very impressed. "Why do you want a bit of the rope?"

"If you have a bit of the rope a man's hanged himself with it brings you luck all your life through."

"That's so," agreed Doris.

"Oh!" said Celia again.

She accepted Rumbolt's death as just one more of those facts that happened every day. She was not fond of Rumbolt, who had never been particularly nice to her.

That evening when her mother came to tuck her up in bed, she asked:

"Mummy, can I have a bit of the rope Rumbolt hanged himself with?"

"Who told you about Rumbolt?" Her mother's voice sounded angry. "I gave particular orders."

Celia's eyes opened very wide.

"Susan told me. Mummy, can I have a bit of the rope? Susan says it's very lucky."

Suddenly her mother smiled—the smile deepened into a laugh.

"What are you laughing at, Mummy?" asked Celia suspiciously.

"Because it's so long since I was nine years old that I've forgotten what it feels like."

Celia puzzled a little before she went to sleep. Susan had once been nearly drowned when she went to the sea for a holiday. The other servants had laughed and said: "You're born to be hanged, my girl."

Hanging and drowning—there must be some connection between them. . . .

"I'd much, much, much rather be drowned," thought Celia sleepily.

Darling Grannie [wrote Celia the next day]: Thank you so much for sending me the Pink Fairy book. It is very good of you. Goldie is well and sends his love. Please give my love to Sarah and Mary and Kate and Poor Miss Bennett. There is an Iceland poppy come out in my garden. The gardener hanged himself in the stable yesterday. Daddy is in bed but not very ill Mummy says. Rouncy is going to let me make twists and cottages too.

Lots and lots and lots of love and kisses

from
Celia

4

Celia's father died when she was ten years old. He died in his mother's house at Wimbledon. He had been in bed for several months, and there had been two hospital nurses in the house. Celia had got used to Daddy being ill. Her mother was always talking of what they would do when Daddy was better.

That Daddy could *die* had never entered her head. She had just been coming up the stairs when the door of the sickroom opened and her mother came out. A mother she had never seen before. . . .

Long afterward she thought of it like a leaf driven before the wind. Her mother's arms were thrown up to heaven, she was moaning, and then she burst open the door of her own room and disappeared within. A nurse followed her out onto the landing, where Celia was staring openmouthed.

"What has happened to Mummy?"

"Hush, my dear. Your father—your father has gone to Heaven."

"Daddy? Daddy dead and gone to Heaven?"

"Yes, now you must be a good little girl. Remember, you'll have to comfort your mother."

The nurse disappeared into Miriam's room.

Stricken dumb, Celia wandered out into the garden. It took her a long time to take it in. Daddy. Daddy gone—dead. . . .

Momentarily her world was shattered.

Daddy—and everything looked just the same. She shivered. It was like the Gun Man—everything all right and then *he* was there. . . . She looked at the garden, the ash tree, the paths—all the same and yet, somehow different. *Things could change—things could happen. . . .*

Was Daddy in Heaven now? Was he happy?

Oh, Daddy. . . .

She began to cry.

She went into the house. Grannie was there—she was sitting in the dining room; the blinds were all down. She was writing letters. Occasionally a tear ran down her cheek, and she attended to it with a handkerchief.

"Is that my poor little girl?" she said when she saw Celia. "There, there, my dear, you mustn't fret. It's God's will."

"Why are the blinds down?" asked Celia.

She didn't like the blinds being down—it made the house dark and queer, as though, it too were different.

"It's a mark of respect," said Grannie.

She began rummaging in her pocket and produced a black-currant and glycerine jujube of which she knew Celia was fond.

Celia took it and said thank you. But she did not eat it. She did not feel it would go down properly.

She sat there holding it and watching Grannie.

Grannie went on writing—writing—letter after letter—on black-edged notepaper.

5

For two days Celia's mother was very ill. The starched hospital nurse murmured phrases to Grannie.

"The long strain—wouldn't allow herself to believe—shock all the worse in the end—must be roused."

They told Celia she could go in and see Mummy.

The room was darkened. Her mother lay on her side, her brown hair with its gray strands lying wildly all around her. Her eyes looked queer, very bright—they stared at something—something beyond Celia.

"Here's your dear little girl," said the nurse in her high irritating *"I know best"* voice.

Mummy smiled at Celia then—but not a real smile—not the kind of smile as if Celia were really there.

Nurse had talked to Celia beforehand. So had Grannie.

Celia spoke in her prim good little girl's voice.

"Mummy, darling, Daddy's happy—he's in Heaven. You wouldn't want to call him back."

Suddenly her mother laughed.

"Oh, yes, I would! If I could call him back, I'd never stop calling—never—day or night. John—John, come back to me."

She had raised herself up on one elbow, her face was wild and beautiful but strange.

The nurse hustled Celia out of the room. Celia heard her go back to the bed and say:

"You've got to live for your children, remember, my dear."

And she heard her mother say in a strange docile voice:

"Yes, I've got to live for my children. You needn't tell me that. I know it."

Celia went downstairs and into the drawing room, to a place on the wall where there hung two colored prints. They were called The Distressed Mother and The Happy Father. Of the latter, Celia did not think much. The ladylike person in the print did not look in the least like Celia's idea of a father—happy or otherwise. But the distraught woman, her hair flying, her arms clasping children in every direction—yes, that was how Mummy had looked. The Distressed Mother. Celia nodded her head with a kind of queer satisfaction.

6

Things happened rapidly—some of them rather exciting things—like being taken by Grannie to buy black clothes.

Celia couldn't help rather enjoying those black clothes. Mourning! She was in mourning! It sounded very important and grown up. She fancied people looking at her in the street. "See that child all dressed in black?" "Yes, she's just lost her father." "Oh! dear, how sad. Poor child." And Celia would strut a little as she walked and droop her head sadly. She felt a little ashamed of feeling like this, but she couldn't help feeling an interesting and romantic figure.

Cyril was at home. He was very grown up now, but occasionally his voice did peculiar things, and then he blushed. He was gruff and uncomfortable. Sometimes there were tears in his eyes, but he was furious if you noticed them. He caught Celia preening herself in front of the glass in her new clothes and was openly contemptuous.

"That's all a kid like you thinks of. New clothes. Oh, well, I suppose you're too young to take things in."

Celia cried and thought he was very unkind.

Cyril shrank from his mother. He got on better with Grannie. He played the man of the family to Grannie, and Grannie encouraged him. She consulted him about the letters she wrote and appealed to his judgment about various details.

Celia was not allowed to go to the funeral, which she thought very unfair. Grannie did not go either. Cyril went with his mother.

She came down for the first time on the morning of the funeral. She looked very unfamiliar to Celia in her widow's bonnet—rather sweet and small—and—and—oh, yes, *helpless* looking.

Cyril was very manly and protective.

Grannie said: "I've got a few white carnations here, Miriam. I thought perhaps you might like to throw them on the coffin as it is being lowered."

But Miriam shook her head, and said in a low voice:

"No, I'd rather not do anything like that."

After the funeral the blinds were pulled up, and life went on as usual.

7

Celia wondered whether Grannie really liked Mummy and whether Mummy really liked Grannie. She didn't quite know what put the idea into her head.

She felt unhappy about her mother. She moved about so quietly, so silently, speaking very little.

Grannie spent a long part of the day receiving letters and reading them. She would say:

"Miriam, I'm sure you'd like to hear this. Mr. Pike speaks so feelingly of John."

But her mother would wince back, and say:

"Please, no, not now."

And Grannie's eyebrows would go up a little and she would fold the letter, saying dryly: "As you please."

But when the next post came in the same thing would happen.

"Mr. Clark is a truly good man," she would say, sniffing a little as she read. "Miriam, you really should hear this. It would help you. He speaks so beautifully of how our dead are always with us."

And suddenly roused from her quiescence Miriam would cry out:

"No, no!"

It was that sudden cry that made Celia feel she knew what her mother was feeling. Her mother wanted to be let alone.

One day a letter came with a foreign stamp on it. . . . Miriam opened it and sat reading it—four sheets of delicate sloping handwriting. Grannie watched her.

"Is that from Louise?" she asked.

"Yes."

There was silence. Grannie watched the letter hungrily.

"What does she say?" she asked at last.

Miriam was folding up the letter.

"I don't think it's meant for any one but me to see," she said quietly. "Louise—understands."

That time Grannie's eyebrows rose right up into her hair.

A few days later Celia's mother went away with Cousin Lottie for a change. Celia stayed with Grannie for a month.

When Miriam came back, she and Celia went home.

And life began again—a new life. Celia and her mother alone in the big house and garden.

Chapter 5

MOTHER AND DAUGHTER

Her mother explained to Celia that things would be rather different now. While Daddy was alive they had thought they were comparatively rich. But now that he was dead the lawyers had found out that there was very little money left.

"We shall have to live very, very simply. I ought really to sell this house and take a little cottage somewhere."

"Oh, no, Mummy—no."

Miriam smiled at her daughter's vehemence.

"Do you love it so much?"

"Oh, *yes*."

Celia was terribly in earnest. Sell *Home?* Oh, she couldn't bear it.

"Cyril says the same. . . . But I don't know that I'm wise. . . . It will mean being very, very economical—"

"Oh, please, Mummy. Please—please—please."

"Very well, darling. After all, it's a happy house."

Yes, it was a happy house. Looking back after long years Celia acknowledged the truth of that remark. It had, somehow, an atmosphere. Happy home and happy years spent in it.

There were changes, of course. Jeanne went back to France. A gardener came only twice a week just to keep the place tidy, and the hothouses fell gradually to pieces. Susan and the parlor maid left. Rouncy remained. She was unemotional but firm.

Celia's mother argued with her. "But you know it will be much harder work. I shall only be able to afford a house parlor maid and no outside help for the boots and knives."

"I'm quite willing, ma'am. I don't like change. I'm used to my kitchen here, and it suits me."

No hint of loyalty—of affection. The mere suggestion of such a thing would have embarrassed Rouncy very much.

So Rouncy remained at reduced wages, and sometimes, Celia realized afterward, her staying tried Miriam more than her going would have done. For Rouncy had been trained in the grand school. For her the recipes beginning "Take a pint of rich cream and a dozen fresh eggs." To cook plainly and economically and give small orders to the tradespeople was beyond the reach of Rouncy's imagination. She still made sheets of rock cakes for the kitchen tea and threw whole loaves into the pig tub when they went stale. To give large and handsome orders to the tradespeople was a kind of pride with her. It reflected credit on the House. She suffered acutely when Miriam took the ordering out of her hands.

As house parlor maid there came an elderly woman called Gregg. Gregg had been parlor maid to Miriam when the latter was first married.

"And as soon as I saw your advertisement in the paper, ma'am, I gave in my notice and came along. I've never been so happy anywhere as I was here."

"It will be very different now, Gregg."

But Gregg was determined to come. She was a first-class parlor maid, but her skill in that direction was not tested. There were no more dinner parties. As a housemaid she was slapdash, indifferent to cobwebs and indulgent to dust.

She would regale Celia with long tales of the glories in past days.

"Twenty-four your Pa and Ma would sit down to dinner. Two soups, two fish courses, four entrées, a joint—a sorbée as they call it, two sweets, lobster salad, and an ice pudding!"

"Those were the days," Gregg implied as she reluctantly brought in the macaroni au gratin that represented Miriam's and Celia's supper.

Miriam got interested in the garden. She knew nothing about gardening and did not trouble to learn. She just made experiments—and the experiments were crowned with wild and quite unjustifiable success. She put flowers and bulbs in at the wrong time of year and in the wrong depth of soil, she sowed seeds wildly. Everything she touched bloomed and lived.

"Your Ma's got the live hand," said old Ash gloomily.

Old Ash was the jobbing gardener who came twice a week. He really knew something about gardening, but was unfortunately gifted with a dead hand. Anything he put in always died. His pruning was unlucky, and the things that didn't "damp off" were victims of the "early frost." He gave Miriam advice which she did not take.

It was his earnest wish to cut up the slope of the lawn into "Some nice beds—crescent shape and diamond, and have some nice bedding-out plants." He was chagrined by Miriam's indignant refusal. When she said she liked the unbroken sweep of green he would reply: "Well, beds look like a gentleman's place. You can't deny it."

Celia and Miriam "did" flowers for the house—vying with each other. They would make great tall bouquets of white flowers, trailing jasmine, sweet-scented syringas, white phlox, and stocks. Then Miriam had a passion for little exotic posies, cherry pie, and sweet flat-faced pink roses.

The smell of old-fashioned pink roses reminded Celia of her mother all through her life.

It annoyed Celia that her own arrangements could never equal her mother's, however much time and trouble she took over them. Miriam could fling flowers together with a wild grace. Her arrangements were original—they were not at all in accord with the flower arrangements of the period.

Lessons were a haphazard arrangement. Miriam said Celia must go on with her arithmetic by herself. She was no good at it herself. Celia did so conscientiously, working through the little brown book that she had started with her father.

Every now and then she stuck in a bog of uncertainty—uncertain in a problem as to whether the answer would be in sheep or men. The papering of rooms so bewildered her that she skipped it altogether.

Miriam had theories of her own as to education. She was a good teacher, clear in explanation, and able to arouse enthusiasm over any subject she selected.

She had a passion for history, and under her guidance Celia was swept from one event to another in the world's life story. The steady progression of English history bored Miriam, but Elizabeth, the Emperor Charles the Fifth, Francis the First of France, Peter the Great—all these became living personages to Celia. The splendor of Rome lived again. Carthage perished. Peter the Great strove to raise Russia from barbarism.

Celia loved being read aloud to, and Miriam would select books dealing with the various historical periods they were studying. She skipped shamelessly when reading aloud—she had a complete impatience for anything tedious. Geography was rather bound up with history. Other lessons they had none, except that Miriam did her best to improve Celia's spelling, which was, for a girl of her age, nothing short of disgraceful.

A German woman was engaged to teach Celia the piano, and she showed an immediate aptitude and love for the study, practicing long beyond the time Fräulein had indicated.

Margaret McCrae had left the neighborhood, but once a week the Maitlands came to tea—Ellie and Janet. Ellie was older than Celia, Janet younger. They played Colors and Grandmother's Steps, and they founded a Secret Society called the Ivy. After inventing passwords, a peculiar handclasp, and writing messages in invisible ink, the Ivy Society rather languished.

There were also the little Pines.

They were thick children, with adenoidy voices, younger than Celia. Dorothy and Mabel. Their only idea in life was eating. They always ate too much and were usually sick before they left. Sometimes Celia would go to lunch with them. Mr. Pine was a great fat red-faced man; his wife was tall and angular with a terrific black fringe. They were very affectionate, and they too were devoted to food.

"Percival, this mutton is delicious—really delicious."

"A little more, my love. Dorothy, a little more?"

"Thank you, Papa."

"Mabel?"

"No, thank you, Papa."

"Come, come, what's this? This mutton is delicious."

"We must congratulate Giles, my love." (Giles was the butcher.)

Neither the Pines nor the Maitlands made much impression on Celia's life. The games she played by herself were still the most real games to her.

As her piano playing improved she would spend long hours in the big schoolroom, turning out old dusty piles of music and reading them. Old songs—"Down the Vale," "A Song of Sleep," "Fiddle and I." She would sing them, her voice rising clear and pure.

She was rather vain about her voice.

When small she had declared her intention of marrying a duke. Nannie had concurred on the condition that Celia learned to eat her dinner faster.

"Because, my dear, in the grand houses the butler would take away your plate long before you'd finished."

"Would he?"

"Yes, in the grand houses, the butler comes round, and he takes everyone's plate away whether they've finished or not!"

After this Celia fairly bolted her food to get into training for the ducal life.

Now, for the first time, her intention wavered. Perhaps she wouldn't marry a duke after all. No, she would be a prima donna—somebody like Melba.

Celia still spent much of her time alone. Although she had the Maitlands and the Pines to tea—they were not nearly so real to her as "the girls."

"The girls" were creations of Celia's imagination. She knew all about them—what they looked like, what they wore, what they felt and thought.

First there was Ethelred Smith—who was tall and very dark and very, *very* clever. She was good at games, too. In fact, Ethel was good at everything. She had a decided "figure" and wore striped shirts. Ethel was everything that Celia was not. She represented what Celia would like to be. Then there was Annie Brown. Ethel's great friend. She was fair and weak and "delicate." Ethel helped her with her lessons, and Annie looked up to and admired Ethel. Next came Isabella Sullivan, who had red hair and brown eyes and was beautiful. She was rich and proud and unpleasant. She always thought that she was going to beat Ethel at croquet, but Celia saw to it that she didn't, though she felt rather mean sometimes when she deliberately made Isabella miss balls. Elsie Green was her cousin—her poor cousin. She had dark curls and blue eyes and was very merry.

Ella Graves and Sue de Vete were much younger—only seven. Ella was very serious and industrious, with bushy brown hair and a plain face. She often won the arithmetic prize, because she worked so hard. She was very fair, and Celia was never quite sure what she looked like, and her character was variable. Vera de Vete, Sue's half sister, was the romantic personality of "the school." She was fourteen. She had straw-colored hair and deep forget-me-not blue eyes. There was mystery about her past—and in the end Celia knew that she would turn out to have been changed at birth and that she was really the Lady Vera, the daughter of one of the proudest noblemen in the land. There was a new girl—Lena, and one of Celia's favorite plays was to be Lena arriving at the school.

Miriam knew vaguely about "the girls" but she never asked questions about them—for which Celia was passionately grateful. On wet days "the girls" gave a concert in the schoolroom, different pieces being allotted to them. It annoyed Celia very much that her fingers stumbled over Ethel's piece, which she was anxious to play well, and that though she always allotted Isabella the most difficult, it went perfectly. "The girls" played cribbage against each other also, and here again Isabella always seemed to have an annoying run of luck.

Sometimes, when Celia went to stay with Grannie, she was taken by her to a musical comedy. They would have a four-wheeler to the station, then train to Victoria, four-wheeler to lunch at the Army and Navy Stores, where Grannie would do immense lists of shopping in the grocery with the special old man who always attended to her. Then they would go up to the restaurant and have lunch, finishing with "a small cup of coffee in a large cup," so that plenty of milk could be added. Then they would go to the confectionery department and buy half a pound of chocolate coffee creams, and *then* into another four-wheeler and off to the theater, which Grannie enjoyed every bit as much as Celia did.

Very often, afterward, Grannie would buy Celia the score of the music. That opened up a new field of activity to "the girls." They now blossomed into musical comedy stars. Isabella and Vera had soprano voices—Isabella's was bigger, but Vera's was sweeter. Ethel had a magnificent contralto—Elsie had a pretty little voice. Annie, Ella, and Sue had unimportant parts, but Sue gradually developed into taking the soubrette roles. *The Country Girl* was Celia's favorite. "Under the Deodars" seemed to her the loveliest song that had ever been written. She sang it until she was hoarse. Vera was given the part of the Princess, so that she could sing it and the heroine's role given to Isabella. *The Cingalee* was another favorite, because it had a good part for Ethel.

Miriam, who suffered from headaches and whose bedroom was below the piano, at last forbade Celia to play for more than three hours on end.

2

At last Celia's early ambition was realized. She had an accordion-pleated dancing dress, and she stayed behind for the skirt-dancing class.

She was now one of the elect. She would no longer dance with Dorothy Pine who only wore a plain white party frock. The accordion-pleated girls only danced with each other—unless they were being self-consciously "kind." Celia and Janet Maitland paired off. Janet danced beautifully. They were engaged for the waltz in perpetuity. And they also partnered each other for the march, but there they were sometimes torn apart, since Celia was a head and a half taller than Janet, and Miss Mackintosh liked her marching pairs to look symmetrical. The polka it was the fashion to dance with the little ones. Each elder girl took a tot. Six girls stayed behind for skirt dancing. It was a source of bitter disappointment to Celia that she always remained in the second row. Janet, Celia did not mind, because Janet danced better than anyone else, but Daphne danced badly and made lots of mistakes. Celia always felt it was very unfair, and the true solution of the mystery, that Miss Mackintosh put the shorter girls in front and the taller ones behind, never once occurred to her.

Miriam was quite as excited as Celia over what color her accordion pleat should be. They had a long earnest discussion, taking into account what the other girls wore, and in the end they decided on a flame-colored one. Nobody else had ever had a dress of that color. Celia was enchanted.

Since her husband's death Miriam went out and entertained very little. She "kept up" only with such people as had children of Celia's age, and a few old friends. All the same, the ease with which she dropped out of things made her a little bitter. The difference that money made. All those people who hadn't been able to make fuss enough of her and John! Nowadays they hardly remembered her existence. She didn't care for herself—she had always been a shy woman. It was for John's sake that she had been sociable. He loved people coming to the house; he loved going out. He had never guessed that Miriam hated it, so well had she played her part. She was relieved now, but all the same, she felt resentful on Celia's account. When the child grew up she would want social things.

The evenings were some of the happiest times mother and daughter spent together. They had supper early, at seven, and afterward would go up to the schoolroom, and Celia would do fancy work, and her mother would read to her. Reading aloud would make Miriam sleepy. Her voice would go queer and blurry, her head would tilt forward. . . .

"Mummy," Celia would say accusingly, "you're going to sleep."

"I'm not," Miriam would declare indignantly. She would sit very upright and read very clearly and distinctly for a couple of pages. Then she would say suddenly:

"I believe you're right," and, shutting the book, she could drop fast asleep.

She only slept for about three minutes. Then she would wake up and start off again with renewed vigor.

Sometimes Miriam would tell stories of her early life instead of reading. Of how she had come, a distant cousin, to live with Grannie.

"My mother had died, and there was no money afterward, so Grannie very kindly offered to adopt me."

She was a little cool about the kindness, perhaps—a coolness that showed in tone, not in words. It masked a memory of childish loneliness, of a longing for her own mother. She had been ill at last, and the doctor called in. He had said: "This child is fretting about something." "Oh, no," Grannie had answered positively. "She's quite a happy, merry little thing." The doctor had said nothing, but when Grannie had gone out of the room he had sat on the bed talking to her in a kindly, confidential manner, and she had suddenly broken down and admitted to long bouts of weeping in bed at night.

Grannie had been very astonished when he had told her.

"Why, she never said anything to me about it."

And after that, it had been better. Just the telling seemed to have taken the ache away.

"And then there was your father." How her voice softened. "He was always kind to me."

"Tell me about Daddy."

"He was grown up—eighteen. He didn't come home very often. He didn't like his stepfather very much."

"And did you love him at once?"

"Yes, from the very first moment I saw him. I grew up loving him. . . . I never dreamt he'd ever think of me."

"Didn't you?"

"No. You see, he was always going about with smart grown-up girls. He was a great flirt—and then he was supposed to be a very good match. I was always expecting him to get married to someone else. He was very kind to me when he came—used to bring me flowers and sweets and brooches. I was just 'little Miriam' to him. I think he was pleased by my being so devoted to him. He told me once that an old lady, the mother of one of his friends, said to him, 'I think, John, you will marry the little cousin.' And he had said, laughing, 'Miriam? Why, she's only a child.' He was rather in love with a very handsome girl then. But somehow or other, it came to nothing. . . . I was the only woman he ever asked to marry him. . . . I remember—I used to think that if he married I should perhaps lie on a sofa pining away, and nobody would know what was the matter with me! I should just gradually fade away! That was the regular romantic idea in my young days—hopeless love—and lying on a sofa. I would die, and no one would ever know until they found a packet of his letters with pressed forget-me-nots in them all bound up in blue ribbon. All very silly—but I don't know, somehow—it helped—all that imagining. . . .

"I remember the day when your father said suddenly, 'What lovely eyes the child has got.' I was so startled. I'd always thought I was terribly plain. I climbed up on a chair and stared and stared at myself in the glass to see what he had meant. In the end I thought perhaps my eyes *were* rather nice. . . ."

"When did Daddy ask you to marry him?"

"I was twenty-two. He'd been away for a year. I'd sent him a Christmas card and a poem that I'd written for him. He kept that poem in his pocketbook. It was there when he died. . . .

"I can't tell you how surprised I was when he asked me. I said, No."

"But, Mummy, *why?*"

"It's difficult to explain. . . . I'd been brought up to be very diffident about myself. I felt that I was 'dumpy'—not a tall, handsome person. I felt, perhaps, he'd be disappointed in me once we were married. I was dreadfully modest about myself."

"And then Uncle Tom—" prompted Celia who knew this part of the story almost as well as Miriam.

Her mother smiled.

"Yes, Uncle Tom. We were down in Sussex with Uncle Tom at the time. He was an old man then—but very wise—very kindly. I was playing the piano, I remember, and he was sitting by the fire. He said: 'Miriam, John's asked you to marry him, hasn't he? And you've refused him.' I said, 'Yes.' 'But you love him, Miriam?' I said, 'Yes,' again. 'Don't say No next time,' he said. 'He'll ask you once more, but he won't ask you a third time. He's a good man, Miriam. Don't throw away your happiness.' "

"And he did ask you, and you said 'Yes.' "

Miriam nodded.

She had that kind of starry look in her eyes that Celia knew well.

"Tell me how you came to live here."

That was another well-known tale.

Miriam smiled.

"We were staying down here in rooms. We had two young babies—your little sister Joy, who died, and Cyril. Your father had to go abroad to India on business. He couldn't take me with him. We decided that this was a very pleasant place and that we'd take a house for a year. I went about looking for one with Grannie.

"When your father came home to lunch, I said to him, 'John, I've bought a house.' He said, '*What?*' Grannie said, 'It's all right, John, it will be quite a good investment.' You see, Grannie's husband, your father's stepfather, had left me a little money of my own. The only house I saw that I liked was this one. It was so peaceful—so happy. But the old lady who owned it wouldn't let—she would only sell. She was a Quaker—very sweet and gentle. I said to Grannie, 'Shall I buy it with my money?'

"Grannie was my trustee. She said, 'House property is a good investment. Buy it.'

"The old Quaker lady was so sweet. She said, 'I think of thee, my dear, being very happy here. Thee and thy husband, and they children. . . . ' It was like a blessing."

How like her mother—that suddenness, that quick decision.

Celia said:

"And I was born here?"

"Yes."

"Oh, Mother, don't let's ever sell it. . . ."

Miriam sighed.

"I don't know if I've been wise. . . . But you love it so. . . . And perhaps—it will be something—always—for you to come back to. . . ."

3

Cousin Lottie came to stay. She was married now and had a house of her own in London. But she needed a change and country air, so Miriam said.

Cousin Lottie was certainly not well. She stayed in bed and was terribly sick.

She talked vaguely about some food that had upset her.

"But she ought to be better now," urged Celia, as a week passed and Cousin Lottie was still sick.

When you were "upset" you had castor oil and stayed in bed, and the next day or the day after you were better.

Miriam looked at Celia with a funny expression on her face. A sort of half-guilty, half-smiling look.

"Darling, I think I'd better tell you. Cousin Lottie is sick because she is going to have a baby."

Celia had never been so astonished in her life. Since the dispute with Marguerite Priestman she had never thought of the baby question again.

She asked eager questions.

"But why does it make you sick? When will it be here? Tomorrow?"

Her mother laughed.

"Oh! No, not till next autumn."

She told her more—how long a baby took to come—something of the process. It all seemed most astonishing to Celia—quite the most remarkable thing she had ever heard.

"Only don't talk about it before Cousin Lottie. You see, little girls aren't supposed to know about these things."

Next day Celia came to her mother in great excitement.

"Mummy, Mummy, I've had a most exciting dream. I dreamt Grannie was going to have a baby. Do you think it will come true? Shall we write and ask her?"

She was astonished when her mother laughed.

"Dreams do come true," she said reproachfully. "It says so in the Bible."

4

Her excitement over Cousin Lottie's baby lasted for a week. She still had a sneaking hope that the baby might arrive now and not next autumn. After all, Mummy might be wrong.

Then Cousin Lottie returned to town, and Celia forgot about it. It was quite a surprise to her the following autumn when she was staying with Grannie when old Sarah came suddenly out into the garden, saying: "Your Cousin Lottie's got a little baby boy. Isn't that nice now?"

Celia had rushed into the house where Grannie was sitting with a telegram in her hand talking to Mrs. Mackintosh, a crony of hers.

"Grannie, Grannie," cried Celia, "has Cousin Lottie really got a baby? How big is it?"

With great decision Grannie measured off the baby's size on her knitting pin—the big knitting pin—since she was making night socks.

"Only as long as that?" It seemed incredible.

"My sister Jane was so small she was put in a soapbox," said Grannie.

"A soapbox, Grannie?"

"They never thought she'd live," said Grannie with relish, adding to Mrs. Mackintosh in a lowered voice, "Five months."

Celia sat quietly trying to visualize a baby of the required smallness.

"What kind of soap?" she asked presently, but Grannie did not answer. She was busy talking to Mrs. Mackintosh in a low, hushed voice.

"You see, the doctors disagreed about Charlotte. Let the labor come on—that's what the specialist said. Forty-eight hours—the cord—actually round the neck . . ."

Her voice dropped lower and lower. She shot a glance at Celia and stopped.

What a funny way Grannie had of saying things. It made them sound, somehow, exciting. . . . She had a funny way, too, of looking at you. As though there were all sorts of things she could tell you, if she liked.

5

When she was fifteen Celia became religious again. It was a different religion this time, very high church. She was confirmed, and she also heard the Bishop of London preach. She was seized immediately by a romantic devotion for him. A picture postcard of him was placed on her mantelpiece, and she scanned the newspapers eagerly for any mention of him. She wove long stories in which she worked in East End parishes, visiting the sick, and one day he noticed her, and finally they were married and went to live at Fulham Palace. In the alternative story she became a nun—there were nuns who weren't Roman Catholics, she had discovered—and she lived a life of great holiness and had visions.

After she was confirmed, she read a good deal in various little books and went to early church every Sunday. She was pained because her mother would not come with her. Miriam only went to church on Whitsunday. Whitsunday was to her the great festival of the Christian Church.

"The holy spirit of God," she said. "Think of it, Celia. That is the great wonder and mystery and beauty of God. The prayer books shy at it, and clergymen hardly ever speak about it. They're afraid to, because they are not sure what it is. The Holy Ghost."

Miriam worshipped the Holy Ghost. It made Celia feel rather uncomfortable. Miriam didn't like churches much. Some of them, she said, had more of the Holy Spirit than others. It depended on the people who went there to worship, she said.

Celia, who was firmly and strictly orthodox, was distressed. She didn't like her mother being unorthodox. There was something of the mystic about Miriam. She had a vision, a perception of unseen things. It was on a par with her disconcerting habit of knowing what you were thinking.

Celia's vision of becoming the wife of the Bishop of London faded. She thought more and more about being a nun.

She thought at last that perhaps she had better break it to her mother. She was afraid her mother would, perhaps, be unhappy. But Miriam took the news very calmly.

"I see, darling."

"You don't mind, Mummy?"

"No, darling. If, when you are twenty-one, you want to be a nun, of course you shall be one. . . ."

Perhaps, Celia thought, she would become a Roman Catholic. Roman Catholic nuns were, somehow, more real.

Miriam said she thought the Roman Catholic religion a very fine one.

"Your father and I nearly became Catholics once. Very nearly." She smiled suddenly. "I nearly dragged him into it. Your father was a good man—as simple as a child—quite happy in his own religion. It was I who was always discovering religions and urging him to take them up. I thought it mattered very much what religion you were."

Celia thought that of course it mattered. But she did not say so, because if she did her mother would begin about the Holy Ghost, and Celia rather fought shy of the Holy Ghost. The Holy Ghost did not come much into any of the little books. She thought of the time when she would be a nun praying in her cell. . . .

6

It was soon after that that Miriam told Celia it was time for her to go to Paris. It had always been understood that Celia was to be "finished" in Paris. She was rather excited at the prospect.

She was well educated as to history and literature. She had been allowed and encouraged to read anything she chose. She was also thoroughly conversant with the topics of the day. Miriam insisted on her reading such newspaper articles as she thought essential to what she called "general knowledge." Arithmetic had been solved by her going twice a week to the local school for instruction in that subject for which she had always had a natural liking.

Of geometry, Latin, algebra, and grammar she knew nothing at all. Her geography was sketchy, being confined to the knowledge acquired through books of travel.

In Paris she would study singing, piano playing, drawing and painting, and French.

Miriam selected a place near the Avenue du Bois which took twelve girls and which was run by an Englishwoman and a Frenchwoman in partnership.

Miriam went to Paris with her and stayed until she was sure her child was going to be happy. After four days Celia had a violent attack of homesickness for her mother. At first she didn't know what was the matter with her—this queer lump in the throat—these tears that came into her eyes whenever she thought of her mother. If she put on a blouse her mother had made for her, the tears would come into her eyes as she thought of her mother stitching at it. On the fifth day she was to be taken out by her mother.

She went down outwardly calm but inwardly in a turmoil. No sooner were they outside and in the cab going to the hotel than Celia burst into tears.

"Oh, Mummy—Mummy."

"What is it, darling? Aren't you happy? If you're not, I'll take you away."

"I don't want to be taken away. I like it. It was just I wanted to *see* you."

Half an hour later her recent misery seemed dreamlike and unreal. It was rather like seasickness. Once you recovered from it, you couldn't remember what you had felt like.

The feeling did not return. Celia waited for it, nervously studying her own feelings. But, no—she loved her mother—adored her, but the mere thought of her no longer made a lump come in her throat.

One of the girls, an American, Maisie Payne, came up to her and said in her soft drawling voice:

"I hear you've been feeling lonesome. My mother's staying at the same hotel as yours. Are you feeling better now?"

"Yes, I'm all right now. It was silly."

"Well, I reckon it was kind of natural."

Her soft drawling voice reminded Celia of her friend in the Pyrenees, Marguerite Priestman. She felt a little tremor of gratitude toward this big black-haired creature. It was increased when Maisie said:

"I saw your mother at the hotel. She's very pretty. And more than pretty—she's kind of distanguay."

Celia thought about her mother, seeing her objectively for the first time—her small eager face, her tiny hands and feet, her small delicate ears, her thin high-bridged nose.

Her mother—oh, there was no one like her mother in the whole world.

Chapter 6

PARIS

Celia stayed for a year in Paris. She enjoyed the time there very much. She liked the other girls, though none of them seemed very real to her. Maisie Payne might have done so, but she left the Easter after Celia arrived. Her best friend was a big fat girl called Bessie West who had the next room to hers. Bessie was a great talker, and Celia was a good listener, and they both indulged in a passion for eating apples. Bessie told long tales of her escapades and adventures between bites of apple— the stories always ending "and then my hair came down."

"I like you, Celia," she said one day. "You're sensible."

"Sensible?"

"You're not always going on about boys and things. People like Mabel and Pamela get on my nerves. Every time I have a violin lesson they giggle and snigger and pretend I'm sweet on old Franz or he's sweet on me. I call that sort of thing common. I like a rag with the boys as well as anyone, but not all this idiotic sniggering business about the music masters."

Celia, who had outgrown her passion for the Bishop of London, was now in the throes of one for Mr. Gerald du Maurier ever since she had seen him in *Alias Jimmy Valentine*. But it was a secret passion of which she never spoke.

The other girl she liked was one whom Bessie usually referred to as "the Moron."

Sybil Swinton was nineteen, a big girl with beautiful brown eyes and a mass of chestnut hair. She was extremely amiable and extremely stupid. She had to have everything explained to her twice. The piano was her great cross. She was bad at reading music, and she had no ear to hear when she played wrong notes. Celia would sit patiently beside her for an hour saying, "No, Sybil, a sharp—your left hand's wrong now— D natural now. Oh, Sybil, can't you hear?" But Sybil couldn't. Her people were anxious for her to "play the piano" like other girls, and Sybil did her best, but music lessons were a nightmare—incidentally they were a nightmare for the teacher also. Madame LeBrun, who was one of the two teachers who visited, was a little old woman with white hair and claw-like hands. She sat very close to you when you played so that your right arm was slightly impeded. She was very keen on sight-reading and used to produce big books of duets *à quatre mains*. Alternately you played the treble or the bass, and Madame LeBurn played the other. Things went most happily when Madame LeBrun was at the treble end of the piano. So immersed was she in her own performance that it would be some time before she discovered that her pupil was playing the accompanying bass some bars in front or behind herself. Then there would be an outcry *"Mais qu'est-ce que vous jouez là, ma petite? C'est affreux—c'est tout ce qu'il y a de plus affreux!"*

Nevertheless, Celia enjoyed her lessons. She enjoyed them still more when she was transferred to M. Kochter. M. Kochter took only those girls who showed talent. He was delighted with Celia. Seizing her hands and pulling the fingers mercilessly apart he would cry, "You see the stretch here? This is the hand of a pianist. Nature is in your favor, Mademoiselle Celia. Now let us see what you can do to assist her." M. Kochter himself played beautifully. He gave a concert twice a year in London, so he told Celia. Chopin, Beethoven, and Brahms were his favorite masters. He would usually give Celia a choice as to what she learned. He inspired her with such enthusiasm that she willingly practiced the six hours a day he required. Practicing was no real fatigue to her. She loved the piano. It had been her friend always.

For singing lessons Celia went to M. Barré—an ex-operatic singer. She had a very high, clear soprano voice.

"Your high notes are excellent," said M. Barré. "They could not be better produced. That is the *voix de tête*. The low notes, the chest notes, they too are weak but not bad. It is the *médium* that we must improve. The *médium*, mademoiselle, comes from the roof of the mouth."

He produced a tape measure.

"Let us now test the diaphragm. Breathe in—hold it—hold it—now let the breath expire suddenly. Capital—capital. You have the breath of a singer."

He handed her a pencil.

"Place that between the teeth—so—in the corner of the mouth. And do not let it fall out when you sing. You can pronounce every word and retain the pencil. Do not say that it is impossible."

On the whole M. Barré was satisfied with her.

"But your French, it puzzles me. It is not the usual French with the English accent—ah, how I have suffered from that—*Mon Dieu!* nobody knows! No, it is, one would swear, an accent *méridional* that you have. Where did you learn French?"

Celia told him.

"Oh, and your maid she came from the South of France? That explains it. Well, well, we will soon get out.

Celia worked hard at her singing. On the whole she pleased him, but occasionally he would rail at her English.

You are like all the rest of the English, you think that to sing is to open the mouth as wide as possible and let the voice come out! Not at all—there is the skin—the skin of the face—all round the mouth. You are not a little choir boy—you are singing the Habanera of Carmen which, by the way, you have brought me in the wrong key. This is transposed for soprano—an operatic song should always be sung in its original key—anything else is an abomination and an insult to the composer—remember that. I particularly want you to learn a mezzo song. Now then, you are Carmen, you have a rose in your mouth, not a pencil, you are singing a song that is meant to allure this young man. Your face—your face—do not let your face be of wood."

The lesson ended with Celia in tears. Barré was kind.

"There, there—it is not your song. No, I see it is not your song. You shall sing the 'Jerusalem' of Gounod. The 'Alléluia' from the Cid. Some day we will return to Carmen."

Music occupied the time of most of the girls. There was an hour's

French every morning, that was all. Celia, who could speak much more fluent and idiomatic French than any of the others, was always horribly humiliated at French. In dictation, while the other girls had two, three, or at most five faults, she would have twenty-five or thirty. In spite of reading innumerable French books, she had no idea of the spelling. Also she wrote much slower than the others. Dictation was a nightmare to her.

Madame would say:

"But it is impossible—*impossible*—that you should have so many faults, Celia! Do you not even know what a past participle is?"

Alas, that was exactly what Celia did not know.

Twice a week she and Sybil went to their painting lesson. Celia grudged the time taken from the piano. She hated drawing, and painting even worse. Flower painting was what the two girls were learning.

Oh, miserable bunch of violets in a glass of water!

"The shadows, Celia, put in the shadows first."

But Celia could never see the shadows. Her best hope was surreptitiously to look at Sybil's painting and try to make hers look like it.

"You seem to see where these beastly shadows are, Sybil. I don't— I never do. It's just a blob of lovely purple."

Sybil was not particularly talented, but certainly at painting it was Celia who was "the Moron."

Something deep down in her hated this copying business—this tearing the secrets out of flowers and scratching and blobbing it down on paper. Violets should be left to grow in gardens or arranged droopingly in glasses. This making something out of something else—it went against her.

"I don't see why you've got to draw things," she said to Sybil one day. "They're there already."

"What do you mean?"

"I don't know quite how to say it, but why make things that are like other things? It's such a waste. If one could draw a flower that didn't exist—imagine one—then it might be worthwhile."

"You mean make up a flower out of your head?"

"Yes, but even then it wouldn't be right. I mean it would still be a flower, and you wouldn't have made a flower—you'd have made a thing on paper."

"But, Celia, pictures, real pictures, art—they're very beautiful."

"Yes, of course—at least—" She stopped. "Are they?"

"Celia!" cried Sybil, aghast at such heresy.

Had they not been taken to the Louvre to look at old masters only yesterday?

Celia felt she had been too heretical. Everybody spoke reverently of Art.

"I expect I'd had too much chocolate to drink," she said. "That's why I thought them stuffy. All those saints looking exactly alike. Of course, I don't mean it," she added. "They're wonderful, really."

But her voice sounded a little unconvinced.

"You *must* be fond of art, Celia, you're so fond of music."

"Music's different. Music's *itself*. It's not copycat. You take an instrument—the violin, or the piano, or the cello, and you make sounds—lovely sounds all woven together. You haven't got to get it like anything else. It's just itself."

"Well," said Sybil, "I think music is just a lot of nasty noises. And very often when I'm playing the wrong notes it sounds to me better than when I play the right ones."

Celia gazed despairingly at her friend.

"You can't be able to *hear* at all."

"Well, from the way you were painting those violets this morning nobody would think you were able to see."

Celia stopped dead—thereby blocking the path of the little *femme de chambre* who accompanied them and who chattered angrily.

"Do you know, Sybil," said Celia, "I believe you're right. I don't think I do see things—not *see* them. That's why I can't spell. And that's why I don't really know what anything is like."

"You always walk straight through puddles," said Sybil.

Celia was reflecting.

"I don't see that it matters—not really—except spelling, I suppose. I mean, it's the feeling a thing gives you that matters—not just its shape and how it happens to be made."

"What *do* you mean?"

"Well, take a rose." Celia nodded toward a flower seller they were passing. "What does it matter how many petals it has and exactly what the shape of them is—it's just the—oh, sort of whole thing that matters—the velvetyness and the smell."

"You couldn't draw a rose without knowing its shape."

"Sybil, you great ass, haven't I told you I don't want to draw? I don't like roses on paper. I like them real."

She stopped in front of the flower woman and for a few sous bought a bunch of drooping dark-red roses.

"Smell," she said, thrusting them in front of Sybil's nose. "Now, doesn't that give you a heavenly sort of pain just here?"

"You've been eating too many apples again."

"I haven't. Oh, Sybil, don't be so literal. Isn't it a heavenly smell?"

"Yes, it is. But it doesn't give me a pain. I don't see why one should want it to."

"Mummy and I tried to do botany once," said Celia. "But we threw the book away, I hated it so. Knowing all the different kinds of flowers and classifying them—and pistils and stamens—horrid, like undressing the poor things. I think it's disgusting. It's—it's indelicate."

"Do you know, Celia, that if you go to a convent, the nuns make you have your bath with a chemise on. My cousin told me."

"Do they? Why?"

"They don't think it's nice to look at your own body."

"Oh." Celia thought a minute. "How do you manage with the soap? You wouldn't get awfully clean if you soaped yourself through a chemise."

2

The girls at the Pensionnat were taken to the opera, and to the Comédie Française, and to skate at the Palais de Glace in winter. Celia enjoyed it all, but it was the music that really filled her life. She wrote to her mother that she wanted to take up the piano professionally.

At the end of the term Miss Schofield gave a party, at which the more advanced of the girls played and sang. Celia was to do both. The singing went off quite all right, but over playing she broke down and stumbled badly through the first movement of Beethoven's Sonate Pathétique.

Miriam came over to Paris to fetch her daughter, and at Celia's wish she asked M. Kochter to tea. She was not at all anxious for Celia to take up music professionally, but she thought she might as well hear what M. Kochter had to say on the matter. Celia was not in the room when she asked him about it.

"I will tell you the truth, madame. She has the ability—the technique—the feeling. She is the most promising pupil I have. But I do not think she has the temperament."

"You mean she has not the temperament to play in public?"

"That is exactly what I do mean, madame. To be an artist one must be able to shut out the world—if you feel it there listening to you, then you must feel it as a stimulus. But Mademoiselle Celia, she will give of her best to an audience of one—of two people—and she will play best of all to herself with the door closed."

"Will you tell her what you have told me, M. Kochter?"

"If you wish, madame."

Celia was bitterly disappointed. She fell back on the idea of singing.

"Though it won't be the same thing."

"You don't love singing as you love your piano?"

"Oh, no."

"Perhaps that's why you're not nervous when you sing?"

"Perhaps it is. A voice seems somehow something apart from one's self—I mean, it isn't you doing it—like it is with your fingers on the piano. Do you understand, Mummy?"

They had a serious discussion with M. Barré.

"She has the ability and the voice, yes. Also the temperament. She has as yet very little expression in her singing—it is the voice of a boy, not a woman. That"—he smiled—"will come. But the voice is charming—pure—steady—and her breathing is good. She can be a singer, yes. A singer for the concert stage—her voice is not strong enough for opera."

When they were back in England, Celia said:

"I've thought about it, Mummy. If I can't sing in opera, I don't want to sing at all. I mean, not professionally."

Then she laughed.

"You didn't want me to, did you, Mummy?"

"No, I certainly didn't want you to become a professional singer."

"But you'd have let me? Would you let me do anything I wanted to if I wanted it enough?"

"Not anything," said Miriam with spirit.

"But nearly anything?"

Her mother smiled at her.

"I want you to be happy, my pet."

"I'm sure I shall always be happy," said Celia with great confidence.

3

Celia wrote to her mother that autumn that she wanted to be a hospital nurse. Bessie was going to be one, and she wanted to be one too. Her letters had been very full of Bessie lately.

Miriam did not reply directly, but toward the end of the term she wrote and told Celia that the doctor had said it would be a good thing for her to winter abroad. She was going to Egypt, and Celia was coming with her.

Celia arrived back from Paris to find her mother staying with Grannie and in the full bustle of departure. Grannie was not at all pleased at the Egyptian idea. Celia heard her talking about it to Cousin Lottie, who had come to lunch.

"I can't understand Miriam. Left as badly off as she is. The idea of rushing off to Egypt—Egypt—about the most expensive place she could go to! That's Miriam all over—no idea of money. And Egypt was one of the last places she went to with poor John. It seems most unfeeling."

Celia thought her mother looked both defiant and excited. She took Celia to shop and bought her three evening dresses.

"The child's not out. You're absurd, Miriam," said Grannie.

"It wouldn't be a bad idea for her to come out there. She's not as though she could have a London season—we can't afford it."

"She's only sixteen."

"Nearly seventeen. My mother was married before she was seventeen."

"I don't suppose you want Celia to marry before she's seventeen."

"No, I don't, but I want her to have her young girl's time."

The evening dresses were very exciting—though they emphasized the one crumpled roseleaf in Celia's life. Alas, the figure that Celia had never ceased to look forward to so eagerly had never materialized. No swelling mounds for Celia to encase in a striped shirt. Her disappointment was bitter and acute. She had wanted "a chest" so badly. Poor Celia—had she only been born twenty years later—how admired her shape would have been! No slimming exercises necessary for that slender yet well-covered frame.

As it was, "plumpers" were introduced into the bodices of Celia's evening dresses—delicate ruchings of net.

Celia longed for a black evening dress, but Miriam said No, not until she was older. She bought her a white taffeta gown, a dress of pale green net with lots of little ribbons running across it, and a pale pink satin with rosebuds on the shoulder.

Then Grannie unearthed from one of the bottom mahogany drawers a piece of brilliant turquoise blue taffeta with suggestions that Poor Miss Bennett should try her hand at it. Miriam managed to suggest tactfully that perhaps Poor Miss Bennett would find a fashionable evening dress a little beyond her. The blue taffeta was made up elsewhere. Then Celia was taken to a hairdresser and given a few lessons in the art of putting up her own hair—a somewhat elaborate process, since it was trained over a "hair frame" in front and arranged in masses of curls behind. Not an easy style for anyone who had, like Celia, long thick hair falling far below her waist.

It was all very exciting, and it never occurred to Celia that her mother seemed rather better than worse in health than usual.

It did not escape Grannie.

"But there," she said, "Miriam's got a bee in her bonnet over this business."

It was many years later that Celia realized exactly what her mother's feelings were at the time. She had had a dull girlhood herself—she was passionately eager that her darling should have all the gaieties and excitements that a young girl's life could hold. And it was going to be difficult for Celia to have a "good time" living buried in the country with few young people of her own age around.

Hence, Egypt—where Miriam had many friends from the time when she and her husband had been there together. To obtain the necessary funds she did not hesitate to sell out some of the few stocks and shares she possessed. Celia was not to be envious of other girls having "good times" which she had never had.

Also, so she confided some years later to Celia, she had been afraid of her friendship for Bessie West.

"I've seen so many girls get interested in another girl and refuse to go out or take any interest in men. It's unnatural—and not right."

"Bessie? But I was never very fond of Bessie."

"I know that now. But I didn't know it then. I was afraid. And all that hospital nurse nonsense. I wanted you to have a good time and pretty clothes and enjoy yourself in a young, natural way."

"Well," said Celia, "I did."

Chapter 7

GROWN UP

Celia enjoyed herself, it is true, but she also went through a lot of agony through being handicapped by the shyness that she had had ever since she was a baby. It made her tongue-tied and awkward, and utterly unable to show when she was enjoying herself.

Celia seldom thought about her appearance. She took it for granted that she was pretty—and she *was* pretty—tall, slender, and graceful, with very fair flaxen hair and Scandinavian fairness and delicacy of coloring. She had an exquisite complexion, though she went pale through nervousness. In the days when to "make up" was shameful,

Miriam put a touch of rouge on her daughter's cheeks every evening. She wanted her to look her best.

It was not her appearance that worried Celia. What weighed her down was the consciousness of her stupidity. She was not clever. It was awful not to be clever. She never could think of anything to say to the people she danced with. She was solemn and rather heavy.

Miriam ceaselessly urged her daughter to talk.

"Say something, darling. Anything. It doesn't matter what silly thing it is. But it's such uphill work for a man to talk to a girl who says nothing but yes and no. Don't let the ball drop."

Nobody appreciated Celia's difficulties more than her mother who had been hampered herself by shyness all her life.

Nobody ever realized that Celia was shy. They thought she was haughty and conceited. Nobody realized how humble this pretty girl was feeling—how bitterly conscious of her social defects.

Because of her beauty Celia had a good time. Also, she danced well. At the end of the winter she had been to fifty-six dances and had at last acquired a certain amount of the art of small talk. She was less gauche now, more self-assured, and was at last beginning to be able to enjoy herself without being tortured by constantly recurring shyness.

Life was rather a haze—a haze of dancing and golden light, and polo and tennis and young men. Young men who held her hand, flirted with her, asked if they might kiss her, and were baffled by her aloofness. To Celia only one person was real, the dark bronzed colonel of a Scottish regiment, who seldom danced and who never bothered to talk to young girls.

She liked jolly little red-haired Captain Gale who always danced three times with her every evening. (Three was the largest number of dances permissible with one person.) It was his joke that she didn't need teaching to dance, but did need teaching to talk.

Nevertheless, she was surprised when Miriam said on the way home:

"Did you know that Captain Gale wanted to marry you?"

"Me?" Celia was very surprised.

"Yes, he talked to me about it. He wanted to know whether I thought he had any chance."

"Why didn't he ask me?" Celia felt a little resentful about it.

"I don't quite know. I think he found it difficult." Miriam smiled. "But you don't want to marry him, do you, Celia?"

"Oh, *no*—but I think I ought to have been asked."

That was Celia's first proposal. Not, she thought, a very satisfactory one.

Not that it mattered. She would never want to marry anyone except Colonel Moncrieff, and he would never ask her. She would remain an old maid all her life, loving him secretly.

Alas for the dark, bronzed Colonel Moncrieff! In six months he had gone the way of Auguste, of Sybil, of the Bishop of London, and Mr. Gerald du Maurier.

2

Grown-up life was difficult. It was exciting but tiring. You always seemed to be in agonies about something or other. The way your hair was done, or your lack of figure, or your stupidity in talking, and people, especially men, made you feel uncomfortable.

All her life Celia never forgot her first country-house visit. Her nervousness in the train, which made pink blotches come out all down her neck. Would she behave properly? Would she (ever-recurring nightmare) be able to *talk*? Would she be able to roll up her curls on the back of her head? Miriam usually did the very back ones for her. Would they think her very stupid? Had she got the right clothes with her?

Nobody could have been kinder than her host and hostess. She was not shy with them.

It felt very grand to be in this big bedroom with a maid unpacking for her and coming in to do her dress up down the back.

She wore a new pink net dress and went down to dinner feeling terribly shy. There were lots of people there. It was awful. Her host was very nice. He talked to her, chaffed her, called her the Pink 'Un because he said she always wore pink dresses.

There was a lovely dinner, but Celia couldn't really enjoy it because she had to be thinking what to say to her neighbors. One was a little fat round man with a very red face, the other a tall man with a quizzical expression and a touch of gray hair.

He talked to her gravely about books and theaters, and then about the country and asked her where she lived. When she told him, he said he might be coming down that way at Easter. He would come and see her if she would allow it. Celia said that would be very nice.

"Then why not look as though it would be nice?" he asked, laughing.

Celia got red.

"You ought to," he said. "Especially as I've made up my mind only a minute ago to go there."

"The scenery's beautiful," said Celia earnestly.

"It isn't the scenery I'm coming to see."

How she wished people wouldn't say things of that kind. She crumbled her bread desperately. Her neighbor looked at her with amusement. What a child she was! It amused him to embarrass her. He gravely proceeded to pay her the most extravagant compliments.

Celia was terribly relieved when at last he turned to the lady on his other side and left her to the little fat man. His name was Roger Raynes, so he told her, and very soon they had got onto the subject of music. Raynes was a singer—not a professional, though he had often sung professionally. Celia became quite happy chatting to him.

She had hardly noticed what there had been to eat, but now an ice cream was coming round—a slender apricot-colored pillar studded with crystalized voilets.

It collapsed just before being handed to her. The butler took it to the sideboard and rearranged it. Then he resumed his round, but, alas, his memory failed him. He missed out Celia!

She was so bitterly disappointed that she hardly heard what the little fat man was saying. He had taken a large helping and seemed to be enjoying it very much. The idea of asking for some ice cream never occurred to Celia. She resigned herself to disappointment.

After dinner they had music. She played Roger Raynes's accompaniments. He had a splendid tenor voice. Celia enjoyed playing for him. She was a good and sympathetic accompanist. Then it was her turn to sing. Singing never made her nervous. Roger Raynes said kindly that she had a charming voice and then continued to talk about his own. He asked Celia to sing again, but she said, Wouldn't he? And he accepted with alacrity.

Celia went to bed quite happy. The house party was not being so dreadful after all.

The next morning passed pleasantly. They went out and looked at the stables and tickled the pigs' backs, and then Roger Raynes asked Celia if she would come and try over some songs with him. She did. After he had sung about six he produced a song called "Love's Lilies," and when they had finished he said:

"Now, tell me your candid opinion—what do you really think of that song?"

"Well—" Celia hesitated—"well, really, I think it's rather dreadful."

"So do I," said Roger Raynes. "At least, I wasn't sure. But you've settled it. You don't like it—so here goes."

And he tore the song in half and flung it into the grate. Celia was very much impressed. It was a brand-new song which, he told her, he had only bought the day before. And because of her opinion he had torn it up relentlessly.

She felt quite grown-up and important.

3

The big fancy-dress ball for which the party was assembled was to take place that night. Celia was to go as Marguerite from *Faust*—all in white with her hair in two plaits hanging down each side. She looked very fair and Gretchen-like, and Roger Raynes told her that he had the music of *Faust* with him, and that they would try over one of the duets tomorrow.

Celia felt rather nervous as they set off for the ball. She always found her program a difficulty. She always seemed to manage badly—to dance with the people she didn't much like, and then when the people she did like came along, there weren't any dances left. But if one pretended to be engaged then the people one liked mightn't come along after all, and then one might have to "sit out" (horror). Some girls seemed to manage cleverly but, Celia realized for the hundredth time gloomily, she *wasn't* clever.

Mrs. Luke looked after Celia well, introducing people to her.

"Major de Burgh."

Major de Burgh bowed. "Have you a dance?"

He was a big man, rather horsey-looking, long fair mustache, rather red face, about forty-five.

He put down his name for three dances and asked Celia to go in to supper with him.

She did not find him very easy to talk to. He said little, but he looked at her a good deal.

Mrs. Luke left the ball early. She was not strong.

"George will look after you and bring you home," she said to Celia. "By the way, child, you seem to have made quite a conquest of Major de Burgh."

Celia felt heartened. She was afraid she had bored Major de Burgh horribly.

She danced every dance, and it was two o'clock when George came up to her, and said:

"Hallo, Pink 'Un, time to take the stable home."

It was not till Celia was in her room that she realized that she was quite unable to extricate herself unaided from her evening frock. She heard George's voice in the corridor still saying good-nights. Could she ask him? Or couldn't she? If she didn't she would have to sit up in her frock till morning. Her courage failed her. When the morning dawned Celia was lying on her bed fast asleep in her evening dress.

4

Major de Burgh came over that morning. He wasn't hunting today, he said, to the chorus of astonishment that greeted him. He sat there saying very little. Mrs. Luke suggested that he might like to see the pigs. She sent Celia with him. At lunch Roger Raynes was very sulky.

The next day Celia went home. She had a quiet morning alone with her host and hostess. The others left in the morning, but she was going by an afternoon train. Somebody called "dear Arthur, so amusing" came to lunch. He was (in Celia's eyes) a very elderly man, and he did not seem amusing. He spoke in a low tired voice.

After lunch, when Mrs. Luke had left the room and he was alone with Celia, he began stroking her ankles.

"Charming," he murmured. "Charming. You don't mind, do you?"

Celia did mind. She minded very much. But she endured it. She supposed that this was a regular part of house parties. She did not want to appear gauche or immature. She set her teeth and sat very stiff.

Dear Arthur slipped a practiced arm round her waist and kissed her. Celia turned on him furiously and pushed him away.

"I can't—oh, please, I can't."

Manners were manners, but there were some things she couldn't endure.

"Such a sweet little waist," said Arthur advancing the practiced arm again.

Mrs. Luke came into the room. She noticed Celia's expression and flushed face.

"Did Arthur behave himself?" she asked on the way to the station. "He's not really to be trusted with young girls—can't leave him alone. Not that there's any real harm in him."

"Have you *got* to let people stroke your ankles?" demanded Celia.

"Got to? Of course not, you funny child."

"Oh," said Celia with a deep sigh. "I'm *so* glad."

Mrs. Luke looked amused and said again:

"You funny child!"

She went on: "You looked charming at the dance. I fancy you'll hear something more of Johnnie de Burgh." She added: "He's extremely well off."

5

The day after Celia got home a big pink box of chocolates arrived addressed to her. There was nothing inside to show whom they came from. Two days later a little parcel came. It contained a small silver box. Engraved on the lid were the words "Marguerite" and the date of the ball.

Major de Burgh's card was enclosed.

"Who is this Major de Burgh, Celia?"

"I met him at the ball."

"What is he like?"

"He's rather old and got rather a red face. Quite nice, but difficult to talk to."

Miriam nodded thoughtfully. That night she wrote to Mrs. Luke. The answer was quite frank—Mrs. Luke was by nature the complete matchmaker.

"He's very well off—very well off indeed. Hunts with the B—. George doesn't like him very much but *there's nothing against him*. He seems to have been *quite* bowled over by Celia. She is a dear child—very naive. She is certainly going to be attractive to men. Men do admire fairness and sloping shoulders so much."

A week later Major de Burgh "happened to be in the neighborhood." Might he come over and call on Celia and her mother?

He did so. He seemed as tongue-tied as ever—sat and stared at Celia a good deal, and tried clumsily to make friends with Miriam.

For some reason, after he had gone, Miriam was upset. Her conduct puzzled Celia. Her mother made disjointed remarks that Celia could not make head or tail of.

"I wonder if it's wise to pray for a thing. . . . How hard it is to know what is right. . . ." Then suddenly, "I want you to marry a good man—a man like your father. Money isn't everything—but comfortable surroundings do mean a lot to a woman. . . .

Celia accepted and replied to these remarks without in any way connecting them with the late visit of Major de Burgh. Miriam was in the habit of making remarks out of the blue, as it were. They had ceased to surprise her daughter.

Miriam said: "I should like you to marry a man older than yourself. They take more care of a woman."

Celia's thoughts flew momentarily to Colonel Moncrieff—now a fast fading memory. She had danced at the ball with a young soldier of six feet four and was inclined at the moment to idealize handsome young giants.

Her mother said: "When we go to London next week, Major de Burgh wants to take us to the theater. That will be nice, won't it?"

"Very nice," said Celia.

6

When Major de Burgh proposed to Celia he took her completely by surprise. Mrs. Luke's remarks, her mother's, none of them had made any impression upon her. Celia saw clearly her own thoughts—she never saw coming events, and not usually her own surroundings.

Miriam had asked Major de Burgh to come for the weekend. Actually he had practically asked himself, and, a little troubled, Miriam had uttered the necessary invitation.

On the first evening Celia was showing the guest the garden. She found him very hard work. He never seemed to be listening to what she was saying. She was afraid that he must be terribly bored. . . . Everything that she was saying was rather stupid, of course—but if only he would *help*—

And then, breaking into what she was saying, he had suddenly seized her hands in his and in a queer, hoarse, utterly unrecognizable voice had said:

"Marguerite—my Marguerite. I want you so. Will you marry me?"

Celia stared. Her face went quite blank—her eyes were blue and wide and astonished. She was quite incapable of speech. Something was affecting her—affecting her powerfully—something that was being communicated through those trembling hands that held her. She felt enveloped in a storm of emotion. It was rather frightening—rather terrible.

She stammered out:

"I—no. I don't know. Oh, no, I can't."

What was he making her feel, this man, this elderly quiet stranger whom as yet she had hardly noticed, save to feel flattered because he "liked her"?

"I've startled you, my darling. My little love. You're so young—so pure. You can't understand what I feel for you. I love you so."

Why didn't she take her hands away and say at once, firmly and truthfully, "I'm very sorry, but I don't care for you in that way"?

Why, instead, just stand there, helpless, looking at him—feeling those currents beating round her head?

He drew her gently toward him, but she resisted—only half resisted—did not draw completely away.

He said gently: "I won't worry you now. Think it over."

He released her. She walked away slowly to the house, went upstairs to her bed, lay down there, her eyes closed, her heart beating.

Her mother came to her there half an hour later.

She sat down on the bed, took Celia's hand.

"Did he tell you, Mother?"

"Yes. He cares for you very much. What—what do you feel about it?"

"I don't know. It's—it's all so queer."

She couldn't say anything else. It was all queer—everything was queer—complete strangers could turn into lovers—all in a minute. She didn't know what she felt or what she wanted.

Least of all did she understand or appreciate her mother's perplexities.

"I'm not very strong. I've been praying so that a good man would come along and give you a good home and make you happy. . . . There's so little money. . . . and I've had dreadful expenses over Cyril lately. . . . There will be so little for you when I am gone. I don't want you to marry anyone rich if you don't care for him. But you're so romantic, and a Fairy Prince—that sort of thing doesn't happen. So few women can marry the man they are romantically in love with."

"You did."

"*I* did—yes—but even then—it isn't always wise—to care too much. It's a thorn in your side always. . . . To be cared for—it's better. . . . You can take life more easily. . . . I've never taken it easily enough. If I knew more about this man. . . . If I was sure I liked him. He might drink. . . . He might be—anything. Would he take care of you—look after you? Be good to you? There *must* be someone to take care of you when I'm gone."

Most of it passed Celia by. Money meant nothing to her. When

Daddy had been alive they had been rich; when he had died they had been poor; but Celia had found no difference between the two states. She had had home and the garden and her piano.

Marriage to her meant love—poetical, romantic love—and living happily ever afterward. All the books she had read had taught her nothing of the problems of life. What puzzled and confused her was that she did not know whether she loved Major de Burgh—Johnnie—or not. A minute before his proposal she would have said if asked that most certainly she did not. But now? He had roused in her something—something hot and exciting and uncertain.

Miriam had decreed that he was to go away and leave Celia to think it over for two months. He had obeyed—but he wrote—and the inarticulate Johnnie de Burgh was a master of the love letter. His letters were sometimes short, sometimes long, never twice the same, but they were the love letters a young girl dreams of getting. By the end of two months Celia had decided that she was in love with Johnnie. She went up to London with her mother prepared to tell him so. When she saw him, a sudden revulsion of feeling swept over her. This man was a stranger whom she did not love. She refused him.

7

Johnnie de Burgh did not take his defeat easily. He asked Celia five times more to marry him. For over a year he wrote to her, accepted "friendship" with her, sent her pretty trifles, and laid persistent siege to her, and his perseverance nearly won the day.

It was all so romantic—so much the way Celia's fancy inclined to being wooed. His letters, the things he said—they were all so exactly right. That was, indeed, Johnnie de Burgh's forte. He was a born lover. He had been the lover of many women, and he knew what appealed to women. He knew how to attack a married woman and how to attract a young girl. Celia was very nearly swept off her feet into marriage with him, but not quite. Somewhere in her was something calm that knew what it wanted and was not to be deceived.

8

It was at this time that Miriam urged the reading of a course of French novels upon her daughter. To keep up your French, she said.

They included the works of Balzac and other French realists.

And there were some modern ones that few English mothers would have given to their daughters.

But Miriam had a purpose.

She was determined that Celia—so dreamy—so much in the clouds—should not be ignorant of life. . . .

Celia read them with great docility and very little interest.

9

Celia had other suitors. Ralph Graham, the original freckled-faced boy of the dancing class. He was now a tea planter in Ceylon. He had always been attracted by Celia, even when she was a child. Returning to find her grown up, he asked her to marry him during the first week of his leave. Celia refused him without hesitation. He had had a friend staying with him, and later the friend wrote to Celia. He had not wanted to "queer Ralph's pitch," but he had fallen in love with her at first sight. Was there any hope for him? But neither Ralph nor his friend made any impression on Celia's consciousness.

But during the year of Johnnie de Burgh's wooing she made a friend—Peter Maitland. Peter was some years older than his sisters. He was a soldier and had been stationed abroad for many years. Now he returned to England for a period of home service. His return coincided with Ellie Maitland's engagement. Celia and Janet were to be bridesmaids. It was at the wedding that Celia got to know Peter.

Peter Maitland was tall and dark. He was shy, but concealed it under a lazy, pleasant manner. The Maitlands were all much the same, good-natured, companionable, and easy-going. They never hurried themselves for anyone or anything. If they missed a train—well, there would be another one sometime. If they were late in getting home for lunch—well, they supposed someone would have kept them something to eat. They had no ambitions and no energies. Peter was the most marked example of the family traits. No one had ever seen Peter hurry. "All the same a hundred years hence," was his motto.

Ellie's wedding was a typical Maitland affair. Mrs. Maitland, who was large and vague and good-natured, never got up till midday and frequently forgot to order any meals. "Getting Mum into her wedding garments" was the chief business of the morning. Owing to Mum's distaste for trying on, her oyster satin was found to be uncomfortably tight. The bride fussed round her—and all was made comfortable by a judicious use of the scissors and a spray of orchids to cover the deficiency. Celia was at the house early—to help—and it certainly seemed at one point as though Ellie was never going to get married that day. At the moment she should have been putting the final touches to her appearance, she was sitting in a chemise placidly manicuring her toenails.

"I meant to have done this last night," she explained. "But somehow I didn't seem to have time."

"The carriage has come, Ellie."

"Has it? Oh, well, somebody had better telephone Tom and tell him I shall be about half an hour late."

"Poor little Tom," she added reflectively. "He's such a dear little fellow. I shouldn't like him to be dithering in the church thinking I'd changed my mind."

Ellie had grown very tall—she was nearly six foot. Her bridegroom was five foot five, and as Ellie described it, "such a merry little fellow—and a sweet little nature."

While Ellie was finally being induced to finish her toilet, Celia wandered into the garden, where Captain Peter Maitland was smoking a placid pipe, not in the least concerned by the tardiness of his sister.

"Thomas is a sensible fellow," he said. "He knows what she is like. He won't expect her to be on time."

He was a little shy talking to Celia, but, as is often the case when two shy people get together, they soon found it easy to talk to each other.

"Expect you find us a rum family?" said Peter.

"You don't seem to have much sense of time," said Celia laughing.

"Well, why spend your life rushing? Take it easy—enjoy yourself."

"Does one ever get anywhere that way?"

"Where is there to get to? One thing is very like another in this life."

When he was at home on leave, Peter Maitland usually refused all invitations. He hated "poodle faking" he said. He did not dance, and he played tennis or golf with men or his own sisters. But after the wedding he seemed to adopt Celia as an extra sister. He and she and Janet used to do things together. Then Ralph Graham, recovering from Celia's refusal, began to be attracted to Janet, and the trio became a foursome. Finally it split into couples—Janet and Ralph and Celia and Peter.

Peter used to instruct Celia in the game of golf.

"We won't hurry ourselves, mind. Just a few holes and take it easy—and sit down and smoke a pipe if it gets too hot."

The program suited Celia very well. She had no "eye" for games—which fact depressed her only a little less than her lack of "a figure." But Peter made her feel that it didn't matter.

"You don't want to be a pro—or a pot hunter. Just get a little fun out of it—that's all."

Peter himself was extraordinarily good at all games. He had a natural flair for athletics. He could have been in the front rank but for his constitutional laziness. But he preferred, as he said, to treat games as games. "Why make a business of the thing?"

He got on very well with Celia's mother. She was fond of all the Maitland family, and Peter, with his lazy, easy charm, his pleasant manners, and his undoubted sweetness of disposition, was her favorite.

"You don't need to worry about Celia," he said when he suggested that they should ride together. "I'll look after her. I will—really—look after her."

Miriam knew what he meant. She felt Peter Maitland was to be trusted.

He knew a little of how the land lay between Celia and her major. Vaguely, in a delicate way, he gave her advice.

"A girl like you, Celia, ought to marry a fellow with a bit of the 'oof.' You're the kind that wants looking after. I don't mean you ought to marry a beastly Jew boy—nothing like that. But a decent fellow who's fond of sports and all that—and who could look after you."

When Peter's leave was up and he rejoined his regiment, which was stationed at Aldershot, Celia missed him very much. She wrote to him, and he to her—easy colloquial letters that were very much like the way he talked.

When Johnnie de Burgh finally accepted his dismissal, Celia felt rather flat. The effort to withstand his influence had taken more out of her than she knew. No sooner had the final break occurred than she wondered whether, after all, she didn't regret. . . . Perhaps she did care for him more than she thought. She missed the excitement of his letters, of his presents, of his continual siege.

She was uncertain of her mother's attitude. Was Miriam relieved or disappointed? Sometimes she thought one and sometimes the other, and as a matter of fact was not far from the truth in so thinking.

Miriam's first sensation had been one of relief. She had never really liked Johnnie de Burgh—she had never quite trusted him—though she could never put her finger on exactly where the distrust lay. Certainly he was devoted to Celia. His past had been nothing outrageous—and indeed Miriam had been brought up in the belief that a man who has sown his wild oats is likely to make a better husband.

The thing that worried her most was her own health. The heart attacks that she once suffered from at long distant intervals were becoming more frequent. From the humming and hawing and diplomatic language of doctors she had formed the conclusion that while she might have long years of life in front of her—she might equally well die suddenly. And then, what was to become of Celia? There was so little money. How little only Miriam knew.

So little—little—money.

COMMENTARY MADE BY J. L——

It would strike us in these days: "But why on earth, if there was so little money, didn't she train Celia for a profession?"

But I don't think that would ever have occurred to Miriam. She was, I should imagine, intensely receptive to new thought and new ideas—

but I don't think that that particular idea had come her way. And if it had, I don't think she would have taken to it readily.

I take it that she knew the peculiar vulnerability of Celia. You may say that that might have been altered with a different training, but I don't believe that that is so. Like all people who live chiefly by the inner vision, Celia was peculiarly impervious to influences from outside. She was stupid when it came to realities.

I think Miriam was aware of her daughter's deficiencies. I think her choice of reading—her insisting on Balzac and other French novelists—was done with an object. The French are great realists. I think she wanted Celia to realize life and human nature for what it is, something common, sensual, splendid, sordid, tragic, and intensely comic. She did not succeed, because Celia's nature matched her appearance—she was Scandinavian in feeling. For her the long Sagas, the heroic tales of voyages and heroes. As she clung to fairy tales in childhood, so she preferred Maeterlinck and Fiona MacLeod and Yeats when she grew up. She read the other books, but they seemed as unreal to her as fairy stories and fantasies seem annoying to a practical realist.

We are as we are born. Some Scandinavian ancestor lived again in Celia. The robust Grannie, the merry and jovial John, the mercurial Miriam—one of these passed on the secret strain that they possessed unknown to themselves.

It is interesting to see how completely her brother drops out of Celia's narrative. And yet Cyril must often have been there—on holidays—on leave.

Cyril went into the army and had gone abroad to India before Celia came out. He never loomed very large in her life—or in Miriam's. He was, I gather, a great source of expense when he was first in the army. Later he married, left the army, and went to Rhodesia to farm. As a personality he faded from Celia's life.

Chapter 8

JIM AND PETER

Both Miriam and her daughter believed in prayer. Celia's prayers had been first conscientious and conscious of sin, and later had been spiritual and ascetic. But she never broke herself of her little-girl habit of praying over everything that happened. Celia never went into a ballroom without murmuring: "Oh, God, don't let me be shy. Oh, please God, don't let me be shy. And don't let my neck get red." At dinner parties she prayed: "Please, God, let me think of something to say." She prayed that she might manage her program well and dance with the people she wanted to. She prayed that it might not rain when they started on a picnic.

Miriam's prayers were more intense and more arrogant. She was, in truth, an arrogant woman. For her darling she did not ask, she demanded things of God! Her prayers were so intense, so burning, that she could not believe they would not be answered. And perhaps most of us, when we say our prayers have been unanswered, really mean that the answer has been No.

She had not been sure whether Johnnie de Burgh was an answer to prayer or not, but she was quite sure that Jim Grant was.

Jim was keen on taking up farming, and his people sent him to a farm near Miriam on purpose. They felt that she would keep an eye on the boy. It would help him to keep out of mischief.

Jim at twenty-three was almost exactly like Jim at thirteen had been. The same good-humored, high-cheekboned face, the same round, intensely dark blue eyes, the same good-humored, efficient manner. The same dazzling smile, and the same way of throwing back his head and laughing.

Jim was twenty-three and heart whole. It was spring and he was a strong, healthy young man. He came often to Miriam's house, and Celia was young and fair and beautiful, and since nature is nature, he fell in love.

To Celia, it was another friendship like her friendship with Peter Maitland, only that she admired Jim's character more. She had always felt that Peter was almost too "slack." He had no ambition. Jim was full of ambition. He was young and intensely solemn about life. The words "life is real, life is earnest," might have been written for Jim. His desire to take up farming was not rooted in a love of the soil. He was interested in the practical scientific side of farming. Farming in England ought to be made to pay much better than it did. It only needed science and will power. Jim was very strong on willpower. He had books about it which he lent to Celia. He was very fond of lending books. He was also interested in theosophy, bimetallism, economics, and Christian Science.

He liked Celia because she listened so attentively. She read all the books and made intelligent comments on them.

If Johnnie de Burgh's courtship of Celia had been physical, Jim Grant's was almost entirely intellectual. At this time in his career, he was simply bursting with serious ideas—almost to the point of being priggish. When Celia liked him best was not when he was seriously discussing ethics or Mrs. Eddy, but when he threw back his head and laughed.

Johnnie de Burgh's love-making had taken her by surprise, but she realized Jim was going to ask her to marry him some time before he did.

Sometimes Celia felt life was a pattern: you wove in and out of it like a shuttle, obedient to the design imposed upon you. Jim, she began to suppose, was her pattern. He was her destiny, appointed from the beginning. How happy her mother looked nowadays.

Jim was a dear—she liked him immensely. Someday soon he would ask her to marry him and then she would feel as she had felt with Major de Burgh (she always thought of him as that in her mind, never as Johnnie)—excited and troubled—her heart beating fast. . . .

Jim proposed to her one Sunday afternoon. He had planned to do so some weeks beforehand. He liked making plans and keeping to them. He felt it was an efficient way of living.

It was a wet afternoon. They were sitting in the schoolroom after tea. Celia had been playing and singing. Jim liked Gilbert and Sullivan.

After the singing they sat on the sofa and discussed socialism and the Good of Man. After that, there was a pause. Celia said something about Mrs. Besant, but Jim answered rather at random.

There was another pause, and then Jim got rather red and said:

"I expect you know I am awfully fond of you, Celia. Would you like to be engaged, or would you rather wait a bit? I think we should be very happy together. We've got so many tastes in common."

He was not so calm as he sounded. If Celia had been older she would have realized this. She would have seen the significance of the slight tremble of his lips, the nervous hand that plucked at a sofa cushion.

As it was—well, what was she to say?

She didn't know—so she said nothing.

"I think you like me?" said Jim.

"I do—oh, I do," cried Celia eagerly.

"That's the most important thing," said Jim. "That people should really like each other. That lasts. Passion"—he got a little pink as he said the word—"doesn't. I think you and I would be ideally happy, Celia. I want to marry young." He paused, then said: "Look here, I think the fairest thing would be for us to be engaged on trial, as it were, for six months. We needn't tell anyone except your mother and mine. Then, at the end of six months, you can make up your mind definitely."

Celia reflected a minute.

"Do you think that's fair? I mean, I mightn't—even then—"

"If you don't—then of course we oughtn't to marry. But you will. I know it's going to be all right."

What comfortable assurance there was in his voice. He was so sure. He *knew*.

"Very well," said Celia and smiled.

She expected him to kiss her, but he didn't. He wanted to badly, but she felt shy. They went on discussing socialism and man—not perhaps quite so logically as they might have done.

Then Jim said it was time to go, and got up.

They stood for a minute awkwardly.

"Well," said Jim, "so long. I'll be over next Sunday—perhaps before. And I'll write." He hesitated. "I—shall—will you give me a kiss, Celia?"

They kissed. Rather awkwardly. . . .

It was exactly like kissing Cyril, Celia thought. Only, she reflected, Cyril never wanted to kiss anybody. . . .

Well, that was that. She was engaged to Jim.

2

Miriam's happiness was so overflowing that it made Celia feel quite enthusiastic over her engagement.

"Darling, I'm so happy about you. He's such a dear boy. Honest and manly, and he'll take care of you. And they are such old friends and were so fond of your dear father. It seems so wonderful that it should have come about like this—their son and our daughter. Oh, Celia, I was so unhappy all the time with Major de Burgh. I felt somehow that it wasn't *right* . . . not the thing for you."

She paused and said suddenly:

"And I've been afraid of myself."

"Of yourself?"

"Yes, I've wanted so badly to keep you with me. . . . Not to have you marry. I've wanted to be selfish. I've said that you would lead a more sheltered life—no cares, no children, no troubles. . . . If it hadn't been that I could have left you so little—so very little to live upon, I would have been sorely tempted. . . . It's very hard, Celia, for mothers not to be selfish."

"Nonsense," said Celia. "You would have been dreadfully humiliated when other girls got married."

She had noted with some amusement her mother's intense jealousy on her behalf. Were another girl better dressed, more amusing in conversation, Miriam immediately displayed a frenzied annoyance quite unshared by Celia. Her mother had hated it when Ellie Maitland got married. The only girls Miriam would speak kindly of were girls so plain or so dowdy as not in any way to rival Celia. This trait in her mother sometimes annoyed Celia but more often warmed her heart toward her. Darling thing, what a ridiculous mother bird she was with her ruffled plumage! So absurdly illogical. . . . But it was sweet of her, all the same. Like all Miriam's actions and feelings, it was so violent.

She was glad her mother was so happy. It had indeed all come about in a very wonderful way. It was nice to be marrying into a family of "old friends." And she certainly did like Jim better than anyone else she knew—much, *much* better. He was just the kind of man she had always imagined having as a husband. Young, masterful, full of ideals.

Did girls always feel depressed when they got engaged? Perhaps they did. It was so final—so irrevocable.

She yawned as she picked up Mrs. Besant. Theosophy depressed her too. A lot of it seemed so silly. . . .

Bimetallism was better. . . .

Everything was rather dull—much duller than it had been two days ago.

3

There was a letter on her plate next morning addressed in Jim's handwriting. A little flush rose in Celia's cheek. A letter from Jim. Her first letter since . . .

She felt, for the first time, a little excited. He hadn't said much, but perhaps in a letter . . .

She took it out in the garden and opened it.

Dearest Celia [wrote Jim]: I got back very late for supper. Old Mrs. Cray was rather annoyed but old Cray was rather amusing. He told her not to fuss—I'd been courting, he said. They really are awfully nice, simple people—their jokes are good-natured. I wish they were a little more receptive to new ideas—in farming, I mean. He doesn't seem to have read *anything* on the subject and to be quite content to run the farm just like his great-grandfather did. I suppose agriculture is always more reactionary than anything else. It's the peasant instinct rooted in the soil.

I feel I ought, perhaps, to have spoken to your mother before I left last night. However, I have written to her. I hope she won't mind my taking you away from her. I know you mean a lot to her, but I think she likes me all right.

I might come over on Thursday—it depends on the weather. If not, Sunday next,

Lots of love,

Yours affectionately,
Jim.

After the letters of Johnnie de Burgh, it was not an epistle calculated to produce great elation of spirits in a girl!

Celia felt annoyed with Jim.

She felt that she could love him quite easily—if only he were a little different!

She tore the letter into small pieces and threw it into a ditch.

4

Jim was not a lover. He was too self-conscious. Besides, he had very definite theories and opinions.

Moreover, Celia was not really the kind of woman to stir in him all that was there to be stirred. An experienced woman, whom Jim's bashfulness would have piqued, could have made him lose his head—with beneficial results.

As it was, his relations with Celia were vaguely unsatisfactory. They seemed to have lost the easy camaraderie of their friendship and to have gained nothing in exchange.

Celia continued to admire Jim's character, to be bored by his conversation, to be maddened by his letters, and to be depressed by life in general.

The only thing she found real pleasure in was her mother's happiness.

She got a letter from Peter Maitland, to whom she had written telling her news under a promise of secrecy.

All the best to you, Celia [wrote Peter]. He sounds a thoroughly sound fellow. You don't say whether's he's got any of the ready. I hope so. Girls don't think of a thing like that, but I assure you,

Celia dear, it matters. I'm much older than you and I've seen
women trailing round with their husbands fagged out and worried
to death over money problems. I'd like you to live like a queen.
You're not the sort that can rough it.

Well, there's not much more to say. I shall have a squint at
your young man when I come home in September and see whether
he's worthy of you. Not that I should ever think anyone was that!

All the best to you, old girl, and may your shadow never grow
less.

Yours always,

Peter.

5

It was a strange fact, yet true nevertheless, that the thing Celia enjoyed
most about her engagement was her prospective mother-in-law.

Her old childish admiration for Mrs. Grant resumed its sway. Mrs.
Grant, she thought now as then, was lovely. Gray-haired now, she had
still the same queen-like grace, the same exquisite blue eyes and swaying
figure, the same well-remembered, clear, beautiful voice, the same dominating personality.

Mrs. Grant realized Celia's admiration for her and was pleased by
it. Possibly she was not quite satisfied about the engagement—something may have seemed to her lacking. She quite agreed with what the
young people had decided—to be openly engaged at the end of six
months and married a year later.

Jim adored his mother, and he was pleased that Celia should so
obviously adore her also.

Grannie was very pleased that Celia was engaged but felt constrained to
throw out many dark hints as to the difficulties of married life, ranging
from poor John Godolphin who developed cancer of the throat on his honeymoon, to old Admiral Collingway who "gave his wife a bad disease, and
then carried on with the governess, and at last, my dear, she couldn't
keep a maid in the house, poor thing. He used to jump out at them
from behind doors—and not a stitch on. Naturally they wouldn't stay."

Celia felt that Jim was much too healthy to get cancer of the throat ("Ah, my dear, but it's the healthy ones who get it," interpolated Grannie), and not even the wildest imagination could picture the sedate Jim as an elderly satyr leaping on maidservants.

Grannie liked Jim but was, secretly, a little disappointed in him. A young man who didn't drink or smoke and who looked embarrassed when jokes were made—what sort of a young man was that? Frankly, Grannie preferred a more virile generation.

"Still," she said hopefully, "I saw him pick up a handful of gravel off the terrace last night, and I thought that pretty—the place where your feet had trodden."

In vain Celia explained that it had been a matter of geological interest. Grannie would hear of no such explanation.

"That's what he told you, dear. But I know young men. Why, young Planterton wore my handkerchief next his heart for seven years, and he only met me once at a ball."

Through the indiscretion of Grannie the news leaked through to Mrs. Luke.

"Well, child, I hear you've fixed things up with a young man. I'm glad you turned Johnnie down. George said I wasn't to say anything to put you off, as he was such a good match. But I always did think he looked exactly like a codfish."

Thus Mrs. Luke.

She went on:

"Roger Raynes is always asking about you. I put him off. Of course, he's quite well off—that's why he never really does anything with his voice. A pity—because he could be a professional. But I don't suppose you'd fancy him—he's such a little roundabout. And he eats steak for breakfast and always cuts himself shaving. I hate men who cut themselves shaving."

6

One day in July, Jim came over in a state of great excitement. A very rich man, a friend of his father's was going on a trip round the world with the especial view of studying agriculture. He had offered to take Jim with him.

Jim talked excitedly for some time. He was grateful to Celia for her prompt interest and acquiescence. He had had a half-guilty feeling that she might be annoyed at his going.

A fortnight later he started off in boisterous spirits, sending Celia a farewell telegram from Dover:

best of love take care of yourself—JIM.

How beautiful an August morning can be. . . .

Celia came out on the terrace in front of the house and looked round her. It was early—there was still dew on the grass—that long green slope that Miriam had refused to have cut up into beds. There was the beech tree—bigger than ever, heavily, deeply green. And the sky was blue—blue—blue like deep sea water.

Never, Celia thought, had she felt so happy. The old familiar "pain" clutched at her. It was so lovely—so lovely—it hurt. . . .

Oh, beautiful, beautiful world! . . .

The gong sounded. She went in to breakfast.

Her mother looked at her. "You look very happy, Celia."

"I am happy. It's such a lovely day."

Her mother said quietly:

"It's not only that. . . . It's because Jim's gone away, isn't it?"

Celia had hardly known it herself till that minute. Relief—wild, joyous relief. She wouldn't have to read theosophy or economics for nine months. For nine glorious delirious months she could live as she pleased—feel as she pleased. She was free—free—free . . .

She looked at her mother, and her mother looked back at her.

Miriam said gently:

"You mustn't marry him. Not if you feel like that. . . . I didn't know. . . ."

Words poured from Celia.

"I didn't know myself. . . . I thought I loved him—yes—he's so much the nicest person I ever met—and so splendid in every way."

Miriam nodded sadly. It was the ruin of all her newfound peace.

"I knew you didn't love him at first—but I thought that you might grow to love him if you were engaged. It's been the other way. . . . You mustn't marry anybody who bores you."

"Bores me!" Celia was shocked. "But he's so clever—he couldn't bore me."

"That's just what he does do, Celia." She sighed and added: "He's very young."

Perhaps the thought came to her that minute that if only these two had not met until Jim was older all might have been well. She was always to feel that Jim and Celia missed love by a very little—but they did miss it . . .

And secretly, in spite of her disappointment and her fear for Celia's future, a little thread ran singing joyfully, "She will not leave me yet. She will not leave me yet. . . ."

7

Once Celia had written to Jim to tell him she could not marry him she felt as though a load of care had slipped off her back.

When Peter Maitland came down in September he was amazed at her good spirits and her beauty.

"So you gave that young fellow the chuck, Celia?"

"Yes."

"Poor chap. Still, I dare say you'll soon find someone more to your mind. I suppose people are always asking you to marry them?"

"Oh, not very many."

"How many?"

Celia thought.

There was that funny little man, Captain Gale, in Cairo, and a silly boy on the boat coming back (if that counted), and Major de Burgh, of course, and Ralph and his tea-planter friend (who was married to another girl now, by the way), and Jim—and then there had been that ridiculous business with Roger Raynes only a week ago.

Mrs. Luke had no sooner heard that Celia's engagement was off than she had telegraphed for Celia to come and stay. Roger was coming, and Roger was always asking George to arrange for him to meet Celia again.

Things had really looked quite promising. They had sung together in the drawing room by the hour.

"If only he could sing his proposal, she might take him," thought Mrs. Luke hopefully.

"Why shouldn't she take him? Raynes is a jolly good chap," said George reproachfully.

It was no good explaining to men. They never could understand what women "saw" or did not "see" in a man.

"A bit of a roundabout, of course," admitted George. "But looks don't matter in a man."

"A man invented that saying," snapped Mrs. Luke.

"Well, come now, Amy, you women don't want a barber's block."

He insisted that "Roger should have his chance."

Roger's best chance would have been to propose to Celia in song. He had a magnificent, moving voice. Listening to him singing, Celia would easily have thought she loved him. But when the music was over, Roger resumed his everyday personality.

Celia was a little nervous of Mrs. Luke's matchmaking. She saw the look in her eye and carefully maneuvered not to be alone with Roger. She didn't want to marry him. Why let him speak at all?

But the Lukes were determined to "give Roger his chance," and Celia found herself being compelled to drive with Roger in the dogcart to a certain picnic.

It had not been an auspicious drive. Roger had talked of the delights of a home life and Celia had said a hotel was more fun. Roger said he had always fancied living somewhere not more than an hour from London—but in country surroundings.

"Where would you hate living most?" asked Celia.

"London. I couldn't live in London."

"Fancy," said Celia. "It's the only place I could bear to live."

She looked at him coolly after uttering this untruth.

"Oh, I dare say I *could* do it," said Roger, sighing, "if I found the ideal woman. I think I have found her. I—"

"I must tell you something so funny that happened the other day," said Celia desperately.

Roger did not listen to the anecdote. As soon as it was over he resumed:

"Do you know, Celia, ever since I met you the first time—"

"Do you see that bird? I do believe it's a goldfinch."

But there was no hope. Between a man who is determined to propose and a woman who is determined not to let him, the man always wins. The wilder Celia's red herrings, the more determined Roger became to keep to the point. He was then bitterly hurt by the curtness of Celia's refusal. She was angry because she had not managed to stave it off and also annoyed with Roger for his genuine surprise at her refusal to marry him. The drive finished in cold silence. Roger said to George that, after all, perhaps he had had a lucky escape—she seemed to have quite a temper. . . .

All this passed through Celia's mind as she mediated Peter's question.

"I suppose seven," she said at last doubtfully. "But only two real ones."

They were sitting on the grass under a hedge on the golf course. From there you looked out over a panorama of cliffs and sea.

Peter had let his pipe go out. He was snapping off daisies' heads with his fingers.

"You know, Celia," he said, and his voice sounded odd and strained, "you can—add me to that list any time you like."

She looked at him in astonishment.

"You, Peter?"

"Yes, didn't you know?"

"No, I never thought of it. You never—seemed like that."

"Well, it's been that way with me almost since the beginning. . . . I think I knew even at Ellie's wedding. Only, you see, Celia, I'm not the right sort of fellow for you. You want a go-ahead, brainy chap—oh, yes, you do. I know what your ideal man is like. He's not a lazy, easygoing fellow like me. I shan't get on in life. I'm not made that way. I shall amble through the service and retire. No fireworks. And I've very little of the ready. Five or six hundred a year—that's all we'd have to live upon."

"I wouldn't mind that."

"I know you wouldn't. But I mind for you. Because you don't know what it's like—and I do. You ought to have the best, Celia—absolutely the best. You're a very lovely girl. You could marry anybody. I'm not going to have you throw yourself away on a tuppeny halfpenny soldier. No proper home, always packing up and moving on. No, I always meant to keep my mouth shut and let you make the kind of marriage a beautiful girl like you ought to make. I just thought that supposing you didn't—then—well, someday, there might be a chance for me. . . ."

Very timidly Celia laid her slender pink hand on the brown one. It closed round hers, held it warmly. How nice it felt—Peter's hand. . . .

"I don't know that I ought to have spoken now. But we're ordered abroad again. I thought I'd like you to know before I go. Supposing Mr. Right doesn't turn up—I'm there—always—waiting. . . ."

Peter—dear, dear Peter. . . . Somehow, Peter belonged to the nursery and the garden and Rouncy and the beech tree. Safety—happiness—home . . .

How happy she was, sitting here looking out over the sea, with her hand in Peter's. She would always be happy with Peter. Dear, easygoing, sweet-tempered Peter.

He had never looked at her all this time. His face looked rather grim—rather tense . . . very brown and dark.

She said:

"I'm very fond of you, Peter. I'd like to marry you. . . ."

He turned then—slowly, as he did everything. He put his arm round her . . . those dark, kind eyes looked into hers.

He kissed her—not awkwardly like Jim—not passionately like Johnnie—but with a deep, satisfying tenderness.

"My little love," he said. "Oh, my little love. . . ."

8

Celia wanted to marry Peter at once and go out to India with him. But Peter refused point-blank.

He insisted obstinately that she was still very young—only nineteen now—and that she must still have every chance.

"I'd feel the most awful swine, Celia, if I went and snatched at you greedily. You may change your mind—you may meet someone you like a lot better than me."

"I shan't—I shan't."

"You don't know. Lots of girls are keen about a fellow when they're nineteen and wonder what they could have seen in him by the time they're twenty-two. I'm not going to rush you. You must have lots of time—you've got to be quite sure you're not making a mistake."

Lots of time. The Maitland habit of thought—never rushing a thing—plenty of time. And so the Maitlands missed trains and trams and appointments and meals and, sometimes, more important things.

Peter talked in the same way to Miriam.

"You know how I love Celia," he said. "You've always known, I think. That's why you trusted me to go about with her. I know I'm not the sort of fellow you thought of her marrying—"

Miriam interrupted.

"I want her to be happy. I think she would be happy with you."

"I'd give my life to make her happy—you know that. But I don't want to rush her. Some fellow with money might come along and if she liked him—"

"Money is not everything. It is true that I hoped Celia would not be poor. Still, if you and she are fond of each other—you have enough to live on by being careful."

"It's a dog's life for a woman. And it's taking her away from you."

"If she loves you—"

"Yes, there's an if about it. You feel that. Celia's got to have every chance. She's too young to know her own mind. I shall have leave in two years' time. If she still feels the same—"

"I hope she will."

"She's so beautiful, you know. I feel she ought to do better. I'm a rotten match for her."

"Don't be to humble," said Miriam suddenly. "Women don't appreciate it."

"No, perhaps you're right."

Celia and Peter were very happy together during the fortnight spent at home. Two years would soon pass.

"And I promise you I'll be faithful to you, Peter. You'll find me waiting for you."

"Now, Celia, that's just what you're not to do—consider yourself promised to me. You're absolutely free."

"I don't want to be."

"Never mind, you are."

She said with sudden resentment:

"If you really loved me, you'd want me to marry you at once and come with you."

"Oh, my love, my little love, don't you understand that it's because I love you so much?"

Seeing his stricken face she knew that he did indeed love her, with a love that feared to grasp at a treasure much desired.

Three weeks later Peter sailed.

A year and three months later Celia married Dermot.

Chapter 9

DERMOT

Peter came gradually into Celia's life; Dermot came with a rush.

Except that he too was a soldier, no greater contrast could have been imagined between two men than between Dermot and Peter.

Celia met him at a regimental ball at York to which she went with the Lukes.

When she was introduced to this tall young man with the intensely blue eyes he said: "I'd like three dances, please."

After they had danced the second, he asked for three more. Her program was full up. He said:

"Never mind. Cut somebody."

He took her program from her and crossed out three names at random.

"There," he said, "don't forget. I'll be early so as to snatch you in time."

Dark, tall, with dark curling hair; very blue eyes that slanted, faun-like, and glanced at you and away quickly. A decided manner, an air of being able to get his own way always—under any circumstances.

At the end of the ball he asked how long Celia was going to be in this part of the world. She told him she was leaving the next day. He asked if she ever went to London.

She told him that she was going to stay with her grandmother next month. She gave him the address.

He said: "I may be in town about then. I'll come and call."

Celia said: "Do."

But she never thought seriously that he would. A month is a long time. He fetched her a glass of lemonade, and she sipped it, and they talked about life, and Dermot said that he believed you could always get everything you wanted if only you wanted it enough.

Celia felt rather guilty over the dances she had cut—it wasn't a habit of hers—only, somehow, she hadn't been able to help it. . . . He was like that.

She felt sorry that she would probably never see him again.

But, to be truthful, she had forgotten all about him when on entering the house at Wimbledon one day she found Grannie leaning forward animatedly in her big chair, talking to a young man whose face and ears were rather pink with embarrassment.

"I hope you haven't forgotten me," mumbled Dermot.

He was by now very shy indeed.

Celia said of course she hadn't, and Grannie, always sympathetic to young men, asked him to stay on to dinner, which he did. And after dinner they went into the drawing room, and Celia sang to him.

Before he left he propounded a plan for the morrow. He had tickets for a matinee—would Celia come in to town and go with him to it? When it turned out that he meant alone, Grannie demurred. She didn't think Celia's mother would like it. The young man, however, managed to get round Grannie. So Grannie gave in, but she said on no account was he to take Celia anywhere to tea afterward. She was to come straight home.

So that was settled, and Celia met him at the matinee and enjoyed it more than any theater she had ever seen, and they had tea at the buffet at Victoria, because Dermot said that didn't count.

He came twice again before Celia returned home.

The third day after Celia had returned she was having tea with the Maitlands when she was summoned to the telephone. Her mother spoke:

"Darling, you simply must come home. Some young man of yours has turned up on a motor bicycle—and you know it worries me to have to talk to young men. Come home quickly and look after him yourself."

Celia went home wondering who it was. Her mother had said that he had mumbled his name so that she hadn't been able to hear it.

It was Dermot. He had a desperate, determined, miserable look, and he seemed quite unable to talk to Celia when he did see her. He just sat muttering monosyllables and not looking at her.

The motor bicycle was a borrowed one, he told her. He had thought it would be refreshing to get out of London and do a few days' tour round. He was putting up at the inn. He had to go off tomorrow morning. Would she come for a walk with him first?

He was in much the same mood the next day—silent—miserable—unable to look at her. Suddenly he said:

"My leave's over, I've got to go back to York. Something's got to be settled. I must see you again. I want to see you always—all the time. I want you to marry me."

Celia stood stock still—utterly startled. While she had recognized that Dermot liked her, it had never entered her head that a young subaltern of twenty-three would contemplate marriage.

She said. "I'm sorry—very sorry—but I couldn't—oh, no, I couldn't."

How could she? She was going to marry Peter. She loved Peter. Yes, she still loved Peter—just the same—but she loved Dermot also. . . .

She realized that she wanted to marry Dermot more than anything in the world.

Dermot was going on:

"Well, I've got to see you, anyway. . . . I expect I've asked you too soon . . . I couldn't wait. . . ."

Celia said:

"You see—I'm—engaged to someone else. . . ."

He looked at her—one of those quick sidelong glances. He said:

"That doesn't matter. You must give him up. You do love me?"

"I—I think I do."

Yes, she loved Dermot better than anything in the world. She would rather be unhappy with Dermot than happy with anyone else. But why put it like that? Why should she be unhappy with Dermot? Because, she supposed, she didn't know at all what he was like. . . . He was a stranger. . . .

Dermot was stammering.

"I—I—oh! that's splendid—we'll get married at once. I can't wait. . . ."

Celia thought: "Peter. I can't bear to hurt Peter. . . ."

But she knew that Dermot could bear to hurt any number of Peters and she knew that what Dermot told her to do she would do.

For the first time she looked right into his eyes which no longer gave a glance and flashed away.

Very, very blue eyes. . . .

Shyly—uncertainly—they kissed. . . .

2

Miriam was lying on the sofa in her bedroom, resting, when Celia came in. One glance at her daughter's face told her that something unusual had happened. Like a flash it went through Miriam's mind. "That young man—I don't like him."

She said, "Darling—what is it?"

"Oh, Mother—he wants to marry me—and I want to marry him, Mother. . . ."

Straight into Miriam's arms—her face buried on Miriam's shoulder.

And above the agonizing beating of her strained heart, Miriam's thought ran frenziedly:

"I don't like it—I don't like it. . . . But that's selfishness—because I don't want her to go."

3

There were difficulties almost at once. Dermot could not override Miriam high-handedly as he overrode Celia. He kept his temper because he did not want to put Celia's mother against him, but he was annoyed at any hint of opposition.

He admitted that he had no money—a bare eighty pounds a year beyond his pay. But he was annoyed when Miriam asked how he and Celia proposed to live. He said he hadn't had time to think yet. Surely they could manage—Celia wouldn't mind being poor. When Miriam said that it wasn't usual for subalterns to marry, he said impatiently that he couldn't help what was usual.

He said, rather bitterly, to Celia: "Your mother seems determined to bring everything down to pounds, shillings, and pence."

He was like an eager child denied the thing it had set its heart on and unwilling to listen to "reason."

When he had gone, Miriam felt very depressed. She saw the prospect of a long engagement with very little hope of marriage for many years to come. Perhaps, she felt, she ought not to have let them be engaged at all. . . . But she loved Celia too dearly to cause her pain.

Celia said: "Mother, I must marry Dermot. I must. I shall never love anybody else. It will come right someday—oh, say it will."

"It seems so hopeless, my darling. You've neither of you got anything. And he's so young. . . ."

"But, someday—if we wait. . . ."

"Well, perhaps. . . ."

"You don't like him, Mother. Why?"

"I do like him. I think he's very attractive—very attractive indeed. But not considerate. . . ."

At night Miriam lay awake going over her small income. Could she make Celia an allowance—however small? If she sold the house . . ."

But, at any rate, she was living rent free—running expenses had been reduced to a minimum. The house was in bad repair, and there was very little demand for such properties at the minute.

She lay awake, tossing and turning. How to get her child her heart's desire?

4

It was awful, having to write to Peter and tell him.

Such a lame letter, too—for what could she say to excuse her treachery?

When Peter's answer came it was exactly like Peter. So like Peter that Celia cried over it.

> Don't blame yourself, Celia [wrote Peter]. It was my fault entirely. My fatal habit of putting things off. We're like that. That's why, as a family, we always miss the bus. I meant it for the best—to give you a chance of marrying some rich fellow. And now you've fallen in love with someone poorer than I am.
>
> The truth of it is you feel he's got more guts than I had. I ought to have taken you at your word when you wanted to marry me and come out with me here. . . . I was a cursed fool. I've lost you, and it's my own fault. He's a better man than I am—your Dermot. . . . He must be a good sort, or you wouldn't have taken a fancy to him. Best of luck to you both—always. And don't grieve about me. It's my funeral, not yours. . . . I could kick myself all round the town for being such a confounded fool.
>
> God bless you, my dear. . . .

Dear Peter—dear, dear Peter. . . .

She thought: "I should have been happy with Peter. Very happy always. . . ."

But with Dermot life was high adventure!

5

The year of Celia's engagement was a stormy period. She would get a letter from Dermot suddenly:

> I see now—your mother was perfectly right. We are too
> poor ever to marry. I shouldn't have asked you. Forget me
> as soon as you can.

And then, two days later, he would arrive on the borrowed motor bicycle, take a tear-stained Celia in his arms, and declare that he couldn't give her up. Something *must* happen.

What happened was the war.

6

The war came to Celia as to most people like an utterly improbably thunderbolt. A murdered archduke, a "war scare" in the newspapers— such things barely entered her consciousness.

And then, suddenly, Germany and Russia were actually at war— Belgium was invaded. The fantastically improbable became possible.

Letters from Dermot:

> It looks as though we're going to be in it. Everyone says if
> we are it will be over by Christmas. They say I'm a pessimist,
> but I think it will be a jolly sight more like two years . . .

And then the accomplished fact—England at war. . . .

Meaning to Celia one thing only—*Dermot may be killed.* . . .

A telegram—he couldn't get away to say good-bye to her—could she and her mother come to him?

The banks were closed but Miriam had a couple of five-pound notes (Grannie's training: "Always have a five-pound note in your bag, dear"). The ticket office at the station refused to take the notes. They went round through the goods yard, crossed the line, and entered the train. Ticket collector after ticket collector—no tickets? "No, ma'am, can't take a five-pound note—" endless writing down of names and address.

All a nightmare—nothing was real but Dermot. . . .

Dermot in khaki—a different Dermot—very jerky and flippant, with haunted eyes. No one knows about this new war—it's the kind of war where *no one might come back*. . . . New engines of destruction. The air—nobody knows about the air. . . .

Celia and Dermot were two children clinging together. . . .

"Let me come through. . . ."

"Oh, God, let him come back to me. . . ."

Nothing else mattered.

7

The awful suspense of those first weeks. The postcards faintly scrawled in pencil.

> *"Not allowed to say where we are. Everything goes well. Love."*

Nobody knew what was happening.

The shock of the first casualty lists.

Friends. Boys that you had danced with—killed. . . .

But Dermot was safe—and that was all that mattered.

War, for most women, is the destiny of one person. . . .

8

After that first week and fortnight of suspense there were things to be done at home. A Red Cross hospital was being opened near Celia's home, but she must pass her First Aid and Nursing exam. There were classes going on near Grannie, and Celia went up to stay.

Gladys, the new, pretty young house parlor maid, opened the door. She and a young cook now ran the establishment. Poor old Sarah was no more.

"How are you, miss?"

"Very well. Where's Grannie?"

A giggle.

"She's out, Miss Celia."

"*Out?*"

Grannie—now just on ninety years of age—more particular than ever about letting injurious fresh air touch her. Grannie *out?*

"She went to the Army and Navy Stores, Miss Celia. She said she'd be back before you came. Oh, I believe there she is now."

An aged four-wheeler had drawn up at the gate. Assisted by the cabman, Grannie descended cautiously onto her good leg.

She came with a firm step up the drive. Grannie looked jaunty, positively jaunty—the bugles on her mantel were swaying and glinting in the September sunshine.

"So you've arrived, Celia darling."

Such a soft old face—like crinkled rose leaves. Grannie was very fond of Celia—and was knitting bed socks for Dermot, to keep his feet warm in the trenches.

Her voice changed as she looked at Gladys. More and more did Grannie enjoy bullying "the maids" (well able to take care of themselves nowadays, and keeping bicycles whether Grannie liked it or not!).

"Now then, Gladys," sharply, "why can't you go and help the man with the things? And no taking them into the kitchen, mind. Put them in the morning room."

No longer did Poor Miss Bennett reign in the morning room.

Piled inside the door were flour, biscuits, dozens of tins of sardines, rice, tapioca, sago. Grinning from ear to ear the cabman appeared. He was carrying five hams. Gladys followed with more hams. Sixteen in all were deposited in the treasure chamber.

"I may be ninety," said Grannie (who wasn't, yet, but anticipated the event as more dramatic), "but I shan't let the Germans starve *me* out!"

Celia was taken with hysterical laughter.

Grannie paid the cabman, gave him an enormous tip, and directed him to feed his horse better.

"Yes, mum, thank you, mum."

He touched his hat and, still grinning, departed.

"Such a day as I've had," said Grannie, untying her bonnet strings. She displayed no signs of fatigue and had obviously enjoyed herself.

"The Stores were packed, my dear."

Apparently with other old ladies, all carrying off hams in four-wheeled cabs.

9

Celia never took up Red Cross work.

Several things happened. First, Rouncy broke up and went home to live with her brother. Celia and her mother did the work of the house with the disapproving aid of Gregg, who "didn't hold" with war and ladies doing things they weren't meant to do.

Then Grannie wrote to Miriam.

> Dearest Miriam: You suggested some years ago that I should make my home with you. I refused then, as I felt too old to make a move. But Dr. Holt (such a *clever* man—and enjoys a good story—I'm afraid his wife doesn't really appreciate him) says my eyesight is failing and that nothing can be done about it. That is God's will and I accept it, but I do not fancy being left *at the mercy of maids.* Such wicked things as one reads of nowadays—*and I have missed several things lately.* Do not mention this when you write—they may *open my letters.* I am posting this *myself.* So I think that it will be best for me to come to you. It will make things easier, as my income will help. I do not like the idea of Celia doing things in the house. The dear child should *reserve her strength.* You remember Mrs. Pinchin's Eva? Just that same delicate complexion. She *overdid things* and is now in a Sanatorium in Switzerland. You and Celia must come and help me to *move.* It will be a terrible business, I'm afraid.

It *was* a terrible business. Grannie had lived in the house at Wimbledon for fifty years, and, true product of a thrifty generation, she had never thrown away anything that might possibly "come in."

There were vast wardrobes and chests of drawers of solid mahogany, each drawer and shelf crammed with neatly rolled bundles of materials and odds and ends put away safely by Grannie and forgotten. There were innumerable "remnants," odd lengths of silks and satins, and prints and cottons. There were dozens of needle books "for the maids at Christmas," with the needles rusted in them. There were old scraps and pieces of gowns. There were letters and papers and diaries and recipes and newspaper cuttings. There were forty-four pincushions and thirty-five pairs of scissors. There were drawers and drawers full of fine linen underclothes all gone into holes, but preserved because of "the good embroidery, my dear."

Saddest of all there was the store cupboard (memory of Celia's youth). The store cupboard had defeated Grannie. She could no longer penetrate into its depths. Stores had lain their undisturbed while fresh stores accumulated on top of them. Weevily flour, crumbling biscuits, moldy jams, liquescent mass of preserved fruits—all these were disinterred from the depths and thrown away while Grannie sat and wept and lamented the "shameful waste." "Surely, Miriam, they would do very nicely for puddings for the kitchen?"

Poor Grannie—so able and energetic and thrifty a housewife—defeated by age and failing sight, and forced to sit and see alien eyes surveying her defeat. . . .

She fought tooth and nail for every one of her treasures that this ruthless younger generation wanted to throw away.

"Not my brown velvet. That's my brown *velvet*. Madame Bonserot made it for me in Paris. So Frenchy! Everyone admired me in it."

"But it's all worn, dear, the nap has gone. It's in holes."

"It would do up. I'm sure it would do up."

Poor Grannie—old, defenseless, at the mercy of these younger folk—so scornful, so full of their "That's no good, throw it away."

She had been brought up never to throw away anything. It might come in someday. They didn't know that, these young folk.

They tried to be kind. They yielded so far to her wishes as to fill a dozen old-fashioned trunks with bits and pieces of stuffs and old motheaten furs—all things that could never be used, but why upset the old lady more than need be?

Grannie herself insisted on packing various faded pictures of old-fashioned gentlemen.

"That's dear Mr. Harty—and Mr. Lord—such a handsome couple as we made dancing together! Everyone remarked on it."

Alas, for Grannie's packing! Mr. Harty and Mr. Lord arrived with the glass shattered in the frames. And yet, once Grannie's packing had been celebrated. Nothing she packed was ever broken.

Sometimes, when she thought no one was looking, Grannie would surreptitiously retrieve little bits of trimming, a jet ornament, a little piece of net ruching, a crochet motif. She would stuff them into that capacious pocket of hers, and would secretly transfer them to one of the great ark-like trunks that stood in her bedroom ready for her personal packing.

Poor Grannie, Moving nearly killed her, but it didn't quite. She had the will to live. It was the will to live that was driving her out of the home she had lived in so long. The Germans were not going to starve her out—and they were not going to get her in an air raid, either. Grannie meant to live and enjoy life. When you had reached ninety years you knew how extraordinarily enjoyable life was. That was what the young people didn't understand. They spoke as though anyone old were half dead and sure to be miserable. Young people, thought Grannie, remembering an aphorism of her youth, thought the old people fools, but old people *knew* that young people were fools! Her aunt Caroline had said that at the age of eighty-five and her aunt Caroline had been right.

Anyway, Grannie didn't think much of young people nowadays. They had no stamina. Look at the furniture removers—four strapping young men—and they actually asked her to empty the drawers of her big mahogany chest of drawers.

"It was carried up with every drawer locked," said Grannie.

"You see, ma'am, it's solid mahogany. And there's heavy stuff in the drawers."

"So there was when it came up! There were men in those days. You're all weaklings nowadays. Making a fuss about a little weight."

The young men grinned, and with some difficulty the chest was got down the stairs and out to the van.

"That's better," said Grannie approvingly. "You see, you don't know what you can do until you try."

Among the various things removed from the house were thirty demi-johns of Grannie's homemade liqueurs. Only twenty-eight were unloaded the other end. . . .

Was this, perhaps, the revenge of the grinning young men?

"Rogues," said Grannie. "That's what they are—rogues. And call themselves teetotallers too. The impudence of it."

But she tipped them handsomely and was not really displeased. It was, after all, a subtle compliment to her homemade liqueur. . . .

10

When Grannie was installed, a cook was found to replace Rouncy. This was a girl of twenty-eight called Mary. She was good-natured and pleasant to elderly people, and chattered to Grannie about her young man and her relations who suffered from an agreeable number of complaints. Grannie delighted ghoulishly in the bad legs, varicose veins, and other ailments of Mary's relations. She gave her bottles of patent medicines and shawls for them.

Celia began to think once more about taking up war work, though Grannie combated the idea vigorously, prophesying the most dire disasters if Celia "overstrained" herself.

Grannie loved Celia. She gave her mysterious warnings against all the dangers of life, and five-pound notes. One of Grannie's fixed beliefs in life was that you should always have a five-pound note "handy."

She gave Celia fifty pounds in five-pound notes and told her to "keep it by her."

"Don't even let your husband know you've got it. A woman never knows when she may need a little nest egg. . . .

"Remember, dear, men are not to be trusted. Gentlemen can be very agreeable, but you can't trust one of them—unless he's such a namby-pamby fellow that he's no good at all."

11

The move and all that had gone with it had successfully distracted Celia's mind from the war and Dermot.

Now that Grannie was settled in, Celia began to chafe at her own inactivity.

How keep herself from thinking of Dermot—out there?

In desperation she married off "the girls"! Isabella married a rich Jew, Elsie married an explorer. Ella became a schoolteacher. She married an elderly man, somewhat of an invalid, who was charmed by her young chatter. Ethel and Annie kept house together. Vera had a romantic morganatic alliance with a royal prince, and they both died tragically in a motor accident on their wedding day.

Planning the weddings, choosing the bridesmaids' gowns, arranging the funeral music for Vera—all this helped to keep Celia's mind from realities.

She longed to be hard at work at something. But it meant leaving home. . . . Could Miriam and Grannie spare her?

Grannie required a good deal of attention. Celia felt she couldn't desert her mother.

But it was Miriam herself who urged Celia to leave home. She understood well enough that work, hard physical work, was the thing that would help Celia at the present time.

Grannie wept, but Miriam stood firm.

"Celia must go."

But, after all, Celia didn't take up any war work.

Dermot got wounded in the arm and came home to a hospital. On his recovery he was passed fit for home service and was sent to the War Office. He and Celia were married.

Chapter 10

MARRIAGE

Celia's ideas about marriage were limited in the extreme.

Marriage, for her, was the "living happily ever afterward" of her favorite fairy tales. She saw no difficulties in it, no possibilities of shipwreck. When people loved each other they were happy. Unhappy marriages, and of course she knew there were many such, were because people didn't love each other.

Neither Grannie's Rabelaisian descriptions of the male character, nor her mother's warnings (so old-fashioned they sounded to Celia) that you had to "keep a man," nor any amount of realistic literature with sordid and unhappy endings really made any impression on Celia at all. "The men" of Grannie's conversation never struck her as being the same species as Dermot. People in books were people in books, and Miriam's warnings struck Celia as peculiarly amusing considering the extraordinary happiness of her mother's own married life.

"You know, Mummy, Daddy never looked at anybody but you."

"No, but then he'd spent a very gay life as a young man."

"I don't believe you like Dermot or trust him."

"I do like him," said Miriam. "I find him extremely attractive."

Celia laughed, and said:

"But you wouldn't think anybody I married good enough for ME—your precious pet lamb pigeony pumpkin—come now, would you? Not the superest of supermen."

And Miriam had to confess that perhaps that was true.

And Celia and Dermot were so happy together.

Miriam told herself that she had been unduly suspicious and hostile toward the man who had taken her daughter away from her.

2

Dermot as a husband was quite different from what Celia had imagined. All the boldness, the masterfulness, the audacity of him fell from him. He was young, diffident, very much in love, and Celia was his first love.

In some ways, indeed, he was rather like Jim Grant. But whereas Jim's diffidence had annoyed Celia because she was not in love with him, Dermot's diffidence made him still dearer to her.

She had been, half-consciously, a little afraid of Dermot. He had been a stranger to her. She had felt that though she loved him she knew nothing about him.

Johnnie de Burgh had appealed to the physical side of her, Jim to the mental, Peter was woven into the very stuff of her life, but in Dermot she found what she had never yet had—a playmate.

There was something that was to be eternally boyish in Dermot—it found and met the child in Celia. Their aims, their minds, their characters were poles apart, but they each wanted a playfellow and found that playfellow in the other.

Married life to them was a game—they played at it enthusiastically.

3

What are the things one remembers in life? Not the so-called important things. No—little things—trivialities . . . staying persistently in the memory—not to be shaken off.

Looking back on her early married life, what did Celia remember?

Buying a frock in a dressmaker's—the first frock Dermot bought her. She tried them on in a little cubicle with an elderly woman to help her. Then Dermot was called in to say which he would like.

They both enjoyed it hugely.

Dermot pretended, of course, that he had often done this before. They weren't going to admit they were newly married before the shop people—not likely!

Dermot even said nonchalantly:

"That's rather like the one I got you in Monte two years ago."

They decided at last on a periwinkle blue with a little bunch of rose-buds on the shoulder.

. Celia kept that frock. She never threw it away.

4

House-hunting! They must, of course, have a furnished house or flat. There was no knowing when Dermot would be ordered abroad again. And it must be as cheap as possible.

Neither Celia nor Dermot knew anything about neighborhoods or prices. They started confidently in the heart of Mayfair!

The next day they were in South Kensington, Chelsea, and Bayswater. They reached West Kensington, Hammersmith, West Hampstead, Battersea, and other outlying neighborhoods the day after.

In the end they were undecided between two. One was a self-contained flat at three guineas a week. It was in a block of mansions in West Kensington. It was scrupulously clean and belonged to an awe-inspiring maiden lady called Miss Banks. Miss Banks radiated efficiency.

"No plate or linen? That simplifies things. I never permit agents to make the inventory. I am sure you will agree with me that it is a sheer waste of money. You and I can check over things together."

It was a long time since anyone had frightened Celia as much as Miss Banks did. Every question she asked served to expose anew Celia's complete lack of knowledge where flat-taking was concerned.

Dermot said they would let Miss Banks know, and they got away into the street.

"What do you think?" asked Celia breathlessly. "It's very clean."

She had never thought about cleanliness before, but two days' investigation of cheap furnished flats had brought the matter home to her.

"Some of those other flats simply *smelled*," she added.

"I know—and it's quite decently furnished, and Miss Banks says it's a good shopping neighborhood. I'm not quite sure I like Miss Banks herself. She's such a tartar."

"She is."

"I feel she knows too much for us."

"Let's go and look at the other again. After all, it's cheaper."

The other was two and half guineas a week. It was the top floor of an old decayed house that had known better days. There were only two rooms and a large kitchen, but they were big rooms, nobly proportioned, and they looked out over a garden which actually had two trees in it.

It was, undeniably, not nearly as clean as the flat of the efficient Miss Banks, but it was, Celia said, quite a nice kind of dirt. The wallpaper showed damp, and the paint was peeling, and the boards needed restaining. But the cretonne covers were clean, though so faded as hardly to show the pattern, and it had big, comfortable, shabby armchairs.

There was another great attraction to it in Celia's eyes. The woman who lived in the basement would be able to cook for them. And she looked a nice woman, fat, good-natured, with a kindly eye that reminded Celia of Rouncy.

"We shouldn't have to look for a servant."

"That's true. You're sure it will be all right for you, though? It's not shut off from the rest of the house, and it isn't—well, it isn't what you've been accustomed to, Celia. I mean your home is so lovely."

Yes, home was lovely. She realized now how lovely it was. The mellow dignity of the Chippendale and the Hepplewhite, the china, the fresh cool chintzes. . . . Home might be getting shabby—the roof leaked, the range was old-fashioned, the carpets were showing wear, but it was still beautiful. . . .

"But as soon as the war is over"—Dermot stuck out his chin in his determined way—"I mean to set to at something and make money for you."

"I don't want money. And besides, you're a captain already. You wouldn't have been a captain for ten years if it hadn't been for the war."

"A captain's pay is no good, really. There's no future in the army. I shall find something better. Now I've got you to work for, I feel I could do anything. And I shall."

Celia felt a thrill at his words. Dermot was so different from Peter. He didn't accept life. He set out to change it. And she felt he would succeed.

She thought:

"I was right to marry him. I don't care what anyone says. Someday they'll admit that I was right."

Because, of course, there *had* been criticism. Mrs. Luke, in particular, had shown heartfelt dismay.

"But, darling Celia—your life will be too *dreadful*. Why, you won't even be able to have a kitchen maid. You'll have simply to pig it."

Farther than no kitchen maid Mrs. Luke's imagination refused to go. It was, for her, the supreme catastrophe. Celia magnanimously forbore to break it to her that they mightn't even have a cook!

Then Cyril, who was fighting in Mesopotamia, had written a long disapproving letter on hearing of her engagement. He said it was an absurd business.

But Dermot was ambitious. He would succeed. He had a quality in him—a driving power—that Celia felt and admired. It was so different from anything she possessed herself.

"Let's have this flat," she said. "I like it best—I really do. And Miss Lestrange is much nicer than Miss Banks."

Miss Lestrange was an amiable woman of thirty with a twinkle in her eye and a good-natured smile.

If this serious young house-hunting couple amused her, she did not show it. She agreed to all their suggestions, imparted a certain amount of tactful information and explained the working of the geyser to an awestricken Celia who had never met such a thing before.

"But you can't have baths often," she said cheerfully. "The ration of gas is only forty thousand cubic feet—and you've got to cook, remember."

So Celia and Dermot took 8 Lanchester Terrace for six months, and Celia started her career as a housewife.

5

The thing that Celia suffered from most in her early married life was loneliness.

Dermot went off to the War Office every morning, and Celia was left with a long empty day on her hands.

Pender, Dermot's batman, served up a breakfast of bacon and eggs, cleaned up the flat, and left to draw the rations. Mrs. Steadman then came up from the basement to discuss the evening meal with Celia.

Mrs. Steadman was warmhearted, talkative, and a willing if somewhat uncertain cook. She was, she admitted herself, "heavy in hand with the pepper." There seemed to be no halfway course with her between completely unseasoned food or something that brought the tears to your eyes and made you choke.

"I've always been like that—ever since a girl," said Mrs. Steadman cheerfully. "Curious, isn't it? And I've no hand for pastry, either."

Mrs. Steadman took motherly command of Celia, who was anxious to be economical and was uncertain how to do it.

"You'd better let me shop for you. A young lady like you would get taken advantage of. You'd never think to stand a herring up on its tail to test its freshness. And some of these fish salesmen are that artful."

Mrs. Steadman shook her head darkly.

Housekeeping was complicated by its being wartime. Eggs were eightpence each. Celia and Dermot lived a good deal on "egg substitutes," soup squares which, no matter what their advertised flavor, Dermot always referred to as "brown-sand soup," and their meat ration.

The meat ration excited Mrs. Steadman more than anything had done for a long time. When Pender returned with the first huge chunk of beef, Celia and Mrs. Steadman walked admiringly round it, while Mrs. Steadman gave tongue freely.

"Isn't that a beautiful sight now? Fairly makes my mouth water. I haven't seen a bit of meat like that since the war began. A picture, that's what I call it. I wish Steadman were at home, I'd get him up to see it— you not objecting, ma'am. It would be a treat for him to see a bit of meat like that. If you're wanting to roast it, I don't think it will go in that tiny gas oven. I'll cook it downstairs for you."

Celia pressed Mrs. Steadman to accept some slices of it when cooked, and after a proper reluctance Mrs. Steadman consented.

"Just for once—though not wishing to impose on you."

So free had been Mrs. Steadman's admiration that Celia herself felt quite excited when "the joint" was placed proudly on the table.

For lunch Celia usually went out and fetched something from a national kitchen nearby. She did not dare to use up the gas ration too early in the week. By using the gas stove only morning and evening, and reducing baths to twice a week, they could just keep within it and allow for firing in the sitting room.

In the matter of butter and sugar Mrs. Steadman was a valuable ally, producing supplies of these commodities much in excess of the ration tickets.

"They know me, you see," she said to Celia. "Young Alfred, he always tips me the wink when I come in. 'Plenty for you, Ma,' he says. But he doesn't go handing it out to every fine lady that comes in. He and I know each other."

Thus cared for by Mrs. Steadman, Celia had her whole day practically to herself.

And she found it increasingly difficult to know what to do with it!

At home there had been the garden, the flowers to do, her piano. There had been Miriam. . . .

Here there was nobody. Such friends as she had in London were either married or gone elsewhere or were engaged in war work. Most of them, too, were frankly too rich now for Celia to keep up with. As an unmarried girl she had been asked freely to houses, to dances, to parties at Ranelagh and Hurlingham. But now, as a married woman, all that ceased. She and Dermot could not entertain people in return. People had never meant much to Celia, but she did feel the inactivity of her days. She proposed to Dermot taking up hospital work.

He negatived the idea violently. He hated the idea of it. Celia gave in to him. In the end he agreed to her taking up a course of typewriting and shorthand. Also bookkeeping which, as Celia pointed out, would be useful to her if she wanted a job afterward.

She found life much pleasanter now she had some work to do. She took an extreme pleasure in bookkeeping—the neatness and accuracy of which pleased her.

And then there was the joy of Dermot's return. They were both so excited and happy in their new life together.

Best of all was the time when they would sit in front of the fire before going to bed, Dermot with a cup of Ovaltine, Celia with a cup of Bovril.

They could as yet hardly believe it was true—that they were really together for always.

Dermot was not demonstrative. He never said, "I love you," hardly ever attempted a spontaneous caress. When he did break through his reserve and say something, Celia treasured it up as something to remember. It was so obviously difficult for him that she prized these chance words and sayings all the more. They always startled her when they came.

They would be sitting talking of the oddities of Mrs. Steadman when suddenly Dermot would clutch her to him and stammer:

"Celia—you're so beautiful—so beautiful. Promise me you'll always be beautiful."

"You'd love me just the same if I weren't."

"No. Not quite. It wouldn't be quite the same. Promise me. Say you'll always be beautiful. . . ."

6

Three months after settling in, Celia went home for a week's visit. She found her mother looking ill and tired. Grannie, on the other hand, was looking blooming and had a splendid repertoire of German atrocity stories.

Miriam was like a drooping flower placed in water. The day after Celia's return she had revived—was her old self again.

"Have you missed me so terribly, Mummy?"

"Yes, darling. Don't talk about it. It had to come someday. And you're happy—you look happy."

"Yes, oh, Mummy, you were quite wrong about Dermot. He's kind—he's so kind that nobody could be kinder. . . . And we have such fun. You know how I adore oysters. For a joke he got a dozen and put them in my bed—said it was an oyster bed—oh, it sounds silly told, but we laughed and laughed. He's such a dear. And so good. I don't think he's ever done a mean or dishonorable thing in his life. Pender, that's his batman, thinks the world of 'the captain.' He's rather critical of me. I don't believe he thinks I'm good enough for his idol. He said the other day, 'The captain's very fond of onions, but we never seem to have them here.' So we had fried ones at once. Mrs. Steadman's on my side. She always wants me to have the food I like. She says men are all very well, but if she once gave into Steadman where would she be? she'd like to know."

Celia sat on her mother's bed, chatting happily.

It was lovely to be home—home looked so much lovelier than she remembered. It was so *clean*—the spotless cloth for lunch, and the shining silver and the polished glasses. How much one took for granted!

The food, too, though very plain, was delicious, appetizingly cooked and served.

Mary, her mother told her, was going to join the W. A. A. C. S.

"I think it's quite right that she should. She's young."

Gregg had proved unexpectedly difficult since the war. She grumbled unceasingly at the food.

"A hot meat dinner every day is what I've been used to—these insides and this fish—it's not right and it's not nourishing."

In vain Miriam tried to explain the restrictions in war time. Gregg was too old to take it in.

"Economy's one thing—proper food's another. And margarine I never have eaten and never will. My father would turn in his grave if he knew his daughter was eating margarine—and in a proper gentleman's house too."

Miriam laughed when telling this to Celia.

"At first I was rather weak and used to give her the butter and eat margarine myself. Then, one day, I wrapped the butter in the margarine paper, and the margarine in the butter paper. I took them both out and told her this was unusually good margarine—just like butter—would she taste it? She did and pulled a face at once. No, indeed, she couldn't eat stuff like that. So then I produced the real margarine in the butter paper and said did she like that better? She tasted it and said, 'Ah, yes, that was the right thing.' So then I told her the truth and I was rather fierce—and since then we share the butter and margarine equally, and we've had no fuss."

Grannie was also adamant on the subject of food.

"I hope, Celia, you take plenty of butter and eggs. They're *good* for you."

"Well, one can't get very much butter, Grannie."

"Nonsense, my dear, it's good for you. You must have it. That beautiful girl, Mrs. Riley's daughter, died only the other day. Starved herself. Out working all day—and all these scraps at home. Pneumonia on top of influenza. I could have told her how it would be."

And Grannie nodded cheerfully over her knitting needles.

Poor Grannie, her sight was failing badly. She only knitted on big pins now, and even then she often dropped a stitch or made a mistake in the pattern. Then she would sit weeping quietly—the tears running down her old roseleaf cheeks.

"It's the waste of time," she would say. "It makes me so mad."

She was getting increasingly suspicious of her surroundings.

When Celia came into her bedroom in the morning she would often find the old lady crying.

"It's my earrings, dearie, my diamond earrings your grandfather gave me. That girl has taken them."

"Which girl?"

"Mary. She tried to poison me too. She put something in my boiled egg. I tasted it."

"Oh, no, Grannie, you couldn't put anything in a *boiled* egg."

"I tasted it, my dear. Bitter on my tongue." Grannie made a face. "A servant girl poisoned her mistress only the other day, I heard about it in the paper. She knows I know about her taking my things. Several things I've missed. And now my beautiful earrings."

Grannie wept again.

"Are you sure, Grannie? Perhaps they're in the drawer all the time."

"It's no use your looking, dear, they're gone."

"Which drawer was it?"

"The right-hand one—where she passed with the tray. I rolled them up in my mittens. But it's no use. I looked carefully."

Then Celia would produce the earrings rolled up in a strip of lace, and Grannie would express delighted surprise and say that Celia was a good, clever girl, but her suspicions of Mary remained unabated.

She would lean forward in her chair and hiss excitedly.

"Celia—your bag. Your handbag. Where is it?"

"In my room, Grannie."

"They're up there now. I heard them."

"Yes, they're doing the room."

"They've been a long time. They're looking for your bag. Always keep it with you."

Writing checks was another thing Grannie found very difficult with her failing eyesight. She would get Celia to stand over her and tell her where to start and when she was reaching the end of the paper.

Then, with a sigh, the check written, she would give it to Celia to take to the bank to cash.

"You'll notice I've made it out for ten pounds, although the bills come to just under nine. But never make out a check for nine pounds, Celia, remember that. It's so easily altered into ninety."

Since Celia herself was cashing the check, she was the only person who could have had the opportunity of altering it, but Grannie had not perceived that. It was merely part of her fury for self-preservation.

Another thing that upset her was when Miriam gently told her that she must have some more dresses made.

"You know, Mother, the one you've got on is almost frayed through."

"My velvet? My beautiful velvet?"

"Yes, you can't see. But it's really in a terrible state."

Grannie would sigh piteously, and tears would come into her eyes.

"My velvet. My good velvet. I got this velvet in Paris."

Grannie was suffering from having been uprooted from her surroundings. She found the country terribly dull after Wimbledon. So few people dropped in, and there was nothing going on. She never went outside into the garden, for fear of the air. She sat in the dining room as she had sat in Wimbledon. Miriam read the papers to her, and after that the days passed slowly for both of them.

Almost Grannie's only relaxation was the ordering in of large quantities of foodstuffs, and after they had arrived the discussion and selection of a good hiding place for them so that they should not be convicted of "hoarding." The tops of the cabinets were filled with tins of sardines and biscuits; tinned tongues and packets of sugar were concealed in unexpected cupboards. Grannie's own trunks were full of tins of golden syrup.

"But, Grannie, you really oughtn't to hoard food."

"Tchah!" Grannie gave a good-humored laugh. "You young people don't know about things. In the siege of Paris people ate rats. *Rats*. Forethought, Celia, I was brought up to have forethought."

And then Grannie's face would go suddenly alert.

"The servants—*they're in your room again. What about your jewelry?*"

7

Celia had been feeling slightly sick for some days. Finally she took to her bed and was prostrate with violent nausea.

She said:

"Mummy, do you think this means I'm going to have a baby?"

"I'm afraid so."

Miriam looked worried and depressed.

"Afraid?" Celia was surprised. "Don't you want me to have a baby?"

"No, I didn't. Not yet. Do you want one yourself very much?"

"Well—" Celia considered—"I hadn't thought about it. We've never talked about having a baby, Dermot and I. I suppose we knew we might have one. I wouldn't like not to have one. I should feel I'd missed something . . ."

Dermot came down for the weekend.

It was not at all like in books. Celia was still being violently sick the whole time.

"Why are you so sick, do you think, Celia?"

"Well, I expect I'm going to have a baby."

Dermot was terribly upset.

"I didn't want you to have one. I feel a brute—an absolute brute. I can't bear you to be sick and miserable."

"But, Dermot, I'm very pleased about it. We'd hate not to have a baby."

"I wouldn't care. I don't want a baby. You'll think of it all the time and not of me."

"I shan't. I shan't."

"Yes, you will. Women do. They're forever being domestic and messing about with a baby. They forget about their husbands altogether."

"I shan't. I shall love the baby because it's your baby—don't you understand? It's because it's *your* baby that it's exciting—not because it's *a* baby. And I shall always love you best—always—always—always. . . ."

Dermot turned away—tears in his eyes.

"I can't bear it. I've done this to you. I could have prevented it. You might even die."

"I shan't die. I'm frightfully strong."

"Your grandmother says you're very delicate."

"Oh, that's just Grannie. She can't bear to believe anyone enjoys rude health."

Dermot took a lot of comforting. His anxiety and misery on her behalf touched Celia deeply.

When they returned to London he waited on her hand and foot, urging her to take patent foods and quack medicines to stop the sickness.

"It gets better after three months. The books say so."

"Three months is a long time. I don't want you to be sick for three months."

"It is rather beastly, but it can't be helped."

Expectant motherhood, Celia felt, was distinctly disappointing. It was so different in books. She had visualized herself sitting sewing little garments while she thought beautiful thoughts about the coming child.

But how could one think beautiful thoughts when one was in the condition of one on a Channel steamer? Intense nausea blots out all thought! Celia was just a healthy but suffering animal.

She was sick not only in the early morning, but all day long at irregular intervals. Apart from the discomfort, it made life somewhat of a nightmare to her, since she never knew when the fit would seize her. Twice she jumped off a bus in the nick of time and was sick in the gutter. Under these circumstances, invitations to people's houses could not safely be accepted.

Celia stayed at home feeling miserably ill, occasionally going for a walk for exercise. She had to give up her secretarial training. Sewing made her giddy. She lay in a chair and read, or listened to the rich obstetric reminiscences of Mrs. Steadman.

"It was when I was carrying Beatrice, I remember. It come over me in the greengrocer's sudden like (I'd dropped in for a half of sprouts). *I've got to have that pear!* Big and juicy, it was—the expensive kind that rich people has for dessert. Before you could say knife, I'd up and ate it! The lad who was serving me, he stared—and no wonder. But the proprietor, he was a family man, he knew what it was. 'That's all right, son,' he said. 'Don't you take no notice.' 'I'm ever so sorry,' I said. 'That's all right,' he said. 'I've got seven myself, and the missus had a fancy for nothing but pickled pork the last time.' "

Mrs. Steadman paused for breath, and added:

"I wish your Ma could be with you, but of course there's the old lady, your grandmother, to be considered."

So did Celia wish her mother could come to her. The days were a nightmare. It was a foggy winter—day after day of fog. So terribly long till Dermot returned.

But he was so sweet when he did. So anxious about her. He had usually some new book he had bought on pregnancy. After dinner he used to read out extracts from it.

"*Women sometimes have a craving for strange and exotic food at these times. In olden days such cravings were always supposed to be satisfied. Nowadays they should be controlled when of a harmful character.* Do you feel any longings for strange exotic foods, Celia?"

"I don't care what I eat."

"I've been reading up about twilight sleep. It seems quite the thing to have."

"Dermot, when do you think I shall stop being sick? It's past four months."

"Oh, it's bound to stop soon. All the books say so."

But in spite of what the books said, it didn't. It went on and on.

Dermot, of his own accord, suggested that Celia should go home.

"It's so dreadful for you here all day."

But Celia refused. He would, she knew, feel hurt if she went. And she didn't want to go. Of course, it was going to be all right; she wouldn't die, as Dermot so absurdly suggested, but—just in case—after all, women sometimes did—she wasn't going to miss a minute of her time with Dermot. . . .

Sick as she was, she still loved Dermot—more than ever.

And he was so sweet to her—and so funny.

Sitting one evening, she watched his lips moving.

"What is it, Dermot? What are you saying to yourself?"

Dermot looked rather sheepish.

"I was just imagining that the doctor said to me, 'We can't save both the mother and the child.' And I said, 'Hack the child in pieces.' "

"Dermot, how brutal of you."

"I hate him for what he's doing to you—if it is a he. I want it to be a she. I wouldn't mind having a blue-eyed long-legged daughter. But I hate the thought of a beastly little boy."

"It's a boy. I want a boy. A boy just like you."

"I shall beat him."

"How horrid you are."

"It's the duty of fathers to beat their children."

"You're jealous, Dermot."

He was jealous, horribly jealous.

"You're beautiful. I want you all to myself."

Celia laughed and said:

"I'm particularly beautiful just now!"

"You will be again. Look at Gladys Cooper. She's had two children, and she's just as lovely as ever. It's a great consolation to me to think of that."

"Dermot, I wish you wouldn't insist so on beauty. It—it frightens me."

"But why? You're going to be beautiful for years and years and years. . . ."

Celia gave a slight grimace and moved uncomfortably.

"What is it? Pain?"

"No, a sort of stitch in my side—very tiresome. Like something knocking."

"It isn't *it*, I suppose. It says in that last book that after the fifth month—"

"Oh, but, Dermot, do you mean that 'flutter under the heart'? It always sounded so poetical and lovely. I thought it would be a lovely feeling. It can't be this."

But it was this!

Her child, Celia said, must be a very active one. It spent its time kicking.

Because of this athletic activity they christened him Punch.

"Punch been very active today?" Dermot would ask as he returned.

"Terrible," Celia would reply. "Not a minute's peace, but I think he's gone to sleep for a bit now."

"I expect," said Dermot, "that he's going to be a professional pugilist."

"No, I don't want his nose broken."

What Celia wished for most was that her mother should come to her, but Grannie had not been well—a touch of bronchitis (attributed by her to having inadvertently opened a window in her bedroom), and though longing to come to Celia, Miriam did not like to leave the old lady.

"I feel I am responsible for Grannie and mustn't leave her—especially as she mistrusts the servants, but—oh, my darling, I want to be with you so much. Can't you come here?"

But Celia would not leave Dermot—at the back of her mind that faint shadowy fear—"I might die."

It was Grannie who took the matter into her own hands. She wrote to Celia in her thin spidery handwriting—now erratically astray on the paper owing to her failing sight.

Dearest Celia: I have insisted on your mother going to you. It is very bad for you in your condition to have desires that are not satisfied. Your dear mother wants to go, I know, but doesn't like leaving me alone with servants. I will not say anything about that, as *one never knows who reads one's letters.*

Be sure, dear child, to keep your feet up a good deal, and remember not to put your hand to your skin if you are looking at
a piece of salmon or lobster. My mother put her hand to her neck
when she was expecting and was looking at a piece of salmon at
the time, and so your aunt Caroline was born with a mark like a
piece of salmon on the side of her neck.

I enclose a five-pound note (half—the other half follows sepa-
rately), and be sure you buy yourself any little delicacy you fancy.

With fond love,

Your loving Grannie.

Miriam's visit was a great delight to Celia. They made her a bed in
the sitting room on the divan, and Dermot was particularly charming
to her. It was doubtful if that would have affected Miriam, but his
tenderness to Celia did.

"I think perhaps it was jealousy that made me not like Dermot," she
confessed. "You know, darling, even now, I can't like anyone who has
taken you away from me."

On the third day of her visit Miriam got a telegram and hurried
home. Grannie died a day later—almost her last words being to tell
Celia never to jump off or on a bus. "Young married women never
think of these things."

Grannie had no idea that she was dying. She fretted because she
was not getting on with the little bootikins she was knitting for Celia's
baby. . . . She died without it having entered her head that she would
not live to see her great-grandchild.

8

Grannie's death made little difference financially to Miriam and Celia.
The larger part of her income had been a life interest from her third
husband's estate. Of the remaining money, various small legacies ac-
counted for more than half of it. The remainder was left to Miriam and
Celia. While Miriam was worse off (since Grannie's income had helped
to keep up the house) Celia was the possessor of a hundred a year of
her own. With Dermot's consent and approval she turned this over to

Miriam to help with the upkeep of "home." More than ever, now, she hated the idea of selling it, and her mother agreed. A country home to which Celia's children could come—so Miriam visualized it.

"And besides, darling, you may need it yourself one of these days—when I am gone. I should like to feel it was there to be a refuge to you."

Celia thought refuge was a funny word to use, but she liked the idea of someday going to live at home with Dermot.

Dermot, however, saw the matter differently.

"Naturally you're fond of your own home, but, all the same, I don't suppose it will ever be of much use to us."

"We might go and live there someday."

"Yes, when we're about a hundred and one. It's too far from London to be any practical use."

"Not when you retire from the army?"

"Even then I shan't want to sit down and stagnate. I shall want a job. And I'm not so sure about staying in the army after the war, but we needn't talk about that now."

Of what use to look forward? Dermot might still be ordered out to France again at any minute. He might be killed. . . .

"But I shall have his child," thought Celia.

But she knew that no child could replace Dermot in her heart. Dermot meant more to her than anyone in the world and always would.

Chapter 11

MOTHERHOOD

Celia's child was born in July, and it was born in the same room where she had been born twenty-two years ago.

Outside the deep green branches of the beech tree tapped against the window.

Putting his fears (curiously intense ones) for Celia out of sight, Dermot had resolutely regarded the role of an expectant mother as a highly amusing one. No attitude could so well have helped Celia through the weary time. She remained strong and active but obstinately seasick.

She went home about three weeks before the baby was due. At the end of that time Dermot got a week's leave and joined her. Celia hoped her baby would be born while he was there. Her mother hoped it would be born after he departed. Men, in Miriam's opinion, were nothing more nor less than a nuisance at such times.

The nurse had arrived and was so briskly cheerful and reassuring that Celia was devoured by secret terrors.

One night at dinner Celia dropped her knife and fork and cried: "Oh, Nurse!"

They went out of the room together. Nurse came back in a minute or two. She nodded to Miriam.

"Very punctual," she said, smiling. "A model patient."

"Aren't you going to telephone for the doctor?" demanded Dermot fiercely.

"Oh, there's no hurry. He won't be needed for many hours yet."

Celia came back and went on with her dinner. Afterward Miriam and the nurse went off together. They murmured of linen, and jingled keys. . . .

Celia and Dermot sat looking at each other desperately. They had joked and laughed, but now their fear was upon them.

Celia said: "I'll be all right. I know I'll be all right."

Dermot said violently: "Of course you will."

They stared at each other miserably.

"You're very strong," said Dermot.

"Very strong. And women have babies every day—one a minute isn't it?"

A spasm of pain contorted her face. Dermot cried out:

"Celia!"

"It's all right. Let's go out. The house seems like a hospital somehow."

"It's that damned nurse does it."

"She's very nice, really."

They went out into the summer night. They felt curiously isolated.

Inside the house was bustle, preparation—they heard Nurse at the telephone, her "Yes, Doctor. . . . No, Doctor. . . . Oh, yes, about ten o'clock will do nicely. . . . Yes, quite satisfactory."

Outside the night was cool and green. . . . The beech tree rustled. . . .

Two lonely children wandered there hand in hand—not knowing how to console each other. . . .

Celia said suddenly:

"I just want to say—not that anything will happen—but in case it did—that I've been so wonderfully happy that nothing in the world matters. You promised you'd make me happy, and you have. . . . I didn't dream anyone *could* be so happy."

Dermot said brokenly:

"I've brought this on you. . . ."

"I know. It's worse for you. . . . But I'm terribly happy about it—about everything. . . ."

She added:

"And afterward—we'll always love each other."

"Always, all our lives. . . ."

Nurse called from the house.

"You'd better come in now, my dear."

"I'm coming."

It was upon them now. They were being torn apart. That was the worst of it, Celia felt. Having to leave Dermot to face this new thing alone.

They clung together—all the terror of separation in their kiss.

Celia thought: "We'll never forget this night—never. . . ."

It was the fourteenth of July.

She went into the house.

2

So tired . . . so tired . . . so very tired. . . .

The room, spinning, hazy—then broadening out and settling into reality. The nurse smiling at her, the doctor washing his hands in a corner of the room. He had known her all her life, and he called out to her jocularly:

"Well, Celia, my dear, you've got a baby."

She had got a baby, had she?

It didn't seem to matter.

She was so tired.

Just that . . . tired. . . .

They seemed to be expecting her to do or say something. . . .

But she couldn't.

She just wanted to be let alone. . . .

To rest. . . .

But there was something . . . someone. . . .

She murmured: "Dermot?"

3

She had dozed off. When she opened her eyes he was there.

But what had happened to him? He looked different—so queer. He was in trouble—had had bad news or something.

She said: "What is it?"

He answered in a queer, unnatural voice: "A little daughter."

"No, I mean—you? What's the matter?"

His face crumpled up—puckered queerly. He was crying—Dermot crying!

He said brokenly: "It's been so awful—so long. . . . You don't know how ghastly it's been. . . ."

He knelt by the bed, burying his face there. She laid a hand on his head.

How much he cared. . . .

"Darling," she said. "It's all right now. . . ."

4

Here was her mother. Instinctively, at the sight of that sweet smiling face, Celia felt better—stronger. As in nursery days she felt "everything would be all right now that Mummy was here."

"Don't go away, Mummy."

"No, darling. I'm going to sit here by you."

Celia fell asleep holding her mother's hand. When she woke up, she said:

"Oh, Mummy, it feels just *wonderful* not to be sick!"

Miriam laughed.

"You're going to see your baby now. Nurse is bringing her."

"Are you sure it isn't a boy?"

"Quite sure. Girls are much nicer, Celia. You've always meant much more to me than Cyril has."

"Yes, but I was so sure it was a boy. . . . Well, Dermot will be pleased. He wanted a girl. He's got his own way."

"As usual," said Miriam dryly. "Here comes Nurse."

Nurse came in very starched and stiff and important—carrying something on a pillow.

Celia steeled herself. Newborn babies were very ugly—frightfully ugly. She must be prepared.

"Oh!" she said in a tone of great surprise.

Was this little creature her baby? She felt excited and frightened as Nurse laid her gently within the crook of her arm. This funny little Red Indian squaw with her dark thatch of hair? Nothing raw beef-like about her. A funny, adorable, comic little face.

"Eight and a half pounds," said Nurse with great satisfaction.

As often before in her life, Celia felt unreal. She was now definitely playing the part of the Young Mother.

But she did not feel at all like either a wife or a mother. She felt like a little girl come home after an exciting but tiring party.

5

Celia called the baby Judy—as being the next best thing to Punch!

Judy was a most satisfactory baby. She put on the requisite weight every week and indulged in the minimum amount of crying. When she did cry it was the angry roar of a miniature tigress.

Having, as Grannie would have put it, "taken her month," Celia left Judy with Miriam and went up to London to look about for a suitable home.

Her reunion with Dermot was particularly joyous. It was like a second honeymoon. Part of Dermot's satisfaction arose from the fact (Celia discovered) that she had left Judy to come up to him.

"I've been so afraid you'd get all domestic and not bother about me any longer."

His jealousy allayed, Dermot joined her energetically in flat hunting whenever he could. Celia now felt quite experienced in the house-hunting business—no longer was she the complete nincompoop who had been frightened away by the efficiency of Miss Banks. She might have been renting flats all her life.

They were going to take an unfurnished flat. It would be cheaper, and Miriam could easily supply them with nearly all the furniture they needed from home.

Unfurnished flats, however, were few and far between. They nearly always had a snag attached to them in the shape of a monstrous premium. As day followed day, Celia got more and more depressed.

It was Mrs. Steadman who saved the situation.

She appeared at breakfast one morning with a mysterious air of engaging in a conspiracy.

"Apologizing, I'm sure, to you, sir," said Mrs. Steadman, "for intruding at such a time, but it came to Steadman's ears last night that No. 18 Lauceston Mansions—just round the corner—is to Be Had. They wrote to the agents about it last night, so if you was to nip round now, ma'am, before anybody Got Wind of it, so to speak—"

There was no need for more. Celia sprang up from the table, pulled on a hat, and departed with the eagerness of a dog on the scent.

At 18 Lauceston Mansions also breakfast was in progress. To the announcement by a slatternly maid of "Somebody to see over the flat, ma'am," Celia, standing in the hall, heard an agitated wail: "But they can hardly have got my letter yet. It's only half-past eight."

A young woman in a kimono came out of the dining room, wiping her mouth. A smell of kipper accompanied her.

"Do you really want to see over the flat?"

"Yes, please."

"Oh, well, I suppose . . ."

Celia was taken round. Yes, it would do excellently. Four bedrooms, two sitting rooms—everything pretty dirty, of course. Rent £80 a year (marvelously cheap). A premium (alas) of a hundred and fifty pounds, and the "lino" (Celia abhorred lino) to be taken at a valuation. Celia offered a hundred premium. The young woman in the kimono refused scornfully.

"Very well," said Celia firmly. "I'll take it."

As she descended the stairs she was glad of her decision. Two separate women came up, each with a house agent's order to view in her hand!

Within three days Celia and Dermot had been offered a premium of two hundred to abdicate their right.

But they stuck to it, paid over their hundred and fifty pounds, and entered into possession of 18 Lauceston Mansions. At last they had a home (a very dirty one) of their own.

In a month's time you would hardly have known the place. Dermot and Celia did all the decorating themselves—they could not afford anything else. They learned by experience interesting facts about distempering, painting, and papering. The finished result was charming, they thought. Cheap chintz papers brightened up the long dingy passages. Yellow distempered walls gave a sunny look to the rooms facing north. The sitting rooms were pale cream—a background for pictures and china. The "lino surrounds" were torn up and presented to Mrs. Steadman, who received them greedily. "I do like a bit of nice lino, ma'am. . . ."

6

In the meantime Celia had successfully passed through another ordeal—that of Mrs. Barman's Bureau. Mrs. Barman's Bureau provided children's nurses.

Arriving at this awe-inspiring establishment, Celia was received by a haughty yellow-haired creature, required to fill in thirty-four answers to questions on an imposing form—the questions being of a kind to induce acute humility in the filler-in. She was then conducted to a small cubicle, rather medical in appearance, and there, curtained in, she was left to await those nurses whom the yellow-haired one saw fit to send her.

By the time the first one came in, Celia's sense of inferiority had deepened to complete abasement, not relieved by the first applicant, a big starched massive woman, aggressively clean and majestic in demeanor.

"Good morning," said Celia weakly.

"Good morning, madam." The majestic one took the chair opposite Celia and gazed at her steadily, conveying somehow as she did so, her sense that Celia's situation was not likely to suit anyone who respected one's self.

"I want a nurse for a young baby," began Celia wishing that she did not feel and (she was afraid) sound amateurish.

"Yes, madam. From the month?"

"Yes, at least two months."

One mistake already—"from the month" was a technical term—not a period of time. Celia felt she had gone down in the majestic one's estimation.

"Quite so, madam. Any other children?"

"No."

"A first baby. How many in family?"

"Er—me and my husband."

"And what establishment do you keep, madam?"

Establishment? What a word to describe one general servant not yet acquired.

"We live very simply," said Celia, blushing. "One maid."

"Nurseries cleaned and waited on?"

"No, you would have to do your own nursery."

"Ah!" The majestic one rose and said more in sorrow than in anger: "I'm afraid, madam, your situation is not quite what I am looking for. At Sir Eldon West's, I had a nursery maid, and the nurseries were attended to by the under housemaid."

Celia cursed the yellow-haired one in her heart. Why fill up a paper of your requirements and your household and then be sent someone who would clearly only accept a post with the Rothschilds if they happened to please her fancy?

A stern black-browed woman came next.

"One baby? Taken from the month? You understand, madam, I take *entire charge*. I do not tolerate interference."

She glared at Celia.

"I'll teach young mothers to come bothering me," said the glare.

Celia said she was afraid she would not do.

"I am devoted to children, madam. I worship them, but I cannot have a mother always interfering."

The black-browed one was got rid of.

There came next a very untidy old woman who described herself as a "Nannie."

As far as Celia could make out she could neither see, hear, nor understand what was said to her.

Rout of the Nannie.

Next came a bad-tempered-looking young woman who scoffed at the idea of doing her own nurseries, followed by an amiable red-cheeked girl who had been a housemaid but thought she'd "get on better with children."

Celia was getting desperate when a woman of about thirty-five came in. She had pince-nez, was extremely neat, and had pleasant blue eyes.

She displayed none of the usual reactions when it came to "doing your own nursery."

"Well, I don't object to that—except the grate. I don't like doing a grate—it musses up your hands—and you don't want rough hands looking after a baby. But otherwise I don't mind seeing to things. I've been to the colonies, and I can turn my hand to anything."

She showed Celia various snapshots of her charges, and Celia ended by engaging her if her references were satisfactory.

With a sigh of relief Celia left Mrs. Barman's Bureau.

Mary Denman's references proved most satisfactory. She was a careful, thoroughly experienced nurse. Celia had next to engage a servant.

This proved to be almost more trying than finding a nurse. Nurses at least were plentiful. Servants were practically nonexistent. They were all in munition factories or in the Waacs or Wrens. Celia saw a girl she liked very much, a plump good-humored damsel called Kate. She did her utmost to persuade Kate to come to them.

Like all the others, Kate jibbed at a nursery.

"It isn't the baby I object to, ma'am. I like children. It's the nurse. After my last place I vowed I'd never go where there was a nurse again. Wherever there's a nurse there's trouble."

In vain Celia represented Mary Denman as a mine of all the virtues. Kate repeated solidly:

"Wherever there's a nurse, there's trouble. That's my experience."

In the end it was Dermot who turned the scale. Celia turned him onto the obdurate Kate, and Dermot, the adept at getting his own way, was successful in getting Kate to give them a trial.

"Though whatever came over me I don't know, because go where there is a nursery I said I never would again. But the captain spoke so nicely, and him knowing the regiment my boy's in in France and everything. Well, I said, we can but try."

So Kate was secured, and on a triumphant October day Celia, Dermot, Denman, Kate, and Judy all moved in to 18 Lauceston Mansions, and family life began.

7

Dermot was very funny with Judy. He was afraid of her. When Celia tried to make him hold her in his arms, he backed away nervously.

"No, I can't. I simply can't. I won't hold the thing."

"You'll have to someday, when she's older. And she's not a thing!"

"She'll be better when she's older. Once she can talk and walk, I dare say I shall like her. She's so awfully fat now. Do you think she'll ever get right?"

He refused to admire Judy's curves or her dimples.

"I want her to be thin and bony."

"Not now—at three months old."

"You really think she will be thin someday?"

"Sure to be. We're both thin."

"I couldn't bear it if she grew up fat."

Celia had to fall back upon the admiration of Mrs. Steadman, who walked round and round the baby rather as she had done round the joint of meat of glorious memory.

"The image of the captain, isn't she? Ah, you can see she was made at home—if you'll pardon the old saying."

On the whole, Celia found domesticity rather fun. It was fun because she did not take it seriously. Denman proved an excellent nurse, capable and devoted to the baby, and extraordinarily pleasant and willing so long as there was a lot of work to do and everything was at sixes and sevens. The moment the household had settled down and things were running smoothly, Denman showed she had another side to her character. She had a fierce temper—directed not toward Judy, whom she adored, but toward Celia and Dermot. All employers were to Denman natural enemies. The most innocent remark would create a sudden storm. Celia would say, "You had your electric light on last night. I hope baby was all right?"

Immediately Denman flared up.

"I suppose I can turn on the light to see the time in the night? I may be treated like a black slave, but there are limits. I've had slaves myself under me in Africa—poor ignorant heathen—but they weren't grudged necessities. If you think I'm wasting the light, I'll trouble you to say so straight out."

Kate, in the kitchen, used to giggle sometimes when Denman talked of slaves.

"Nurse won't never be satisfied—not till she's got a dozen niggers under her. She's always talking of the niggers in Africa, I wouldn't have a nigger in my kitchen—nasty black things."

Kate was a great comfort. Good-humored, placid, and untroubled by storms, she went her way, cooking, cleaning, and indulging in reminiscences of "places."

"I'll never forget my first place—no, never. A slip of a girl I was—not seventeen. They starved me something cruel. A kipper, that's all they'd let me have for lunch, and margarine instead of butter. I got so thin you could hear my bones rubbing together. Mother was in a way about me."

Looking at the robust and daily increasing plumpness of Kate, Celia could hardly believe this story.

"I hope you get enough to eat here, Kate?"

"Don't you worry, ma'am, that's all right—and you've no call to do things yourself. You'll only muss yourself up."

But Celia had acquired a guilty passion for cooking. Having made the startling discovery that cooking was mainly following a recipe carefully, she plunged headlong into the sport. Kate's disapproval forced her to confine most of her activities to Kate's days out, when she would go and have an orgy in the kitchen and produce exciting delicacies for Dermot's tea and dinner.

It was in the nature of the unsatisfactory quality of life that Dermot should frequently arrive home on these days with indigestion and demand weak tea and thin toast instead of lobster cutlets and vanilla soufflé.

Kate herself kept firmly to plain cooking. She was unable to follow a recipe because she scorned to measure any quantities.

"A bit of this, and that—that's what I take," she said. "That's the way my mother did. Cooks never measure."

"Perhaps it would be better if they did," suggested Celia.

"You've got to do it by eye," said Kate firmly. "That's the way I've always seen my mother do."

What fun it was, thought Celia.

A house (or rather a flat) of one's very own—a husband—a baby—a servant.

At last, she felt, she was being grown up—a real person. She was even learning the correct jargon. She had made friends with two other young wives in the mansions. These were very earnest over the qualities of good milk, where you got the cheapest Brussels sprouts, and the iniquities of servants.

"I looked her straight in the face, and I said, 'Jane, I never permit insolence,' just like that. Such a look she gave me."

They never seemed to talk about anything except these subjects.

Secretly, Celia felt afraid that she would never be truly domestic.

Luckily Dermot didn't mind. He often said he hated domestic women. Their homes, he said, were always so uncomfortable.

And, really there seemed to be something in what he said. Women who talked of nothing but servants seemed to be always having "insolence" from them and their "treasures" departed at inconvenient moments and left them to do all the cooking and the housework. And women who spent the whole morning shopping and selecting edibles seemed to have worse food than anybody else.

There was, Celia thought, a lot too much fuss made over all this business of domesticity.

People like her and Dermot had far more fun. She wasn't Dermot's housekeeper—she was his playmate.

And some day Judy would run about and talk, and adore her mother like Celia adored Miriam.

And in summer, when London got hot and stuffy, she would take Judy home, and Judy would play in the garden and invent games of princesses and dragons, and Celia would read her all the old fairy stories in the nursery bookcase. . . .

Chapter 12

PEACE

The armistice came as a great surprise to Celia. She had got so used to the war that she had felt it would never end. . . .

It was just a part of life. . . .

And now the war was over!

While the war had been on it hadn't been any use making plans. You had to let the future take care of itself and live for the day—just hoping and praying that Dermot wouldn't be sent out to France again.

But now—it was different.

Dermot was full of plans. He wasn't going to stay in the army. There wasn't any future in the army. As soon as possible he would get demobilized and would go into the City. He knew of an opening in a very good firm.

"But, Dermot isn't it safer to stay in the army? I mean, there's the pension and all that."

"I should stagnate if I stayed in the army. And what good is a miserable pension? I mean to make money—a good deal of money. You don't mind taking a risk, do you, Celia?"

No, Celia didn't mind. That disposition to take risks was what she admired most about Dermot. He was not afraid of life.

Dermot would never run away from life. He would face it and force it to do his will.

Ruthless, her mother had called him once. Well, that was true in a way. He *was* ruthless to life—no sentimental considerations would ever influence him. But he was not ruthless to her. Look how tender he had been before Judy was born. . . .

2

Dermot took his risk.

He left the army and went into the City, starting on a small salary, but with a prospect of good money in the future.

Celia had wondered whether he would find office life irksome, but he did not seem to do so. He seemed entirely happy and satisfied in his new life.

Dermot liked doing new things.

He liked new people too.

Celia was sometimes shocked that he never wanted to go and see the two old aunts in Ireland who had brought him up.

He sent them presents and wrote to them regularly once a month, but he never wanted to see them.

"Weren't you fond of them?"

"Of course I was—especially of Aunt Lucy. She was just like a mother to me."

"Well, then, don't you want to see them? We could have them to stay, if you liked."

"Oh, that would be rather a nuisance."

"A nuisance? If you're fond of them?"

"Well, I know they're all right. Quite happy and all that. I don't exactly want to *see* them. After all, when you grow up, you grow out of your relations. That's only nature. Aunt Lucy and Aunt Kate don't really mean anything to me now. I've outgrown them."

Dermot was extraordinary, Celia thought.

But perhaps he thought her equally extraordinary for being so attached to places and people she had known all her life.

As a matter of fact, he didn't think her extraordinary. He didn't think about it at all. Dermot never thought about what people were like. Talking about thoughts and feelings seemed to him a waste of time.

He liked realities—not ideas.

Sometimes Celia would ask him questions like, "What would you do if I ran away with someone?" or "What would you do if I died?"

Dermot never knew what he would do. How could he know till it happened?

"But can't you just sort of imagine?"

No, Dermot couldn't. Imagining things that weren't so seemed to him a great waste of time.

Which, of course, was quite true.

Nevertheless, Celia couldn't stop doing it. She was made that way.

3

One day Dermot hurt Celia.

They had been to a party. Celia was still rather scared of parties in case a fit of tongue-tied shyness should come over her. Sometimes it did and sometimes it didn't.

But this party (or so she thought) had gone remarkably well. She *had* been a little tongue-tied at first, and then she had ventured on a remark that had made the man she was talking to laugh.

Emboldened, Celia had found her tongue, and after that she fairly chattered. Everybody had laughed and talked a great deal, Celia as much as anybody. She had said things that sounded to her quite witty and which even seemed to have appeared witty to other people. She came home in a happy glow.

"I'm not so stupid. I'm not so stupid after all," she said to herself happily.

She called through the dressing-room door to Dermot.

"I think that was a nice party. I enjoyed it. How lucky that I caught that ladder in my stocking in time."

"It wasn't too bad."

"Oh, Dermot didn't you like it?"

"Well, I've got a bit of indigestion."

"Oh, darling, I'm so sorry. I'll get you some bicarbonate."

"Oh, it's all right now. What was the matter with you this evening?"

"With me?"

"Yes, you were quite different."

"I suppose I was excited. Different in what way?"

"Well, you're usually so sensible. Tonight you were talking and laughing and quite unlike yourself."

"Didn't you like it? I thought I was getting on so well."

A queer, cold feeling began to form in Celia's inside.

"Well, I thought it sounded rather silly—that's all."

"Yes," said Celia slowly. "I suppose I was being silly. . . . But people seemed to like it—they laughed."

"Oh, people!"

"And, Dermot—I enjoyed it myself. . . . It's awful, but I believe I like being silly sometimes."

"Oh, well, that's all right, then."

"But I won't be again. Not if you don't like it."

"Well, I do rather hate it when you sound silly. I don't like silly women."

It hurt—oh, yes, it hurt. . . .

A fool—she was a fool. Of course she was a fool, she'd always known it. But she'd hoped, somehow—that Dermot wouldn't mind. That he'd be—what did she mean exactly?—tender to her over it. If you loved a person, their faults and failings endeared them more to you—not less. You said, "Now, isn't that *like* so and so?" But you said it, not with exasperation but with tenderness.

But then men didn't deal much in tenderness. . . .

A queer little pang of fright swept over Celia.

No, men weren't tender. . . .

They weren't like mothers. . . .

A sudden misgiving assailed her. She didn't really know anything about men. She didn't really know anything about Dermot. . . .

"The men!" Grannie's phrase came back to her. Grannie had seemed perfectly confident of knowing exactly what men liked and didn't like.

But Grannie, of course, wasn't silly. . . . She had often laughed at Grannie, but Grannie wasn't silly.

And she, Celia, was. . . . She'd always known it really, deep down. But she had thought, with Dermot, it wouldn't matter. Well, it *did* matter.

In the darkness the tears ran down her cheeks unchecked. . . .

She'd have her cry over—there, in the night, under the shelter of the darkness. And in the morning, she'd be different. She would never be silly in public again.

She'd been spoiled, that's what it was. Everyone had always been so kind to her—encouraged her. . . .

But she didn't want Dermot to look as just for one moment he had looked. . . .

It reminded her of something—something long ago.

No, she couldn't remember.

But she'd be very careful not to be silly anymore.

Chapter 13

Companionship

There were several things, Celia found, that Dermot didn't like about her.

Any sign of helplessness annoyed him.

"Why do you want me to do things for you when you can perfectly well do them for yourself?"

"Oh, Dermot, but it's so nice having you do them for me."

"Nonsense, you'd get worse and worse if I'd let you."

"I expect I should," said Celia sadly.

"It isn't as though you can't do all these things perfectly. You're perfectly sensible and intelligent and capable."

"I expect," said Celia, "that it goes with slightly sloping Victorian shoulders. You want, automatically, to cling—like ivy."

"Well," said Dermot good-humoredly, "you can't cling to me. I'm not going to let you."

"Do you mind very much, Dermot, my being dreamy and fancying things and imagining things that might happen and what I should do if they did?"

"Of course I don't mind, if it amuses you."

Dermot was always fair. He was independent himself, and he respected independence in other people. He had, presumably, his own ideas about things, but he never put them into words or wanted to share them with anyone else.

The trouble was that Celia wanted to share everything. When the almond tree in the court below came into flower it gave her a queer ecstatic feeling just under her heart, and she longed to put her hand into Dermot's and drag him to the window and make him feel the same. But Dermot hated having his hand taken. He hated being touched at all unless he was in a recognizably amorous mood.

When Celia burned her hand on the stove and immediately after pinched a finger in the kitchen window she longed to go and put her head on Dermot's shoulder and be comforted. But she felt that that sort of thing would annoy Dermot—and she was perfectly right. He disliked being touched, or leaned on for comfort, or asked to enter into other people's emotion.

So Celia fought heroically against her passion for sharing, her weakness for caresses, her longing for reassurance.

She told herself that she was babyish and foolish. She loved Dermot, and Dermot loved her. He loved her, probably, more deeply than she loved him since he needed less expression of love to satisfy him.

She had passion and comradeship from him. It was unreasonable to expect affection as well. Grannie would have known better. "The men" were not like that.

2

At weekends Dermot and Celia went into the country together. They took sandwiches with them and then went by rail or bus to a chosen spot and then walked across country and came home by another train or bus.

All the week Celia looked forward to the weekends. Dermot came back from the City every day thoroughly tired, sometimes with a head-ache—sometimes with indigestion. After dinner he liked to sit and read. Sometimes he told Celia of incidents that had happened during the day, but on the whole he preferred not to talk. He usually had some technical book that he wanted to read uninterrupted.

But at weekends Celia got her comrade back. They walked through woods and made ridiculous jokes, and sometimes, going up hill, Celia would say, "I'm very fond of you, Dermot," and put her hand through his arm. This was because Dermot raced up hills and Celia got out of breath. Dermot didn't mind his arm being held if it was only a joke and really to help her up the hill.

One day Dermot suggested that they should play golf. He was very bad, he said, but he could play a little. Celia got out her clubs and cleaned the rust off them—and she thought of Peter Maitland. Dear Peter—dear, *dear* Peter. That warm affection she felt for Peter would stay with her to the end of her life. Peter was part of things. . . .

They found an obscure golf links where the green fees were not too high. It was fun to play golf again. She was frightfully rusty, but then Dermot wasn't much good either. He hit terrific long shots but they were pulled or sliced wildly.

It was great fun playing together.

It didn't just remain fun, though. Dermot, in games as in work, was efficient and painstaking. He bought a book and studied it deeply. He practiced swings at home and bought some cork balls to practice with.

The next weekend they didn't play a round. Dermot did nothing but practice shots. He made Celia do the same.

Dermot began to live for golf. Celia tried to live for golf too, but not with much success.

Dermot's game improved by leaps and bounds. Celia's stayed much the same. She wished, passionately, that Dermot was a little more like Peter Maitland. . . .

Yet she had fallen in love with Dermot, attracted by precisely those qualities which differentiated him from Peter.

3

One day Dermot came in and said:

"Look here, I'm going down to Dalton Heath with Andrews next Sunday. Is that all right?"

Celia said of course it was all right.

Dermot came back enthusiastic.

Golf was wonderful, played on a first-rate course. Celia must come down next week and see Dalton Heath. Women couldn't play at the weekends, but she could walk around with him.

They went once or twice more to their little cheap course, but Dermot took no further pleasure in it. He said that sort of place was no good to him.

A month later he told Celia that he was going to join Dalton Heath.

"I know it's expensive. But, after all, I can economize in other ways. Golf is the only recreation I've got, and it's going to make all the difference to me. Both Andrews and Weston belong there."

Celia said slowly:

"What about me?"

"It wouldn't be any good your belonging. Women can't play at weekends and I don't suppose you'd care to go down by yourself in the week."

"I mean, what am I going to do at the weekends? You'll be playing with Andrews and people."

"Well, it would be rather silly to join a golf club and not use it."

"Yes, but we've always spent the weekends together, you and I."

"Oh, I see. Well, you can get someone to go about with, can't you? I mean, you've got lots of friends of your own."

"No, I haven't. Not now. The few friends I had who lived in London have all married and gone away."

"Well, there's Doris Andrews, and Mrs. Weston, and people."

"Those aren't exactly my friends. They're your friends' wives. It isn't quite the same thing. Besides, that isn't it at all. You don't understand. I like being with *you*. I like doing things with you. I liked our walks and our sandwiches, and playing golf together, and all the fun. You're tired all the week, and I don't worry you or bother you to do things in the evening, but I looked forward to the weekends. I loved them. Oh, Dermot, I like being with you, and now we shall never do anything together anymore."

She wished her voice wouldn't tremble. She wished she could keep the tears back from her eyes. Was she being dreadfully unreasonable? Would Dermot be cross? Was she being selfish? She was clinging—yes, undoubtedly she was clinging. Ivy again!

Dermot was trying hard to be patient and reasonable.

"You know, Celia, I don't think that's quite fair. I never interfere with what you want to do."

"But I don't want to do things."

"Well, I shouldn't mind if you did. If any weekend you'd said that you wanted to go off with Doris Andrews or some old friend of yours, I should have been quite happy. I'd have hunted up somebody and gone off somewhere else. After all, when we married we did agree that each side should be free and do just what they wanted to do."

"We didn't agree or talk about anything of the kind," said Celia. "We just loved each other and wanted to marry each other and thought it would be perfectly heavenly always to be together."

"Well, so it is. It isn't that I don't love you. I love you just as much as ever. But a man likes doing things with other men. And he needs exercise. If I was wanting to go off with other women, well, then you might have something to complain about. But I never want to be bothered with any other woman but you. I hate women. I just want to play a decent game of golf with another man. I do think you're rather unreasonable about it."

Yes, probably she was being unreasonable . . .

What Dermot wanted to do was so innocent—so natural. . . .

She felt ashamed. . . .

But he didn't realize how terribly she was going to miss those weekends together. . . . She didn't only want Dermot in her bed at night. She loved Dermot as play-fellow even better than Dermot as lover. . . .

Was it true what she had so often heard women say—that men only wanted women as bedfellows and housekeepers? . . .

Was that the whole tragedy of marriage—that women wanted to be companions, and that men were bored by it?

She said something of the kind. Dermot, as always, was honest.

"I think, Celia, that that *is* true. Women always want to do things with men—and a man would always rather have another man."

Well, she had got it flat. Dermot was right, and she was wrong. She *had* been unreasonable. She said so, and his face cleared.

"You are so sweet, Celia. And I expect you'll really enjoy it better in the end. I mean you'll find people to go about with who enjoy talking about things and feelings. I know I'm rather bad at all that kind of thing. And we'll be just as happy. In fact, I shall probably only play golf either Saturday or Sunday. The other day we'll go out together as we did before."

The next Sunday he went off, radiant. On Sunday he suggested of his own accord that he and she should go for a ramble.

They did, but it was not the same. Dermot was perfectly sweet, but she knew that his heart was at Dalton Heath. Weston had asked him to play but he had refused.

He was full of conscious pride in his sacrifice.

The next weekend Celia urged him to play golf both days, and he went off happily.

Celia thought: "I must learn to play by myself again. Or else—I must find some friends."

She had scorned "domestic women." She had been proud of her companionship with Dermot. Those domestic women—absorbed in their children, their servants, their house running—relieved when Tom or Dick or Fred went off to play golf at the weekend because there was no mess about the house—"It makes it so much easier for the servants, my dear—" Men were necessary as breadwinners, but they were an inconvenience in the house. . . .

Perhaps, after all, domesticity paid best.

It looked like it.

Chapter 14

IVY

How lovely to be at home. Celia lay full length on the green grass—it felt deliciously warm and alive. . . .

The beech tree rustled overhead. . . .

Green—green—all the world was green. . . .

Trailing a wooden horse behind her, Judy came toiling up the slope of the lawn. . . .

Judy was adorable with her firm legs, her rosy cheeks and blue eyes, her thickly curling chestnut brown hair. Judy was her own little girl, just as she had been her mother's little girl.

Only, of course, Judy was quite different. . . .

Judy didn't want to have stories told to her—which was a pity, because Celia could think of heaps of stories without any effort at all. And, anyway, Judy didn't like fairy stories.

Judy wasn't any good at make-believe. When Celia told Judy how she herself had pretended that the lawn was a sea and her hoop a river horse, Judy had merely stared and said: "But it's grass. And you bowl a hoop. You can't ride it."

It was so obvious that she thought Celia must have been a rather silly little girl that Celia felt quite dashed.

First Dermot had found out that she was silly, and now Judy!

Although only four years old Judy was full of common sense. And common sense, Celia found, can be often very depressing.

Moreover, Judy's common sense had a bad effect upon Celia. She made efforts to appear sensible in Judy's eyes—clear blue appraising eyes—with the result that she often made herself out sillier than she was.

Judy was a complete puzzle to her mother. All the things that Celia had loved doing as a child bored Judy. Judy could not play for three minutes in the garden by herself. She would come marching into the house declaring that there was "nothing to do."

Judy liked doing real things. She was never bored in the flat at home. She polished tables with a duster, assisted in bed making, and helped her father to clean his golf clubs.

Dermot and Judy had suddenly become friends. A thoroughly satisfying communion had grown up between them. Though still deploring Judy's well-covered frame, Dermot could not but be charmed by her evident delight in his company. They talked to each other seriously, like grown-up people. When Dermot gave Judy a club to clean, he expected her to do it properly. When Judy said, "Isn't that nice?" about anything—a house she had built of bricks—or a ball she had made of wool, or a spoon she had cleaned—Dermot never said it was unless he thought so. He would point out errors or faulty construction.

"You'll discourage her," Celia would say.

But Judy was not in the least discouraged, and her feelings were never hurt. She liked her father better than her mother because her father was more difficult to please. She liked doing things that were difficult.

Dermot was rough. When he and Judy romped together, Judy nearly always got damaged—games with Dermot always ended in a bump or a scratch or a pinched finger. Judy didn't care. Celia's gentler games seemed to her tame.

Only when she was ill did she prefer her mother to her father.

"Don't go away, Mummy. Don't go away. Stay with me. Don't let Daddy come. I don't want Daddy."

Dermot was quite satisfied for his presence not to be desired. He didn't like ill people. Anybody ill or unhappy embarrassed him.

Judy was like Dermot about being touched. She hated to be kissed or picked up. One good-night kiss from her mother she bore, but nothing more. Her father never kissed her. When they said good night they grinned at each other.

Judy and her grandmother got on very well together. Miriam was delighted with the child's spirit and intelligence.

"She's extraordinarily quick, Celia. She takes a thing in at once."

Miriam's old love of teaching revived. She taught Judy her letters and small words. Both grandmother and grandchild enjoyed the lessons.

Sometimes Miriam would say to Celia:

"But she's not you, my precious. . . ."

It was as though she were excusing herself for her interest in youth. Miriam loved youth. She had the teacher's joy in an awakening mind. Judy was an abiding excitement and interest to her.

But her heart was all Celia's. The love between them was stronger than ever. When Celia arrived she would find her mother looking a tiny old woman—gray—faded. But in a day or two she would revive, the color would come back to her cheeks, the sparkle to her eyes.

"I've got my girl back," she would say happily.

She always asked Dermot down too, but she was always delighted when he didn't come. She wanted Celia to herself.

And Celia loved the feeling of stepping back into her old life. To feel that happy tide of reassurance sweeping over her—the feeling of being loved—of being *adequate*. . . .

For her mother, she was perfect. . . . Her mother didn't want her to be different. . . . She could just be herself.

It was so restful to be yourself. . . .

And then she could let herself go—in tenderness—in *saying* things. . . .

She could say, "I am so happy," without having to catch back the words at Dermot's frown. Dermot hated you to say what you were feeling. He felt it, somehow, to be indecent. . . .

At home Celia could be as indecent as she liked. . . .

She could realize better at home how happy she was with Dermot and how much she loved him and Judy. . . .

And after an orgy of loving and saying all the things that came into her head, she could go back and be a sensible, independent person such as was approved of by Dermot.

Oh, dear home—and the beech tree—and the grass—growing—growing—against her cheek.

She thought dreamily: "It's alive—it's a Great Green Beast—the whole earth is a Great Green Beast . . . it's kind and warm and alive. . . . I'm so happy—I'm so happy. . . . I've got everything I want in the world. . . ."

Dermot drifted happily in and out of her thoughts. He was a kind of motif in her melody of life. Sometimes she missed him terribly.

She said to Judy one day:

"Do you miss Daddy?"

"No," said Judy.

"But you'd like him to be here?"

"Yes, I suppose so."

"Aren't you sure? You're so fond of Daddy."

"Of course I am, but he's in London."

That settled it for Judy.

When Celia got back, Dermot was very pleased to see her. They had a happy, lover-like evening. Celia murmured:

"I've missed you a lot. Have you missed me?"

"Well, I haven't thought about it."

"You mean you haven't thought about me?"

"No. What would be the good? Thinking of you wouldn't bring you here."

That, of course, was quite true and very sensible.

"But you're pleased now that I am here?"

His answer satisfied her.

But later, when he was asleep, and she lay awake, dreamily happy, she thought:

"It's awful, but I believe I wish that Dermot could sometimes be a tiny bit *dishonest*. . . .

"If he could have said, 'I missed you terribly, darling,' how comforting and warming it would have been, and it really wouldn't have mattered if it had been true or not."

No, Dermot was Dermot. Her funny, devastatingly truthful Dermot. Judy was just like him. . . .

It was wiser, perhaps, not to ask them questions if you didn't fancy the truth for an answer.

She thought drowsily:

"I wonder if I shall get jealous of Judy someday. . . . She and Dermot understand each other so much better than he and I do."

Judy, she had fancied, was sometimes jealous of her. She liked her father's attention to be entirely focused on herself.

Celia thought: "How queer. Dermot was so jealous of her before she was born—and even when she was a tiny baby. It's funny the way things turn out the opposite way from what you expect. . . .

"Darling Judy . . . darling Dermot . . . so alike—so funny—and so sweet . . . and *hers*. No—not hers. *She* was *theirs*. One liked it better that way. It felt warmer—more comfortable. She belonged to them."

2

Celia invented a new game. It was really, she thought, a new phase of "the girls." "The girls" themselves were moribund. Celia tried to resurrect them, gave them babies and stately homes in parks and interesting careers—but it was all no good. "The girls" refused to come to life again.

Celia invented a new person. Her name was Hazel. Celia followed her career from childhood upward with great interest. Hazel was an unhappy child—a poor relation. She acquired a sinister reputation with nursemaids by a habit of chanting, "Something's going to happen—something's going to happen"; and as something usually did happen—even if it was only a nursery maid's pricked finger—Hazel found herself established as a kind of witch's familiar. She grew up with the knowledge of how easy it was to impose on the credulous. . . .

Celia followed her with great interest into a world of spiritualism, fortune telling, séances, and so on. Hazel ended up at a fortune-telling establishment in Bond Street, where she acquired a great reputation, aided by a little coterie of impoverished society "spies."

Then she fell in love with a young Welsh naval officer, and there were scenes on Welsh villages, and slowly it began to be apparent (to everyone but Hazel herself) that side by side with her fraudulent practices went a genuine gift.

At last Hazel herself found it out and was terrified. But the more she tried to cheat the more her uncanny guesses came right. . . . The power had got hold of her and wouldn't let her go.

Owen, the young man, was more nebulous, but in the end he proved himself to be a plausible rotter.

Whenever Celia had a little leisure, or when she was wheeling Judy to the Park, the story went on in her mind.

It occurred to her one day that she might write it down. . . .

She might, in fact, make a book of it. . . .

She bought six penny exercise books and a lot of pencils, because she was careless about pencils, and started. . . .

It wasn't quite so easy when it came to writing down. Her mind had always gone on about six paragraphs farther than the one she was writing down—and then by the time she got to that, the exact wording had gone out of her head.

But still she made progress. It wasn't quite the story she had had in her head, but it was something that read recognizably like a book. It had chapters and all that. She bought six more exercise books.

She didn't tell Dermot about it for some time, not, in fact, till she had successfully wrestled with an account of a Welsh Revivalist meeting at which Hazel had "testified."

That particular chapter had gone much better than Celia hoped. She felt so flushed by victory that she wanted to tell somebody.

"Dermot," she said, "do you think I could write a book?"

Dermot said cheerfully:

"I think that's an excellent idea. I should, if I were you."

"Well, as a matter of fact, I have—that is, I've begun. I'm halfway through."

"Good," said Dermot.

He had put down a book on economics when Celia spoke. Now he picked it up again.

"It's about a girl who's a medium—but doesn't know she is. And she gets tangled up in a bogus fortune-telling place, and she cheats at séances. And then she falls in love with a young man in Wales and she goes to Wales and queer things happen."

"I suppose there's some kind of story?"

"Of course there is. I'm saying it badly—that's all."

"Do you know anything about mediums or séances or things?"

"No," said Celia rather stricken.

"Well, isn't it a bit risky to write about them, then? And you've never been to Wales, have you?"

"No."

"Well, hadn't you better write about something you do know about? London or your part of the country. It seems to me you're simply making difficulties for yourself."

Celia felt abashed. As usual, Dermot was right. She had behaved like a simpleton. Why on earth choose subjects she knew nothing about? That revivalist meeting, too. She had never been to a revivalist meeting. Why on earth try to describe one?

All the same, she couldn't give up Hazel and Owen now. . . . They were *there*. . . . No, but something must be done about them.

For the next month Celia read every conceivable work she could find on spiritualism, séances, mediumistic powers, and fraudulent practices. Then, slowly and laboriously, she rewrote all the first part of the book. She did not enjoy her task. All the sentences seemed to run haltingly, and she even got into the most amazingly complicated grammatical tangles for no apparent reason.

That summer Dermot very obligingly agreed to go to Wales for his fortnight's holiday. Celia could then look about for "local color." They duly carried out the project, but Celia found local color extremely elusive. She took round a little notebook with her, so as to be able to put down anything that struck her. But she was by nature remarkably unobservant, and days passed when it seemed quite impossible to put down anything at all.

She had an awful temptation to abandon Wales and to turn Owen into a Scotsman called Hector who lived in the Highlands.

But then Dermot pointed out to her that the same difficulty would arise. She knew nothing about the Highlands either.

In despair Celia abandoned the whole thing. It just wouldn't go anymore. Besides, she was already playing in her mind with a family of fishing folk on the Cornish coast. . . .

Amos Polridge was already quite well known to her. . . .

She didn't tell Dermot, because she felt guilty, realizing perfectly well that she knew nothing about fishermen or the sea. It would be useless writing it down, but it was fun to think about. There would be an old grandmother too—very toothless and rather sinister. . . .

And sometime or other she would finish the Hazel book. Owen could perfectly well be a rotten young stockbroker in London.

Only, or so it seemed to her, Owen didn't want to be that. . . .

He sulked and became so vague that he really didn't exist at all.

3

Celia had become quite used to being poor and living carefully.

Dermot expected to make money someday. In fact, he was quite sure of it. Celia never expected to be rich. She was quite content to remain as they were but hoped it wouldn't be too much of a disappointment to Dermot.

What neither of them expected was a real financial calamity. But the boom after the war was over. It was followed by the slump.

Dermot's firm went into liquidation, and he was out of a job.

They had fifty pounds a year of Dermot's and a hundred pounds a year of Celia's, they had two hundred pounds saved in War Loan and there was the shelter of Miriam's house for Celia and Judy.

It was a bad time. It affected Celia principally through Dermot. Dermot took misfortune—especially undeserved misfortune (for he had worked well) such as this, hard. It made him bitter and bad tempered. Celia dismissed Kate and Denman and proposed to run the flat by herself until such times as Dermot got another job. Denman, however, refused to be dismissed.

Fiercely and angrily she said: "I'm stopping. It's no good arguing. I'll wait for my wages. I'm not going to leave my little love now."

So Denman remained. She and Celia did turn and turn about with housework, cooking, and Judy. One morning Celia took Judy to the Park and Denman cooked and cleaned. The next morning Denman went and Celia remained.

Celia found a queer enjoyment in this. She liked to be busy. In the evening she found time to go on with Hazel. She finished the book painstakingly, consulting her Welsh notes, and sent it to a publisher. It might bring in something.

It was, however, promptly returned, and Celia tossed it into a drawer and did not try again.

Celia's chief difficulty in life was Dermot. Dermot was utterly unreasonable. He was so sensitive to failure that he was quite unbearable to live with. If Celia was cheerful, he told her she might show a little more appreciation of his difficulties. If she was silent, he said she might try to brighten him up.

Celia felt desperately that if only Dermot would help, they might make a kind of picnic of it all. Surely to laugh at trouble was the best way of meeting it.

But Dermot couldn't laugh. His pride was involved.

However unkind and unreasonable he was, Celia did not feel hurt as she had done over the party episode. She understood that he was suffering, and suffering on her account more than his own.

Sometimes he came near to expressing himself.

"Why don't you go away—you and Judy? Take her to your mother's. I'm no good just now. I know I'm not fit to live with. I told you once before—I'm no good in trouble. I can't stand trouble."

But Celia would not leave him. She wished she could make it easier for him, but there seemed nothing she could do.

And as day followed day and Dermot was unsuccessful in finding a job, his mood grew blacker and blacker.

Then, at last, when Celia felt her courage failing her entirely, and she had almost decided to go to Miriam as Dermot so constantly suggested she should, the tide turned.

Dermot came into the flat one afternoon a changed man. He looked his young boyish self again. His dark blue eyes danced and sparkled.

"Celia—it's splendid. You remember Tommy Forbes? I looked him up—just on chance—and he jumped at me. Was just looking for a man like me. Eight hundred a year to start with, and in a year or two I may be making anything up to fifteen hundred or two thousand. Let's go out somewhere and celebrate."

What a happy evening! Dermot so different—so childlike in his zest and excitement. He insisted on buying Celia a new frock.

"You look lovely in that hyacinth blue. I—I still love you frightfully, Celia."

Lovers—yes, they were still lovers.

That night, lying awake, Celia thought: "I hope—I hope things will always go well for Dermot. He minds so much when they don't."

"Mummy," said Judy suddenly the next morning, "what's a fair-weather friend? Nurse says her friend in Peckham is one." ·

"It means somebody who is nice to you when everything is all right but doesn't stand by you in trouble."

"Oh," said Judy. "I see. Like Daddy."

"No, Judy, of course not. Daddy is unhappy and not very gay when he is worried, but if you or I were ill or unhappy, Daddy would do anything for us. He's the most loyal person in the world."

Judy looked thoughtfully at her mother and said:

"I don't like people who are ill. They go to bed and can't play. Margaret got something in her eye yesterday in the Park. She had to stop running and sit down. She wanted me to sit with her, but I wouldn't."

"Judy, that was very unkind."

"No, it wasn't. I don't like sitting down. I like running about."

"But if you had something in your eye you would like someone to sit and talk to you—not go off and leave you."

"I wouldn't mind. . . . And, anyway, I hadn't got something in my eye. It was Margaret."

Chapter 15

PROSPERITY

Dermot was prosperous. He was making nearly two thousand a year. Celia and he had a lovely time. They both agreed that they ought to save, but they also agreed that they wouldn't start just yet.

The first thing they bought was a secondhand car.

Then Celia longed to live in the country. It would be so much nicer for Judy, and she herself hated London. Always before, Dermot had negatived the idea on the score of expense—railway fares for him, food being cheaper in town, etc.

But now he admitted that he liked the idea. They would find a cottage not too far from Dalton Heath.

They eventually settled in the lodge of a big estate that was being cut up for building. Dalton Heath golf course was ten miles away. They also bought a dog—an adorable Sealyham called Aubrey.

Denman refused to accompany them to the country. Having been angelic all through the bad times, she became a positive fiend with the advent of prosperity. She was rude to Celia, went about tossing her head in the air, and finally gave notice saying that as some she knew were getting stuck up it was time she made a change.

They moved in spring, and the most exciting thing to Celia was the lilacs. There were hundreds of lilacs, all shades of mauve and purple. Wandering out into the garden in the early morning with Aubrey at her heels, Celia felt that life had become almost perfect. No more dirt and dust and fog. This was Home. . . .

Celia adored the country life and the long rambling walks with Aubrey. There was a small school nearby where Judy went in the mornings. Judy took to school as a duck takes to water. She was very shy with individuals, but completely unabashed by large numbers.

"Can I go to a really big school one day, Mummy? Where there are hundreds and hundreds and hundreds of girls? What's the biggest school in England?"

Celia had one passage of arms with Dermot over their little home. One of the front top rooms was to be their bedroom. Dermot wanted the other for his dressing room. Celia insisted that it should be Judy's nursery.

Dermot was annoyed.

"I suppose you'll have it your own way. I shall be the only person in the house who is never to have a bit of sun in his room."

"Judy ought to have a sunny room."

"Nonsense, she's out all day. That room at the back is quite large—plenty of room for her to run about in."

"There's no sun in it."

"I don't see why sun for Judy is more important than sun for me."

But Celia, for once, stood firm. She wanted badly to give Dermot his sunny room, but she didn't.

In the end Dermot was perfectly good-natured about his defeat. He adopted it as a grievance—but quite good-temperedly—and pretended to be a down-trodden husband and father.

2

They had a good many neighbors near them—most of them with children. Everyone was friendly. The only thing that made a difficulty was Dermot's refusal to go out to dinner.

"Look here, Celia, I come down from London tired out, and you want me to dress up and go out and not get home and to bed till past midnight. I simply can't do it."

"Not every night, of course. But I don't see that one night a week would matter."

"Well, I don't want to. You go, if you like."

"I can't go alone. People don't ask you to dinner except in pairs. And it sounds so odd for me to say that you never go out at night— because, after all, you're quite young."

"I'm sure you could manage to go without me."

But that wasn't so easy. In the country, as Celia said, people were asked in couples or not at all. Still, she saw the justice of what Dermot said. He was earning the money—he ought to have the say in their joint life. So she refused the invitations, and they sat at home, Dermot reading books on financial subjects, and Celia sometimes sewing, sometimes sitting with her hands clasped, thinking about her family of Cornish fishermen.

3

Celia wanted to have another child.

Dermot didn't.

"You always said there was no room in London," said Celia. "And of course we were very poor. But we've got enough now, and there's heaps of room and two wouldn't be any more trouble than one."

"Well, we don't want one just now. All the fuss and bother and crying and bottles all over again."

"I believe you'll always say that."

"No, I shan't. I'd like to have two more children. But not now. There's heaps of time. We're quite young still. It will be a sort of adventure for when we're getting bored with things. Let's just enjoy ourselves now. You don't want to begin sick again." He paused. "I tell you what I did look at today."

"Oh, Dermot!"

"A car. This secondhand little beast is pretty rotten. Davis put me onto this. It's a sports model—only done eight thousand miles."

Celia thought:

"How I love him! He's such a boy. So eager. . . . And he's worked so hard. Why shouldn't he have the things he likes? . . . We'll have another baby someday. In the meantime let him have his car. . . . After all, I care more for him than for any baby in the world. . . ."

4

It puzzled Celia that Dermot never wanted any of his old friends to stay.

"But you used to be so fond of Andrews."

"Yes—but we've grown out of touch with each other. We never meet nowadays. One changes. . . ."

"And Jim Lucas—you and he used to be inseparable when we were engaged."

"Oh, I can't be bothered with any of the old army crowd."

One day Celia had a letter from Ellie Maitland—Ellie Peterson, as she now was.

"Dermot, my old friend Ellie Peterson is home from India. I was her bridesmaid. Shall I ask her and her husband down for the weekend?"

"Yes, of course, if you like. Does he play golf?"

"I don't know."

"Rather a bore if he doesn't. However, it won't really matter, you won't want me to stay at home and entertain them, will you?"

"Couldn't we play tennis?"

There were a number of courts for the use of residents on the estate.

"Ellie used to be awfully keen on tennis, and Tom plays, I know. He used to be good."

"Look here, Celia, I simply can't play tennis. It absolutely ruins my game. And there's the Dalton Heath Cup in three weeks' time."

"Does nothing matter but golf? It makes it so difficult."

"Don't you think, Celia, that it's ever so much better if everyone does as they like? I like golf—you like tennis. You have your friends down and do as you like with them. You know I never interfere with anything you want to do."

That was true. It all sounded perfectly all right. But somehow it made things difficult in practice. When you were married, Celia reflected, you were somehow so tied up with your husband. Nobody considered you as a separate unity. It would be all right if it were only Ellie coming down, but surely Dermot ought to do something about Ellie's husband.

After all, when Davis (with whom Dermot played nearly every weekend) and his wife came to stay, she, Celia, had to entertain Mrs. Davis all day. Mrs. Davis was nice but dull. She just sat about and had to be talked to.

But she didn't say these things to Dermot because she knew he hated to be argued with. She asked the Petersons down and hoped for the best.

Ellie had changed very little. She and Celia enjoyed talking over old times. Tom was a little quiet. He had gone a little gray. He seemed a nice little man, Celia thought. He had always seemed a little absent-minded but very pleasant.

Dermot behaved angelically. He explained that he was obliged to play golf on Saturday (Ellie's husband didn't play), but he devoted Sunday to entertaining his guests and took them on the river, a form of spending an afternoon which Celia knew he hated.

When they had gone he said to her: "Now then, have I been noble or have I not?"

Noble was one of Dermot's words. It always made Celia laugh.

"You have. You've been an angel."

"Well, don't make me do it again for a long time, will you?"

Celia didn't. She rather wanted to invite another friend and her husband down two weeks later, but she knew the man wasn't a golfer, and she didn't want Dermot to have to make a sacrifice a second time. . . .

It was so difficult, thought Celia, living with a person who was sacrificing himself. Dermot was rather trying as a martyr. He was much better to live with when he was enjoying himself. . . .

And, anyway, he was unsympathetic about old friends. Old friends, in Dermot's opinion, were usually a bore.

Judy was obviously in sympathy with her father over this, for a few days later when Celia mentioned her friend Margaret, Judy merely stared.

"Who's Margaret?"

"Don't you remember Margaret? You used to play with her in the Park in London?"

"No, I didn't. I never played with a Margaret anywhere."

"Judy, you must remember. It's only a year ago."

But Judy couldn't remember any Margaret at all. She couldn't remember anyone she had played with in London.

"I only know the girls at school," said Judy comfortably.

5

Something rather exciting happened. It began by Celia being rung up and asked to take someone's place at a dinner party at the last minute.

"I know you won't mind, dear. . . ."

Celia didn't mind. She was delighted.

She enjoyed the evening frightfully.

She wasn't shy. She found it easy to talk. There was no need to watch whether she were being "silly" or not. Dermot's critical eyes were not upon her.

She felt as though she had been suddenly wafted back to girlhood.

The man on her right had traveled a lot in the East. Above everything in the world Celia longed to travel.

She felt sometimes that if the chance were to be given her she would leave Dermot and Judy and Aubrey and everything and dash off into the blue. . . . To wander. . . .

The man at her side spoke of Baghdad, of Kashmir, of Ispahan and Teheran and Shiraz (such lovely words—nice to say them even without any meaning attached). He told her, too, of wandering in Baluchistan where few travelers had been.

The man on her left was an elderly, kindly person. He liked the bright young creature at his side who turned to him at last with a rapturous face still full of the glamor of far lands.

He had something to do with books, she gathered, and she told him, laughing a good deal, about her one unlucky venture. He said he'd like to see her manuscript. Celia told him that it was very bad.

"All the same, I'd like to see it. Will you show it to me?"

"Yes, if you like, but you'll be disappointed."

He thought that probably he would. She didn't look like a writer— this young creature with her Scandinavian fairness. But, just because she attracted him, it would interest him to see what she had written.

Celia came home at 1 A.M. to find Dermot happily asleep. She was so excited that she woke him up.

"Dermot—I've had such a lovely evening. Oh! I have enjoyed myself! There was a man there who told me all about Persia and Baluchistan, and there was a nice publisher man—and they made me sing after dinner. I sang awfully badly, but they didn't seem to mind. And then we went out in the garden, and I went with the traveling man to see the lily pond—and he tried to kiss me—but quite nicely—and it was all so lovely—with the moon and the lilies and everything that I would have liked him to—but I didn't because I knew you wouldn't have liked it."

"Quite right," said Dermot.

"But you don't mind, do you?"

"Of course not," said Dermot kindly. "I'm glad you enjoyed yourself. But I don't know why you've got to wake me up to tell me about it."

"Because I have enjoyed myself so much." She added apologetically, "I know you don't like me to say so."

"I don't mind. It just seems to me rather silly. I mean, one can enjoy one's self without having to *say* so."

"I can't," said Celia honestly. "I have to say so a great deal, otherwise I'd burst."

"Well," said Dermot, turning over, "you've told me now."

And he went to sleep again.

Dermot was like that, thought Celia, a little sobered as she undressed, rather damping but quite kind. . . .

6

Celia had forgotten all about her promise to show the publisher man her book. To her great surprise he walked in upon her the following afternoon and reminded her of her promise.

She hunted out a bundle of dusty manuscripts from a cupboard in the attic, reiterating her statement that it was very stupid.

A fortnight later she had a letter asking her to come up to town to see him.

From behind a very untidy table strewn with bundles of manuscript he twinkled at her from behind his glasses.

"Look here," he said, "I understood this was a book. There's only a little more than half of it here. Where's the rest? Have you lost it?"

Puzzled, Celia took the manuscript from him.

Her mouth fell open with dismay.

"I've given you the wrong one. This is the old one I never finished."

Then she explained. He listened attentively, then told her to send him the revised version. He would keep the unfinished one for the moment.

A week later she was summoned again. This time her friend's eyes were twinkling more than ever.

"The second edition's no good," he said. "You won't find a publisher to look at it—quite right too. But your original story is not bad at all—do you think you could finish it?"

"But it's all wrong. It's full of mistakes."

"Now look here, my dear child, I'm going to talk to you quite plainly. You're not a heaven-sent genius. I don't think you'll ever write a masterpiece. But what you certainly *are* is a born storyteller. You think of spiritualism and mediums and Welsh Revivalist meetings in a kind of romantic haze. You may be all wrong about them, but you see them as ninety-nine percent of the reading public (who know nothing about them either) see them. That ninety-nine percent won't enjoy reading about carefully acquired facts—they want fiction—which is plausible untruth. It must be plausible, mind. You'll find it will be the same with your Cornish fisher folk that you told me about. Write your book about them, but, for heaven's sake, don't go near Cornwall or fishermen until you've finished. Then you'll write the kind of grimly realistic stuff that people expect when they read about Cornish fisher folk. You don't want to go there and find out that Cornish fishermen are not a breed by themselves but something quite closely allied to a Walworth plumber. You'll never write well about anything you really know about, because you've got an honest mind. You can be imaginatively dishonest but not practically dishonest. You can't write lies about something you know, but you'll be able to tell the most splendid lies about something you don't know. You've got to write about the fabulous (fabulous to you) and not about the real. Now, go away and do it."

A year later Celia's first novel was published. It was called *Lonely Harbor*. The publishers corrected any glaring inaccuracies.

Miriam thought it splendid, and Dermot thought it rather awful.

Celia knew that Dermot was right, but she was grateful to her mother.

"Now," thought Celia, "I'm pretending to be a writer. I think it's almost queerer than pretending to be a wife or a mother."

Chapter 16

LOSS

Miriam was ailing. Every time that Celia saw her mother, her heart had a sudden squeezed feeling.

Her mother looked so small and pathetic.

And she was so lonely in that big house.

Celia wanted her mother to come and live with them, but Miriam refused energetically.

"It never works. It wouldn't be fair to Dermot."

"I've asked Dermot. He's quite willing."

"That is nice of him. But I shouldn't dream of doing it. Young people *must* be left alone."

She spoke vehemently. Celia did not protest.

Presently Miriam said:

"I've wanted to tell you—for some time. I was wrong about Dermot. When you married him, I didn't trust him. I didn't think he was honest or loyal. . . . I thought there would be other women."

"Oh, Mother, Dermot never looks at anything but a golf ball."

Miriam smiled.

"I was wrong . . . I'm glad . . . I feel now that when I go I'm leaving you with someone who will look after you and take care of you."

"He will. He does."

"Yes—I'm satisfied. . . . He's very attractive—he is attractive to women, Celia, remember that. . . ."

"He's a frightfully stay-at-home person, Mummy."

"Yes, that's lucky. And I think he really loves Judy. She is exactly like him. She's not like you. She's Dermot's child."

"I know."

"So long as I feel that he will be kind to you. . . . I didn't think so at first. I thought he was cruel—ruthless—"

"He isn't. He's frightfully kind. He was sweet before Judy was born. He's just one of those people who hate to say things. It's all there underneath. He's like a rock."

Miriam sighed.

"I've been jealous. I haven't been willing to recognize his good qualities. I want you so much to be happy, my darling."

"I am, Mother dear, I am."

"Yes, I think you are. . . ."

Celia said after a minute or two:

"There's really nothing I want in the world—except another baby, perhaps. I'd like a boy as well as a girl."

She had expected her mother to be in sympathy with her wish, but a slight frown crossed Miriam's forehead.

"I don't know that you will be wise. You care for Dermot so much—and children take you away from a man. They are supposed to bring you together, but it isn't so . . . no, it isn't so."

"But you and Father—"

Miriam sighed.

"It was difficult. Pulling—always pulling both ways. It's difficult."

"But you and Father were perfectly happy. . . ."

"Yes—but I minded. . . . There were heaps of things I minded. Giving up things for the sake of the children annoyed him sometimes. He loved you all, but we were happiest when he and I went away together for a little holiday. . . . Don't ever leave your husband too long alone, Celia. Remember, a man forgets. . . ."

"Father would never have looked at anyone but you."

Her mother answered musingly.

"No, perhaps he wouldn't. But I was always on the look out. There was a parlor maid—a big handsome girl—the type I had often heard your father admire. She was handing him the hammer and some nails. As she did it she put her hand over his. I saw her. Your father hardly noticed—he just looked surprised. I don't suppose he thought anything of it—probably imagined it was just an accident—men are very simple. . . . But I sent that girl away—at once. Just gave her a good reference and said she didn't suit me."

Celia was shocked.

"But Father would never—"

"Probably not. *But I wasn't taking any risks.* I've seen so many things. A wife who's in bad health and a governess or companion takes charge—some young, bright girl. Celia, promise me you'll be very careful what kind of governesses you have for Judy."

Celia laughed and kissed her mother.

"I won't have any fine big girls," she promised. "They shall be thin and old and wear glasses."

2

Miriam died when Judy was eight years old. Celia was abroad at the time. Dermot had got ten days' leave at Easter, and he had wanted Celia to go to Italy with him. Celia had been a little unwilling to leave England. The doctor had told her that her mother's health was bad. She had a companion who looked after her, and Celia went down to see her every few weeks.

Miriam, however, would not hear of Celia's remaining behind and letting Dermot go alone. She came up to London and stayed with Cousin Lottie (a widow now), and Judy and her governess came to stay there also.

At Como, Celia got a telegram advising her return. She took the first train available. Dermot wanted to go too, but Celia persuaded him to stay behind and finish his holiday. He needed a change of air and scene.

It was as she was sitting in the dining car on her way through France that a curious cold certainty seemed to invade her body.

She thought:

"Of course, I shall never see her again. She's dead. . . ."

She found on arrival that Miriam had died just about that hour.

3

Her mother . . . her little gallant mother . . .

Lying there so still and strange with flowers and whiteness and a cold, peaceful face. . . .

Her mother, with her fits of gaiety and depression—her enchanting changeableness of outlook—her steadfast love and protection. . . .

Celia thought: "I'm alone now. . . ."

Dermot and Judy were strangers. . . .

She thought: "There's no one to go to any more. . . ."

Panic swept over her . . . and then remorse. . . .

How full her mind had been of Dermot and Judy all these last years. . . . She had thought so little of her mother . . . her mother had just been *there* . . . always *there*—at the back of everything. . . .

She knew her mother through and through, and her mother knew her. . . .

As a tiny child she had found her mother wonderful and satisfying. . . .

And wonderful and satisfying her mother had always remained. . . .

And now her mother had gone. . . .

The bottom had fallen out of Celia's world. . . .

Her little mother. . . .

Chapter 17

DISASTER

Dermot meant to be kind. He hated trouble and unhappiness, but he wanted to be kind. He wrote from Paris, suggesting Celia should come over and have a day or two to cheer her up.

Perhaps it was kindness, perhaps it was because he funked going home to a house of mourning. . . .

That, however, was what he had to do. . . .

He arrived at the Lodge just before dinner. Celia was lying on her bed. She was awaiting his coming with passionate intensity. The strain of the funeral was over, and she had been anxious not to upset Judy by an atmosphere of grief. Little Judy, so young and cheerful and important over her own affairs. Judy had cried about Grandmamma but had soon forgotten. Children ought to forget.

Soon Dermot would be here, and then she could let go.

She thought passionately: "How wonderful that I've got Dermot. If it weren't for Dermot I should want to die too. . . ."

Dermot was nervous. It was sheer nervousness that made him come into the room and say:

"Well, how's everybody, bright and jolly?"

At another time Celia would have recognized the cause that made him speak flippantly. Just at the moment it was as though he had hit her in the face.

She shrank back and burst into tears.

Dermot apologized and tried to explain.

In the end Celia went to sleep holding his hand, which he withdrew with relief when he saw she was really asleep.

He wandered off and joined Judy in the nursery. She waved a cheerful spoon at him. She was drinking a cup of milk.

"Hullo, Daddy. What shall we play?"

Judy wasted no time.

"It mustn't be noisy," said Dermot. "Your mother's asleep."

Judy nodded comprehendingly.

"Let's play Old Maid."

They played Old Maid.

2

Life went on as usual. At least, not quite as usual.

Celia went about as usual. She displayed no outward signs of grief. But all the spring had gone out of her for the time being. She was like a run-down clock. Both Dermot and Judy felt the change, and they didn't like it.

Dermot wanted some people to stay a fortnight later, and Celia cried out before she could stop herself.

"Oh, not just now. I just can't bear to have to talk to a strange woman all day."

But immediately afterward she repented and went to Dermot, telling him that she didn't mean to be silly. Of course he must have his friends. So they came, but the visit wasn't a great success.

A few days later Celia had a letter from Ellie. Its contents surprised and grieved her very much.

> My Dear Celia [wrote Ellie]: I feel I should like to tell you myself (since you'll probably hear a garbled version otherwise) that Tom has gone off with a girl we met on the boat

coming home. It has been a terrible grief and shock to me.
We were so happy together, and Tom loved the children. It
seems like some terrible dream. I feel absolutely broken-
hearted. I don't know what to do. Tom has been such a
perfect husband—we never even quarreled.

Celia was very upset over her friend's trouble.

"What a lot of sad things there are in the world," she said to Dermot.

"That husband of hers must be rather a rotter," said Dermot. "You
know, Celia, you sometimes seem to think that I'm selfish—but you
might have much worse things to put up with. At any rate, I am a good,
straight, undeceiving husband, aren't I?"

There was something comic in his tone. Celia kissed him and
laughed.

Three weeks later she went home, taking Judy with her. The house
had got to be turned out and gone through. It was a task she dreaded.
But no one else could do it.

Home without her mother's welcoming smile was unthinkable. If
only Dermot could have come with her.

Dermot himself tried in his own fashion to cheer her up.

"You'll enjoy it really, Celia. You'll find lots of old things you've
forgotten all about. And it will be lovely down there this time of year.
It will do you good to have a change. Here am I having to grind along
in an office every day."

Dermot was so inadequate! He persistently ignored the significance
of emotional stress. He shied away from it like a frightened horse.

Celia cried out—angry for once:

"You talk as though it was a holiday!"

He looked away from her.

"Well," he said, "so it will be in a way. . . ."

Celia thought: "He's *not* kind . . . he's *not*. . . ."

A great wave of loneliness passed over her. She felt afraid. . . .

How cold the world was—without her mother. . . .

3

Celia went through a bad time in the next few months. She had lawyers to see, all kind of business questions to settle.

Her mother had, of course, left hardly any money. There was the question of the house to consider—whether to keep it or sell it. It was in a very bad state—there had been no money for repairs. A fairly large sum would have to be spent on it almost immediately if the whole place were not to go to rack and ruin. In any case, it was doubtful if a purchaser would consider it in its present condition.

Celia was torn by indecision.

She could not bear to part with it—yet common sense whispered that it was the best thing to do. It was too far from London for her and Dermot to live in it—even if the idea had appealed to Dermot (and Celia was sure it would not appeal to him). The country, to Dermot, meant a first-class golf course.

Was it not, then, mere sentiment on her part to insist on clinging to the place?

Yet she could not bear to give it up. Miriam had made such valiant struggles to keep it for her. It was she herself who had dissuaded her mother from selling it long ago. . . . Miriam had kept it for her—for her and her children.

Did Judy care for it as she had done? She thought not. Judy was so aloof—so unattached—she was like Dermot. People like Dermot and Judy lived in places because they were convenient. In the end Celia asked her daughter. Celia often felt that Judy, at eight years old, was far more sensible and practical than herself.

"Will you get a lot of money for it if you sell it, Mummy?"

"No, I'm afraid not. You see, it's an old-fashioned house—and it's right in the country—not near a town."

"Well, then, perhaps you'd better keep it," said Judy. "We can come here in the summer."

"Are you fond of being here, Judy? Or do you like the Lodge best?"

"The Lodge is very small," said Judy. "I'd like to live in the Dormy House. I like big—big—houses."

Celia laughed.

It was true what Judy had said—she would get very little for the house if she sold it now. Surely even as a business proposition it would be better to wait until country houses were less of a drug in the market. She went into the question of the minimum repairs that were absolutely necessary. Perhaps, when they were completed, she could find a tenant for the house furnished.

The business side of things had been worrying, but it had kept her mind away from sad thoughts.

Now there came the part she had dreaded—the turning out. If the house was to be let, it must first be cleared. Some of the rooms had been locked up for years—there were old trunks, drawers, and cupboards, all crammed with memories of the past.

4

Memories. . . .

It was so lonely—so strange in the house.

No Miriam. . . .

Only trunks full of old clothes—drawers full of letters and photographs. . . .

It hurt—it hurt horribly.

A japanned box with a stork on it that she had loved as a child. Inside it folded letters. One from Mummy. "My own precious lamb pigeony pumpkin. . . ." The scalding tears fell down Celia's cheeks. . . .

A pink silk evening dress with little rosebuds—shoved into a trunk— in case it might be "renovated"—and forgotten. One of her first evening dresses. . . . She remembered the last time she had worn it. . . . Such a gauche, eager, idiotic creature. . . .

Letters belonging to Grannie—a whole trunk full. She must have brought them with her when she came. Photograph of an old gentleman in a Bath chair, "Always your devoted admirer," and some initials scrawled on it. Grannie and "the men." Always "the men" even when they were reduced to Bath chairs on the sea front. . . .

A mug with a picture of two cats on it that Susan had once given her for a birthday present. . . .

Back—back into the past. . . .

Why did it hurt so?

Why did it hurt so abominably?

If only she wasn't alone in the house. . . . If only Dermot could be with her!

But Dermot would say: "Why not burn the lot without looking through them?"

So sensible, but somehow she couldn't. . . .

She opened more locked drawers.

Poems. Sheets of poems in flowing faded handwriting. Her mother's handwriting as a girl. . . . Celia looked through them.

Sentimental—stilted—very much of the period. Yes, but something—some quick turn of thought, some sudden originality of phrase—that made them essentially her mother's. Miriam's mind—that quick, darting, bird-like mind. . . .

"*Poem to John on his birthday. . . .*"

Her father—her bearded, jolly father. . . .

Here was a daguerroetype of him as a solemn clean-shaven boy.

Being young—growing old—how mysterious—how frightening it all was. Was there any particular moment at which you were more you than at any other moment?

The future. . . . Where was she, Celia, going in the future?. . . .

Well, it was clear enough. Dermot growing a little richer . . . a larger house . . . another child . . . two, perhaps. Illnesses—childish ailments—Dermot growing a little more difficult, a little more impatient still of anything interfering with what he wanted to do. . . . Judy growing up—vivid, decided, intensely alive. . . . Dermot and Judy together. . . . herself, rather fatter—faded—treated with just a touch of amused contempt by those two. . . . "Mother, you *are* rather silly, you know. . . ." Yes, more difficult to disguise that you were silly as your looks left you. (A sudden flash of memory: "Don't ever grow less beautiful, will you, Celia?") Yes, but that was all over now. They'd lived together long enough for such things as the beauty of a face to have lost its meaning. Dermot was in her blood and she in his. They *belonged*—essentially strangers, they belonged. She loved him because he was so different—because though she knew by now exactly how he reacted to things, she did not know and never would know *why* he reacted as he did. Probably he felt the same about her. No, Dermot accepted things as they were. He never thought about them. It seemed to him a waste of time. Celia thought: "It's right—it's absolutely right to marry the person you love. Money and outside things don't count. I should always have been happy with Dermot even if we'd had to live in a tiny cottage and I'd had to do all the cooking and everything." But Dermot wasn't going to be poor. He was a success. He would go on succeeding. He was that kind of person. His digestion, of course, *that* would get worse. He would continue to play golf. . . . And they'd go on and on and on—probably at Dalton Heath or somewhere like it. . . . She'd never see things—faraway things—India, China, Japan—the wilds of Baluchistan—Persia, where the names were like music: Ispahan, Teheran, Shiraz. . . .

Little shivers ran over her. . . . If one could be free—quite free—nothing, no belongings, no houses, or husband or children, nothing to hold you, and tie you, and pull at your heart. . . .

Celia thought: "I want to run away. . . ."

Miriam had felt like that.

For all her love of her husband and children she had wanted, sometimes, to get out. . . .

Celia opened another drawer. Letters. Letters from her father to her mother. She picked up the top one. It was dated the year before his death.

Dearest Miriam: I hope you will soon be able to join me. Mother seems very well and is in good spirits. Her eyesight is failing, but she knits just as many bedsocks for her beaux!

I had a long talk with Armour about Cyril. He says the boy is *not* stupid. He is just indifferent. I talked to Cyril too, and, I hope, made some impression.

Try and be with me by Friday, my dearest—our twenty-second anniversary. I find it hard to put into words all that you have meant to me—the dearest, most devoted wife any man could have. I am humbly grateful to God for you, my darling.

Love to our little Poppet.

Your devoted husband,
John.

Tears came again to Celia's eyes.

Someday she and Dermot would have been married twenty-two years. Dermot wouldn't write a letter like that, but, deep down, he would perhaps feel the same.

Poor Dermot. It had been sad for him having her so broken and battered this last month. He didn't like unhappiness. Well, once she had got through with this task she would put grief behind her. Miriam, alive, had never come between her and Dermot. Miriam, dead, must not do so. . . .

She and Dermot would go forward together—happy and enjoying things.

That was what would please her mother best.

She took all her father's letters out of the drawer, and making a pile of them on the hearth, she set a match to them. They belonged to the dead. The one she had read she kept.

At the bottom of the drawer was a faded old pocketbook embroidered in gold thread. Inside it was a folded sheet of paper, very old and worn. On it was written: "Poem sent me by Miriam on my birthday."

Sentiment. . . .

The world despised sentiment nowadays. . . .

But to Celia, at that moment, it was somehow unbearably sweet. . . .

5

Celia felt ill. The loneliness of the house was getting on her nerves. She wished she had someone to speak to. There were Judy and Miss Hood, but they belonged to such an alien world that being with them brought more strain than relief. Celia was anxious that no shadow should cloud Judy's life. Judy was so vivid—so full of enjoyment of everything. When she was with Judy, Celia made a point of being gay. They had strenuous games together with balls, and battledores, and shuttle-cocks.

It was after Judy had gone to bed that the silence of the house wrapped itself round Celia like a pall. It seemed so empty—so empty. . . .

It brought back so vividly those happy, cozy evenings spent talking

to her mother—about Dermot, about Judy, about books and people
and ideas.

Now, there was no one to talk to. . . .

Dermot's letters were infrequent and brief. He had gone round in
seventy-two—he had played with Andrews—Rossiter had come down
with his niece. He had got Marjorie Connell to make a fourth. They'd
played at Hillborough—a rotten course. Women were a nuisance in
golf. He hoped Celia was enjoying herself. Would she thank Judy for
her letter?

Celia began to sleep badly. Scenes came up out of the past and kept
her awake. Sometimes she awoke frightened—not knowing what it was
that had frightened her. She looked at herself in the glass and knew she
looked ill.

She wrote to Dermot and begged him to come down for a weekend.
He wrote back:

Dear Celia: I've looked up the train service and it really isn't worth
it. I'd either have to go back Sunday morning or else land in town
about two in the morning. The car's not running very well now,
and I'm having her overhauled. I know you'll realize that I feel it
a bit of a strain working all the week. I feel dog-tired by the weekend—and don't want to embark on train journeys.

In another three weeks I shall get off for my holiday. I think
your idea of Dinard is quite a good one. I'll write about rooms.
Don't do too much and overtire yourself. Get out a good deal.

You remember Marjorie Connell, rather nice dark girl, niece
of the Barretts? She's just lost her job. I may be able to get her
one here. She's quite efficient. I took her to the theater one night
as she was down on her luck.

Take care of yourself and go easy. I think you're right not to
sell the house now. Things may improve and you might get a
better price later. I don't see that it's ever going to be much use
to us, but if you feel sentimental about it I don't suppose it would
cost much to shut it up with a caretaker—and you might let it
furnished. The money you get in from the books would pay the
rates and a gardener, and I'll help toward it, if you like. I'm

working frightfully hard and come home with a headache most nights.

It will be good to get right away.

Love to Judy.

> Your loving,
> Dermot.

The last week Celia went to the doctor and asked him to give her something to make her sleep. He had known her all her life. He asked her questions, examined her, then he said:

"Can't you get someone to be with you?"

"My husband is coming in a week's time. We are going abroad together."

"Ah, excellent! You know, my dear, you're heading for a breakdown. You're very run-down—you've had a shock, and you've been fretting. Very natural. I know how attached you were to your mother. Once you get away with your husband into fresh surroundings you'll be as right as rain."

He patted her on the shoulder, gave her a prescription, and dismissed her.

Celia counted the days one by one. When Dermot came, everything would be all right. He was to arrive the day before Judy's birthday. They were to celebrate that, and then they were to start for Dinard.

A new life. . . . Grief and memories left behind. . . . She and Dermot going forward into the future.

In four days Dermot would be here. . . .

In three days. . . .

In two days. . . .

Today!

6

Something was wrong. . . . Dermot had come, but it wasn't Dermot. It was a stranger who looked at her—quick sideways glances—and looked away again. . . .

Something was the matter. . . .

He was ill. . . .

In trouble. . . .

No, it was different from that.

He was—a stranger. . . .

7

"Dermot, is anything the matter?"

"What should be the matter?"

They were alone together in Celia's bedroom. Celia was doing up Judy's birthday presents with tissue paper and ribbon.

Why was she so frightened? Why this sick feeling of terror?

His eyes—his queer shifty eyes—that looked away from her and back again. . . .

This wasn't Dermot—upright, handsome, laughing Dermot. . . .

This was a furtive, shrinking person . . . he looked—almost—like a criminal. . . .

She said suddenly:

"Dermot, there isn't anything—with money—I mean, you haven't done anything—?"

How put it into words? Dermot, who was the soul of honor, an embezzler? Fantastic—fantastic!

But that shifty evasive glance. . . .

As though she would care what he had done!

He looked surprised.

"Money? Oh, no, money's all right. I'm—I'm doing very well."

She was relieved.

"I thought—it was absurd of me. . . ."

He said:

"There is something. . . . I expect you can guess."

But she couldn't. If it wasn't money (she had had a fleeting fear the firm might have failed) she couldn't imagine what it could be.

She said: "Tell me."

It wasn't—it couldn't be *cancer*. . . .

Cancer attacked strong people, young people, sometimes.

Dermot stood up. His voice sounded strange and stiff.

"It's—well, it's Marjorie Connell. I've seen a lot of her, I'm very fond of her."

Oh, the relief! *Not* cancer. . . . But Marjorie Connell—why on earth Marjorie Connell? Had Dermot—Dermot who never looked at a girl—

She said gently:

"It doesn't matter, Dermot, if you've been rather silly. . . ."

A flirtation. Dermot wasn't used to flirting. All the same, she was surprised. Surprised and hurt. While she had been so miserable—so longing for Dermot's comfort and presence—he had been flirting with Marjorie Connell. Marjorie was quite a nice girl and rather good-looking. Celia thought: "Grannie wouldn't have been surprised." And the idea flashed through her mind that perhaps Grannie *had* known men rather well, after all.

Dermot said violently:

"You don't understand. It's not at all as you think. There has been nothing—nothing—"

Celia flushed.

"Of course. I didn't think there had. . . ."

He went on:

"I don't know how to make you see. It isn't her fault. . . . She's very distressed about it—about you. . . . Oh, God!"

He sat down and buried his face in his hands. . . .

Celia said wonderingly:

"You really care for her—I see. Oh, Dermot, I am so sorry. . . ."

Poor Dermot, overtaken by this passion. He was going to be so unhappy. She mustn't—she simply mustn't be beastly about it. She must help him to get over it—not reproach him. It hadn't been his fault. She hadn't been there—he'd been lonely—it was quite natural. . . .

She said again:

"I'm so dreadfully sorry for you."

He got up again.

"You don't understand. You needn't be sorry for *me*. . . . I'm a rotter. I feel a cur. I couldn't be decent to you. I shall be no more use to you and Judy. . . . You'd better cut me right out. . . ."

She stared. . . .

"You mean," she said, "you don't love me any longer? Not at all? But we've been so happy. . . . Always so happy together."

"Yes, in a way—a quiet way. . . . This is quite different."

"I think to be quietly happy is the best thing in the world."

Dermot made a gesture.

She said wonderingly:

"You want to go away from us? Not to see me and Judy anymore? But you're Judy's father. . . . She loves you."

"I know. . . . I mind terribly about her. But it's no good. I'm never any use doing anything I don't want to do. . . . I can't behave decently when I'm unhappy. . . . I should be a brute."

Celia said slowly:

"You're going away—with *her*?"

"Of course not. She's not that kind of a girl. I would never suggest such a thing to her."

He sounded hurt and offended.

"I don't understand—you just want to leave *us*?"

"Because I can't be any good to you. . . . I should be simply foul."

"But we've been so happy—so happy . . ."

Dermot said impatiently:

"Yes, of course, we have—in the past. But we've been married eleven years. After eleven years one needs a change."

She winced.

He went on, his voice persuasive, more like himself:

"I'm making quite a good income, I'd allow you plenty for Judy—and you're making money yourself now. You could go abroad—travel—do all sorts of things you've always wanted to do. . . ."

She put up her hand as though he had struck her.

"I'm sure you'd enjoy it. You'd really be much happier than you would be with me. . . ."

"Stop!"

After a minute or two she said quietly:

"It was on this night, nine years ago, that Judy began to be born. Do you remember? Doesn't it mean anything to you? Isn't there any difference between me and—a mistress you would try to pension off?"

He said sulkily:

"I've said I was sorry about Judy. . . . But, after all, we both agreed that the other should be perfectly free. . . ."

"Did we? When?"

"I'm sure we did. It's the only decent way to regard marriage."

Celia said:

"I think, when you've brought a child into the world—it would be more decent to stick to it."

Dermot said:

"All my friends think that the ideal of marriage should be freedom. . . ."

She laughed. His friends. How extraordinary Dermot was—only he would have dragged in his friends.

She said:

"You are free. . . . You can leave us if you choose . . . if you really choose . . . but won't you wait a little—won't you be sure? There's eleven years' happiness to remember—against a month's infatuation. Wait a year—make sure of things—before bursting up everything. . . ."

"I don't want to wait. I don't want the strain of waiting. . . ."

Suddenly Celia stretched out and caught at the door handle.

All this wasn't real—couldn't be real. . . . She called out: "Dermot!"

The room went black and whirled round her.

She found herself lying on the bed. Dermot was standing beside her with a glass of water. He said:

"I didn't mean to upset you."

She stopped herself laughing hysterically . . . took the water and drank it. . . .

"I'm all right," she said. "It's all right. . . . You must do as you please. . . . You can go away now. I'm all right. . . . You do as you like. But let Judy have her birthday tomorrow."

"Of course. . . ."

He said: "If you're sure you're all right . . ."

He went slowly through the open door into his room and shut it behind him.

Judy's birthday tomorrow. . . .

Nine years ago she and Dermot had wandered in the garden—had been parted—she had gone down into pain and fear—and Dermot had suffered. . . .

Surely—surely—no one in the world could be so cruel as to choose this day to tell her. . . .

Yes, Dermot could. . . .

Cruel . . . cruel . . . cruel. . . .

Her heart cried out passionately:

"How could he—how could he—be so cruel to *me*? . . ."

8

Judy must have her birthday.

Presents—special breakfast—picnic—sitting up to dinner—games.

Celia thought: "There's never been a day so long—so long—I shall go mad. If only Dermot would play up a little more."

And Judy noticed nothing. She noticed her presents, her fun, the readiness of everyone to do what she wanted.

She was so happy—so unconscious—it tore at Celia's heart.

9

The next day Dermot left.

"I'll write from London, shall I? You'll stay here for the present?"

"Not here—no, not here."

Here, in the emptiness, the loneliness, without Miriam to comfort her?

Oh, Mother, Mother, come back to me, Mother. . . .

Oh, Mother, if you were here. . . .

Stay here alone? In this house so full of happy memories—memories of Dermot?

She said: "I'd rather come home. We'll come home tomorrow."

"As you please. I'll stay in London. I thought you were so fond of it down here."

She didn't answer. Sometimes you couldn't. People either saw or they didn't see.

When Dermot had left, she played with Judy. She told her they were not going to France after all. Judy accepted the pronouncement calmly, without interest.

Celia felt terribly ill. Her legs ached, her head swam. She felt like an old, old woman. The pain in her head increased till she could have screamed. She took aspirin, but it was no use. She felt sick, and the thought of food repelled her.

10

Celia was afraid of two things: she was afraid of going mad, and she was afraid of Judy noticing anything. . . .

She didn't know whether Miss Hood noticed anything. Miss Hood was so quiet. It was a comfort to have Miss Hood—so calm and incurious.

Miss Hood managed the going home. She seemed to think it quite natural that Celia and Dermot weren't going to France after all.

Celia was glad to get back to the Lodge. She thought: "This is better. I mayn't go mad after all."

Her head felt better but her body worse—as though she had been battered all over. Her legs felt too weak to walk. . . . That and the deathly sickness made her limp and unresisting. . . .

She thought: "I'm going to be ill. Why does your mind affect your body so?"

Dermot came down two days after her return.

It was still not Dermot. . . . Queer—and frightening—to find a stranger in the body of your husband. . . .

It frightened Celia so much that she wanted to scream. . . .

Dermot talked stiffly about outside matters.

"Like someone who's come to call," thought Celia.

Then he said:

"Don't you agree that it is the best thing to do—to part, I mean?"

"The best thing—for whom?"

"Well, for all of us."

"I don't think it's the best thing for Judy or me. You know I don't."

Dermot said: "Everybody can't be happy."

"You mean it's you who are going to be happy and Judy and I who aren't. . . . I don't see really why it should be you and not us. Oh, Dermot, can't you go and do what you want to do, and not insist on talking about it. You've got to choose between Marjorie and me—no, that's not it—you're tired of me and perhaps that's my fault—I ought to have seen it coming—I ought to have tried more, but I was so sure you loved me—I believed in you as I believed in God. That was stupid—Grannie would have told me so. No, what you have to choose between is Marjorie and Judy. You *do* love Judy—she's your own flesh and blood— and I can never be to her what you can be. There's a tie between you two that there isn't between her and me. I love her, but I don't understand her. I don't want you to abandon Judy—I don't want her life maimed. I wouldn't fight for myself, but I will fight for Judy. It's a mean thing to do, to abandon your own child. I believe—if you do it—you won't be happy. Dermot, dear Dermot, won't you *try?* Won't you give a year out of your life? If, at the end of a year, you can't do it, you feel you must go to Marjorie—well, then, you must go. But I'd feel then that you'd tried."

Dermot said: "I don't want to wait. . . . A year is a long time. . . ."

Celia gave a discouraged gesture.

(If only she didn't feel so deathly sick.)

She said: "Very well—you've chosen. . . . But if ever you want to come back—you'll find us waiting, and I won't reproach you. . . . Go, and be—be happy, and perhaps you'll come back to us someday. . . . I think you will. . . . I think that underneath everything it's really me and Judy you love. . . . And I think, too, that underneath you're straight and loyal. . . ."

Dermot cleared his throat. He looked embarrassed.

Celia wished he would go away. All this talking. . . . She loved him so—it was agony to look at him—if only he would go away and do what he wanted to do—not ram the agony of it home to her. . . .

"The real point is," said Dermot, "how soon can I get my freedom?"

"You are free. You can go now."

"I don't think you understand what I am talking about. All my friends think there should be a divorce as soon as possible."

Celia stared.

"I thought you told me there wasn't—there wasn't—well, any grounds for a divorce."

"Of course there aren't. Marjorie is as straight as a die."

A wild desire to laugh passed over Celia. She repressed it.

"Well, then?" she said.

"I'd never suggest anything of that kind to her," said Dermot in a shocked voice. "But I believe that, if I were free, she would marry me."

"But you're married to me," said Celia, puzzled.

"That's why there must be a divorce. It can all be put through quite easily and quickly. It will be no bother to you. And all the expense will fall on me."

"You mean that you and Marjorie *are* going away together after all?"

"Do you think I'd drag a girl like that through the divorce court? No, the whole thing can be managed quite easily. Her name need never appear."

Celia got up. Her eyes blazed.

"You mean—you mean—oh, I think that's disgusting! If I loved a man I'd go away with him even if it was wrong. I might take a man from his wife—I don't think I would take a man from his child—still, one never knows. But I'd do it *honestly*. I'd not skulk in the shadow and let someone else do the dirty work and play safe myself. I think both you and Marjorie are disgusting—disgusting. If you really loved each other and couldn't live without each other I would at least respect you. I'd divorce you if you wanted me to—although I think divorce is wrong. But I won't have anything to do with lying and pretending and making a put-up job of it."

"Nonsense, everybody does."

"I don't care."

Dermot came up to her.

"Look here, Celia, I'm going to have a divorce. I won't wait for it, and I won't have Marjorie dragged into it. And you've got to agree to it."

Celia looked him full in the face.

"I won't," she said.

Chapter 18

FEAR

It was here, of course, that Dermot made his mistake.

If he had appealed to Celia, if he had thrown himself on her mercy, if he had told her that he loved Marjorie and wanted her and couldn't live without her, Celia would have melted and agreed to anything he wanted—no matter how repugnant to her own feelings. Dermot unhappy she could not have resisted. She had always given him anything he wanted, and she would not have been able to keep from doing so again.

She was on the side of Judy against Dermot, but if he had taken her the right way, she would have sacrificed Judy to him, although she would have hated herself for doing so.

But Dermot took an entirely different line. He claimed what he wanted as a right and tried to bully her into consenting.

She had always been so soft, so malleable, that he was astonished at her resistance. She ate practically nothing, she did not sleep, her legs felt so weak she could hardly walk, she suffered tortures from neuralgia and earache, but she stood firm. And Dermot tried to bully her into giving her consent.

He told her that she was behaving disgracefully, that she was a vulgar, clutching woman, that she ought to be ashamed of herself, that he was ashamed of her. It had no effect.

Outwardly, that is. Inwardly his words cut her like wounds. That Dermot—Dermot—could think she was like that.

She grew worried about her physical condition. Sometimes she lost the thread of what she was saying—her thoughts, even, became confused. . . .

She would wake up in the night in a condition of utter terror. She would feel sure that Dermot was poisoning her—to get her out of the way. In the daytime she knew these for the wildest night fancies, but, all the same, she locked up the packet of weed killer that stood in the potting shed. As she did so, she thought: "That isn't quite sane—I mustn't go mad—I simply mustn't go mad. . . ."

She would wake up in the night and wander about the house looking for something. One night she knew what it was. She was looking for her mother. . . .

She must find her mother. She dressed and put on a coat and hat. She took her mother's photograph. She would go to the police station and ask them to trace her mother. Her mother had disappeared, but the police would find her. . . . And once she had found her mother everything would be all right. . . .

She walked for a long time—it was raining and wet. . . . She couldn't remember what she was walking for. Oh, yes, the police station—where was the police station? Surely in a town, not out in the open country.

She turned and walked in the other direction. . . .

The police would be kind and helpful. She would give them her mother's name—what was her mother's name? . . . Odd, she couldn't remember. . . . What was her own name?

How frightening—she couldn't remember. . . .

Sybil, wasn't it? Or Yvonne—how awful not to be able to remember. . . .

She *must* remember her own name. . . .

She stumbled over a ditch. . . .

The ditch was full of water. . . .

You could drown yourself in water. . . .

It would be better to drown yourself than to hang yourself. If you lay down in the water. . . .

Oh, how cold it was!—she couldn't—no, she couldn't. . . .

She would find her mother. . . . Her mother would put everything right.

She would say, "I nearly drowned myself in a ditch," and her mother would say, "That would have been very silly, darling."

Silly—yes, silly. Dermot had thought her silly—long ago. He had said so and his face had reminded her of something.

Of course! Of the Gun Man!

That was the horror of the Gun Man. All the time Dermot had really been the Gun Man. . . .

She felt sick with fear. . . .

She must get home . . . she must hide. . . . The Gun Man was looking for her. . . . Dermot was stalking her down. . . .

She got home at last. It was two o'clock. The house was asleep. . . .

She crept up the stairs. . . .

Horror, the Gun Man was there—behind that door—she could hear him breathing. . . . Dermot, the Gun Man. . . .

She daren't go back to her room. Dermot wanted to be rid of her. He might come creeping in. . . .

She ran wildly up one flight of stairs. Miss Hood, Judy's governess, was there. She burst in.

"Don't let him find me—don't let him . . ."

Miss Hood was wonderfully kind and reassuring.

She took her down to her room and stayed with her.

Just as Celia was falling asleep she said suddenly:

"How stupid, I couldn't have found my mother. I remember—*she's dead*. . . ."

2

Miss Hood got the doctor in. He was kind and emphatic Celia was to put herself in Miss Hood's charge.

He himself had an interview with Dermot. He told him plainly that Celia was in a very grave condition. He warned him of what might happen unless she were to be left entirely free from worry.

Miss Hood played her part very efficiently. As far as possible, she never left Celia and Dermot alone. Celia clung to her. With Miss Hood she felt safe. . . . She was *kind*. . . .

One day Dermot came in and stood by the bed.

He said: "I'm sorry you're ill. . . ."

It was Dermot who spoke to her—not the stranger.

A lump came in her throat. . . .

The next day Miss Hood came in with a rather worried face.

Celia said quietly: "He's gone, hasn't he?"

Miss Hood nodded. She was relieved that Celia took it so quietly.

Celia lay there motionless. She felt no grief—no pang. . . . She was just numb and peaceful. . . .

He had gone. . . .

Someday she must get up and start life again—with Judy. . . .

It was all over. . . .

Poor Dermot. . . .

She slept—she slept almost continuously for two days.

3

And then he came back.

It was Dermot who came back—not the stranger.

He said he was sorry—that as soon as he had gone he had been miserable. He said he thought that Celia was right—that he ought to stick to her and Judy. At any rate, he would try. . . . He said: "But you must get well. I can't bear illness . . . or unhappiness. It was partly because you were unhappy this spring that I got to be friends with Marjorie. I wanted someone to play with. . . ."

"I know. I ought to have 'stayed beautiful,' as you always told me."

Celia hesitated, then she said: "You—you do really mean to give it a chance? I mean, I can't stand any more. . . . If you'll honestly try—for three months. At the end of it, if you can't, then that's that. But—but—I'm afraid to go queer again. . . ."

He said that he'd try for three months. He wouldn't even see Marjorie. He said he was sorry.

4

But it didn't stay like that.

Miss Hood, Celia knew, was sorry that Dermot had come back.

Later, Celia admitted that Miss Hood had been right.

It began gradually.

Dermot became moody.

Celia was sorry for him, but she didn't dare to say anything.

Slowly things went worse and worse.

If Celia came into a room, Dermot went out of it.

If she spoke to him, he wouldn't answer. He talked only to Miss Hood and Judy.

Dermot never spoke to her or looked at her. He took Judy out in the car sometimes.

"Is Mummy coming?" Judy would ask.

"Yes, if she likes."

When Celia was ready, Dermot would say:

"Mummy had better drive you. I believe I'm busy."

Sometimes Celia would say *No*, she was busy, and then Dermot and Judy would go off.

Incredibly, Judy noticed nothing—or so Celia thought.

But occasionally Judy said things that surprised her.

They had been talking about being kind to Aubrey, who was the adored dog of the house by now, and Judy said suddenly:

"You're kind—you're very kind. Daddy's not kind, but he's very, very jolly. . . ."

And once she said reflectively:

"Daddy doesn't like you much. . . ." Adding with great satisfaction, "But he likes *me*."

One day Celia spoke to her.

"Judy, your father wants to leave us. He thinks he would be happier living with somebody else. Do you think it would be kinder to let him go?"

"I don't want him to go," said Judy quickly. "Please, please, Mummy, don't let him go. He's very happy playing with me—and besides—besides, he's my father."

"He's my father!" Such pride, such certainty in those words!

Celia thought: "Judy or Dermot? I've got to be on one side or the other. . . . And Judy's only a child, I *must* be on her side. . . ."

But she thought: "I can't stand Dermot's unkindness much longer. I'm losing grip again. . . . I'm getting frightened. . . ."

Dermot had disappeared again—the stranger was here in Dermot's place. He looked at her with hard, hostile eyes. . . .

Horrible when the person you loved most in the world looked at you like that. Celia could have understood infidelity, she couldn't understand the affection of eleven years turning suddenly—overnight as it were—to dislike. . . .

Passion might fade and die, but had there never been anything else? She had loved him and lived with him and borne his child, and gone through poverty with him—and he was quite calmly prepared never to see her again. . . . Oh, frightening—horribly frightening. . . .

She was the Obstacle. . . . If she were dead . . .

He wished her dead. . . .

He must wish her dead; otherwise she wouldn't be so afraid.

5

Celia looked in at the nursery door. Judy was sleeping soundly. Celia shut the door noiselessly and came down to the hall and went to the front door.

Aubrey hurried out of the drawing room.

"Hallo," said Aubrey: "A walk? At this time of night? Well, I don't mind if I do. . . ."

But his mistress thought otherwise. She took Aubrey's face between her hands and kissed him on the nose.

"Stay at home. Good dog. Can't come with missus."

Can't come with missus—no, indeed! No one must come where missus was going. . . .

She knew now that she couldn't bear any more. . . . She'd got to escape. . . .

She felt exhausted after that long scene with Dermot. . . . But she also felt desperate. . . . She must escape. . . .

Miss Hood had gone to London to see a sister come home from abroad. Dermot had seized the opportunity to "have things out."

He admitted at once he'd been seeing Marjorie. He'd promised—but he hadn't been able to keep the promise. . . .

None of that mattered, Celia felt, if only he wouldn't begin again battering at her. . . . But he had. . . .

She couldn't remember much now. . . . Cruel, hurting words—those hostile stranger's eyes. . . . Dermot, whom she loved, hated her. . . .

And she couldn't bear it. . . .

So this was the easiest way out. . . .

She had said when he had explained that he was going away but would come back two days later: "You won't find me here." By the flicker in his eyelids she had felt sure that he knew what she meant. . . .

He had said quickly: "Well, of course, if you like to go away."

She hadn't answered. . . . Afterward, when it was all over, he would be able to tell everybody (and convince himself) that he hadn't understood her meaning. . . . It would be easier for him like that. . . .

He had known . . . and she had seen just that momentary flicker—of hope. He hadn't, perhaps, known that himself. He would be shocked to admit such a thing . . . *but it had been there.* . . .

He did not, of course, prefer that solution. What he would have liked was for her to say that, like him, she would welcome "a change." He wanted her to want her freedom too. He wanted, that is, to do what he wanted, and at the same time to feel comfortable about it. He would like her to be happy and contented traveling about abroad so that he could feel, "Well, it's really been an excellent solution for both of us."

He wanted to be happy, and he wanted to feel his conscience quite at ease. He wouldn't accept facts as they were—he wanted things to be as he would like them to be.

But death *was* a solution. . . . It wasn't as though he'd feel himself to blame for it. He would soon persuade himself that Celia had been in a bad way ever since the death of her mother. Dermot was so clever at persuading himself. . . .

She played for a minute with the idea that he would be sorry—that he would feel a terrible remorse . . . She thought for a moment, like a child: "When I'm dead he'll be sorry. . . ."

But she knew that wasn't so. . . . Once admit to himself that he was in any way responsible for her death, and he would go to pieces. . . . His very salvation would depend on his deceiving himself. . . . And he would deceive himself. . . .

No, she was going away—out of it all.

She couldn't bear any more.

It hurt too much. . . .

She no longer thought of Judy—she had got past that. . . . Nothing mattered to her now but her own agony and her longing for escape. . . .

The river. . . .

Long ago there had been a river through a valley—and primroses . . . long ago before anything happened. . . .

She had walked rapidly. She came now to the point where the road
crossed over the bridge.

The river, running swiftly, ran beneath it. . . .

There was no one about. . . .

She wondered where Peter Maitland was. He was married—he'd
married after the war. Peter would have been kind. She would have
been happy with Peter . . . happy and safe. . . .

But she would never have loved him as she loved Dermot. . . .

Dermot—Dermot. . . .

So cruel. . . .

The whole world was cruel, really—cruel and treacherous. . . .

The river was better. . . .

She climbed up on the parapet and jumped. . . .

BOOK THREE

THE ISLAND

Chapter 1

SURRENDER

That, to Celia, was the end of the story.

Everything that happened afterward seemed to her not to count. There were proceedings in a police court—there was the cockney young man who pulled her out of the river—there was the magistrate's censure—the paragraphs in the Press—Dermot's annoyance—Miss Hood's loyalty—all that seemed unimportant and dreamlike to Celia as she sat up in bed telling me about it.

She didn't think of commiting suicide again.

She admitted that it had been very wicked of her to try. She was doing exactly what she blamed Dermot for doing—abandoning Judy.

"I felt," she said, "that the only thing I could do to make up was to live only for Judy and never think of myself again. . . . I felt ashamed. . . ."

She and Miss Hood and Judy had gone abroad to Switzerland.

There Dermot had written to her, enclosing the necessary evidence for divorce.

She hadn't done anything about it for some time.

"You see," she said, "I felt too bewildered. I just wanted to do anything he asked, so that I should be left in peace. . . . I was afraid—afraid of more things happening to me. I've been afraid ever since. . . .

"So I didn't know what to do about it. . . . Dermot thought I didn't do anything because I was vindictive. . . . It wasn't that. I'd promised Judy not to let her father go. . . . And here I was ready to give in just through sheer disgusting cowardice. . . . I wished—oh, how I wished—

that he and Marjorie would go away together—then I could have divorced them. . . . I could have said to Judy afterward: 'I had no choice. . . .' Dermot wrote to me saying all his friends thought I was behaving disgracefully . . . all his friends . . . that same phrase!

"I waited. . . . I wanted just to rest—somewhere safe—where Dermot couldn't get at me. I was terrified of his coming and storming at me again. . . . You can't give in to a thing because you're terrified. It isn't decent. I know I'm a coward—I've always been a coward—I hate noise or scenes—I'll do anything—*anything* to be left in peace. . . . But I *didn't* give in out of fear. I stuck it out. . . .

"I got strong again in Switzerland. . . . I can't tell you how wonderful it was. Not to want to cry every time you walked up a hill. Not to feel sick whenever you looked at food. And that awful neuralgia in my head went away. Mental misery and physical misery is too much to have together. . . . You can bear one *or* the other—not both. . . .

"In the end, when I felt really strong and well again, I went back to England. I wrote to Dermot. I said I didn't believe in divorce. . . . I believed (though it might be old-fashioned and wrong in his eyes) in staying together and bearing things for the sake of the children. I said that people often told you that it was better for children if parents who didn't get on together parted. I said that I didn't think that was true. Children needed their parents—both parents—because they were their own flesh and blood—quarrels or bickering didn't matter half so much to children as grown-up people imagine—perhaps even it's a good thing. It teaches them what life is like. . . . My home was *too* happy. It made me grow up a fool. . . . I said too, that he and I never had quarreled. We had always got on well together. . . .

"I said I didn't think love affairs with other people ought to matter very much. . . . He could be quite free—so long as he was kind to Judy and a good father to her. And I told him again that I knew he meant more to Judy than I could ever mean. She only wanted me physically—like a little animal when she was ill, but it was he and she who belonged together in mind.

"I said if he came back I wouldn't reproach him—or ever throw things in his face. I asked if we couldn't just be kind to each other because we'd both suffered.

"I said the choice lay with him, but he must remember that I didn't want or believe in divorce, and that if he chose that, the responsibility rested with him only.

"He wrote back and sent me fresh evidence. . . .

"I divorced him. . . .

"It was all rather beastly . . . divorce is. . . .

"Standing up before a lot of people . . . answering questions . . . intimate questions . . . chambermaids. . . .

"I hated it all. It made me sick.

"It must be easier to be divorced. You don't have to be *there*. . . .

"So, you see, I gave in, after all. Dermot got his way. I might as well have given way at the beginning and saved myself a lot of pain and horror. . . .

"I don't know whether I'm glad I didn't give in earlier or not. . . .

"I don't even know why I did give in—because I was tired and wanted peace—or because I became convinced it was the only thing to be done, or because, after all, I wanted to give in to Dermot. . . .

"I think, sometimes, it was the last. . . .

"That's why, ever since, I've felt guilty when Judy looked at me. . . .

"In the end, you see, I betrayed Judy for Dermot."

Chapter 2

REFLECTION

Dermot had married Marjorie Connell a few days after the decree was made absolute.

I was curious about Celia's attitude to the other woman. She had touched on it so little in her story—almost as though the other woman hadn't existed. She never once took up the attitude that a weak Dermot had been led astray, although that is the most common attitude for a betrayed wife.

Celia answered my question at once and honestly.

"I don't think he was—led astray, I mean. Marjorie? What did I think about her? I can't remember. . . . It didn't seem to matter. It was Dermot and me that mattered—not Marjorie. It was his being cruel to me that I couldn't get over. . . ."

And there, I think, I see what Celia will never be able to see. Celia was essentially tender in her attitude toward suffering. A butterfly pinned in his hat would never have upset Dermot as a child. He would have assumed firmly that the butterfly liked it!

That is the line he took with Celia. He was fond of Celia, but he wanted Marjorie. He was an essentially moral young man. To enable Dermot to marry Marjorie, Celia had to be got rid of. Since he was fond of Celia, he wanted her to like the idea too. When she didn't, he was angry with her. Because he felt badly about hurting her, he hurt her all the more and was unnecessarily brutal about it . . . I can understand—I can almost sympathize. . . .

If he had let himself believe he was being cruel to Celia he couldn't have done it. . . . He was, like many brutally honest men, dishonest about himself. He thought himself a finer fellow than he really was. . . .

He wanted Marjorie, and he had to get her. He'd always got everything that he wanted—and life with Celia hadn't improved him.

He loved Celia, I think, for her beauty and her beauty only. . . .

She loved him enduringly and for life. He was, as she once put it, in her blood. . . .

And, also, she clung. And Dermot was the type of man who cannot endure being clung to. Celia had very little devil in her, and a woman with very little devil in her has a poor chance with men.

Miriam had devil. For all her love for her John, I don't believe he always had an easy life with her. She adored him, but she tried him too. There's a brute in man that likes being stood up to. . . .

Miriam had something that Celia lacked. What is vulgarly called guts, perhaps.

When Celia stood up to Dermot it was too late. . . .

She admitted that she had come to think differently about Dermot now that she was no longer bewildered by his sudden apparent inhumanity.

"At first," she said, "it seemed as though I had always loved him and done anything he wanted, and then—the first time that I *really* needed him and was in trouble, he turned round and stabbed me in the back. That's rather journalese, but it expresses what I felt.

"There are words in the Bible that say it exactly." She paused, then quoted:

"*For it is not an open enemy that hath done me this dishonour: for then I could have borne it; . . . But it was even thou, my companion: my guide, and mine own familiar friend.*

"It was that, you see, that hurt. 'Mine own familiar friend.'

"If *Dermot* could be treacherous, then anyone could be treacherous. The world itself became unsure. I couldn't trust anyone or anything anymore. . . .

"That's horribly frightening. You don't know how frightening that is. Nothing anywhere is safe.

"You see—well, you see the Gun Man everywhere. . . .

"But, of course, it was my fault really, for trusting Dermot too much. You shouldn't trust anyone as much as that. It's unfair.

"All these years, while Judy has been growing up, I've had time to think. . . . I've thought a great deal. . . . And I've seen that the real trouble was that *I* was stupid. . . . Stupid and arrogant!

"I loved Dermot—and I didn't keep him. I ought to have seen what he liked and wanted, and been that. . . . I ought to have realized (as he himself said) that he would 'want a change.' . . . Mother told me not to go away and leave him alone. . . . I did leave him alone. I was so arrogant I never thought of such a possibility as happened. I was so sure that I was the person he loved and always would love. As I said, it's unfair to trust people too much, to try them too high, to put them on pedestals just because you like them there. I never saw Dermot clearly. . . . I could have . . . if I hadn't been so arrogant—thinking that nothing that happened to other women could ever happen to me. . . . I was stupid.

"So I don't blame Dermot now—he was just made that way. I ought to have known and been on my guard and not been so cocksure and pleased with myself. If a thing matters to you more than anything in life, you've got to be clever about it. . . . I wasn't clever about it. . . .

"It's a very common story. I know that now. You've only got to read the papers—especially the Sunday ones that go in for that sort of thing. Women who put their heads in gas ovens—or take overdoses of sleeping draughts. The world is like that—full of cruelty and pain—because people are stupid.

"I was stupid. I lived in a world of my own. Yes, I was stupid."

Chapter 3

FLIGHT

"And since?" I asked Celia. "What have you done since? That's some time ago."

"Yes, ten years. Well, I've traveled. I've seen the places I've wanted to see. I've made a lot of friends. I've had adventures. I think, really, I've enjoyed myself quite a lot."

She seemed rather hazy about it all.

"There were Judy's holidays, of course. I always felt guilty with Judy. . . . I think she knew I did. She never said anything, but I thought that, secretly, she blamed me for the loss of her father. . . . And there, of course, she was right. She said once: 'It was *you* Daddy didn't like. He was fond of *me*.' I failed her. A mother ought to keep a child's father fond of her. That's part of a mother's job. I hadn't. Judy was unconsciously cruel sometimes, but she did me good. She was so uncompromisingly honest.

"I don't know whether I've failed with Judy or succeeded. I don't know whether she loves me or doesn't love me. I've given her material things. I haven't been able to give her the other things—the things that matter to me—because she doesn't want them. I've done the only thing I could. Because I love her, I've let her alone. I haven't tried to force my views and my beliefs upon her. I've tried to make her feel I'm there if she wants me. But, you see, she didn't want me. The kind of person I am is no good to the kind of person she is—except, as I said before, for material things. . . . I love her, just as I loved Dermot, but I don't understand her. I've tried to leave her free, but at the same time not to give in to her out of cowardice. . . . Whether I've been any use to her I shall never know. I hope I have—oh, how I hope I have. . . . I love her so. . . ."

"Where is she now?"

"She's married. That's why I came here. I mean, I wasn't free before. I had to look after Judy. She was married at eighteen. He's a very nice man—older than she is—straight, kind, well off, everything I could wish. I wanted her to wait, to be sure, but she wouldn't wait. You can't fight people like her and Dermot. They have to have their own way. Besides, how can you judge for someone else? You might ruin their lives when you thought you were helping them. One mustn't interfere. . . .

"She's out in East Africa. She writes me occasionally, short happy letters. They're like Dermot's, they tell you nothing except facts, but you can feel it's all right."

2

"And then," I said, "you came here. Why?"

She said slowly:

"I don't know whether I can make you understand. . . . Something a man said to me once made an impression on me. I'd told him a little of what had happened. He was an understanding person. He said: 'What are you going to do with your life? You're still young.' I said that there was Judy and traveling and seeing things and places.

"He said: 'That won't be enough. You'll have either to take a lover or lovers. You will have to decide which it's to be.'

"And, you know, that frightened me, because I knew he was right. . . .

"People, ordinary unthinking people, have said, 'Oh, my dear, some day you'll marry again—some nice man who'll make it all up to you.'

"Marry? I'd be terrified to marry. Nobody can hurt you except a husband—nobody's near enough. . . .

"I didn't mean ever to have anything more to do with men. . . .

"But that young man frightened me. . . . I wasn't old . . . not old enough. . . .

"There might be a—a lover? A lover wouldn't be so terrifying as a husband—you'd never get to depend so on a lover—it's all the little shared intimacies of life that hold you so with a husband and tear you to pieces when you part. . . . A lover you just have occasional meetings with—your daily life is your own. . . .

"Lover—or lovers. . . .

"Lovers would be best. You'd be—almost safe—with lovers!

"But I hoped it wouldn't come to that. I hoped I'd learn to live alone. I tried."

She didn't speak for some moments. "I tried," she had said. Those two words covered a good deal.

"Yes?" I said at last.

She said slowly:

"It was when Judy was fifteen that I met someone. . . . He was rather like Peter Maitland. . . . Kind, not very clever. He loved me. . . .

"He told me that what I needed was gentleness. He was—very good to me. His wife had died when their first baby was born. The baby died too. So, you see, he'd been unhappy too. He understood what it was like.

"We enjoyed things together . . . we seemed to be able to share things. And he didn't mind if I was myself. I mean, I could say I was enjoying myself and be enthusiastic without his thinking me silly. . . . He was—it's an odd thing to say, but he really was—like a *mother* to me. A mother, not a father! He was so gentle. . . ."

Celia's voice had grown gentle. Her face was a child's—happy, confident. . . .

"Yes?"

"He wanted to marry me. I said I could never marry anyone. . . . I said I'd lost my nerve. He understood that too. . . .

"That was three years ago. He's been a friend—a wonderful friend. . . . He's always been there when I wanted him. I've felt *loved*. . . . It's a happy feeling. . . .

"After Judy's wedding he asked me again to marry him. He said that he thought I could trust him now. He wanted to take care of me. He said we'd go back home—to *my* home. It's been shut up with a caretaker all these years—I couldn't bear to go there, but I've always felt it's there waiting for me. . . . Just waiting for me. . . . He said we'd go there and live, and that all this misery would seem like a bad dream. . . .

"And I—I felt I wanted to. . . .

"But, somehow, I couldn't. I said we'd be lovers if he liked. It didn't matter now that Judy was married. Then, if he wanted to be free, he could leave me any minute. I could never be an obstacle, and so he'd never have to hate me because I stood in the way of his wanting to marry someone else. . . .

"He wouldn't do that. He was very gentle but firm. He had been a doctor, you know, a surgeon, rather a celebrated one. He said I'd got to get over this nervous terror. He said once I was actually married to him it would be all right . . .

"At last—I said I would. . . ."

3

I didn't speak and in a minute or two Celia went on:

"I felt happy—really happy. . . .

"At peace again and as though I were safe. . . .

"And then *it* happened. It was the day before we were to be married.

"We'd driven out of town to dinner. It was a hot night. . . . We were sitting in a garden by the river. He kissed me and said I was beautiful. . . . I'm thirty-nine, and worn and tired, but he said I was beautiful.

"*And then he said the thing that frightened me—that broke up the dream.*"

"What did he say?"

"He said: 'Don't ever be less beautiful. . . .'

"He said it just in the same voice that Dermot had said it. . . ."

4

"I expect you don't understand—nobody could. . . .

"*It was the Gun Man all over again.* . . .

"Everything happy and at peace, and then you feel *He's* there. . . .

"It all came back again—the terror. . . .

"I couldn't face it—not going through it all again . . . being happy for years—and then, perhaps, being ill or something . . . and the whole misery coming over again. . . .

"*I couldn't risk going through it again.*

"I think what I really mean is that I couldn't face being frightened of going through it again . . . being terrified that the same experience would come nearer and nearer—every day of happiness would make it more frightening. . . . I couldn't face the suspense. . . .

"And so I ran away. . . .

"Just like that. . . .

"I left Michael—I don't think he knew why I went—I just made some excuse—I went through the little inn and asked for the station. It was about ten minutes' walk. I just hit off a train.

"When I got to London I went home and fetched my passport and went and sat in the ladies' waiting room at Victoria till morning. I was afraid Michael might find me and persuade me. . . . I might have been persuaded, because, you see, I did love him. . . . He was so sweet to me always.

"But I can't face going through everything again. . . .

"*I can't.* . . .

"It's too ghastly to live in fear. . . .

"And it's awful to have no trust left. . . .

"I simply couldn't trust *anyone* . . . not even Michael.

"It would be Hell for them as well as for me. . . ."

5

"That's a year ago. . . .

"I never wrote to Michael. . . .

"I never gave him any explanation. . . .

"I've treated him disgracefully. . . .

"I don't mind. Ever since Dermot, I've been hard. . . . I haven't cared whether I've hurt people or not. When you've been hurt too much yourself you don't care. . . .

"I traveled about, trying to be interested in things and make my own life. . . .

"Well, I've failed. . . .

"I can't live alone. . . . I can't make up stories about people anymore—it doesn't seem to come. . . .

"So it means being alone all the time even if you're in the middle of a crowd. . . .

"And I can't live with someone. . . . I'm too miserably afraid. . . .

"I'm beaten. . . .

"I can't face the prospect of living, perhaps, another thirty years. I'm not, you see, sufficiently brave. . . ."

Celia sighed. . . . Her lids drooped. . . .

"I remembered this place, and I came here on purpose. . . . It's a very nice place. . . ."

She added:

"This is a very long stupid, story. . . . I seem to have been talking a lot . . . it must be morning. . . ."

Celia fell asleep. . . .

Chapter 4

BEGINNING

Well, you see, that's where we are—except for the one incident I referred to at the beginning of the story.

The whole point is, is that significant, or isn't it?

If I'm right, the whole of Celia's life led up to and came to its climax in that one minute.

It happened when I was saying good-bye to her on the boat.

She was dead sleepy. I'd wakened her up and made her dress. I wanted to get her away from the island quickly.

She was like a tired child—obedient and very sweet and completely bemused.

I thought—I may be wrong—but I thought that the danger was over. . . .

And then, suddenly, as I was saying good-bye, she seemed to wake up. She, as it were, *saw* me for the first time.

She said: "I don't know your name even. . . ."

I said: "It doesn't matter—you wouldn't know it. I used to be a fairly well-known portrait painter."

"Aren't you now?"

"No," I said, "something happened to me in the war."

"What?"

"This. . . ."

And I pushed forward my stump where the hand ought to have been.

2

The bell rang and I had to run . . .

So I've only got my impression.

But that impression is very clear.

Horror—and then *relief*. . . .

Relief's a poor word—it was more than that—*Deliverance* expresses it better.

It was the Gun Man again, you see—her symbol for fear. . . .

The Gun Man had pursued her all these years. . . .

And now, at last, she had met him face to face. . . .

And he was just an ordinary human being.

Me. . . .

3

That's how I see it.

It is my fixed belief that Celia went back into the world to begin a new life. . . .

She went back at thirty-nine—to grow up. . . .

And she left her story and her fear—with me. . . .

I don't know where she went. I don't even know her name. I've *called* her Celia because that name seems to suit her. I could find out, I suppose, by questioning hotels. But I can't do that. . . . I suppose I shall never see her again. . . .

· THE BURDEN ·

"For my yoke is easy, and my burden is light"
—ST. MATTHEW, CH.II,V.30

"Lord, Thy most pointed pleasure take
And stab my spirit broad awake;
Or, Lord, if too obdurate I,
Choose Thou, before that spirit die,
A piercing pain, a killer sin,
And to my dead heart run them in!"
—R. L. STEVENSON

Prologue

The church was cold. It was October, too early for the heating to be on. Outside, the sun gave a watery promise of warmth and good cheer, but here within the chill gray stone there was only dampness and a sure foreknowledge of winter.

Laura stood between Nannie, resplendent in crackling collars and cuffs, and Mr. Henson, the curate. The vicar was in bed with mild influenza. Mr. Henson was young and thin, with an Adam's apple and a high nasal voice.

Mrs. Franklin, looking frail and attractive, leaned on her husband's arm. He himself stood upright and grave. The birth of his second daughter had not consoled him for the loss of Charles. He had wanted a son. And it seemed now, from what the doctor had said, that there would not be a son. . . .

His eyes went from Laura to the infant in Nannie's arms gurgling happily to itself.

Two daughters . . . Of course Laura was a nice child, a dear child and, as babies go, the new arrival was a splendid specimen, but a man wanted a son.

Charles—Charles, with his fair hair, his way of throwing back his head and laughing. Such an attractive boy, so handsome, so bright, so intelligent. Really a very unusual boy. It seemed a pity that if one of his children had to die, it hadn't been Laura. . . .

His eyes suddenly met those of his elder daughter, eyes that seemed large and tragic in her small pale face, and Franklin flushed guiltily—what had he been thinking of? Suppose the child should guess what had been in his mind. Of course he was devoted to Laura—only—only, she wasn't, she could never be Charles.

Leaning against her husband, her eyes half closed, Angela Franklin was saying to herself:

'My boy—my beautiful boy—my darling. . . . I still can't believe it. Why couldn't it have been Laura?'

She felt no guilt in that thought as it came to her. More ruthless and more honest than her husband, closer to primeval needs, she admitted the simple fact that her second child, a daughter, had never meant, and could never mean to her what her firstborn had. Compared with Charles, Laura was an anticlimax—a quiet disappointing child, well-behaved, giving no trouble, but lacking in—what was it?—personality.

She thought again: 'Charles—nothing can ever make up to me for losing Charles.'

She felt the pressure of her husband's hand on her arm, and opened her eyes—she must pay attention to the Service. What a very irritating voice poor Mr. Henson had!

Angela looked with half-amused indulgence at the baby in Nannie's arms—such big solemn words for such a tiny mite.

The baby, who had been sleeping, blinked and opened her eyes. Such dazzling blue eyes—like Charles's eyes—she made a happy gurgling noise.

Angela thought: 'Charles's smile.' A rush of mother love swept over her. Her baby—her own lovely baby. For the first time Charles's death receded into the past.

Angela met Laura's dark sad gaze, and thought with momentary curiosity: 'I wonder just what that child is thinking?'

Nannie also was conscious of Laura standing quiet and erect beside her.

'Such a quiet little thing,' she thought. 'A bit too quiet for my taste—not natural for any child to be as quiet and well-behaved as she is. There has never been much notice taken of her—maybe not as much as there ought to have been—I wonder now—'

The Reverend Eustace Henson was approaching the moment that always made him nervous. He had not done many christenings. If only the vicar were here. He noticed with approval Laura's grave eyes and serious expression. A well-behaved child. He wondered suddenly what was passing through her mind.

It was as well that neither he, nor Nannie, nor Arthur and Angela Franklin knew.

It wasn't fair. . . .

Oh, it wasn't fair. . . .

Her mother loved this baby sister as much as she loved Charles.

It wasn't *fair*. . . .

She hated the baby—she hated it, hated it, hated it!

'*I'd like her to die.*'

Standing by the font, the solemn words of baptism were ringing in her ears—but far more clear, far more real—was the thought translated into words:

'I'd like her to die. . . .'

There was a gentle nudge. Nannie was handing her the baby, whispering:

"Careful, now, take her—steady—and then you hand her to the clergyman." Laura whispered back: "I know."

Baby was in her arms. Laura looked down at her. She thought: 'Supposing I opened my arms and just let her fall—on to the stones. Would it kill her?'

Down on to the stones, so hard and gray—but then babies were so well wrapped up, so—so *padded*. Should she? Dare she?

She hesitated and then the moment was gone—the baby was now in the somewhat nervous arms of the Reverend Eustace Henson, who lacked the practiced ease of the vicar. He was asking the names and repeating them after Laura. Shirley, Margaret, Evelyn. . . . The water trickled off the baby's forehead. She did not cry, only gurgled as though an even more delightful thing than usual had happened to her. Gingerly, with inward shrinking, the curate kissed the baby's forehead. The vicar always did that, he knew. With relief he handed the baby back to Nannie.

The christening was over.

PART ONE

LAURA—1929

Chapter One

1

Below the quiet exterior of the child standing beside the font, there raged an ever-growing resentment and misery.

Ever since Charles had died she had hoped . . . Though she had grieved for Charles's death (she had been very fond of Charles), grief had been eclipsed by a tremulous longing and expectation. Naturally, when Charles had been there, Charles with his good looks and his charm and his merry carefree ways, the love had gone to Charles. That, Laura, felt, was quite right, was fair. She had always been the quiet, the dull one, the so often unwanted second child that follows too soon upon the first. Her father and mother had been kind to her, affectionate, but it was Charles they had loved.

Once she had overheard her mother say to a visiting friend:

"Laura's a dear child, of course, but rather a dull child."

And she had accepted the justice of that with the honesty of the hopeless. She *was* a dull child. She was small and pale and her hair didn't curl, and the things she said never made people laugh—as they laughed at Charles. She was good and obedient and caused nobody trouble, but she was not and, she thought, never would be, *important*.

Once she had said to Nannie: "Mummy loves Charles more than she loves me. . . ."

Nannie had snapped immediately:

"That's a very silly thing to say and not at all true. Your mother loves both of her children equally—fair as fair can be she is, always. Mothers always love all their children just the same."

"Cats don't," said Laura, reviewing in her mind a recent arrival of kittens.

"Cats are just animals," said Nannie. "And anyway," she added, slightly weakening the magnificent simplicity of her former pronouncement, "God loves you, remember."

Laura accepted the dictum. God loved you—He had to. But even God, Laura thought, probably loved Charles best. . . . Because to have made Charles must be far more satisfactory than to have made her, Laura.

'But of course,' Laura had consoled herself by reflecting, 'I can love myself best. I can love myself better than Charles or Mummy or Daddy or anyone.'

It was after this that Laura became paler and quieter and more unobtrusive than ever, and was so good and obedient that it made even Nannie uneasy. She confided to the housemaid an uneasy fear that Laura might be 'taken' young.

But it was Charles who died, not Laura.

2

"Why don't you get that child a dog?" Mr. Baldock demanded suddenly of his friend and crony, Laura's father.

Arthur Franklin looked rather astonished, since he was in the middle of an impassioned argument with his friend on the implications of the Reformation.

"What child?" he asked, puzzled.

Mr. Baldock nodded his large head toward a sedate Laura who was propelling herself on a fairy bicycle in and out of the trees on the lawn. It was an unimpassioned performance with no hint of danger or accident about it. Laura was a careful child.

"Why on earth should I?" demanded Mr. Franklin. "Dogs, in my opinion, are a nuisance, always coming in with muddy paws, and ruining the carpets."

"A dog," said Mr. Baldock, in his lecture-room style, which was capable of rousing almost anybody to violent irritation, "has an extraordinary power of bolstering up the human ego. To a dog, the human being who owns him is a god to be worshipped, and not only worshipped but, in our present decadent state of civilization, also loved.

"The possession of a dog goes to most people's heads. It makes them feel important and powerful."

"Humph," said Mr. Franklin, "and would you call that a good thing?"

"Almost certainly *not,*" said Mr. Baldock. "But I have the inveterate weakness of liking to see human beings happy. I'd like to see Laura happy."

"Laura's perfectly happy," said Laura's father. "And anyway she's got a kitten," he added.

"Pah," said Mr. Baldock. "It's not at all the same thing. As you'd realize if you troubled to think. But that's what is wrong with you. You never think. Look at your argument just now about economic conditions at the time of the Reformation. Do you suppose for one moment—"

And they were back at it, hammer and tongs, enjoying themselves a great deal, with Mr. Baldock making the most preposterous and provocative statements.

Yet a vague disquiet lingered somewhere in Arthur Franklin's mind, and that evening, as he came into his wife's room where she was changing for dinner, he said abruptly:

"Laura's quite all right, isn't she? Well and happy and all that?"

His wife turned astonished blue eyes on him, lovely dark cornflower-blue eyes, like the eyes of her son Charles.

"Darling!" she said. "Of course! Laura's always all right. She never even seems to have bilious attacks like most children. I never have to worry about Laura. She's satisfactory in every way. Such a blessing."

A moment later, as she fastened the clasp of her pearls round her neck, she asked suddenly: "Why? Why did you ask about Laura this evening?"

Arthur Franklin said vaguely:

"Oh, just Baldy—something he said."

"Oh, *Baldy*!" Mrs. Franklin's voice held amusement. "You know what *he's* like. He likes starting things."

And on an occasion a few days later when Mr. Baldock had been to lunch, and they came out of the dining room, encountering Nannie in the hall, Angela Franklin stopped her deliberately and asked in a clear slightly raised voice:

"There's nothing wrong with Miss Laura, is there? She's quite well and happy?"

"Oh, yes, Madam." Nannie was positive and slightly affronted. "She's a *very* good little girl, never gives *any* trouble. Not like Master Charles."

"So Charles does give you trouble, does he?" said Mr. Baldock.

Nannie turned to him deferentially.

"He's a regular boy, sir, always up to pranks! He's getting on, you know. He'll soon be going to school. Always high-spirited at this age, they are. And then his digestion is weak, he gets hold of too many sweets without my knowing."

An indulgent smile on her lips and shaking her head, she passed on.

"All the same, she adores him," said Angela Franklin as they went into the drawing room.

"Obviously," said Mr. Baldock. He added reflectively: "I always have thought women were fools."

"Nannie isn't a fool—very far from it."

"I wasn't thinking of Nannie."

"Me?" Angela gave him a sharp, but not too sharp, glance, because after all it was Baldy, who was celebrated and eccentric and was allowed a certain licence in rudeness, which was, actually, one of his stock affectations.

"I'm thinking of writing a book on the problem of the second child," said Mr. Baldock.

"Really, Baldy! You don't advocate the only child, do you? I thought that was supposed to be unsound from every point of view."

"Oh! I can see a lot of point in the family of ten. That is, if it was allowed to develop in the legitimate way. Do the household chores, older ones look after the younger ones, and so on. All cogs in the household machine. Mind you, they'd have to be really of some use—not just made to think they were. But nowadays, like fools, we split 'em up and segregate 'em off, each with their own 'age group'! Call it education! Pah! Flat against nature!"

"You and your theories," said Angela indulgently. "But what about the second child?"

"The trouble about the second child," said Mr. Baldock didactically, "is that it's usually an anticlimax. The first child's an adventure. It's frightening and it's painful; the woman's sure she's going to die, and the husband (Arthur here, for example) is equally sure you're going to die. After it's all over, there you are with a small morsel of animate flesh yelling its head off, which has caused two people all kinds of hell to produce! Naturally they value it accordingly! It's new, it's ours, it's wonderful! And then, usually rather too soon, Number Two comes along—all the caboodle over again—not so frightening this time, much more boring. And there it is, it's yours, but it's not a new experience, and since it hasn't cost you so much, it isn't nearly so wonderful."

Angela shrugged her shoulders.

"Bachelors know everything," she murmured ironically. "And isn't that equally true of Number Three and Number Four and all the rest of them?"

"Not quite. I've noticed that there's usually a gap before Number Three. Number Three is often produced because the other two are getting independent, and it would be 'nice to have a baby in the nursery again.' Curious taste; revolting little creatures, but biologically a sound instinct, I suppose. And so they go on, some nice and some nasty, and some bright and some dull, but they pair off and pal up more or less, and finally comes the afterthought which like the firstborn gets an undue share of attention."

"And it's all very unfair, is that what you're saying?"

"Exactly. That's the whole point about life, it is unfair!"

"And what can one do about it?"

"Nothing."

"Then really, Baldy, I don't see what you're talking about."

"I told Arthur the other day. I'm a soft-hearted chap. I like to see people being happy. I like to make up to people a bit for what they haven't got and can't have. It evens things up a bit. Besides, if you don't—" he paused a moment—"it can be dangerous. . . ."

3

"I do think Baldy talks a lot of nonsense," said Angela pensively to her husband when their guest had departed.

"John Baldock is one of the foremost scholars in this country," said Arthur Franklin with a slight twinkle.

"Oh, I know *that*." Angela was faintly scornful. "I'd be willing to sit in meek adoration if he was laying down the law on Greeks and Romans, or obscure Elizabethan poets. But what can he know about children?"

"Absolutely nothing, I should imagine," said her husband. "By the way, he suggested the other day that we should give Laura a dog."

"A dog? But she's got a kitten."

"According to him, that's not the same thing."

"How very odd . . . I remember him saying once that he disliked dogs."

"I believe he does."

Angela said thoughtfully: "Now Charles, perhaps, ought to have a dog. . . . He looked quite scared the other day when those puppies at the Vicarage rushed at him. I hate to see a boy afraid of dogs. If he had one of his own, it would accustom him to it. He ought to learn to ride, too. I wish he could have a pony of his own. If only we had a paddock!"

"A pony's out of the question, I'm afraid," said Franklin.

In the kitchen, the parlor maid, Ethel, said to the cook:

"That old Baldock, he's noticed it too."

"Noticed what?"

"Miss Laura. That she isn't long for this world. Asking Nurse about it, they were. Ah, she's got the look, sure enough, no mischief in her, not like Master Charles. You mark my words, *she* won't live to grow up."

But it was Charles who died.

Chapter Two

1

Charles died of infantile paralysis. He died at school; two other boys had the disease but recovered.

To Angela Franklin, herself now in a delicate state of health, the blow was so great as to crush her completely. Charles, her beloved, her darling, her handsome merry high-spirited boy.

She lay in her darkened bedroom, staring at the ceiling, unable to weep. And her husband and Laura and the servants crept about the muted house. In the end the doctor advised Arthur Franklin to take his wife abroad.

"Complete change of air and scene. She *must* be roused. Somewhere with good air—mountain air. Switzerland, perhaps."

So the Franklins went off, and Laura remained under the care of Nannie, with daily visits from Miss Weekes, an amiable but uninspiring governess.

To Laura, her parents' absence was a period of pleasure. Technically, she was the mistress of the house! Every morning she 'saw the cook' and ordered meals for the day. Mrs. Brunton, the cook, was fat and good-natured. She curbed the wilder of Laura's suggestions and managed it so that the actual menu was exactly as she herself had planned it. But Laura's sense of importance was not impaired. She missed her parents the less because she was building in her own mind a fantasy for their return.

It was terrible that Charles was dead. Naturally they had loved Charles best—she did not dispute the justice of that, but now—*now*—it was *she* who would enter into Charles's kingdom. It was Laura now who was their only child, the child in whom all their hopes lay and to whom would flow all their affection. She built up scenes in her mind of the day of their return. Her mother's open arms . . .

"Laura, my darling. You're all I have in the world now!"

Affecting scenes, emotional scenes. Scenes that in actual fact were wildly unlike anything Angela or Arthur Franklin were likely to do or say. But to Laura, they were warming and rich in drama, and by slow degrees she began to believe in them so much that they might almost already have happened.

Walking down the lane to the village, she rehearsed conversations: raising her eyebrows, shaking her head, murmuring words and phrases under her breath.

So absorbed was she in this rich feast of emotional imagination, that she failed to observe Mr. Baldock, who was coming toward her from the direction of the village, pushing in front of him a gardening basket on wheels, in which he brought home his purchases.

"Hullo, young Laura."

Laura, rudely jostled out of an affecting drama where her mother had gone blind and she, Laura, had just refused an offer of marriage from a viscount ("I shall never marry. My mother means *everything* to me"), started and blushed.

"Father and mother still away, eh?"

"Yes, they won't be coming back for ten days more."

"I see. Like to come to tea with me tomorrow?"

"Oh, yes."

Laura was elated and excited. Mr. Baldock, who had a Chair at the University fourteen miles away, had a small cottage in the village where he spent the vacations and occasional weekends. He declined to behave in a social manner, and affronted Bellbury by refusing, usually impolitely, their many invitations. Arthur Franklin was his only friend—it was a friendship of many years standing. John Baldock was not a friendly man. He treated his pupils with such ruthlessness and irony that the best of them were goaded into distinguishing themselves, and the rest perished by the wayside. He had written several large and abstruse volumes on obscure phases of history, written in such a way that very few people could understand what he was driving at. Mild appeals from his publishers to write in a more readable fashion were turned down with a savage glee, Mr. Baldock pointing out that the people who could appreciate his books were the only readers of them who were worthwhile! He was particularly rude to women, which enchanted many of them so much that they were always coming back for more. A man of savage prejudices, and overriding arrogance, he had an un- expectedly kindly heart which was always betraying his principles.

Laura knew that to be asked to tea with Mr. Baldock was an honor, and preened herself accordingly. She turned up neatly dressed, brushed, and washed, but nevertheless with an underlying apprehension, for Mr. Baldock was an alarming man.

Mr. Baldock's housekeeper showed her into the library, where Mr. Baldock raised his head, and stared at her.

"Hullo," said Mr. Baldock. "What are you doing here?"

"You asked me to tea," said Laura.

Mr. Baldock looked at her in a considering manner. Laura looked back at him. It was a grave, polite look that successfully concealed her inner uncertainty.

"So I did," said Mr. Baldock, rubbing his nose. "Hm . . . yes, so I did. Can't think why. Well, you'd better sit down."

"Where?" said Laura.

The question was highly pertinent. The library into which Laura had been shown was a room lined with bookshelves to the ceiling. All the shelves were wedged tight with books, but there still existed large numbers of books which could find no places in the shelves, and these were piled in great heaps on the floor and on tables, and also occupied the chairs.

Mr. Baldock looked vexed.

"I suppose we'll have to do something about it," he said grudgingly.

He selected an armchair that was slightly less encumbered than the others and, with many grunts and puffs, lowered two armsful of dusty tomes to the floor.

"There you are," he said, beating his hands together to rid them of dust. As a result, he sneezed violently.

"Doesn't anyone ever dust in here?" Laura asked, as she sat down sedately.

"Not if they value their lives!" said Mr. Baldock. "But mind you, it's a hard fight. Nothing a woman likes better than to come barging in flicking a great yellow duster, and armed with tins of greasy stuff smelling of turpentine or worse. Picking up all my books, and arranging them in piles, by size as likely as not, no concern for the subject matter! Then she starts an evil-looking machine, that wheezes and hums, and out she goes finally, as pleased as Punch, having left the place in such a state that you can't put your hand on a thing you want for at least a month. Women! What the Lord God thought he was doing when he created woman, I can't imagine. I daresay He thought Adam was looking a little too cocky and pleased with himself; Lord of the Universe, and naming the animals and all that. Thought he needed taking down a peg or two. Daresay that was true enough. But creating woman was going a bit far. Look where it landed the poor chap! Slap in the middle of Original Sin."

"I'm sorry," said Laura apologetically.

"What do you mean, sorry?"

"That you feel like that about women, because I suppose I'm a woman."

"Not yet you're not, thank goodness," said Mr. Baldock. "Not for a long while yet. It's got to come, of course, but no point in looking ahead toward unpleasant things. And by the way, I *hadn't* forgotten that you were coming to tea today. Not for a moment! I just pretended that I had for a reason of my own."

"What reason?"

"Well—" Mr. Baldock rubbed his nose again. "For one thing I wanted to see what you'd say." He nodded his head. "You came through that one very well. Very well indeed. . . ."

Laura stared at him uncomprehendingly.

"I had another reason. If you and I are going to be friends, and it rather looks as though things are tending that way, then you've got to accept me as I am—a rude, ungracious old curmudgeon. See? No good expecting pretty speeches. 'Dear child—so pleased to see you—been looking forward to your coming.' "

Mr. Baldock repeated these last phrases in a high falsetto tone of unmitigated contempt. A ripple passed over Laura's grave face. She laughed.

"That would be funny," she said.

"It would indeed. Very funny."

Laura's gravity returned. She looked at him speculatively.

"Do you think we *are* going to be friends?" she inquired.

"It's a matter for mutual agreement. Do you care for the idea?"

Laura considered.

"It seems—a little odd," she said dubiously. "I mean, friends are usually children who come and play games with you."

"You won't find me playing 'Here We Go Round the Mulberry Bush,' and don't you think it!"

"That's only for babies," said Laura reprovingly.

"Our friendship would be definitely on an intellectual plane," said Mr. Baldock.

Laura looked pleased.

"I don't really know quite what that means," she said, "but I think I like the sound of it."

"It means," said Mr. Baldock, "that when we meet we discuss subjects which are of interest to both of us."

"What kind of subjects?"

"Well—food, for instance. I'm fond of food. I expect you are, too. But as I'm sixty-odd, and you're—what is it, ten?—I've no doubt that our ideas on the matter will differ. That's interesting. Then there will be other things—colors—flowers—animals—English history."

"You mean things like Henry the Eighth's wives?"

"Exactly. Mention Henry the Eighth to nine people out of ten, and they'll come back at you with his wives. It's an insult to a man who was called the Fairest Prince in Christendom, and who was a statesman of the first order of craftiness, to remember him only by his matrimonial efforts to get a legitimate male heir. His wretched wives are of no importance *whatever* historically."

"Well, I think his wives were very important."

"There you are!" said Mr. Baldock. "Discussion."

"I should like to have been Jane Seymour."

"Now why her?"

"She died," said Laura ecstatically.

"So did Nan Bullen and Katherine Howard."

"They were executed. Jane was only married to him for a year, and she had a baby and died, and everyone must have been terribly sorry."

"Well—that's a point of view. Come in the other room and see if we've got anything for tea."

2

"It's a wonderful tea," said Laura ecstatically.

Her eyes roamed over currant buns, jam roll, éclairs, cucumber sandwiches, chocolate biscuits, and a large indigestible-looking rich black plum cake.

She gave a sudden little giggle.

"You *did* expect me," she said. "Unless—do you have a tea like this every day?"

"God forbid," said Mr. Baldock.

They sat down companionably. Mr. Baldock had six cucumber sandwiches, and Laura had four éclairs, and a selection of everything else.

"Got a good appetite, I'm glad to see, young Laura," said Mr. Baldock appreciatively as they finished.

"I'm always hungry," said Laura, "and I'm hardly ever sick. Charles used to be sick."

"Hm . . . Charles. I suppose you miss Charles a lot?"

"Oh yes, I do. I do, *really*."

Mr. Baldock's bushy gray eyebrows rose.

"All right. All right. Who says you don't miss him?"

"Nobody. And I do—I really *do*."

He nodded gravely in answer to her earnestness, and watched her. He was wondering.

"It was terribly sad, his dying like that." Laura's voice unconsciously reproduced the tones of another voice, some adult voice, which had originally uttered the phrase.

"Yes, very sad."

"Terribly sad for Mummy and Daddy. Now—I'm all they've got in the world."

"So that's it?"

She looked at him uncomprehendingly.

She had gone into her private dream world. "*Laura, my darling. You're all I have—my only child—my treasure....*"

"Bad butter," said Mr. Baldock. It was one of his expressions of perturbation. "Bad butter! Bad butter!" He shook his head vexedly.

"Come out in the garden, Laura," he said. "We'll have a look at the roses. Tell me what you do with yourself all day."

"Well, in the morning Miss Weekes comes and we do lessons."

"That old Tabby!"

"Don't you like her?"

"She's got Girton written all over her. Mind you never go to Girton, Laura!"

"What's Girton?"

"It's a woman's college. At Cambridge. Makes my flesh creep when I think about it!"

"I'm going to boarding school when I'm twelve."

"Sinks of iniquity, boarding schools!"

"Don't you think I'll like it?"

"I daresay you'll *like* it all right. That's just the danger! Hacking other girls' ankles with a hockey stick, coming home with a crush on the music mistress, going on to Girton or Somerville as likely as not. Oh well, we've got a couple of years still, before the worst happens. Let's make the most of it. What are you going to do when you grow up? I suppose you've got some notions about it?"

"I did think that I might go and nurse lepers—"

"Well, that's harmless enough. Don't bring one home and put him in your husband's bed, though. St. Elizabeth of Hungary did that. Most misguided zeal. A Saint of God, no doubt, but a very inconsiderate wife."

"I shall never marry," said Laura in a voice of renunciation.

"No? Oh, I think I should marry if I were you. Old maids are worse than married women in my opinion. Hard luck on some man, of course, but I daresay you'd make a better wife than many."

"It wouldn't be right. I must look after Mummy and Daddy in their old age. They've got nobody but me."

"They've got a cook and a house parlor maid and a gardener, and a good income, and plenty of friends. *They'll* be all right. Parents have to put up with their children leaving them when the time comes. Great relief sometimes." He stopped abruptly by a bed of roses. "Here are my roses. Like 'em?"

"They're beautiful," said Laura politely.

"On the whole," said Mr. Baldock, "I prefer them to human beings. They don't last as long for one thing."

Then he took Laura firmly by the hand.

"Good-bye, Laura," he said. "You've got to be going now. Friendship should never be strained too far. I've enjoyed having you to tea."

"Good-bye, Mr. Baldock. Thank you for having me. I've enjoyed myself very much."

The polite slogan slipped from her lips in a glib fashion. Laura was a well-brought-up child.

"That's right," said Mr. Baldock, patting her amicably on the shoulder. "Always say your piece. It's courtesy, and knowing the right passwords that makes the wheels go round. When you come to my age, you can say what you like."

Laura smiled at him and passed through the iron gate he was holding open for her. Then she turned and hesitated.

"Well, what is it?"

"Is it really settled now? About our being friends, I mean?"

Mr. Baldock rubbed his nose.

"Yes," he said with a sigh. "Yes, I think so."

"I hope you don't mind very much?" Laura asked anxiously.

"Not too much. . . . I've got to get used to the idea, mind."

"Yes, of course. *I've* got to get used to it, too. But I think—I think— it's going to be nice. Good-bye."

"Good-bye."

Mr. Baldock looked after her retreating figure, and muttered to himself fiercely: "*Now* look what you've let yourself in for, you old fool!"

He retraced his steps to the house, and was met by his housekeeper Mrs. Rouse.

"Has the little girl gone?"

"Yes, she's gone."

"Oh dear, she didn't stay very long, did she?"

"Quite long enough," said Mr. Baldock. "Children and one's social inferiors never know when to say good-bye. One has to say it for them."

"Well!" said Mrs. Rouse, gazing after him indignantly as he walked past her.

"Good night," said Mr. Baldock. "I'm going into my library, and I don't want to be disturbed again."

"About supper—"

"Anything you please." Mr. Baldock waved an arm. "And take away all that sweet stuff, and finish it up, or give it to the cat."

"Oh, thank you, sir. My little niece—"

"Your niece, or the cat, or *anyone*."

He went into the library and shut the door.

"Well!" said Mrs. Rouse again. "Of all the crusty old bachelors! But there, I understand his ways! It's not everyone that would."

Laura went home with a pleasing feeling of importance.

She popped her head through the kitchen window where Ethel, the house parlor maid, was struggling with the intricacies of a crochet pattern.

"Ethel," said Laura. "I've got a Friend."

"Yes, dearie," said Ethel, murmuring to herself under her breath. "Five chain, twice into the next stitch, eight chain—"

"I *have* got a Friend." Laura stressed the information.

Ethel was still murmuring:

"Five double crochet, and then three times into the next—but that makes it come out wrong at the end—now where have I slipped up?"

"I've got a *Friend*," shouted Laura, maddened by the lack of comprehension displayed by her confidante.

Ethel looked up, startled.

"Well, rub it, dearie, rub it," she said vaguely.

Laura turned away in disgust.

Chapter Three

Angela Franklin had dreaded returning home but, when the time came, she found it not half so bad as she had feared.

As they drove up to the door, she said to her husband:

"There's Laura waiting for us on the steps. She looks quite excited."

And, jumping out as the car drew up, she folded her arms affectionately round her daughter and cried:

"Laura darling. It's lovely to see you. Have you missed us a lot?"

Laura said conscientiously:

"Not very much. I've been very busy. But I've made you a raffia mat."

Swiftly there swept over Angela's mind a sudden remembrance of Charles—of the way he would tear across the grass, flinging himself upon her, hugging her. "Mummy, Mummy, Mummy!"

How horribly it hurt—remembering.

She pushed aside memories, smiled at Laura and said:

"A raffia mat? How nice, darling."

Arthur Franklin tweaked his daughter's hair.

"I believe you've grown, Puss."

They all went into the house.

What it was Laura had expected, she did not know. Here were Mummy and Daddy home, and pleased to see her, making a fuss of her, asking her questions. It wasn't *they* who were wrong, it was herself. She wasn't—she wasn't—what wasn't she?

She herself hadn't said the things or looked or even felt as she had thought she would.

It wasn't the way she had planned it. She hadn't—really—taken

Charles's place. There was something missing with her, Laura. But it would be different tomorrow, she told herself, or if not tomorrow, then the next day, or the day after. The heart of the house, Laura said to herself, suddenly recalling a phrase that had taken her fancy from an old-fashioned children's book she had come across in the attic.

That was what she was now, surely, the heart of the house.

Unfortunate that she should feel herself, with a deep inner misgiving, to be just Laura as usual.

Just Laura. . . .

2

"Baldy seems to have taken quite a fancy to Laura," said Angela. "Fancy, he asked her to tea with him while we were away."

Arthur said he'd like very much to know what they had talked about.

"I think," said Angela after a moment or two, "that we ought to *tell* Laura. I mean, if we don't, she'll hear something—the servants or someone. After all, she's too old for gooseberry bushes and all that kind of thing."

She was lying in a long basket chair under the cedar tree. She turned her head now toward her husband in his deck chair.

The lines of suffering still showed in her face. The life she was carrying had not yet succeeded in blurring the sense of loss.

"It's going to be a boy," said Arthur Franklin. "I know it's going to be a boy."

Angela smiled, and shook her head.

"No use building on it," she said.

"I tell you, Angela, I know."

He was positive—quite positive.

A boy like Charles, another Charles, laughing, blue-eyed, mischievous, affectionate.

Angela thought: 'It may be another boy—but it won't be Charles.'

"I expect we shall be just as pleased with a girl, however," said Arthur, not very convincingly.

"Arthur, you know you want a son!"

"Yes," he sighed, "I'd like a son."

A man wanted a son—needed a son. Daughters—it wasn't the same thing.

Obscurely moved by some consciousness of guilt, he said:

"Laura's really a dear little thing."

Angela agreed sincerely.

"I know. So good and quiet and helpful. We shall miss her when she goes to school."

She added: "That's partly why I hope it won't be a girl. Laura might be a teeny bit jealous of a baby sister—not that she'd have any need to be."

"Of course not."

"But children are sometimes—it's quite natural; that's why I think we ought to tell her, prepare her."

And so it was that Angela Franklin said to her daughter:

"How would you like a little baby brother?"

"Or sister?" she added rather belatedly.

Laura stared at her. The words did not seem to make sense. She was puzzled. She did not understand.

Angela said gently: "You see, darling, I'm going to have a baby . . . next September. It will be nice, won't it?"

She was a little disturbed when Laura, murmuring something incoherent, backed away, her face crimsoning with an emotion that her mother did not understand.

Angela Franklin felt worried.

"I wonder," she said to her husband. "Perhaps we've been wrong? I've never actually told her anything—about—about *things*, I mean. Perhaps she hadn't any idea . . ."

Arthur Franklin said that considering that the production of kittens that went on in the house was something astronomical, it was hardly likely that Laura was completely unacquainted with the facts of life.

"Yes, but perhaps she thinks people are different. It may have been a shock to her."

It had been a shock to Laura, though not in any biological sense. It was simply that the idea that her mother would have another child had never occurred to Laura. She had seen the whole pattern as simple and straightforward. Charles was dead, and she was her parents' only child. She was, as she had phrased it to herself, '*all they had in the world.*'

And now—now—there was to be another Charles.

She never doubted, any more than Arthur and Angela secretly doubted, that the baby would be a boy.

Desolation struck through to her.

For a long time Laura sat huddled upon the edge of a cucumber frame, while she wrestled with disaster.

Then she made up her mind. She got up, walked down the drive and along the road to Mr. Baldock's house.

Mr. Baldock, grinding his teeth and snorting with venom, was penning a really vitriolic review for a learned journal of a fellow historian's life work.

He turned a ferocious face to the door, as Mrs. Rouse, giving a perfunctory knock and pushing it open, announced:

"Here's little Miss Laura for you."

"Oh," said Mr. Baldock, checked on the verge of a tremendous flood of invective. "So it's you."

He was disconcerted. A fine thing it would be if the child was going to trot along here at any odd moment. He hadn't bargained for *that*. Drat all children! Give them an inch and they took an ell. He didn't like children, anyway. He never had.

His disconcerted gaze met Laura's. There was no apology in Laura's look. It was grave, deeply troubled, but quite confident in a divine right to be where she was. She made no polite remarks of an introductory nature.

"I thought I'd come and tell you," she said, "that I'm going to have a baby brother."

"Oh," said Mr. Baldock, taken aback.

"We-ell . . ." he said, playing for time. Laura's face was white and expressionless. "That's news, isn't it?" He paused. "Are you pleased?"

"No," said Laura. "I don't think I am."

"Beastly things, babies," agreed Mr. Baldock sympathetically. "No teeth and no hair, and yell their heads off. Their mothers like them, of course, have to—or the poor little brutes would never get looked after, or grow up. But you won't find it so bad when it's three or four," he added encouragingly. "Almost as good as a kitten or a puppy by then."

"Charles died," said Laura. "Do you think it's likely that my new baby brother may die too?"

He shot her a keen glance, then said firmly:

"Shouldn't think so for a moment," and added: "Lightning never strikes twice."

"Cook says that," said Laura. "It means the same thing doesn't happen twice?"

"Quite right."

"Charles—" began Laura, and stopped.

Again Mr. Baldock's glance swept over her quickly.

"No reason it should be a baby brother," he said. "Just as likely to be a baby sister."

"Mummy seems to think it will be a brother."

"Shouldn't go by that if I were you. She wouldn't be the first woman to think wrong."

Laura's face brightened suddenly.

"There was Jehoshaphat," she said. "Dulcibella's last kitten. He's turned out to be a girl after all. Cook calls him Josephine now," she added.

"There you are," said Mr. Baldock encouragingly. "I'm not a betting man, but I'd put my money on its being a girl myself."

"Would you?" said Laura fervently.

She smiled at him, a grateful and unexpectedly lovely smile that gave Mr. Baldock quite a shock.

"Thank you," she said. "I'll go now." She added politely: "I hope I haven't interrupted your work?"

"It's quite all right," said Mr. Baldock. "I'm always glad to see you if it's about something important. I know you wouldn't barge in here just to chatter."

"Of course I wouldn't," said Laura earnestly.

She withdrew, closing the door carefully behind her.

The conversation had cheered her considerably. Mr. Baldock, she knew, was a very clever man.

"He's much more likely to be right than Mummy," she thought to herself.

A baby sister? Yes, she could face the thought of a sister. A sister would only be another Laura—an inferior Laura. A Laura lacking teeth and hair, and any kind of sense.

3

As she emerged from the kindly haze of the anaesthetic, Angela's cornflower-blue eyes asked the eager question that her lips were almost afraid to form.

"Is it—all right—is it—?"

The nurse spoke glibly and briskly after the manner of nurses.

"You've got a lovely daughter, Mrs. Franklin."

"A daughter—a daughter . . ." The blue eyes closed again.

Disappointment surged through her. She had been so sure—so sure. . . . Only a second Laura . . .

The old tearing pain of her loss reawakened. Charles, her handsome laughing Charles. Her boy, her son . . .

Downstairs, Cook was saying briskly:

"Well, Miss Laura. You've got a little sister, what do you think of *that*?"

Laura replied sedately to Cook:

"I knew I'd have a sister. Mr. Baldock said so."

"An old bachelor like him, what should he know?"

"He's a very clever man," said Laura.

Angela was rather slow to regain her full strength. Arthur Franklin was worried about his wife. The baby was a month old when he spoke to Angela rather hesitatingly.

"Does it matter so much? That it's a girl, I mean, and not a boy?"

"No, of course not. Not really. Only—I'd felt so sure."

"Even if it had been a boy, it wouldn't have been Charles, you know?"

"No. No, of course not."

The nurse entered the room, carrying the baby.

"Here we are," she said. "Such a lovely girl now. Going to your Mumsie-wumsie, aren't you?"

Angela held the baby slackly and eyed the nurse with dislike as the latter went out of the room.

"What idiotic things these women say," she muttered crossly.

Arthur laughed.

"Laura darling, get me that cushion," said Angela.

Laura brought it to her, and stood by as Angela arranged the baby more comfortably. Laura felt comfortably mature and important. The baby was only a silly little thing. It was she, Laura, on whom her mother relied.

It was chilly this evening. The fire that burned in the grate was pleasant. The baby crowed and gurgled happily.

Angela looked down into the dark blue eyes, and a mouth that seemed already to be able to smile. She looked down, with sudden shock, into Charles's eyes. Charles as a baby. She had almost forgotten him at that age.

Love rushed blindingly through her veins. *Her* baby, *her* darling. How could she have been so cold, so unloving to this adorable creature? How could she have been so blind? A gay beautiful child, like Charles.

"My sweet," she murmured. "My precious, my darling."

She bent over the child in an abandonment of love. She was oblivious of Laura standing watching her. She did not notice as Laura crept quietly out of the room.

But perhaps a vague uneasiness made her say to Arthur:

"Mary Wells can't be here for the christening. Shall we let Laura be proxy godmother? It would please her, I think."

Chapter Four

1

"Enjoy the christening?" asked Mr. Baldock.

"No," said Laura.

"Cold in that church, I expect," said Mr. Baldock. "Nice font though," he added. "Norman—black Tournai marble."

Laura was unmoved by the information.

She was busy formulating a question:

"May I ask you something, Mr. Baldock?"

"Of course."

"Is it wrong to pray for anyone to die?"

Mr. Baldock gave her a swift sideways look.

"In my view," he said, "it would be unpardonable interference."

"Interference?"

"Well, the Almighty is running the show, isn't He? What do you want to stick *your* fingers into the machinery for? What business is it of yours?"

"I don't see that it would matter to God very much. When a baby has been christened and everything, it goes to heaven, doesn't it?"

"Don't see where else it could go," admitted Mr. Baldock.

"And God is fond of children. The Bible says so. So He'd be pleased to see it."

Mr. Baldock took a short turn up and down the room. He was seriously upset, and didn't want to show it.

"Look here, Laura," he said at last. "You've got—you've simply *got* to mind your own business."

"But perhaps it is my business."

"No, it isn't. *Nothing's* your business but *yourself*. Pray what you like about yourself. Ask for blue ears, or a diamond tiara, or to grow up and win a beauty competition. The worst that can happen to you is that the answer to your prayer might be 'Yes.' "

Laura looked at him uncomprehendingly.

"I mean it," said Mr. Baldock.

Laura thanked him politely, and said she must be going home now.

When she had gone, Mr. Baldock rubbed his chin, scratched his head, picked his nose, and absentmindedly wrote a review of a mortal enemy's book simply dripping with milk and honey.

Laura walked back home, thinking deeply.

As she passed the small Roman Catholic church, she hesitated. A daily woman who came in to help in the kitchen was a Catholic, and stray scraps of her conversation came back to Laura, who had listened to them with the fascination accorded to something rare and strange, and also forbidden. For Nannie, a staunch chapelgoer, held very strong views about what she referred to as the Scarlet Woman. Who or what the Scarlet Woman was, Laura had no idea, except that she had some undefined connection with Babylon.

But what came to her mind now was Molly's chat of praying for her Intention—a candle had entered into it in some way. Laura hesitated a little longer, drew a deep breath, looked up and down the road, and slipped into the porch.

The church was small and rather dark, and did not smell at all like the parish church where Laura went every Sunday. There was no sign of the Scarlet Woman, but there was a plaster figure of a lady in a blue cloak, with a tray in front of her, and wire loops in which candles were burning. Nearby was a supply of fresh candles, and a box with a slot for money.

Laura hesitated for some time. Her theological ideas were confused and limited. God she knew, God who was committed to loving her by the fact that He was God. There was also the Devil, with horns and a tail, and a specialist in temptation. But the Scarlet Woman appeared to occupy an in-between status. The Lady in the Blue Cloak looked beneficent, and as though she might deal with Intentions in a favorable manner.

Laura drew a deep sigh and fumbled in her pocket where reposed, as yet untouched, her weekly sixpence of pocket money.

She pushed it into the slit and heard it drop with a slight pang. Gone irrevocably! Then she took a candle, lit it, and put it into the wire holder. She spoke in a low polite voice.

"This is my Intention. Please let baby go to Heaven." She added: "As soon as you possibly can, please."

She stood there for a moment. The candles burned, the Lady in the Blue Cloak continued to look beneficent. Laura had for a moment or two a feeling of emptiness. Then, frowning a little, she left the church and walked home.

On the terrace was the baby's pram. Laura came up to it and stood beside it, looking down on the sleeping infant.

As she looked, the fair downy head stirred, the eyelids opened, and blue eyes looked up at Laura with a wide unfocused stare.

"You're going to Heaven soon," Laura told her sister. "It's lovely in Heaven," she added coaxingly. "All golden and precious stones."

"And harps," she added, after a minute. "And lots of angels with real feathery wings. It's much nicer than here."

She thought of something else.

"You'll see Charles," she said. "Think of that! You'll see Charles."

Angela Franklin came out of the drawing-room window.

"Hullo, Laura," she said. "Are you talking to baby?"

She bent over the pram. "Hullo, my sweetie. Was it awake, then?"

Arthur Franklin, following his wife out on to the terrace, said:

"Why do women have to talk such nonsense to babies? Eh, Laura? Don't you think it's odd?"

"I don't think it's nonsense," said Laura.

"Don't you? What do you think it is, then?" He smiled at her teasingly.

"I think it's love," said Laura.

He was a little taken aback.

Laura, he thought, was an odd kid. Difficult to know what went on behind that straight, unemotional gaze.

"I must get a piece of netting, muslin or something," said Angela.

"To put over the pram when it's out here. I'm always so afraid of a cat jumping up and lying on her face and suffocating her. We've got too many cats about the place."

"Bah," said her husband. "That's one of those old wives' tales. I don't believe a cat has ever suffocated a baby."

"Oh, they have, Arthur. You read about it quite often in the paper."

"That's no guarantee of truth."

"Anyway, I shall get some netting, and I must tell Nannie to look out of the window from time to time and see that she's all right. Oh dear, I wish our own nanny hadn't had to go to her dying sister. This new young nanny—I don't really feel happy about her."

"Why not? She seems a nice enough girl. Devoted to baby and good references and all that."

"Oh yes, I know. She *seems* all right. But there's something . . . There's that gap of a year and a half in her references."

"She went home to nurse her mother."

"That's what they always say! And it's the sort of thing you can't check. It might have been for some reason she doesn't want us to know about."

"Got into trouble, you mean?"

Angela threw him a warning glance, indicating Laura.

"Do be careful, Arthur. No, I don't mean that. I mean—"

"What do you mean, darling?"

"I don't really know," said Angela slowly. "It's just—sometimes when I'm talking to her I feel that there's something she's anxious we shouldn't find out."

"Wanted by the police?"

"Arthur! That's a very silly joke."

Laura walked gently away. She was an intelligent child and she perceived quite plainly that they, her father and mother, would like to talk about Nannie unhampered by her presence. She herself was not interested in the new nanny; a pale, dark-haired, soft-spoken girl, who showed herself kindly to Laura, though plainly quite uninterested by her.

Laura was thinking of the Lady with the Blue Cloak.

2

"Come *on*, Josephine," said Laura crossly.

Josephine, late Jehoshaphat, though not actively resisting, was displaying all the signs of passive resistance. Disturbed in a delicious sleep against the side of the greenhouse, she had been half dragged, half carried by Laura, out of the kitchen garden and round the house to the terrace.

"There!" Laura plopped Josephine down. A few feet away, the baby's pram stood on the gravel.

Laura walked slowly away across the lawn. As she reached the big lime tree, she turned her head.

Josephine, her tail lashing from time to time, in indignant memory, began to wash her stomach, sticking out what seemed a disproportionately long hind leg. That part of her toilet completed, she yawned and looked round her at her surroundings. Then she began halfheartedly to wash behind the ears, thought better of it, yawned again, and finally got up and walked slowly and meditatively away, and round the corner of the house.

Laura followed her, picked her up determinedly, and lugged her back again. Josephine gave Laura a look and sat there lashing her tail. As soon as Laura had got back to the tree, Josephine once more got up, yawned, stretched, and walked off. Laura brought her back again, remonstrating as she did so.

"It's sunny here, Josephine. It's *nice!*"

Nothing could be clearer than that Josephine disagreed with this statement. She was now in a very bad temper indeed, lashing her tail, and flattening back her ears.

"Hullo, young Laura."

Laura started and turned. Mr. Baldock stood behind her. She had not heard or noticed his slow progress across the lawn. Josephine, profiting by Laura's momentary inattention, darted to a tree and ran up it, pausing on a branch to look down on them with an air of malicious satisfaction.

"That's where cats have the advantage over human beings," said Mr. Baldock. "When they want to get away from people they can climb a tree. The nearest we can get to that is to shut ourselves in the lavatory."

Laura looked slightly shocked. Lavatories came into the category of things which Nannie (the late Nannie) had said 'little ladies don't talk about.'

"But one has to come out," said Mr. Baldock, "if for no other reason than because other people want to come in. Now that cat of yours will probably stay up that tree for a couple of hours."

Immediately Josephine demonstrated the general unpredictability of cats by coming down with a rush, crossing toward them, and proceeding to rub herself to and fro against Mr. Baldock's trousers, purring loudly.

"Here," she seemed to say, "is exactly what I have been waiting for."

"Hullo, Baldy." Angela came out of the window. "Are you paying your respects to the latest arrival? Oh dear, these *cats*. Laura dear, do take Josephine away. Put her in the kitchen. I haven't got that netting yet. Arthur laughs at me, but cats do jump up and sleep on babies' chests and smother them. I don't want the cats to get the habit of coming round to the terrace."

As Laura went off carrying Josephine, Mr. Baldock sent a considering gaze after her.

After lunch, Arthur Franklin drew his friend into the study.

"There's an article here—" he began.

Mr. Baldock interrupted him, without ceremony and forthrightly, as was his custom.

"Just a minute. I've got something *I* want to say. Why don't you send that child to school?"

"Laura? That is the idea—after Christmas, I believe. When she's eleven."

"Don't wait for that. Do it now."

"It would be midterm. And, anyway, Miss Weekes is quite—"

Mr. Baldock said what he thought of Miss Weekes with relish.

"Laura doesn't want instruction from a desiccated blue-stocking, however bulging with brains," he said. "She wants distraction, other girls, a different set of troubles if you like. Otherwise, for all you know, you may have a tragedy."

"A tragedy? What sort of tragedy?"

"A couple of nice little boys the other day took their baby sister out of the pram and threw her in the river. The baby made too much work for Mummy, they said. They had quite genuinely made themselves believe it, I imagine."

Arthur Franklin stared at him.

"Jealousy, you mean?"

"Jealousy."

"My dear Baldy, Laura's not a jealous child. Never has been."

"How do you know? Jealousy eats inward."

"She's never shown any sign of it. She's a very sweet, gentle child, but without any very strong feelings, I should say."

"*You'd* say!" Mr. Baldock snorted. "If you ask me, you and Angela don't know the first thing about your own child."

Arthur Franklin smiled good-temperedly. He was used to Baldy.

"We'll keep an eye on the baby," he said, "if that's what's worrying you. I'll give Angela a hint to be careful. Tell her not to make too much fuss of the newcomer, and a bit more of Laura. That ought to meet the case." He added with a hint of curiosity: "I've always wondered just what it is you see in Laura. She—"

"There's promise there of a very rare and unusual spirit," said Mr. Baldock. "At least so I think."

"Well—I'll speak to Angela—but she'll only laugh."

But Angela, rather to her husband's surprise, did not laugh.

"There's something in what he says, you know. Child psychologists all agree that jealousy over a new baby is natural and almost inevitable. Though frankly *I* haven't seen any signs of it in Laura. She's a placid child, and it isn't as though she were wildly attached to *me* or anything like that. I must try and show her that I depend upon her."

And so, when about a week later, she and her husband were going for a weekend visit to some old friends, Angela talked to Laura.

"You'll take good care of baby, won't you, Laura, while we're away? It's nice to feel I'm leaving you here to keep an eye on everything. Nannie hasn't been here very long, you see."

Her mother's words pleased Laura. They made her feel old and important. Her small pale face brightened.

Unfortunately, the good effect was destroyed almost immediately by a conversation between Nannie and Ethel in the nursery, which she happened to overhear.

"Lovely baby, isn't she?' said Ethel, poking the infant with a crudely affectionate finger. "There's a little ducksie-wucksie. Seems funny Miss Laura's always been such a plain little thing. Don't wonder her pa and ma never took to her, as they took to Master Charles and this one. Miss Laura's a nice little thing, but you can't say more than that."

That evening Laura knelt by her bed and prayed.

The Lady with the Blue Cloak had taken no notice of her Intention. Laura was going to headquarters.

"*Please, God*," she prayed, "*let baby die and go to Heaven soon. Very soon.*"

She got into bed and lay down. Her heart beat, and she felt guilty and wicked. She had done what Mr. Baldock had told her not to do, and Mr. Baldock was a very wise man. She had had no feeling of guilt about her candle to the Lady in the Blue Cloak—possibly because she had never really had much hope of any result. And she could see no harm in just bringing Josephine on to the terrace. She wouldn't have put Josephine actually on to the pram. That, she knew, *would* have been wicked. But if Josephine, of her own accord . . . ?

Tonight, however, she had crossed the Rubicon. God was all-powerful. . . .

Shivering a little, Laura fell asleep.

Chapter Five

Angela and Arthur Franklin drove away in the car.

Up in the nursery, the new nanny, Gwyneth Jones, was putting the baby to bed.

She was uneasy tonight. There had been certain feelings, portents, lately, and tonight—

"I'm just imagining it," she said to herself. "Fancy! That's all it is."

Hadn't the doctor told her that it was quite possible she might never have another fit?

She'd had them as a child, and then never a sign of anything of the kind until that terrible day . . .

Teething convulsions, her aunt had called those childhood seizures. But the doctor had used another name, had said plainly and without subterfuge what the malady was. And he had said, quite definitely: "You mustn't take a place with a baby or children. It wouldn't be safe."

But she'd paid for that expensive training. It was her trade—what she knew how to do—certificates and all—well paid—and she loved looking after babies. A year had gone by, and there had been no recurrence of trouble. It was all nonsense, the doctor frightening her like that.

So she'd written to the bureau—a different bureau, and she'd soon got a place, and she was happy here, and the baby was a little love.

She put the baby into her cot and went downstairs for her supper. She awoke in the night with a sense of uneasiness, almost terror. She thought:

'I'll make myself a drop of hot milk. It will calm me down.'

She lit the spirit lamp and carried it to the table near the window.

There was no final warning. She went down like a stone, lying there on the floor, jerking and twisting. The spirit lamp fell to the floor, and the flame from it ran across the carpet and reached the end of the muslin curtains.

2

Laura woke up suddenly.

She had been dreaming—a bad dream—though she couldn't remember the details of it. Something chasing her, something—but she was safe now, in her own bed, at home.

She felt for the lamp by her bedside, and turned it on, and looked at her own little clock. Twelve o'clock. Midnight.

She sat up in bed, feeling a curious reluctance to turn out the light again.

She listened. What a queer creaking noise. . . . 'Burglars perhaps,' thought Laura, who like most children was perpetually suspecting burglars. She got out of bed and went to the door, opened it a little way, and peered cautiously out. Everything was dark and quiet.

But there was a smell, a funny smoky smell, Laura sniffed experimentally. She went across the landing and opened the door that led to the servants' quarters. Nothing.

She crossed to the other side of the landing, where a door shut off a short passage leading to the nursery and the nursery bathroom.

Then she shrank back, appalled. Great wreaths of smoke came curling toward her.

"It's on fire. The house is on fire!"

Laura screamed, rushed to the servants' wing, and called:

"Fire! The house is on fire!"

She could never remember clearly what came after. Cook and Ethel—Ethel running downstairs to telephone, Cook opening that door across the landing and being driven back by the smoke, Cook soothing her with: "It'll be all right." Incoherent murmurs: "The engine will come—they'll get them out through the window—don't you worry, my dear."

But it would not be all right. Laura knew.

She was shattered by the knowledge that her prayer had been answered. God had acted—acted with promptitude and with indescribable terror. This was His way, His terrible way, of taking baby to Heaven.

Cook pulled Laura down the front stairs with her.

"Come on now, Miss Laura—don't wait about—we must all get outside the house."

But Nannie and baby could not get outside the house. They were up there, in the nursery, trapped!

Cook plunged heavily down the stairs, pulling Laura after her. But as they passed out through the front door to join Ethel on the lawn, and Cook's grip relaxed, Laura turned back and ran up the stairs again.

Once more she opened the landing door. From somewhere through the smoke she heard a far-off fretful whimpering cry.

And suddenly, something in Laura came alive—warmth, passionate endeavor, that curious incalculable emotion, love.

Her mind was sober and clear. She had read or been told that to rescue people in a fire you dipped a towel in water and put it round your mouth. She ran into her room, soaked the bath towel in the jug, rolled it round her, and crossing the landing plunged into the smoke. There was flame now across the passage, and the timbers were falling. Where an adult would have estimated danger and chances, Laura went bull-headed with the unknowing courage of a child. She *must* get to baby, she must save baby. Otherwise baby would burn to death. She stumbled over the unconscious body of Gwyneth, not knowing what it was. Choking, gasping, she found her way to the crib; the screen round it had protected it from the worst of the smoke.

Laura grabbed at the baby, clutched her close beneath the sheltering wet towel. She stumbled toward the door, her lungs gasping for air.

But there was no retracing her steps. Flames barred her way.

Laura had her wits still. The door to the tank room—she felt for it, found it, pushed through it to a rickety stair that led up to the tank room in the loft. She and Charles had got out that way once on to the roof. If she could crawl across the roof . . .

As the fire engines arrived, an incoherent couple of women in night attire rushed to them crying out:

"The baby—there's a baby and the nurse in that room up there."

The fireman whistled and pursed his lips. That end of the house was blazing with flame. 'Goners,' he said to himself. 'Never get *them* out alive!'

"Everyone else out?" he asked.

Cook, looking round, cried out: "Where's Miss Laura? She came out right after me. Wherever can she be?"

It was then that a fireman called out: "Hi, Joe, there's someone on the roof—the other end. Get a ladder up."

A few moments later, they set their burden down gently on the lawn—an unrecognizable Laura, blackened, her arms scorched, half unconscious, but tight in her grip a small morsel of humanity, whose outraged howls proclaimed her angrily alive.

3

"If it hadn't been for Laura—" Angela stopped, mastering her emotions.

"We've found out all about poor Nannie," she went on.

"It seems she was an epileptic. Her doctor warned her not to take a nurse's post again, but she did. They think she dropped a spirit lamp when she had a fit. I always knew there was something wrong about her—something she didn't want me to find out."

"Poor girl," said Franklin, "she's paid for it."

Angela, ruthless in her mother love, swept on, dismissing the claims of Gwyneth Jones to pity.

"And baby would have been burned to death if it hadn't been for Laura."

"Is Laura all right again?" asked Mr. Baldock.

"Yes. Shock, of course, and her arms were burned, but not too badly. She'll be quite all right, the doctor says."

"Good for Laura," said Mr. Baldock.

Angela said indignantly: "And you pretending to Arthur that Laura was so jealous of the poor mite that she might do her a mischief! Really—you bachelors!"

"All right, all right," said Mr. Baldock. "I'm not often wrong, but I dare say it's good for me sometimes."

"Just go and take a look at those two."

Mr. Baldock did as he was told. The baby lay on a rug in front of the nursery fire, kicking vaguely and making indeterminate gurgling noises.

Beside her sat Laura. Her arms were bandaged, and she had lost her eyelashes which gave her face a comical appearance. She was dangling some colored rings to attract the baby's attention. She turned her head to look at Mr. Baldock.

"Hullo, young Laura," said Mr. Baldock. "How are you? Quite the heroine, I hear. A gallant rescue."

Laura gave him a brief glance, and then concentrated once more on her efforts with the rings.

"How are the arms?"

"They did hurt rather a lot, but they've put some stuff on, and they're better now."

"You're a funny one," said Mr. Baldock, sitting down heavily in a chair. "One day you're hoping the cat will smother your baby sister—oh yes, you did—can't deceive me—and the next day you're crawling about the roof hugging the child to safety at the risk of your own life."

"Anyway, I *did* save her," said Laura. "She isn't hurt a bit—not a bit." She bent over the child and spoke passionately. "I won't ever let her be hurt, not ever. I shall look after her all my life."

Mr. Baldock's eyebrows rose slowly.

"So it's love now. You love her, do you?"

"Oh, *yes!*" The answer came with the same fervor. "I love her better than anything in the world!"

She turned her face to him, and Mr. Baldock was startled. It was, he thought, like the breaking open of a cocoon. The child's face was radiant with feeling. In spite of the grotesque absence of lashes and brows, the face had a quality of emotion that made it suddenly beautiful.

"I see," said Mr. Baldock. "*I* see . . . And where shall we go from here, I wonder?"

Laura looked at him, puzzled, and slightly apprehensive.

"Isn't it all right?" she asked. "For me to love her, I mean?"

Mr. Baldock looked at her. His face was thoughtful.

"It's all right for *you*, young Laura," he said. "Oh yes, it's all right for you. . . ."

He relapsed into abstraction, his hand tapping his chin.

As a historian he had always mainly been concerned with the past, but there were moments when the fact that he could not foresee the future irritated him profoundly. This was one of them.

He looked at Laura and the crowing Shirley, and his brow contracted angrily. 'Where will they be,' he thought, 'in ten years' time—in twenty years—in twenty-five? Where shall *I* be?'

The answer to that last question came quickly.

'Under the turf,' said Mr. Baldock to himself. 'Under the turf.'

He knew that, but he did not really believe it, any more than any other positive person full of the vitality of living really believes it.

What a dark and mysterious entity the future was! In twenty-odd years what would have happened? Another war, perhaps? (Most unlikely!) New diseases? People fastening mechanical wings on themselves, perhaps, and floating about the streets like sacrilegious angels! Journeys to Mars? Sustaining oneself on horrid little tablets out of bottles, instead of on steaks and succulent green peas!

"What are you thinking about?" Laura asked.

"The future."

"Do you mean tomorrow?"

"Farther forward than that. I suppose you're able to read, young Laura?"

"Of course," said Laura, shocked. "I've read nearly all the Doctor Dolittles, and the books about Winnie-the-Pooh and—"

"Spare me the horrid details," said Mr. Baldock. "How do you read a book? Begin at the beginning and go right through?"

"Yes. Don't you?"

"No," said Mr. Baldock. "I take a look at the start, get some idea of what it's all about, then I go on to the end and see where the fellow has got to, and what he's been trying to prove. And then, *then* I go back and see *how* he's got there and what's made him land up where he did. Much more interesting."

Laura looked interested but disapproving.

"I don't think that's the way the author meant his book to be read," she said.

"Of course he didn't."

"I think you should read the book the way the author meant."

"Ah," said Mr. Baldock. "But you're forgetting the party of the second part, as the blasted lawyers put it. There's the reader. The reader's got *his* rights, too. The author writes his book the way *he* likes. Has it all his own way. Messes up the punctuation and fools around with the sense any way he pleases. And the reader reads the book the way *he* wants to read it, and the author can't stop him."

"You make it sound like a battle," said Laura.

"I like battles," said Mr. Baldock. "The truth is, we're all slavishly obsessed *by* Time. Chronological sequence has no significance whatever. If you consider Eternity, you can jump about in Time as you please. But no one does consider Eternity."

Laura had withdrawn her attention from him. She was not considering Eternity. She was considering Shirley.

And watching that dedicated devoted look, Mr. Baldock was again conscious of a vague feeling of apprehension.

PART TWO

SHIRLEY—1946

Chapter One

1

Shirley walked at a brisk pace along the lane. Her racket with the shoes attached was tucked under one arm. She was smiling to herself and was slightly out of breath.

She must hurry, she would be late for supper. Really, she supposed, she ought not to have played that last set. It hadn't been a good set, anyway. Pam was such a rabbit. Pam and Gordon had been no match at all for Shirley and—what was his name? Henry, anyway. Henry what, she wondered?

Considering Henry, Shirley's feet slowed up a little.

Henry was something quite new in her experience. He wasn't in the least like any of the local young men. She considered them impartially. Robin, the vicar's son. Nice, and really very devoted, with rather a pleasant old-world chivalry about him. He was going in for Oriental Languages at the S.O.A.S. and was slightly highbrow. Then there was Peter—Peter was really terribly young and callow. And there was Edward Westbury, who was a good deal older, and worked in a bank, and was rather heavily political. They all belonged here in Bellbury. But Henry came from outside, and had been brought along as somebody's nephew. With Henry had come a sense of liberty and detachment.

Shirley savored the last word appreciatively. It was a quality she admired.

In Bellbury, there was no detachment, everybody was heavily involved with everybody else.

There was altogether too much family solidarity in Bellbury. Everybody in Bellbury had roots. They belonged.

Shirley was a little confused by these phrases, but they expressed, she thought, what she meant.

Now Henry, definitely, didn't belong. The nearest he would get to it, she thought, was being somebody's nephew, and even then it would probably be an aunt by marriage—not a real aunt.

'Ridiculous, of course,' said Shirley to herself, 'because after all, Henry must have a father and a mother, and a home like everybody else.' But she decided that his parents had probably died in an obscure part of the world, rather young. Or possibly he had a mother who spent all her time on the Riviera, and had had a lot of husbands.

'Ridiculous,' said Shirley again to herself. 'Actually you don't know the first thing about Henry. You don't even know what his surname is—or who brought him this afternoon.'

But it was typical of Henry, she felt, that she should not know. Henry, she thought, would always appear like that—vague, with an insubstantial background—and then he would depart again, and still nobody would know what his name was, or whose nephew he had been. He was just at attractive young man, with an engaging smile, who played tennis extremely well.

Shirley liked the cool way in which, when Mary Crofton had pondered: "Now how had we better play?" Henry had immediately said: "I'll play with Shirley against you two," and had there upon spun a racket saying: "Rough or smooth?"

Henry, she was quite sure, would always do exactly as he pleased.

She had asked him: "Are you down here for long?" and he had replied vaguely: "Oh, I shouldn't think so."

He hadn't suggested their meeting again.

A momentary frown passed over Shirley's face. She wished he had done so. . . .

Again she glanced at her watch, and quickened her steps. She was really going to be very late. Not that Laura would mind. Laura never minded. Laura was an angel. . . .

The house was in sight now. Mellow in its early Georgian beauty, it had a slightly lopsided effect, due, so she understood, to a fire which had consumed one wing of it, which had never been rebuilt.

Irresistibly Shirley's pace slackened. Somehow today, she didn't want to get home. She didn't want to go inside those kindly enclosing walls, the late sun streaming in through the west windows on to the gentle faded chintzes. The stillness there was so peaceful; there would be Laura with her warm welcoming face, her watchful protecting eyes, and Ethel stumping in with the supper dishes. Warmth, love, protection, home. . . . All the things, surely, most valuable in life? And they were hers, without effort or desire on her part, surrounding her, pressing on her. . . .

'Now that's a curious way of putting it,' thought Shirley to herself. 'Pressing on me? What on earth do I mean by that?'

But it was, exactly, what she was feeling. Pressure—definite, steady pressure. Like the weight of the knapsack she had carried once on a walking tour. Almost unnoticed at first, and then steadily making itself felt, bearing down, cutting into her shoulders, weighing down on her. A burden. . . .

'Really, the things I think of!' said Shirley to herself, and running up to the open front door, she went in.

The hall was in semi-twilight. From the floor above, Laura called down the well of the staircase in her soft, rather husky voice:

"Is that you, Shirley?"

"Yes, I'm afraid I'm frightfully late, Laura."

"It doesn't matter at all. It's only macaroni—the *an gratin* kind. Ethel has got it in the oven."

Laura Franklin came round the bend of the staircase, a slim fragile creature, with an almost colorless face and deep brown eyes set at an unusual angle that made them, in some curious way, look tragic.

She came down, smiling at Shirley.

"Enjoy yourself?"

"Oh yes," said Shirley.

"Good tennis?"

"Not bad."

"Anybody exciting? Or just Bellbury?"

"Mostly Bellbury."

Funny how when people asked you questions, you didn't want to answer them. And yet the answers were so harmless. Naturally Laura liked to know how she'd enjoyed herself.

If people were fond of you, they always wanted to know—

Would Henry's people want to know? She tried to visualize Henry at home, but failed. It sounded ridiculous, but she couldn't somehow *see* Henry in a home. And yet he must have one!

A nebulous picture swam before her eyes. Henry strolling into a room where his mother, a platinum blonde just back from the South of France, was carefully painting her mouth a rather surprising color. "Hullo, Mother, so you're back?"—"Yes, have you been playing tennis?"—"Yes." There would be no curiosity, practically no interest. Henry and his mother would both be quite indifferent to what the other had been doing.

Laura asked curiously:

"What are you saying to yourself, Shirley? Your lips are moving, and your eyebrows are going up and down."

Shirley laughed:

"Oh, just an imaginary conversation."

Laura raised delicate eyebrows.

"It seemed to please you."

"It was quite ridiculous really."

The faithful Ethel put her head round the dining room door and said: "Supper's in."

Shirley cried: "I must wash," and ran upstairs.

After supper, as they sat in the drawing room, Laura said: "I got the prospectus from the St. Katherine's Secretarial College today. I gather it's one of the best of its kind. What do you feel about it, Shirley?"

A grimace marred the loveliness of Shirley's young face.

"Learn shorthand and typing and then go and take a job?"

"Why not?"

Shirley sighed, and then laughed.

"Because I'm a lazy devil. I'd much rather stay at home and do nothing. Laura darling, I've been at school for *years*! Can't I have a bit of a break?"

"I wish there was something you really wished to train for, or were keen about." A frown showed itself for a moment on Laura's forehead.

"I'm a throwback," said Shirley. "I just want to sit at home and dream of a big handsome husband, and plenty of family allowances for a growing family."

Laura did not respond. She was still looking worried.

"If you do a course at St. Katherine's, it's a question, really, of where you should live in London. Would you like to be a P.G.—with Cousin Angela, perhaps—"

"*Not* Cousin Angela. Have a heart, Laura."

"Not Angela then, but with some family or other. Or there are hostels, I believe. Later, you could share a flat with another girl."

"Why can't I share a flat with you?" demanded Shirley.

Laura shook her head.

"I'd stay here."

"Stay here? Not come to London with me?"

Shirley sounded indignant and incredulous.

Laura said simply: "I don't want to be bad for you, darling."

"Bad for me? How could you be?"

"Well—possessive, you know."

"Like the kind of mother who eats her young? Laura, you're never possessive."

Laura said dubiously: "I hope I'm not, but one never knows." She added with a frown: "One doesn't know in the least what one is really like. . . ."

"Well, I really don't think you need have qualms, Laura. You're not in the least the domineering kind—at least not to me. You don't boss or bully, or try to arrange my life for me."

"Well, actually, that is exactly what I am doing—arranging for you to take a secretarial course in London when you don't in the least want to!"

The sisters both laughed.

2

Laura straightened her back and stretched her arms.

"Four dozen," she said.

She had been bunching sweet peas.

"We ought to get a good price from Trendle's," she said. "Long stalks, and four flowers on each stem. The sweet peas have been a success this year, Horder."

Horder, who was a gnarled, dirty, and gloomy-looking old man growled a qualified assent.

"Not too bad this year, they ain't," he said grudgingly.

Horder was a man very sure of his position. An elderly, retired gardener, who really knew his trade, his price at the end of five years of war was above rubies. Everyone had competed for him. Laura by sheer force of personality had got him, though Mrs. Kindle, whose husband was rumored to have made a fortune out of munitions, had offered him much more money.

But Horder had preferred to work for Miss Franklin. Known her father and mother, he had; proper folk, gentlefolk. He remembered Miss Laura as a little bit of a thing. These sentiments alone would not have retained his services. The truth was that he liked working for Miss Laura. Proper drove you, she did, not much chance for slackness. If she'd been out, she knew just how much you ought to have got on with. But then, too, she appreciated what you'd done. She was free with her praise and her admiration. Generous, too, in elevenses and frequent cups of hot, strong, sugary tea. Wasn't everyone who was free with their tea and sugar nowadays, seeing it was rationed. And she was a fine quick worker herself, Miss Laura was, she could bunch quicker than he could—and that was saying something. And she'd got ideas— always looking toward the future—planning this and that—going in for new-fangled notions. Them cloches, for instance. Horder had taken a poor view of cloches. Laura admitted to him that of course she might be wrong. . . . On this basis, Horder graciously consented to give the new-fangled things a trial. The tomatoes had achieved results that surprised him.

"Five o'clock," said Laura, glancing at her watch. "We've got through very well."

She looked round her, at the metal vases and cans filled with to-morrow's quota, to be taken into Milchester, where she supplied a florist and a greengrocer.

"Wonderful price vedges fetch," old Horder remarked appreciatively. "Never wouldn't have believed it."

"All the same, I'm sure we're right to start switching over to cut flowers. People have been starved for them all through the war, and everybody's growing vegetables now."

"Ah!" said Horder, "things aren't what they used to be. In your pa and ma's time, growing things for the market wouldn't have been thought of. I mind this place as it used to be—a picture! Mr. Webster was in charge, he came just before the fire, he did. That fire! Lucky the whole house didn't burn down."

Laura nodded, and slipped off the rubber apron she had been wearing. Horder's words had taken her mind back many years. *"Just before the fire—"*

The fire had been a kind of turning point in her life. She saw herself dimly before it—an unhappy jealous child, longing for attention, for love.

But on the night of the fire, a new Laura had come into existence—a Laura whose life had become suddenly and satisfyingly full. From the moment that she had struggled through smoke and flames with Shirley in her arms, her life had found its object and meaning—to care for Shirley.

She had saved Shirley from death. Shirley was hers. All in a moment (so it seemed to her now) those two important figures, her father and mother, had receded into the middle distance. Her eager longing for their notice, for their need of her, had diminished and faded. Perhaps she had not so much loved them as craved for *them* to love *her*. Love was what she had felt so suddenly for that small entity of flesh named Shirley. Satisfying all cravings, fulfilling her vaguely understood need. It was no longer she, Laura, who mattered—it was Shirley. . . .

She would look after Shirley, see that no harm came to her, watch out for predatory cats, wake up at night and be sure that there was no second fire; fetch and carry for Shirley, bring her toys, play games with her when she was older, nurse her if she were ill. . . .

The child of eleven couldn't, of course, foresee the future: the Franklins, taking a brief holiday together, flying to Le Touquet and the plane crashing on the return journey. . . .

Laura had been fourteen then, and Shirley three. There had been no near relatives; old Cousin Angela had been the nearest. It was Laura who had made her plans, weighing them carefully, trimming them to meet with approval, and then submitting them with all the force of indomitable decision. An elderly lawyer and Mr. Baldock had been the executors and trustees. Laura proposed that she should leave school and live at home, an excellent nanny would continue to look after Shirley. Miss Weekes should give up her cottage and come to live in the house, educating Laura, and being normally in charge of the household. It was an excellent suggestion, practical and easy to carry out, only feebly opposed by Mr. Baldock on the grounds that he disliked Girton women, and that Miss Weekes would get ideas in her head, and turn Laura into a blue-stocking.

But Laura had no doubts about Miss Weekes—it would not be Miss Weekes who would run things. Miss Weekes was a woman of intellect, with an enthusiasm that ran to passion for mathematics. Domestic administration would not interest her. The plan had worked well. Laura was splendidly educated, Miss Weekes had an ease of living formerly denied to her, Laura saw to it that no clashes occurred between Mr. Baldock and Miss Weekes. The choice of new servants if needed, the decision for Shirley to attend, first a kindergarten school, later a convent in a nearby town, though apparently all originated by Miss Weekes, were in reality Laura's suggestions. The household was a harmonious one. Later Shirley was sent to a famous boarding school. Laura was then twenty-two.

A year after that, the war broke out, and altered the pattern of existence. Shirley's school was transferred to new premises in Wales. Miss Weekes went to London and obtained a post in a Ministry. The house was requisitioned by the Air Ministry to house officers; Laura transferred herself to the gardener's cottage, and worked as a land-girl on an adjacent farm, managing at the same time to cultivate vegetables in her own big walled garden.

And now, a year ago, the war with Germany had ended. The house had been derequisitioned with startling abruptness. Laura had to attempt the reestablishment of it as something faintly like a home. Shirley had come home from school for good, declining emphatically to continue her studies by going to a university.

She was not, she said, the brainy kind! Her headmistress in a letter to Laura confirmed this statement in slightly different terms:

"I really do not feel that Shirley is the type to benefit by a university education. She is a dear girl, and very intelligent, but definitely not the academic type."

So Shirley had come home, and that old standby, Ethel, who had been working in a factory which was now abandoning war work, gave up her job and arrived back, not as the correct house parlor maid she had once been, but as a general factotum and friend. Laura continued and elaborated her plans for vegetable and flower production. Incomes were not what they had been with present taxation. If she and Shirley were to keep their home, the garden must be made to pay for itself and, it was to be hoped, show a profit.

That was the picture of the past that Laura saw in her mind, as she unfastened her apron and went into the house to wash. All through the years, the central figure of the pattern had been Shirley.

A baby Shirley, staggering about, telling Laura in stuttering unintelligible language what her dolls were doing. An older Shirley, coming back from kindergarten, pouring out confused descriptions of Miss Duckworth, of Tommy this and Mary that, of the naughty things Robin had done, and what Peter had drawn in his reading book, and what Miss Duck had said about it.

An older Shirley had come back from boarding school, brimming over with information: the girls she liked, the girls she hated, the angelic disposition of Miss Geoffrey, the English mistress, the despicable meannesses of Miss Andrews, the mathematics mistress, the indignities practiced by all on the French mistress. Shirley had always chatted easily and unselfconsciously to Laura. Their relationship was in a way a curious one—not quite that of sisters, since the gap in years separated them, yet not removed by a generation, as a parent and child would be. There had never been any need for Laura to ask questions. Shirley would be bubbling over—"Oh, Laura, I've got such lots to tell you!"

And Laura would listen, laugh, comment, disagree, approve, as the case might be.

Now that Shirley had come home for good, it had seemed to Laura that everything was exactly the same. Every day saw an interchange of comment on any separate activities they had pursued. Shirley talked unconcernedly of Robin Grant, of Edward Westbury; she had a frank affectionate nature, and it was natural to her, or so it had seemed, to comment daily on what happened.

But yesterday she had come back from tennis at the Hargreaves and had been oddly monosyllabic in her replies to Laura's questions.

Laura wondered why. Of course, Shirley was growing up. She would have her own thoughts, her own life. That was only natural and right. What Laura had to decide was how best that could be accomplished. Laura sighed, looked at her watch again, and decided to go and see Mr. Baldock.

Chapter Two

Mr. Baldock was busy in his garden when Laura came up the path. He grunted and immediately asked:

"What do you think of my begonias? Pretty good?"

Mr. Baldock was actually an exceedingly poor gardener, but was inordinately proud of the results he achieved and completely oblivious of any failures. It was expected of his friends not to refer to these latter. Laura gazed obediently on some rather sparse begonias and said they were very nice.

"Nice? They're magnificent!" Mr. Baldock, who was now an old man and considerably stouter than he had been eighteen years ago, groaned a little as he bent over once more to pull at some weeds.

"It's this wet summer," he grumbled. "Fast as you clear the beds, up the stuff comes again. Words fail me when it comes to what I think of bindweed! You may say what you like, but *I* think it is directly inspired by the devil!" He puffed a little, then said, his words coming shortly between stertorous breaths: "Well, young Laura, what is it? Trouble? Tell me about it."

"I always come to you when I'm worried. I have ever since I was six."

"Rum little kid you were. Peaky face and great big eyes."

"I wish I knew whether I was doing right."

"Shouldn't bother if I was you," said Mr. Baldock. "Garrrrr! Get up, you unspeakable brute!" (This was to the bindweed.) "No, as I say, I shouldn't bother. Some people know what's right and wrong, and some people haven't the least idea. It's like an ear for music!"

"I don't think I really meant right or wrong in the moral sense, I think I meant was I being wise?"

"Well, that's quite a different thing. On the whole, one does far more foolish things than wise ones. What's the problem?"

"It's Shirley."

"Naturally it's Shirley. You never think of anything or anyone else."

"I've been arranging for her to go to London and train in secretarial work."

"Seems to me remarkably silly," said Mr. Baldock. "Shirley is a nice child, but the last person in the world to make a competent secretary."

"Still, she's got to do something."

"So they say nowadays."

"And I'd like her to meet people."

"Blast and curse and damn that nettle," said Mr. Baldock, shaking an injured hand. "People? What d'you mean by *people?* Crowds? Employers? Other girls? Young men?"

"I suppose really I mean young men."

Mr. Baldock chuckled.

"She's not doing too badly down here. That mother's boy, Robin, at the vicarage seems to be making sheep's eyes at her, young Peter has got it badly, and even Edward Westbury has started putting brilliantine on what's left of his hair. Smelled it in church last Sunday. Thought to myself: 'Now, who's *he* after?' And sure enough there he was when we came out, wriggling like an embarrassed dog as he talked to her."

"I don't think she cares about any of them."

"Why should she? Give her time. She's very young, Laura. Come now, why do you really want to send her away to London, or are you going too?"

"Oh no. That's the whole point."

Mr. Baldock straightened up.

"So that's the point, is it?" He eyed her curiously. "What exactly is in your mind, Laura?"

Laura looked down at the gravel path.

"As you said just now, Shirley is the only thing that matters to me. I—I love her so much that I'm afraid of—well, of hurting her. Of trying to tie her to me too closely."

Mr. Baldock's voice was unexpectedly gentle.

"She's ten years younger than you are, and in some ways she's more like a daughter than a sister to you."

"I've mothered her, yes."

He nodded.

"And you realize, being intelligent, that maternal love is a possessive love?"

"Yes, that's exactly it. And I don't want it to be like that. I want Shirley to be free and—well—free."

"And that's at the bottom of pushing her out of the nest? Sending her out in the world to find her feet?"

"Yes. But what I'm so uncertain about is—am I wise to do so?"

Mr. Baldock rubbed his nose in an irritable way.

"You women!" he said. "Trouble with all of you is, you make such a song and dance about things. How is one ever to know what's wise or not? If young Shirley goes to London and picks up with an Egyptian student and has a coffee-colored baby in Bloomsbury, you'll say it's all your fault, whereas it will be entirely Shirley's and possibly the Egyptian's. And if she trains and gets a good job as a secretary and marries her boss, then you'll say you were justified. All bunkum! You *can't* arrange other people's lives for them. Either Shirley's got some sense or she hasn't. Time will show. If you think this London idea is a good plan, go ahead with it, but don't take it so seriously. That's the whole trouble with you, Laura, you take life seriously. It's the trouble with a lot of women."

"And you don't?"

"I take bindweed seriously," said Mr. Baldock, glaring down balefully at the heap on the path. "*And* greenfly. And I take my stomach seriously, because it gives me hell if I don't. But I never dream of taking other people's lives seriously. I've too much respect for them, for one thing."

"You don't understand. I couldn't bear it if Shirley made a mess of her life and was unhappy."

"Fiddle de dee," said Mr. Baldock rudely. "What does it matter if Shirley's unhappy? Most people are, off and on. You've got to stick being unhappy in this life, just as you've got to stick everything else.

You need courage to get through this world, courage and a gay heart."

He looked at her sharply.

"What about yourself, Laura?"

"Myself?" said Laura, surprised.

"Yes. Suppose *you're* unhappy? Are you going to be able to bear that?"

Laura smiled.

"I've never thought about it."

"Well, why not? Think about yourself a bit more. Unselfishness in a woman can be as disastrous as a heavy hand in pastry. What do *you* want out of life? You're twenty-eight, a good marriageable age. Why don't you do a bit of man-hunting?"

"How absurd you are, Baldy."

"Thistles and ground elder!" roared Mr. Baldock. "You're a woman, aren't you? A not bad-looking, perfectly normal woman. Or aren't you normal? What's your reaction when a man tries to kiss you?"

"They haven't very often tried," said Laura.

"And why the hell not? Because you're not doing your stuff." He shook a finger at her. "You're thinking the whole time of something else. There you stand in a nice neat coat and skirt looking the nice modest sort of girl my mother would have approved of. Why don't you paint your lips pillar-box red and varnish your nails to match?"

Laura stared at him.

"You've always said you hated lipstick and red nails."

"Hate them? Of course I hate them. I'm seventy-nine! But they're a symbol, a sign that you're in the market and ready to play at Nature's game. A kind of mating call, that's what they are. Now look here, Laura, you're not everybody's fancy. You don't flaunt a banner of sex, looking as though you weren't able to help it, as some women do. There's one particular kind of man who might come and hunt you out without your doing anything about it—the kind of man that has the sense to know that you're the woman for him. But it's long odds against that happening. You've got to do your bit. You've got to remember that you're a woman, and play the part of a woman and look about for your man."

"Darling Baldy, I love your lectures, but I've always been hopelessly plain."

"So you *want* to be an old maid?"

Laura flushed a little.

"No, of course I don't. I just don't think it's likely that I shall marry."

"Defeatism!" roared Mr. Baldock.

"No, indeed it isn't. I just think it's impossible that anyone should fall in love with me."

"Men can fall in love with anything," said Mr. Baldock rudely. "With hare lips, and acne, and prognathous jaws and with numbskulls and cretins! Just think of half the married women you know! No, young Laura, you just don't want to bother! You want to love—not to be loved—and I dare say you've got something there. To be loved is to carry a heavy burden."

"You think I do love Shirley too much? That I am possessive?"

"No," said Mr. Baldock slowly, "I don't think you are possessive. I acquit you of *that*"

"Then—can one love anyone too much?"

"Of course one can!" he roared. "One can do anything too much. Eat too much, drink too much, love too much . . ."

He quoted:

> "I've known a thousand ways of love
> And each one made the loved one rue."

"Put that in your pipe, young Laura, and smoke it."

2

Laura walked home, smiling to herself. As she entered the house, Ethel appeared from the back premises, and spoke in a confidential whisper:

"There's a gentleman waiting for you—a Mr. Glyn-Edwards, quite a young gentleman. I put him in the drawing room. Said he'd wait. He's all right—not vacuums I mean, or hard-luck stories."

Laura smiled a little, but she trusted Ethel's judgment.

Glyn-Edwards? She could not recall the name. Perhaps it was one of the young flying officers who had been billeted here during the war.

She went across the hall and into the drawing room.

The young man who rose quickly as she came in was a complete stranger to her.

That, indeed, in the years to come, was to remain her feeling about Henry. He was a stranger. Never for one moment did he become anything else.

The young man was smiling, an eager, rather charming smile which suddenly wavered. He seemed taken aback.

"Miss Franklin?" he said. "But you're not—" His smile suddenly widened again, confidently. "I expect she's your sister."

"You mean Shirley?"

"That's it," said Henry, with evident relief. "Shirley. I met her yesterday—at a tennis party. My name's Henry Glyn-Edwards."

"Do sit down," said Laura. "Shirley ought to be back soon. She went to tea at the vicarage. Won't you have some sherry? Or would you rather have gin?"

Henry said he would prefer sherry.

They sat there talking. Henry's manner was just right, it had that touch of diffidence that is disarming. A charm of manner that was too assured might have aroused antagonism. As it was, he talked easily and gaily, without awkwardness, but deferring to Laura in a pleasant well-bred manner.

"Are you staying in Bellbury?" Laura asked.

"Oh no. I'm staying with my aunt over at Endsmoor."

Endsmoor was well over sixty miles away, the other side of Milchester. Laura felt a little surprised. Henry seemed to see that a certain amount of explanation was required.

"I went off with someone else's tennis racket yesterday," he said. "Awfully stupid of me. So I thought I'd run over to return it and find my own. I managed to wangle some petrol."

He looked at her blandly.

"Did you find your racket all right?"

"Oh yes," said Henry. "Lucky, wasn't it? I'm afraid I'm awfully vague about things. Over in France, you know, I was always losing my kit."

He blinked disarmingly.

"So as I *was* over here," he said, "I thought I'd look up Shirley."

Was there, or was there not, some faint sign of embarrassment?

If there was, Laura liked him none the worse for it. Indeed, she preferred that to too much assurance.

This young man was likeable, eminently so. She felt the charm he exuded quite distinctly. What she could not account for was her own definite feeling of hostility.

Possessiveness again, Laura wondered? If Shirley had met Henry the day before, it seemed odd that she should not have mentioned him.

They continued to talk. It was now past seven. Henry was clearly not bound by conventional hours of calling. He was obviously remaining here until he saw Shirley. Laura wondered how much longer Shirley was going to be. She was usually home before this.

Murmuring an excuse to Henry, Laura left the room and went into the study where the telephone was. She rang up the vicarage.

The vicar's wife answered.

"Shirley? Oh yes, Laura, she's here. She's playing clock golf with Robin. I'll get her."

There was a pause, and then Shirley's voice, gay, alive.

"Laura?"

Laura said dryly:

"You've got a follower."

"A follower? Who?"

"His name's Glyn-Edwards. He blew in an hour and a half ago, and he's still here. I don't think he means to leave without seeing you. Both his conversation and mine are wearing rather thin!"

"Glyn-Edwards? I've never heard of him. Oh dear—I suppose I'd better come home and cope. Pity. I'm well on the way to beating Robin's record."

"He was at the tennis yesterday, I gather."

"Not *Henry?*"

Shirley's voice sounded breathless, slightly incredulous. The note in it surprised Laura.

"It could be Henry," she said dryly. "He's staying with an aunt over at—"

Shirley, breathless, interrupted:

"It *is* Henry. I'll come at once."

Laura put down the receiver with a slight sense of shock. She went back slowly into the drawing room.

"Shirley will be back soon," she said, and added that she hoped Henry would stay to supper.

3

Laura leaned back in her chair at the head of the dinner table and watched the other two. It was still only dusk, not dark, and the windows were uncurtained. The evening light was kind to the two young faces that bent toward each other so easily.

Watching them dispassionately, Laura tried to understand her own mounting feeling of uneasiness. Was it simply that she had taken a dislike to Henry? No, it could hardly be that. She acknowledged Henry's charm, his likeability, his good manners. Since, as yet, she knew nothing about him, she could hardly form a considered judgment. He was perhaps a little too casual, too offhand, too detached? Yes, that explained it best—detached.

Surely the core of her feeling was rooted in Shirley. She was experiencing the sharp sense of shock which comes when you discover an unknown facet in someone about whom you are assured you know everything. Laura and Shirley were not unduly demonstrative to each other, but stretching back over the years was the figure of Shirley, pouring out to Laura her hates, her loves, her desires, her frustrations.

But yesterday, when Laura had asked casually: "Anybody exciting? Or just Bellbury?" Shirley had replied nonchalantly: "Oh, mostly Bellbury."

Laura wondered why Shirley hadn't mentioned Henry. She remembered the sudden breathlessness just now in Shirley's voice as she had said, over the telephone *"Henry?"*

Her mind came back to the conversation going on so close to her.

Henry was just concluding a sentence. . . .

"—if you liked. I'd pick you up in Carswell."

"Oh, I'd love it. I've never been much to race meetings. . . ."

"Marldon's a tin-pot one, but a friend of mine's got a horse running. We might . . ."

Laura reflected calmly and dispassionately that this was a courtship. Henry's unexplained appearance, the wangled petrol, the inadequate excuse—he was sharply attracted by Shirley. She did not tell herself that this all might come to nothing. She believed, on the contrary, that she saw events casting their shadows before them.

Henry and Shirley would marry. She knew it, she was sure of it. And Henry was a stranger. . . . She would never really know Henry any better than she knew him now.

Would Shirley ever know him?

Chapter Three

1

"I wonder," said Henry, "if you ought to come and meet my aunt."

He looked at Shirley doubtfully.

"I'm afraid," he said, "that it will be an awful bore for you."

They were leaning over the rail of the paddock, gazing unseeingly at the only horse, Number Nineteen, which was being led monotonously round and round.

This was the third race meeting Shirley had attended in Henry's company. Where other young men's ideas ran to the pictures, Henry's seemed to be concerned with sport. It was all on a par with the exciting difference between Henry and other young men.

"I'm sure I shouldn't be bored," said Shirley politely.

"I don't really see how you could help it," said Henry. "She does horoscopes and has queer ideas about the Pyramids."

"Do you know, Henry, I don't even know what your aunt's name is?"

"Don't you?" said Henry, surprised.

"Is it Glyn-Edwards?"

"No. It's Fairborough. Lady Muriel Fairborough. She's not bad really. Doesn't mind how you come and go. And always very decent at stumping up in a crisis."

"That's a very depressed-looking horse," said Shirley, looking at Number Nineteen. She was nerving herself to say something quite different.

"Wretched brute," agreed Henry. "One of Tommy Twisdon's worst. Come down over the first hurdle, I should think."

Two more horses were brought into the ring, and more people arrived to lean over the rails.

"What's this? Third race?" Henry consulted his card. "Are the numbers up yet? Is Number Eighteen running?"

Shirley glanced up at the board behind her.

"Yes."

"We might have a bit on that, if the price is all right."

"You know a lot about horses, don't you, Henry? Were you—were you brought up with horses?"

"My experience has mostly been with bookmakers."

Shirley nerved herself to ask what she had been wanting to ask.

"It's funny, isn't it, how little I really know about you? Have you got a father or mother, or are you an orphan, like me?"

"Oh! My father and mother were killed in the Blitz. They were in the Café de Paris."

"Oh! Henry—how awful!"

"Yes, wasn't it?" agreed Henry, without, however, displaying undue emotion. He seemed to feel this himself, for he added: "Of course it's over four years ago now. I was quite fond of them and all that, but one can't go on remembering things, can one?"

"I suppose not," said Shirley doubtfully.

"Why all this thirst for information?" asked Henry.

"Well—one likes to know about people," Shirley spoke almost apologetically.

"Does one?" Henry seemed genuinely surprised.

"Anyway," he decided, "you'd better come and meet my aunt. Put it all on a proper footing with Laura."

"Laura?"

"Well, Laura's the conventional type, isn't she? Satisfy her that I'm respectable and all that."

And very shortly afterward, a polite note arrived from Lady Muriel, inviting Shirley to lunch, and saying Henry would call for her in the car.

2

Henry's aunt bore a strong resemblance to the White Queen. Her costume was a jumble of different and brightly colored wool garments, she knitted assiduously, and she had a bun of faded brown hair, streaked with gray, from which untidy wisps descended in all directions.

She managed to combine the qualities of briskness and vagueness.

"So nice you could come, my dear," she said warmly, shaking Shirley by the hand and dropping a ball of wool. "Pick it up, Henry, there's a good boy. Now tell me, when were you born?"

Shirley said that she was born on September 18th, 1928.

"Ah yes. Virgo—I thought so. And the time?"

"I'm afraid I don't know."

"Tck! How annoying! You must find out and let me know. It's most important. Where are my other needles—the number eights? I'm knitting for the Navy—a pullover with a high neck."

She held out the garment.

"It will have to be for a very large sailor," said Henry.

"Well, I expect they have all sizes in the Navy," said Lady Muriel comfortably. "And in the Army, too," she added inconsequently. "I remember Major Tug Murray—sixteen stone—special polo ponies to be up to his weight—and when he rode anyone off there was nothing they could do about it. Broke his neck when he was out with the Pytchley," she added cheerfully.

A very old and shaky butler opened the door and announced that luncheon was served.

They went into the dining room. The meal was an indifferent one, and the table silver was tarnished.

"Poor old Melsham," said Lady Muriel when the butler was out of the room. "He really can't see *at all*. And he shakes so when he hands things, that I'm never sure if he'll get round the table safely. I've told him again and again to put things on the sideboard, but he won't. And he won't let any of the silver be put away, though of course he can't see to clean it. And he quarrels with all the queer girls which are all one gets nowadays—not what he's been accustomed to, he says. Well, I mean, what is? With the war and all."

They returned to the drawing room, and Lady Muriel conducted a brisk conversation on biblical prophecies, the measurements of the Pyramids, how much one should pay for illicit clothing coupons, and the difficulties of herbaceous borders.

After which she rolled up her knitting with great suddenness, and announced that she was going to take Shirley round the garden and dispatched Henry with a message to the chauffeur.

"He's a dear boy, Henry," she said as she and Shirley set forth. "Very selfish, of course, and frightfully extravagant. But what can you expect—brought up as he has been?"

"Does he—take after his mother?" Shirley felt her way cautiously.

"Oh dear me, no. Poor Mildred was always most economical. It was quite a passion with her. I can't think why my brother ever married her—she wasn't even a pretty girl, and deadly dull. I believe she was very happy when they were out on a farm in Kenya among the serious farming kind. Later, of course, they got into the gay set, which didn't suit her nearly as well."

"Henry's father—" Shirley paused.

"Poor dear Ned. He went through the Bankruptcy Court three times. But such good company. Henry reminds me of him sometimes. That's a very special kind of alstroemeria—it doesn't do everywhere. I've had a lot of success with it."

She tweaked off a dead bloom and glanced sideways at Shirley.

"How pretty you are, my dear—you mustn't mind my saying so. And very young, too."

"I'm nearly nineteen."

"Yes . . . I see . . . Do you do things—like all these clever girls nowadays?"

"I'm not clever," said Shirley. "My sister wants me to take a secretarial course."

"I'm sure that would be very nice. Secretary to an M.P. perhaps. Everyone says that's *so* interesting; I've never seen why. But I don't suppose you'll do anything long—you'll get married."

She sighed.

"Such an odd world nowadays. I've just had a letter from one of my oldest friends. Her girl has just married a dentist. A *dentist*. In my young days, girls didn't marry dentists. Doctors, yes, but not dentists."

She turned her head.

"Ah, here comes Henry. Well, Henry, I suppose you're going to take Miss—Miss—"

"Franklin."

"Miss Franklin away from me."

"I thought we'd run over to Bury Heath."

"Have you been getting petrol out of Harman?"

"Just a couple of gallons, Aunt Muriel."

"Well, I won't have it, do you hear? You must wangle your own petrol. I have trouble enough getting mine."

"You don't really mind, darling. Come now."

"Well—just this once. Good-bye, my dear. Now mind you send me those particulars about time of birth—don't forget—then I can get your horoscope worked out properly. You should wear green, dear—all Virgo people should wear green."

"I'm Aquarius," said Henry. "January 20th."

"Unstable," snapped his aunt, "remember that, my dear. All Aquariuses—most undependable."

"I hope you weren't too bored," said Henry as they drove away.

"I wasn't bored at all. I think your aunt's sweet."

"Oh, I wouldn't go as far as that. But she's not too bad."

"She's very fond of you."

"Oh, not really. She doesn't mind having me about."

He added: "My leave's nearly over. I ought to be demobbed soon."

"What are you going to do then?"

"I don't really know. I thought of the Bar."

"Yes?"

"But that's rather a sweat. I think perhaps I might go into a business of some kind."

"What kind?"

"Well, it rather depends where one has a pal to give one a start. I've got one or two banking connections. And I know a couple of tycoons who'd graciously allow me to start at the bottom." He added: "I've not got much money, you know. Three hundred a year to be exact. Of my own, I mean. Most of my relations are as mean as hell—no good for a touch. Good old Muriel comes to the rescue now and again, but she's a bit straitened herself nowadays. I've got a godmother who's reasonably generous if one puts it to her the right way. It's all a bit unsatisfactory, I know. . . ."

"Why," said Shirley, puzzled by this sudden flood of information, "are you telling me all this?"

Henry blushed. The car wobbled in a drunken manner.

He spoke in an indistinct mumble.

"Thought you knew . . . Darling—you're so lovely . . . I want to marry you . . . You must marry me—you *must*—you *must*. . . ."

3

Laura looked at Henry with a kind of desperation.

It was exactly, she thought, like climbing up a steep hill on an icy day—you slipped back as fast as you advanced.

"Shirley is too young," she said, "far too young."

"Come now, Laura, she's nineteen. One of my grandmothers was married at sixteen, and had twins before she was eighteen."

"That was a long time ago."

"And lots of people have married young in the war."

"And have already lived to regret it."

"Don't you think you're taking rather a gloomy view? Shirley and I shan't regret."

"You don't know that."

"Oh, but I do," he grinned at her. "I'm positive. I do really love Shirley madly. And I shall do everything I can to make her happy."

He looked at her hopefully. He said again:

"I really do love her."

As before, his patent sincerity disarmed Laura. He did love Shirley.

"I know, of course, that I'm not particularly well off—"

There again he was disarming. For it wasn't the financial angle that worried Laura. She had no ambition for Shirley to make what is called a 'good match.' Henry and Shirley would not have a large income to start life on, but they would have enough, if they were careful. Henry's prospects were no worse than those of hundreds of other young men released from the services with their way to make. He had good health, good brains, great charm of manner. Yes, perhaps that was it. It was his charm that made Laura mistrust him. No one had any right to have as much charm as Henry had.

She spoke again, a tone of authority in her voice.

"No, Henry. There can be no question of marriage as yet. A year's engagement, at least. That gives you both time to be sure you know your own minds."

"Really, Laura dear, you might be at least fifty. A heavy Victorian father rather than a sister."

"I have to stand in the place of a father to Shirley. That gives time for you to find a job and get yourself established."

"How depressing it all sounds." His smile was still charming. "I don't believe you want Shirley to marry *anybody*."

Laura flushed.

"Nonsense."

Henry was pleased with the success of his stray shaft. He went away to find Shirley.

"Laura," he said, "is being tiresome. Why shouldn't we get married? I don't want to wait. I hate waiting for things. Don't you? If one waits too long for anything, one loses interest. Of course we could go off and get quietly married at a registry office somewhere. How about it? It would save a lot of fuss."

"Oh no, Henry, we couldn't do *that*."

"I don't see why not? As I say, it would save a lot of fuss all round."

"I'm underage. Wouldn't we have to have Laura's consent?"

"Yes, I suppose you would. She's your legal guardian, isn't she? Or is it old what's his name?"

"I don't believe I actually know. Baldy is my trustee."

"The trouble is," said Henry, "that Laura doesn't like me."

"Oh, she does, Henry. I'm sure she does."

"No, she doesn't. She's jealous, of course."

Shirley looked troubled.

"Do you really think so?"

"She never *has* liked me—from the beginning. And I've taken a lot of trouble to be nice to her." Henry sounded injured.

"I know. You're sweet to her. But after all, Henry, we have sprung this rather suddenly on her. We've only known each other—what?— three weeks. I suppose it doesn't *really* matter if we have to wait a year."

"Darling, *I* don't want to wait a year. I want to marry you now— next week—tomorrow. Don't you want to marry me?"

"Oh, Henry, I do—I do."

4

Mr. Baldock had duly been asked to dinner to meet Henry. Afterward Laura had demanded breathlessly:

"Well, what do you think of him?"

"Now, now, slowly. How can I judge across a dinner table? Nice manners, doesn't treat me as an old fogey. Listens to me deferentially."

"Is that all you've got to say? Is he good enough for Shirley?"

"Nobody, my dear Laura, will ever be good enough for Shirley in your eyes."

"No, perhaps that's true . . . But do you like him?"

"Yes, I like him. What I'd call an agreeable fellow."

"You think he'll make her a good husband."

"Oh, I wouldn't go as far as that. I should strongly suspect that as a husband he might prove unsatisfactory in more ways than one."

"Then we can't let her marry him."

"We can't stop her marrying him, if she wants to. And I dare say he won't prove much more unsatisfactory than any other husband she might choose. I shouldn't think he'd beat her, or put arsenic in her coffee, or be rude to her in public. There's a lot to be said, Laura, for having a husband who's agreeable and got good manners."

"Do you know what I think about him? I think he's utterly selfish and—and ruthless."

Mr. Baldock raised his eyebrows.

"I shouldn't wonder if you weren't right."

"Well, then?"

"Yes, but she *likes* the fellow, Laura. She likes him very much. In fact, she's crazy about him. Young Henry mayn't be your cup of tea, and strictly speaking, he isn't my cup of tea, but there's no doubt that he *is* Shirley's cup of tea."

"If she could only see what he's really like!" cried Laura.

"Well, she'll find out," prophesied Mr. Baldock.

"When it's too late! I want her to see what he's like *now!*"

"Dare say it wouldn't make any difference. She means to have him, you know."

"If she could go away somewhere . . . On a cruise or to Switzerland—but everything's so difficult now since the war."

"If you ask me," said Mr. Baldock, "it's never any good trying to stop people marrying each other. Mind you, I'd have a try if there were some serious reason; if he had a wife and five children, or epileptic fits, or was wanted for embezzlement. But shall I tell you exactly what would happen if you did succeed in separating them and sending Shirley off on a cruise or to Switzerland or to a South Sea island?"

"Well?"

Mr. Baldock wagged an emphatic forefinger at her.

"She'd come back having teamed up with another young man of exactly the same kind. People know what they want. Shirley wants Henry, and if she can't get Henry, she'll look around until she finds a young man as like Henry as possible. I've seen it happen again and again. My very best friend was married to a woman who made his life hell on earth, nagged at him, bullied him, ordered him around, never a moment's peace, everybody wondering why he didn't take a hatchet to her. Then he had a bit of luck! She got double pneumonia and died! Six months later, he was looking like a new man. Several really nice women taking an interest in him. Eighteen months later, what has he done? Married a woman who was even a worse bitch than the first one. Human nature's a mystery."

He took a deep breath.

"So stop walking up and down looking like a tragedy queen, Laura. I've told you already you take life too seriously. You can't run other people's lives for them. Young Shirley has got her own row to hoe. And if you ask me, she can take care of herself a good deal better than you can. It's *you* I'm worried about, Laura. I always have been. . . ."

Chapter Four

Henry surrendered as charmingly as he did everything else.

"All right, Laura. If it must be a year's engagement . . . We're in your hands. I daresay it would be very hard on you to part with Shirley without having time to get used to the idea."

"It isn't that—"

"Isn't it?" His eyebrows rose, his smile was faintly ironical. "Shirley's your ewe lamb, isn't she?"

His words left Laura with an uneasy sensation.

The days after Henry had left were not easy to get through.

Shirley was not hostile, but aloof. She was moody, unsettled, and though not openly resentful, a faint air of reproach hung about her. She lived for the arrival of the post, but the post, when it did come, proved unsatisfactory.

Henry was not a letter-writer. His letters were brief scrawls.

"Darling, how's everything? I miss you a lot. I rode in a point-to-point yesterday. Didn't do any good. How's the dragon? Yours always, Henry."

Sometimes a whole week passed without a letter.

Once Shirley went up to London and they had a short and unsatisfactory meeting.

He refused the invitation she brought him from Laura.

"I don't want to come down and stay for the weekend! I want to marry you, and have you to myself for always, not come down and 'walk out' with you under Laura's censorious eye. Don't forget, Laura will turn you against me if she possibly can."

"Oh, Henry, she'd never do anything like that. Never—she hardly ever mentions you."

"Hopes you'll forget about me, I expect."

"As if I should!"

"Jealous old cat."

"Oh, Henry, Laura's a darling."

"Not to me."

Shirley went back home unhappy and restless.

In spite of herself, Laura began to feel worn down.

"Why don't you ask Henry down for a weekend?"

Shirley said sullenly:

"He doesn't want to come."

"Not want to come? How extraordinary."

"I don't think it's so extraordinary. He knows you don't like him."

"I do like him." Laura tried to make her voice convincing.

"Oh, Laura, you don't!"

"I think Henry's a very attractive person."

"But you don't want me to marry him."

"Shirley—that isn't true. I only want you to be quite, quite sure."

"I *am* sure."

Laura cried desperately:

"It's only because I love you so much. I don't want you to make any mistake."

"Well, don't love me so much. I don't *want* to be eternally loved!" She added: "The truth is, you're jealous."

"Jealous?"

"Jealous of Henry. You don't want me to love anyone but you."

"Shirley!"

Laura turned away, her face white.

"You'll never want me to marry *anyone*."

Then, as Laura moved away, walking stiffly, Shirley rushed after her in warmhearted apology.

"Darling, I didn't mean it, I didn't mean it. I'm a beast. But you always seem so against—Henry."

"It's because I feel he's selfish." Laura repeated the words she had used to Mr. Baldock. "He isn't—he isn't—*kind*. I can't help feeling that in some ways he could be—ruthless."

"Ruthless," Shirley repeated the word thoughtfully without any symptom of distress. "Yes, Laura, in a way you're right. Henry could be ruthless."

She added: "It's one of those things that attracts me in him."

"But think—if you were ill—in trouble—would he look after you?"

"I don't know that I'm so keen on being looked after. I can look after myself. And don't worry about Henry. He loves me."

'Love?' thought Laura. 'What is love? A young man's thoughtless greedy passion? Is Henry's love for her anything more than that? Or is it true, and *am* I jealous?'

She disengaged herself gently from Shirley's clinging arms and walked away deeply disturbed.

'Is it true that I don't want her to marry anybody? Not just Henry? Anybody? I don't think so now, but that's because there is no one else she wants to marry. If someone else were to come along, should I feel the same way as I do now, saying to myself: Not *him*—not *him*? Is it true that I love her too much? Baldy warned me. . . . I love her too much, and so I don't want her to marry—I don't want her to go away— I want to keep her—never to let her go. What have I got against Henry really? Nothing. I don't know him, I've never known him. He's what he was at first—a stranger. All I do know is that he doesn't like me. And perhaps he's right not to like me.'

On the following day, Laura met young Robin Grant coming out of the vicarage. He took his pipe out of his mouth, greeted her, and strolled beside her into the village. After mentioning that he had just come down from London, he remarked casually:

"Saw Henry last night. Having supper with a glamorous blonde. Very attractive. Mustn't tell Shirley."

He gave a whinny of laughter.

Although Laura recognized the information for exactly what it was, a piece of spite on Robin's part, since he himself had been deeply attracted to Shirley, yet it gave her a qualm.

Henry, she thought, was not a faithful type. She suspected that he and Shirley had come very near to a quarrel on the occasion when they had recently met. Supposing that Henry was becoming friendly with another girl? Supposing that Henry should break off the engagement . . . ?

'That's what you wanted, isn't it?' said the sneering voice of her thoughts. 'You don't want her to marry him? That's the real reason you insisted on a long engagement, isn't it? Come now!'

But she wouldn't really be pleased if Henry broke with Shirley. Shirley loved him. Shirley would suffer. If only she herself was sure, quite sure, that it was for Shirley's good—

'What you mean,' said the sneering voice, 'is for your own good. You want to keep Shirley. . . .'

But she didn't want to keep Shirley that way—not a heartbroken Shirley, not a Shirley unhappy and longing for her lover. Who was she to know what was best, or not best for Shirley?

When she got home, Laura sat down and wrote a letter to Henry:

"Dear Henry," she wrote, "I have been thinking things over. If you and Shirley really want to marry, I don't feel I ought to stand in your way. . . ."

A month later Shirley, in white satin and lace, was married to Henry in Bellbury parish church by the vicar (with a cold in his head) and given away by Mr. Baldock in a morning coat very much too tight for him. A radiant bride hugged Laura good-bye, and Laura said fiercely to Henry:

"Be good to her, Henry. You *will* be good to her?"

Henry, lighthearted as ever, said: "Darling Laura, what do you think?"

Chapter Five

1

"Do you really think it's nice, Laura?"

Shirley, now a wife of three months' standing, asked the question eagerly.

Laura, completing her tour of the flat (two rooms, kitchen, and bath), expressed warm approval.

"I think you've made it lovely."

"It was awful when we moved in. The dirt! We've done most of it ourselves—not the ceilings, of course. It's been such fun. Do you like the red bathroom? It's supposed to be constant hot water, but it isn't usually hot. Henry thought the redness would make it seem hotter—like hell!"

Laura laughed.

"What fun you seem to have had."

"We're frightfully lucky to have found a flat at all. Actually some people Henry knew had it, and they passed it on to us. The only awkward thing is that they don't seem to have paid any bills while they were here. Irate milkmen and furious grocers turn up all the time, but of course it's nothing to do with us. It's rather mean to bilk tradesmen, I think—especially small tradesmen. Henry doesn't think it matters."

"It may make it more difficult for you to get things on credit," said Laura.

"I pay our bills every week," said Shirley virtuously.

"Are you all right for money, darling? The garden's been doing very well lately. If you want an extra hundred."

"What a pet you are, Laura! No, we're all right. Keep it in case there's an emergency—I might have a really serious illness."

"Looking at you, that seems an absurd idea."

Shirley laughed gaily.

"Laura, I'm terribly happy."

"Bless you!"

"Hullo, here's Henry."

Turning the latchkey, Henry entered, and greeted Laura with his usual happy air.

"Hullo, Laura."

"Hullo, Henry. I think the flat's lovely."

"Henry, what's the new job like?"

"New job?" asked Laura.

"Yes. He chucked the other one. It was awfully stuffy. Nothing but sticking on stamps and going to the post."

"I'm willing to start at the bottom," said Henry, "but *not* in the basement."

"What's this like?" Shirley repeated impatiently.

"Promising, I think," said Henry. "Of course it's early days to say."

He smiled charmingly at Laura and told her how very pleased they were to see her.

Her visit went off very well, and she returned to Bellbury feeling that her fears and hesitations had been ridiculous.

2

"But Henry, how *can* we owe so much?"

Shirley spoke in a tone of distress. She and Henry had been married just over a year.

"I know," Henry agreed, "that's what I always feel! That one *can't* owe all that. Unfortunately," he added sadly, "one always does."

"But how are we going to be able to pay?"

"Oh, one can always stave things off," said Henry vaguely.

"It's a good thing I got that job at the flower place."

"Yes, it is, as it turns out. Not that I want you ever to feel you've got to work. Only if you like it."

"Well, I do like it. I'd be bored to death doing nothing all day. All that happens is that one goes out and buys things."

"I must say," said Henry, picking up a sheaf of accounts rendered, "this sort of thing is very depressing. I do hate Lady Day. One's hardly got over Christmas, and income tax, and all that." He looked down at the topmost bill in his hand. "This man, the one who did the bookcases, is asking for his money in a very rude sort of way. I shall put him straight into the wastepaper basket." He suited the action to the word, and went on to the next one. " 'Dear sir, we must respectfully draw your attention—' Now that's a nice polite way of putting it."

"So you'll pay that one?"

"I shan't exactly pay it," said Henry, "but I shall file it, ready to pay."

Shirley laughed—

"Henry, I do adore you. But what are we really going to *do?*"

"We needn't worry tonight. Let's go out to dinner somewhere really expensive."

Shirley made a face at him.

"Will that help?"

"It won't help our financial position," Henry admitted. "On the contrary! But it will cheer us up."

3

"Dear Laura,

"Could you possibly lend us a hundred pounds? We're in a bit of a jam. I've been out of a job for two months now, as you probably know (Laura didn't know), but I'm on the verge of landing something really good. In the meantime we've taken to sneaking out by the service lift to avoid the duns. Really very sorry to sponge like this, but I thought I'd better do the dirty work as Shirley mightn't like to.

"Yours ever,
"Henry."

4

"I didn't know you'd borrowed money from Laura!"

"Didn't I tell you?" Henry turned his head lazily.

"No, you didn't." Shirley spoke grimly.

"All right, darling, don't bite my head off. Did Laura tell you?"

"No, she didn't. I saw it in the passbook."

"Good old Laura, she stumped up without any fuss at all."

"Henry, why did you borrow money from *her*? I wish you hadn't. Anyway, you oughtn't to have done it without telling me about it first."

Henry grinned.

"You wouldn't have let me do it."

"You're quite right. I wouldn't."

"The truth is, Shirley, the position was rather desperate. I got fifty out of old Muriel. And I made sure that I'd get at least a hundred out of Big Bertha—that's my godmother. Unfortunately, she turned me down flat. Feeling her surtax, I gather. Nothing but a lecture. I tried one or two other sources, no good. In the end, it boiled down to Laura."

Shirley looked at him reflectively.

'I've been married two years,' she thought. 'I see now just what Henry's like. He'll never keep a job very long, and he spends money like water. . . .'

She still found it delightful to be married to Henry, but she perceived that it had its disadvantages. Henry had by now had four different jobs. It never seemed difficult for him to get a job—he had a large circle of wealthy friends—but it seemed quite impossible for him to keep a job. Either he got tired of it and chucked it, or it chucked him. Also, Henry spent money like water, and never seemed to have any difficulty in getting credit. His idea of settling his affairs was by borrowing. Henry did not mind borrowing. Shirley did.

She sighed:

"Do you think I'll ever be able to change you, Henry?" she asked.

"Change me?" said Henry, astonished. "Why?"

5

"Hullo, Baldy."

"Why, it's young Shirley." Mr. Baldock blinked at her from the depths of his large shabby armchair. "I wasn't asleep," he added aggressively.

"Of course not," said Shirley tactfully.

"Long time since we've seen you down here," said Mr. Baldock. "Thought you'd forgotten us."

"I never forget you!"

"Got your husband with you?"

"Not this time."

"I see." He studied her. "Looking rather thin and pale, aren't you?"

"I've been dieting."

"You women!" He snorted. "In a spot of trouble?" he inquired.

Shirley flared out at him.

"Certainly *not!*"

"All right, all right. I just wanted to know. Nobody ever tells me anything nowadays. And I'm getting deaf. Can't overhear as much as I used to. It makes life very dull."

"Poor Baldy."

"And the doctor says I mustn't do any more gardening—no stooping over flowerbeds—blood rushes to my head or something. Damned fool—croak, croak, croak! That's all they do, these doctors!"

"I *am* sorry, Baldy."

"So you see," said Mr. Baldock wistfully. "If you *did* want to tell me anything—well—it wouldn't go any further. We needn't tell Laura."

There was a pause.

"In a way," said Shirley, "I did come to tell you something."

"Thought you did," said Mr. Baldock.

"I thought you might give me—some advice."

"Shan't do that. Much too dangerous."

Shirley paid no attention.

"I don't want to talk to Laura. She doesn't really like Henry. But you like Henry, don't you?"

"I like Henry all right," said Mr. Baldock. "He's a most entertaining fellow to talk to, and he's a nice sympathetic way of listening to an old man blowing off steam. Another thing that I like about him is that he never worries."

Shirley smiled.

"He certainly never worries."

"Very rare in the world nowadays. Everybody I meet has nervous dyspepsia from worrying. Yes, Henry's a pleasant fellow. I don't concern myself about his moral worth as Laura would."

Then he said gently:

"What's he been up to?"

"Do you think I'm a fool, Baldy, to sell out my capital?"

"Is that what you have been doing?"

"Yes."

"Well, when you married, the control of it passed to you. It's yours to do what you like with."

"I know."

"Henry suggest it to you?"

"No. . . . Really no. It was entirely my doing. I didn't want Henry to go bankrupt. I don't think Henry himself would have minded going bankrupt at all. But I would. Do you think I was a fool?"

Mr. Baldock considered.

"In one way, yes, in another way not at all."

"Expound."

"Well, you haven't got very much money. You may need it badly in the future. If you think your attractive husband can be relied upon to provide for you, you can just think again. In that way, you're a fool."

"And the other way?"

"Looking at it the other way, you've paid out your money to buy yourself peace of mind. That may have been quite a wise thing to do." He shot a sharp glance at her. "Still fond of your husband?"

"Yes."

"Is he a good husband to you?"

Shirley walked slowly round the room. Once or twice she ran her finger absently along a table or the back of a chair, and looked at the dust upon it. Mr. Baldock watched her.

She came to a decision at last. Standing by the fireplace, her back turned to him, she said:

"Not particularly."

"In what way?"

In an unemotional voice Shirley said:

· "He's having an affair with another woman."

"Serious?"

"I don't know."

"So you came away?"

"Yes."

"Angry?"

"Furious."

"Going back?"

Shirley was silent a moment. Then she said:

"Yes, I am."

"Well," said Mr. Baldock, "it's your life."

Shirley came over to him and kissed the top of his head. Mr. Baldock grunted.

"Thank you, Baldy," she said.

"Don't thank me, I haven't done anything."

"I know," said Shirley. "That's what's so wonderful of you!"

Chapter Six

The trouble was, Shirley thought, that one got tired.

She leaned back against the plush of the Underground seat.

Three years ago, she hadn't known what tiredness was. Living in London might be a partial cause. Her work had at first been only part-time, but she now worked full-time at the flowershop in the West End. After that, there were usually things to buy, and then the journey home in the rush hour, and then the preparing and cooking of the evening meal.

It was true that Henry appreciated her cooking!

Her eyes closed as she leaned back. Someone trod heavily on her toes and she winced.

She thought: 'But I am tired. . . .'

Her mind went back fitfully over the three and a half years of her married life. . . .

Early bliss . . .

Bills . . .

More bills. . . .

Sonia Cleghorn . . .

Rout of Sonia Cleghorn. Henry penitent, charming, affectionate . . .

More money difficulties . . .

Bailiffs . . .

Muriel to the rescue . . .

Expensive and unnecessary but quite delightful holiday at Cannes. . . .

The Hon. Mrs. Emlyn Blake . . .

Deliverance of Henry from the toils of Mrs. Emlyn Blake . . .

Henry grateful, penitent, charming . . .

Fresh financial crisis . . .

Big Bertha to the rescue . . .

The Lonsdale girl . . .

Financial worries . . .

Still the Lonsdale girl . . .

Laura . . .

Staving off Laura . . .

Failure to stave off Laura . . .

Row with Laura . . .

Appendicitis. Operation. Convalescence . . .

Return home . . .

Final phase of the Lonsdale girl . . .

Her mind lingered and dwelled on that last item.

She had been resting in the flat. It was the third flat they had lived in, and was filled with furniture bought on the hire purchase system— this last suggested by the incident of the bailiffs.

The bell had rung, and she felt too lazy to get up and open the door. Whoever it was would go away. But whoever it was didn't go away. They rang again and again.

Shirley rose angrily to her feet. She went to the door, pulled it open and stood face to face with Susan Lonsdale.

"Oh, it's you, Sue."

"Yes. Can I come in?"

"Actually I'm rather tired. I've just come back from hospital."

"I know. Henry told me. You poor darling. I've brought you some flowers."

Shirley took the out-thrust bunch of daffodils without any marked expression of gratitude.

"Come in," she said.

She went back to the sofa and put her feet up. Susan Lonsdale sat down in a chair.

"I didn't want to worry you while you were still in hospital," she said. "But I do feel, you know, that we ought to get things settled."

"In what way?"

"Well—Henry."

"What about Henry?"

"Darling, you're not going to be an ostrich, are you? Head in the sand and all that?"

"I don't think so."

"You do know, don't you, that Henry and I have got quite a thing about each other?"

"I should have to be blind and deaf not to know that," said Shirley coldly.

"Yes—yes, of course. And, I mean, Henry's awfully fond of you. He'd hate to upset you in any way. But there it is."

"There what is?"

"What I'm really talking about is divorce."

"You mean that Henry wants a divorce?"

"Yes."

"Then why hasn't he mentioned it?"

"Oh, Shirley darling, you know what Henry's like. He does so hate having to be *definite*. And he didn't want to upset you."

"But you and he want to get married?"

"Yes. I'm *so* glad you understand."

"I suppose I understand all right," said Shirley slowly.

"And you'll tell him that it's all right?"

"I'll talk to him, yes."

"It's awfully sweet of you. I do feel that in the end—"

"Oh, go away," said Shirley. "I'm just out of hospital and I'm *tired*. Go away—at once—do you hear?"

"Well, really," said Susan, rising in some dudgeon. "I do think—well, one might at least be *civilized*."

She went out of the room and the front door banged.

Shirley lay very still. Once a tear crept slowly down her cheek. She wiped it away angrily.

'Three years and a half,' she thought. 'Three years and a half . . . and it's come to this.' And then, suddenly, without being able to help it, she began to laugh. That sentiment sounded so like a line in a bad play.

She didn't know if it was five minutes later or two hours when she heard Henry's key in the door.

He came in looking gay and lighthearted as usual. In his hand was an enormous bunch of long-stemmed yellow roses.

"For you, darling. Nice?"

"Lovely," said Shirley. "I've already had daffodils. Not so nice. Rather cheap and past their prime, as a matter of fact."

"Oh, who sent you those?"

"They weren't *sent*. They were brought. Susan Lonsdale brought them."

"What cheek," said Henry indignantly.

Shirley looked at him in faint surprise.

"What did she come here for?" he asked.

"Don't you know?"

"I suppose I can guess. That girl's becoming a positive pest."

"She came to tell me that you want a divorce."

"That *I* want a divorce? From *you?*"

"Yes. Don't you?"

"Of course I don't," said Henry indignantly.

"You don't want to marry Susan?"

"I should hate to marry Susan."

"She wants to marry you."

"Yes, I'm afraid she does." Henry looked despondent. "She's always ringing me up and writing me letters. I don't know what to do about her."

"Did you tell her you wanted to marry her?"

"Oh, one says things," said Henry vaguely. "Or rather they say things and one agrees. . . . One has to, more or less." He gave her an uneasy smile. "You wouldn't divorce me, would you, Shirley?"

"I might," said Shirley.

"Darling—"

"I'm getting rather—tired, Henry."

"I'm a brute. I've given you a rotten deal." He knelt down beside her. The old alluring smile flashed out. "But I do love you, Shirley. All this other silly nonsense doesn't count. It doesn't mean anything. I'd never want to be married to anyone but you. If you'll go on putting up with me?"

"What did you really feel about Susan?"

"Can't we forget about Susan? She's such a *bore*."

"I'd just like to understand."

"Well—" Henry considered. "For about a fortnight I was mad about her. Couldn't sleep. After that, I still thought she was rather wonderful. After that I thought she was beginning, perhaps, to be just the least bit of a *bore*. And then she quite definitely *was* a bore. And just lately she's been an absolutely *pest*."

"Poor Susan."

"Don't worry about Susan. She's got no morals and she's a perfect bitch."

"Sometimes, Henry, I think you're quite heartless."

"I'm not heartless," said Henry indignantly. "I just don't see why people have to cling so. Things are fun if you don't take them seriously."

"Selfish devil!"

"Am I? I suppose I am. You don't really mind, do you, Shirley?"

"I shan't leave you. But I'm rather fed up, all the same. You're not to be trusted over money, and you'll probably go on having these silly affairs with women."

"Oh no, I won't. I swear I won't."

"Oh, Henry, be honest."

"Well, I'll try not to, but do try and understand, Shirley, that none of these affairs mean anything. There's only you."

"I've a good mind to have an affair myself!" said Shirley.

Henry said that he wouldn't be able to blame her if she did.

He then suggested that they should go out somewhere amusing, and have dinner together.

He was a delightful companion all the evening.

Chapter Seven

1

Mona Adams was giving a cocktail party. Mona Adams loved all cocktail parties, and particularly her own. Her voice was hoarse, since she had had to scream a good deal to be heard above her guests. It was being a very successful cocktail party.

She screamed now as she greeted a latecomer.

"Richard! How wonderful! Back from the Sahara—or is it the Gobi?"

"Neither. Actually it's the Fezzan."

"Never heard of it. But how good to see you! What a lovely tan. Now who do you want to talk to? Pam, Pam, let me introduce Sir Richard Wilding. You know, the traveler—camels and big game and deserts—those thrilling books. He's just come back from somewhere in—in—Tibet."

She turned and screamed once more at another arrival.

"Lydia! I'd no idea you were back from Paris. *How* wonderful!"

Richard Wilding was listening to Pam, who was saying feverishly:

"I saw you on television—only last night! How thrilling to meet you. Do tell me now—"

But Richard Wilding had no time to tell her anything.

Another acquaintance had borne down upon him.

He fetched up at last, with his fourth drink in his hand, on a sofa beside the loveliest girl he had ever seen.

Somebody had said:

"Shirley, you must meet Richard Wilding."

Richard had at once sat down beside her. He said:

"How exhausting these affairs are! I'd forgotten. Won't you slip away with me, and have a quiet drink somewhere?"

"I'd love to," said Shirley. "This place gets more like a menagerie every minute."

With a pleasing sense of escape, they came out into the cool evening air.

Wilding hailed a taxi.

"It's a little late for a drink," he said, glancing at his watch, "and we've had a good many drinks, anyway. I think dinner is indicated."

He gave the address of a small, but expensive restaurant off Jermyn Street.

The meal ordered, he smiled across the table at his guest.

"This is the nicest thing that's happened to me since I came back from the wilds. I'd forgotten how frightful London cocktail parties were. Why do people go to them? Why did I? Why do you?"

"Herd instinct, I suppose," said Shirley lightly.

She had a sense of adventure that made her eyes bright. She looked across the table at the bronzed attractive man opposite her.

She was faintly pleased with herself at having snatched away the lion of the party.

"I know all about you," she said. "*And* I've read your books!"

"I don't know anything about you—except that your Christian name is Shirley. What's the rest of it?"

"Glyn-Edwards."

"And you're married." His eyes rested on her ringed finger.

"Yes. And I live in London and work in a flowershop."

"Do you like living in London, and working in a flowershop and going to cocktail parties?"

"Not very much."

"What would you like to do—or be?"

"Let me see." Shirley's eyes half closed. She spoke dreamily. "I'd like to live on an island—an island rather far away from anywhere. I'd like to live in a white house with green shutters and do absolutely nothing all day long. There would be fruit on the island and great curtains of flowers, all in a tangle . . . color and scent . . . and moon-

light every night . . . and the sea would look dark purple in the evenings. . . ."

She sighed and opened her eyes.

"Why does one always choose islands? I don't suppose a real island
would be nice at all."

Richard Wilding said softly: "How odd that you should say what
you did."

"Why?"

"I could give you your island."

"Do you mean you own an island?"

"A good part of one. And very much the kind of island you described. The sea is wine-dark there at night, and my villa is white with
green shutters, and the flowers grow as you describe, in wild tangles of
color and scent, and nobody is ever in a hurry."

"How lovely. It sounds like a dream island."

"It's quite real."

"How can you ever bear to come away?"

"I'm restless. Someday I shall go back there and settle down and
never leave it again."

"I think you'd be quite right."

The waiter came with the first course and broke the spell. They began
talking lightly of everyday things.

Afterward Wilding drove Shirley home. She did not ask him to come
in. He said: "I hope—we'll soon meet again?"

He held her hand a fraction longer than necessary, and she flushed
as she drew it away.

That night she dreamed of an island.

2

"Shirley?"

"Yes?"

"You know, don't you, that I'm in love with you?"

Slowly she nodded.

She would have found it hard to describe the last three weeks. They had had a queer, unreal quality about them. She had walked through them in a kind of permanent abstraction.

She knew that she had been very tired—and that she was still tired, but that out of her tiredness had come a delicious hazy feeling of not being really anywhere in particular.

And in that state of haziness, her values had shifted and changed.

It was as though Henry and everything that pertained to Henry had become dim and rather far away. Whereas Richard Wilding stood boldly in the foreground—a romantic figure rather larger than life.

She looked at him now with grave considering eyes.

He said:

"Do you care for me at all?"

"I don't know."

What *did* she feel? She knew that every day this man came to occupy more and more of her thoughts. She knew that his proximity excited her. She recognized that what she was doing was dangerous, that she might be swept away on a sudden tide of passion. And she knew that, definitely, she didn't want to give up seeing him. . . .

Richard said:

"You're very loyal, Shirley. You've never said anything to me about your husband."

"Why should I?"

"But I've heard a good deal."

Shirley said:

"People will say anything."

"He's unfaithful to you and not, I think, very kind."

"No, Henry's not a kind man."

"He doesn't give you what you ought to have—love, care, tenderness."

"Henry loves me—in his fashion."

"Perhaps. But you want something more than that."

"I used not to."

"But you do now. You want—your island, Shirley."

"Oh! the island. That was just a daydream."

"It's a dream that could come true."

"Perhaps. I don't think so."

"It *could* come true."

A small chilly breeze came across the river to the terrace on which they were sitting.

Shirley got up, pulling her coat tightly around her.

"We mustn't talk like this anymore," she said. "What we're doing is foolish, Richard, foolish and dangerous."

"Perhaps. But you don't care for your husband, Shirley, you care for me."

"I'm Henry's wife."

"You care for *me*."

She said again:

"I'm Henry's wife."

She repeated it like an article of faith.

3

When she got home, Henry was lying stretched out on the sofa. He was wearing white flannels.

"I think I've strained a muscle." He made a faint grimace of pain.

"What have you been doing?"

"Played tennis at Roehampton."

"You and Stephen? I thought you were going to play golf."

"We changed our minds. Stephen brought Mary along, and Jessica Sandys made a fourth."

"Jessica? Is that the dark girl we met at the Archers the other night?"

"Er—yes—she is."

"Is she your latest?"

"Shirley! I told you, I promised you . . ."

"I know, Henry, but what are promises? She *is* your latest—I can see it in your eye."

Henry said sulkily:

"Of course, if you're going to imagine things . . ."

"If I'm going to imagine things," Shirley murmured, "I'd rather imagine an island."

"Why an island?"

Henry sat up on the sofa and said: "I really *do* feel stiff."

"You'd better have a rest tomorrow. A quiet Sunday for a change."

"Yes, that might be nice."

But the following morning Henry declared that the stiffness was passing off.

"As a matter of fact," he said, "we agreed to have a return."

"You and Stephen and Mary—and Jessica?"

"Yes."

"Or just you and Jessica?"

"Oh, all of us," he said easily.

"What a liar you are, Henry."

But she did not say it angrily. There was even a slight smile in her eyes. She was remembering the young man she had met at the tennis party four years ago, and how what had attracted her to him had been his detachment. He was still just as detached.

The shy embarrassed young man who had come to call the following day, and who had sat doggedly talking to Laura until she herself returned, was the same young man who was now determinedly in pursuit of Jessica.

'Henry,' she thought, 'has really not changed at all.'

'He doesn't want to hurt me,' she thought, 'but he's just like that. He always has to do just what he wants to do.'

She noticed that Henry was limping a little, and she said impulsively:

"I really don't think you ought to go and play tennis—you must have strained yourself yesterday. Can't you leave it until next weekend?"

But Henry wanted to go, and went.

He came back about six o'clock and dropped down on his bed looking so ill that Shirley was alarmed. Notwithstanding Henry's protests, she went and rang up the doctor.

Chapter Eight

1

As Laura rose from lunch the following afternoon the telephone rang.

"Laura? It's me, Shirley."

"Shirley? What's the matter? Your voice sounds queer."

"It's Henry, Laura. He's in hospital. He's got polio."

'Like Charles,' thought Laura, her mind rushing back over the years. 'Like Charles . . .'

The tragedy that she herself had been too young to understand acquired suddenly a new meaning.

The anguish in Shirley's voice was the same anguish that her own mother had felt.

Charles had died. Would Henry die?

She wondered. Would Henry die?

2

"Infantile paralysis is the same as polio, isn't it?" she asked Mr. Baldock doubtfully.

"Newer name for it, that's all—why?"

"Henry has gone down with it."

"Poor chap. And you're wondering if he's going to get over it?"

"Well—yes."

"And hoping he won't?"

"Really, really. You make me out a monster."

"Come now, young Laura—the thought was in your mind."

"Horrible thoughts do pass through one's mind," said Laura. "But I wouldn't wish anyone dead—really I wouldn't."

"No," said Mr. Baldock thoughtfully. "I don't believe you would—nowadays—"

"What do you mean—nowadays? Oh, you don't mean that old business of the Scarlet Woman?" She couldn't help smiling at the remembrance. "What I came in to tell you was that I shan't be able to come in and see you every day for a bit. I'm going up to London by the afternoon train—to be with Shirley."

"Does she want you?"

"Of course she'll want me," said Laura indignantly. "Henry's in hospital. She's all alone. She needs someone with her."

"Probably—yes, probably. Quite right. Proper thing to do. It doesn't matter about *me*."

Mr. Baldock, as a semi-invalid, got a lot of pleasure out of an exaggerated self-pity.

"Darling, I'm terribly sorry, but—"

"But Shirley comes first! All right, all right . . . who am I? Only a tiresome old fellow of eighty, deaf, semiblind—"

"Baldy—"

Mr. Baldock suddenly grinned and closed one eyelid.

"Laura," he said, "you're a pushover for hard-luck stories. Anyone who's sorry for himself doesn't need you to be sorry for him as well. Self-pity is practically a full-time occupation."

3

"Isn't it lucky I didn't sell the house?" said Laura.

It was three months later. Henry had not died, but he had been very near death.

"If he hadn't insisted upon going out and playing tennis after the first signs, it wouldn't have been so serious. As it is—"

"It's bad—eh?"

"It's fairly certain that he'll be a cripple for life."

"Poor devil."

"They haven't told him that, of course. And I suppose there's just a chance . . . but perhaps they only say that to cheer up Shirley. Anyway, as I said, it's lucky I haven't sold the house. It's queer—I had a feeling

all along that I oughtn't to sell it. I kept saying to myself it was ridiculous, that it was far too big for me, that since Shirley hadn't any
children they would never want a house in the country. And I was quite
keen to take on this job, running the Children's Home in Milchester.
But as it is, the sale hasn't gone through, and I can withdraw and the
house will be there for Shirley to bring Henry to when he gets out of
hospital. That won't be for some months, of course."

"Does Shirley think that's a good plan?"

Laura frowned.

"No, for some reason she's most reluctant. I think I know why."

She looked up sharply at Mr. Baldock.

"I might as well know—Shirley may have told you what she
wouldn't like to tell me. She's got practically none of her own money
left, has she?"

"She hasn't confided in me," said Mr. Baldock, "but no, I shouldn't
think she had." He added: "I should imagine Henry's gone through
pretty well all he ever had, too."

"I've heard a lot of things," said Laura. "From friends of theirs and
other people. It's been a terribly unhappy marriage. He's gone through
her money, he's neglected her, he's constantly had affairs with other
women. Even now, when he's so ill, I can't bring myself to forgive him.
How could he treat Shirley like that? If anyone deserved to be happy,
Shirley did. She was so full of life and eagerness and—and trust." She
got up and walked restlessly about the room. She tried to steady her
voice as she went on:

"Why did I ever let her marry Henry? I could have stopped it, you
know, or at any rate delayed it so that she would have had time to see
what he was like. But she was fretting so—she wanted him. I wanted
her to have what she wanted."

"There, there, Laura."

"And it's worse than that. I wanted to show that I wasn't possessive.
Just to prove that to myself, I let Shirley in for a lifetime of unhappiness."

"I've told you before, Laura, you worry too much about happiness
and unhappiness."

"I can't bear to see Shirley suffer! *You* don't mind, I suppose."

"Shirley, Shirley! It's you I mind about, Laura—always have. Ever since you used to ride round the garden on that fairy cycle of yours looking as solemn as a judge. You've got a capacity for suffering, and you can't minimize it as some can, by the balm of self-pity. You don't think about yourself at all."

"What do I matter? It isn't *my* husband who's been struck down with infantile paralysis!"

"It might be, by the way you're going on about it! Do you know what I want for you, Laura? Some good everyday happiness. A husband, some noisy, naughty children. You've always been a tragic little thing ever since I've known you—you need the other thing, if you're ever going to develop properly. Don't take the sufferings of the world upon your shoulders—our Lord Jesus Christ did that once for all. You can't live other people's lives for them, not even Shirley's. Help her, yes; but don't *mind* so much."

Laura said, white-faced: "You don't understand."

"You're like all women, have to make such a song and dance about things."

Laura looked at him for a moment in silence, and then turned on her heel and went out of the room.

"Bloody old fool, that's what I am," said Mr. Baldock aloud to himself. "Oh well, I've been and done it now, I suppose."

He was startled when the door opened, and Laura came swiftly through it, and across to his chair.

"You *are* an old devil," she said, and kissed him.

When she went out again, Mr. Baldock lay still and blinked his eyes in some embarrassment.

It had become his habit lately to mutter to himself, and he now addressed a prayer to the ceiling.

"Look after her, Lord," he said. "I can't. And I suppose it's been presumption on my part to try."

4

On hearing of Henry's illness, Richard Wilding had written to Shirley a letter expressing conventional sympathy. A month later he had written again, asking her to see him. She wrote back:

"I don't think we had better meet. Henry is the only reality now in my life. I think you will understand. Good-bye."

To that he replied:

"You have said what I expected you to say. God bless you, my dear, now and always."

So that, Shirley thought, was the end of that....

Henry would live, but what confronted her now were the practical difficulties of existence. She and Henry had practically no money. When he came out of hospital, a cripple, the first necessity would be a home.

The obvious answer was Laura.

Laura, generous, loving, took it for granted that Shirley and Henry would come to Bellbury. Yet, for some curious reason, Shirley was deeply reluctant to go.

Henry, a bitter rebellious invalid, with no trace of his former light-heartedness, told her she was mad.

"I can't see what you've got against it. It's the obvious thing to do. Thank goodness Laura has never given the house up. There's plenty of room. We can have a whole suite to ourselves, and a bloody nurse or man attendant, too, if I've got to have one. I can't see *what* you are dithering about."

"Couldn't we go to Muriel?"

"She's had a stroke, you know that. She'll probably be having another quite soon. She's got a nurse looking after her and is quite ga-ga, and her income's halved with taxation. It's out of the question. What's wrong with going to Laura? She's offered to have us, hasn't she?"

"Of course she has. Again and again."

"Then that's all right. Why don't you want to go there? You know Laura adores you."

"She loves *me*—but—"

"All right! Laura adores you and doesn't like me! All the more fun for her. She can gloat over my being a helpless cripple and enjoy herself."

"Don't say that, Henry. You know Laura isn't like that."

"What do I care what Laura is like? What do I care about anything. Do you realize what I'm going through? Do you realize what it's like to be helpless, inert, not able to turn over in bed? And what do you care?"

"I care."

"Tied to a cripple! A lot of fun for you!"

"It's all right for me."

"You're like all women, delighted to be able to treat a man like a child. I'm dependent on you, and I expect you enjoy it."

"Say anything you like to me," said Shirley. "I know just how awful it is for you."

"You don't know in the least. You can't. How I wish I was dead! Why don't these bloody doctors finish one off? It's the only decent thing to do. Go on, say some more soothing, sweet things."

"All right," said Shirley, "I will. This will make you really mad. It's worse for me than it is for you."

Henry glared at her; then, reluctantly, he laughed.

"You called my bluff," he said.

5

Shirley wrote to Laura a month later.

"Darling Laura. It's very good of you to have us. You mustn't mind Henry and the things he says. He's taking it very hard. He's never had to bear anything he didn't want to before, and he gets in the most dreadful rages. It's such an awful thing to happen to anyone like Henry."

Laura's answer, quick and loving, came by return.

Two weeks later, Shirley and her invalid husband came home.

Why, Shirley wondered, as Laura's loving arms went round her, had she ever felt she did not want to come here?

This was her own place. She was back within the circle of Laura's care and protection. She felt like a small child again.

"Laura darling, I'm so glad to be here. . . . I'm so tired . . . so dread-fully tired. . . ."

Laura was shocked by her sister's appearance.

"My darling Shirley, you've been through such a lot . . . don't worry anymore."

Shirley said anxiously: "You mustn't mind Henry."

"Of course I shan't mind anything Henry says or does. How could I? It's dreadful for a man, especially a man like Henry, to be completely helpless. Let him blow off steam as much as he likes."

"Oh, Laura, you *do* understand. . . ."

"Of course I understand."

Shirley gave a sigh of relief. Until this morning, she had hardly real-ised herself the strain under which she had been living.

Chapter Nine

1

Before going abroad again, Sir Richard Wilding went down to Bellbury.

Shirley read his letter at breakfast; and then passed it to Laura, who read it.

"Richard Wilding. Is that the traveler man?"

"Yes."

"I didn't know he was a friend of yours."

"Well—he is. You'll like him."

"He'd better come to lunch. Do you know him well?"

"For a time," said Shirley, "I thought I was in love with him."

"Oh!" said Laura, startled.

She wondered . . .

Richard arrived a little earlier than they had expected. Shirley was up with Henry, and Laura received him, and took him out into the garden.

She thought to herself at once: 'This is the man Shirley ought to have married.'

She liked his quietness, his warmth and sympathy, and his authoritativeness.

Oh! if only Shirley had never met Henry, Henry with his charm, his instability and his underlying ruthlessness.

Richard enquired politely after the sick man. After the conventional questions and answers, Richard Wilding said:

"I only met him a couple of times. I didn't like him."

And then he asked brusquely:

"Why didn't you stop her marrying him?"

"How could I?"

"You could have found some way."

"Could I? I wonder."

Neither of them felt that their quick intimacy was unusual.

He said gravely:

"I might as well tell you, if you haven't guessed, that I love Shirley very deeply."

"I rather thought so."

"Not that it's any good. She'll never leave the fellow now."

Laura said dryly:

"Could you expect her to?"

"Not really. She wouldn't be Shirley if she did." Then he said: "Do you think she still cares for him?"

"I don't know. Naturally she's dreadfully sorry for him."

"How does he bear up?"

"He doesn't," said Laura sharply. "He's no kind of endurance or fortitude. He just—takes it out of her."

"Swine!"

"We ought to be sorry for him."

"I am in a way. But he always treated her very badly. Everybody knows about it. Did you know?"

"She never said so. Of course I've heard things."

"Shirley's loyal," he said. "Loyal through and through."

"Yes."

After a moment or two's silence Laura said, her voice suddenly harsh:

"You're quite right, you know. I ought to have stopped that marriage. Somehow. She was so young. She hadn't had time. Yes, I made a terrible mess of things."

He said gruffly:

"You'll look after her, won't you?"

"Shirley is the only person in the world I care about."

He said:

"Look, she's coming now."

They both watched Shirley as she came across the lawn toward them.

He said:

"How terribly thin and pale she is. My poor child, my dear brave child . . ."

2

Shirley walked with Richard after lunch by the side of the brook.

"Henry's asleep. I can get out for a little."

"Does he know I'm here?"

"I didn't tell him."

"Are you having a bad time of it?"

"I am—rather. There's nothing I can say or do that's any help to him. That's what's so awful."

"You didn't mind my coming down?"

"Not if it's to say—good-bye."

"It's good-bye all right. You'll never leave Henry now?"

"No. I shall never leave him."

He stopped and took her hands in his.

"Just one thing, my dear. If you need me—at any time—just send the one word: 'Come.' I'll come from the ends of the earth."

"Dear Richard."

"It's good-bye then, Shirley."

He took her in his arms. Her starved and tired body trembled into life. She kissed him wildly, desperately.

"I love you, Richard, I love you, I love you. . . ."

Then she whispered:

"Good-bye. No, don't come with me. . . ."

She tore herself away and ran back toward the house.

Richard Wilding swore under his breath. He cursed Henry Glyn-Edwards and the disease called polio.

3

Mr. Baldock was confined to bed. More than that, he had two nurses in attendance. He loathed them both.

Laura's visits were the only bright spot in his day.

The nurse who was on duty retired tactfully, and Mr. Baldock told Laura all her failings.

His voice rose in a shrill falsetto:

"So damned arch. *'And how are we this morning?'* There's only one of me, I told her. The other one is a damned slab-faced, grinning ape."

"That was very rude of you, Baldy."

"Bah! Nurses are thick-skinned. They don't mind. Held up her finger, and said: 'Naughty, naughty!' *How* I'd like to boil the woman in oil!"

"Now don't get excited. It's bad for you."

"How's Henry? Still playing up?"

"Yes. Henry really is a *fiend!* I try to be sorry for him, but I can't."

"You women! Hard-hearted! Sentimental about dead birds and things like that, and hard as nails when a poor fellow is going through hell."

"It's Shirley who's going through hell. He just—goes for her."

"Naturally. Only person he can take it out on. What's a wife for, if you can't let loose on her in times of trouble?"

"I'm terribly afraid she'll have a breakdown."

Mr. Baldock snorted contemptuously: "Not she. Shirley's tough. She's got guts, Shirley has."

"She's under a terrible strain."

"Yes, I expect so. Well, she would marry the fellow."

"She didn't know he was going to get polio."

"*That* wouldn't have stopped her? What's all this I hear about some romantic swashbuckler coming down here to stage a fond farewell?"

"Baldy, how *do* you get hold of things?"

"Keep my ears open. What's a nurse for, if you can't get the local scandal out of her?"

"It was Richard Wilding, the traveler."

"Oh yes, rather a good chap by all accounts. Made a silly marriage before the war. Glorified Piccadilly tart. Had to get rid of her after the war. Very cut up about it, I believe—silly ass to marry her. These idealists!"

"He's nice—very nice."

"Soft about him?"

"He's the man Shirley ought to have married."

"Oh, I thought maybe you fancied him yourself. Pity."

"I shall never marry."

"Ta-ra-ra-boom-di-ay," said Mr. Baldock rudely.

4

The young doctor said: "You ought to go away, Mrs. Glyn-Edwards. Rest and a change of air is what you need."

"I can't possibly go away."

Shirley was indignant.

"You're very run-down. I'm warning you." Dr. Graves spoke impressively. "You'll have a complete breakdown if you're not careful."

Shirley laughed.

"I shall be all right."

The doctor shook his head doubtfully.

"Mr. Glyn-Edwards is a very trying patient," he said.

"If he could only—resign himself a little," said Shirley.

"Yes, he takes things badly."

"You don't think that *I'm* bad for him? That I—well—irritate him?"

"You're his safety valve. It's hard on you, Mrs. Glyn-Edwards, but you're doing good work, believe me."

"Thank you."

"Continue with the sleeping pills. It's rather a heavy dose, but he must have rest at night when he works himself up so much. Don't leave them where he can get at them, remember."

Shirley's face grew paler.

"You don't think that he'd—"

"No, no, no," the doctor interrupted her hastily. "I should say definitely not the type to do away with himself. Yes, I know he says he wants to sometimes, but that's just hysteria. No, the danger with this type of drug is that you may wake up in a half-bemused condition, forget you've had your dose and take another. So be careful."

"Of course I will."

She said good-bye and went back to Henry.

Henry was in one of his most unpleasant moods.

"Well, what does he say—everything proceeding satisfactorily! Patient just a *little* irritable, perhaps. No need to worry about *that!*"

"Oh, Henry." Shirley sank down in a chair. "Couldn't you sometimes—be a little kind?"

"Kind—to you?"

"Yes. I'm so tired, so dreadfully tired. If you could just be—sometimes—kind."

"*You've* got nothing to complain about. You're not a twisted mass of useless bones. *You're* all right."

"So you think," said Shirley, "that I'm all right?"

"Did the doctor persuade you to go away?"

"He said I ought to have a change and a rest."

"And you're going, I suppose! A nice week at Bournemouth!"

"No, I'm not going."

"Why not?"

"I don't want to leave you."

"*I* don't care whether you go or not. What use are you to me?"

"I don't seem to be any use," said Shirley dully.

Henry turned his head restlessly.

"Where's my sleeping stuff? You never gave it to me last night."

"Yes, I did."

"You didn't. I woke up and I asked for it. That nurse pretended I'd had it."

"You had had it. You forget."

"Are you going to the vicarage thing tonight?"

"Not if you don't want me to," said Shirley.

"Oh, better go! Otherwise everyone says what a selfish brute I am. I told nurse she could go, too."

"I'll stay."

"You needn't. Laura will look after me. Funny—I've never liked Laura much, but there's something about her that's very soothing when you're ill. There's a sort of—strength."

"Yes. Laura's always been like that. She *gives* you something. She's better than me. I only seem to make you angry."

"You're very annoying sometimes."

"Henry—"

"Yes?"

"Nothing."

When she came in before going out to the vicarage whist drive, she thought at first that Henry was asleep. She bent over him. Tears pricked her eyelids. Then as she turned to go, he plucked at her sleeve.

"Shirley."

"Yes, darling?"

"Shirley—don't hate me."

"Hate you? How could I hate you?"

He muttered: "You're so pale, so thin. . . . I've worn you out. I couldn't help it. . . . I can't help it. I've always hated anything like illness or pain. In the war, I used to think I wouldn't mind being killed, but I could never understand how fellows could bear to be burned or disfigured or—or maimed."

"I see. I understand. . . ."

"I'm a selfish devil, I know. But I'll get better—better in mind, I mean—even if I never get better in body. We might be able to make a go of it—of everything—if you'll be patient. Just don't leave me."

"I'll never leave you, never."

"I do love you, Shirley. . . . I do. . . . I always have. There's never really been anyone but you—there never will be. All these months— you've been so good, so patient. I know I've been a devil. Say you forgive me."

"There's nothing to forgive. I love you."

"Even if one is cripple—one might enjoy life."

"We will enjoy life."

"Can't see how!"

With a tremor in her voice, Shirley said:

"Well, there's always eating."

"And drinking," said Henry.

A faint ghost of his old smile showed.

"One might go in for higher mathematics."

"Crossword puzzles for me."

He said:

"I shall be a devil tomorrow, I expect."

"I expect you will. I shan't mind now."

"Where are my pills?"

"I'll give them to you."

He swallowed them obediently.

"Poor old Muriel," he said suddenly.

"What made you think of her?"

"Remembering taking you over there the first time. You had on a yellow stripy dress. I ought to have gone and seen old Muriel more often, but she had got to be such a bore. I hate bores. Now *I'm* a bore."

"No, you're not."

From the hall below, Laura called: "Shirley!"

She kissed him. She ran down the stairs, happiness surging up in her, happiness and a kind of triumph.

In the hall below, Laura said that nurse had started.

"Oh, am I late? I'll run."

She ran down the drive turning her head to call:

"I've given Henry his sleeping pills."

But Laura had gone inside again, and was closing the door.

PART THREE

LLEWELLYN—1956

Chapter One

1

Llewellyn Knox threw open the shutters of the hotel windows and let in the sweet-scented night air. Below him were the twinkling lights of the town, and beyond them the lights of the harbor.

For the first time for some weeks, Llewellyn felt relaxed and at peace. Here, perhaps, in the island, he could pause and take stock of himself and of the future. The pattern of the future was clear in outline, but blurred as to detail. He had passed through the agony, the emptiness, the weariness. Soon, very soon now, he should be able to begin life anew. A simpler, more undemanding life, the life of a man like any other man—with this disadvantage only: he would be beginning it at the age of forty.

He turned back into the room. It was austerely furnished but clean. He washed his face and hands, unpacked his few possessions, and then left his bedroom, and walked down two flights of stairs into the hotel lobby. A clerk was behind a desk there, writing. His eyes came up for a moment, viewed Llewellyn politely, but with no particular interest or curiosity, and dropped once more to his work.

Llewellyn pushed through the revolving doors and went out into the street. The air was warm with a soft, fragrant dampness.

It had none of the exotic languor of the tropics. Its warmth was just sufficient to relax tension. The accentuated tempo of civilization was left behind here. It was as though in the island one went back to an earlier age, an age where the people went about their business slowly, with due thought, without hurry or stress, but where purpose was still purpose. There would be poverty here, and pain, and the various ills of the flesh, but not the jangled nerves, the feverish haste, the apprehensive thoughts of tomorrow, which are the constant goads of the higher civilizations of the world. The hard faces of the career women, the ruthless faces of mothers, ambitious for their young, the worn gray faces of business executives fighting incessantly so that they and theirs should not go down and perish, the anxious tired faces of multitudes fighting for a better existence tomorrow or even to retain the existence they had—all these were absent from the people who passed him by. Most of them glanced at him, a good-mannered glance that registered him as a foreigner, and then glanced away, resuming their own lives. They walked slowly, without haste. Perhaps they were just taking the air. Even if they were bent upon some particular course, there was no urgency. What was not done today could be done tomorrow; friends who awaited their arrival would always wait a little longer, without annoyance.

A grave, polite people, Llewellyn thought, who smiled seldom, not because they were sad, but because to smile one must be amused. The smile here was not used as a social weapon.

A woman with a baby in her arms came up to him and begged in a mechanical, lifeless whine. He did not understand what she said, but her outstretched hand, and the melancholy chant of her words conformed, he thought, to a very old pattern. He put a small coin in her palm and she thanked him in the same mechanical manner and turned away. The baby lay asleep against her shoulder. It was well nourished, and her own face, though worn, was not haggard or emaciated. Probably, he thought, she was not in want, it was simply that begging was her trade. She pursued it mechanically, courteously, and with sufficient success to provide food and shelter for herself and the child.

He turned a corner and walked down a steep street toward the harbor. Two girls, walking together, came up and passed him. They were talking and laughing, and, without turning their heads, it was apparent that they were very conscious of a group of four young men who walked a little distance behind them.

Llewellyn smiled to himself. This, he thought, was the courting pattern of the island. The girls were beautiful with a proud dark beauty that would probably not outlast youth. In ten years, perhaps less, they would look like this elderly woman who was waddling up the hill on her husband's arm, stout, good-humored, and still dignified in spite of her shapelessness.

Llewellyn went on down the steep, narrow street. It came out on the harbor front. Here there were cafés with broad terraces where people sat and drank little glasses of brightly colored drinks. Quite a throng of people were walking up and down in front of the cafés. Here again their gaze registered Llewellyn as a foreigner, but without any overwhelming interest. They were used to foreigners. Ships put in, and foreigners came ashore, sometimes for a few hours, sometimes to stay—though not usually for long, since the hotels were mediocre and not much given to refinements of plumbing. Foreigners, so the glances seemed to say, were not really their concern. Foreigners were extraneous and had nothing to do with the life of the island.

Insensibly, the length of Llewellyn's stride shortened. He had been walking at his own brisk transatlantic pace, the pace of a man going to some definite place, and anxious to get there with as much speed as is consistent with comfort.

But there was, now, no definite place to which he was going. That was as true spiritually as physically. He was merely a man amongst his fellow kind.

And with that thought there came over him that warm and happy consciousness of brotherhood which he had felt increasingly in the arid wastes of the last months. It was a thing almost impossible to describe—this sense of nearness to, of feeling with, his fellowmen. It had no purpose, no aim, it was as far removed from beneficence as anything could be. It was a consciousness of love and friendliness that gave nothing, and took nothing, that had no wish to confer a benefit or to receive one. One might describe it as a moment of love that embraced utter comprehension, that was endlessly satisfying, and that yet could not, by very reason of what it was, last.

How often, Llewellyn thought, he had heard and said those words: *"Thy loving kindness to us and to all men."*

Man himself could have that feeling, although he could not hold
it long.

And suddenly he saw that here was the compensation, the promise
of the future, that he had not understood. For fifteen or more years he
had been held apart from just that—the sense of brotherhood with other
men. He had been a man set apart, a man dedicated to service. But
now, now that the glory and the agonizing exhaustion were done with,
he could become once more a man among men. He was no longer
required to serve—only to live.

Llewellyn turned aside and sat down at one of the tables in a café.
He chose an inside table against the back wall where he could look over
the other tables to the people walking in the street, and beyond them
to the lights of the harbor, and the ships that were moored there.

The waiter who brought his order asked in a gentle, musical voice:
"You are American? Yes?"

Yes, Llewellyn said, he was American.

A gentle smile lit up the waiter's grave face.

"We have American papers here. I bring them to you."

Llewellyn checked his motion of negation.

The waiter went away, and came back with a proud expression on
his face, carrying two illustrated American magazines.

"Thank you."

"You are welcome, señor."

The periodicals were two years old, Llewellyn noted. That again
pleased him. It emphasized the remoteness of the island from the up-
to-date stream. Here at least, he thought, there would not be recognition.

His eyes closed for a moment, as he remembered all the various
incidents of the last months.

"Aren't you—isn't it? I *thought* I recognized you. . . ."

"Oh, do tell me—you *are* Dr. Knox?"

"You're Llewellyn Knox, aren't you? Oh, I do want to tell you how
terribly grieved I was to hear—"

"I knew it must be you! What are your plans, Dr. Knox? Your illness
was so terrible. I've heard you're writing a book? I do hope so. Giving
us a message?"

And so on, and so on. On ships, in airports, in expensive hotels, in obscure hotels, in restaurants, on trains. Recognized, questioned, sympathized with, fawned upon—yes, that had been the hardest. Women . . . Women with eyes like spaniels. Women with that capacity for worship that women had.

And then there had been, of course, the Press. For even now he was still news. (Mercifully, *that* would not last long.) So many crude brash questions: What are your plans? Would you say now that—? Can I quote you as believing—? Can you give us a message?

A message, a message, always a message! To the readers of a particular journal, to the country, to men and women, to the world—

But he had never had a message to give. He had been a messenger, which was a very different thing. But no one was likely to understand that.

Rest—that was what he had needed. Rest and time. Time to take in what he himself was, and what he should do. Time to take stock of himself. Time to start again, at forty, and live his own life. He must find out what had happened to him, to Llewellyn Knox, the man, during the fifteen years he had been employed as a messenger.

Sipping his little glass of colored liqueur, looking at the people, the lights, the harbor, he thought that this would be a good place to find out all that. It was not the solitude of a desert he wanted, he wanted his fellow kind. He was not by nature a recluse or an ascetic. He had no vocation for the monastic life. All he needed was to find out who and what was Llewellyn Knox. Once he knew that, he could go ahead and take up life once more.

It all came back, perhaps, to Kant's three questions:

What do I know?

What can I hope?

What ought I to do?

Of these questions, he could answer only one, the second.

The waiter came back and stood by his table.

"They are good magazines?" he asked happily.

Llewellyn smiled.

"Yes."

"They were not very new, I am afraid."

"That does not matter."

"No. What is good a year ago is good now."

He spoke with calm certainty.

Then he added:

"You have come from the ship? The *Santa Margherita*? Out there?"

He jerked his head toward the jetty.

"Yes."

"She goes out again tomorrow at twelve, that is right?"

"Perhaps. I do not know. I am staying here."

"Ah, you have come for a visit? It is beautiful here, so the visitors say. You will stay until the next ship comes in? On Thursday?"

"Perhaps longer. I may stay here some time."

"Ah, you have business here!"

"No, I have no business."

"People do not usually stay long here, unless they have business. They say the hotels are not good enough, and there is nothing to do."

"Surely there is as much to do here as anywhere else?"

"For us who live here, yes. We have our lives and our work. But for strangers, no. Although we have foreigners who have come here to live. There is Sir Wilding, an Englishman. He has a big estate here—it came to him from his grandfather. He lives here altogether now, and writes books. He is a very celebrated señor, and much respected."

"You mean Sir Richard Wilding?"

The waiter nodded.

"Yes, that is his name. We have known him here many, many years. In the war he could not come, but afterward he came back. He also paints pictures. There are many painters here. There is a Frenchman who lives in a cottage up at Santa Dolmea. And there is an Englishman and his wife over on the other side of the island. They are very poor, and the pictures he paints are very odd. She carves figures out of stone as well—"

He broke off and darted suddenly forward to a table in the corner at which a chair had been turned up, to indicate that it was reserved. Now he seized the chair and drew it back a little, bowing a welcome at the woman who came to occupy it.

She smiled her thanks at him as she sat down. She did not appear to give him an order, but he went away at once. The woman put her elbows on the table and stared out over the harbor.

Llewellyn watched her with a stirring of surprise.

She wore an embroidered Spanish scarf of flowers on an emerald green background, like many of the women walking up and down the street, but she was, he was almost sure, either American or English. Her blonde fairness stood out amongst the other occupants of the café. The table at which she was sitting was half obliterated by a great hanging mass of coral-colored bougainvillaea. To anyone sitting at it, it must have given the feeling of looking out from a cave smothered in vegetation on to the world, and more particularly over the lights of the ships, and their reflections in the harbor.

The girl, for she was little more, sat quite still, in an attitude of passive waiting. Presently the waiter brought her her drink. She smiled her thanks without speaking. Then, her hands cupped round the glass, she continued to stare out over the harbor, occasionally sipping her drink.

Llewellyn noticed the rings on her fingers, a solitaire emerald on one hand, and a cluster of diamonds on the other. Under the exotic shawl she was wearing a plain high-necked black dress.

She neither looked at, nor paid any attention to, the people sitting round her, and none of them did more than glance at her, and even so without any particular attention. It was clear that she was a well-known figure in the café.

Llewellyn wondered who she was. It struck him as a little unusual that a young woman of her class should be sitting there alone, without any companion. Yet she was obviously perfectly at ease and had the air of someone performing a well-known routine. Perhaps a companion would shortly come and join her.

But the time went on, and the girl still sat alone at her table. Occasionally she made a slight gesture with her head, and the waiter brought her another drink.

It was almost an hour later when Llewellyn signaled for his check and prepared to leave. As he passed near her chair, he looked at her.

She seemed oblivious both of him and of her immediate surroundings. She stared now into her glass, now out to sea, and her expression did not change. It was the expression of someone who is very far away.

As Llewellyn left the café and started up the narrow street that led back to his hotel, he had a sudden impulse to go back, to speak to her, to warn her. Now why had that word 'warn' come into his head? Why did he have the idea that she was in danger?

He shook his head. There was nothing he could do about it at the moment, but he was quite sure that he was right.

2

Two weeks later found Llewellyn Knox still on the island. His days had fallen into a pattern. He walked, rested, read, walked again, slept. In the evenings after dinner he went down to the harbor and sat in one of the cafés. Soon he cut reading out of his daily routine. He had nothing more to read.

He was living now with himself only, and that, he knew, was what it should be. But he was not alone. He was in the midst of others of his kind, he was at one with them, even if he never spoke to them. He neither sought nor avoided contact. He had conversations with many people, but none of them meant anything more than the courtesies of fellow human beings. They wished him well, he wished them well, but neither of them wanted to intrude into the other's life.

Yet to this aloof and satisfying friendship there was an exception. He wondered constantly about the girl who came to the café and sat at the table under the bougainvillaea. Though he patronized several different establishments on the harbor front, he came most often to the first one of his choice. Here, on several occasions, he saw the English girl. She arrived always late in the evening and sat at the same table, and he had discovered that she stayed there until almost everyone else had left. Though she was a mystery to him, it was clear to him that she was a mystery to no one else.

One day he spoke of her to the waiter.

"The señora who sits there, she is English?"

"Yes, she is English."

"She lives in the island?"

"Yes."

"She does not come here every evening?"

The waiter said gravely:

"She comes when she can."

It was a curious answer, and Llewellyn thought about it afterward.

He did not ask her name. If the waiter had wanted him to know her name, he would have told it to him. The boy would have said: "She is the señora so and so, and she lives at such-and-such a place." Since he did not say that, Llewellyn deduced that there was a reason why her name should not be given to a stranger.

Instead he asked:

"What does she drink?"

The boy replied briefly: "Brandy," and went away.

Llewellyn paid for his drink and said good night. He threaded his way through the tables and stood for a moment on the pavement before joining the evening throng of walkers.

Then, suddenly, he wheeled round and marched with the firm decisive tread of his nationality to the table by the coral bougainvillaea.

"Do you mind," he said, "if I sit down and talk to you for a moment or two?"

Chapter Two

Her gaze came back very slowly from the harbor lights to his face. For a moment or two her eyes remained wide and unfocused. He could sense the effort she made. She had been, he saw, very far away.

He saw, too, with a sudden quick pity, how very young she was. Not only young in years (she was, he judged, about twenty-three or four), but young in the sense of immaturity. It was as though a normally maturing rosebud had had its growth arrested by frost—it still presented the appearance of normality, but actually it would progress no further. It would not visibly wither. It would just, in the course of time, drop to the ground, unopened. She looked, he thought, like a lost child. He appreciated, too, her loveliness. She was very lovely. Men would always find her lovely, always yearn to help her, to protect her, to cherish her. The dice, one would have said, were loaded in her favor. And yet she was sitting here, staring into unfathomable distance, and somewhere on her easy, assured happy path through life she had got lost.

Her eyes, wide now and deeply blue, assessed him.

She said, a little uncertainly: "Oh—?"

He waited.

Then she smiled.

"Please do."

He drew up a chair and sat.

She asked: "You are American?"

"Yes."

"Did you come off the ship?"

Her eyes went momentarily to the harbor again. There was a ship alongside the quay. There was nearly always a ship.

"I did come on a ship, but not that ship. I've been here a week or two."

"Most people," she said, "don't stay as long as that."

It was a statement, not a question.

Llewellyn gestured to a waiter who came.

He ordered a Curaçao.

"May I order you something?"

"Thank you." she said. And added: "He knows."

The boy bowed his head in assent and went away.

They sat for a moment or two in silence.

"I suppose," she said at last, "you were lonely? There aren't many Americans or English here."

She was, he saw, settling the question of why he had spoken to her.

"No," he said at once. "I wasn't lonely. I find I'm—glad to be alone."

"Oh, one is, isn't one?"

The fervor with which she spoke surprised him.

"I see," he said. "That's why you come here?"

She nodded.

"To be alone. And now I've come and spoiled it?"

"No," she said. "You don't matter. You're a stranger, you see."

"I see."

"I don't even know your name."

"Do you want to?"

"No. I'd rather you didn't tell me. I won't tell you my name, either."

She added doubtfully:

"But perhaps you've been told that already. Everyone in the café knows me, of course."

"No, they haven't mentioned it. They understand, I think, that you would not want it told."

"They do understand. They have, all of them, such wonderful good manners. Not *taught* good manners—the natural thing. I could never have believed till I came here that natural courtesy could be such a wonderful—such a *positive* thing."

The waiter came back with their two drinks. Llewellyn paid him.

He looked over to the glass the girl held cupped in her two hands.

"Brandy?"

"Yes. Brandy helps a lot."

"It helps you to feel alone? Is that it?"

"Yes. It helps me to feel—free."

"And you're not free?"

"Is anybody free?"

He considered. She had not said the words bitterly—as they are usually spoken. She had been asking a simple question.

"*The fate of every man is bound about his neck*—is that what you feel?"

"No, I don't think so. Not quite. I can understand feeling rather like that, that your course was charted out like a ship's, and that you must follow it, again rather like a ship, and that so long as you do, you are all right. But I feel more like a ship that has, quite suddenly, gone off its proper course. And then, you see, you're lost. You don't know where you are, and you're at the mercy of the wind and sea, and you're not free, you're caught in the grip of something you don't understand—tangled up in it all." She added: "What nonsense I'm talking. I suppose it's the brandy."

He agreed.

"It's partly the brandy, no doubt. Where does it take you?"

"Oh, *away* . . . that's all—away. . . ."

"What is it, really, that you have to get away from?"

"Nothing. Absolutely nothing. That's the really—well, wicked part of it. I'm one of the fortunate ones. I've got everything." She repeated somberly: "Everything. . . . Oh, I don't mean I've not had sorrows, losses, but it's not that. I don't hanker and grieve over the past. I don't resurrect it and live it over again. I don't want to go back, or even forward. I just want to go *away* somewhere. I sit here drinking brandy and presently I'm out there, beyond the harbor, and going farther and farther—into some kind of unreal place that doesn't really exist. It's rather like the dreams of flying you have as a child—no weight—so light—floating."

The wide unfocused stare was coming back to her eyes. Llewellyn sat watching her.

Presently she came to herself with a little start.

"I'm sorry."

"Don't come back. I'm going now." He rose. "May I, now and then, come and sit here and talk to you? If you'd rather not, just say so. I shall understand."

"No, I should like you to come. Good night. I shan't go just yet. You see, it's not always that I can get away."

2

It was about a week later when they talked together again.

She said as soon as he sat down: "I'm glad you haven't gone away yet. I was afraid you might have gone."

"I shan't go away just yet. It's not time yet."

"Where will you go when you leave here?"

"I don't know."

"You mean—you're waiting for orders?"

"You might put it like that, yes."

She said slowly:

"Last time, when we talked, it was all about me. We didn't talk about you at all. Why did you come here—to the island? Had you a reason?"

"Perhaps it was for the same reason as you drink brandy—to get away, in my case from people."

"People in general, or do you mean special people?"

"Not people in general. I meant really people who know me—or knew me—as I was."

"Did something—happen?"

"Yes, something happened."

She leaned forward.

"Are you like me? Did something happen that put you off course?"

He shook his head with something that was almost vehemence.

"No, not at all. What happened to me was an intrinsic part of the pattern of my life. It had significance and intention."

"But what you said about people—"

"They don't understand, you see. They are sorry for me, and they want to drag me back—to something that's finished."

She wrinkled a puzzled brow.

"I don't quite—"

"I had a job," he said smiling. "Now—I've lost it."

"An important job?"

"I don't know." He was thoughtful. "I thought it was. But one can't really know, you see, what *is* important. One has to learn not to trust one's own values. Values are always relative."

"So you gave up your job?"

"No." His smile flashed out again. "I was sacked."

"Oh." She was taken aback. "Did you—mind?"

"Oh yes, I minded. Anyone would have. But that's all over now."

She frowned at her empty glass. As she turned her head, the boy who had been waiting replaced the empty glass with a full one.

She took a couple of sips, then she said:

"Can I ask you something?"

"Go ahead."

"Do you think happiness is very important?"

He considered.

"That's a very difficult question to answer. If I were to say that happiness is vitally important, and that at the same time it doesn't matter at all, you'd think I was crazy."

"Can't you be a little clearer?"

"Well, it's rather like sex. Sex is vitally important, and yet doesn't matter. You're married?"

He had noticed the slim gold ring on her finger.

"I've been married twice."

"Did you love your husband?"

He left it in the singular, and she answered without quibbling.

"I loved him more than anything in the world."

"When you look back on your life with him, what are the things that come first to your mind, the moments that you will always remember? Are they of the first time you slept together—or are they of something else?"

Laughter came to her suddenly, and a quick enchanting gaiety.

"His hat," she said.

"Hat?"

"Yes. On our honeymoon. It blew away and he bought a native one, a ridiculous straw thing, and I said it would be more suitable for *me*. So I put it on, and then he put on mine—one of those silly bits of nonsense women wear, and we looked at each other and laughed. All trippers change hats, he said, and then he said: 'Good Lord, I do love you . . .' " Her voice caught. "I'll never forget."

"You see?" said Llewellyn. "Those are the magical moments—the moments of belonging—of everlasting sweetness—not sex. And yet if sex goes wrong, a marriage is completely ruined. So, in the same way, food is important—without it you cannot live, and yet, so long as you *are* fed, it occupies very little of your thoughts. Happiness is one of the foods of life, it encourages growth, it is a great teacher, but it is not the purpose of life, and is, in itself, not ultimately satisfying."

He added gently:

"Is it happiness that you want?"

"I don't know. I ought to be happy. I have everything to make me happy."

"But you want something more?"

"*Less*," she said quickly, "I want *less* out of life. It's too much—it's all too much."

She added, rather unexpectedly:

"It's all so *heavy*."

They sat for some time in silence.

"If I knew," she said at last, "if I knew in the least what I really wanted, instead of just being so negative and idiotic."

"But you do know what you want; you want to escape. Why don't you, then?"

"Escape?"

"Yes. What's stopping you? Money?"

"No, it's not money. I have money—not a great deal, but sufficient."

"What is it then?"

"It's so many things. You wouldn't understand." Her lips twisted in a sudden, ruefully humorous smile. "It's like Chekhov's three sisters, always moaning about going to Moscow; they never go, and never will, although I suppose they *could* just have gone to the station and taken a train to Moscow any day of their lives! Just as I could buy a ticket and sail on that ship out there, that sails tonight."

"Why don't you?"

He was watching her.

"You think you know the answer," she said.

He shook his head.

"No, I don't know the answer. I'm trying to help you find it."

"Perhaps I'm like Chekhov's three sisters. Perhaps I don't really want to go."

"Perhaps."

"Perhaps escape is just an idea that I play with."

"Possibly. We all have fantasies that help us to bear the lives we live."

"And escape is my fantasy?"

"I don't know. *You* know."

"I don't know anything—anything at all. I had every chance, I did the wrong thing. And then, when one has done the wrong thing, one has to stick to it, hasn't one?"

"I don't know."

"Must you go *on* saying that over and over?"

"I'm sorry, but it's true. You're asking me to come to a conclusion on something I know nothing about."

"It was a general principle."

"There isn't such a thing as a general principle."

"Do you mean"—she stared at him—"that there isn't such a thing as absolute right and wrong?"

"No, I didn't mean that. Of course there's absolute right and wrong, but that's a thing so far beyond our knowledge and comprehension, that we can only have the dimmest apprehension of it."

"But surely one knows what is right?"

"You have been taught it by the accepted canons of the day. Or, going further, you can feel it of your own instinctive knowledge. But even that's a long way off. People were burned at the stake, not by sadists or brutes, but by earnest and high-minded men, who believed that what they did was right. Read some of the law cases in ancient

Greece, of a man who refused to let his slaves be tortured so as to get at the truth, as was the prevalent custom. He was looked upon as a man who deliberately obscured justice. There was an earnest God-fearing clergyman in the States who beat his three-year-old son, whom he loved, to death, because the child refused to say his prayers."

"That's all horrible!"

"Yes, because time has changed our ideas."

"Then, what can we do?"

Her lovely bewildered face bent toward him.

"Follow your pattern, in humility—and hope."

"Follow one's pattern—yes, I see that, but my pattern—it's wrong somehow." She laughed. "Like when you're knitting a jumper and you've dropped a stitch a long way back."

"I wouldn't know about that," he said. "I've never knitted."

"Why wouldn't you give me an opinion just now?"

"It would only have been an opinion."

"Well?"

"And it might have influenced you. . . . I should think you're easily influenced."

Her face grew somber again.

"Yes. Perhaps that's what was wrong."

He waited for a moment or two, then he said in a matter-of-fact voice:

"What exactly *is* wrong?"

"Nothing." She looked at him despairingly. "Nothing. I've got everything any woman could want."

"You're generalizing again. You're not any woman. You're you. Have *you* got everything you want?"

"Yes, yes, *yes!* Love and kindness and money and luxury, and beautiful surroundings and companionship—everything. All the things that I would have chosen for myself. No, it's *me*. There's something wrong with *me*."

She looked at him defiantly. Strangely enough, she was comforted when he answered matter-of-factly:

"Oh yes. There's something wrong with *you*—that's very clear."

3

She pushed her brandy glass a little way away from her.

She said: "Can I talk about myself?"

"If you like."

"Because if I did, I might just see where—it all went wrong. That would help, I think."

"Yes. It might help."

"It's all been very nice and ordinary—my life, I mean. A happy childhood, a lovely home. I went to school and did all the ordinary things, and nobody was ever nasty to me; perhaps if they had been, it would have been better for me. Perhaps I was a spoiled brat—but no, I don't really think so. And I came home from school and played tennis and danced, and met young men, and wondered what job to take up—all the usual things."

"Sounds straightforward enough."

"And then I fell in love and married." Her voice changed slightly.

"And lived happily . . ."

"No." Her voice was thoughtful. "I loved him, but I was unhappy very often." She added: "That's why I asked you if happiness really mattered."

She paused, and then went on:

"It's so hard to explain. I wasn't very happy, but yet in a curious way it was all right—it was what I'd chosen, what I wanted. I didn't—go into it with my eyes shut. Of course I idealized him—one does. But I remember now, waking up very early one morning—it was about five o'clock, just before dawn. That's a cold, truthful time, don't you think? And I knew then—saw, I mean—what the future would become, I knew I shouldn't be really happy, I saw what he was like, selfish and ruthless in a gay kind of charming way, but I saw, too, that he was charming, and gay and lighthearted—and that I loved him, and that no one else would do, and that I would rather be unhappy, married to him, than smug and comfortable without him. And I thought I could, with luck, and if I wasn't too stupid, make a go of it. I accepted the fact that I loved him more than he would ever love me, and that I mustn't—ever—ask him for more than he wanted to give."

She stopped a moment, and then went on:

"Of course I didn't put it to myself as clearly as all that. I'm describing now what was then just a feeling. But it was *real*. I went back again to thinking him wonderful and inventing all sorts of noble things about him that weren't in the least true. But I'd had my *moment*—the moment when you do see what lies ahead of you, and you can turn back or go on. I did think in those cold early morning minutes when you see how difficult and—yes—frightening things are—I did think of turning back. But instead I chose to go on."

He said very gently:

"And you regret—?"

"No, *no!*" She was vehement. "I've never regretted. Every minute of it was worthwhile! There's only one thing to regret—that he died."

The deadness was gone from her eyes now. It was no longer a woman drifting away from life toward fairyland, who leaned forward facing him across the table. It was a woman passionately alive.

"He died too soon," she said. "What is it Macbeth says? *'She should have died hereafter.'* That's what I feel about him. He should have died hereafter."

He shook his head.

"We all feel that when people die."

"Do we? I wouldn't know. I know he was ill. I realize he'd have been a cripple for life. I realize he bore it all badly and hated his life, and took it out on everybody and principally on me. But he didn't *want* to die. In spite of everything he didn't want to die. That's why I resent it so passionately for him. He'd what amounts to a genius for living— even half a life, even a quarter, he would have enjoyed. Oh!" She raised her arms passionately. "I *hate* God for making him die."

She stopped then, and looked at him doubtfully. "I shouldn't have said that—that I hated God."

He said calmly: "It's much better to hate God than to hate your fellow men. You can't hurt God."

"No. But He can hurt you."

"Oh no, my dear. We hurt each other, and hurt ourselves."

"And make God our scapegoat?"

"That is what He has always been. He bears our burdens—the burden of our revolts, of our hates, yes, and of our love."

Chapter Three

1

In the afternoons, Llewellyn had formed the habit of going for long walks. He would start up from the town on a widely curving, zig-zagging road that led steadily upward until the town and the bay lay beneath him, looking curiously unreal in the stillness of the afternoon. It was the hour of the siesta, and no gaily colored dots moved on the waterfront, or on the occasionally glimpsed roads and streets. Up here on the hills, the only human creatures Llewellyn met were goatherds, little boys who wandered singing to themselves in the sunshine, or sat playing games of their own with little heaps of stones. These would give Llewellyn a grave good afternoon, without curiosity. They were accustomed to foreigners who strode energetically along, their shirts open at the neck, perspiring freely. Such foreigners were, they knew, either writers or painters. Though not numerous, they were, at least, no novelty. As Llewellyn had no apparatus of canvas or easel or even sketchbook with him, they put him down as a writer, and said to him politely: "Good afternoon."

Llewellyn returned their greetings and strode on.

He had no particular purpose in his wandering. He observed the scenery, but it had for him no special significance. Significance was within him, not yet clear and recognized, but gradually gaining form and shape.

A path led him through a grove of bananas. Once within its green spaces, he was struck by how immediately all sense of purpose or direction had to be abandoned. There was no knowing how far the bananas extended, and where or when he would emerge. It might be a tiny path, or it might extend for miles. One could only continue on one's way. Eventually one would emerge at the point where the path had led one. That point was already in existence, fixed. He himself could not determine it. What he could determine was his own progression—his feet trod the path as a result of his own will and purpose. He could turn back or he could continue. He had the freedom of his own integrity. To travel hopefully . . .

Presently with almost disconcerting suddenness, he came out from the green stillness of the bananas on to a bare hillside. A little below him, to one side of a path that zigzagged down the side of a hill, a man sat painting at an easel.

His back was to Llewellyn, who saw only the powerful line of shoulders outlined beneath the thin yellow shirt and a broad-brimmed battered felt hat stuck on the back of the painter's head.

Llewellyn descended the path. As he drew abreast, he slackened speed, looking with frank interest at the work proceeding on the canvas. After all, if a painter settled himself by what was evidently a well-trodden path, it was clear that he had no objection to being overlooked.

It was a vigorous bit of work, painted in strong bands of color, laid on with an eye to broad effect, rather than detail. It was a pleasing piece of craftsmanship, though without deep significance.

The painter turned his head sideways and smiled.

"Not my life work," he said cheerfully. "Just a hobby."

He was a man of perhaps between forty and fifty, with dark hair just tinged with gray. He was handsome, but Llewellyn was conscious not so much of his good looks as of the charm and magnetism of his personality. There was a warmth to him, a kindly radiating vitality that made him a person who, if met only once, would not easily be forgotten.

"It's extraordinary," said the painter meditatively, "the pleasure it gives one to squeeze out rich, luscious colors on to a palette and splash 'em all over a canvas! Sometimes one knows what one's trying to do, and sometimes one doesn't, but the pleasure is always there." He gave a quick upward glance. "You're not a painter?"

"No. I just happen to be staying here."

"I see." The other laid a streak of rose color unexpectedly on the blue of his sea. "Funny," he said. "That looks good. I thought it might. Inexplicable!"

He dropped his brush on to the palette, sighed pushed his dilapidated hat farther back on his head, and turned slightly sideways to get a better view of his companion. His eyes narrowed in sudden interest.

"Excuse me," he said, "but aren't you Dr. Llewellyn Knox?"

2

There was a moment's swift recoil, not translated into physical motion, before Llewellyn said tonelessly:

"That's so."

He was aware a moment later of how quick the other man's perceptions were.

"Stupid of me," he said. "You had a breakdown in health, didn't you? And I suppose you came here to get away from people. Well, you needn't worry. Americans seldom come to the island, the local inhabitants aren't interested in anybody but their own cousins and their cousins' cousins, and the births, deaths, and marriages of same, and I don't count. I live here."

He shot a quick glance at the other.

"That surprise you?"

"Yes, it does."

"Why?"

"Just to live—I should not have thought you would be contented with that."

"You're right, of course. I didn't come here originally to live. I was left a big estate here by a great-uncle of mine. It was in rather a bad way when I took it on. Gradually it's beginning to prosper. Interesting."

He added: "My name's Richard Wilding."

Llewellyn knew the name; traveler, writer—a man of varied interests and widely diffused knowledge in many spheres, archaeology, anthropology, entomology. He had heard it said of Sir Richard Wilding that there was no subject of which he had not some knowledge, yet withal he never pretended to be a professional. The charm of modesty was added to his other gifts.

"I have heard of you, of course," said Llewellyn. "Indeed, I have enjoyed several of your books very much indeed."

"And I, Dr. Knox, have attended your meetings—one of them; that is to say, at Olympia a year and a half ago."

Llewellyn looked at him in some surprise.

"That seems to surprise you," said Wilding, with a quizzical smile.

"Frankly, it does. Why did you come, I wonder?"

"To be frank, I came to scoff, I think."

"That does not surprise me."

"It doesn't seem to annoy you, either."

"Why should it?"

"Well, you're human, and you believe in your mission—or so I assume."

Llewellyn smiled a little.

"Oh yes, you can assume that."

Wilding was silent for a moment. Then he said, speaking with a disarming eagerness:

"You know, it's extraordinarily interesting to me to meet you like this. After attending the meeting, the thing I desired most was actually to meet you."

"Surely there would have been no difficulty about doing that?"

"In a certain sense, no. It would have been obligatory on you! But I wanted to meet you on very different terms—on such terms that you could, if you wanted to, tell me to go to the devil."

Llewellyn smiled again.

"Well, those conditions are fulfilled now. I have no longer any obligations."

Wilding eyed him keenly.

"I wonder now, are you referring to health or to viewpoint?"

"It's a question, I should say, of function."

"Hm—that's not very clear."

The other did not answer.

Wilding began to pack up his painting things.

"I'd like to explain to you just how I came to hear you at Olympia. I'll be frank, because I don't think you're the type of man to be offended by the truth when it's not offensively meant. I disliked very much—still do—all that that meeting at Olympia stood for. I dislike more than I can tell you the idea of mass religion relayed, as it were, by loudspeaker. It offends every instinct in me."

He noted the amusement that showed for a moment on Llewellyn's face.

"Does that seem to you very British and ridiculous?"

"Oh, I accept it as a point of view."

"I came therefore, as I have told you, to scoff. I expected to have my finer susceptibilities outraged."

"And you remained to bless?"

The question was more mocking than serious.

"No. My views in the main are unchanged. I dislike seeing God put on a commercial basis."

"Even by a commercial people in a commercial age? Do we not always bring to God the fruits in season?"

"That is a point, yes. No, what struck me very forcibly was something that I had not expected—your own very patent sincerity."

Llewellyn looked at him in genuine surprise.

"I should have thought that might be taken for granted."

"Now that I have met you, yes. But it might have been a racket—a comfortable and well-paid racket. There are political rackets, so why not religious rackets? Granted you've got the gift of the gab, which you certainly have, I imagine it's a thing you could do very well out of, if you put yourself over in a big way or could get someone to do that for you. The latter, I should imagine?"

It was half a question.

Llewellyn said soberly: "Yes, I was put over in a big way."

"No expense spared?"

"No expense spared."

"That, you know, is what intrigues me. How you could stand it? That is, after I had seen and heard you."

He slung his painting things over his shoulder.

"Will you come and dine with me one night? It would interest me enormously to talk to you. That's my house down there on the point.

The white villa with the green shutters. But just say so, if you don't want to. Don't bother to find an excuse."

Llewellyn considered for a moment before he replied:

"I should like to come very much."

"Good. Tonight?"

"Thank you."

"Nine o'clock. Don't change."

He strode away down the hillside. Llewellyn stood for a moment looking after him, then he resumed his own walk.

3

"So you go to the villa of the Señor Sir Wilding?"

The driver of the ramshackle Victoria was frankly interested. His dilapidated vehicle was gaily adorned with painted flowers, and his horse was decked with a necklace of blue beads. The horse, the carriage, and the driver seemed equally cheerful and serene.

"He is very sympathetic, the Señor Sir Wilding," he said. "He is not a stranger here. He is one of us. Don Estobal, who owned the villa and the land, he was old, very old. He let himself be cheated, all day long he read books, and more books came for him all the time. There are rooms in the villa lined with books to the ceiling. It is incredible that a man should want so many books. And then he dies, and we all wonder, will the villa be sold? But then Sir Wilding comes. He has been here as a boy, often, for Don Estobal's sister married an Englishman, and her children and her children's children would come here in the holidays from their schools. But after Don Estobal's death the estate belongs to Sir Wilding, and he comes here to inherit, and he starts at once to put all in order, and he spends much money to do so. But then there comes the war, and he goes away for many years, but he says always that if he is not killed, he will return here—and so at last he has done so. Two years ago it is now since he returned here with his new wife, and has settled here to live."

"He has married twice then?"

"Yes." The driver lowered his voice confidentially. "His first wife was a bad woman. She was beautiful, yes, but she deceived him much with other men—yes, even here in the island. He should not have married her. But where women are concerned, he is not clever—he believes too much."

He added, almost apologetically:

"A man should know whom to trust, but Sir Wilding does not. He does not know about women. I do not think he will ever learn."

Chapter Four

His host received Llewellyn in a long, low room, lined to the ceiling with books. The windows were thrown open, and from some distance below there came the gentle murmur of the sea. Drinks were set on a low table near the window.

Wilding greeted him with obvious pleasure, and apologized for his wife's absence.

"She suffers badly from migraine," he said. "I hoped that with the peace and quiet of her life out here it might improve, but it hasn't done so noticeably. And doctors don't really seem to have the answer for it."

Llewellyn expressed his sorrow politely.

"She's been through a lot of trouble," said Wilding. "More than any girl should be asked to bear. And she was so young—still is."

Reading his face, Llewellyn said gently:

"You love her very much."

Wilding sighed:

"Too much, perhaps, for my own happiness."

"And for hers?"

"No love in the world could be too much to make up to her for all she has suffered."

He spoke vehemently.

Between the two men there was already a curious sense of intimacy which had, indeed, existed from the first moment of their meeting. It was as though the fact that neither of them had anything in common with the other—nationality, upbringing, way of life, beliefs—made them therefore ready to accept each other without the usual barriers of reticence or conventionality. They were like men marooned together on a desert island, or afloat on a raft for an indefinite period. They could speak to each other frankly, almost with the simplicity of children.

Presently they went into dinner. It was an excellent meal, beautifully served, of a very simple character. There was wine which Llewellyn refused.

"If you'd prefer whiskey . . ."

The other shook his head.

"Thank you—just water."

"Is that—excuse me—a principle with you?"

"No. Actually it is a way of life that I need no longer follow. There is no reason—now—why I should not drink wine. Simply I am not used to it."

As he uttered the word 'now,' Wilding raised his head sharply. He looked intensely interested. He almost opened his mouth to speak, then rather obviously checked himself, and began to talk of extraneous matters. He was a good talker, with a wide range of subjects. Not only had he traveled extensively, and in many unknown parts of the globe, but he had the gift of making all he himself had seen and experienced equally real to the person who was listening to him.

If you wanted to go to the Gobi Desert, or to the Fezzan, or to Samarkand, when you had talked of those places with Richard Wilding, you had been there.

It was not that he lectured, or in any way held forth. His conversation was natural and spontaneous.

Quite apart from his enjoyment of Wilding's talk, Llewellyn found himself increasingly interested by the personality of the man himself. His charm and magnetism were undeniable, and they were also, so Llewellyn judged, entirely unself-conscious. Wilding was not exerting himself to radiate charm; it was natural to him. He was a man of parts, too, shrewd, intellectual without arrogance, a man with a vivid interest in ideas and people as well as in places. If he had chosen to specialize in some particular subject—but that, perhaps, was his secret: he never had so chosen, and never would. That left him human, warm, and essentially approachable.

And yet, it seemed to Llewellyn, he had not quite answered his own question—a question as simple as that put by a child. "Why do I like this man so much?"

The answer was not in Wilding's gifts. It was something in the man himself.

And suddenly, it seemed to Llewellyn, he got it. It was because, with all his gifts, the man himself was fallible. He was a man who could, who would, again and again prove himself mistaken. He had one of those warm, kindly emotional natures that invariably meet rebuffs because of their untrustworthiness in making judgments.

Here was no clear, cool, logical appraisal of men and things; instead there were warmhearted impulsive beliefs, mainly in people, which were doomed to disaster because they were based on kindliness always rather than on fact. Yes, the man was fallible, and being fallible, he was also lovable. Here, thought Llewellyn, is someone whom I should hate to hurt.

They were back again now in the library, stretched out in two big armchairs. A wood fire had been lit, more to convey the sense of a hearth, than because it was needed. Outside the sea murmured, and the scent of some night-blooming flower stole into the room.

Wilding was saying disarmingly:

"I'm so interested, you see, in people. I always have been. In what makes them tick, if I might put it that way. Does that sound very cold-blooded and analytical?"

"Not from you. You wonder about your fellow human beings because you care for them and are therefore interested in them."

"Yes, that's true." He paused. Then he said: "If one can help a fellow human being, that seems to me the most worthwhile thing in the world."

"If," said Llewellyn.

The other looked at him sharply.

"That seems oddly skeptical, coming from you."

"No, it's only a recognition of the enormous difficulty of what you propose."

"Is it so difficult? Human beings want to be helped."

"Yes, we all tend to believe that in some magical manner others can attain for us what we can't—or don't want to—attain for ourselves."

"Sympathy—and belief," said Wilding earnestly. "To believe the best of someone is to call the best into being. People respond to one's belief in them. I've found that again and again."

"For how long?"

Wilding winced, as though something had touched a sore place in him.

"You can guide a child's hand on the paper, but when you take your hand away the child still has to learn to write himself. Your action may, indeed, have delayed the process."

"Are you trying to destroy my belief in human nature?"

Llewellyn smiled as he said:

"I think I'm asking you to have pity on human nature."

"To encourage people to give of their best—"

"Is forcing them to live at a very high altitude; to keep up being what someone expects you to be is to live under a great strain. Too great a strain leads eventually to collapse."

"Must one then expect the worst of people?" asked Wilding satirically.

"One should recognize that probability."

"And you a man of religion!"

Llewellyn smiled:

"Christ told Peter that before the cock crew, he would have denied Him thrice. He knew Peter's weakness of character better than Peter himself knew it, and loved him none the less for it."

"No," said Wilding, with vigour, "I can't agree with you. In my own first marriage"—he paused, then went on—"my wife was—could have been—a really fine character. She'd got into a bad set; all she needed was love, trust, belief. If it hadn't been for the war—" He stopped. "Well, it was one of the lesser tragedies of war. I was away, she was alone, exposed to bad influences."

He paused again before saying abruptly: "I don't blame her. I make allowances—she was the victim of circumstances. It broke me up at the time. I thought I'd never feel the same man again. But time heals. . . ."

He made a gesture.

"Why I should tell you the history of my life I don't know. I'd much rather hear about your life. You see, you're something absolutely new to me. I want to know the 'why' and 'how' of you. I was impressed when I came to that meeting, deeply impressed. Not because you swayed your audience—that I can understand well enough. Hitler did it. Lloyd George did it. Politicians, religious leaders, and actors, they can all do it in a greater or lesser degree. It's a gift. No, I wasn't interested in the *effect* you were having, I was interested in *you*. Why was this particular thing worthwhile to you?"

Llewellyn shook his head slowly.

"You are asking me something that I do not know myself."

"Of course, a strong religious conviction." Wilding spoke with slight embarrassment, which amused the other.

"You mean, belief in God? That's a simpler phrase, don't you think? But it doesn't answer your question. Belief in God might take me to my knees in a quiet room. It doesn't explain what you are asking me to explain. Why the public platform?"

Wilding said rather doubtfully:

"I can imagine that you might feel that in that way you could do more good, reach more people."

Llewellyn looked at him in a speculative manner.

"From the way you put things, I am to take it that you yourself are not a believer?"

"I don't know, I simply don't know. Yes, I do believe in a way. I want to believe . . . I certainly believe in the positive virtues—kindness, helping those who are down, straight dealing, forgiveness."

Llewellyn looked at him for some moments.

"The Good Life," he said. "The Good Man. Yes, that's much easier than to attempt the recognition of God. That's *not* easy, it's very difficult, and very frightening. And what's even more frightening is to stand up to God's recognition of *you*."

"Frightening?"

"It frightened Job." Llewellyn smiled suddenly: "He hadn't an idea, you know, poor fellow, as to what it was all about. In a world of nice rules and regulations, rewards and punishments, doled out by Almighty God strictly according to merit, he was singled out. (Why? We don't know. Some quality in him in advance of his generation? Some power of perception given him at birth?) Anyway, the others could go on being rewarded and punished, but Job had to step into what must have seemed to him a new dimension. After a meritorious life, he was *not* to be rewarded with flocks and herds. Instead, he was to pass through unendurable suffering, to lose his beliefs, and see his friends back away from him. He had to endure the whirlwind. And then, perhaps, having been groomed for stardom, as we say in Hollywood, he could hear the voice of God. And all for what? So that he could begin to recognize what God actually *was*. 'Be still and know that I am God.' A terrifying experience. The highest pinnacle that man, so far, had reached. It didn't, of course, last long. It couldn't. And he probably made a fine mess trying to tell about it, because there wasn't the vocabulary, and you can't describe in terrestrial terms an experience that is spiritual. And whoever tidied up the end of the Book of Job hadn't an idea what it was all about either, but he made it have a good moral happy ending, according to the lights of the time, which was very sensible of him."

Llewellyn paused.

"So you see," he said, "that when you say that perhaps I chose the public platform because I could do more good, and reach more people, that simply is miles off the course. There's no numerical value in reaching people as such, and 'doing good' is a term that really hasn't any significance. What *is* doing good? Burning people at the stake to save their souls? Perhaps. Burning witches alive because they are evil personified? There's a very good case for it. Raising the standard of living for the unfortunate? We think nowadays that that is important. Fighting against cruelty and injustice?"

"Surely you agree with that?"

"What I'm getting at is that these are all problems of *human* conduct. What is good to do? What is right to do? What is wrong to do? We are human beings, and we have to answer those questions to the best of our ability. We have our life to live in this world. But all that has nothing to do with spiritual experience."

"Ah," said Wilding. "I begin to understand. I think you yourself went through some such experience. How did it come about? What happened? Did you always know, even as a child—?"

He did not finish the question.

"Or had you," he said slowly, "no idea?"

"I had no idea," said Llewellyn.

Chapter Five

No idea . . . Wilding's question had taken Llewellyn back into the past. A long way back.

He himself as a child . . .

The pure clear tang of the mountain air was in his nostrils. The cold winters, the hot, arid summers. The small closely knit community. His father, that tall, gaunt Scot, austere, almost grim. A God-fearing, upright man, a man of intellect, despite the simplicity of his life and calling, a man who was just and inflexible, and whose affections, though deep and true, were not easily shown. His dark-haired Welsh mother, with the lilting voice which made her most ordinary speech sound like music . . . Sometimes, in the evenings, she would recite in Welsh the poem that her father had composed for the Eisteddfod long years ago. The language was only partly understood by her children, the meaning of the words remained obscure, but the music of the poetry stirred Llewellyn to vague longings for he knew not what. A strange intuitive knowledge his mother had, not intellectual like his father, but a natural innate wisdom of her own.

Her dark eyes would pass slowly over her assembled children and would linger longest on Llewellyn, her firstborn, and in them would be an appraisement, a doubt, something that was almost fear.

That look would make the boy himself restless. He would ask apprehensively: "What is it, Mother? What have I done?"

Then she would smile, a warm, caressing smile, and say:

"Nothing, bach. It's my own good son you are."

And Angus Knox would turn his head sharply and look, first at his wife, and then at the boy.

It had been a happy childhood, a normal boy's childhood. Not luxurious, indeed spartan in many ways. Strict parents, a disciplined way
of life. Plenty of home chores, responsibility for the four younger children, participation in the community activities. A godly but narrow way
of life. And he fitted in, accepted it.

But he had wanted education, and here his father had encouraged
him. He had the Scot's reverence for learning, and was ambitious for
this eldest son of his to become something more than a mere tiller of
the soil.

"I'll do what I can to help you, Llewellyn, but that will not be much.
You'll have to manage mostly for yourself."

And he had done so. Encouraged by his teacher, he had gone ahead
and put himself through college. He had worked on vacations, waiting
in hotels and camps, he had done evening work washing dishes.

With his father he had discussed his future. Either a teacher or a
doctor, he decided. He had had no particular sense of vocation, but
both careers seemed to him congenial. He finally chose medicine.

Through all these years, was there no hint of dedication, of special
mission? He thought back, trying to remember.

There had been *something* . . . yes, looking back from today's viewpoint, there had been something. Something not understood by himself
at the time. A kind of fear—that was the nearest he could get to it.
Behind the normal facade of daily life, a fear, a dread of something that
he himself did not understand. He was more conscious of this fear when
he was alone, and he had, therefore, thrown himself eagerly into community life.

It was about that time he became conscious of Carol.

He had known Carol all his life. They had gone to school together.
She was two years younger than he was, a gawky, sweet-tempered child,
with a brace on her teeth and a shy manner. Their parents were friends,
and Carol spent a lot of time in the Knox household.

In the year of taking his finals, Llewellyn came home and saw Carol
with new eyes. The brace was gone, and so was the gawkiness. Instead
there was a pretty coquettish young girl, whom all the boys were anxious to date up.

Girls had so far not impinged much on Llewellyn's life. He had worked too hard, and was, moreover, emotionally undeveloped. But now the manhood in him suddenly came to life. He started taking trouble with his appearance, spent money he could ill afford on new ties, and bought boxes of candy to present to Carol. His mother smiled and sighed, as mothers do, at the signs that her son had entered on maturity! The time had come when she must lose him to another woman. Too early to think of marriage as yet, but if it had to come, Carol would be a satisfactory choice. Good stock, carefully brought up, a sweet-tempered girl, and healthy—better than some strange girl from the city whom she did not know. 'But not good enough for my son,' said her mother's heart, and then she smiled at herself, guessing that that was what all mothers had felt since time immemorial! She spoke hesitantly to Angus of the matter.

"Early days yet," said Angus. "The lad has his way to make. But he might do worse. She's a good lass, though maybe not overloaded with brains."

Carol was both pretty and popular, and enjoyed her popularity. She had plenty of dates, but she made it fairly clear that Llewellyn was the favorite. She talked to him sometimes in a serious way about his future. Though she did not show it, she was slightly disconcerted by his vagueness and what seemed to her his lack of ambition.

"Why, Lew, surely you've got *some* definite plans for when you've qualified?"

"Oh! I shall get a job all right. Plenty of openings."

"But don't you have to specialize nowadays?"

"If one has any particular bent. I haven't."

"But, Llewellyn Knox, you want to get on, don't you?"

"Get on—where?" His smile was slightly teasing.

"Well—get *somewhere.*"

"But that is life, isn't it, Carol? From here to here." His finger traced a line on the sand. "Birth, growth, school, career, marriage, children, home, hard work, retirement, old age, death. From the frontier of this country to the frontier of the next."

"That's not what I mean at all, Lew, and you know it. I mean getting *somewhere*, making a name for yourself, making good, getting right to the top, so that everyone's proud of you."

"I wonder if all that makes any difference," he said abstractedly.

"I'll say it makes a difference!"

"It's *how* you go through your journey that matters, I think, not where it takes you."

"I never heard such nonsense. Don't you *want* to be a success?"

"I don't know. I don't think so."

Carol was a long way away from him suddenly. He was alone, quite alone, and he was conscious of fear. A shrinking, a terrible shrinking. "Not me—someone else." He almost said the words aloud.

"Lew! Llewellyn!" Carol's voice came thinly to him from a long way away, coming toward him through the wilderness. "What's the matter? You look downright queer."

He was back again, back with Carol, who was staring at him with a perplexed, frightened expression. He was conscious of a rush of tenderness toward her. She had saved him, called him back from that barren place. He took her hand.

"You're so sweet." He drew her toward him, kissed her gently, almost shyly. Her lips responded to his.

He thought: 'I can tell her now . . . that I love her . . . that when I'm qualified we can get engaged. I'll ask her to wait for me. Once I've got Carol, I'll be safe.'

But the words remained unspoken. He felt something that was almost like a physical hand on his breast, pushing him back, a hand that forbade. The reality of it alarmed him. He got up.

"Someday, Carol," he said, "someday I—I've got to talk to you."

She looked up at him and laughed, satisfied. She was not particularly anxious for him to come to the point. Things were best left as they were. She enjoyed in an innocent happy fashion her own young girl's hour of triumph, courted by the young males. Someday she and Llewellyn would marry. She had felt the emotion behind his kiss. She was quite sure of him.

As for his queer lack of ambition, that did not really worry her. Women in this country were confident of their power over men. It was women who planned and urged on their men to achieve; women, and the children that were their principal weapons. She and Llewellyn would want the best for their children, and that would be a spur to urge Llewellyn on.

As for Llewellyn, he walked home in a serious state of perturbation. What a very odd experience that had been. Full of recent lectures on psychology, he analyzed himself with misgiving. A resistance to sex perhaps? Why had he set up this resistance? He ate his supper staring at his mother, and wondering uneasily if he had an Oedipus Complex.

Nevertheless, it was to her he came for reassurance before he went back to college.

He said abruptly:

"You like Carol, don't you?"

Here it comes, she thought with a pang, but she said steadfastly:

"She's a sweet girl. Both your father and I like her well."

"I wanted to tell her—the other day—"

"That you loved her?"

"Yes. I wanted to ask her to wait for me."

"No need of that, if she loves you, bach."

"But I couldn't say it, the words wouldn't come."

She smiled. "Don't let that worry you. Men are mostly tongue-tied at these times. There was your father sitting and glowering at me, day after day, more as though he hated me than loved me, and not able to get a word out but 'How are you?' and 'It's a fine day.' "

Llewellyn said sombrely: "It was more than that. It was like a hand shoving me back. It was as though I was—*forbidden*."

She felt then the urgency and force of his trouble. She said slowly:

"It may be that she's not the real girl for you. Oh—" she stifled his protest. "It's hard to tell when you're young and the blood rises. But there's something in you—the true self, maybe—that knows what should and shouldn't be, and that saves you from yourself, and the impulse that isn't the true one."

"Something in oneself . . ." He dwelt on that.

He looked at her with sudden desperate eyes.

"I don't know really—anything about myself."

2

Back at college, he filled up every moment, either with work or in the company of friends. Fear faded away from him. He felt self-assured once more. He read abstruse dissertations on adolescent sex manifestations, and explained himself to himself satisfactorily.

He graduated with distinction, and that, too, encouraged him to have confidence in himself. He returned home with his mind made up, and his future clear ahead. He would ask Carol to marry him, and discuss with her the various possibilities open to him now that he was qualified. He felt an enormous relief now that his life unfolded before him in so clear a sequence. Work that was congenial and which he felt himself competent to do well, and a girl he loved with whom to make a home and have children.

Arrived at home, he threw himself into all the local festivities. He went about in a crowd, but within that crowd he and Carol paired off and were accepted as a pair. He was seldom, if ever, alone, and when he went to bed at night he slept and dreamed of Carol. They were erotic dreams and he welcomed them as such. Everything was normal, everything was fine, everything was as it should be.

Confident in this belief, he was startled when his father said to him one day:

"What's wrong, lad?"

"Wrong?" He stared.

"You're not yourself."

"But I am! I've never felt so fit!"

"You're well enough physically, maybe."

Llewellyn stared at his father. The gaunt, aloof old man, with his deep-set burning eyes, nodded his head slowly.

"There are times," he said, "when a man needs to be alone."

He said no more, turning away, as Llewellyn felt once more that swift illogical fear spring up. He *didn't* want to be alone—it was the last thing he wanted. He couldn't, he *mustn't* be alone.

Three days later he came to his father and said:

"I'm going camping in the mountains. By myself."

Angus nodded. "Ay."

His eyes, the eyes of a mystic, looked at his son with comprehension. Llewellyn thought: 'I've inherited something from him—something that *he* knows about, and I don't know about yet.'

3

He had been alone here, in the desert, for nearly three weeks. Curious things had been happening to him. From the very first, however, he had found solitude quite acceptable. He wondered why he had fought against the idea of it so long.

To begin with, he had thought a great deal about himself and his future and Carol. It had all unrolled itself quite clearly and logically, and it was not for some time that he realized that he was looking at his life from *outside*, as a spectator and not a participator. That was because none of that mapped-out planned existence was real. It was logical and coherent, but in fact it did not exist. He loved Carol, he desired her, but he would not marry her. He had something else to do. As yet he did not know what. After he had acknowledged that fact, there came another phase—a phase he could only describe as one of emptiness, great echoing emptiness. He was nothing, and contained nothing. There was no longer any fear. By accepting emptiness, he had cast out fear.

During this phase, he ate and drank hardly anything.

Sometimes he was, he thought, slightly lightheaded.

Like a mirage in front of him, scenes and people appeared.

Once or twice he saw a face very clearly. It was a woman's face, and it roused in him an extraordinary excitement. It had fragile, very beautiful bones, with hollowed temples, and dark hair springing back from the temples, and deep, almost tragic eyes. Behind her he saw, once, a background of flames, and another time the shadowy outline of what looked like a church. This time, he saw suddenly that she was only a child. Each time he was conscious of suffering. He thought: 'If I could only help . . .' But at the same time he knew that there was no help possible, and that the very idea was wrong and false.

Another vision was of a gigantic office desk in pale shining wood, and behind it a man with a heavy jowl and small, alert, blue eyes. The man leaned forward as though about to speak, and to do so emphasized what he was about to say by picking up a small ruler and gesticulating with it.

Then again he saw the corner of a room at a curious angle. Near it was a window, and through the window the outlines of a pine tree with snow on it. Between him and the window, a face obtruded, looking down on him—a round, pink-faced man with glasses, but before Llewellyn could see him really clearly, he, too, faded away.

All these visions must, Llewellyn thought, be the figments of his own imagination. There seemed so little sense or meaning to them, and they were all faces and surroundings that he had never known.

But soon there were no more pictorial images. The emptiness of which he was so conscious was no longer vast and all-encompassing. The emptiness drew together, it acquired meaning and purpose. He was no longer adrift in it. Instead, he held it within himself.

Then he knew something more. He was waiting.

4

The dust storm came suddenly—one of those unheralded storms that arose in this mountainous desert region. It came whirling and shrieking in clouds of red dust. It was like a live thing. It ended as suddenly as it had begun.

After it, the silence was very noticeable.

All Llewellyn's camping gear had been swept away by the wind, his tent carried flapping and whirling like a mad thing down the valley. He had nothing now. He was quite alone in a world suddenly peaceful and as though made anew.

He knew now that something he had always known would happen was about to happen. He knew fear again, but not the fear he had felt before, that had been the fear of resistance. This time he was ready to accept—there was emptiness within him, swept and garnished, ready to receive a Presence. He was afraid only because in all humility he knew what a small and insignificant entity he was.

It was not easy to explain to Wilding what came next.

"Because, you see, there aren't any words for it. But I'm quite clear as to *what* it was. It was the recognition of God. I can express it best by saying that it was as though a blind man who believed in the sun from literary evidence, and who had felt its warmth on his hand, was suddenly to open his eyes and *see* it.

"I had *believed* in God, but now I *knew*. It was direct personal knowledge, quite indescribable. And a most terrifying experience for any human being. I understood then why, in God's approach to man, He has to incarnate Himself in human flesh.

"Afterward—it only lasted a few seconds of time—I turned around and went home. It took me two or three days, and I was very weak and exhausted when I staggered in."

He was silent for a moment or two.

"My mother was dreadfully worried over me! She couldn't make it all out. My father, I think, had an inkling. He knew, at least, that I had had some vast experience. I told my mother that I had had curious visions that I couldn't explain, and she said: 'They have the "sight" in your father's family. His grandmother had it, and one of his sisters.'

"After a few days of rest and feeding up, I was strong again. When people talked of my future, I was silent. I knew that all that would be settled for me. I had only to accept—I had accepted—but *what* it was I had accepted, I didn't yet know.

"A week later, there was a big prayer meeting held in the neighborhood. A kind of Revivalist Mission is how I think you describe it. My mother wanted to go, and my father was willing, though not much interested. I went with them."

Looking at Wilding, Llewellyn smiled.

"It wasn't the sort of thing *you* would have cared for—crude, rather melodramatic. It didn't move me. I was a little disappointed that that was so. Various people got up to testify. Then the command came to me, clear and quite unmistakable.

"I got up. I remember the faces turning to me.

"I didn't know what I was going to say. I didn't think—or expound my own beliefs. The words were there in my head. Sometimes they got ahead of me, I had to speak faster to catch up, to say them before I lost them. I can't describe to you what it was like—if I said it was like flame and like honey, would you understand at all? The flame seared me, but the sweetness of the honey was there too, the sweetness of obedience. It is both a terrible and a lovely thing to be the messenger of God."

"Terrible as an army with banners," murmured Wilding.

"Yes. The psalmist knew what he was talking about."

"And—afterwards?

Llewellyn Knox spread out his hands.

"Exhaustion, utter and complete exhaustion. I must have spoken, I suppose, for about three-quarters of an hour. When I got home, I sat by the fire shivering, too dead to lift a hand or to speak. My mother understood. She said: 'It is like my father was, after the Eisteddfod.' She gave me hot soup and put hot-water bottles in my bed."

Wilding murmured: "You had all the necessary heredity. The mystic from the Scottish side, and the poetic and creative from the Welsh—the voice, too. And it's a true creative picture—the fear, the frustration, the emptiness, and then the sudden uprush of power, and after it, the weariness."

He was silent for a moment, and then asked:

"Won't you go on with the story?"

"There's not so much more to tell. I went and saw Carol the next day. I told her I wasn't going to be a doctor after all, that I was going to be a preacher of some kind. I told her that I had hoped to marry her, but that now I had to give up that hope. She didn't understand. She said: 'A doctor can do just as much good as a preacher can do.' And I said it wasn't a question of doing good. It was a command, and I had to obey it. And she said it was nonsense saying I couldn't get married. I wasn't a Roman Catholic, was I? And I said: 'Everything I am, and have, has to be God's.' But of course she couldn't see that—how could she, poor child? It wasn't in her vocabulary. I went home and told my mother, and asked her to be good to Carol, and begged her to understand. She said: 'I understand well enough. You'll have nothing left over to give a woman,' and then she broke down and cried, and said: 'I knew—I always knew—there was *something*. You were different from the others. Ah, but it's hard on the wives and mothers.'

"She said: 'If I lost you to a woman, that's the way of life, and there would have been your children for me to hold on my knee. But this way, you'll be gone from me entirely.'

"I assured her that wasn't true, but all the time we both knew that it was in essence. Human ties—they all had to go."

Wilding moved restlessly.

"You must forgive me, but I can't subscribe to that, as a way of life. Human affection, human sympathy, service to humanity—"

"But it isn't a way of life that I am talking about! I am talking of the man singled out, the man who is something more than his fellows, and who is also very much less—that is the thing he must never forget, how infinitely less than they he is, and must be."

"There I can't follow you."

Llewellyn spoke softly, more to himself than to his listener.

"That, of course, is the danger—that one will forget. That, I see now, is where God showed mercy to me. I was saved in time."

Chapter Six

1

Wilding looked faintly puzzled by Llewellyn's last words.

He said with a faint trace of embarrassment: "It's good of you to have told me all you have. Please believe that it wasn't just vulgar curiosity on my part."

"I know that. You have a real interest in your fellowman."

"And you are an unusual specimen. I've read in various periodicals accounts of your career. But it wasn't those things that interested me. Those details are merely factual."

Llewellyn nodded. His mind was still occupied with the past. He was remembering the day when the elevator had swept him up to the thirty-fifth floor of a high building. The reception room, the tall, elegant blonde who had received him, the square-shouldered, thickset young man, to whom she had handed him over, and the final sanctuary; the inner office of the magnate. The gleaming pale surface of the vast desk, and the man who rose from behind the desk to proffer a hand and utter a welcome. The big jowl, the small, piercing blue eyes. Just as he had seen them that day in the desert.

". . . certainly glad to make your acquaintance, Mr. Knox. As I see it, the country is ripe for a great return to God . . . got to be put over in a big way . . . to get results we've got to spend money . . . been to two of your meetings . . . I certainly was impressed . . . you'd got them right with you, eating up every word . . . it was great . . . great!"

God and Big Business. Did they seem incongruous together? And yet, why should they? If business acumen was one of God's gifts to man, why should it not be used in his service?

He, Llewellyn, had had no doubts or qualms, for this room and this man had already been shown to him. It was part of the pattern, *his* pattern. Was there sincerity here, a simple sincerity that might seem as grotesque as the early carvings on a font? Or was it the mere grasping of a business opportunity? The realization that God might be made to pay?

Llewellyn had never known, had not, indeed, troubled himself even to wonder. It was part of his pattern. He was a messenger, nothing more, a man under obedience.

Fifteen years . . . from the small open-air meetings of the beginning, to lecture rooms, to halls, to vast stadiums.

Faces, blurred gigantic masses of faces, receding into the distance, rising up in serried rows. Waiting, hungering . . .

And his part? Always the same.

The coldness, the recoil of fear, the emptiness, the waiting.

And then Dr. Llewellyn Knox rises to his feet and . . . the words come, rushing through his mind, emerging through his lips. . . . Not his words, never his words. But the glory, the ecstasy of speaking them, that was his.

(That, of course, was where the danger had lain. Strange that he should not have realized that until now.)

And then the aftermath, the fawning women, the hearty men, his own sense of semicollapse, of deadly nausea, the hospitality, the adulation, the hysteria.

And he himself, responding as best he could, no longer the messenger of God, but the inadequate human being, something far less than those who looked at him with their foolish worshipping gaze. For virtue had gone out of him, he was drained of all that gives a man human dignity, a sick exhausted creature, filled with despair, black, empty, hollow despair.

"Poor Dr. Knox," they said, "he looks so tired."

Tired. More and more tired . . .

He had been a strong man physically, but not strong enough to outlast fifteen years. Nausea, giddiness, a fluttering heart, a difficulty in drawing breath, blackouts, fainting spells—quite simply, a worn-out body.

And so the sanatorium in the mountains. Lying there motionless, staring out through the window at the dark shape of the pine tree cutting the line of the sky, and the round, pink face bending over him, the eyes behind the thick glasses, owlish in their solemnity.

"It will be a long business; you'll have to be patient."

"Yes, doctor?"

"You've a strong constitution fortunately, but you've strained it unmercifully. Heart, lungs—every organ in your body has been affected."

"Are you breaking it to me that I'm going to die?"

He had asked the question with only mild curiosity.

"Certainly not. We'll get you right again. As I say, it will be a long business, but you'll go out of here a fit man. Only—"

The doctor hesitated.

"Only what?"

"You must understand this, Dr. Knox. You'll have to lead a quiet life in future. There must be no more public life. Your heart won't stand it. No platforms, no exertion, no speeches."

"After a rest—"

"No, Dr. Knox, however long you rest, my verdict will be the same."

"I see." He thought about it. "I see. Worn out?"

"Just that."

Worn out. Used by God for His purpose, but the instrument, being human and frail, had not lasted long. His usefulness was over. Used, discarded, thrown away.

And what next?

That was the question? What next?

Because, after all, who was he, Llewellyn Knox?

He would have to find out.

2

Wilding's voice came in, pat upon his thoughts.

"Is it in order for me to ask you what your future plans are?"

"I have no plans."

"Really? You hope, perhaps, to go back—"

Llewellyn interrupted, a slight harshness in his voice.

"There is no going back."

"Some modified form of activity?"

"No. It's a clean break—has to be."

"They told you that?"

"Not in so many words. Public life is out, was what they stressed. No more platform. That means finish."

"A quiet living somewhere? Living is not your term, I know, but I mean minister to some church?"

"I was an Evangelist, Sir Richard. That's a very different thing."

"I'm sorry. I think I understand. You've got to start an entirely new life."

"Yes, a private life, as a man."

"And that confuses and alarms you?"

Llewellyn shook his head.

"Nothing like that. I see, I've seen it plainly in the weeks I've been here, that I've escaped a great danger."

"What danger?"

"Man cannot be trusted with power. It rots him—from within. How much longer could I have gone on without the taint creeping in? I suspect that already it had begun to work. Those moments when I spoke to those vast crowds of people—wasn't I beginning to assume that it was *I* who was speaking, *I* who was giving them a message, I who knew just what they should or should not do, I who was no longer just God's messenger, but God's representative? You see? Promoted to Vizier, exalted, a man set above other men!" He added quietly: "God in His goodness has seen fit to save me from that."

"Then your faith has not been diminished by what has happened to you?"

Llewellyn laughed.

"Faith? That seems an odd word to me. Do we believe in the sun, the moon, the chair we sit in, the ground we walk upon? If one has knowledge, what need of belief? And do disabuse your mind of the idea that I've suffered some kind of tragedy. I haven't, I've pursued my appointed course—am still pursuing it. It was right for me to come here—to the island; it will be right for me to leave it when the time comes."

"You mean you will get another—what did you call it?—command?"

"Oh no, nothing so definite. But little by little a certain course of action will appear not only to be desirable, but inevitable. Then I shall go ahead and act. Things will clarify themselves in my mind. I shall know where I have to go and what I have to do."

"As easy as that?"

"I think so—yes. If I can explain it, it's a question of being in *harmony*. A wrong course of action—and by wrong I don't mean wrong in the sense of evil, but of being mistaken—is felt at once: it's like falling out of step if you're dancing, or singing a false note—it jars." Moved by a sudden memory, he said: "If I was a woman, I daresay it would feel like getting a stitch wrong when you were knitting."

"What about women? Will you, perhaps, go back home? Find your early love?"

"The sentimental ending? Hardly. Besides," he smiled, "Carol has been married for many years now. She has three children, and her husband is going ahead in real estate in a big way. Carol and I were never meant for each other. It was a boy and girl affair that never went deep."

"Has there been no other woman in all these years?"

"No, thank God. If there had been, if I had met her then—"

He left the sentence unfinished, puzzling Wilding a little by so doing. Wilding could have no clue to the picture that sprang up before Llewellyn's mental vision—the wings of dark hair, the frail delicate temple-bones, the tragic eyes.

Someday, Llewellyn knew, he would meet her. She was as real as the office desk and the sanatorium had been. She existed. If he had met her during the time of his dedication he would have been forced to give her up. It would have been required of him. Could he have done it? He doubted himself. His dark lady was no Carol, no light affair born of the springtime and a young man's quickened senses. But that sacrifice had not been demanded of him. Now he was free. When they met. . . .

He had no doubt that they would meet. Under what circumstances, in what place, at what moment of time—all that was unknown. A stone font in a church, tongues of fire, those were the only indications he had. Yet he had the feeling that he was coming very near, that it would not be long now.

The abruptness with which the door between the bookcases opened, startled him. Wilding turned his head, rose to his feet with a gesture of surprise.

"Darling, I didn't expect—"

She was not wearing the Spanish shawl, or the high-necked black dress. She had on something diaphanous and floating in pale mauve, and it was the color, perhaps, that made Llewellyn feel that she brought with her the old-fashioned scent of lavender. She stopped when she saw him; her eyes, wide and slightly glazed, stared at him, expressing such a complete lack of emotion that it was almost shocking.

"Dearest, is your head better? This is Dr. Knox. My wife."

Llewellyn came forward, took her limp hand, said formally: "I'm very pleased to make your acquaintance, Lady Wilding."

The wide stare became human; it showed, very faintly, relief. She sat in the chair that Wilding pushed forward for her and began talking rapidly, with a staccato effect.

"So you're Dr. Knox? I've read about you, of course. How odd that you should come here—to the island. Why did you? I mean, what made you? People don't usually, do they, Richard?" She half turned her head, hurried on, inconsequently:

"I mean they don't stay in the island. They come in on boats, and go out again. Where? I've often wondered. They buy fruit and those silly little dolls and the straw hats they make here, and then they go back with them to the boat, and the boat sails away. Where do they go back to? Manchester? Liverpool? Chichester, perhaps, and wear a plaited straw hat to church in the cathedral. That would be funny. Things are funny. People say: 'I don't know whether I'm going or coming.' My old nurse used to say it. But it's true, isn't it? It's life. Is one going or coming? I don't know."

She shook her head and suddenly laughed. She swayed a little as she sat. Llewellyn thought: 'In a minute or two, she'll pass out. Does he know, I wonder?'

But a quick sideways glance at Wilding decided that for him. Wilding, that experienced man of the world, had no idea. He was leaning over his wife, his face alight with love and anxiety.

"Darling, you're feverish. You shouldn't have got up."

"I felt better—all those pills I took; it's killed the pain, but it's made me dopey." She gave a slight, uncertain laugh, her hands pushed the pale, shining hair back from her forehead. "Don't fuss about me, Richard. Give Dr. Knox a drink."

"What about you? A spot of brandy? It would do you good."

She made a quick grimace:

"No, just lime and soda for me."

She thanked him with a smile as he brought her glass to her.

"You'll never die of drink," he said.

For a moment her smile stiffened.

She said:

"Who knows?"

"I know. Knox, what about you? Soft drink? Whiskey?"

"Brandy and soda, if I may."

Her eyes were on the glass as he held it.

She said suddenly: "We could go away. Shall we go away, Richard?"

"Away from the villa? From the island?"

"That's what I meant."

Wilding poured his own whiskey, came back to stand behind her chair.

"We'll go anywhere you please, dearest. Anywhere and at any time. Tonight if you like."

She sighed, a long, deep sigh.

"You're so—good to me. Of course I don't want to leave here. Anyway, how could you? You've got the estate to run. You're making headway at last."

"Yes, but that doesn't really matter. You come first."

"I might go away—by myself—just for a little."

"No, we'll go together. I want you to feel looked after, someone beside you—always."

"You think I need a keeper?" She began to laugh. It was slightly uncontrolled laughter. She stopped suddenly, hand to her mouth.

"I want you to feel—always—that I'm there," said Wilding.

"Oh, I do feel it—I do."

"We'll go to Italy. Or to England, if you like. Perhaps you're homesick for England."

"No," she said. "We won't go anywhere. We'll stay here. It would be the same wherever we went. Always the same."

She slumped a little in her chair. Her eyes stared somberly ahead of her. Then suddenly she looked up over her shoulder, up into Wilding's puzzled, worried face.

"Dear Richard," she said. "You are so wonderful to me. So patient always."

He said softly: "So long as you understand that to me nothing matters but you."

"I know that—oh, I do know it."

He went on:

"I hoped that you would be happy here, but I do realize that there's very little—distraction."

"There's Dr. Knox," she said.

Her head turned swiftly toward the guest, and a sudden gay, impish smile flashed at him. He thought: 'What a gay, what an enchanting creature she could be—has been.'

She went on: "And as for the island and the villa, it's an earthly paradise. You said so once, and I believed you, and it's true. It *is* an earthly paradise."

"Ah!"

"But I can't quite take it. Don't you think, Dr. Knox"—the slight staccato tempo returned—"that one has to be rather a strong character to stand up to paradise? Like those old Primitives, the blessed sitting in a row under the trees, wearing crowns—I always thought the crowns looked so heavy—casting down their golden crowns before the glassy sea—that's a hymn, isn't it? Perhaps God let them cast down the crowns because of the weight. It's heavy to wear a crown all the time. One can have too much of everything, can't one? I think—" She got up, stumbled a little. "I think, perhaps, I'll go back to bed. I think you're right, Richard, perhaps I am feverish. But crowns are heavy. Being here is like a dream come true, only I'm not in the dream anymore. I ought to be somewhere else, but I don't know where. If only—"

She crumpled very suddenly, and Llewellyn, who had been waiting for it, caught her in time, relinquishing her a moment later to Wilding.

"Better get her back to her bed," he advised crisply.

"Yes, yes. And then I'll telephone to the doctor."

"She'll sleep it off," said Llewellyn.

Richard Wilding looked at him doubtfully.

Llewellyn said: "Let me help you."

The two men carried the unconscious girl through the door by which she had entered the room. A short way along a corridor brought them to the open door of a bedroom. They laid her gently on the big carved wooden bed, with its hangings of rich dark brocade. Wilding went out into the corridor and called: "Maria—Maria."

Llewellyn looked swiftly round the room.

He went through a curtained alcove into a bathroom, looked into the glass-paneled cupboard there, then came back to the bedroom.

Wilding was calling again: "Maria," impatiently.

Llewellyn moved over to the dressing table.

A moment or two later Wilding came into the room, followed by a short, dark woman. The latter moved quickly across the room to the bed and uttered an exclamation as she bent over the recumbent girl.

Wilding said curtly:

"See to your mistress. I will ring up the doctor."

"It is not necessary, señor. I know what to do. By tomorrow morning she will be herself again."

Wilding, shaking his head, left the room reluctantly.

Llewellyn followed him, but paused in the doorway.

He said: "Where does she keep it?"

The woman looked at him; her eyelids flickered.

Then, almost involuntarily, her gaze shifted to the wall behind his head. He turned. A small picture hung there, a landscape in the manner of Corot. Llewellyn raised it from its nail. Behind it was a small wall safe of the old-fashioned type, where women used to keep their jewels, but which would hold little protection against a modern cracksman. The key was in the lock. Llewellyn pulled it gently open and glanced inside. He nodded and closed it again. His eyes met those of Maria in perfect comprehension.

He went out of the room and joined Wilding, who was just replacing the telephone on its cradle.

"The doctor is out, at a confinement, I understand."

"I think," said Llewellyn, choosing his words carefully, "that Maria knows what to do. She has, I think, seen Lady Wilding like this before."

"Yes . . . yes . . . Perhaps you are right. She is very devoted to my wife."

"I saw that."

"Everybody loves her. She inspires love—love, and the wish to protect. All these people here have a great feeling for beauty, and especially for beauty in distress."

"And yet they are, in their way, greater realists than the Anglo-Saxon will ever be."

"Possibly."

"They don't shirk facts."

"Do we?"

"Very often. That is a beautiful room of your wife's. Do you know what struck me about it? There was no smell of perfume such as many women delight in. Instead, there was only the fragrance of lavender and eau-de-cologne."

Richard Wilding nodded.

"I know. I have come to associate lavender with Shirley. It brings back to me my days as a boy, the smell of lavender in my mother's linen cupboard. The fine white linen, and the little bags of lavender that she made and put there, clean, pure, all the freshness of spring. Simple country things."

He sighed and looked up to see his guest regarding him with a look he could not understand.

"I must go," said Llewellyn, holding out his hand.

Chapter Seven

"So you still come here?"

Knox delayed his question until the waiter had gone away.

Lady Wilding was silent for a moment. Tonight she was not staring out at the harbor. Instead she was looking down into her glass. It held a rich golden liquid.

"Orange juice," she said.

"I see. A gesture."

"Yes. It helps—to make a gesture."

"Oh, undoubtedly."

She said: "Did you tell him that you had seen me here?"

"No."

"Why not?"

"It would have caused him pain. It would have caused you pain. And he didn't ask me."

"If he had asked you, would you have told him?"

"Yes."

"Why?"

"Because the simpler one is over things, the better."

She sighed.

"I wonder if you understand at all?"

"I don't know."

"You do see that I can't hurt him? You do see how good he is? How he believes in me? How he thinks only of me?"

"Oh yes. I see all that. He wants to stand between you and all sorrow, all evil."

"But that's too much."

"Yes, it's too much."

"One gets into things. And then, one can't get out. One pretends—
day after day one pretends. And then one gets tired, one wants to shout:
'Stop loving me, stop looking after me, stop worrying about me, stop
caring and watching.' " She clenched both hands. "I *want* to be happy
with Richard. I want to! Why can't I? Why must I sicken of it all?"

"*Stay me with flagons, comfort me with apples, for I am sick of love.*"

"Yes, just that. It's *me*. It's my fault."

"Why did you marry him?"

"Oh, that!" Her eyes widened. "That's simple. I fell in love with
him."

"I see."

"It was, I suppose, a kind of infatuation. He has great charm, and
he's sexually attractive. Do you understand?"

"Yes, I understand."

"And he was romantically attractive too. A dear old man, who's
known me all my life, warned me. He said to me: 'Have an affair with
Richard, but don't marry him.' He was quite right. You see, I was very
unhappy, and Richard came along. I—daydreamed. Love and Richard
and an island and moonlight. It helped, and it didn't hurt anybody.
Now I've got the dream—but I'm not the me I was in the dream. I'm
only the me who dreamed it—and that's no good."

She looked across the table, straight into his eyes.

"Can I ever become the me of the dream? I'd like to."

"Not if it was never the real you."

"I could go away—but where? Not back into the past because that's
all gone, broken up. I'd have to start again, I don't know how or where.
And, anyway, I couldn't hurt Richard. He's already been hurt too
much."

"Has he?"

"Yes, that woman he married. She was just a natural tart. Very attractive and quite good-natured, but completely amoral. He didn't see
her like that."

"He wouldn't."

"And she let him down—badly—and he was terribly cut up about
it. He blamed himself, thought he'd failed her in some way. He's no
blame for her, you know, only pity."

"He has too much pity."

"Can one have too much pity?"

"Yes, it makes you unable to see straight."

"Besides," he added, "it's an insult."

"What *do* you mean?"

"It implies just what the Pharisee's prayer implied. 'Lord, I thank Thee I am not as this man.' "

"Aren't *you* ever sorry for anyone?"

"Yes. I'm human. But I'm afraid of it."

"What harm could it do?"

"It might lead to action."

"Would that be wrong?"

"It might have very bad results."

"For you?"

"No, no, not for me. For the other person."

"Then what should one do if one's sorry for a person?"

"Leave them where they belong—in God's hands."

"That sounds terribly implacable—and harsh."

"It's not nearly so dangerous as yielding to facile pity."

She leaned toward him.

"Tell me, are you sorry for me—at all?"

"I am trying not to be."

"Why not?"

"In case I should help you to feel sorry for yourself."

"You don't think I am—sorry for myself?"

"Are you?"

"No," she said slowly. "Not really. I've got all—mixed up somehow, and that must be my own fault."

"It usually is, but in your case it may not be."

"Tell me—you're wise, you go about preaching to people—what ought I to do?"

"You know."

She looked at him and suddenly, unexpectedly, she laughed. It was a gay, gallant laugh.

"Yes," she said. "I know. Quite well. *Fight*."

PART FOUR

AS IT WAS IN THE BEGINNING— 1956

Chapter One

Llewellyn looked up at the building before he entered it.

It was drab like the street in which it stood. Here, in this quarter of London, war damage and general decay still reigned. The effect was depressing. Llewellyn himself felt depressed. The errand which he had come to perform was a painful one. He did not exactly shrink from it, but he was aware that he would be glad when he had discharged it to the best of his ability.

He sighed, squared his shoulders, and went up a short flight of steps and through a swing door.

The inside of the building was busy, but busy in an orderly and controlled fashion. Hurrying but disciplined feet sped along the corridors. A young woman in a dull blue uniform paused beside him.

"What can I do for you?"

"I wish to see Miss Franklin."

"I'm sorry. Miss Franklin can't see anyone this morning. I will take you to the secretary's office."

He insisted gently on seeing Miss Franklin.

"It is important," he said, and added: "If you will please give her this letter."

The young woman took him into a minute waiting room and sped away. Five minutes later a round woman with a kindly face and an eager manner came to him.

"I'm Miss Harrison, Miss Franklin's secretary. I'm afraid you will have to wait a few minutes. Miss Franklin is with one of the children who is just coming out of the anaesthetic after an operation."

Llewellyn thanked her and began to ask questions. She brightened at once, and talked eagerly about the Worley Foundation for Sub-Normal Children.

"It's quite an old foundation, you know. Dates back to 1840: Nathaniel Worley, our founder, was a mill owner." Her voice ran on. "So unfortunate—the funds dwindled, investments brought in so much less . . . and rising costs . . . of course there were faults of administration. But since Miss Franklin has been superintendent . . ."

Her face lightened up, the speed of her words increased.

Miss Franklin was clearly the sun in her heaven. Miss Franklin had cleaned the Augean stables, Miss Franklin had reorganized this and that, Miss Franklin had battled with authority and won, and now, equally clearly, Miss Franklin reigned supreme, and all was for the best in the best of possible worlds. Llewellyn wondered why women's enthusiasms for other women always sounded so pitifully crude. He doubted if he should like the efficient Miss Franklin. She was, he thought, of the order of Queen Bees. Other women buzzed round them, and they waxed and throve on the power thus accorded to them.

Then at last he was taken upstairs and along a corridor, and Miss Harrison knocked at a door and stood aside, and motioned to him to go in to what was evidently the Holy of Holies—Miss Franklin's private office.

She was sitting behind a desk, and she looked frail and very tired.

He stared at her in awe and amazement as she got up and came toward him.

He said, just under his breath: "You . . ."

A faint, puzzled frown came between her brows, those delicately marked brows that he knew so well. It was the same face—pale, delicate, the wide sad mouth, the unusual setting of the dark eyes, the hair that sprang back from the temples, triumphantly, like wings. A tragic face, he thought, yet that generous mouth was made for laughter, that severe, proud face might be transformed by tenderness.

She said gently: "Dr. Llewellyn? My brother-in-law wrote to me that you would be coming. It's very good of you."

"I'm afraid the news of your sister's death must have been a great shock to you."

"Oh, it was. She was so young."

Her voice faltered for one moment, but she had herself well under control. He thought to himself: "She is disciplined, has disciplined herself."

There was something nun-like about her clothes. She wore plain black with a little white at the throat.

She said quietly:

"I wish it could have been I who died—not her. But perhaps one always wishes that."

"Not always. Only—if one cares very much—or if one's own life has some quality of the unbearable about it."

The dark eyes opened wider. She looked at him questioningly, she said:

"You're really Llewellyn Knox, aren't you?"

"I was. I call myself Dr. Murray Llewellyn. It saves the endless repetition of condolences, makes it less embarrassing for other people and for me."

"I've seen pictures of you in the papers, but I don't think I would have recognized you."

"No. Most people don't now. There are others faces in the news—and perhaps, too, I've shrunk."

"Shrunk?"

He smiled.

"Not physically, but in importance."

He went on:

"You know that I've brought your sister's small personal possessions. Your brother-in-law thought you would like to have them. They are at my hotel. Perhaps you will dine with me there, or if you prefer, I will deliver them to you here?"

"I shall be glad to have them. I want to hear all you can tell me about—about Shirley. It is so long since I saw her last. Nearly three years. I still can't believe—that she's *dead*."

"I know how you feel."

"I want to hear all you can tell me about her, but—but—don't say consoling things to me. You still believe in God, I suppose. Well, I don't! I'm sorry if that seems a crude thing to say, but you'd better understand what I feel. If there *is* a God, He is cruel and unjust."

"Because He let your sister die?"

"There's no need to discuss it. Please don't talk religion to me. Tell me about Shirley. Even now I don't understand how the accident happened."

"She was crossing the street and a heavy lorry knocked her down and ran over her. She was killed instantly. She did not suffer any pain."

"That's what Richard wrote me. But I thought—perhaps he was trying to be kind, to spare me. He is like that."

"Yes, he is like that. But I am not. You can take it as the truth that your sister was killed outright, and did not suffer."

"How did it happen?"

"It was late at night. Your sister had been sitting in one of the open-air cafés facing the harbor. She left the café, crossed the road without looking, and the lorry came round the corner and caught her."

"Was she alone?"

"Quite alone."

"But where was Richard? Why wasn't he with her? It seems so extraordinary. I shouldn't have thought Richard would have let her go off by herself at night to a café. I should have thought he would have looked after her, taken care of her."

"You mustn't blame him. He adored her. He watched over her in every way possible. On this occasion he didn't know she had left the house."

Her face softened.

"I see. I've been unjust."

She pressed her hands together.

"It's so cruel, so unfair, so *meaningless*. After all Shirley had been through. To have only three years of happiness."

He did not answer at once, just sat watching her.

"Forgive me, you loved your sister very much?"

"More than anyone in the world."

"And yet, for three years you never saw her. They invited you, repeatedly, but you never came?"

"It was difficult to leave my work here, to find someone to replace me."

"That, perhaps; but it could have been managed. Why didn't you want to go?"

"I did. I did!"

"But you had some reason for not going?"

"I've told you. My work here—"

"Do you love your work so much?"

"Love it? No." She seemed surprised. "But it's worthwhile work. It answers a need. These children were in a category that was not catered for. I think—I really think—that what I'm doing is useful."

She spoke with an earnestness that struck him as odd.

"Of course it's useful. I don't doubt it."

"This place was in a mess, an incredible mess. I've had a terrific job getting it on its feet again."

"You're a good administrator. I can see that. You've got personality. You can manage people. Yes, I'm sure that you've done a much-needed and useful job here. Has it been fun?"

"Fun?"

Her startled eyes looked at him.

"It's not a word in a foreign language. It could be fun—if you loved them."

"Loved who?"

"The children."

She said slowly and sadly:

"No, I don't love them—not really—not in the way you mean. I wish I did. But then—"

"But then it would be pleasure, not duty. That's what you were thinking, wasn't it? And duty is what you must have."

"Why should you think that?"

"Because it's written all over you. Why, I wonder?"

He got up suddenly and walked restlessly up and down.

"What have you been doing all your life? It's so baffling, so extraordinary, to know you so well and to know nothing at all about you. It's—it's heartrending. I don't know where to begin."

His distress was so real that she could only stare.

"I must seem quite mad to you. You don't understand. How should you? But I came to this country to meet you."

"To bring me Shirley's things?"

He waved an impatient hand.

"Yes, yes, that's all I thought it was. To do an errand that Richard hadn't got the heart to do. I'd no idea—not the faintest—that it would be *you*."

He leaned across the desk toward her.

"Listen, Laura, you've got to know sometime—you might as well know now. Years ago, before I started on my mission, I saw three scenes. In my father's family there's a tradition of second sight. I suppose I have it too. I saw three things as clearly as I see you now. I saw an office desk, and a big-jowled man behind it. I saw a window looking out on pine trees against the sky and a man with a round pink face and an owlish expression. In due course I met and lived through those scenes. The man behind the big desk was the multimillionaire who financed our religious crusade. Later I lay in a sanatorium bed, and I looked at those snow-covered pine trees against the sky, and a doctor with a round pink face stood by my bed and told me that my life and mission as an evangelist were over.

"The third thing I saw was *you*. Yes, Laura, *you*. As distinctly as I see you now. Younger than you are now, but with the same sadness in your eyes, the same tragedy in your face. I didn't see you in any particular setting, but very faintly, like an insubstantial backcloth, I saw a church, and after that a background of leaping flames."

"Flames?"

She was startled.

"Yes. Were you ever in a fire?"

"Once. When I was a child. But the church—what kind of a church? A Catholic church, with Our Lady in a blue cloak?"

"Nothing so definite as that. No color—or lights. Cold gray, and—yes, a font. You were standing by a font."

He saw the color die out of her face. Her hands went slowly to her temples.

"That means something to you, Laura. What does it mean?"

"Shirley Margaret Evelyn, in the name of the Father and the Son and the Holy Ghost . . ." Her voice trailed off.

"Shirley's christening. I was Shirley's proxy godmother. I held her, and I wanted to drop her down on the stones! I wanted her to be dead! That's what was in my mind. I wished her to be dead! That's what was in my mind. I wished her to be dead. And now—now—she *is* dead."

She dropped her face suddenly on her hands.

"Laura, dearest, I see—oh, I see. And the flames? That means something too?"

"I prayed. Yes, prayed. I lit a candle for my Intention. And do you know what my Intention was? I wanted Shirley to die. And now—"

"Stop, Laura. Don't go on saying that. The fire—what happened?"

"It was the same night. I woke up. There was smoke. The house was on fire. I thought my prayer had been answered. And then I heard the baby give a queer little cry, and then suddenly it was all different. The only thing I wanted was to get her out safe. And I did. She wasn't even singed. I got her out on to the grass. And then I found it was all gone— the jealousy, the wanting to be first—all gone, and I loved her, loved her terribly. I've loved her ever since."

"My dear—oh! my dear."

Again he leaned across the desk toward her.

He said urgently:

"You do see, don't you, that my coming here—"

He was interrupted as the door opened.

Miss Harrison came in breathlessly:

"The specialist is here—Mr. Bragg. He's in A ward, and is asking for you."

Laura rose.

"I'll come at once." Miss Harrison withdrew, and Laura said hurriedly:

"I'm sorry. I must go now. If you'll arrange to send me Shirley's things . . ."

"I'd rather you came to dine with me at my hotel. It's the 'Windsor,' near Charing Cross Station. Can you come tonight?"

"I'm afraid tonight's impossible."

"Then tomorrow."

"It's difficult for me to get away in the evenings—"

"You are off duty then. I've already inquired about that."

"I have other arrangements—commitments. . . ."

"It's not that. You're afraid."

"Very well then, I'm afraid."

"Of me?"

"I suppose so, yes."

"Why? Because you think I'm mad?"

"No. You're not mad. It's not that."

"But still you are afraid. Why?"

"I want to be let alone. I don't want my—my way of life disturbed. Oh! I don't know what I'm talking about. And I must go."

"But you'll dine with me—when? Tomorrow? The day after? I shall wait here in London until you do."

"Tonight, then."

"And get it over!" He laughed and suddenly, to her own surprise, she laughed with him. Then, her gravity restored, she went quickly to the door. Llewellyn stood aside to let her pass, and opened the door for her.

"Windsor Hotel, eight o'clock. I'll be waiting."

Chapter Two

1

Laura sat before her mirror in the bedroom of her tiny flat. There was a queer smile on her lips as she studied her face. In her right hand she held a lipstick, and she looked down now at the name engraved on the gilt case. *Fatal Apple.*

She wondered again at the unaccountable impulse that had taken her so suddenly into the luxurious perfumed interior of the shop that she passed every day.

The assistant had brought out a selection of lipsticks, trying them for her to see on the back of a slim hand with long exotic fingers and deep carmine nails.

Little smears of pink and cerise and scarlet and maroon and cyclamen, some of them hardly distinguishable from one another except by their names—such fantastic names they seemed to Laura.

Pink Lightning, Buttered Rum, Misty Coral, Quiet Pink, Fatal Apple.

It was the name that attracted her, not the color.

Fatal Apple . . . it carried with it the suggestion of Eve, of temptation, of womanhood.

Sitting before the mirror, she carefully painted her lips.

Baldy! She thought of Baldy, pulling up bindweed and lecturing her so long ago. What had he said "Show you're a woman, hang out your flag, go after your man . . ."

Something like that. Was that what she was doing now?

And she thought: 'Yes, it's exactly that. Just for this evening, just for this once, I want to be a woman, like other women, decking herself out, painting herself up to attract her man. I never wanted to before. I didn't think I was that kind of person. But I am, after all. Only I never knew it.'

And her impression of Baldy was so strong that she could almost fancy him standing behind her, nodding his great heavy head in approval, and saying in his gruff voice:

"That's right, young Laura. Never too late to learn."

Dear Baldy . . .

Always, all through her life, there had been Baldy, her friend. Her one true and faithful friend.

Her mind went back to his deathbed, two years ago. They had sent for her, but when she had got there the doctor had explained that he was probably too far gone to recognize her. He was sinking fast and was only semiconscious.

She had sat beside him, holding his gnarled hand between her own, watching him.

He had lain very still, grunting occasionally and puffing as though some inner exasperation possessed him. Muttered words came fitfully from his lips.

Once he opened his eyes, looked at her without recognition and said: "Where *is* the child? Send for her, can't you? And don't talk tommyrot about its being bad for her to see anyone die. Experience, that's all. . . . And children take death in their stride, better than we do."

She had said:

"I'm here, Baldy. I'm here."

But closing his eyes he had only murmured indignantly:

"Dying, indeed? I'm not dying. Doctors are all alike—gloomy devils. I'll show him."

And then he had relapsed into his half-waking state, with the occasional murmur that showed where his mind was wandering, amongst the memories of his life.

"Damned fool—no historical sense . . ." Then a sudden chortle! "Old Curtis and his bonemeal. My roses better than his any day."

Then her name came.

"Laura—ought to get her a dog. . . ."

That puzzled her. A dog? Why a dog?

Then, it seemed, he was speaking to his housekeeper:

"—and clear away all that disgusting sweet stuff—all right for a child—makes me sick to look at it . . ."

Of course—those sumptuous teas with Baldy, that had been such an event of her childhood. The trouble that he had taken. The éclairs, the meringues, the macaroons. . . . Tears came into her eyes.

And then suddenly his eyes were open, and he was looking at her, recognizing her, speaking to her. His tone was matter of fact:

"You shouldn't have done it, young Laura," he said reprovingly. "You shouldn't have done it, you know. It will only lead to trouble."

And in the most natural manner in the world, he had turned his head slightly on his pillow and had died.

Her friend . . .

Her only friend.

Once again Laura looked at her face in the mirror. She was startled, now, at what she saw. Was it only the dark crimson line of the lipstick outlining the curve of her lips? Full lips—nothing really ascetic about them. Nothing ascetic about her in this moment of studying herself.

She spoke, half aloud, arguing with someone who was herself and yet not herself.

"Why shouldn't I try to look beautiful? Just this once? Just for to-night? I know it's too late, but why shouldn't I know what it feels like. Just to have something to remember. . . ."

2

He said at once: "What's happened to you?"

She returned his gaze equably. A sudden shyness had invaded her, but she concealed it. To regain her poise, she studied him critically.

She liked what she saw. He was not young—actually he looked older than his years (which she knew from the Press accounts of him)—but there was a boyish awkwardness about him that struck her as both strange and oddly endearing. He showed an eagerness allied with timidity, a queer, hopeful expressiveness, as though the world and everything in it was fresh and new to him.

"Nothing's happened to me." She let him help her off with her coat.

"Oh, but it has. You're different—quite different—from what you were this morning!"

She said brusquely: "Lipstick and makeup, that's all!"

He accepted her word for it.

"Oh, I see. Yes, I did think your mouth was paler than most women's usually are. You looked rather like a nun."

"Yes—yes—I suppose I did."

"You look lovely now, really lovely. You *are* lovely, Laura. You don't mind my saying so?"

She shook her head. "I don't mind."

'Say it often,' her inner self was crying. 'Say it again and again. It's all I shall ever have.'

"We're having dinner up here—in my sitting room. I thought you'd prefer it. But perhaps—you don't mind?"

He looked at her anxiously.

"I think it's perfect."

"I hope the dinner will be perfect. I'm rather afraid it won't. I've never thought much about food until now, but I would like it to be just right for you."

She smiled at him as she sat down at the table, and he rang for the waiter.

She felt as though she was taking part in a dream.

For this wasn't the man who had come to see her this morning at the Foundation. This was a different man altogether. A younger man, callow, eager, unsure of himself, desperately anxious to please. She thought suddenly: 'This was what he was like when he was in his twenties. This is something he's missed—and he's gone back into the past to find it.'

For a moment sadness, desperation, swept over her. This wasn't real. This was a might-have-been that they were acting out together. This was young Llewellyn and young Laura. It was ridiculous and rather pathetic, unsubstantial in time, but oddly sweet.

They dined. The meal was mediocre, but neither of them noticed it. Together they were exploring the *Pays du Tendre*. They talked, laughed, hardly noticed what they said.

Then, when the waiter finally left, setting coffee on the table, Laura said:

"You know about me—a good deal, anyway, but I know nothing about you. Tell me."

He told her, describing his youth, his parents, and his upbringing.

"Are they still alive?"

"My father died ten years ago, my mother last year."

"Were they—was she—very proud of you?"

"My father, I think, disliked the form my mission took. Emotional religion repelled him, but he accepted, I think, that there was no other way for me. My mother understood better. She was proud of my world fame—mothers are—but she was sad."

"Sad?"

"Because of the things—the human things—that I was missing. And because my lack of them separated me from other human beings; and, of course, from her."

"Yes. I see that."

She thought about it. He went on, telling her his story, a fantastic story it seemed to her. The whole thing was outside her experience, and in some ways it revolted her. She said:

"It's terribly commercial."

"The machinery? Oh yes."

She said: "If only I could understand better. I want to understand. You feel—you felt—that it was really important, really worthwhile."

"To God?"

She was taken aback.

"No—no, I didn't mean that. I meant—to *you*."

He sighed.

"It's so hard to explain. I tried to explain to Richard Wilding. The question of whether it was worthwhile never arose. It was a thing I had to do."

"And suppose you'd just preached to an empty desert, would that have been the same?"

"In my sense, yes. But I shouldn't have preached so well, of course." He grinned. "An actor can't act well to an empty house. An author needs people to read his books. A painter needs to show his pictures."

"You sound—that's what I can't understand—as though the *results* didn't interest you."

"I have no means of knowing what the results were."

"But the figures, the statistics, the converts—all those things were listed and put down in black and white."

"Yes, yes, I know. But that's machinery again, human calculations. I don't know the results that God wanted, or what he got. But understand this, Laura: if, out of all the millions who came to hear me, God wanted one—just one—soul, and chose that means to reach that soul, it would be enough."

"It sounds like taking a steam hammer to crack a nut."

"It does, doesn't it, by human standards? That's always our difficulty, of course; we have to apply human standards of values—or of justice and injustice—to God. We haven't, can't have, the faintest knowledge of what God really requires from man, except that it seems highly probable that God requires man to become something that he could be, but hasn't thought of being yet."

Laura said:

"And what about you? What does God require of you—now?"

"Oh—just to be an ordinary sort of guy. Earn my living, marry a wife, raise a family, love my neighbors."

"And you'll be satisfied—with that?"

"Satisfied? What else should I want? What more should any man want? I'm handicapped, perhaps. I've lost fifteen years—of ordinary life. That's where you'll have to help me, Laura."

"I?"

"You know that I want to marry you, don't you? You realize, you must realize, that I love you."

She sat, very white, looking at him. The unreality of their festive dinner was over. They were themselves now. Back in the now and here that they had made for themselves.

She said slowly: "It's impossible."

He answered her without due concern: "Is it? Why?"

"I can't marry you."

"I'll give you time to get used to the idea."

"Time will make no difference."

"Do you mean that you could never learn to love me? Forgive me, Laura, but I don't think that's true. I think that, already, you love me a little."

Emotion rose up in her like a flame.

"Yes, I could love you. I do love you. . . ."

He said very softly: "That's wonderful, Laura . . . dearest Laura, my Laura."

She thrust out a hand, as though to hold him away from her.

"But I can't marry you. I can't marry anybody."

He stared at her hard.

"What's in your head? There's something."

"Yes. There's something."

"Vowed to good works? To celibacy?"

"No, no, *no!*"

"Sorry. I spoke like a fool. Tell me, my dearest."

"Yes. I must tell you. It's a thing I thought I should never tell anybody."

"Perhaps not. But you must certainly tell me."

She got up and went over to the fireplace. Without looking at him, she began to speak in a quiet matter-of-fact voice.

"Shirley's first husband died in my house."

"I know. She told me."

"Shirley was out that evening. I was alone in the house with Henry. He had sleeping tablets, quite a heavy dose, every night. Shirley called back to me when she went out that she had given him his tablets, but I had gone back into the house. When I came, at ten o'clock, to see if he wanted anything, he told me that he hadn't had his evening dose of tablets. I fetched them and gave them to him. Actually, he *had* had his tablets—he'd got sleepy and confused, as people often do with that particular drug, and imagined that he hadn't had them. The double dose killed him."

"And you feel responsible?"

"I was responsible."

"Technically, yes."

"More than technically. I *knew* that he had taken his dose. I heard when Shirley called to me."

"Did you know that a double dose would kill him?"

"I knew that it might."

She added deliberately:

"I hoped that it would."

"I see." Llewellyn's manner was quiet, unemotional. "He was incurable, wasn't he? I mean, he would definitely have been a cripple for life."

"It was not a mercy killing, if that is what you mean."

"What happened about it?"

"I took full responsibility. I was not blamed. The question arose as to whether it might have been suicide—that is, whether Henry might have deliberately told me that he had not had his dose in order to get a second one. The tablets were never left within his reach, owing to his extravagant fits of despair and rage."

"What did you say to that suggestion?"

"I said that I did not think that it was likely. Henry would never have thought of such a thing. He would have gone on living for years— years, with Shirley waiting on him and enduring his selfishness and bad temper, sacrificing all her life to him. I wanted her to be happy, to have her life and live it. She'd met Richard Wilding not long before. They'd fallen in love with each other."

"Yes, she told me."

"She might have left Henry in the ordinary course of events. But a Henry ill, crippled, dependent upon her—*that* Henry she would never leave. Even if she no longer cared for him, she would never have left him. Shirley was loyal, she was the most loyal person I've ever known. Oh, can't you see? I couldn't bear her whole life to be wasted, ruined. I didn't care what they did to me."

"But actually they didn't do anything to you."

"No. Sometimes—I wish they had."

"Yes, I daresay you do feel like that. But there's nothing really they could do. Even if it wasn't a mistake, if the doctor suspected some merciful impulse in your heart, or even an unmerciful one, he would know that there was no case, and he wouldn't be anxious to make one. If there had been any suspicion of Shirley having done it, it would have been a different matter."

"There was never any question of that. A maid actually heard Henry say to me that he hadn't had his tablets and ask me to give them to him."

"Yes, it was all made easy for you—very easy." He looked up at her. "How do you feel about it now?"

"I wanted Shirley to be free to—"

"Leave Shirley out of it. This is between you and Henry. How do you feel about Henry? That it was all for the best?"

"No."

"Thank God for that."

"Henry didn't want to die. I killed him."

"Do you regret?"

"If you mean—would I do it again?—yes."

"Without remorse?"

"Remorse? Oh yes. It was a wicked thing to do. I know that. I've lived with it ever since. I can't forget."

"Hence the Foundation for Sub-Normal Children? Good works? A course of duty, stern duty. It's your way of making amends."

"It's all I *can* do."

"Is it any use?"

"What do you mean? It's worthwhile."

"I'm not talking of its use to others. Does it help *you*?"

"I don't know. . . ."

"It's punishment you want, isn't it?"

"I want, I suppose, to make amends."

"To whom? Henry? But Henry's dead. And from all I've heard, there's nothing that Henry would care less about than sub-normal children. You must face it, Laura, *you can't make amends.*"

She stood motionless for a moment, like one stricken. Then she flung back her head, the color rose in her cheeks. She looked at him defiantly, and his heart leapt in sudden admiration.

"That's true," she said. "I've been trying, perhaps, to dodge that. You've shown me that I can't. I told you I didn't believe in God, but I do, really. I know that what I've done was evil. I think I believe, in my heart of hearts, that I shall be damned for it. Unless I repent—and I don't repent. I did what I did with my eyes open. I wanted Shirley to have her chance, to be happy, and she *was* happy. Oh, I know it didn't last long—only three years. But if for three years she was happy and contented, and even if she did die young, then it's worth it."

As he looked at her, the greatest temptation of his life came to Llewellyn—the temptation to hold his tongue, never to tell her the truth. Let her keep her illusion, since it was all she had. He loved her. Loving her, how could he strike her brave courage down into the dust? She need never know.

He walked over to the window, pulled aside the curtain, stared out unseeing into the lighted streets.

When he turned, his voice was harsh.

"Laura," he said, "do you know how your sister died?"

"She was run over—"

"That, yes. But how she came to be run over—that you don't know. She was drunk."

"Drunk?" she repeated the word almost uncomprehendingly. "You mean—there had been a party?"

"No party. She crept secretly out of the house and down to the town. She did that now and again. She sat in a café there, drinking brandy. Not very often. Her usual practice was to drink at home. Lavender water and eau-de-cologne. She drank them until she passed out. The servants knew; Wilding didn't."

"Shirley—drinking? But she never drank? Not in that way! Why?"

"She drank because she found her life unbearable, she drank to escape."

"I don't believe you."

"It's true. She told me herself. When Henry died, she became like someone who had lost their way. That's what she was—a lost, bewildered child."

"But she loved Richard, and Richard loved her."

"Richard loved her, but did she ever love him? A brief infatuation—that's all it ever was. And then, weakened by sorrow and the long strain of looking after an irascible invalid, she married him."

"And she wasn't happy. I still can't believe it."

"How much did you know about your sister? Does a person ever seem the same to two different people? You see Shirley always as the helpless baby that you rescued from fire, you see her as weak, helpless, in need always of love, of protection. But I see her quite differently, although I may be just as wrong as you were. I see her as a brave, gallant, adventurous young woman, able to take knocks, able to hold her own, needing difficulties to bring out the full capabilities of her spirit. She was tired and strained, but she was winning her battle, she was making a good job of her chosen life, she was bringing Henry out of despair into the daylight, she was triumphant that night that he died. She loved Henry, and Henry was what she wanted; her life was difficult, but passionately worthwhile.

"And then Henry died, and she was shoved back—back into layers of cotton-wool and soft wrapping, and anxious love, and she struggled and she couldn't get free. It was then that she found that drink helped. It dimmed reality. And once drink has got a hold on a woman, it isn't easy to give it up."

"She never told me she wasn't happy—never."

"She didn't want you to know that she was unhappy."

"And *I* did that to her—*I?*"

"Yes, my poor child."

"Baldy knew," Laura said slowly. "That's what he meant when he said: 'You shouldn't have done it, young Laura.' Long ago, long ago he warned me. *Don't interfere.* Why do we think we know what's best for other people?" Then she wheeled sharply toward him. "She didn't— mean to? It wasn't suicide?"

"It's an open question. It could be. She stepped off the pavement straight in front of the lorry. Wilding, in his heart of hearts, thinks it was."

"No. Oh, no!'

"But *I* don't think so. I think better of Shirley than that. I think she was often very near to despair, but I don't believe she ever really aban- doned herself to it. I think she was a fighter, I think she continued to fight. But you don't give up drinking in the snap of a finger. You relapse every now and then. I think she stepped off that pavement into eternity without knowing what she was doing or where she was going."

Laura sank down on to the sofa.

"What shall I do? Oh! What shall I do?"

Llewellyn came and put his arms round her.

"You will marry me. You'll start again."

"No, no, I can never do that."

"Why not? You need love."

"You don't understand. I've got to pay. For what I've done. Everyone has to pay."

"How obsessed you are by the thought of payment."

Laura reiterated: "Everyone has to pay."

"Yes, I grant you that. But don't you see, my dearest child—" He hesitated before this last bitter truth that she had to know. "For what you did, someone has already paid. *Shirley paid.*"

She looked at him in sudden horror.

"Shirley paid—for what I did?"

He nodded.

"Yes. I'm afraid you've got to live with that. Shirley paid. And Shirley is dead, and the debt is canceled. You have got to go forward, Laura. You have got, not to forget the past, but to keep it where it belongs, in your memory, but not in your daily life. You have got to accept not punishment but happiness. Yes, my dear, happiness. You have got to stop giving and learn to take. God deals strangely with us—He is giving you, so I fully believe, happiness and love. Accept them in humility."

"I can't. I can't!"

"You must."

He drew her to her feet.

"I love you, Laura, and you love me—not as much as I love you, but you do love me."

"Yes, I love you."

He kissed her—a long, hungry kiss.

As they drew apart, she said, with a faint shaky laugh:

"I wish Baldy knew. He'd be pleased!"

As she moved away, she stumbled and half fell.

Llewellyn caught her.

"Be careful—did you hurt yourself?—you might have struck your head on that marble chimney piece."

"Nonsense."

"Yes, nonsense—but you're so precious to me. . . ."

She smiled at him. She felt his love and his anxiety.

She was wanted, as in her childhood she had longed to be wanted.

And suddenly, almost imperceptibly, her shoulders sagged a little, as though a burden, a light burden, but still a burden, had been placed on them.

For the first time, she felt and comprehended the weight of love. . . .

CPSIA information can be obtained at www.ICGtesting.com
Printed in the USA
LVOW06s0949151213

365391LV00001B/103/P

9 780312 274726